西方语言学与应用语言学视野

西方语言学视野

Construing Experience through Meaning

A Language-based Approach to Cognition

通过意义识解经验

——基于语言研究认知

M. A. K. Halliday

Christian M. I. M. Matthiessen

著

杨信彰　导读

世界图书出版公司

北京·广州·上海·西安

图书在版编目（CIP）数据

通过意义识解经验——基于语言研究认知 = Construing Experience through Meaning：A Language-based Approach to Cognition：英文/（美）韩礼德（Halliday，M. A. K.），（美）马蒂亚森（Matthiessen，C.）著. —北京：世界图书出版公司北京公司，2008.9
（西方语言学与应用语言学视野. 西方语言学视野）
ISBN 978-7-5062-9244-3

I. 通... II. ①韩…②马… III. 语言学—研究—英文 IV. HO

中国版本图书馆 CIP 数据核字（2008）第 074838 号

通过意义识解经验——基于语言研究认知

Construing Experience through Meaning：A Language-based Approach to Cognition

著　者：M. A. K. Halliday，Christian M. I. M. Matthiessen
导　读：杨信彰
责任编辑：梁沁宁
封面设计：然则设计公司

出版发行：世界图书出版公司北京公司　　　http：//www.wpcbj.com.cn
地　址：北京市朝内大街 137 号（邮编 100010，电话 010-64077922）
销　售：各地新华书店及外文书店
印　刷：三河市国英印务有限公司

开　本：787 × 1092　1/16
印　张：43.5
字　数：1096 千
版　次：2008 年 9 月第 1 版　2008 年 9 月第 1 次印刷
书　号：ISBN 978-7-5062-9244-3/H·1052
版权登记：京权图字 01-2006-5519
定　价：88.00 元

西方语言学视野

西方语言学视野

目　　录

总　序

　　世界图书出版公司是国内最早通过版权贸易出版影印海外科技图书和期刊的出版机构，为我国的教学和科研作出了重要的贡献。作为读者，我自己也是得益于这项工作的人之一。现在世界图书出版公司北京公司打算引进出版一套"西方语言学视野"系列丛书，一定也会受到广大研究语言、教学语言的人士的欢迎。

　　世界图书出版公司的宗旨是，把中国介绍给世界，把世界介绍给中国。我认为，从总体上讲，在今后相当长一段时间内，把世界介绍给中国这项任务还是主要的。西方的语言学在过去几十年里的发展和变化是很快的，新理论、新方法、新成果很多，特别是在语言学和其他学科的交叉方面。跟我们的近邻日本相比，据我所知，我们翻译、引进西方语言学著作无论在速度还是数量上都是有差距的。不错，从《马氏文通》开始，我们就在不断地引进和学习西方的语言学理论和方法，有人会问，这样的引进和学习还要继续到哪一天？其实，世界范围内各种学术传统的碰撞、交流和交融是永恒的，我们既要有奋起直追的勇气、独立创新的精神，也要有宽广平和的心态。要使我们的语言研究领先于世界，除了要继承我们传统中的优秀部分，还必须将别人先进的东西学到手，至少学到一个合格的程度，然后再加上我们自己的创新。

　　这套丛书叫"西方语言学视野"，顾名思义，就是要开拓我们的视野。理论和方法姑且不谈，单就关注的语言而言，我们的视野还不够开阔，对世界上各种各样其他民族的语言是个什么状况，有什么特点，关心不够，了解得更少，这肯定不利于我们探究人类语言的普遍规律。我们需要多引进一些语言类型学方面的书，看来出版社已经有这方面的考虑和计划。我发现这套丛书中有一本是《历史句法学的跨语言视角》，另一本是《语法化的世界词库》，都是从各种语言的比较来看语言演变的普遍规律。还有一本是《语言与认知的空间——认知多样性探索》，大概是从语言的多样性来看认知方式的多样性。这都是值得我们参考学习的。

　　请专家给每本引进的书写一个导读，这是一个帮助一般读者阅读原著的好办法。种种原因不能通读原著的人，至少也可以从导读中了解到全书的概貌和要点。最后希望世界图书出版公司能不断给这套丛书增添新的成员，以满足读者的需求。

沈家煊

2007 年 2 月

《通过意义识解经验
——基于语言研究认知》导读

杨信彰

一、引言

本书涉及两个领域：一个是对人类认知能力的研究；另一个是语篇生成的研究。这两个领域涉及了多门学科。随着认知科学的出现，学者开始关注认知能力和语篇生成之间的密切关系。

20世纪60年代起，人类学、人工智能、语言学、神经科学、哲学、心理学和修辞学领域的学者提出了对语言研究产生很大影响的认知科学理论。认知科学被看做是对智能及其计算过程的研究（Simon & Kaplan，1989：2）。认知的标准模式包括短期记忆和长期记忆。Gardner（1985：6）认为认知科学是为了回答长期的认识问题，特别是与知识的本质、成分、资源、发展和安排相关的问题。在语言研究上，许多学者认为语言能表现心理表征或连贯的思想，反映着人类的认知能力，研究主要集中在语言范畴化的结构特征、类典型、多义性、完形、图式、意象、认知模型、隐喻、象似性、认知语法、构式语法、语言与思维的关系等。学者们强调人类经验的影响，研究经验在语言结构上的体现。

系统功能语言学一直都在研究人类的认知能力，本书所做的研究充分地说明了这一点。正如本书的副标题所表示的那样，本书从语言的角度来观察人类认知能力的发展，而不是从认知的角度来考察认知能力在语言中的反映。可以说，本书是第一部从系统功能语言学的角度探讨语言与认知关系的专著。

本书可供从事语言学、文学、哲学、教育学、心理学、社会学、神经科学和计算机人工智能研究的人员参考。

二、作者简介

Halliday是世界著名的语言学家。他曾在英国伦敦大学学习汉语语言文学，获学士学位；1947年至1950年先后于北京大学和岭南大学在罗常培先生和王力先生的指导下学习；1951年至1955年跟随剑桥大学弗斯（Firth）教授攻读博士学位。Halliday先后在剑桥大学、爱丁堡大学、伦敦大学、耶鲁大学、布朗大学、埃克塞斯大学和肯尼亚内罗毕大学任教。他于1973年到1974年担任美国斯坦福大学行为科学高级研究员，1976至1987年任悉尼大学语言学系主任。Halliday长期从事语言研究，既重视系统概念又重视功能概念，从功能和系统的角度审视语言在人类社会中的作用。他的思想受弗斯和马林诺夫斯基影响很大，理论体系十分严密。Halliday 的系统功能语言学学说在世界语言学界产生了很大的影响。在我国，系统功能语言学的研究也不断深入，研究成果日益增多。

Matthiessen 于 1984 年获加州大学洛杉矶分校的语言学硕士学位，论文题目为"选择英语的时态（Choosing Tense in English）"。他于 1989 年获得加州大学洛杉矶分校的哲学博士学位，博士论文题目为"语言研究的语篇生成"（Text-generation as a Linguistic Research Task）。1980 年至 1988 年，Matthiessen 在南加州大学信息科学研究所任助理研究员和研究员，主要进行系统功能语言学理论和应用、英语语篇生成等研究，1988 年至 1994 年先后在悉尼大学语言学系任讲师，高级讲师，1994 年至 2002 年任麦考瑞大学语言学系副教授，2002 年至今任教授。Matthiessen 在多语生成、计算机话语分析、会话和言语生成、系统功能语言学理论、英语语法、语义学和话语等方面进行了大量的研究，成果颇丰。

三、内容概览

本书共有五大部分十五章，主要论点是语言具有两个互补的功能：（1）识解经验；（2）构建社会过程。本书主要论述语言识解经验、构建"概念基块"的功能，强调经验的范畴和关系不是天生的。这些功能不是被动地反映在语言里的，而是语言积极构建的，词汇语法在其中发挥很重要的作用。此外，语言是一个层次化的符号系统，能够将经验转换成意义。总体来说，本书以语法为出发点描写了经验转换成意义的过程。

四、章节提要

序言

Halliday 和 Matthiessen 在序言中概述了本书的写作意图。他们认为本书的研究是系统功能语言学的一部分，目的是把语言理论应用到研究和实践中，同时回答普通人和语言学家提出的问题，在语境中观察语言，注重研究语言的功能。他们认为心理图谱实际上是符号图谱，并且把语言看做人类构建世界心理图谱的资源，把认知看做意义而不是思维。他们用语言过程来解释认知，而不是用认知过程来解释语言，并认为连通主义等的认知研究方法与语义方法能够互补。序言中还提到，所有的计算机运算其实是意义的运算，人工智能研究需要了解自然语言的语义操作。

第一部分　引论

第一章　理论基础

第一部分为引论，由第一章构成。Halliday 和 Matthiessen 把经验看做理解和表征现实、做出行动的资源。构建经验通常被看做知识（knowledge），但本书提出了一种与此互补的解释，把经验看做意义（meaning），即用语言构建的东西。因此，经验的识解是个语义系统，语言是解释的出发点。语言不仅在储存和交换经验中起着重要作用，在识解经验中也起着重要作用。经验的识解是普通语言学和认知科学共同关注的问题，但本书提出的视角与认知科学不同，把信息视为意义而不是知识，把语言解释为社会符号系统而不是人脑系统。

系统功能语言学还关注计算机自然语言处理，尤其是语篇生成。作者从语义的角度解释了语篇生成过程中语法环境的概念成分。语法环境包括知识基块、语篇规划成分和表示作者与读者关系的成分，对应于系统功能语言学的概念元功能、语篇元功能和人际元功能。概念功能是把语言当做现实的理论，也是反映识解经验的资源；人际功能用语言构建人际关系，是与他人互动的资源；语篇功能将概念意义和人际意义组织成为话语，成为语境化的意义。由于本书集中讨论的是概念元功能，语法的经验环境被解释成意义，因此把语法的经验环境称做意义基块，而不是知识基块。在构建意义基块的模式时，本书采用的是自语法而上的角度，而不是把经验和语言分开，用概念术语堆积的经验向下解释。

Halliday 和 Matthiessen 指出，虽然"知识"和"意义"表示的是同一种现象，但采用的是不同角度的解释。可以说，一切知识都是用符号系统构成的，其中语言是最重要的符号系统。本章把经验看做我们用语言手段识解的现实，并强调知识的表征都是先用语言构建的。语言是人类经验的基础，意义是人类上层意识的主要方式。作者采用系统功能语法来描述"意义基块"。他们使用叶尔姆斯列夫（Hjelmslev）的层次理论，把语义和语法归入内容层，把音系或书写归入表达层，各层通过体现关系发生联系。语义由词汇语法来体现，词汇语法由音系体现。各层次之间没有时间或因果关系。

Halliday 和 Matthiessen 还认为语义研究的一个重要任务是解释内容层的语法隐喻现象。语法隐喻是成人语言使用的基础。他们采用构成主义观点，认为语法与意义的关系是非自动和非任意的，因为语法能识解现实世界，构建经验。这一章还解释了符号生成过程：首先是人类语言的演变，其次是个人的发展，然后是意义表达行为的展开，即以语篇的形式构建意义。这些是意义不断产生、传递、重构、扩展和变化的三个复合过程。语言能不断扩展，不断变化，从语法化向词汇化逐渐晶化。而传统语法只考虑某些显性的语法范畴，以单词为基础，从语义上描写和解释单词的屈折变化。Halliday 和 Matthiessen 认为在系统功能语法中这些显性范畴的作用较小。系统功能语法不仅考虑显性范畴，还考虑了隐性范畴，认为从小句探讨语义才是重要的。

本章最后讨论意义呈现问题，指出语法具有多种呈现方式，是一个多重的意义呈现系统。意义组织的理论描写在人工智能和计算语言学中被称为知识呈现（know-ledge representation），在功能语言学中被称为意义呈现（meaning representation）。意义通过两个循环来体现：首先体现在词汇语法中，然后体现在语言表达中。

第二部分　概念基块

第二章　普通概念潜势概览

第二部分由第二章至第七章构成。第二章把任何可识解为人类一部分经验的东西称为现象。经验现象分为成分（element）、图形（figure）和序列（sequence）。图形由成分构成，序列由图形构成。成分是图形的组成部分，各个成分起着不同的作用。图形通过相互依赖关系构成序列。一个序列包含一系列相关的图形，序列中的图形之间存在着时间、因果等各种关系。如果一个序列有两个图形，其中一个图形扩展或投射另一个图形。图形呈现经验，由过程、参与者和有关的环境构成。现实世界中有各种各样的过程，但这些过程需要由符号来识解。图形分为做事与发生图形、感知图形、说话图形和存在与拥有图形。图形由成分构成，成分体现各种图形角色。这些成分包括一个核心过程、一至三个过程参与者以及七个以上的环境成分，在语法上由小句的及物性成分来呈现。动词词组体现过程，名词词组体现参与者，副词词组或介词短语体现环境。此外，图形还有另一种成分，叫做连接词语（relator）。连接词语识解图形之间扩展的逻辑语义关系，由连词词组体现。

Halliday 和 Matthiessen 对图形中的参与者进行了详细的分类。参与者分为宏观参与者和简单参与者。宏观参与者都是隐喻的，简单参与者分为简单事物和简单品质。简单事物分为简单的隐喻事物和简单的普通事物。简单的普通事物再细分为有意识的和无意识的两种。简单品质分为隐喻的和普通的两种。普通品质分为普通投射品质和普通扩展品质。环境有两个同现的特征：一个是可区分出投射环境和扩展环境，其中扩展环境分为详述、延伸和增强；另一个有关环境的经验复杂度，可区分出宏观环境和简单环境。过程在图形中起核心作用，包含着图形展开的时间特性。除了隐喻过程之外，过程成分要么是带极性的，要么是带情态的，可能包含相（phase）或体（aspect），而且涉及时（tense）。这些分类勾画了概念基块中识解我们周围和内心经验的各种资源。

范畴化近年来得到语言学，尤其是认知科学的关注。系统功能语言学没有沿用亚里斯多德的传统，它关注的是意义在自然语篇中的构建。因此，概念基块不仅被看做识解经验的资源，还被看做识解概念基块本身的资源。这一章认为，范畴化是一种创造性行为，能把经验转换成意义。概念基块中最普遍的组织是语义类型。此外，从构造的视角看，意义是用空间隐喻识解的。概念基块可看做灵活的多维语义空间。本章还从个体发育（ontogenetic）的角度，阐述了儿童语言发展中把经验识解为意义的过程。

Halliday 和 Matthiessen 还把精密度和分类联系起来，认为从通俗分类到科学分类的转变增加了精密度，改变了分类的原则。概念基块的精密度从低到高的变化是用词汇语法识解的。概念基块把现象识解为有机的整体，也把许多有机的整体识解为成分。这些成分可能是同类的现象。分类存在着两类扩展关系：延伸关系和详述关系。部分整体义关系属于延伸关系，上下义关系属于详述关系。

第三章　序列

第三章专门讨论了序列。序列表现图形间的关系。Halliday 和 Matthiessen 在这里说明了自然逻辑和命题逻辑的差别，并且论述了语义序列中的经验识解类型。他们认为存在两种序列关系：一种是通过添加另一个图形来扩展一个序列，两个图形处于相同的现象层次；另一种是将一个图形投射到二级层面，即符号层。

这一章随后讨论了投射关系和扩展关系。投射关系在二级层面建立图形。被投射的图形以内容的形式投射出来。被投射的图形要么是意义，要么是措辞。他们认为思想内容是意义，在说话人头脑中未体现出来，而说话内容是体现出来的措辞。前者叫做思想（idea），后者叫做言辞（locution）。言辞是说话的投射，思想是意识的投射。投射图形和被投射图形在序列中可能是平级的引述（quoting）关系，也可能是不同级的报告（reporting）关系。在报告中，被投射图形依赖于投射图形；在引述中，两者是独立的图形。投射图形和被投射图形没有时间的限制，主要受现实的投射顺序影响。在人际会话中，所交换的东西可能是符号的，用语言识解的信息，也可能是物质的，独立于语言的物质和服务。信息可以是给予或者索求，此时编码为命题的形式。物质和服务也可以是给予或者索求，但语言只起中间作用，作为一种提供或者命令，此时编码为提议的形式。需要注意的是，第三章指出投射在人工智能和计算语言学的听者模型中起着重要作用，对于扩展标准逻辑也有特殊作用。

扩展关系指的是通过连接词建立两个图形的逻辑语义关系，构成一个序列。扩展分为详述、延伸和增强三种。在语法上，扩展关系的典型体现方式是使用连词或连接性词语。图形是一个成分有限的单位，但序列可以无限扩大。序列通过关系把事件联系起来，使我们的经验有一种顺序。因此，序列能构成有组织的语篇，可用来储存信息，产生语篇类型。

序列和语篇都是语义现象。Halliday 和 Matthiessen 指出，语篇利用了概念基块，是在语境中具有功能的语言，因此序列是语篇组织的一种原则。许多语篇类型可被看做是通过逻辑语义关系扩展的"宏图形"（macro-figures）。序列体现为小句复合体（clause complex），但是序列可能比一个小句复合体大，一个小句复合体也可能是一个图形。

第四章　图形

第四章专门讨论了图形。图形是经验的一个基本片断。从成分上说，图形是现象的单位，由功能不同的成分构成。图形发生的时间与过程有关。Halliday 和 Matthiessen 认为，图形系统把经验识解为四个方面：做事（包括发生）、感知、说话和状态（包括拥有）。每一种图形都有自己的一套参与者角色。这四种语义类型体现在及物性结构中时，做事和发生体现为物质过程，感知体现为心理过程，说话体现为言语过程，存在和拥有体现为关系过程。

感知分为认知、渴望、感觉和情感。认知和渴望类的感知能把思想投射为存在。认知感知投射命题，渴望感知投射提议。感觉和情感类感知可为事实提供空间。区分这四种感知主要根据以下 11 个方面：投射思想、现象、情态隐喻、动词使役、方向、识解行为、相、同源归属过程、识解为归属的属性、程度可变性、具体化。情感感知靠近品质归属，感觉感知靠近行为过程。状态和拥有图形识解参与者之间的关系。因此，一个参与者可以详述、延伸或者增强另一个参与者。具体来说，参与者可通过精密度、体现或示例来详述另一个参与者，用组合成分、拥有或者联系来延伸另一个参与者，用时间、空间、条件等环境来增强另一个参与者。做事是一种涉及时间和能量的变化过程。如果这个过程是创造性的，其结果是一个存在的实体；如果是决定性的，其结果则可能是一个做事/发生的图形或存在/拥有的图形。在有些情况下，结果还有可能呈现为体现图形的小句。

英语中的过程参与者在不同的图形中是不同的。感知图形的两个参与者是感知者（sensor）和现象（phenomenon）。说话图形的参与者是说话者（sayer）和受话者（receiver），此外，还有讲话内容（verbiage），也可能有个对象（target）。做事图形的参与者是动作者（actor）和目标（goal），可能还有个受益者（beneficiary）。状态图形有两个参与者，有时只有一个。我们还可以归纳出适用于所有过程的中心参与者：中介（medium）。中介在语法上是必要成分，与过程一起构成整个图像的中心。中介要实现过程需涉及另一个参与者：施事（agent）。本章还讨论了参与者的程度问题，除典型的参与者目标之外，还有一个非典型的参与者范围（range）。

环境是图形中的一个成分，分为简单环境和宏环境。简单环境由副词短语体现，宏环境由介词短语体现。环境也可分为投射环境和扩展环境。扩展环境还可以细分为详述、延伸和增强三种。

第五章　成分

第五章讨论了成分。成分是图形的组成部分。图形中有过程、参与者和环境等三种成分，还有能让图形构成序列的连接语。在一致式的情况下，过程由动词词组体现，参与者由名词词组体现，环境由副词词组或介词短语体现，连接语由连词词组体现。但成分本身也可能是个复合体。过程是图形的中心成分，英语过程的一个突出特征是时间。Halliday 和 Matthiessen 在这一章里还说明了参与者和过程的异同之处。从语法上看，名词词组由事物和品质构成，可体现参与者。从结构上看，事物和品质的分界点位于类别词和事物之间。事物在时空上比较稳定，但在语义组织上比较复杂，可以细分成许多类别。事物的类别表示了经验现象的分类。与其他成分相比，事物在图形中能起各种角色，成为经验范畴化的基础。本章还说明事物可详细分为许多细微范畴，系统地建立事物之间的分类关系。

品质在经验内容上比较简单，表示了年龄、大小、重量、颜色、响度等方面的程度。根据投射和扩展这两个跨现象类型，品质可分为投射品质和扩展品质，两者的差别在于同源关系的模式上。扩展品质通过详述、延伸或增强来扩展相关的事物。

在语法上，环境成分体现为副词词组和介词短语。一般来说，副词词组的功能是作为方式环境。在小句的概念结构中，副词词组还可以表示结果属性、空间位置、时间位置、品质和原因环境。

投射和扩展出现于现象的各个范畴，成为识解经验的原则，也是语义系统创造新意义的基本资源，它们在概念基块的许多环境中能生成各种组织。同时，投射和扩展也可以识解为事物。可见，概念基块包括序列、图形和成分，完全能识解日常生活中的经验，组织和交换普通的常识。现象通常是以一致式识解的，但一致式无法满足先进技术和理论的符号要求。在构建科学知识时，系统需要使用隐喻的力量。

第六章　语法隐喻

第六章专门讨论语法隐喻。语法隐喻能扩展系统的语义潜能。传统方法从下级探讨隐喻：一个词汇项可能既有字面意义，也有隐喻意义。从上级看，一种现象可以用字面方式来表达，也可用隐喻方式来表达。词汇隐喻和语法隐喻不是两个不同的现象，它们都是我们通过扩展语义来识解经验的隐喻策略，两者都涉及将一个域重构为另一个域。从语法上说，词汇隐喻往往出现在正常的组合里。序列可能体现为小句和词组，当序列体现为小句复合体，过程体现为动词时，我们说这是一致式，因为语言就是这样演变的。如果序列不是由小句复合体体现，过程不是由动词体现，这就是隐喻。隐喻形式多出现在书面语中，是重构经验的资源。语言先出现的是一致式，儿童先学会的也是一致式。一致式和隐喻式的不同在于语篇意义的变化，隐喻加大了与日常经验的距离。

语法隐喻是语言的内在本质，跨范畴化是语法的一个特征。每个词都属于某个大类，有些词能通过某些手段转换成另一种词类。本章根据语法类别和功能把成分的语法隐喻分为 13 种。从级阶上看，这些成分隐喻有三类：从图形重构为成分、从序列重构为图形、从带过程的图形重构为带过程作为事物的图形。

Halliday 和 Matthiessen 还论述了隐喻、跨范畴化和级阶转移之间的关系，说明语篇中语法隐喻的典型表现包括级阶转移和类别转移在内的一系列特征。语法隐喻的主要趋势是向"事物"移动，其次是从"事物"向"品质"移动。名词词组具有通过扩展识解事物分类的无限潜力。此外，语法隐喻还能增强语篇意义。但由于使用语法隐喻，经验范畴会被模糊化，配置关系会变得含糊而丢失一些经验意义；不过由于参与者的语义特征能够得到扩展，表征经验信息的潜能也可得到加强。作者认为不能把语法隐喻简单看做是意义的不同体现方式，它还是对经验的不同识解。语法隐喻在构建科学经验中起着重要作用。

第七章　与汉语的比较

第七章比较了英汉语言的概念语义。两种语言都具有人类语言的共性，也有一些相同的特征。英语和汉语概念基块的构建有许多共同之处，例如：序列、图形和成分的体现在英汉语中也是相同的；汉语的名词化和英语一样突出。但二者也有以下区别：英汉语的极性、人称和名词指称语都体现在语法上，而过程、事物和品质的类别体现在词汇上；汉语的相（phase）更多采用语法手段，而英语的时态更多采用语法手段；英语的词汇化意义是任选的，语法化意义是必需的，但汉语的词汇化意义和许多语法化意义是任选的，在词汇语法上，汉语倾向于避免使用不必要的特指；在英语中，时间在语法上识解为时态，但在汉语中，时间在语法上识解为体（aspect）；此外，汉语的品质已包括了归属关系；英汉语的成分差别最大，英语事物的分类比过程丰富，但汉语的过程比事物具体。

第三部分　语言处理系统中作为资源的意义基块

第八章　概念基块的构建

　　第八章通过分析天气预报和食谱的概念意义，探讨了在语场中概念基块的构建和特征。语境包括语场、语旨和语式。Halliday 和 Matthiessen 认为语场的特征是部署和组织概念基块。语场有两个层面：第一个层面是社会活动，第二个层面是话题。在语义上与语场相关的关联项是域（domain）。域模型是构建某个语场的概念语义模型，是普通模型的变异。域模型与普通模型的关系是示例。本章详细分析了天气预报语言。首先分析了天气预报的语场、语旨和语式。生成语篇时，对语场的描写能显示哪些概念意义受到触发，哪些选择被前景化。然后通过分析序列、图形和成分来归纳天气预报语篇的主要特征。在天气预报语篇中，被识解为序列的意义属于限制性意义。语篇中几乎没有投射，大都使用延伸逻辑关系，而且都是添加或转折的延伸关系。本章运用概念基块的语义框架分析了天气预报的概念语义特征。在分析的例子中，所有的图形都是状态的图形，表示存在和归属。存在图形包括已存在、将存在、继续存在和停止存在的图形。归属图形涉及天气特征和时间、空间和某些外部原因。天气预报语篇的成分可分为过程、参与者和环境。例子中的过程都是状态过程，表示存在、属性、延伸或拥有。例子中的参与者都是事物和识解为事物的品质。这些事物可分为存在物、载体、施事和属性等。从分析中可以看出，天气预报图形识解的经验域属于状态和拥有。

　　本章还分析了食谱语言。食谱属于一种程序性语篇。我们在食谱中可看到许多与厨师、食品、器具、时间单位、烹饪事件、操作、归属、颜色等有关的表征，但很少出现语法隐喻。就图形来说，改变状态的操作居多，也有些烹饪状态的图形。烹饪的语义分类非常窄，状态都是内包式和归属的状态，物体都是具体的物体，做事也是具体的动作。厨师总是烹饪图形里的施事，食品是唯一的中介。此外，食谱中还有设备和时间单位这样的事物。环境成分大都是地点、品质、手段、时间长度等。

第九章　概念基块在语篇处理中的使用

　　第九章涉及概念基块在语篇处理中的作用，讨论了生成系统如何生成语篇。目前的语篇生成系统有 Penman 系统、COMMUNAL 系统、KPML 系统、MULTEX 系统、WAG 系统等。语篇生成系统的理论框架可建立在层次化资源的基础上。资源可层次化为语境和语言两个层次，语言又可分为语义、词汇语法和音系/书写三个层次。在这种层次组织中，层次间的体现关系由层次间的预先选择所体现，不同层次之间的预先选择可能呈不同的形式。Halliday 和 Matthiessen 认为生成过程有三个阶段：情景确定、语义生成和词汇语法生成。作者通过对一份食谱生成过程三个阶段的分析，说明了食谱语篇的生成过程。语篇的确定引导语义生成，词汇语法为食谱生成器提供呈现信息的资源，并考虑它的人际和语篇意义。

　　概念基块支持语篇基块。语篇元功能与概念元功能不同，其横向展开方式呈波浪状，其功能关注的是符号现实，把语篇作为过程。英语语法的整个主位系统包括主位识别（theme identification）和主位述谓（theme predication）。在这两个小句系统产生的结构里，识别型关系过程被用来把图形构建成等式。

本章的后半部分还用实例说明语篇基块和概念基块的关系。概念意义是一个由各种关系连接的大网络。语篇产生时，网络中的一些结点被用来呈现意义。语篇信息可看做语篇基块的模式。语篇压力影响概念基块的组织方式。语篇元功能还是解释概念隐喻的有力手段。

第四部分　理论和描写的其他方法

第十章　意义研究的其他方法

第十章把系统功能语言学对概念基块的研究和其他方法进行了比较。据本章介绍，西方对意义的看法有两种：一种是采用逻辑和哲学的角度，把语言看做一个规则系统；另一种则从修辞和民族学的角度，把语言看做资源。20 世纪 50 年代，逻辑和哲学传统与认知主义联系起来，产生了认知科学。但是，修辞民族学传统也研究知识的模型和表征。近来，人类学家和人类语言学家在研究通俗分类，布拉格学派也在探索推理（intellectualization）。Halliday 和 Matthiessen 认为他们主要采用的是修辞民族学传统，但也考虑了逻辑哲学传统。这两种传统在意义的确定、意义的基本单位、语义理论的元功能范围以及语义组织等方面的区别很大，但具有互补性。

本章回顾了形式语义学和认知语义学对于意义的分析。形式语义学采用结构分析，只关注语言的表征意义，而且认为意义位于语言外部的世界。Halliday 和 Matthiessen 认为，我们需要做的是识解我们的经验。解释是个符号过程，我们不仅考虑具体的自然识解，也要考虑作为符号结构的社会文化。在美国，认知语义学分为两个学派：具有逻辑哲学倾向的东海岸学派和具有修辞民族学倾向的西海岸学派。东海岸学派的 Jack-endoff 提出了概念语义学，从生成语言学的角度探讨语义和认知。西海岸学派的 Lakoff，Langacker，Chafe，Talmy 等学者所作的研究也与概念基块的组织有关。

Fawcett 从系统功能语言学的角度，提出了大脑的认知模式。他的模式在内容层只有一个系统－结构循环，语义与世界知识相互分离。但在本书提出的模式中，有两个系统－结构循环：一个位于语义，一个位于词汇语法。世界知识被识解为意义，而不是知识。这一章还讨论了自然语言处理对于意义的研究。语义研究可采取三种角度：第一种是研究语义层的内部组织；第二种是研究语义层与上层的语境和下层的词汇语法的接口；第三种是研究语言和非符号系统的关系。这些方法研究了语义层的不同方面，具有互补性。

第十一章　歪曲和转换

第十一章讨论参考框架问题。西方有两种观点：一种认为语言歪曲现实，歪曲思维；另一种认为句法歪曲语义。针对这两种观点，Halliday 和 Matthiessen 在这一章说明这些观点误解了符号系统的本质，阻碍了基于语言的活动的发展。符号系统不是一种能揭示或者掩盖东西的外衣，而是把经验转换成意义的手段。

这一章还专门对图形中的品质进行了讨论。中动物质小句和中动关系小句与品质的语义分类有关。这两种小句体现了做事与发生、状态和拥有的图形，在话语中起着互补的作用。Halliday 和 Matthiessen 认为对此有三种态度：第一种态度认为动词确实是形容词；第二种认为形容词是动词；第三种则把形容词看做名词性实词，可作为独立的词类或与名词合在一起。本章认为，把品质的语法体现形式分析成不是它们的实际样子在理论上或描写上没有任何好处。相反，这会把描写复杂化。如果认为语言歪曲事物或思维，最后将以歪曲语言告终。

第十二章　图形与过程

第十二章讨论了图形和过程的关系。过程可看做参与者的组织者，也可看做在时间上可例示的事件。这两种观点表示了两种不同的侧面：一种是及物性的侧面，另一种是时间的侧面。两者之间有着一定的联系，及物性结构的某个成分会决定时间侧面。本章同时还审视了一些学者提出的过程的时间类型。Vendler 提出的活动/完成/成就/状态类型与本书提出的做事、感知、说话和状态图形类型有一定的对应关系。Vendler 的区分主要与动词有关，但在确定过程是一种活动、完成或成就时，Vendler 忽视了参与者和环境的重要性。另外，这些类型之间的关系不够系统。Halliday 和 Matthiessen 认为 Vendler 的类型在确定识解时的选择是副现象的。过程的时间侧面是各种系统因素引起的一种解释，涉及过程所处图形的配置、参与者的本质和品质、过程本身的相。除了时间上的区别之外，本章还结合控制力（control）这一概念，说明了控制力与意图、力量和确定权这些概念的密切关系，从而整体考虑了图形中的参与者和过程，而不是仅仅考虑过程。

人类的经验十分丰富。系统功能语言学对图形的研究强调各种图形界限的流动性，在语法中把图形识解为过程系统。本章还说明了书中提出的方法和认知科学、自然语言处理等其他方法的异同，指出系统往往具有互补作用，可以提供不止一个识解类似经验的方法。从语境的多样性来看，系统是多系统的。在特定的语境下，整个语义系统的一些部分会进行系统性的部署，而其他部分则保持闲置。

第五部分　语言与经验的识解

第十三章　作为多功能系统与过程的语言

第十三章把概念基块置于广阔的社会符号环境中加以考虑。语言是创造意义的系统，其意义潜势具有概念元功能、人际元功能和语篇元功能。概念元功能包括经验成分和逻辑成分。由于语言的源泉在于语法，这三个元功能也是语法的三个方面。从概念元功能来看，语法是有关人类经验的理论。从人际元功能来看，语法不是理论而是行为方式。从语篇元功能来看，语法能创建信息。经验的基本成分是变化，语法把变化的经验以过程配置的形式识解出来。语法的基本单位是小句，它把过程分为几个成分。英语小句的成分有过程本身、参与者以及环境，但并非所有的过程都是相同的。语法区分出物质过程、心理过程、关系过程、言语过程、行为过程和存在过程。物质过程、心理过程和关系过程是三种主要的过程，三者之间区别较大。其他三种过程则处于临界之中。

语法提供的是一个灵活的语义空间。由于语法的发展伴随着人类的发展，因此充满着异常、矛盾和妥协。语法还把每一种过程与不同的参与者联系起来，参与者代表时空中实体的典型，分类十分精密。语法的另一个特征是通过扩展名词词组来识解事物的分类。

这一章还分析了语言的不确定性，认为语言的不确定性是特殊的标记性现象。不确定性是符号系统发展的一个必然现象。概括化的范畴都没有明确的界限，也没有固定的标准和稳定的关系。人类的生存条件丰富多彩，其生存靠的不是确定的单一经验结构，所以我们需要以不确定的方式看待事物。Halliday 和 Matthiessen 认为概念基块存在五种不确定性：模糊性、混合、重叠、中性化、互补性。概率让我们看到某些词汇语法模式在某种语域重现率高，构成语域的特征。因此，要研究语域变体，需要使用大型语料库。不确定性给语篇生成和计算机分析研究带来了困难，人类很难建造一种能承担人类符号任务的机器。但是，不确定性是语法的典型特征，系统有各种不同的概率特征，承载着不同的信息量。语域变异体现了社会活动的多样性。

本章还说明概念基块具有多系统性（polysystemicness），能支持对经验的不同识解。概念意义的潜势不是只有一个语义系统，而是存在着以内部互补和语域变异的方式相互存在的几个语义系统。不同的语域变体构成了我们经验的不同方面。这些方面关注经验的不同领域，相互补充。

第十四章 识解概念模型：日常生活和认知科学中的意识

第十四章主要探讨概念基块的模型。文化模式分为民间模式、专家模式和科学模式。从民间模式到科学模式中间有许多变异。这些模式是文化语境高级意义的配置，在概念基块中可得到语义识解。科学模式受语境的制约很大，我们可以从它的语境、语旨和语式中找出其特征。Halliday 和 Matthiessen 认为模式是一种文化结构。民间模式的发展没有特别的目的，与学术语境没有联系，但科学模式作为推理的资源，在学术机构中是有特殊目的的。民间模式和科学模式在概念基块中是同一个系统的两个变体。Halliday 和 Matthiessen 审视了科学语域的发展历程和民间模式向科学模式转变的过程，认为新语域的出现是为了满足人们以系统知识和实验科学的形式重构经验的需要。

这一章还专门讨论了人类感知的经验，并指出概念基块能识解意识。有意识的过程是经验识解中的主要图形。在语法上，被投射小句不是思维或言语小句的一个成分。另外，在一致式中，感知图形由心理小句体现，但是有些心理小句是隐喻的，表示了情态。例如，投射心理小句 I think 在概念意义上体现了感知图形，把说话者识解为说话时的感知者，但同时也构建了说话者对被投射句中命题内容的判断。在概念模式中，我们把自己识解为有意识的感知者；在人际模式中，我们把自己构建为与受众互动的说话者。隐喻把两者联系起来，概念识解表示了人际关系的构建。日常语法对感知的识解贡献很大，它的有些特征还对主流认知科学的模式很有意义。语法以心理过程的形式把意识和经验的其他部分分开，投射思想；但感知也可以通过言语过程的形式外在化，投射言辞。语法把感知识解为有界的语义域，词汇通过词汇隐喻丰富了这方面的内容，空间隐喻则增加了语法识解感知的能力。

本章把经验识解的民间模式称为一致式，把科学模式称为隐喻式。但在语法隐喻中，小句复合体被压缩成小句，小句复合体中的小句被压缩成名词词组，这使思想投射与对行为的感知之间失去了差别。

　　本章还运用实例分析了认知科学论著中的语法隐喻，发现科学的认知领域由感知过程所决定，感知被隐喻为抽象的"事物"。这表明主流认知科学基本上是民间模式的一种变体，只是拉开了与一致式经验的隐喻距离。主流认知科学的模式关注的是个人大脑中被组织为一个概念系统的信息。科学模式演变出学术的心理学模式和心理分析模式。这两种模式改变了现有的大脑概念，把感知图形重构为做事、状态、拥有图形，强调理据是一种重要的潜意识心理因素。但是，思维的科学模式未能像英语语法那样扩展感知。

　　本章认为英语的语义和语法系统存在着两种互补的视角，为认知科学所识解的信息和所研究的个人思维提供了两种不同的解释。其中一个视角是从概念资源的角度识解心理过程之外的过程，另一个视角是从人际资源的角度把意义看做是在建立互动关系的同时又在识解经验。这两个视角都依赖投射，能帮助我们了解人类经验这些复杂和重要的方面。这两个方面对于个人思维的研究和认知科学非常重要。Halliday 和 Matthiessen 同时也指出，认知科学不应当只是认知的，也应当是符号的，因为意义这个概念能使我们看到感知和言语、感知和理论的关系。民间模式通过各种视角识解和构建了人的复杂性，通过语言折射出这种复杂性，扩展了人的思维。

第十五章　语言与意义构建

　　第十五章探讨语义系统和其他系统的关系。语言能够创造意义，因为它以三个不同而又互补的方式与我们的现实世界联系了起来。语言构建了时空环境的模型，识解和建立了我们的概念基块。语言不是任意的，是我们人类进化的一部分，是我们物质、生物、社会和生存方式的符号反映。语言也不是自动的，它通过体现与语境产生了联系，也正是语言的语境化特征使我们把语言和符号等其他系统联系了起来。

　　语言中构建意义的主要资源分为两个层次系统：一个是词汇语法系统，另一个是语义系统。语义系统是外层，是经验转化为意义的接口。词汇语法系统是内层，策划转化的方式。Halliday 和 Matthiessen 认为社会符号系统有两种：一种是通过语言体现的社会符号系统，包括科学、哲学、美学等理论以及法律、金融系统、行为准则等社会机构中涉及语言的方面；另一种是寄生在语言上的符号系统，包括视觉艺术、歌舞、衣着方式、烹饪、生活空间的布置等创建意义的行为。语言还通过生物符号系统与其生物环境产生联系。大脑也被视做是生物符号系统，作者认为大脑是在构建现实模式的过程中进化的。

　　这一章还通过对儿童成长过程的观察说明个人是个生物人，也是社会人和社会符号人。儿童在语言能力的发展过程中经历了概括化、抽象和隐喻三个阶段。儿童的语言在发展过程中从原始母语转变为具有概括化的语言，从常识性的口语转变为抽象的书面语，再从非专业化的书面语转变为具有隐喻特征的科技语言。这说明我们在从婴孩成长为成年人的过程中不断经历了经验的重新识解和重新范畴化。

五、小结

　　本书旨在探索人类识解世界经验的机制。经验的构建通常被看做以概念分类、图式、脚本等形式呈现的知识，但 Halliday 和 Matthiessen 在本书中提出一种互补的观点，即把经验看做意义，认为经验是一种用语言构建的东西而不是知识。也就是说，本书关注的是把经验识解为语义系统。语言在储存、交换和识解经验中起着重要作用，因此被作为解释的基础。

　　本书既有理论又有描写。Halliday 和 Matthiessen 认为理论和描写应该平行发展，两者需要不停地互动。书中主要描写英语概念语义的最普遍特征，并用菜谱和天气预报这两种普通的语篇类型作为示例，也运用本书提出的模式对英汉语言进行了比较。此外，本书还从系统功能语言学的角度提出了相应的理论问题，并把这些问题与人工智能、认知科学和认知语言学等领域进行了比较分析。因此，本书给读者提供了一个新的视角，让我们了解到系统功能语言学对认知问题的研究，也为今后我们从系统功能语言学的角度探索人类认知现象提供了一种新的方法。

六、参考文献

Croft, W. & D. A. Cruse. *Cognitive Linguistics*. Cambridge：Cambridge University Press. 2004.

Gardner, H. *The Mind's New Science：A History of the Cognitive Revolution*. New York：Basic Books. 1985.

Halliday, M. A. K. *Language as Social Semiotic：The Social Interpretation of Language and Meaning*. London：Edward Arnold. 1978.

Halliday, M. A. K. *An Introduction to Functional Grammar. 2nd edition*. London：Arnold. 1994.

Halliday, M. A. K. & Christian M. I. M. Matthiessen. *Construing Experience through Meaning：A Language-based Approach to Cognition*. London & New York：Continuum. 1999.

Langacker, R. W. *Foundations of Cognitive Grammar*. Stanford University Press. 1987.

McKeown, K. R. *Text Generation：Using Discourse Strategies and Focus Constrains to Generate Natural Language Text*. Cambridge：Cambridge University Press. 1985.

Matthiessen, C. M. I. M. & J. A. Bateman. *Text Generation and Systemic-Functional Linguistics：Experiences from English and Japanese*. London：Pinter Publishers. 1991.

Popping, R. *Computer-assisted Text Analysis*. London：SAGE Publications. 2000.

Simon, H. A. & C. A. Kaplan. Foundations of cognitive linguistics. In Michael I. Posner ed. *Foundations of Cognitive Science*. MA：MIT Press. 1989.

Teich, E. *Systemic Functional Grammar in Natural Language Generation：Linguistic Description and Computational Representation*. London & New York：CASSELL. 1999.

胡壮麟等. 《系统功能语言学概论》. 北京大学出版社，2005.

唐青叶. 功能与认知研究的新发展——《通过意义识解经验》评介. 《外国语》，2004 年第 3 期.

杨信彰. 功能语言学对认知因素的解释. 见：黄国文等编. 《功能语言学的理论与应用》. 高等教育出版社，2005 年 9 月.

Contents

Preface

This book was conceived dialogically: it started as notes on discussions between the two authors when CM was working at the University of Southern California's Information Sciences Institute and MAKH was visiting there as a consultant. (The earliest draft is reproduced as Figure 0-1 on page xiii.) It then developed diachronically — from time to time — and diatopically — from place to place: the dialogue continued at a summer school in the midwestern United States; on a tour round England with long walks in Yorkshire and in Devon; during a visit to Singapore sustained by tropical fruit; in Japan against the background of the fireworks of autumn colours; and in Australia on beaches and riversides in northern New South Wales. Critical moments were times spent on the campus of Bloomington, Indiana; outside the village pub, the Buck, at Buckden, Yorkshire; and in the countryside around Bellingen, N.S.W. The text suggests something of the interval that elapsed during this 3-B; the chapters were not of course written in the order in which they appear, and in any case they have all been revised many times before reaching their present form, but we have not attempted to hide the rather sporadic manner in which the book came into being.

What has remained constant, throughout this history, is the way we have conceptualized our topic and its location in a neighbourhood of related theoretical enquiries. It can be located, perhaps, along the dimensions of a three-dimensional space. First, we see it as a contribution to the growing body of work in systemic functional linguistics, work which extends across general theory of language, lexicogrammar and semantics, text structure and discourse analysis, child language development, language education, and natural language processing by computer. Secondly, we have tried to orient it (like systemic functional theory itself) towards the outside: that is, to theorize language in a way that is relevant to applications in research and practice, focussing on other people's questions about language at least as much as on questions generally formulated by linguists. And thirdly, it is outward-facing in another sense: looking from language out towards its context, to what people do with language (whether this is modelled as social action, as cognitive process or as some form of abstract value system). Intersecting these three dimensions we have tried to represent language as the resource whereby the human species, and each individual member of that species, constructs the functioning mental map of their phenomenal world: of their experience of **process**, both what goes on out there and what goes on in the realms of their own consciousness.

It seems to us that our dialogue is relevant to current debates in cognitive science. In one sense, we are offering it as an alternative to mainstream currents in this area, since we are saying that cognition "is" (that is, can most profitably be modelled as) not thinking but meaning: the "mental" map is in fact a semiotic map, and "cognition" is just a way of talking about language. In modelling knowledge as meaning, we are treating it as a linguistic construct: hence, as something that is construed in the lexicogrammar. Instead of explaining language by reference to cognitive processes, we explain cognition by reference to linguistic processes. But at the same time this is an "alternative" only if it is assumed that the "cognitive" approach is in some sense natural, or unmarked. It seems to us that current approaches to neural networks, "connectionist" models and the like, are in fact more compatible with a semantic approach, where "understanding" something is transforming it into meaning, and to "know" is to have performed that transformation. There is a significant strand in the study of language — not only in systemic functional theory but also for example in Lamb's relational networks — whereby "knowledge" is modelled semiotically: that is, as system-&-process of meaning, in abstract terms which derive from the modelling of grammar.

The semantic perspective enables us to emphasize four aspects of human consciousness which have been rather less foregrounded in cognitive approaches. One is that of meaning as a **potential**, a systemic resource which is deployed in — and ongoingly modified by — individual acts of meaning in language. (Whereas most theoretical work in linguistics since the mid century has focussed strongly on syntagmatic relations — what goes with what, systemic theory has foregrounded the paradigmatic — what is meant in relation to what might be). The second is that of meaning as **growth**, a semogenic resource which is constantly expanding in power by opening up new domains and refining those that are already within its compass. The third is that of meaning as a **joint construction**, a shared resource which is the public enterprise of a collective (whereas "thinking" is essentially a private phenomenon "located" within the individual). The fourth is that of meaning as a form of **activity**, a resource of energy which is powered by the grammar at the heart of every language.

Because we are viewing language from round about, so to speak, rather than from a disciplinary vantagepoint within linguistics, we have tried to stress what language *does* rather than what it is (our notion of the "ideation base" is that of construing experience through meaning, as embodied in our main title). We have hoped that what we say about it will resonate with findings from other sources: particularly perhaps those of neuroscience, with its new understanding of the nature and evolution of human "higher order" consciousness. The context within which we have more specifically located ourselves is that of computer science; not so much that of natural language processing as a specialized activity within computing, and certainly not with any suggestion that meaning can be reduced to computation or the brain to a sophisticated computational device (we prefer Edelman's analogy of the brain as a complex jungle), but rather taking the view (following Sugeno) that all computing is essentially computing with meaning and that "intelligent" computing requires learning to operate with the semantic practices of natural language.

We naturally hope that our approach will be found relevant by those who are engaging with language from other points of departure, such as education, literature, philosophy, psychology and sociology. At the same time we should perhaps caution against carrying over terminological preoccupations from any of these other disciplines. Terms such as "system", "functional", "semiotic", "ideational" which have conceptual and often ideological loadings in one context or another are defined here within the conceptual framework of systemic functional linguistics; we have tried as far as possible to make them explicit within our own text, and at the least to give references to other sources which will make their theoretical status clear. (We should perhaps make special mention of the word "semantic", which in lay parlance means almost the opposite of what it means in linguistics; when a learned judge says that "the difference is semantic" s/he is saying that two expressions are equivalent in meaning, whereas to us this indicates precisely that their meanings differ. Somewhat ironically, the person saying this is likely to be unintentionally right — that is, the two wordings in fact usually do differ in meaning, often rather more significantly than is being allowed for!)

Condensed into one short paragraph, our own point of departure is the following. Language evolved, in the human species, in two complementary functions: construing experience, and enacting social processes. In this book we are concerned with the first of these, which we refer to as constructing the "ideation base"; and we stress that the categories and relations of experience are not "given" to us by nature, to be passively reflected in our language, but are actively constructed by language, with the lexicogrammar as the driving force. By virtue of its unique properties as a stratified semiotic system, language is able to transform experience into meaning. In our attempt to describe this process, we have deliberately used the grammar as the source of modelling, because we wanted to show how such a process could take place. We have confined ourselves, in principle, to how it takes place in English; the theoretical concepts we have used are general to all languages, but the descriptive categories should be interpreted in the context of a description of English (there is a brief discussion of Chinese in Chapter 6). We could, obviously, have located our discourse within any of a large number of other possible frameworks; and we could have oriented it more towards issues in language education, in sociology, in the construction of knowledge and so on. But we found that it was easier to make it explicit by locating it in the general context of computational research, since it is here that the notion of modelling natural language is most clearly expounded.

Even in this context, the idea of modelling meaning is still relatively new. When we began the work that has evolved into the present study, the prevailing ideology was that of "knowledge representation"; this was conceived of as a piecemeal accumulation of individual concepts with certain valences attached and having little or no overall organization. It was not until the latter part of the 80s that the conception of a semantic system began to gain ground in natural language processing, and it is this concept that we have tried to develop here. At the same time we could perhaps observe that it has been a concern of systemic theory since the 1960s to model the "content plane" in terms of a stratal pairing within language, with "semantics" as the "upper model" that is construed by the lexicogrammar as a whole.

We would like to acknowledge our debt to the many colleagues with whom we have been able to exchange ideas while working on the present book. In particular, we are deeply grateful to Ruqaiya Hasan, to Jim Martin and to John Bateman for detailed comments on various earlier drafts; and to Bill Mann for envisioning and making possible the entire enterprise of deploying systemic grammar in a text generation task. John Bateman has shown the power of a "meaning base" in developing various areas within natural language processing; and Zeng Licheng has extended our work, both in theory and in application, implementing many of the central categories that make up the metalinguistic resource which we draw on and which is being developed and deployed collectively.

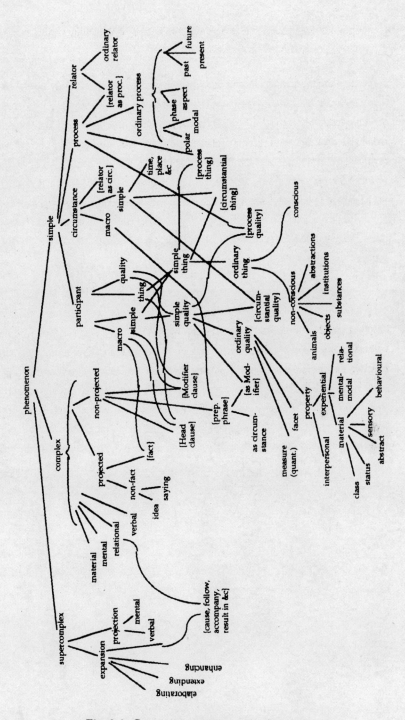

Fig. 0-1: Construing experience: the first design

Part I:

Introduction

1. Theoretical preliminaries

1.1 Meaning base

In this book we are concerned with how human beings construe experience. This means, first and foremost, not experience as an instantial product — the particulars of the world that is around us and inside our heads, the particular individuals, the events of last Friday, and so on — but experience as a resource, as a potential for understanding, representing and acting on reality. It is in terms of this potential that the particulars of daily life are interpreted: they make sense because they are instantiations of this potential.

The construction of experience is usually thought of as **knowledge**, having the form of conceptual taxonomies, schemata, scripts and the like. We shall offer an interpretation that is complementary to this, treating experience not as knowing but as **meaning**; and hence as something that is construed in language. In other words, we are concerned with the construal of human experience as a semantic system; and since language plays the central role not only in storing and exchanging experience but also in construing it, we are taking language as our interpretative base.

Our focus will be both theoretical and descriptive. We consider it important that theory and description should develop in parallel, with constant interchange between them. The major descriptive component is an account of the most general features of the ideational semantics of English, which is then exemplified in two familiar text types (recipes and weather forecasts). We have also made a brief reference to the semantics of Chinese. Theoretical issues have been raised throughout as they became relevant to the discussion. Our theoretical base is drawn from systemic-functional linguistics, a particular functional approach to language developed over the last thirty years or so.[1] We will introduce the theoretical abstractions we need, in the course of our presentation.

---

[1] For a historical survey, see Matthiessen & Halliday (forthc.); for general discussions of various aspects of systemic linguistics, see e.g. Benson & Greaves (1985, 1988), Benson, Cummings & Greaves (1988), Eggins (1994), Fawcett (1980, 1988a), Fawcett & Young (1988), Halliday (1976), Halliday (1978a), Halliday (1985), Halliday (1993b), Halliday & Hasan (1985), Halliday & Martin (1981), Halliday & Martin (1993), Halliday & Fawcett (1987), Martin (1992), Martin, Matthiessen & Painter (1997), Matthiessen & Halliday (forthc.), Steiner (1991). For discussions of systemic linguistics in natural language processing, see e.g. Bateman (1996), Fawcett, Tucker & Lin (1992), Matthiessen &

We feel that our topic is central to general linguistics, and also to cognitive science, an interdisciplinary formation that includes both natural language processing and artificial intelligence in its domain; and we have tried to address our discourse to researchers in both these areas. But at the same time our own approach, both in theory and in method, is in contradistinction to that of cognitive science: we treat "information" as meaning rather than as knowledge and interpret language as a semiotic system, and more specifically as a social semiotic, rather than as a system of the human mind. This perspective leads us to place less emphasis on the individual than would be typical of a cognitivist approach; unlike thinking and knowing, at least as these are traditionally conceived, meaning is a social, intersubjective process. If experience is interpreted as meaning, its construal becomes an act of collaboration, sometimes of conflict, and always of negotiation.

While our general concern is with ideational semantics, we shall also sharpen the focus by considering in particular one specific research application of this, namely natural language processing by computer, in particular text generation as an example of this.[2] What we are putting forward is a **semantic** interpretation of the ideational component of the "environment" of a grammar in text generation. Typically, the environment of the grammar consists of two or three parts: (i) a knowledge base, representing the experiential domains within which the grammar is required to operate, together with (ii) a text planner, assigning appropriate rhetorical structure to the discourse in terms of some theory of "register" or functional variation in language, and perhaps also (iii) a third component specifying features of the writer-audience relationship. These three components correspond to the three "metafunctions" of systemic theory (see further Section 1.4 below), (i) ideational, (ii) textual and (iii) interpersonal.

Since we are confining ourselves to the ideational metafunction, this might suggest that what we are doing is modelling the knowledge base for a text processing system. However, as already noted, our approach contrasts with representations of knowledge in that in our own work the experiential environment of the grammar is being interpreted not as knowledge but as meaning. We have therefore referred to this as a **meaning base** instead of a knowledge base.

What is the significance of this switch of metaphor from knowing to meaning? A meaning base differs from a knowledge base in the *direction* from which it is construed. In modelling the meaning base we are building it 'upwards' from the grammar,

---

Bateman (1991), Davey (1978), Patten (1988), Teich (1995), Winograd (1972, 1983), Zeng (1996).

[2] Since our focus is on the resources needed to support language processing in general, the ideation base would relate to other aspects of this work such as parsing and machine translation.

instead of working 'downwards' from some interpretation of experience couched in conceptual terms, and seen as independent of language. We contend that the conception of 'knowledge' as something that exists independently of language, and may then be coded or made manifest in language, is illusory. All knowledge is constituted in semiotic systems, with language as the most central; and all such representations of knowledge are constructed from language in the first place. (Hence when we consider the knowledge enshrined in a particular discipline, we understand this by examining the language of the discipline — the particular ways of meaning that it has evolved. The most obvious example is perhaps that of scientific taxonomies; but aspects of the grammar are no less crucial: this will appear below in our discussion of models of agency and of grammatical metaphor, among other features.)

This suggests that it should be possible to build outwards from the grammar, making the explicit assumption that the (abstract structure of) categories and relations needed for modelling and interpreting any domain of experience will be derivable from those of language. Our contention is that there is no ordering of experience other than the ordering given to it by language. We could in fact define experience in linguistic terms: *experience is the reality that we construe for ourselves by means of language*.

Thus "knowledge" and "meaning" are not two distinct phenomena; they are different metaphors for the same phenomenon, approaching it with a different orientation and different assumptions. But in almost all recent work in this area, the cognitive approach has predominated, with language treated as a kind of code in which pre-existing conceptual structures are more or less distortedly expressed. We hope here to give value to the alternative viewpoint, in which language is seen as the foundation of human experience, and meaning as the essential mode of higher-order human consciousness. This may have more to offer both in theoretical power and in relation to the many practical tasks for which we need to engage with "knowledge". What we are doing is mapping back on to language those patterns that were themselves linguistic in their origin.

1.2 Functional grammatics and functional semantics

For the task of constructing such a "meaning base", we shall use a **systemic** grammar. A systemic grammar is one of the class of **functional** grammars, which means (among other things) that it is semantically motivated, or "natural". In contradistinction to **formal** grammars, which are autonomous, and therefore semantically arbitrary, in a systemic grammar every category (and "category" is used here in the general sense of an organizing theoretical concept, not in the narrower sense of 'class' as in formal grammars) is based on meaning: it has a semantic as well as a formal, lexicogrammatical reactance.[3] Looked at from the formal angle, of course, this means that it is likely to appear complex; many of the categories are "cryptotypic", manifested only through a long chain of realizations (a "realizational chain"). Hence it takes a long time and a great deal of effort to get such a grammar off the ground in any context (such as natural language processing) requiring total explicitness. Once airborne, however, because it is semantically natural it has considerable potential as the basis on which to represent higher level organization — provided, that is, such organization is interpreted in linguistic terms, as meaning rather than as knowledge. For a recent view of formal and functional approaches to the description of language, see de Beaugrande (1994).

We might refer to the Hjelmslevian notion of the "content plane" as incorporating both a grammar and a semantics (e.g., Hjelmslev, 1943). Grammar and semantics are the two strata or levels[4] of content in the three-level systemic theory of language, and they are related in a natural, non-arbitrary way. The third level is the level of expression, either phonology or graphology. We can draw this model of language as in Figure 1-1. Here the relationship is not one of 'consists of' or 'is a subset of': the concentric circles show the stratal environment of each level — thus lexicogrammar appears in the environment of semantics and provides the environment for phonology. This ordering of levels is known as **stratification**. We have used circles for all three levels to represent the fact that they are all based on the same fundamental principles of organization: each level is a network of inter-related options, either in meaning, wording or sounding, which are realized as structures, based on the principle of rank. These principles will become clear later in our discussion.

Language, therefore, is a resource organized into three **strata** differentiated according to order of abstraction. These strata are related by means of realization. Semantics, or the system of meaning, is realized by lexicogrammar, or the system of wording (that is, grammatical structures and lexical items); and lexicogrammar is realized by phonology, or the system of sounding.[5] For instance, a sequence of **figures** (a sequence of

---

[3] The reactance of a category is its distinctive treatment; cf. Whorf (1956), and also Section 1.8 below.

[4] Note that the sense of *level* here is that of 'stratum' (the term made very explicit in Lamb's, e.g. 1965, stratificational linguistics; see also Lockwood, 1972). In linguistics in general, the term level is used sometimes in this sense, but sometimes in the sense of 'rank' (as in *phrase level*) — the hierarchy of units according to their constituency potential. (The ambiguity resides in the overlap between two grammatical relations, those of elaboration ('be') and of extension ('have'), a distinction that will be introduced later in our account of the relations that construct sequences: see Chapter 3, Section 3.7.2 and Chapter 4, Section 4.2.3.2.)

[5] This is the traditional formulation; more properly: semantics is realized by the realization of lexicogrammar in phonology. For further discussion of realization in reference to the model presented here, see Halliday (1992) and Matthiessen & Halliday (forthc.).

configurations of processes with participants and attendant circumstances) at the level of semantics is realized by a complex of **clauses** at the level of grammar; this, in turn, has its own realization in the phonology — for example, a particular complex of clauses might be realized by a particular sequence of tones (pitch contours). Between lexicogrammar and phonology runs the line of symbolic arbitrariness: prototypically the relation between these two levels is conventional, whereas that between semantics and lexicogrammar is prototypically natural. What this means is that experience is construed *twice* in the content plane, once semantically and once lexicogrammatically. The ideational meaning base that we are concerned with in this book is a construct that is 'located' within the semantic system — that is, at the highest level — and realized in the lexicogrammar.

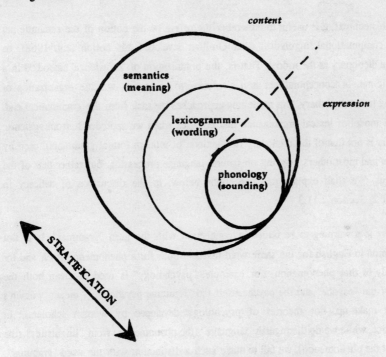

Fig. 1-1: Language as tri-stratal system

A word needs to be said here about the interpretation of the **term "grammar"** itself. As used in systemic theory, this term stands for **lexicogrammar**. The lexical region, or **lexis**, is not a separate component, but simply the most "delicate" end of the (unified) lexicogrammar (Cross, 1992, 1993; Halliday, 1961; Hasan, 1985a, 1987; Matthiessen, 1991b; Nesbitt, 1994).[6] There is a complementarity here. Lexis and grammar are not two

---

[6] The "lexicon" in the sense of 'dictionary' is just one view that can be taken on lexis — an item-based compilation from the lexical stock. The thesaurus is another view, one that is more indicative of the systemic organization of lexis. See Matthiessen (1991) and Nesbitt (1994) for further discussion.

different phenomena; they are different ways looking at the same phenomenon. Some aspects of this phenomenon of "wording" in language are foregrounded by viewing it as grammar, others by viewing it as lexis. Some models of language used in computational linguistics are lexis based (see for example, Mel'chuk, 1982; and Sinclair, 1992; cf. also Becker's, 1975, notion of the phrasal dictionary and the work inspired by Becker's ideas, e.g. Hovy's, 1988b, text-generator Pauline): all (or most) of what is usually treated grammatically is subsumed under the concept of lexis. Systemic theory, by contrast, takes the opposite stance, subsuming all (or most) of what is usually treated lexically (e.g. in a dictionary) under the concept of grammar. It is outside our present scope to argue this case in detail; but one of the reasons for doing this is to take maximum advantage of the naturalness of the grammar in the overall modelling of the system.

In this context, it is useful to remember the origin of the notion of the semantic net within computational linguistics: when Quillian developed this notion (e.g. 1968), he used the dictionary as the model. That is, the organization of 'knowledge' embodied in a semantic net, or 'conceptual' net as it also came to be known, was the organization of meaning in the dictionary. Our modelling approaches the task from the grammatical end. But the model of lexical organization that emerges when we approach it from systemic grammar is not that of the dictionary (the lexicon of modern formal grammars), used by Quillian and most others working on natural language processing, but rather that of the thesaurus. We shall explain this conception below, in the discussion of delicacy in Chapter 2, Section 2.11.3.

There is a warning to be issued in connection with the term "grammar". It is not uncommon in English for the same word to stand both for a phenomenon itself and for the study of that phenomenon. For example, "psychology" is used to mean both the study of the "psyche" and the psyche itself (so "feminine psychology" means women's psychic make-up, not theories of psychology developed by women scholars). In linguistics, while we do distinguish "language" (the phenomenon) from "linguistics" (the study of the phenomenon), we fail to make such a distinction with the word "grammar", which means both the grammar of a language and the study of grammar. To avoid such pathological ambiguity, we find it helpful to refer to the study of grammar by a special name, **grammatics** (see Halliday, 1996). We will use this term from time to time in order to make it quite clear that we are talking about the model, the theory used to interpret the phenomenon, and not the phenomenon itself.

Thus we can say that a **grammatics** is a theory of grammar; while a **grammar** is (among other things) a theory of experience. But to show that a grammar is a theory of experience we use a functional, semantically motivated grammatics, since this allows us to seek explanations of the form of the grammar in terms of the functions to which language is adapted. But this closeness of fit between the semantics (i.e. the meaning) and the grammar does not mean that our grammatics can take over the semantic domain.

Adopting a functional approach enables us to extend the domain of grammar in significant ways in the direction of semantics — not thereby reducing the scope of the semantics but rather enabling us to investigate how experience is construed in semantic terms — to develop the "meaning base" model that is the topic of the present book.

One essential task for our semantics is that of modelling a particular phenomenon of the content plane that is known as **grammatical metaphor**. This is the phenomenon whereby a set of agnate (related) forms is present in the language having different mappings between the semantic and the grammatical categories, for example:

```
alcohol's dulling effect on the brain
alcohol has a dulling effect on the brain
alcohol has the effect of dulling the brain
alcohol affects the brain by dulling it
the effect of alcohol is to dull the brain
the effect of alcohol is to make the brain dull
if one takes/drinks alcohol it makes the brain dull
if one takes/drinks alcohol the/one's brain becomes dull &c.
```

Since this phenomenon of grammatical metaphor is fundamental to adult uses of language, we shall take it as a central thrust of our book (see especially Chapter 6). One way in which we shall seek to demonstrate the validity and power of a semantic approach is by using it to handle grammatical metaphor, and to show how this pervasive aspect of the lexicogrammar expands the potential of the meaning base. (Grammatical metaphor is fundamental in particular to those registers for which natural language processing systems are devised. For example, if our task is to build a text generator capable of producing economic reports, we have to be able to generate text such as the following: *While the March drop in retail sales points to a sharp reduction of growth in consumer credit, the shortfall of tax refunds could be partly offsetting.*)

1.3 Metafunctional diversification; the ideational metafunction

The content plane of a natural language is functionally diverse: it extends over a spectrum of three distinct modes of meaning, ideational, interpersonal and textual. These highly generalized functions of the linguistic system are referred to in our theory as **metafunctions**. The **ideational** metafunction is concerned with construing experience — it is language as a theory of reality, as a resource for reflecting on the world. (For the distinction of the ideational into **logical** and **experiential** see Chapter 13, Section 13.2.) The **interpersonal** metafunction is concerned with enacting interpersonal relations through language, with the adoption and assignment of speech roles, with the negotiation of attitudes, and so on — it is language in the praxis of intersubjectivity, as a resource for interacting with others. The **textual** metafunction is an enabling one; it is concerned with organizing ideational and interpersonal meaning as discourse — as meaning that is contextualized and shared. But this does not mean processing some pre-existing body of information; rather it is the ongoing creation of a semiotic realm of reality (cf. Matthiessen, 1992, and Section 1.3 below.)

Let us illustrate these categories briefly in reference to the clause. Consider the following passage concerned with the ontological status of the Velveteen Rabbit, taken from a children's story; this toy rabbit is confronted by two flesh-&-blood ones:

> (1) One summer evening, the Rabbit saw two strange beings creep out of the bracken. (2) They were rabbits like himself, but quite furry. (3) Their seams didn't show at all, and they changed shape when they moved.
>
> (4) "Can you hop on your hind legs?" asked the furry rabbit.
>
> (5) "I don't want to," said the little Rabbit.
>
> (6) The furry rabbit stretched out his neck and looked.
>
> (7) "He hasn't got any hind legs!" he called out. (8) "And he doesn't smell right! (9) He isn't a rabbit at all! (10) He isn't real!"
>
> (11) "I *am* Real!" said the little Rabbit.
>
> (12) "The Boy said so!"
>
> (13) Just then ... (M. Williams, The Velveteen Rabbit)

Each grammatical unit represents a number of selections such as 'relational', 'declarative' and 'unmarked theme' from a large network of systems of choice. These selections are realized structurally and by means of items of wording. We can illustrate this with an informal commentary on sentences (1) and (11).

Sentence (1), *One summer evening, the Rabbit saw two strange beings creep out of the bracken,* is a simple clause.

> **Ideationally,** a clause construes experience by categorizing and configuring it as a figure. (1) is a mental clause of perception, with the structure 'Time: nominal group (*one summer evening*) + Senser: nominal group (*the Rabbit*) + Process: verbal group (*saw*) + Phenomenon: clause, nonfinite (*two strange beings creep out of the bracken*)'.

Interpersonally, the clause enacts a relationship between speaker and addressee as a move in a potential exchange; its mood is declarative, with the structure 'Mood (Subject (*The Rabbit*) ^ Finite (*saw*))', and its polarity is positive. It is the Mood element that embodies the arguability status of the clause: *the Rabbit saw ... did he?; the Rabbit saw ... didn't he?*

Textually, the clause presents the ideational and interpersonal information as a message — a contribution to the text evolving in its context. It is structured as 'Theme (*One summer evening*) ^ Rheme (*the Rabbit saw two strange beings creep out of the bracken*)'; the Theme provides a local environment created for this clause, positioning it in the unfolding text. The Theme is a marked one (Theme = Subject would be unmarked): more specifically it is a temporal one, which indicates that the story has shifted time frame and a new episode is about to start. This time frame is carried forward by default in the ensuing clauses, where the Velveteen rabbit and the real rabbits take turns at being Theme.

The clause integrates these three metafunctional perspectives as shown in Figure 1-2.

	One summer evening	the Rabbit	saw		two strange beings creep out of the bracken
textual	Theme	Rheme			
interpersonal	Adjunct	Subject	Finite/ Predicator		Complement
	Resi-	Mood		-due	
ideational	Time	Senser	Process		Phenomenon
	nom. gp.	nom. gp.	verbal gp.		clause: nonfinite

Fig. 1-2: Metafunctional integration in the structure of the clause (1)

Each metafunctional contribution constitutes one layer in the box diagram. The final row in the diagram does not represent a layer within the function structure of the clause but rather the sequence of classes realizing the functionally specified elements within the configuration of functions. This sequence of classes is called a **syntagm** to distinguish it from the (function) **structure** (see Halliday, 1966). It specifies constraints on the units serving within the clause — the units on the rank below the clause on the grammatical **rank scale**. The rank scale determines the overall constituency potential in the grammar: in English, clauses consist of groups (/ phrases), groups consist of words, and words consist of morphemes.[7] The units below the clause on the rank scale are all groups (nominal, verbal, adverbial, etc.) or phrases (prepositional phrases), or else clauses that are shifted downwards on the rank scale to serve as if they were groups or phrases. Such down-ranking is known as **rankshift** (Halliday, 1961; 1985; Matthiessen & Halliday, forthc.). This has the powerful effect of expanding the resources of grammar by allowing the meaning potential of a higher-ranking unit to enrich that of a unit of lower rank. Thus the Phenomenon of the clause above is realized by a rankshifted clause — *two strange beings creep out of the bracken;* we indicate the rankshifted status of a clause by special brackets (⟦ ⟧): *One summer evening the Rabbit saw* ⟦*two strange beings creep out of the bracken*⟧. Such rankshifted clauses construe what we call macro-phenomena.

Sentence (11) is formed by two clauses linked by a relation of quoting, *"I am real"* and *said the little Rabbit.* Let's consider the quoted clause.

> **Ideationally**, the clause is an ascriptive relational clause: 'Carrier: nominal group (*I*) + Process: verbal group (*am*) + Attribute: nominal group (*real*)'. That is, the Attribute 'real' is ascribed to the Carrier 'I'; 'I' is construed as a member of the class of real ones — a construal that is in conflict with the view taken by the other rabbits.

> **Interpersonally**, the clause is declarative. The polarity has been switched from that of the previous clause — from negative to positive; and this switch is the issue of the argument:

> | He | isn't | real. |
> |----|-------|-------|
> | I | *am* | Real. |

> The **textual** metafunction gives the option of presenting the Finite, which carries the polarity choice, as the news of the message to be attended to; the italicized *am* suggests that that is precisely what the Velveteen Rabbit does. That is, he shifts the New element of this unit of information to a marked position, in this case to indicate that the news is the contrast between positive *am* and negative *isn't*. In addition, there is also a thematic choice: Subject = *I* serves as unmarked Theme. Subject/ Theme = 'Velveteen Rabbit' is in fact the combination that runs through the quoted clauses in this passage until the Velveteen Rabbit brings in the boy instead: *the boy said so.*

The three metafunctional perspectives are diagrammed together in Figure 1-3.

---

[7] For a discussion of analogous compositional hierarchies in material systems, see Sheldrake (1988: Ch. 5).

	I	am	real
textual	Given	New	Given
	Theme	Rheme	
interpersonal	Subject	Finite/ Predicator	Complement
	Mood	Residue	
ideational	Carrier	Process	Attribute
	nom. gp.	verbal gp.	nom. gp.: adjectival

Fig. 1-3: Metafunctional integration in the structure of the clause (2)

As already hinted at earlier, the present book is concerned with just one portion of the higher-level environment of the grammar: that having to do with the ideational metafunction. In other words, we are concerned with that portion of the semantics which "controls" the ideational systems in the grammar: primarily, that of transitivity in the clause and those of projection and expansion in the clause complex. Transitivity is the grammar of processes: actions and events, mental processes and relations. It is that part of grammar which constitutes a theory of "goings-on". Projection and expansion are the fundamental relations *between* processes: this is the part of the grammar that constitutes a theory of how one happening may be related to another. Thus our aim is towards a general ideational semantics. We may call this the **ideational meaning base**, or **ideation base** for short. It is complemented by meaning bases supporting the other two metafunctions — the interaction base (supporting the interpersonal metafunction) and the text base (supporting the textual metafunction). The overall meaning base thus encompasses three complementary domains:

> **the ideation base**: The ideational semantic resources construe our experience of the world that is around us and inside us. The phenomena of our experience are construed as units of meaning that can be ranked into hierarchies and organized into networks of semantic types. The units of meaning are structured as configurations of functions (roles) at different ranks in the hierarchy. For instance, figures are configurations consisting of elements — a process, participants and circumstances; these figures are differentiated into a small number of general types — figures of doing & happening, of sensing, of saying, and of being & having.

> **the interaction base**: The interaction base provides the resources for speaker and listener to enact a social and intersubjective relationship, through the assignment of discursive roles, the expression of evaluations and attitudes. The

base includes both the semantic strategies speaker and listener deploy in dialogic exchanges and the social personae of the interactants. This second component is a model of the interpersonal and ideational distance between speaker and listener.

the text base: The text base provides the resources that enable the speaker to produce contextualized discourse and to guide the listener in interpreting it. These include resources for engendering a wide variety of diverse rhetorical structures, for differentiating among the different values and statuses of the components of the unfolding text, and for ongoingly expanding the text so as to create and maintain the semiotic flow.

The three bases are shown in relation to the metafunctional components of the grammar (at the rank of clause) in Figure 1-4. Here the three bases are shown as different metafunctional domains within the overall meaning base, with the textual one as internal to the meaning base and oriented towards both the ideation base and the interaction base. We will return to the relationship between the ideation base and the text base in Chapter 9, Section 9.3 below (for a recent discussion of computational modelling of the coordination of these three metafunctions, see Zeng, 1993).

There is no separate component of "pragmatics" within our interpretative frame. Since it emerged as a distinct field of scholarly activity, pragmatics has by and large been associated with two aspects of language. On the one hand, it has dealt with those aspects of the meaning of a text which depend on specific instances — particulars of the situation and of the interactants, and inferences drawn from these. But just as, in grammatics, we do not distinguish between the grammar of the **system** and the grammar of the **instance** — a systemic theory is a theory of both, and necessarily (therefore) of the relationship between them — so in semantics we would not want to separate the system from its instantiation in text. In this aspect, pragmatics appears as another name for the semantics of instances. And on the other hand, pragmatics has served as an alternative term for the interpersonal and textual domains of semantics. Here the distinction that is being labelled is one of metafunction, not of instantiation; but it seems undesirable to obscure the relationship between ideational meaning on the one hand and interpersonal and textual meaning on the other hand by locating them within different disciplines.

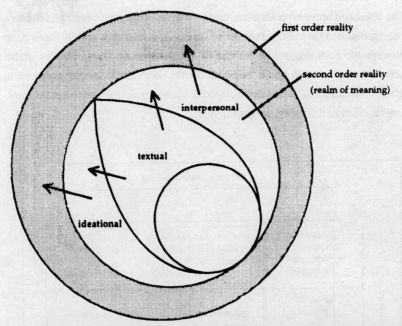

first order reality

second order reality
(realm of meaning)

interpersonal

textual

ideational

Fig. 1-4: The three bases of the environment as seen from grammar

Since our approach is via the grammar, we have taken the boundaries of the grammar as criterial, using the clause complex — the highest rank of ideational organization — to define the scope of the ideational-semantic representation. This is not a *necessary* constraint; but it is one that is clearly motivated in terms of the overall design, and which may turn out to define the optimal moment of interfacing between the ideational and the other components. This will depend on subsequent work on the text base and the interaction base. The constraint does not imply, however, that the scope of ideational semantics does not extend over sequences longer than a clause complex (see Chapter 3).

1.4 The scope of the ideation base

We have said that the ideation base is a resource for construing our experience of the world. Such construal is both paradigmatic and syntagmatic. (i) In paradigmatic construal, we construe a phenomenon as being of some particular type — some selection from a set of potential types. The ideation base is in fact organized as a network of inter-related types of phenomena. (ii) In syntagmatic construal, we construe a phenomenon as having some particular composition — as consisting of parts in some structural configuration. For example, if some phenomenon is construed as belonging to the type 'creative doing', it will configure as an Actor, a Process, and a Goal which is brought into existence through the actualization of the Process. These two modes of construal are related: on the one hand, syntagmatic organization **realizes** paradigmatic organization; on the other hand, types in the network of paradigmatic organization correspond to fragments of syntagmatic specification — this is one way in which such types are differentiated.

The distinction between paradigmatic organization and syntagmatic organization opens up one dimension of the ideation base. As we have said, syntagmatic specifications occur in paradigmatic environments, as realizations of paradigmatic types. But the global organization of the ideation base is paradigmatic; the paradigmatic network is ordered in **delicacy** (subsumption, classification, specialization), from the least delicate (most general) to the most delicate (most specific types).

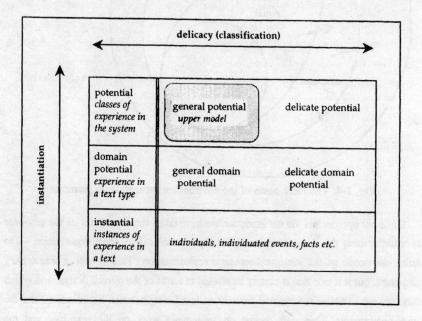

Fig. 1-5: The overall dimensions of the ideation base

The ideation base has one other primary dimension, that of **instantiation**. The ideation base is not just a repository of particular facts and other instantial meanings but also a systemic network of meaning potential. For any given domain the ideation base incorporates not only the known particulars of that domain but also the resources necessary for assimilating new information. Instantiation refers to the move from the semantic potential within the general system to instances of this potential within a particular text (cf. Halliday, 1973, 1977, 1992).[8] Intermediate between these two on the instantiation cline are patterns of instantiation that recur in particular situation types — semantic domains located within the overall meaning potential as situated variants of it (see further Chapter 8, Section 8.1).

---

[8] The two domains of information have been called TBox and Abox in the KL-ONE tradition. We avoid these terms since they are misleading — the potential is not restricted to terminological information, nor is the instantial restricted to assertions.

In general, the ideation base can thus be thought of as a large semantic 'space' organized in terms of these two basic dimensions: see Figure 1-5 above. (Note that it is important to keep delicacy and instantiation distinct. In early work on semantic networks, they were sometimes neutralized (cf. Woods', 1975, review). The difference is essentially that between being a type of x (delicacy) and being a token of x (instantiation). Both may be construed by intensive ascription: cf. Chapter 4, Section 4.2.3.2.)

We will be concerned in the first instance with the general **potential**; but we shall move along the dimension of instantiation to illustrate with two domain models, weather forecasts and recipes. The more general semantic potential is realized by selections in the grammar; but as we move towards the more delicate part of the ideation base, we come to types of phenomenon that are realized primarily by lexical means.

1.5 Guiding principles

We have mentioned two corollaries of using a functional grammar. One was that the grammar is 'natural': that is, the forms of the grammar are non-autonomous, non-arbitrary in their relation to meaning. The other was that the grammar is explained in functional terms: specifically, in systemic grammar, in terms of the interaction among various functional constructions of meaning or 'metafunctions': ideational, interpersonal, and textual. These will be followed up in more detail in Part II.

As already pointed out, these two corollaries together define the concept of the 'ideation base' which is what we are setting out to explore in the present book.

We can now enumerate certain guiding principles that we are following in this endeavour. These constitute so to speak our own 'discourse dynamics': not in the sense that our argument is explicitly *presented* along these directional lines (that would be impossible, since all would demand different principles of ordering), but in the sense that they gave direction to the thinking that has gone into our argument as we developed it.

1.5.1 Approach from grammar

In approaching the semantic environment from within grammar, as opposed to approaching it from some postulated cognitive or conceptual plane (i.e. in constructing it as meaning rather than as knowing), we are following the principle from which semantics first evolved in western thought. By the time of Aristotle there had emerged the grammatical concept of a word, and of word classes; for example, 'noun'. This concept was born in the work of the Sophists, in their study of rhetoric, out of the dialectic between form and function. A noun was that 'about which something is said', thus embodying the *functional* concept of a syntactic (Theme-Rheme) structure; and that 'which inflects for number and case but not for gender', embodying the *formal* concept of a morphological (case and number) paradigm. The category of noun once established, the question arises of why does a noun appear sometimes in singular sometimes in plural number, sometimes in nominative sometimes in accusative, genitive or dative case? These questions are answered with semantic explanations: a noun is the name of a person, other living creature or inanimate object; a noun is in the plural if it refers to more than one of these entities; it is in the nominative case if it refers to the 'doer' in some kind of action, the accusative if it refers to the 'done-to', and so on. The semantics was construed by exegesis out of the grammar: both the general conception of *meaning* as a linguistic phenomenon and the specific *meanings* that were constructed by words, their classes and their variants.

Here we can see both similarities with and differences from our own present approach. We are also constructing meaning out of the grammar. But there are two significant differences.

(i) One is that we are not starting from the word, but from larger units of grammatical organization: clauses and clause complexes (sentences) — the largest units, in fact, that are constructed on grammatical principles.[9]

(ii) The other is that we are starting not from the overt categories and markers of the grammar, like case and case inflexions, but from the often covert, cryptogrammatical relations that are less immediately accessible to conscious reflection yet constitute the real foundation on which the grammar construes the world of our experience.[10]

We could sum this up by saying that grammar provides the mode of entry into semantics provided the motivating 'grammatics' is broad enough and deep enough. But to say this already suggests that there are other, more fundamental guiding principles at work underlying our own current practice. We started by saying that to adopt this approach means interpreting grammar as 'natural', in the sense that its formal organization is typically iconic rather than conventional in relation to meaning. We need to pursue this line of thinking a little further, bringing in the arrows of time.

---

[9] In systemic terms, the largest that can be exhaustively represented as system networks on the paradigmatic axis. Cf. Chapter 3 below.

[10] This formulation specifically relates to the ideational metafunction. If we were concerned with the interaction base it would be the cryptogrammar of language as action: enacting social and personal relationships, power structures of all kinds, institutional attitudes and value systems and the like.

1.5.2 Meaning constructed in grammar

In what we have said so far we could seem to be taking an 'essentialist' or 'correspondence' approach to grammar and meaning, according to which 'meaning' pre-exists the forms in which it is 'encoded' (cf. Lakoff's, 1988, argument against the 'objectifying' view of meaning). In such a view, the grammar is said to be natural because it evolves to serve an already developed model of experience, a "real world" that has previously been construed. In fact we are not taking an 'essentialist' or 'correspondence' approach, and there will be many places throughout our discussion where such an interpretation is clearly ruled out, as being incompatible with our own conception of semantics (see for example the discussion of sequences in Chapter 3 below). The view we are adopting is a **constructivist** one, familiar from European linguistics in the work of Hjelmslev and Firth. According to this view, it is the grammar itself that construes experience, that constructs for us our world of events and objects. As Hjelmslev (1943) said, reality is unknowable; the only things that are known are our construals of it — that is, meanings. Meanings do not 'exist' before the wordings that realize them. They are formed out of the impact between our consciousness and its environment.

1.5.3 Semogenesis

We need, therefore, a further guiding principle in the form of some model of the processes by which meaning, and particular meanings, are created; let us call these **semogenic** processes. Since these processes take place through time, we need to identify the time frames, of which there are (at least) three.[11]

(i) First, there is the *evolution* of human language (and of particular languages as manifestations of this). Known histories represent a small fraction of the total time scale of this evolution, perhaps 0.1%; they become relevant only where particular aspects of this evolutionary change have taken place very recently, e.g. the evolution of scientific discourse. This is the **phylogenetic** time frame.

(ii) Secondly, there is the *development* of the individual speaker (speaking subject). A speaker's history may — like that of the biological individual — recapitulate some of the evolutionary progression along epigenetic lines. But the individual experience is one of *growth*, not evolution, and follows the typical cycle of growth, maturation and decay. This is the **ontogenetic** time frame.

---

[11] There may be more, but these are the ones that matter here.

(iii) Thirdly, there is the *unfolding* of the act of meaning itself: the instantial construction of meaning in the form of a text. This is a stochastic process in which the potential for creating meaning is continually modified in the light of what has gone before; certain options are restricted or disfavoured, while others are emprobabled or opened up. We refer to this as the **logogenetic** time frame, using logo(s) in its original sense of 'discourse'.

These are the three major processes of **semohistory**, by which meanings are continually created, transmitted, recreated, extended and changed. Each one provides the *environment* within which the 'next' takes place, in the order in which we have presented them; and, conversely, each one provides the material out of which the previous one is constructed: see Figure 1-6.

semogenic processes:

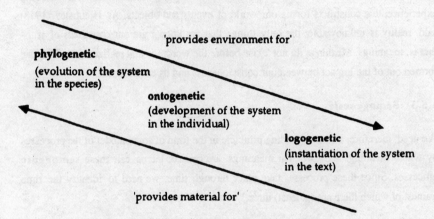

phylogenetic
(evolution of the system
in the species)

'provides environment for'

ontogenetic
(development of the system
in the individual)

logogenetic
(instantiation of the system
in the text)

'provides material for'

Fig. 1-6: The three semohistories related

As the upward pointing arrow suggests, the individual's (transfinite) meaning potential is constructed out of (finite) instances of text; the (transfinite) meaning potential of the species is constructed out of (finite) instances of individual 'meaners'. Following the downward arrow, the system of the language (the meaning potential of the species) provides the environment in which the individual's meaning emerges; the meaning potential of the individual provides the environment within which the meaning of the text emerges.

The sense in which grammar is said to construe experience will be somewhat different in each of these three time frames.

1.5.4 Semantics in relation to grammar

In all these histories, the wordings and the meanings emerge together. The relationship is that of the two sides of the Stoic-Saussurean sign — best represented, perhaps, in the familiar Chinese figure yin & yang (which is in fact just that, a representation of the sign):

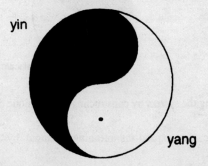

Thus, to return to our earlier illustration of the noun: what evolved, in the history of the system, was an entity on the content plane which had a structure as follows:

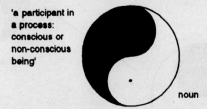

The relationship between the two sides of the sign is that of **realization**: thus the meaning 'participant in a process: conscious or non-conscious being' **is realized** as the wording (class of wording) 'noun'.

Suppose we now consider the semogenic processes whereby this potential expands. (i) We may, for example, construe new participants by creating new thing/name complexes: thus

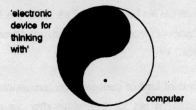

Of course, the 'thing' may have been 'there' all along but it is only newly observed and semanticized:

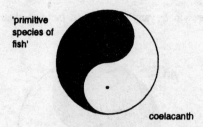

Here we are extending the system by constructing new semiotic domains.

(ii) Secondly, we may expand the meaning potential by increasing the semantic delicacy; for example

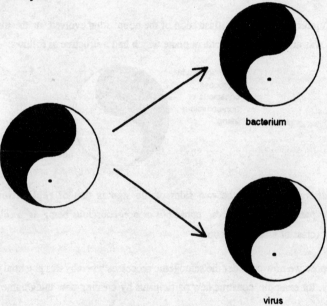

Here the semiotic domain has not been extended but rather has been brought into sharper focus, so that further shades of meaning are differentiated. A finer grid has been applied to the given semantic space.

(iii) There is also a third kind of semogenic process which arises from the nature of the sign itself. Our "sign" is not the Saussurean sign: we are not talking about the relationship between a word and its phonological representation (between content and expression, in Hjelmslev's terms). The relationship is *within* the content plane, between a meaning and a wording — the non-arbitrary relationship between the system of semantics and the system of lexicogrammar.

This process, then, takes the form of deconstructing the two components of the sign. How is this possible? This can happen because, once a 'pair' of this kind has come into being, each component takes on an existence of its own. To pursue the example of the complex 'participant ↘ noun' above: the category of 'participant' becomes detached from that of noun, so that we can have participants realized by other things than nouns, and nouns realizing other things than participants.

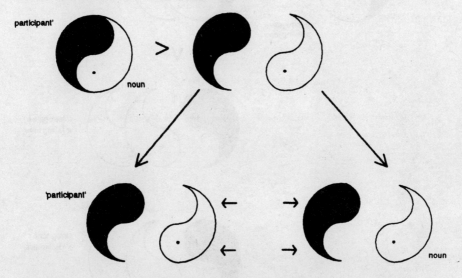

We now have three meanings instead of one: participants constructed by nouns, as hitherto, but now contrasting (a) with participants constructed by something other than nouns, and (b) with nouns constructing something other than participants. (Of course, neither of these two entails the other; there might be just many to one, not many to many. To take this actual example, there are many cases of nouns realizing things other than participants; but relatively few cases of participants being realized otherwise than by a noun.)

A common variant of this process is that of the dissociation of associated features in the wording. We could represent this as:

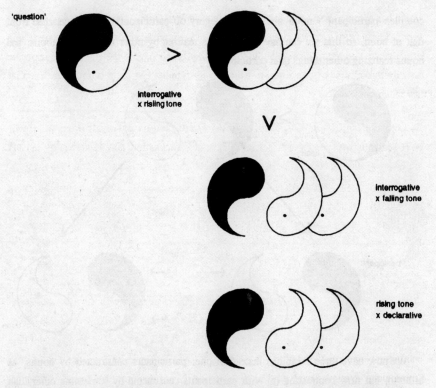

Here again one meaning has been replaced by three: we now have (say) question₁ ⬊ interrogative x rising tone, question₂ ⬊ interrogative x falling tone, and question₃ ⬊ declarative x rising tone, e.g. *is she cóming? is she còming? she's cóming?*

Typically processes of this type leave their traces in the form of marking, as marked/ unmarked oppositions. The original member of the set remains the unmarked one. (One could say 'the unmarked term in the system'; but this formulation assumes that the offspring combine with the parent to form a system. Sometimes they do, but not always.) In these first set of examples, the unmarked mapping is that of participant ⬊ noun; when the noun realizes some other element in the figure, it is a marked variant (see on grammatical metaphor, Chapter 6 below). Presumably many 'unmarked' variants originate in this way, although in most instances we no longer have the evidence which would enable us to judge.

1.6 Codifying

Semogenic processes of the kinds just described take place in all three dimensions of semohistory: as the system of language evolves, as children develop their language, and as the language of a text unfolds. Hence language embodies the potential for its own ongoing expansion; and since the system at any moment is the repository of its own history, we can sometimes recognize disjunctions or interstices that offer a likely context for new meanings to appear. For example, the 'double *-ing* ' form of the English verb, which has recently been establishing itself (e.g. *being raining,* as in *it seemed better to stay at home with it being raining*), could have been predicted from a knowledge of the present state and recent history of the tense system. A change of this kind will propagate steadily throughout the system: sometimes very rapidly, but more often in an irregular and rather uneven flow.

Let us refer to this process as that of **codifying**, noting that as always it is at once both semantic and lexicogrammatical: there is no implication that meanings are already there and waiting to be codified. Consider a series of examples such as the following:

What happens here is that a meaning has gradually crystallized, as it were, out of the total meaning potential of the system so that it can be deployed in codified form instead of being constructed afresh each time. In *an animal that has four legs,* each of the component elements *animal, four & legs* is codified separately, as are the various grammatical relations involved; but the complex is not codified as a whole. When we come to *quadruped,* it is. Again, this codifying progression takes place in all the three dimensions of history: *quadruped* evolves later in the system, is learnt later by a child, and typically at least appears later in the text (cf. *an animal that has four legs is called a quadruped*). This process of codifying may take place at any point along the cline from grammar to lexis, from **grammaticalization** at one end (cf. Hopper & Traugott, 1993) to **lexicalization** at the other. Perhaps the most highly coded meanings are those which are fully grammaticalized: that is, organized into grammatical systems, such as tense and polarity in English. This does not mean that they must be overtly signalled in syntax or morphology; some of them are, but others are uncovered only through systematic analysis (cf. Section 1.8 below on covert categories), such as the different types of process configurations in English.

Lexicalization may take the form of the instantaneous creation of new lexicalized meanings; like *sputnik* in 1958 or *gazumping* sometime in the seventies. But more often it is the end point of a process of **lexical compacting**, as in the example of *quadruped* above. Since lexicalized meanings do not form clearly defined and bounded systems in the way that grammaticalized ones do, we might consider meanings of this kind less highly codified, although the process of codification is the same in both cases.

Somewhere between the two extremes of grammar and lexis we may recognize the emergence of **distinct grammatical structures** and **lexical classes**. In the course of the history of English the meaning 'it is precipitating' became highly codified, in that types of precipitation came to be lexicalized as verbs (*rain, hail, snow, sleet, thunder, lighten*) in a unique class having no participants associated with it: e.g., *it's raining*, where the *it* functions as Subject but has no role in transitivity. (Note humorous back-formation on model of Actor-Process: *What's it doing? — Raining.*)

In general the process of creating meaning involves constructing some kind of **lexicogrammatical generalization** -- some form of wording that is in some respect unique. It is not possible to quantify the degree to which any semantic feature or domain has been codified at any one moment in semohistory; but meanings that are more highly codified are those that have been to a greater extent condensed and/or compacted, where 'compacting' is generalizing on the syntagmatic axis (e.g. *animal that has four legs > quadruped*), while 'condensing' is generalizing on the paradigmatic axis (forming into a system at some point along the scale of delicacy). The evolution of language (i.e. of specific languages in their various registers), the learning of language by children, and the production of language in the form of discourse constitute the historical contexts in which meanings are continuously being created along these lines.

Of course, not every instance of the *use* of language involves the creation of new meanings. The greater part of most discourse consists of wordings which have been constructed on countless previous occasions — in the language, in the individual, and even in the course of the text.[12] When we come across the sentence *Rain is expected in the northern part of the region, falling as snow over high ground* we recognize probably all of it as something that is ready to hand: not only has it occurred in the English language many times before, but the same writer has probably written it many times before, and many of these instances could be seen as forming part of the same discourse (that is, day-by-day weather reports in a sense constitute one continuous text). The **storing** of meanings for repetitive use and reuse is just as important as the potential for creating new ones. The production of discourse by an individual speaker or writer can be seen as a dialectic between these two semiotic activities: between (i) *recycling* elements, figures and sequences that that individual has used many times before, and so for him or her are already fully codified, and (ii) *constructing new ones that are being codified for the first time* (and some of which may remain codified for future use — especially with a child who is learning the system). Much recent work in

---

[12] Note that text construction is *not* a matter of 'old words in new sentences'. Obviously, the higher (more complex) the unit, the more likely it is to be being newly created: sequences are less often repeated than figures, figures than elements. But (as we have seen) new elements are being created all the time (again, 'new' in relation to any of the histories above; for example, the COBUILD project in lexicological research at the University of Birmingham reports each week on the number of words that have been identified in English as occurring for the first time); while whole sequences are frequently stored and used over again. Both creating new meanings and reusing old ones are, of course, equally meaningful (even 'creative') activities; effective semiosis depends on both.

AI and much of linguistics generally has tended to foreground either one or the other of these two activities, whereas the creation of meaning involves ongoing interaction between the two.

Thus an interpretation of semantics must account not merely for the system at some particular point in its evolution but also for the processes by which it got there and the changes that will shape it in the future. As far as text is concerned, the changes in semantic styling that take place in the course of a text cannot be dismissed as simply ad hoc devices for making the text shorter (or longer!), more interesting or whatever; they should be seen as the operation of general semogenic principles in the specific context which is engendering and being engendered by that text. If we are attempting to model a learning system, in which the computer constructs its own general-purpose grammar from large samples of text data, it will be essential both to model these processes in their own terms and to set up the semantic and lexicogrammatical representations in terms that are compatible with them. We certainly do not claim to have produced a model with which one could achieve this goal. But we have kept in mind, as a guiding principle, the need to interpret the system in ways which allow for its possible histories —how it got the way it is, rather than (as seems to us sometimes to be the case) in ways which make it difficult to see how any system could have arrived at that particular state.

1.7 Realization

We have retained the term 'realization' to refer to the **interstratal relationship** between the semantics and the lexicogrammar: the lexicogrammar 'realizes' the semantics, the semantics 'is realized by' the grammar. We shall have more to say about this relationship in general (i.e. as extending to other strata) later on. In any stratal system (i.e. any system where there are two strata such that one is the realization of the other) there is no temporal or causal ordering between the strata. It makes no sense to ask which comes first or which causes which. That would be like taking an expression such as $x = 2$ and asking which existed first, the x or the 2, or which caused the other to come into being (it is *not* like the chicken and the egg, which *are* temporally ordered even though in a cycle). There is a sense in which realization is the *analogue,* in semiotic systems, of cause-&-effect in physical systems; but it is a relationship among levels of meaning and not among sequences of events. (In terms of the figures of being we shall discuss in Chapter 4, the relationship is an intensive one, not a causal circumstantial one.)

Every scientific theory is itself a stratal-semiotic system, in which the relation among the different levels of abstraction is one of realization. This is to be expected, since all such theories are modelled on natural language in the first place; and, as we have seen, the semantics of natural language is itself a theory of daily experience.

Thus when we move from the lexicogrammar into the semantics, as we are doing here, we are not simply relabelling everything in a new terminological guise. We shall stress the fundamental relationship between (say) clause complex in the grammar and sequence in the semantics, precisely because the two originate as one: a theory of logical relationships between processes. But, as we have shown, what makes such a theory (i.e. an ideation base as the construal of experience) possible is that it is a stratal construction that can also be deconstructed, every such occasion being a gateway to the creation of further meanings which reconstrue in new and divergent ways. Thus a sequence is not 'the same thing as' a clause complex; if it was, language would not be a dynamic open system of the kind that it is. This issue will be foregrounded particularly in our discussion of grammatical metaphor (see Chapter 6).

1.8 Grammatical evidence

Since we are taking the grammar as a point of departure for exploring the organization of semantics, it may be helpful to say a few general words about the various ways in which semantic categories may be reflected at the lexicogrammatical level.

In traditional grammar, only certain grammatical categories were taken into consideration; these categories were (i) overt and (ii) word-based (cf. Section 1.5.1 above). In particular, inflectional categories of the word such as tense, case, and number were described and then interpreted semantically. In a functional grammar, while such categories are not ignored, they tend to play a less significant role, appearing at the end point of realizational chains. For instance, it is not possible to base a functional interpretation of number in English simply on the presence or absence of 'plural' as a nominal suffix (as in *grammar+s*); the category of number is rather more complex, involving two complementary systems (see Halliday, 1985: 161-2). Similarly, the general properties of the construal of time embodied in the English tense system are not revealed by only looking at the overt suffixal past tense marker (as in *laugh+ed*); again the scope of the semantics of tense in English is far greater than this overt word category would suggest (see Halliday, 1985: 182-4; Matthiessen, 1996). In general, our move into semantics from grammar differs from the traditional one along the following lines.

(i) We consider not only overt categories but also covert ones. The understanding of covert categories in the grammar is due to Whorf (1956: 88 ff), who made the distinction between **overt** categories or phenotypes and **covert** categories or cryptotypes; he is worth quoting at some length:

> An overt category is a category having a formal mark which is present (with only infrequent exceptions) in every sentence containing a member of the category. The mark need not be part of the same word to which the category may be said to be attached in a paradigmatic sense; i.e. it need not be a suffix, prefix, vowel change, or

other 'inflection', but may be a detached word or a certain patterning of the whole sentence. ...

A covert category is marked, whether morphemically or by sentence pattern, only in certain types of sentence and not in every sentence in which a word or element belonging to the category occurs. The class membership of the word is not apparent until there is a question of using it or referring to it in one of these special types of sentence, and then we find that this word belongs to a class requiring some sort of distinctive treatment, which may even be the negative treatment of excluding that type of sentence. This distinctive treatment we may call the **reactance** of the category. ... A covert category may also be termed a **cryptotype**, a name which calls attention to the rather hidden, cryptic nature of such word-groups, especially when they are not strongly contrasted in idea, nor marked by frequently occurring reactances such as pronouns. They easily escape notice and may be hard to define, and yet may have profound influence on linguistic behaviour. ... Names of countries and cities in English form a cryptotype with the reactance that they are not referred to by personal pronouns as objects of the prepositions 'in, at, to, from'. We can say 'I live in Boston' but not 'That's Boston — I live in it'.

There are many examples of cryptotypes in this sense, both as classes and as systems (i.e., cryptoclasses and cryptosystems), in our ideational semantics. For example:

process types: doing & happening/ sensing/ saying/ being & having
transitivity model: ergative/ transitive
projections: locutions/ ideas
expansions: elaboration/ extension/ enhancement
number: plural/ non-plural; singular/ non-singular

The concept of **reactance** is particularly significant for our purposes where it involves a relationship between an ideational category and features of other metafunctions, interpersonal or textual. For instance, the interpersonal grammar provides for participants, within the ideational dimension of the clause, to function as Subjects; but this potential is not in general open to circumstances, and this is a principal reason for distinguishing these two classes within the ideational metafunction. Among reactances from the interpersonal and textual components of the grammar, we could mention the following:

interpersonal:

can/ cannot serve as Subject
can/ cannot serve as 'focus' of alternative question
can/ cannot serve as Wh element

<u>textual</u>:

can/ cannot serve as Theme

can/ cannot serve as 'focus' of theme predication (*it is ... that ...*)

can/ cannot be presumed by substitution/ ellipsis

(ii) The gateway to semantics is the **clause** rather than the word. Consequently, grammatical categories will typically be interpreted 'from above', within their context in the clause or the group, rather than 'from below' within their context in the word. This has rather far-reaching consequences for the understanding of the semantic systems realized by the grammar. Systems that are approached 'from above' in this way include:

projection — clause complex: traditionally a form of 'subordination' within clause; reinterpreted as distinction between hypotaxis in clause complex vs. rankshift in clause, laying the foundation for a semantic distinction between reports and facts.

transitivity — clause: traditionally a word category, transitive = verb taking object/ intransitive = verb not taking object; reinterpreted as (i) process types (material/ mental/ verbal/ relational) and (ii) an ergative system (middle/ effective) in the clause.

tense — group: traditionally a mixture, because the model was taken over from Latin with richer word-rank realizations than English, but more recently in this century often a word category, past/ non-past; reinterpreted (relative to this) as (i) past/ present/ future and (ii) recursive, with secondary tense.

Taking the clause as starting point facilitates the exploration of cryptotypes: the chain of realization often starts cryptotypically in the clause, whereas the final stages of realization at word and morpheme rank are more overt — although, as noted in connection with tense and number, the overt marking is seldom the only factor involved.

A functional grammatics thus allows us to approach semantics from a deeper and more wide-angled perspective. To this general property, *systemic* functional grammar adds another characteristic— its paradigmatic orientation (cf. Matthiessen, 1987, for a discussion of how the development of the semantic environment of a generation grammar can be based on paradigmatic choice). For instance, while more formally oriented accounts may approach transitivity patterns essentially in terms of sequences of grammatical classes such as 'nominal group + verb (+ nominal group)' and speak of classes of verb followed by one nominal group ('mono-transitive') or two nominal groups ('di-transitive'), a systemic grammar interprets such sequences in terms of systems of distinct and contrasting process types (see Halliday, 1985: Ch. 5; Davidse, 1991; Martin, 1996 a, b).

Section 2.11.5 in Chapter 2 below provides a summary of grammatical evidence for semantic types.

1.9 Ways of representing semantic organization

We have dealt with various theoretical aspects of the nature of meaning in the ideation base and we now turn to the final issue of our introduction, the question of how to represent our theoretical account of the organization of meaning in some representational system. In AI and computational linguistics, this is usually formulated as **knowledge representation**; from our complementary point of view, the task is one of **meaning representation**. For a systemic functional review of knowledge representation, see also Steiner (1991: Section 2.6.5).

Representation is, of course, an inherently semiotic phenomenon, and we can gain some insight into it by considering it first within language itself, before turning to representation in our own 'metalanguage' (see the beginning of Section 1.9.1 below). Meaning is realized stratally in two cycles (see Figure 1-1 above). We have noted that the first cycle, the realization in lexicogrammar, is natural, in the sense of being non-arbitrary: for example, the grammatical constituency structure of a clause provides a natural representation of the semantic configuration of a process, participants and circumstances. By attending to grammatical representations, we can thus learn a good deal about the more abstract organization of meaning at the higher stratum of semantics. We can learn about the different modes of meaning — logical, experiential, interpersonal, and textual — by exploring their different modes of representation in the grammar — chaining, constituency, prosody, and wave (see Halliday, 1979a; Matthiessen & Halliday, forthcoming). Grammar is thus a hybrid system for representing meaning in the sense of embodying different modes of representation; but it is this that allows it to maintain a natural relationship with respect to semantics, with each mode of representation realizing a different mode of meaning.

Grammatical representations are in turn represented in linguistic **expressions** — prototypically, in sounding. Here the relationship is more complex than it is between semantics and grammar, in that it is both natural and conventional. In the interpersonal and textual domains of content, it is often natural: thus interpersonal content tends to be represented prosodically by movements or variant levels in pitch, and textual content tends to be represented by prominence achieved phonologically (e.g. by the major pitch movement in an intonation contour) or sequentially (e.g. by using distance from initial position in the clause as a scale of prominence). In the ideational domain, the representation is usually conventional; but, even here there is a relationship of analogy, where we find in the sounding modes of organization similar to those of wording (and therefore of meaning). Systemically, we find that the system construes a phonetic space — notably the vowel space; and that this provides a model for semantic space.

Structurally, we find that sound is structured both as chains of segments (e.g. rhythmic units interpreted as syllable complexes) and as configurations of segmental constituents (e.g. syllables interpreted as configurations of phonemes).

The phonological representations are still abstract; they have to be manifested in bodily movements — in the ongoing movement of the parameters of the articulatory system. The sound system thus categorizes bodily processes; and in this respect, it is similar to the semantic system: both are ways of construing human experience. Meaning is thus represented by modes of organization that are similar to its own. This parallelism is even more foregrounded where the modality of expression is spatial, as in the Sign Languages of deaf communities (see Johnston, 1989; 1992 on AUSLAN). Here the domain of expression is a 4-dimensional signing space-time in a field of perception shared by signer and addressee (though clearly perceived from different angles). The spatial orientation and the shared perception increase the potential for iconicity in the expression; Johnston (1992) points out: "Despite an oral-aural language being suited to iconically encode sounds, the fact that our experience as a whole is visual, temporal and spatial means that a language which has itself visual and temporal resources for representation has greater means than an auditory one to map onto itself those very visual and spatial qualities of the world it wishes to represent." Johnston's insight into the power of representation embodied in Sign is central also to the general challenge of representation in metalanguage.

1.9.1 Stratification of metalanguage

We noted above that the semantics/ lexicogrammar of natural language is itself a 'realization' (an abstract construction) of daily experience. Likewise, the system we use to explore the semantics/ lexicogrammar — our theory of semantics and our grammatics — is a 'realization' of that part of daily experience that is constituted by semantics and lexicogrammar; that is, it is an abstract construction of language. This system is itself a semiotic one — a **metalanguage**; in Firth's more everyday terms, it is language turned back on itself (cf. Matthiessen & Nesbitt, 1996). So whereas a language is (from an ideational point of view) a resource for construing our experience of the world, a metalanguage is a resource for construing our experience of language.

Metalanguage has the same basic properties as any semiotic system. This means that it is stratified. It construes language in abstract **theoretical terms**; but this construal is in turn realized as some form of **representation** — either language itself, in discursive constructions of theory, or some form of designed semiotic (system networks, constituency rules, conceptual networks, logical formulae, and so on). In the environment of computational work, this level is in turn realized in some form of **implementation** (stated in a programming 'language' such as LISP, Prolog or C). We could summarize as follows (see Figure 1-7):

- metalanguage construes language at various strata (theoretical construal, representation, and implementation)

- metalanguage construes language in terms of resources (the circles) and processes using the resources (the arrows), where processes include description, deduction and compilation.

- the relationship between theoretical construal and representation should preferably be a natural one (note the 'should be'!), while the relationship between representation and implementation is likely to be more arbitrary (for instance, it should not matter whether LISP, Prolog or C is used).

- the range of phenomena accounted for in metalanguage tends to decrease at lower levels. (A primary goal of research is always to expand it.)

If we recognize stratification as an aspect of the design of metalanguage, we are in a position to locate aspects of the overall construal of meaning at the appropriate stratum. Early work on knowledge representation in the 1960s and 1970s tended not to make this stratal differentiation; it was under-differentiated from a meta-theoretical point of view. Responding to this situation, Brachman (1979) proposed a number of levels to separate out different aspects of the overall statement of knowledge. He identifies implementational, logical, epistemological, conceptual, and linguistic levels. While these are not all metalinguistic strata in our sense, it is still clear that he is concerned with the need to sort out different semiotic domains of generalization: the different 'levels' are subject to different kinds of tasks and constraints. Brachman's comments on the implementational level are worth noting:

> In implementation level networks, links are merely pointers, and nodes are simply destinations for links. These primitives make no important substantive claims about the structure of knowledge, since this level takes a network to be only a data structure out of which to build logical forms. While a useful data-organizing technique, this kind of network gives us no more hint about how to represent (factor) knowledge than do list structures.

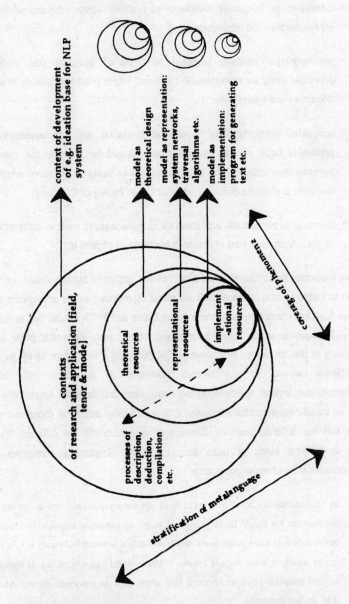

Fig. 1-7: The relationship between language and metalanguage

Thus any account of the ideation base has to be metalinguistically stratified. It has to be constructed as a **theoretical model** out of the resources the theory provides and according to the constraints imposed by these resources. From a systemic-functional point of view, this means that the ideation base is construed as a multidimensional, elastic semantic space. This space is organized as a meaning potential, with an extensive system of semantic alternatives; these alternatives are ordered in delicacy. Each set of alternatives is a cline in semantic space rather than a set of discrete categories, and any alternative may be constituted structurally as a configuration of semantic roles. The meaning potential is thus differentiated axially into (i) **systems of options** in meaning and (ii) **structural configurations** of roles by which these options are constituted.

The meaning potential itself is one pole on the dimension of instantiation: it is instantiated in the unfolding of text, with patterns of typical instantiation (specific domains of meaning) lying somewhere in between the potential and the instance. At the same time, this overall ideation base can be expanded by various semogenic strategies, among which we are foregrounding that of grammatical metaphor.

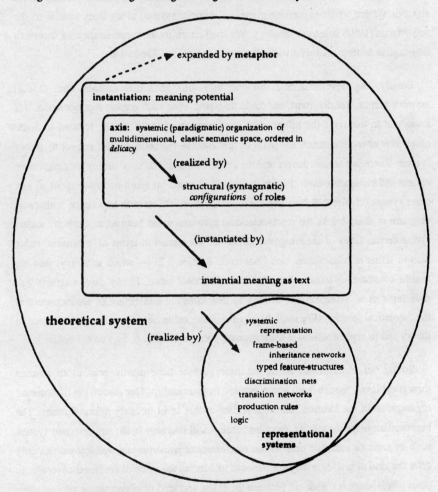

Fig. 1-8: Stratification in the account of the ideation base

The theoretical model makes considerable demands on the representational system or systems in which it is realized. Such a system must be able to handle the axial differentiation of the meaning base so that it represents not only structural configurations but also variation in delicacy, the indeterminacy between options in meaning, the move in instantiation from potential to instance, and other theoretical specifications. There are a considerable number of alternative representational systems, some of which we will refer to below. See Figure 1-8 above for a diagrammatic summary of the relationship between theory and representation in the construal of the ideation base.

As we have already noted, the representational semiotic may also be language itself — the theory may be represented discursively in the register(s) of linguistics. In this case, the relationship between theory and language is similar to the relationship between 'theme' and 'language' in Hasan's (1985/9) theory of verbal art — a relationship where theory might be construed as a connotative semiotic (in Hjelmslev's, 1943, conception: a semiotic system whose expression plane is a semiotic system) along lines similar to the way Martin (1992) construes ideology. We shall return to the representation of theory in language in another context towards the end of the book (Chapter 14).

Finally, the representational semiotic may also be a diagrammatic one — e.g. network graphs, tree diagrams, our circle diagrams. With such graphic representation, it is important to ask (i) if the information represented graphically can be restated in some other form of representation and (ii) if its realizational relationship with respect to theory is clear. There is a certain danger that the graphic representation is simply assumed to be natural and transparent even though it depends as much on semiotic conventions as any other system (cf. Kress & van Leeuwen, 1990, 1996).[13] Our own experience with circle diagrams is that, unless the representational convention has been made explicit, readers favour certain types of meaning: the circles are interpreted in terms of 'extension' rather than in terms of 'elaboration' (see Chapter 2, Section 2.2) — which is to say, they are read in constituency terms rather than in realizational terms. In any case, diagrams will only serve us as 'visualizations' as long as they construe a metaphor of abstract space at the theoretical stratum. (We shall discuss the relationship between metaphorical space in theory and its representation in diagrammatic form in Chapter 6, Section 6.7 below.)

So far our observations about the meaning base have mostly been at an abstract theoretical level, though with some graphic representations. Our discussion of semantic organization in the ideation base will remain at this level in fairly informal terms. The best metalanguage for talking about language is still language itself; any designed system such as logic or semantic nets whose mathematical properties are well-known can only offer the kind of precision they are intended to have at the price of restricted coverage. In other words, there is a trade-off between the extent and kind of observations we can make and the formality of the semiotic system used for the task. Moreover we consider it important to explore the domain of meaning substantially and in some detail before

---

[13] It has been noted in NLP that in the early days of semantic networks there were too many ways of using 'links' and 'nodes' (cf. Woods, 1975; also Brachman's, 1978, 1979, emphasis of the need to define networks algebraically).

judging what forms of representation are most suitable. And for certain aspects of the task it should be possible to use more than one form of representation. (The Penman Upper Model [see Bateman et al, 1990] derived from an early version of our ideation base was represented first in NIKL and then in LOOM, both frame-based inheritance networks; and O'Donnell, 1994, has now re-expressed this model in systemic form.)

At this point we shall briefly outline the major representational options, to wit:

(i) Logic (Section 1.9.2);

(ii) Discrimination networks (Section 1.9.3);

(iii) Componential analysis (Section 1.9.4);

(iv) Semantic nets, in particular frame-based inheritance networks (Section 1.9.5);

(v) Systemic representation (Section 1.9.6).

It is possible to use some kind of 'hybrid' representation; combinations of logic and semantic nets have been used in computational linguistics and AI, where they are seen to complement each other (e.g. KRYPTON [Brachman, Fikes & Levesque, 1983], KL-ONE [Brachman & Schmolze, 1985], NIKL, LOOM [Brill, 1990]). In this connection, natural language can itself be thought of as a 'hybrid' system of representation; we have already noted its hybrid nature in the modes of realization of the different metafunctions. The list above could also be extended: thus it would be relevant to consider feature structures, typed feature structures, and fuzzy logic. The 'typed feature structure' system, which is widely used in NLP, is not so much an alternative to the systemic representation, but rather an additional representational level that could be inserted between the theoretically informed systemic representation and the lower level of program code (cf. the work on representing systemic functional information in typed feature structures reported in Bateman & Momma, 1991). Fuzzy logic foregrounds the ideational indeterminacy that we shall be emphasizing throughout our account (cf. Zadeh, 1987; Sugeno, 1993).

The choice of representation will always depend on the task at hand. A particular task might foreground inferencing based on collections of 'instantial facts' in a data base; or it might foreground taxonomic organization and inferencing based on hyponymy (classification), and so on. Similarly, the need to analyse ideational meaning in text for educational purposes and the need to process ideational meaning in an NLP system will share certain demands on the representational system; but they will also make demands that point in fairly different directions, e.g. towards perspicuity on the one hand and towards automatic manipulation on the other.

1.9.2 Logic

Logic is attractive because its properties are well understood in terms of both formation-rules ('syntax') and interpretation ('semantics') and it can be used to support inferencing.

To take a trivial example, if one proposition implies another and the first is asserted, the second can be deduced:

$(p \rightarrow q) \& p \models q$

e.g. 'it's raining' -> 'the market is closed' & 'it's raining' $\models$ 'the market is closed'

However, there are a number of serious problems that have made it very hard to use logic as the only form of representation of the meaning base.

(1) We need a form of representation that can handle not only 'propositions' (propositional logic), their internal organization (predicate logic), and their temporalization and modalization (temporal and modal logic), but also paradigmatic organization, including taxonomic relations. Standard logic is not designed for the representation of taxonomies (cf. Samlowski, 1976). One type of logic, **sorted** logic, has been developed to represent taxonomic inheritance, with variables assigned to sorts or types; but it does not constitute a full-fledged representation of paradigmatic order.

(2) Logic operates with a very simple **ontology**: in standard logic, propositions (p, q, r etc.), truth functions (&, ->, ~ etc.), individual constants (a, b, c, etc.), variables (x, y, z, etc.), quantifiers, ($\forall$, $\exists$, $\exists$!, etc.) and predicates (F, G, etc.). These ontological categories are insufficient for the task of representing semantic organization (cf. Jackendoff, 1983: Ch. 3 and Section 4.1); for example, the truth functions cover a very small range of the spectrum of logical relations in natural language (cf. Chapter 3, Section 3.1 below), predicates fail to distinguish among things, qualities and processes, and it is not clear how circumstances can be accommodated.[14] It is possible to increase the power of logic e.g. by adding temporal, modal, and intensional components, or by allowing for nonmonotonic reasoning to handle unmarked cases and exceptions; but this is a slow process since the formal properties that are valued have to be retained. It has often been noted, of course, that logic falls far short of being able to represent linguistic theories of meaning; Simon Dik's (e.g. 1986, 1987) response has been to explore a functional logic that consists of a range of different sublogics reflecting the semantic diversity of language as a knowledge representation system.

---

[14] The problem with the ontology of logic arises primarily when logic is used as the first level of representation and semantic types are represented directly by logical ones, as was done in generative semantics, for example. However, a more indirect relationship can be constructed whereby there is no one-to-one correspondence between semantic types and logical ones. Thus using Prolog as the coding system at the level of programming does not impose its ontology on the ideation base. Here a 'line of arbitrariness' relative to the higher levels of organization is maintained. Compare Brachman's (1979) cautionary note: "A network implemented as some level should be *neutral* toward the level above it. For example, logical nets are "epistemologically neutral", in that they do not force any choice of epistemological primitives on the language user. Making "concepts" in logical nets, then, is a mixing of levels."

(3) From the point of view of language, logic misinterprets and displaces a number of semantic categories. We have referred to the lack of ontological distinctions, which also has undesirable consequences for semantic structure (see Jackendoff, 1983: Section 4.1), but in addition to this, logic merges determination and quantification so that their distinctive contribution to texture is obscured. Quantifier scope has the effect of scrambling semantic structure and so distorting its relationship to the grammar (cf. Keenan & Faltz, 1985). Moreover, the interpersonal resource of polarity (positive/ negative) is interpreted in terms of negation as a truth function. While this may be appropriate for statements (as opposed to other speech functions) in certain registers (viz. those concerned with deductive reasoning, where logic was first designed and is still used today), it is certainly not appropriate for language in general (see e.g. Givón, 1979: Ch. 3).

This last point about negation illustrates the general relationship between logic and language (a point to be taken up again in Chapter 3, Section 3.1). As a semiotic for reasoning, logic is registerially quite constrained: it operates under a number of contextual assumptions about valid reasoning. In contrast, language is a very general system; it can support many more types of reasoning in a wide range of different contexts. There is obviously a trade-off here between degree of axiomatization and generality. Logic has its own contexts of application; problems only set in when we try to use this designed and highly constrained semiotic to interpret an evolved and much less constrained semiotic system such as language. For a highly pertinent discussion of logic and natural language, see Ellis (1993).

To conclude the discussion of logic, we can try to identify the areas of language that have been the source of designed logical systems: see Table 1(1). Modern knowledge representations such as NIKL and LOOM tend to be hybrid systems just like language itself: they incorporate both logic and inheritance networks. As already noted above, these different subsystems are all integrated in natural language; as a knowledge representation system, natural language can be characterized as being 'hybrid' in the sense of being diversified into different modes of representation for different modes of meaning (knowledge) — and the same holds true of designed systems from the 1980s onwards.

1.9.3 Discrimination networks

In AI, discrimination networks have often been used to encode taxonomic distinctions, as in the example of discriminations in the area of sensing shown in Figure 1-9. The nature of the discriminations may vary from one node to another; but each discrimination network is a strict taxonomy.

Table 1(1): Lexicogrammatical systems giving rise to logical systems

	grammatical end	lexical end
logical	expansion — laws, rules of inferencing ==> the logical connectives of propositional logic (&, /, ⇔, ⇒); projection — propositional attitudes ==> intensional logic	
experiential	transitivity — predication ==> [i] the predicate-argument structures of predicate logic ((arg1, arg2 PREDICATE)); [ii] the frames of knowledge representation tense — temporal logic	lexical taxonomy — taxonomic organization of predicates ==> [i] taxonomies in early artificial languages; [ii] inheritance networks in modern AI/NLP
interpersonal	modality — judgement of truth value ==> [i] modal operators in modal logic (Np, Mp) [cf. also projection above]; [ii] partitions within networks	
textual	reference — constants vs. variables, quantification over variables ==> quantifiers in predicate logic (∀ ∃ ∃! ι).	

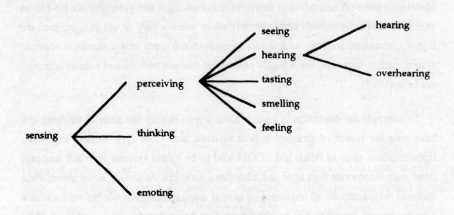

Fig. 1-9: Example of discrimination network

Strict taxonomies of this kind have, of course, a long history: it was this type of organization that Roget (1852) relied on in compiling his Thesaurus. One of its limitations is that words in natural language do not have a unique taxonomic location; Roget overcame this limitation by allowing any word to occur in any number of places. From the present point of view, strict taxonomies display two major drawbacks.

(1) They are one-dimensional; and while one-dimensional organization may suffice for certain domains, in the overall semantic system multi-dimensional organization is the norm.

(2) They only allow us to represent paradigmatic organization; but we need to be able to represent syntagmatic organization as well. (In a way, this is the reverse of the problem presented by logic; and as we shall see presently, hybrid forms of representation have been developed to combine taxonomy and logic.)

1.9.4 Componential analysis

Discrimination networks do not, then, provide the answer to our need. The problem of **multi-dimensional** organization in phonological systems was solved by the introduction of oppositions that can intersect (such as front/ back, open/ closed, and rounded/ unrounded for vowels); in Trubetzkoy's (1939) theory, the oppositions were treated as classificatory dimensions and the values as 'sound properties'. In the late 1940s, however, Roman Jakobson (1949) reinterpreted these properties as components or distinctive features of the phoneme (see e.g. Fischer-Jørgensen, 1975: 144-7); this was in effect a reification of the earlier sound properties. Phonemes were said to *consist of* components (just as longer phonological sequences consisted of phonemes) instead of being said to *realize* terms in phonological systemic oppositions. In other words, a paradigmatic abstraction (sound property in an opposition) was given a syntagmatic status (component of a phoneme). Jakobson's notion of component or distinctive feature was then taken over into generative phonology.

In the 1950s, componential analysis was developed by Goodenough (1956), Lounsbury (1956) and others as a model of semantic organization, particularly in the study of folk taxonomies. In the following decade, Katz and Fodor (1963) used semantic markers as components of meaning in dictionary definitions within a generative grammar.

In componential analysis semantic oppositions are treated in the same way as phonological ones. So just as rounding in a vowel system is characterized by means of two components, +rounded/ -rounded, and a vowel such as /i/ is said to consist of +high, + front & -rounded, so a semantic dimension such as sex is interpreted as +male/ -male and an item such as 'girl' is said to consist of -male, -adult & +human. This approach provides for multidimensional matrices — for example:

	+ male		- male	
+ adult		man	woman	
- adult		boy	girl	
	- human	+ human		

Components may be organized taxonomically; for instance, ±adult, ±male and ±human all presuppose +animate. Componential analysis has been applied to various domains such as kinship and cuisine.

A comprehensive critique of componential analysis has been provided by Wierzbicka (1975). Many of the problems with componential analysis arise from misinterpreting the 'components' as if they were *constituents* of some structure, rather than being *paradigms* of abstract features; or, if they are recognized as paradigmatic, from failing to organize them into networks of systems (cf. Leech, 1974). Without this step, a componential analysis remains "flat", in that it fails to construe any kind of multidimensional semantic space (cf. Chapter 2, Section 2.11.1 below).

1.9.5 Frame-based inheritance networks

In AI and computational linguistics, paradigmatic and syntagmatic organization are combined in current frame-based inheritance networks. The ancestor of these is the **semantic net** developed originally by R. Quillian in the 1960s. Quillian's model was a linguistic one — the dictionary. He constructed a network of nodes and relations; nodes represented word senses and relations were drawn from dictionary definitions, including 'is-a' (hyponymy or instantiation) and 'has-a' (meronymy). Apart from the greater definitional rigour achieved in subsequent networks, two later developments are particularly significant for our purposes:

> (i) nodes were given organization in the form of **frames** — configurations of roles with specifications of possible fillers of these roles ('value restrictions');

> (ii) the 'is-a' relation was given special status in the network, defined as a **subsumption** relation over nodes.

Together these two are essential aspects of a **frame-based inheritance network** such as KL-ONE, NIKL and LOOM (see e.g. papers in Brachman & Levesque, 1985, and Sowa, 1991). Concept frames at a given point in the subsumption hierarchy inherit any role information associated with concepts higher up the hierarchy. For instance, Figure 1-10 shows a fragment of the subsumption hierarchy of figures and elements. Certain concepts have roles associated with them — doing/ Actor; directed doing/ Goal; and spear/ Means. Since 'directed doing' is subsumed under (classified under) 'doing', it inherits the Actor role; and since 'spear' is subsumed under both 'directed doing' and 'doing', it inherits both the Actor and Goal roles. In addition, the possible class of filler is specified for each role as a value restriction. These are shown as pointers from the roles to other concepts in the subsumption hierarchy, in this case pointers to types of element.

Although the example in Figure 1-10 is a strict taxonomy, that is not a restriction imposed on networks used in e.g. NIKL and LOOM. Any concept may be subsumed by more than one other concept, co-inheriting their properties. Further, simultaneous distinctions are allowed; that is, it is easy to represent cross-classification. When two or

more concepts specify another concept, they may constitute a disjoint covering, which
means that their disjunction is exclusive.

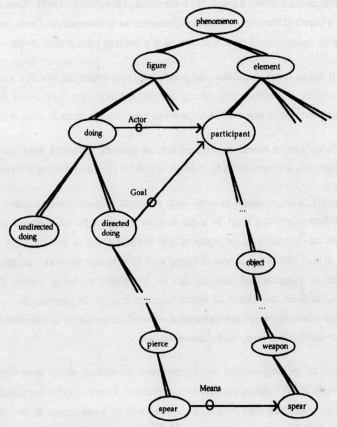

Fig. 1-10: Concept frames in subsumption hierarchy, supporting inheritance

1.9.6 Systemic representation

Representations within systemic theory have been designed to realize theoretical
abstractions such as the ones shown in Figure 1-8 above. But the design task has not
been completed; representations are still being explored so as to expand their coverage of
the theoretical resources. In general, explicit systemic representations lag behind systemic
theory (cf. Matthiessen, 1988a), particularly in certain areas such as that of grammatical
metaphor; but this is for a good reason. While the relationship between theory and
representation is a dialogic one, the stratum of theory is the domain where demands on
representation first develop and have to be sorted out relative to the overall theoretical
system.

Systemic representations include (i) system networks and (ii) realization statements.
(i) A **system network** is an acyclic directed graph, consisting of systems partially
ordered in delicacy (see e.g. Fawcett, 1984; Henrici, 1966; on the use of system networks

in semantics, see Halliday, 1973, 1984b; Hasan, 1989, 1996: Ch. 5); on formal and computational issues, cf. also Bateman & Momma, 1991; Patten & Ritchie, 1987; Kasper, 1988; Mellish, 1988; Brew (1991); Henschel, 1994; Teich, 1995). Each system constitutes a choice (alternation, opposition) between two or more terms. These terms are represented by features, and a system as a whole is a Boolean combination of features:

> (1) It has an **entry condition**, the condition under which the systemic choice is available. The entry condition may be a single feature or a complex of features, conjunct and/ or disjunct. These features must serve as terms in other systems.[15]

> (2) It has a set of **terms**, the options that are available given the entry condition. The terms are represented by features, which are related by exclusive disjunction.

Collectively, a set of related systems form a system network (since features in the entry conditions to systems must be terms in other systems). As an example, consider the systemic representation of the componential analysis given in Section 1.9.4 above: see Figure 1-11. (This is not a typical example of how system networks are deployed.) The features of componential analysis can be interpreted as being related through extension — they are the 'atoms' of which meanings consist. In contrast, the systemic interpretation relates them through elaboration — word meanings lie at the intersections of systemic values in an elastic multidimensional space.

Systems can be implemented or re-represented in various ways; apart from the implementation in the Penman system, we can mention Patten's (1988) implementation of systems as production rules (where one system will be implemented as two or more production rules), Kasper's (e.g. 1987) re-representation in terms of feature structures in Kay's (e.g. 1979) Functional Unification Grammar, Zeng's (1996) re-representation in terms of the frame-based inheritance system LOOM, and Bateman & Momma's (1991) re-representation in terms of Typed Feature Structures.

If we use systemic representation to encode information in the ideation base, we *factor out* the logic of subsumption and alternatives from the syntagmatic realization: this logic is represented in the system network. If each feature is interpreted as a type, this gives us a lattice of types. In European structuralist terms, the network is a representation of the paradigmatic organization of a linguistic system. However, it is also

---

[15] The exception is a special type of system, the **logical recursive system**. (The logical system and the kind of structure realizing its selection are the appropriate form of representation for sequences in the ideation base.) Non-logical systems are purely declarative — terms such as "choice" and "entry condition" do not imply a procedural interpretation; they merely indicate that the system network can be traversed. For the interpretation of logical recursive systems, see Bateman (1989). Recently, Zeng (1996) has developed a new kind of system, a **multiple-view system**, for representing different but comparable systemic organization across languages or semiotic systems.

necessary to show how feature choices are realized structurally; i.e., what are the structural properties of the types. This is the province of the realization statement.

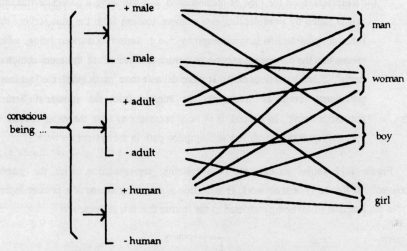

Fig. 1-11: Components re-interpreted as systemic terms

(ii) A **realization statement** is a minimal specification of a piece of structure or configuration of roles presented in a paradigmatic context; it is always associated with a particular systemic feature. For instance, the realization statement '+ Senser' occurs in the context of 'sensing' in the system of figures; it is the syntagmatic realization of that feature: a figure of sensing is a configuration of roles one of which is Senser.

The general form of a realization statement is 'realization operator + one or more realization operands', as in 'insert Senser' and 'conflate Medium and Senser'. The operators used to specify functional structuring are insert, conflate, and preselect. The first operand is always a semantic function (role); additional operands may be functions or features. The realization statements we will make use of in our representation of ideation base information are as follows:[16]

(1) **Presence** of functions in the structure: the presence of a function in a function structure is specified by **inserting** the function into the structure; the operation of insertion is symbolized by '+'; e.g. +Actor, +Senser, etc.

(2) **Conflation** of one function with another: one function from one perspective is conflated with a function from another perspective — they are identified with one another. Conflation is symbolized by '/'; for example, Medium/Senser

---

[16] The same set is used at the lexicogrammatical stratum, but two additional types are also needed: order and expand. See Matthiessen & Bateman (1991); Matthiessen & Halliday (forthc.).

means that Medium (ergative perspective) and Senser (transitive perspective) apply to the same element of a figure.

(3) **Restriction** on the type of phenomenon that can serve a particular function: this is stated by **preselecting** one or more features from the unit serving that function; preselection is symbolized by ':', e.g. Senser: conscious being, which means that the participant serving as Senser is restricted to the type 'conscious being'. (Since 'conscious being' is more delicate than 'participant', the fact that a participant serves as Senser can be inferred from the statement 'Senser: conscious being'. In general, it is only necessary to state the most delicate or specific restriction along any subsumption path in the system network.)

Figure 1-12 shows an example of a systemic representation, with the graphic conventions for the system network. Preselection is shown by means of a pointer leading from the function (role) being restricted to the feature that it is restricted to.

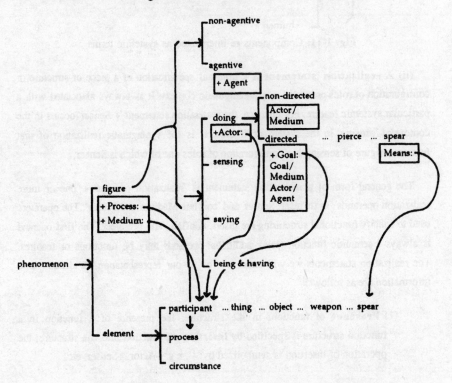

Fig. 1-12: Example of systemic representation, graphic mode

The example is basically the same as we used to illustrate the frame-based inheritance network in Figure 1-10 above. As the two examples illustrate, there is a basic similarity between frame-based inheritance networks and system networks, in their common concern with types and subtypes. These types are related by Boolean operators: a given type may be a subtype of a single type, a conjunction of other types or a disjunction of other types. Types are distinguished in terms of structural properties: each type will typically have some structural consequence, in specifying some aspect of a configuration of roles (functions, slots). Each role may in turn be restricted as to what type can serve that role (value restriction, preselection). Table 1(2) below summarizes how this general organization is manifested (1) in frame-based inheritance networks used for representing 'knowledge' and (2) in system networks used for representing lexical and grammatical information.

Table 1(2): Frame-based inheritance networks and systemic representation

	frame-based inheritance network	**systemic representation**
basic notation	frame-based inheritance network	system network
nodes	concept frames (with roles)	features (with associated realization statements)
network logic	Boolean — classes	Boolean — systems (with input & output features)
relation between node and structure specification	identical (with a concept frame as node)	feature — realized by specifications of contributions to structure

unit:
    structure
	concept frame:
	    configuration of roles
		semantic unit:
		    configuration of functions

role restriction	value restriction of role fillers	preselection of functions

The example in Figure 1-12 is a representation of a fragment of the ideational potential. However, given the summary of the theoretical account of the ideation base at the beginning of this section (cf. Figure 1-8), there are additional representational challenges. We shall mention four such challenges briefly here.

(i) The first representational challenge is the need to handle the dimension of **instantiation**. As a process, instantiation can be represented as involving traversal of the system network and activation of realization statements (cf. Matthiessen & Bateman, 1991: Section 6.5, on the grammatical generation algorithm). The instance is thus a set of features (semantic types) selected, with associated realizational specifications — an instantial pattern over the semantic potential. However, instantiation also defines a scale between the potential and the instance, with intermediate patterns of instantiation. We will introduce these later as register-specific domain models (see Chapter 8). Such patterns of instantiation will need to be represented: perhaps as systemic probabilities, or as domain-partitions within the overall ideation base (cf. Matthiessen, 1993b, for some discussion).

(ii) The second representational challenge is the need to model how the overall ideation base is expanded by **grammatical metaphor**. It must be shown how metaphor adds junctional types to the ordinary types illustrated in Figure 1-12. We shall not solve this representational problem in the present book; but we shall suggest ways of thinking about it (see Section 6.8).

(iii) The third representational challenge comes from outside the account of the ideation base itself: the ideation base has to be related to the **other metafunctional modes of meaning**, the interaction base and the text base. The interaction base will include alternative 'projections' of the ideation base to account for the relationship between speaker and addressee. We shall not attempt to take up this particular challenge; the text base is discussed briefly in Chapter 9, Section 9.3 below.

(iv) The fourth representational challenge concerns the **non-discreteness** of the various systems that construe semantic space (see Chapter 13, Section 13.3). The semantic types represented by the features of systems in the system network do not constitute discrete Aristotelian categories; they are values on semantic clines (cf. Halliday, 1961) — core regions, to use the metaphor of semantic space. We can bring this out by adopting a topological view on meaning (cf. Martin & Matthiessen, 1991); we can also explore the possibility of interpreting features as names of fuzzy sets (cf. Matthiessen, 1995a).

In what follows we shall use mainly the systemic form of representation, although it will be helpful at points to refer to frame-based inheritance networks. Our representational practice is informal; the representations would be defined formally if required to support various operations such as inference of inherited properties. We should also emphasize again that representation is at one stratal move below theoretical specification; while it takes us closer to a form of specification that can be implemented in an NLP system, the total coverage decreases. There are various types of theoretical information that can be stated in terms of language or a diagrammatic representation but which we do not yet know how to represent in terms explicit enough to be implemented in a computational system. One instance that arises at various points in our discussion is that of topological specifications and the related notion of clines (scales) between types. It is thus essential to construe our interpretation of the ideation base multi-stratally: representation at any single level is bound to be partial, and will be so whichever type of representation we choose to deploy. But this is not an undesirable state: the theory should always push towards the expansion of the representational resources.

1.10 Organization of the remainder of the book

Here in Part I, we have now introduced the major themes of our book: the notion of a meaning base and the approach to it from grammar. We shall elaborate on these as follows in Parts II through V.

II. The meaning base: We begin by presenting an overview of our description of the meaning base. We then discuss the major semantic categories — sequences, figures and elements — in more detail, and explore the semantics of grammatical metaphor. After our description of the ideational semantics of English, we turn to Chinese to identify the major similarities and differences.

III. The meaning base as a resource in text generation: Next, we show how the meaning base can be used as a resource in a language processing system, particularly in a text generation system. First we discuss how two particular 'domains' can be modelled in the terms introduced in Part II. Then we locate the meaning base in the overall organization of a text generation system, discussing for example how it interacts with the grammar.

IV. Theoretical and descriptive alternatives: After having presented the details of the meaning base and shown how it can be used, we compare and contrast certain key points with other approaches within linguistics and computational linguistics, in theoretical as well as descriptive terms.

V. Language and the construal of experience: In the final part, we take our account of the meaning base as the basis for a discussion of the role of language in the construal of experience. We look at how children learn about the world — how their 'world view' expands and changes as their linguistic resources develop.

Part II:

The ideation base

2. Overview of the general ideational potential

In this second part of the book, we shall describe the ideation base — how the phenomena of our experience are construed as categories and relationships of meaning. Our primary concern here is descriptive rather than theoretical or representational; but, at the same time, theory and representation have to be grounded in a comprehensive description if they are to account for the full range of meanings in the meaning base. The descriptive scope of our account is essentially the most general part of the ideation base potential (cf. Chapter 1, Section 1.4); Figure 1-5 showed how this relates to the overall ideation base. In Chapter 8, we shall then illustrate how domain models can be developed and related to the general potential.

We shall present the meaning base first in summary fashion, in the form of a system network accompanied by a brief explanation and exemplification. This will include an initial account of grammatical metaphor as this is interpreted in the systemic model, showing how it may be formally defined by reference to the systemic organization. For greater clarity, the system network is introduced and built up in a number of steps, allowing for a brief commentary to be inserted at each step.

2.1 Phenomena

A phenomenon is the most general experiential category — anything that can be construed as part of human experience. The phenomena of experience are of three orders of complexity: elementary (a single **element**), configurational (configuration of elements, i.e. a **figure**) and complex (a complex of figures, i.e. a **sequence**) — see Plate 1.

While figures are said to consist of elements and sequences are said to consist of figures, the 'consist-of' relation is not the same: elements are **constituent** parts of figures, functioning in different roles; but figures form sequences through **interdependency** relations. We will return to these different types of organization below. The *typical* representation of sequences, figures and elements in the **grammar** is as in Figure 2-1.

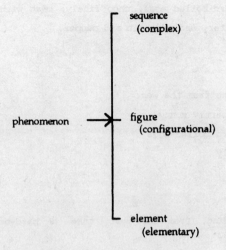

Plate 1: Types of phenomenon

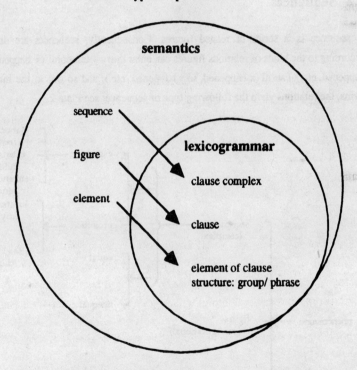

Fig. 2-1: Typical realization of sequences, figures and elements

Examples:

sequences —

```
Rain ending from the west, becoming partly sunny.
```

```
Take 8 hard-boiled eggs, chop finely, mash with 3 tablespoons of
   soft butter, and add salt and pepper.
```

figures —

```
rain ending from the west
becoming partly sunny
take 8 hard-boiled eggs
chop finely
```

elements —

```
rain, ending, from the west, take, 8 hard-boiled eggs, chop,
finely
```

2.2 Sequences

A sequence is a series of related figures. Consequently, sequences are differentiated according to the kinds of relations figures can enter into — temporal (x happened, then y happened, etc.), causal (x happened, so y happened, etc.), and so on; in the most general terms, the relations yield the following type of sequence: see Plate 2.

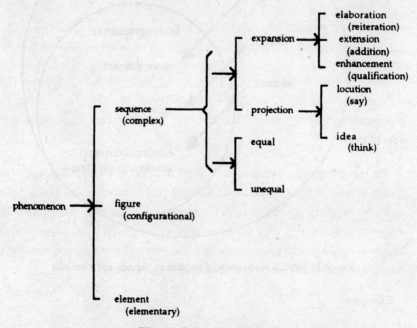

Plate 2: Types of sequence

In any pair of figures related in sequence, one figure may (i) expand the other, by reiterating it, adding to it or qualifying it; or (ii) project (report, quote) the other by saying it or thinking it. In either case, the two may be either equal or unequal in status, or semantic weight. Some examples:

(1) expansion: add & unequal

```
The heat wave in the    although northern Florida
Southwest will weaken   will remain hot.
slightly,
```

(2) expansion: add & equal

```
Highs will be mid-80s to           but parts of Texas could
mid-90s,                           reach the 100s.
```

(3) expansion: reiterate & unequal

```
The rest of the South will         with only isolated showers
be mostly dry and sunny,           in Florida.
```

Sequences are organized by interdependency relations and they are indefinitely expandable. Consider the following two examples, which are substeps in procedures:

```
If the rotor is not pointing to the mark, pull the distributor
part way out, turn the rotor some, and reinsert the distributor
until the rotor points to within a half inch of the mark.

Add the remaining ingredients, stir to coat the chicken well and
continue until a thick sauce has formed and the chicken is tender.
```

These procedures illustrate the 'logic' of the organization of sequences. The organization of the second sequence can be diagrammed as in Figure 2-2. The interdependency relations linking the units in the chain are marked by arrows between pairs of links.

The phenomenon diagrammed in the figure is organized as a temporal sequence ('and [then]') of three process configurations, 'add', 'stir', and 'continue to stir', two of which are further expanded, one purposively ('[in order] to') the other temporally ('until'). The temporally related unit is itself an additive sequence ('and [also]'). The sequence might have been expanded further, since it is organized as a chain of interdependent units; and in this respect it contrasts with the configuration in Fig. 2-4a below.

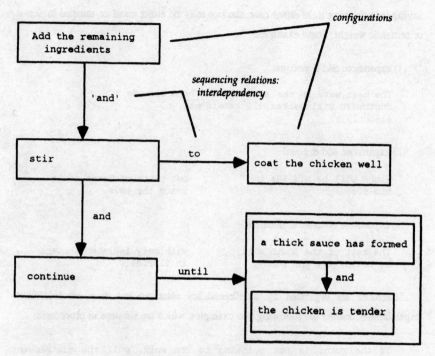

Fig. 2-2: Representation of a sequence

2.3 Figures

A figure is a representation of experience in the form of a configuration, consisting of a process, participants taking part in this process and associated circumstances. There are, of course, indefinitely many kinds of process in the non-semiotic world; but these are construed semiotically, according to the way in which they configure participants, into a small number of process types — being, doing, sensing, and saying. The first three of these have clearly defined subcategories: see Plate 3.

Then, each figure may be either projected (by another figure, or in some other way) or else not; and if projected, it may be an idea or locution or something else — but that 'something else' embodies grammatical metaphor and will be discussed later on. Examples:

(1) (being: ascribing) & non-projected

Rain and thunderstorms will extend today from New England to the upper lake region and North Dakota.

Morning skies will be partly cloudy today.

The taste is very pleasant and salty and it has a high iron content.

(2) (sensing: thinking) & non-projected

Cloudy skies are forecast today for the New York metropolitan
area.

Variable cloudiness is expected tomorrow.

(3) (doing: doing (to)) & non-projected

A warm front may bring scattered showers or thunderstorms to the
northern Tennessee Valley.

Rain will fall in the North West.

Melt the butter in a saucepan and add the onion.

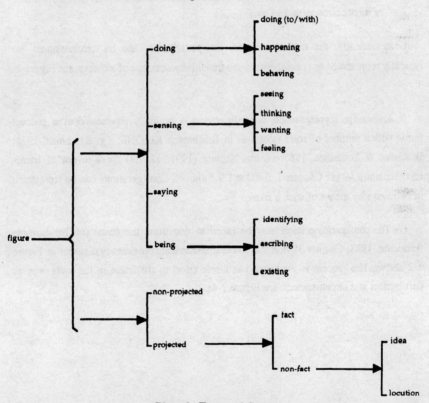

Plate 3: Types of figure

The principle of organization of a figure is different from that of a sequence. As we
have seen, a sequence is constructed by interdependency relations of expansion and
projection. In contrast, a figure is constructed as an organic configuration of parts. Each
part stands in a specific relation to the figure as a whole. The parts of a given
configuration are (i) a nuclear process, (ii) one to three participants of different kinds

taking part in the process, and (iii) up to around seven circumstances of different kinds associated with it.[1]

Participants are inherent in the process; they bring about its occurrence or mediate it. There are a number of specific ways in which a participant may take part in a process; it may act out the process, it may sense it, it may receive it, it may be affected by it, it may say it, and so on. The different configurations of participants are the bases for a typology of process types. The distinction between participants and circumstances is a cline rather than a sharp division, but it is semantically quite significant.

Circumstances are typically less closely associated with the process and are usually not inherent in it. They specify the spatial or temporal location of the process, its extent in space or time (distance or duration), its cause, the manner of its occurrence, and so on.

Grammatically, the nuclear process, its participants, and its circumstances are typically represented as constituents in the transitivity structure of a clause: see Figure 2-3.

In knowledge representation, a configuration is typically represented as a concept frame with a number of roles (slots; as in Brachman's KL-ONE; e.g. Brachman, 1978; Brachman & Schmolze, 1985; cf. also Steiner (1991: 121-31) for a review of frame-representation — see Chapter 1, Section 1.9.5 above). Configurations can be represented in two ways by means of such a frame.

(i) The configuration itself may be taken to constitute the frame (cf. for example Anderson, 1983: Chapter 3), much as in the grammatical constituency diagram in Figure 1-2 above. The process is represented as a role (slot) in the frame in the same way as participants and circumstances: see Figure 2-4a.

---

[1] Both participants and circumstances have been discussed extensively in terms of (deep) cases in linguistics and computational linguistics, but usually without a distinction between the two. The process is typically not given a deep case.

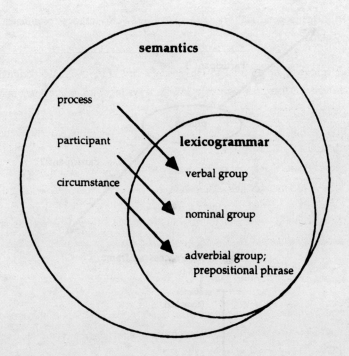

Fig. 2-3: Typical realization of processes, participants and circumstances

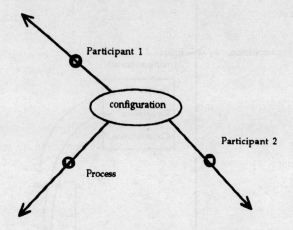

Fig. 2-4a: Configuration as frame

(ii) Alternatively, the process part of the configuration can be treated as the frame itself, rather than as one of the roles of the frame: see Figure 2-4b.

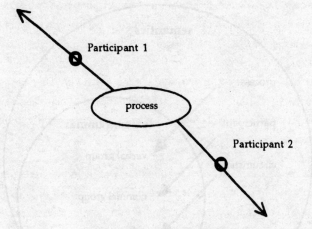

Fig. 2-4b: Process as frame

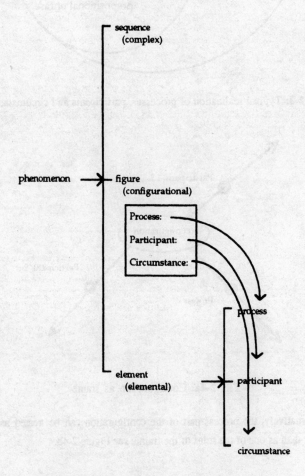

Fig. 2-5: Figure with role types and role fillers

In either case, the roles have restrictions on what semantic types they can be realized by — so-called "value restrictions". These restrictions are themselves types from other parts of the semantic taxonomy not included in the figure. The two representations make different claims about a configuration. In particular, the first approach allows the process to be a role that is filled by another concept frame which may have its own internal organization. As we will see, the process part of a configuration may indeed have internal organization. At the same time, the second approach is simpler and it may be sufficient for many purposes.

If we use the first approach, we can see that a configurational frame is made up of three kinds of roles, (i) the process role, (ii) participant roles, and (iii) circumstance roles. Each type has a default filler from the hierarchy of simple phenomena, respectively processes, participants, and circumstances: see Figure 2-5 above.

As already mentioned, there is a typology of figures based largely on the nature of the particular types of the process, participant, and circumstance roles; the most general part of this is shown in Figure 2-6. Each type of figure has its own set of more delicately specified roles with particular value restrictions. For example, figures of doing have an Actor, which in turn is a participant (rather than some other kind of phenomenon). (Notice that the specification of the filler of the Phenomenon role in a sensing figure is more general than 'participant' — any type of phenomenon can be sensed: see Chapter 4, Section 4.2.1.1.)

Table 2(1): Participant roles and their fillers for figures of three types

figure	roles	most general semantic type serving in role			project-ions
		phenomenon:	**participant:**	**conscious being**	
doing	Actor	figure (non-projected — act)	participant		
	Goal		participant		
	Recipient		participant:	often conscious	
saying	Sayer		participant: symbol source (= semiotic thing / ...	... conscious being)	
	Receiver		participant:	often conscious being	
	Verbiage		participant: generic or speech-functional name of saying		locution
sensing	Senser		participant:	conscious being	
	Phenom-enon	phenomenon:	participant / figure (projected — fact / non-projected — act)		idea

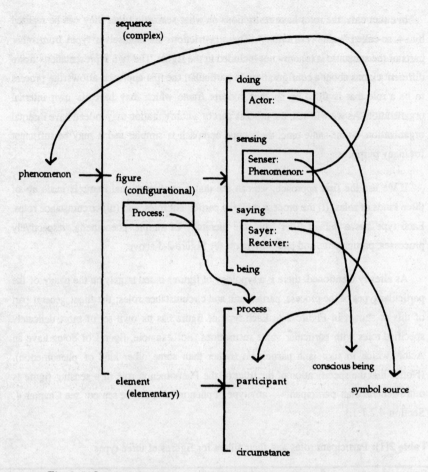

Fig. 2-6: Subtypes of figures and the participant role value restrictions

The role restrictions for sensing, saying, and doing are summarized in Table 2(1) below. These role restrictions represent a kind of metaphysics of English transitivity. For example, according to English, ideas and locutions cannot act on things, but there is no general restriction on what kinds of *things* may act on other things. Not only persons, but also inanimate things and abstractions may kill people (a figure of doing): *the rifleman/ the rock/ his stupidity killed cousin Henry.* In contrast, if we had built our model according to the demands of the transitivity grammar of Navajo, we would have had to rank things in terms of their capacity to act upon other things; e.g., an inanimate cannot act upon an animate thing (Witherspoon, 1977).

2.4 Elements

As we have seen, elements fill the roles of figures. Participant roles are filled by participants (things or qualities), circumstance roles by circumstances (times, places, causes, etc.), and the process role by a process. There are correlations here between the taxonomy of configurational phenomena and that of simple phenomena: Table 2(1) above summarizes the value restrictions on the fillers of the different participant roles of the four process types. The elements of a figure are of three kinds: (i) the **process** itself (action/event, process of consciousness, or relation), (ii) a **participant** in that process, or (iii) a circumstantial element or **circumstance**. Example:

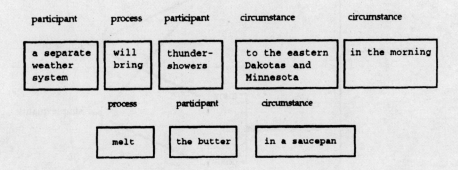

As already noted above, processes are realized by verbal groups, participants by nominal groups, and circumstances by adverbial groups or prepositional phrases. In addition to the three types of element that serve in figures, there is one further type of element — the **relator**: see Plate 4. Relators serve to construe logico-semantic relations of expansion between figures in a sequence (cf. Chapter 3, Section 3.4); they are realized by conjunction groups. We shall discuss them briefly in Chapter 5, Section 5.1, and then again in the context of grammatical metaphor in Chapter 6.

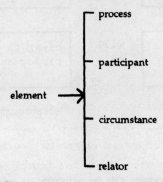

Plate 4: Types of element

2.5 Participants

Participant roles in figures are filled by elements of the type 'participant'; they are phenomena capable of taking on a participant role in a process configuration, e.g. bringing it about or being affected by it. They are further differentiated according to two parameters: see Plate 5.

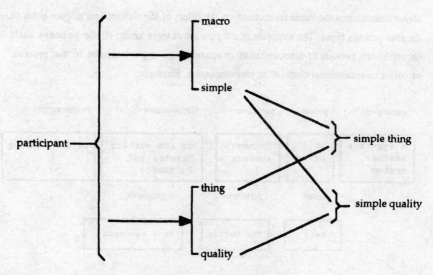

Plate 5: Participants

Macro-participants are all metaphorical and will be left out of consideration for the time being. Simple participants may be things or qualities; for example,

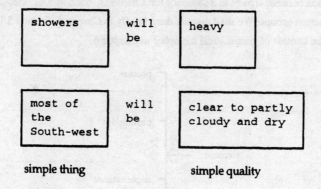

2.6 Simple things

Some 'simple things' are metaphorical; the remainder are referred to as 'ordinary', and these are either conscious or non-conscious (this is the distinction that is actually made in the semantic system, not animate/inanimate or human/non-human): see Plate 6.

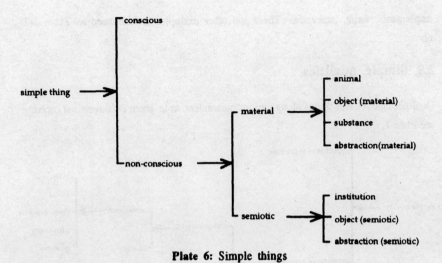

Plate 6: Simple things

Table 2(2): Examples of participants

	general	meteorological	culinary
conscious	person, man, woman, boy, girl, baby		cook ['you']
material: animal: higher	horse, stallion, mare, foal; dog, bitch, puppy		[only as ingredients]
material: animal: lower	ant, butterfly, slug		
material: object	house, rock, car, hammer	scattered clouds	[ingredients:] potato, onion, stem, root, [implements:] knife, pan
material: substance	water, air, tea, sand	air, cloud, sunshine	[ingredients:] fat, sugar, purée
material: abstraction	history, mathematics	a slow-moving weather system	heat, taste, colour
semiotic: institution	government, school	weather bureau	
semiotic: object	book, document, report, film, picture, painting, symbol	forecast	recipe
semiotic: abstraction	notion, idea, fact, principle	chance	

Non-conscious ordinary things are distinguished along more than one dimension, but the categorization given here can be taken as primary, in the sense that it is the one that seems to have the clearest reactances in the grammar.

Most of the participants in the meteorological texts are in fact metaphorical; but there are a few which illustrate these categories: *a slow-moving weather system* (abstraction), *ice* (substance), *scattered clouds* (object), *weather bureau* (institution). In contrast, most of the participants in the culinary texts are non-metaphorical (we refer to this as **congruent**). They are concrete objects and substances that can be chopped, added, sprinkled, and poured: *vegetable fat, sugar, purée, spinach, stems;* or used as implements: *knife, saucepan*. These and other examples are tabulated in Table 2(2) above.

2.7 Simple qualities

Qualities characterize things along various parameters, as in *green cabbage : red cabbage*: see Plate 7.

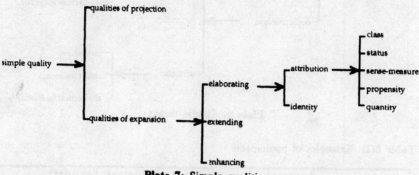

Plate 7: Simple qualities

Again, a number of simple qualities are metaphorical; of the remainder, the "ordinary" qualities, one subtype is qualities of projection and the other is qualities of expansion. (As we will show in subsequent chapters, the categories of projection and expansion are very prevalent in the organization of the ideation base. We discuss their application to qualities in Chapter 5, Section 5.3.3.2 below.) Examples from the weather report texts: *likely* in *rain is likely* (qualities of projection); *hot, humid, sunny, dry* (qualities of expansion: sense-measure); *one to three inches of [rain]* (qualities of expansion: quantity); *metropolitan* (qualities of expansion: class); *high [pressure]* (qualities of expansion: sense-measure [abstract]). These examples and others are tabulated in Table 2(3).

Table 2(3): Examples of qualities

				general	meteor-ological	culin-ary
qualities of projection				happy, angry; likely, certain	likely	
qualities of expansion	elaborat-ing	identity		similar, different		
		attribut-ion	class	wooden, stone, medieval, urban, rural	metropol-itan	
			status	dead, alive; male, female		
			sense-measure	heavy, light; green, red, blue; soft, hard; rough, smooth; loud, quiet	hot, humid, sunny, dry	brown, soft
			propens-ity	difficult, naughty, helpful		
			quantity	few, many; one, two		one, two
	extend-ing			additional, alternative, contrasting		
	enhanc-ing			previous, subsequent; interior, external		

2.8 Circumstances

Circumstances fill circumstantial roles in figures. We can recognize two simultaneous distinctions; see Plate 8. One concerns the type of circumstantial relation construed; the primary contrast is between circumstances of projection and circumstances of expansion and within the latter we distinguish those of elaboration, extension and enhancement. The other concerns the experiential complexity of the circumstance; circumstances are either 'simple' or 'macro', the former being more truly elemental while the latter are more like figures. We shall discuss these distinctions in Chapter 5, Section 5.5 below and just mention a few common types here.

Among simple circumstances, the most usual are those of time, place, manner-quality and intensity, all of which are circumstances of enhancement. Examples: *[skies will be partly cloudy] today* (locative: time), *increasingly* (manner: intensity), *widespread* (locative: place), *easily, carefully* (manner: quality).

Macro circumstances are those which are made up of a special type of figure having another participant inside it, for example (circumstances of enhancement): (locative: place [abstract]) *in the low to mid 60s,* (locative: place) *from the northeast,* (manner: quality) *at 15 to 25 m.p.h.,* (locative: place) *throughout the northern Rockies,* (locative: place) *in a casserole,* (locative: place) *in a hot oven,* (extent: duration) *for 10-15 minutes,* (manner: means)*with a clean absorbent cloth.*

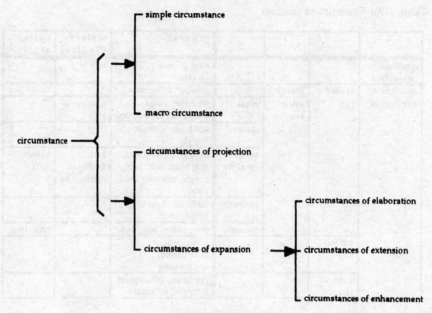

Plate 8: Circumstances

2.9 Processes

Processes serve in the most central or nuclear role in a figure; they embody the temporal properties of a figure unfolding in time: see Plate 9. Other than metaphorical processes, the process element is either polar (positive/negative) or modal (some intermediate degree between positive and negative); it may embody phase, or aspect; and it will refer to past, present or future time. Polarity and modality derive from the interpersonal perspective on the process.

Examples from the meteorological texts: *[yesterday] was [sunny]* (past polar); *[skies] will be [clear tonight]* (future polar); *[scattered showers] may develop [south west]* (future modal); *[temperatures] are expected to be [in the high 80s]* (present polar phasal); *[coastal sections] could get [an inch or more of rain]* (future modal).

Examples from the culinary texts: *[this soup] comes [from Northern Thailand]* (present polar); *simmer [for 15 minutes]* (polar), *continue to boil* (polar phasal); *continue cooking and stirring [for 15 minutes]* (polar phasal); *[they] will not require [any further cooking]* (future polar).

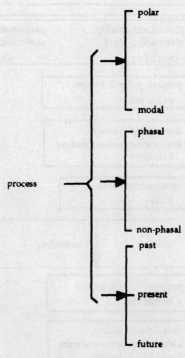

Plate 9: Processes

2.10 Summary

Plate 10 below shows the lattice as described up to this point, incorporating all the categories introduced above (but still omitting those embodying any grammatical metaphor). Here is an example of a meteorological text interpreted in terms of the semantic features presented so far (see Figure 2-7).

```
New York Area
Morning skies will be partly cloudy today, becoming
partly sunny by afternoon. High temperatures will be in the
low 70s. Skies will be clear tonight. Low temperatures will be in
the middle 50s.
```

We interpret the first sentence (in bold) as a sequence of two figures; they are related by an extending relation (shown by the arrow in the diagram in Figure 2-7). Both are figures of 'being'; sensory qualities ('cloudy', 'sunny') are ascribed. The first figure consists of four elements (whose features are shown in boxes): one process, two participants and one circumstance. The second figure consists of three elements: one process, one participant and one circumstance.

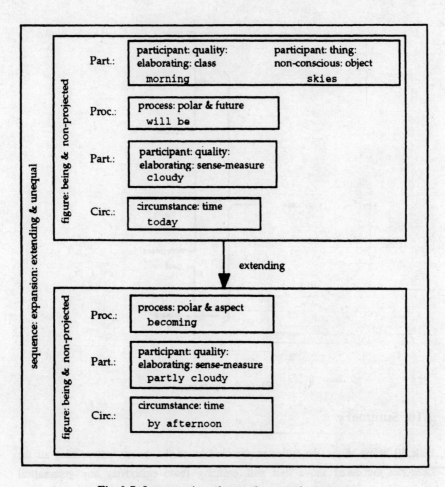

Fig. 2-7: Interpretation of part of meteorological text

2.11 Construing experience in the ideation base

We have presented an initial sketch of the ideation base as a resource for construing our experience of the world around us and inside us. The focus of this sketch was the most general system of semantic types such as 'figure', 'being-&-having', 'participant', 'conscious being'. These semantic types are categories to which phenomenological instances are ascribed; they thus embody the fundamental principle of generalizing across individual phenomenological variation. And they are located somewhere in delicacy between the most general type, the all-inclusive class of 'phenomenon', and the most delicate types we can recognize as being codified lexically in English.

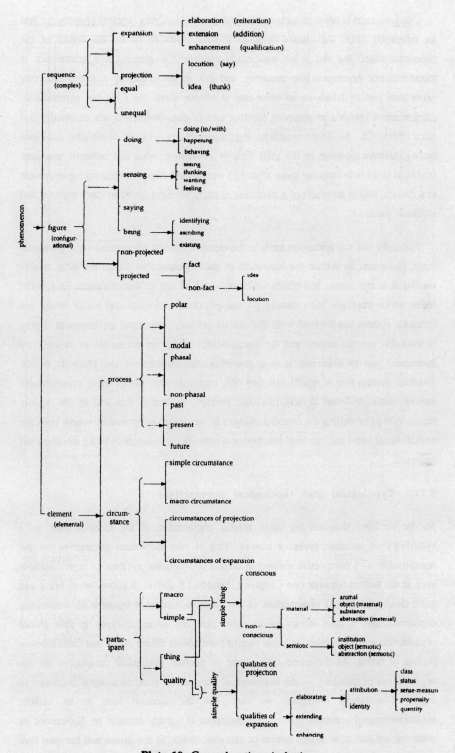

Plate 10: General options in lattice

Categorization is often thought of as a process of classifying together phenomena that are inherently alike, the classes being as it were given to us by the nature of the experience itself. But this is not what really happens. Categorizing is a creative act: it transforms our experience into meaning, and this means imposing a categorical order rather than putting labels on an order that is already there. As Ellis has expressed it, categorization consists in grouping together sets of phenomena that are essentially not alike (1993: Ch. 3). There would be indefinitely many ways of construing analogies among different elements in the total flux of experience; what our semantic resources enable us to do is to construe those analogies which yield categories resonating with what as a species, and as members of a particular culture, we have found to carry material and symbolic value.

Naturally our categorization tends to be oriented towards phenomena on a particular scale, those that lie within the bandwidth of those phenomena which are most readily accessible to our senses and which we engage with in day to day existence. This is the realm which impinges most closely on our physical, biological and social being; the semantic system has evolved with this as its primary semogenic environment. Lying beyond this are the micro- and the macro-worlds which are accessible to us only by instrument and by inference. It is a powerful demonstration of the potential of the semantic system that it readily fashions new meanings that model these experientially remote domains. What is less obvious, perhaps, is that it has had to be equally resourceful in modelling the ongoing changes in our social environment, where both the overall social order and our local interpersonal networks are constantly being modified and realigned.

2.11.1 Typological and topological perspectives

So far we have sketched the most general organization of the ideation base as a **typology** of semantic types or classes. This is one theoretical perspective on the organization — a perspective realized in certain conventional systems of representation, such as the system network (see Chapter 1, Section 1.9 above). It allows us to bring out quite clearly the global organization of the ideation base as a resource for construing experience; and it also allows us to show how the semantic types in this global organization are interrelated, as in the case of participants filling Actor and Goal roles in figures of doing. At the same time, there is another theoretical perspective on the organization of meaning — the **topological** perspective. Here meaning is construed in terms of a spatial metaphor: we can view the ideation base as an elastic, multidimensional semantic space. This metaphor is already familiar in discussions of meaning; we find it in Trier's notion of semantic fields, in the distinction between core meanings and more peripheral meanings, in specifications of semantic distance, and so on.

The notion of a vowel space (with its 'cardinal vowels') provides a familiar analogy. As a material construction, it is limited to the three dimensions of physical space; but as a physiological space, it accommodates variation along a number of dimensions, and brings an elasticity to the expression plane that is in some extent analogous to the metaphorical elasticity that we are ascribing to the plane of the content.

We shall relate typology and topology to one another as *complementary* perspectives on meaning, and then we shall say a few words about the value of keeping the topological perspective in view. Let us start with our analogy from the expression plane: a vowel system can be construed both typologically as a set of systems, e.g. two systems 'front/ back' & 'open/ closed' defining four vowel values, and topologically as a two-dimensional space with four focal (core, cardinal vowel) locations. These two perspectives are related to one another in Figure 2-8. Each system in the typology corresponds to a dimension in the topology. We can thus say that the two simultaneous systems correspond to a two-dimensional space. The systemic terms, or values, correspond to regions within the vowel space along one of its dimensions; an intersection of two systemic terms such as 'front' & 'open' is a region located along two dimensions. If we add further systems in the typology, e.g. rounding ('rounded/ unrounded'), nasality ('nasal/ non-nasal') and tongue root position ('neutral position/ advanced position'), these will correspond to further dimensions in the vowel space. With tongue root position we are still maintaining a reasonably congruent relationship between our representation of the vowel space and the oral cavity in which vowels are articulated, since advanced tongue root position is simply a global shift of the whole space; but with nasality we are beginning to use our representation more metaphorically, since the control of airflow through the nose is not a feature of the oral cavity.

We can now consider a comparable example from the content plane of language — from the ideation base. In our description of sequences, we recognized two simultaneous systems: the relative status of the figures ('equal/ unequal') and the kind of relationship between them ('projecting/ expanding'). This account constitutes the typological perspective on this region of the ideation base; it is mapped onto the topological perspective in Figure 2-9. Sequences are thus construed as a two-dimensional region within the overall semantic space. The correspondences are the same as those already noted for the vowel space.

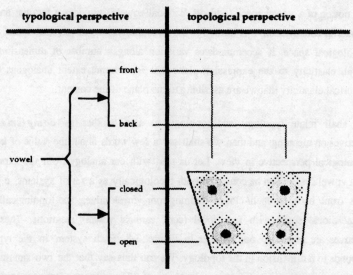

Fig. 2-8: Correspondence between typological and topological perspectives on vowels

What is the relationship between these two perspectives on meaning? So far in work on semantics only the typological perspective has been able to be realized in a formal system (cf. Chapter 1, Section 1.9 above); the power of the topological perspective still derives largely from the metaphor of space within theories of meaning. For present purposes, we can say that the topological organization construes a semantic space, creating the correspondences shown in Table 2(4).

Both perspectives are valuable. The typological perspective allows us to gain insight into the organization of meaning through the network, both as theoretical metaphor and as a system of formal representation (again, cf. Chapter 1, Section 1.9). The topological perspective gives us complementary benefits — in the first instance, the general notion of a multidimensional elastic space. We have indicated in the rightmost column some implications that derive from adopting the topological perspective. The general motif here is that of indeterminacy (see further Chapter 13, Section 13.3). For example, we can show how regions of meaning overlap (e.g. doing & happening overlapping with sensing in an area of 'sensing as activity'). We will use informal topological diagrams at various points in our discussion to bring out this central feature of the ideational system (see e.g. Figure 4-5 in Chapter 4 below).

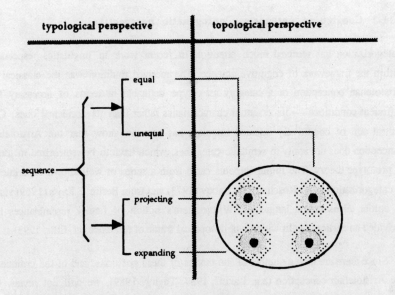

Fig. 2-9: Correspondence between typological and topological perspectives on sequences

The last row in the table above also represents indeterminacy, but this is indeterminacy of a particular kind, relating to the probabilistic nature of the semantic system. The types in the semantic system are instantiated according to probability values; these are manifested as relative frequencies in text. The equivalent in the spatial interpretation of meaning would be curvature or **'chreodization'**. Chreodization embodies time and represents the change of systemic probabilities over time (see e.g. Waddington, 1977, Sheldrake, 1988: Ch. 6, for discussion).

Table 2(4): Typological and topological correspondences

typological	topological	
	topological equivalent	**implication of topological perspective**
typology —	topology —	(multidimensional) space with extent (which can be extended) and regions located within it (which are at different distances from one another)
system (systemic variable, parameter)	dimension in space	continuous rather than discrete (cline, scale),
simultaneous systems	intersecting dimensions — multidimensionality	
systemic term (semantic type)	region (along dimension in space)	more or less central locations in the region along the relevant dimension, related to other regions in relative proximity with indeterminate boundaries
probability of systemic term — partial association	chreodization of dimension — curves in space	

2.11.2 Construing categories: ontogenetic perspective

Categorization has received much attention in recent work in linguistics, especially within the framework of cognitive science. The received tradition was the classical or Aristotelian conception of a category as a type definable in terms of necessary and sufficient conditions — its essential characteristics rather than its accidental ones. One central aim of cognitively oriented linguists has been to show that the Aristotelian conception does not apply to semantic categories, which have to be retheorized in terms of prototype theory. The initial impetus came from a series of well-known experiments in categorization by E. Rosch and by Labov (1973) and from Berlin & Kay's (1969) study of colour terms across languages; Wittgenstein's notion of family resemblances had provided an earlier insight within a philosophical frame of reference (cf. Ellis, 1993).

Since there are now a number of summaries of these positions, and of the critique of the Aristotelian conception (e.g. Lakoff, 1987; Taylor, 1989), we will not review the discussion here. From a systemic-functional point of view, the intellectual context was rather different. Systemic-functional theory was not oriented towards philosophy and logic (see further Part IV on different theoretical orientations in work on meaning), and the Aristotelian conception of a category did not figure as a traditional frame of reference that therefore had to be rejected. Already at the outset of the theoretical work that was to become systemic-functional theory, a major descriptive focus was on intonation (see e.g. Halliday, 1963a, b, 1967), a domain that clearly cannot be construed in Aristotelian terms; and the notion of **cline** was part of the theory already in the first major statement (see Halliday, 1961). Further, the system was conceived of as a probabilistic one even in proto-systemic work (see e.g. Halliday, 1956).

Systemic-functional work on 'categorization' has thus not engaged with the philosophical tradition; nor has it tended to proceed by experimental methods. Rather, it has been concerned with how meaning is construed in naturally occurring text, e.g. in child language studies (Halliday, 1975 onwards; Painter, 1996) and in factual writing (e.g. Halliday & Martin, 1993; Harvey, in prep.). Here one of the questions has been what resources are available in the semantic system for construing new meanings — for 'category development', both in the ontogenetic time frame and in the logogenetic time frame. One central semantic motif that has emerged from these studies is that of elaboration: both in relational clauses (realizing figures of being & having) and in complexes, especially nominal ones (the traditional notion of apposition, realizing sequences of participants). Here elaboration is at work e.g. in 'distilling' new meanings over extended passages. That is, the semantic system includes a theory of how meanings are construed; and this theory is itself a resource for construing new meanings. Thus when a young child says *cats also aren't people* (see below and Halliday, 1991, for the construal of cats), he is using a type of figure of being & having to construe a taxonomic relationship in the ideation base, so that the membership of 'cats' (construed as Carrier) in the class of 'people' (construed as Attribute) can be probed, in this case to 'outclassify' cats from the class of people. Figures of being & having of the intensive and ascriptive kind thus construe, among other things, the taxonomic relation among classes or types in the semantic system.

The ideation base is thus a resource both for construing experience and for *construing its own construal of experience*. It has the potential for expanding itself precisely because it includes a theory of how meanings are construed. When children begin to make the transition from **proto-language** into language (that is, when they begin to develop the system of the mother tongue, typically early in the second year of life), these resources for **self-construal** are not yet in place. The first things that are construed by naming are individuals; there is as yet no potential for taxonomies of general classes. But children soon take the critical step of generalizing across individuals (see e.g. Halliday, 1993a, on generalization). From a lexicogrammatical point of view, this means that naming has been generalized from individual names ("proper nouns") to class names ("common nouns"). Painter (1996) provides a key to the understanding of how linguistic resources are deployed in 'categorization' in language development, drawing on her longitudinal case study of one child, Stephen, between 2 1/2 and 5 years.

The first stage in categorization is **naming** individuals as members of classes; instances of the visual experience **shared** by the young child and his father or mother are ascribed to some general class of experience by means of a figure of being. At about 2 1/2, Stephen produced examples such as: Stephen (examining pattern on a rug): *That's a square. What's that?* — Mother: *That's a circle.* Here some perceived phenomenon of experience is brought "into intersubjective focus" by being referred to exophorically — pointing verbally, so to speak, to some feature of the material setting, sometimes accompanied by or replaced by a pointing as a gesture. This phenomenon is construed by Stephen as the Carrier of the figure of being, and is ascribed as a member of some general class of experience, construed as the Attribute of the figure. Stephen is 'importing' experience of instances into the semantic system by ascribing them to general classes in that system. This is an act of naming, and later this act itself gets named by *call* (see also Halliday, 1977, on calling as an early example of language being turned back on itself).

Children thus build up experience as meaning, in contexts such as the one exemplified above. Construing experience as meaning means locating classes such as squares and circles somewhere in the semantic system, both locally as terms in systems and also more globally in the ordering of these systems in delicacy. Painter comments: "... through the naming utterances where Stephen was practising signification, he was also necessarily construing the things of his experience into taxonomies". So Stephen also construes the attributes of semantic classes, attributes that will help him sort out the organization of the semantic system. Examples from about 2 1/2: (1) Mother: *What cars have you got there?* — Stephen: *There's a fire engine one with a ladder on;* (2) Mother: *What did you see at the zoo?* — Stephen: *Elephants; they got big trunks.*

When Stephen's meaning potential has gained critical semantic mass, he begins to construe its own internal organization explicitly in an effort to sort out taxonomic relations within the system. Painter gives the following example from about a year later in his life, at approximately 3 1/2 years (Stephen is examining animal jigsaw puzzle pieces):

```
Stephen: There isn't a fox; and there isn't - is a platypus an
animal?
Mother: Yes
Stephen: And is a seal is an animal (sic)?
Mother: Yes (shepherding S to bathroom)
Stephen: And is er- er- er- er-
Mother: You do your teeth while you're thinking
```

Again, the resource for construing 'categories' is the intensive ascriptive figure of being; but now both the Carrier and the Attribute are meanings internal to the semantic system. That is, Stephen construes a taxonomic relationship between e.g. 'seal' and 'animal' by construing them as Carrier + Attribute:

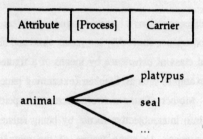

Painter comments: "The importance of this development is that it constitutes a move on Stephen's part from using language to make sense of non-linguistic phenomena to using language to make sense of the valeur relations of the meaning system itself." We can diagram the contrast between these two steps in construing experience as categories of meaning as in Figure 2-10.

visually shared experience

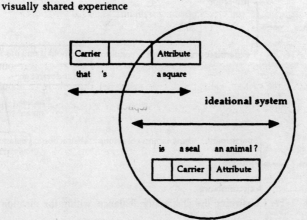

Fig. 2-10: Construing categories externally and internally

In his fourth year, Stephen begins to provide causal evidence for categorization, by adding an enhancing figure. The figure that is linked causally specifies attributes that are critical to the construal. For example: Mother refers to Bond airship as 'spaceship balloon' — Stephen: *Not a spaceship - an airship - cause a spaceship has bits like this to stand it up;* Stephen (pointing at page numbers): *That's fifteen because it's got a five; that's fourteen because it's got a four.* These causal relations are internal (Halliday & Hasan, 1976), i.e. oriented towards the interpersonal act of communication itself ('I know it is an x, because it has feature y'), rather than external ('it is an x, because it has feature y'). In other words, Stephen is attending to the act of construal itself — 'I construe it as x because of y'. At this stage in the development of Stephen's construal of experience, the construal has become something that is not only shared, but can also be explicitly negotiated and argued about.

Also in his fourth year, Stephen begins to extend his deployment of figures of being to include not only the *ascriptive mode* ('a is a member of x') but also the *identifying mode* ('y equals x') so that he can explicitly relate meanings in his ideation base in the form of **definitions**. For example, in *Balance means ⟦you hold it on your fingers and it doesn't go⟧*, he construes a single class of abstract participant, 'balance', as something defined in terms of a sequence of figures, 'you hold it on your fingers and it doesn't fall off': see Figure 2-11. He is now in a position to construe new meanings in terms of the semantic system itself; that is, they do not necessarily have to be 'imported' from direct extra-linguistic experience. As Painter points out, this is yet another expansion of his semantic resources preparing him for educational learning in later life where experience is very often vicarious experience, constructed entirely in educational discourse.

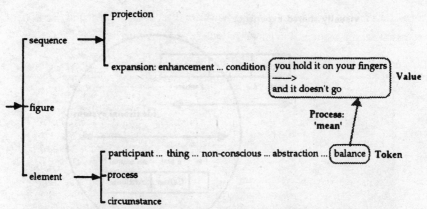

Fig. 2-11: Construing the abstraction 'balance' within the ideation base

Stephen's definition of 'balance' is on a developmental path towards the kinds of definition used in educational and scientific discourse — definitions such as the dictionary definition of 'cat': *a cat is a carnivorous mammal long domesticated and kept by man as a pet or for catching rats and mice* (adapted from Webster's Seventh New Collegiate Dictionary; cf. Nigel's construal of 'cat' discussed below). The definition of 'cat' involves a move to a less delicate category ('carnivore' or 'carnivorous mammal', which can be reconstrued as 'mammal that eats meat' — cf. 'cats like things that go' in the Nigel dialogues below) plus a qualification by a downranked sequence of figures of doing: see Figure 2-12. In both examples, the definition construes a token-value relation (Chapter 4, see Section 4.2.3.2) between a fairly delicate semantic type that is lexicalized within the lexicogrammar and a restatement of this type by means of other resources in the ideation base. The restatement draws more on the resources towards the grammatical end of the scale, so that in the definition a *lexicalized token* is construed as a *grammaticalized value*.[2] This entails a shift from construing experience through depth in the experiential taxonomy towards construing experience through expansion in a logical sequence. In the first example, this only involves a downranked sequence of figures; in the second example, this involves a move towards a less delicate category plus a downranked sequence of figures. The first example can actually be interpreted as meaning 'the condition when you hold it on your fingers and it doesn't fall off', showing that the downranked sequence has the class meaning of 'condition'. See Harvey (in

---

[2] The ideational potential for construing such relations of restatement within the ideation base does not at all imply that meaning is analysed by means of **decomposition** into semantic primitives. (i) Semantic types (such as 'balance', 'cat') are not decomposed into their defining glosses within the ideation base; rather, they are construed as standing in an intensive token-value relationship to these glosses. (ii) The semantic types are construed internally to the ideation base according to their location in the elaborating taxonomy and can be restated in various ways. (iii) The semantic types may also construe extra-linguistic categories of experience; that is, they may have signification outside the ideation base.

prep.) for a review of studies of the development of definitions, a survey of different types of definition, and a general account of their role in technical discourse.

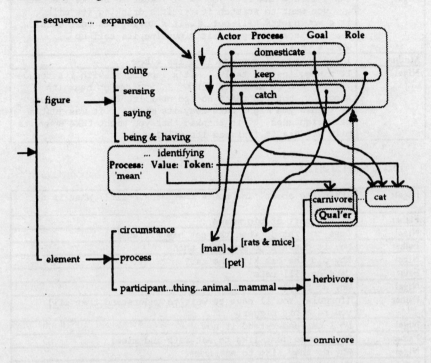

Fig. 2-12: Construing 'cat' within the ideation base according to a dictionary definition

We will leave her account here (see also Painter, 1993, for Stephen's further development), and refer to one additional example from a child's language development to see how one particular category may be ongoingly construed over time. The example is that of Nigel construing the category of cats, taken from Halliday (1984c) and discussed in Halliday (1991). The following dialogues occur over a period of 8 months, from 2;10 to 3;6:

Text 1: Nigel at 2;10;22

Nigel	And you (= I) saw a cat in Chania Falls.
Mother	Yes, you saw a cat in Chania Falls.
Nigel	And you picked the cat up. Mummy, do cats like meat?
Mother	Yes, they do.
Nigel	Do cats like bones? Do cats like marrow?

Text 2: Nigel at 2;10;26

Nigel	Can I stroke the cat? You (= 'I') want to stroke the cat ... you want to scratch it ... it's drinking its milk ... it's moving its tail out ... it's moving its tail outside ... it's scratching ... it's putting its tail up ... what's this?
Mother	I don't know; I suppose it's its elbow.
Nigel	It's waggling its tail ... it's lapping it with its tongue ... you can go near its elbow ... you *can* go near its elbow ... but you can't go too near its face ... because it thinks you might take away its milk ... it was just a bit frightened ... it thinked that you might take away its milk ... has it finished its milk?

Text 3: Nigel at 2;11;5

Nigel	(thinking about "The house that Jack built") What is a rat?
Father	It's a sort of big mouse.
Nigel	Does the rat go when the cat has killed it?
Father	No, it doesn't go any more then.
Nigel	Why did the cat kill the rat?
Father	Cats do kill rats.
Nigel	Why do they?
Father	(formula) You'll have to wait to understand that till you're a bit bigger.
Nigel	No I can understand it now.
Father	Well, cats just like to eat rats and mice.
Nigel	Why do they like to eat them?
Father	They just do.

Text 4: Nigel at 2;11; 15

Nigel	Why did the cat go out? Mummy, why did the cat go out?
Mother	It gets fed up, having its tail squashed.

Text 5: Nigel at 3;0;26

Nigel	How do the cat's claws come out?
Father	They come out from inside its paws. Look, I'll show you.
Nigel	Does it go with its claws?
Father	Not if it's going along the ground.
Nigel	And not if it's climbing up a tree.
Father	Yes; if it's climbing up a tree it does go with its claws.

Text 6: Nigel at 3;2;7

Nigel	Will the cat eat the grape?
Father	I don't think so. Cats like things that go, not things that grow.

Text 7: Nigel at 3;5;12

| Nigel | Cats have no else to stop you from trossing them ... cats have no other way to stop children from hitting them ... so they bite. Cat, don't go away! -- when I come back I'll tell you a story. (He does so.) |

Text 8: Nigel at 3;6;12

Nigel	Can I give the cat some artichoke?
Mother	Well she won't like it.
Nigel	Cats like things that go; they don't like things that grow.

Text 9: Nigel at 3;6;14

Nigel	I wish I was a puppet so that I could go out into the snow in the night. Do puppets like going out in the snow?
Father	I don't know. I don't think they mind.
Nigel	Do cats like going out in the snow?
Father	Cats don't like snow.
Nigel	Do they die? (He knows that some plants do.)
Father	No they don't die; they just don't like it.
Nigel	Why don't puppets mind snow?
Father	Well (hesitating) ... puppets aren't people.
Nigel	Yes but ... cats also aren't people.
Father	No, but cats are alive; they go. Puppets don't go.
Nigel	Puppets do go.
Father	Yes, but you have to make them go; like trains.
Nigel	Trains have wheels. Puppets have legs.
Father	Yes, they have legs; but the legs don't go all by themselves. You have to make them go.

Here the location of 'cat' in Nigel's overall ideation base is construed directly by means of figures of being & having (as in the earlier examples taken from Painter) — *cats are alive; cats also aren't people*; but the location of the category is also construed relative to other categories through the participant roles it takes on in various figures. For example, it is related in the figures of doing in certain ways to the young investigator himself , in other ways to other animals and food, and in yet other ways to the parts of its own body; and in one clause Nigel takes on the role of Actor with the cat as Recipient: see Table 2(5).

Table 2(5): Cats in figures of doing

Goal:	Actor :			
	Nigel	cat	creature: 'mouse'	food: vegetable & fruit; milk
Nigel		(bite + [children])		
cat	pick up; stroke, scratch; (you/ children) + tross, hit take away + possession: milk	scratch move, put up, waggle; lap + body part: tail		
creature: 'mouse'		kill; eat		
food: vegetable & fruit; milk		eat + grape drink, finish + milk		

This small sample suggests that cats are construed in terms of a fairly clear **semantic world order**: Nigel can act on cats, whereas they can act on 'mice' (i.e. rats [= 'a sort of big mouse'] and mice) and on food, and they can (intentionally) act on themselves. On the other hand, 'mice' and food are construed only as Goal relative to the cat as Actor. (This kind of order is also important in Text 9 in the construal of puppets: puppets move only through human agency.)

The construal of cats is filled out in other types of figure: they can be construed as Sensers (so endowed with consciousness) in processes of thinking and liking; they can be construed as Phenomenon (with the child as Senser); and they can be construed as Receiver (with the child as Sayer). The construal of cats as participants in figures is also filled out by expansion in sequences, whereby the cat's actions can be qualified by conditions, reasons, and so on: 'it does not go with its claws —> if it's going along on the ground'; 'does the rat go —> when the cat has killed it'; [implicit:] 'the cat killed the rat —> because cats just like to eat rats and mice'.

The network of relations that emerges from these everyday dialogic construals of cats is diagrammed in part in Figure 2-13 above (which uses some of the general semantic types identified in our survey of the ideation base, together with a number introduced ad hoc for the present example). This is of course only a small fragment of an ongoing construal of experience where 'cat' is just one category in the overall system; but it does indicate how experience is construed as a network of related categories. The network is not fixed or rigid, of course; it is constantly being reviewed, renovated, and expanded.

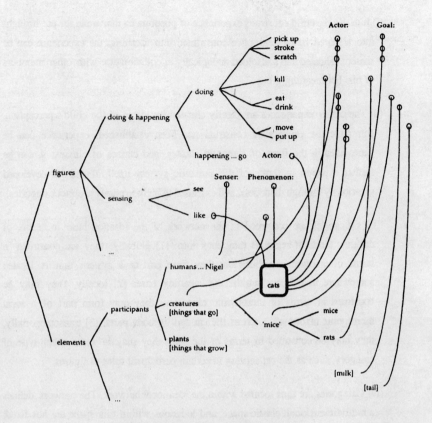

Fig. 2-13: The networking of cats

Figure 2-13 shows the various participant roles as elements in various types of figure. As well as being figures in their own right, such configurations can also be used as qualifications of a class of participant, such as cat — as figures serving to qualify that category with respect to its own role in the figure. Here the figure is being viewed in a participant perspective; this is achieved by downranking the figure so that it acquires the status of a property (cf. Section 2.11.3 [3] below). Grammatically, this perspective would be realized in the nominal group as a Qualifier of some Thing — e.g. *a cat is a creature that drinks milk, kills & eats mice, climbs up trees ... .* In other words, these relationships can also be construed explicitly as parts of definitions, as we showed above.

Finally, we may note that the figures in which 'cat' serves a participant role may form sequences, as in *it gets fed up, having its tail squashed.* Such sequences are also part of the construal of cats. Indeed, Nigel tries (unsuccessfully, as it happens) to find out why cats kill rats and mice, so that he might establish a causal sequence.

We can now sum up what can be learnt about construal from the ontogenetic perspective:

(i) Initially the child construes experience of phenomena that are in, or are brought into, a shared visual field; once constituted into meaning, the experience can be shared, validated and scaffolded dialogically in collaboration with other members of his/ her meaning group.

(ii) The earlier experiences are clearly situated by virtue of the child's perception. But once the process of construal has been established, experience can be generalized in the form of semantic classes, and classes of classes; it can be further explored in terms of the semantic system itself; it can be developed vicariously through discourse, and extended to include purely abstract categories.

(iii) Categories are construed in the network of the ideation base in terms of different kinds of relations they enter into: [1] globally, they are construed in terms of taxonomic elaboration: they form part of a system that is located somewhere in delicacy within the meaning base; [2] locally, they may be construed in terms of meronymic extension: they may form part of a local meronymic taxonomy, such as the cat and its body parts; [3] transcategorially, they may be construed in terms of the roles they play in some other type of category, such as the cat serving in certain participant roles of figures.

(iv) Categories are thus located within the ideational network. The network defines a multidimensional, elastic space; and locations within this space are not fixed, clearly bounded regions but rather regions with core or focal areas and more peripheral areas that shade into one another.

(v) The ideation base is a resource for construing extra-linguistic experience (such as visual experience). But it is also a semogenic resource for construing itself, since it is built up out of the kinds of relations it itself construes — relations such as intensive ascription. Once critical semantic mass has been built up, new categories can be construed internally within the system of the ideation base.

2.11.3 Construing as locating in a network of relations

We have seen how Nigel construed the category of 'cat' by probing its location in a network of relations in his ideation base. From the typological point of view, construing experience in terms of categories means locating them somewhere in this network of relations. When we examine this network more closely, we find that there are actually three types of network involved: (1) taxonomic in the strict sense (i.e. based on hyponymy, 'a is a kind of x/ x subsumes a, b, c'), (2) taxonomic in the extended sense (i.e. based on meronymy, 'd is a part of y/ y has parts d, e, f'), and (3) eco-functional (i.e. based on selection, 'g has function m in environment z/ environment z comprises functions m, n, p, and function m may be filled by g, h, j'). Of these three, the first provides the global organizing principle of elaboration in delicacy; while the third relates paradigmatic organization to organization on the syntagmatic axis.

[1] Taxonomic elaboration

Any option (category, semantic type) is thus located in the network relative to other options, first within its own system, and secondly in terms of the location of that system relative to others. For example, 'participant' is one option in the system 'participant/ process/ circumstance'; and that system is a more delicate elaboration of 'element'. We noted above in reference to Painter's work that the resources of figures of being are deployed in construing taxonomic relations. There is also a generalized set of nominal categories for construing steps in the delicacy hierarchy — e.g. *type, kind, class*; and some taxonomic regions have specific categories of their own, for example: *brand, model, make, issue; genus, species, family.*

Delicacy is a uniform ordering from most general to most delicate; but along this scale, semantic systems differ both in the number of distinctions at any one degree of delicacy and in the overall delicacy that is achieved. There are specific differences associated with particular taxonomic regions. For instance, humans and higher animals are much more highly elaborated than lower animals. But there are also general differences in the nature and degree of taxonomic elaboration associated with different 'bands' in delicacy. Such general taxonomic principles are probably best known for folk-taxonomies in the domains of plants and animals, diseases, and the like (e.g., Berlin, Breedlove & Raven, 1973; Conklin, 1962; Frake, 1962; Slaughter, 1986); these fall within 'element: participant: thing' in the ideation base. The maximum steps in delicacy in a folk taxonomy are kingdom (unique beginner), life form, basic (generic) level, specific level, and varietal level. These steps are by no means always present in every particular taxonomy; and they have different characteristics, summarized in Table 2(6) (for taxonomic examples, see Leech, 1974).

Berlin (1972: 53) characterizes the elaboration of labelled taxonomies as follows:

Generic names are fundamental and will occur first. These will be followed by the major life-form names and specific names. At yet a later period, intermediate taxa and varietal taxa will be labelled. Finally the last category to be lexically designated ... of any ethnobotanical lexicon will be the unique beginner. The suggested sequence can be seen diagrammatically as follows:

$$
\text{generic} \rightarrow \left\{ \begin{array}{c} \text{life-form} \\ \\ \text{specific} \end{array} \right\} \rightarrow \left\{ \begin{array}{c} \text{intermediate} \\ \\ \text{varietal} \end{array} \right\} \rightarrow \text{unique beginner}
$$

... no temporal ordering is implied for some categories. Thus no claim is made as to the priority in time of specific names over major life form names. On the other hand a claim is made that a language must have encoded *at least* one major life-form name and one specific name before the appearance of intermediate and varietal named taxa.

The most favoured 'band' in delicacy is that of the basic level: it is taxonomically most highly elaborated, it tends to be learnt first by children, and it construes categories with syndromes of usually salient functional and perceptual properties. This is where Nigel's categorization of 'cats' fits in and also Stephen's probing of 'seal', 'platypus', etc.. It has been pointed out that basic level categories are most distinct in terms of how human beings interact with them (for a review, see e.g. Taylor, 1989). For example, there are various ways in which we interact with cats in particular; but no distinctive modes of interaction with animals in general. Indeed, Nigel's exploration of 'cats' suggests that an important aspect of construing this basic level category is what roles he can take on in relation to the cat of his immediate experience (including telling it a story!). In addition, the 'basic' degree in delicacy may have a special status in the instantiation of categories in text. In her study of lexicalization in the pear stories, Downing (1980) found that the basic level was by far the most preferred one; these are the figures for concrete, nonhuman things (p. 106):

subordinate	basic	superordinate
5%	93%	2 %

Such findings are interesting because they give some indication of what factors to consider in lexicalization in text generation: a given phenomenon can, in principle, be construed at any point along the scale of delicacy. They are also interesting because they point to the relationship between the system and the instance: from the perspective of the system, we can observe that the basic degree of delicacy is most highly elaborated; from the perspective of the instance, we can observe that it is most frequent. However, we have to allow for considerable variation within a language — in particular, functional or registerial variation within the system according to the context of use, as in the variation between the spoken system of everyday life and the written system of science to which we turn next. (We also have to allow for variation across languages. We shall discuss some differences between Chinese and English in Chapter 7 below.)

Table 2(6): Model of folk taxonomy

kingdom (unique beginner)	life form (kind)	generic (basic)	specific	varietal
	few in number; polytypic	large in number; core in folk taxonomy	most in sets of two or three	rare in folk taxonomies
	primary lexemes		seondary lexemes	
		highly salient; among the first learned by children		

```
                                          ┌ alsatian
                 ┌ bird                   │   alsatian
                 │                ┌ feline ┤ terrier
                 ├ fish           │   cat  │   terrier
 ┌ creature ──→  ├ insect         ├ canine │ spaniel
 │  creature     │                │   dog  └   spaniel
 │               │         ┌ mammal┤ equine  ...
→┤               └ mammal ─┤ animal│   horse
 │                 animal  │       ├ bovine
 │                 ...     │       │   cow
 │                         │       ├ lupine
 │                         │       │   wolf         ┌ western
 │               ┌ herb    │       └ ...            │   whitepine
 │               │         └ oak            ┌ whitepine ┤ ...
 └ plant ──→     ├ bush    ┌ oak            │   ...
                 ├ tree ──→┤ pine ──→       ┤
                 └ ...     ├ beech          └ ...
                          └ ...
```

The ideation base embodies not only folk taxonomies but also a range of taxonomic models such as those used by experts and by scientists (see Chapter 14, Section 14.1). These are all variants within the overall ideational system. We will come back to the principle of variation in our discussion of recipes and weather forecasts (see Chapter 8) and in our discussion of the polysystemic nature of the ideation base (see Chapter 13, Section 13.4). Here we will just say a few words about the significance of such variation for the taxonomic aspect of categorization.

The move from folk taxonomies towards scientific ones involves both an increase in steps in delicacy and a change in the criteria used for classification. Wignell, Martin & Eggins (1990) give examples from the classification of roses and of birds of prey (see their discussion for original references). For roses, folk taxonomy and scientific taxonomy can be contrasted as in Table 2(7).

Table 2(7): Roses

scientific taxonomic order:	Latin	English: scientific	English: folk	folk taxonomic order:
kingdom			plant	*unique beginner*
division	Spermatophyta	seed plants		
class	Angiospermae	flowering plants	(flowers)*	*life form*
sub-class	Dicotyledoneae	dicots		
order	Rosales	rose order		
family	Rosaceae	rose family		
genus	Rosa	rose	**rose**	*basic level*
species	Rosa setigera	wild climbing rose		*specific*
variety	Rosa setigera tomentosa	special wild climbing rose		*varietal*

* Note: this is only a partial equivalence

For birds of prey, they contrast a folk taxonomy with a "birdwatchers' vernacular taxonomy". We superimpose these to give a sense of the difference; see Figure 2-14.

These examples show the difference in degree of delicacy quite clearly; an increase in delicacy reflects the move in the direction of scientific knowledge. At the same time, the criteria for categorization also change, from overt criteria that are accessible to the naked eye to covert criteria available only through the application of scientific techniques. The change in taxonomic criteria is very clear from a review of the early taxonomic stage of science in Europe in the 16th and 17th centuries: see Slaughter (1986).

So far, our discussion of taxonomic elaboration has focussed on those steps in delicacy that tend to be construed lexically in the lexicogrammar. But in the overall meaning base, lexically construed folk and scientific taxonomies do not start at the highest degree of generality in delicacy; they are ordered in delicacy after those systems that are construed grammatically. For example, while 'plant' is the "unique beginner" of a particular folk taxonomy, there are several steps in the construal of things that are more general than this — steps that are constructed in the grammar, in categories such as 'thing', 'conscious/ non-conscious thing', 'countable/ non-countable thing' and the like.

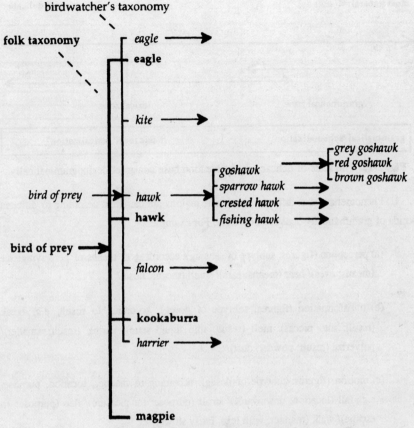

Fig. 2-14: Folk and expert taxonomies

In general, then, we can say that the move in delicacy in the ideation base from 'most general' to 'most delicate' is construed lexicogrammatically as the move from 'grammar' to 'lexis': see Figure 2-15. This is of fundamental significance in the construal of semantic categories. The early part of the scale of delicacy is construed in the grammatical 'zone'. This zone provides the resources of grammatical schematization for construing more delicate categories: those categories are realized lexically but construed according to the systemic parameters of the grammar. For example, the grammar of the nominal group provides a schema for construing various delicate categories of things, by classifying, describing, ordering and other such strategies.

Semantic types in different taxonomic regions are distinguished according to different criteria; and they have different sets of roles. But the different criteria and sets of roles are construed within the grammar. We can exemplify these, taking domains a little more delicate than those presented in Plate 9 above.

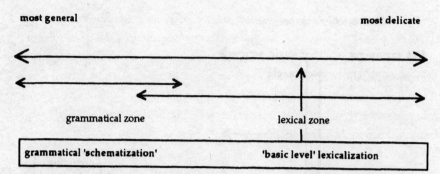

Fig. 2-15: The scale of delicacy in the ideation base construed lexicogrammatically

(i) Phenomena within different taxonomic regions are classified according to different kinds of grammatically construed **criteria**. For example:

(a) perception (figures: subtype of sensing): according to means of perceiving: see (means: eyes)/ hear (means: ears)/ smell (means: nose)/ ...

(b) transformation (figures: subtype of doing): according to result, e.g. break (result: into pieces)/ melt (result: into liquid state)/ shrink (result: smaller)/ pulverize (result: powder, dust)/ ...

(c) motion (figures: subtype of doing): according to manner, location, purpose, e.g. fall (location: downwards)/ stroll (purpose: for pleasure)/ flee (purpose: to escape)/ walk (manner: with legs, fairly slowly)/ ...

(d) higher animals (elements: subtype of conscious thing, at the taxonomic depth of species): according to epithets of age and sex, e.g. cow (sex: female, age: adult), bull (sex: male, age: adult), calf (age: nonadult).

(e) artefacts (elements: a subtype of object): according to material, purpose, e.g. containers (purpose: to contain substances) — barrel (material: wood), basket (material: cane or other woven material), basin (material: metal), bowl (material: earthenware or glass).

(ii) Phenomena within different domains have different grammatically construed **structural roles** associated with them. For example:

(a) perception: perceiver & phenomenon being perceived;

(b) concrete thing (elements: subtype of object): various epithets, specifically of physical dimensions such as size, shape, weight, colour and age.

(c) weight (elements: subtype of quality): tensor, showing degree of intensity.

Within the lexical zone, we have already referred to the differentiation according to the degrees in delicacy; in particular, the 'basic' degree of delicacy stood out as most highly elaborated. There are also grammatical reactances indicating the taxonomic differentiation between the 'basic' degree of delicacy and lower degrees of delicacy, at least in cases where the taxonomic relationship is of a particular kind. For example, the less delicate category may be construed by a mass noun whereas the more delicate, basic degree categories may be construed as count nouns: see Table 2(8).

Wierzbicka (1985: 321-2) identifies this phenomenon and shows that it is not arbitrary. Her explanation is in fact that the relationship between e.g. 'furniture' and 'chair, table' as supercategory and subcategory is not the normal 'kind of' relationship between e.g. 'bird' and 'swallow, magpie', but rather a grouping of different kinds according to similarity in use:

> Thus, supercategories such as *bird* or *tree* are 'taxonomic', i.e. they belong to hierarchies of kinds (where each 'kind' is identified on the basis of similarity between its members); supercategories such as *crockery*, *cutlery* or *kitchenware* are not taxonomic — they include things of different kinds, grouped on the basis of contiguity and/ or similarity of function, not on the basis of similarity of form.

We take delicacy to include both types of the relationship of supercategory to subcategory — both the "taxonomic" and the "non-taxonomic" ones. However, it would seem that with the relationship between 'furniture' and 'chair', 'table' &c. we are on the borderline between elaboration and extension. We now turn to meronymic extension in the ideation base.

[2] Meronymic extension

The ideation base construes phenomena as organic wholes that may take on roles in other kinds of phenomena; but it also deconstrues many such organic wholes into their component parts. When these component parts are phenomena of the same type — participants (e.g., chair: legs, seat, back), figures (e.g., baking a cake: stages in the procedure), this is known as **meronymy** (or meronymic taxonomy; cf. *meros* 'part'; see e.g. Cruse, 1986: Ch. 7).[3] We find local taxonomies of this kind, often interlocked with hyponymies; for example, see Figure 2-16. Taxonomies thus embody the two types of expanding relationships we mentioned at the beginning of this section — extension and elaboration. The meronymic type of taxonomy is extension, whereas the hyponymic type is elaboration.

---

[3] This has sometimes been called *partonymy*, in apparent ignorance of the established term *meronymy*.

Table 2(8): Count and mass nouns in taxonomic relation

kind ('life form') ↘ mass noun	basic degree of delicacy ↘ count noun
furniture	chair(s), couch(es), table(s), bed(s), ...
silverware; cutlery	spoon(s), fork(s), knife (knives), ...
bedlinen	sheet(s), blanket(s), pillow case(s), ...
clothing	shirt(s), sock(s), vest(s), ... ; pants, trousers, slacks, ...

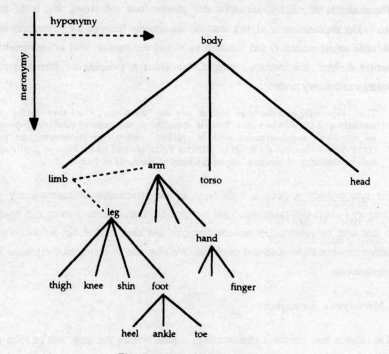

Fig. 2-16: Meronymic taxonomy

And this is in fact how we shall model them — as *local* meronymic taxonomies, *applicable to some particular region of the hyponymic taxonomy*, and not as one global meronymy superimposed on our taxonomy. There would seem to be far too many discontinuities to create a global meronymy; meronymies tend to occur only where there are contiguous parts of an independent whole.[4] Thus while concrete objects are regularly construed meronymically (with the human body as both a representative example and a model for other meronymies), substances are not; substances are extended through measure ('unit of') rather than through part ('part of'). Similarly, taxonomies tend to be more extended meronymically for concrete regions than for abstract ones (although

---

[4] On a fairly large scale these discontinuities are embodied in the differentiation among the natural sciences specializing in domains such as the body, the atom and the universe.

even things in an abstract region can have parts, e.g. aspect of an idea). Thus there is a generalized set of categories such as part, element, component, aspect; and also a generalized set 'facets' of spatial or temporal orientation, top, bottom, side, front, back, middle, centre; beginning, middle, end. There are more specific variants for parts of particular concrete things, such as facade, roof, wall [of a building]; ceiling, floor, wall [of a room]; slope, peak [of a mountain]; limb, trunk, root, bark [of a tree]; skin, core, pips [of an apple]; crust, crumb [of bread]; preface, epilogue [of a book].

The examples of meronymies given above come from the region of 'participant' within the ideation base. It is not clear to what extent, or in what sense, meronymic taxonomies extend beyond that region. We can certainly recognize that processes have phases (cf. the discussion of phase in Chapter 4, Section 4.4) — 'begin to do, keep doing, stop doing'; but it is not immediately clear that these form a process meronymy analogous to the parts of a participant. Although we might reconstrue *he began to dance* metaphorically as *the beginning of his dance* on the model of 'the beginning of the book', this is a metaphorical reification of the process 'dance' and we have to be cautious in interpreting the implications for the congruent process 'dance'. If we probe a little further, we can see that process phase is concerned with the occurrence of a process in time — its temporal unfolding: 'begin to do' means 'begin to be actualized (to occur) as doing in time'. In contrast, participant meronymy is not tied to the existence of a participant in referential space.

Turning to figures, we can note that a given figure may be restated in a definition as a sequence of less delicate figures: see Table 2(9).[5]

---

[5] Adapted from J. Anderson & E. Hanna. 1985. The new Doubleday Cookbook. Garden City, NY: Doubleday & Company, Inc.

Table 2(9): Figure defined as sequence of less delicate figures

Token = figure	Value = sequence [of figures]
sb caramelize sugar	sb heat sugar —> until it melts —> and turns golden
sb baste food	sb ladle or brush drippings, liquid, butter, or sauce over food —> as it cooks —> in order to add flavour —> and to prevent dryness
sb cream butter or other fat	sb beat butter or other fat either solo or with sugar or other ingredients —> until it is smooth and creamy
sb marinate meat, ...	sb steep meat, fish, fowl, vegetables or other savoury food in a spicy liquid several hours —> until food absorbs the flavouring
sb steep tea leaves, ...	sb let tea leaves, coffee grounds, herbs, or spices stand in hot liquid —> until their flavour is extracted

We can interpret the figures to the right as consisting of a sequence of (less delicate) figures. There is certainly a change in focus — some happening either may be construed as a single *figure* (at a fairly high degree of delicacy) or may be 'blown up' as a *sequence* of figures (at a lower degree of delicacy); and this change of focus is a significant option offered by the ideation base. It has been recognized in work on knowledge representation; and it is a significant variable in the move between commonsense models and uncommonsense ones. However, while sharing this change in focus with prototypical participant-based meronymies, the relationship between figure and sequence is unlike these meronymies in other respects. Prototypical meronymies do not involve a change in delicacy; and the categories they relate together are phenomena of the same kind (as noted above). Here the relationship is again one of restatement; for example: '[[for somebody to caramelize sugar]]means [[that s/he heats it until it melts and turns golden brown]].

While the choice of 'level' in hyponymic elaboration is the choice in **delicacy of categorization**, the choice of level in a meronymic taxonomy is the choice in **delicacy of focus**. The focus is typically on the whole (i.e., the most inclusive region within the meronymy) even if a specific part is particularly important (cf. Langacker, 1984). We can see this in the way the involvement of elements in figures is represented:

```
He switched on the light (with his right hand)
[rather than: His right hand switched on the light]

She held the ticket with her teeth
[rather than: Her teeth held the ticket]

He patted the dog (on its head)
[rather than: His hand patted the dog's head]

He saw the alien (with his own eyes)
```

[rather than: His own eyes saw the alien]

Let's paper [the walls of] the living room

He put the vase on [the top of] the table

That is: the whole is involved in the figure as a participant, and if the part comes into the picture as well it tends to be construed as a circumstance (Means, Location) or as a separate participant (Goal, as in Nigel's observations about the cat quoted above: *it's putting up its tail*, rather than *its tail is putting up* — it is the whole organism that is endowed with agency).[6] There is clearly room for alternative choices; for example, figurative representations of conscious processing may construe the whole person as a privileged body part (and in some languages, e.g. Akan, this is a regular, non-figurative feature of certain figures of sensing):

His death broke her heart ('devastated her')
His behaviour turns my stomach ('upsets me')
The news blew my mind ('surprised me')

As an example, in the major portion of his novel *The Inheritors*, dealing with life before homo sapiens, Golding always represents the act of perception as involving a sense organ rather than the whole person. This is a departure from the norm of the language; it owes its effect, that of deconstructing the whole person as a potentially independent agent, precisely to this departure from the norm, as in *his nose examined this stuff and did not like it* (see Halliday, 1973: 117, 124).

Such figurative construals all depend on extension — a whole is being construed in terms of a part (*synecdoche; pars pro toto*). They occur in various environments; additional examples are:

I'm happy to see so many new faces in the audience.
I've got too many mouths to feed.
The man at table 5 is the chicken curry.

---

[6] There are two tendencies at work here. One is a general tendency within the ideational metafunction to involve wholes rather than parts, especially where the whole obviously functions organically (like a person). The other is a pressure from the textual metafunction: since in English, first position in the clause has a distinct in the configuration as text (as 'point of departure': grammatically, the Theme of the clause — cf. Figure 1-2 in Chapter 1, Section 1.3 above), these wordings allow the "whole person" to function as the point of departure rather than just a part of the body. Compare here pairs such as *he has brown hair/ his hair is brown, I have a headache/ my head aches* where the first is typically preferred.

In discourse, the whole may serve as the anaphoric domain of a part ('bridging', cf. Clark, 1975):

> The view of the mountain was breath-taking. *The slopes* were covered with snow and reflected the last purple rays of the sun.

[3] Eco-functional selection

Taxonomic elaboration and meronymic extension form complementary networks of relations that together make up the paradigmatic organization of the ideation base. They define, as we have noted, options in delicacy of categorization and in delicacy of focus. The third type of network involved in the organization of the ideation base which we identified above serves to relate paradigmatic organization and syntagmatic organization. Specifically, it relates syntagmatic functions or roles associated with paradigmatic types to the paradigmatic types that can serve in these functions. For example, the syntagmatic function 'Senser' is associated with the paradigmatic type 'sensing', and it is related to the paradigmatic type 'conscious being', since only participants of this subtype can serve as Sensers. Figure 2-6 above shows this relation, together with a set of other such relations. We shall refer to such network relations as **eco-functional selection** in order to indicate that they specify the syntagmatic environment of semantic types by showing them as selections for syntagmatic functions. Such selections have been referred to as "pre-selections", but in order to avoid any connotations of temporal sequence, we prefer the term "selection" for such relations in the ideation base.[7]

Selections are bidirectional. We have already seen that functions associated with paradigmatic types constitute 'structural properties' by which these types are distinguished and that selections provide further information about these 'properties'. Thus Figure 1-12 above illustrates how a figure of spearing is characterized by reference to the function of Means, which selects for the thing 'spear'. Conversely, semantic types which are selected are characterized by the functional environment within which they are selected. Thus the weapon 'spear' is characterized by its potential for serving as Means in a figure of spearing. Similarly, part of the meaning of a 'conscious being' is that it has the potential for serving in the Senser role of a figure of sensing (cf. Figure 2-6).

The network of selection is **inter-axial** in that it relates syntagmatic specifications to paradigmatic ones; it 'cuts across' the paradigmatic organization of the ideation base, establishing correspondences between paradigmatic types through the syntagmatic functions associated with them, as we have just illustrated by reference to Figures 1-12

---

[7] As noted in Chapter 1, Section 1.9.6, preselection corresponds to the notion of 'value restriction' in frame-based inheritance networks.

and 2-6. We can trace one further example from sequence via figure to element: see Figure 2-17.

Construing a category thus includes locating it not only taxonomically and meronymically but also eco-functionally, as in the case of 'conscious being' just referred to. We noted above in connection with the cat example how the fact that a participant serves a participant role in a figure can be viewed either from the perspective of the figure or from the perspective of the participant (i.e. as a property of the participant). If cats kill mice, the ideation base accommodates the view from the angle of the figure: 'cats kill mice'; but it also accommodates the view from the angle of the participant: 'animals that kill mice'. Here the figure in which cats participate as actors has been construed as if it was a property, so that the category of cats might be construed within the system of the ideation base by means of the definition 'cats are animals that kill mice'. (In formal systems of representation, this can be expressed by means of lambda abstraction.) There is a general semogenic strategy at work here. We referred to 'sequences', 'figures' and 'elements' as three **orders of complexity** in Section 2.1. The shift in perspective means that configurations of meanings that are of a particular order of complexity can be accessed through selection not only in their normal environment (within phenomena of the next higher order of complexity) but also within phenomena of lower orders of complexity. Through this semogenic strategy of opening up the possible domains of selection, a great deal of experiential complexity can be imported into the construal of a participant.

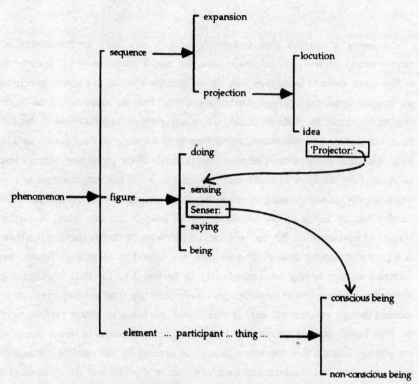

Fig. 2-17: Successive links in selection network

2.11.4 Construal and stratification

A phenomenon of experience is construed as a category in the ideation base by being given a location in the three semantic networks described in the preceding section. This taxonomic, meronymic and eco-functional location is the category's **value** (*valeur*) in relation to the other categories within the ideation base. By being assigned a value internal to the ideational system, a semantic category is also being related to categories that lie beyond semantics itself. On the one hand it is being related to categories within systems that lie outside language but which the semantic system interfaces with; on the other hand it is being related to the grammatical categories in terms of which it is realized. Figure 2-18 shows these three stratal angles on the process of construal. Let us explore these relationships in turn.

We saw in the examples of how categories are first developed that young children will typically construe concrete phenomena that are part of the field of visual perception they share with their interactants. In other words, they are construing into linguistic meanings their experience of the material world as it is construed in the categories from another semiotic system, viz. (visual) perception. These extra-linguistic categories are construed as the **signification** of the semantic categories of the ideation base — always in some particular situation when the child first engages with them. To construe experience of concrete phenomena as meaning is thus to construe some signification which lies outside the ideation base as a value which is internal to the ideation base system. Part of the power of categorization is that extra-linguistic phenomena that are quite varied in signification can be construed as alike in value.

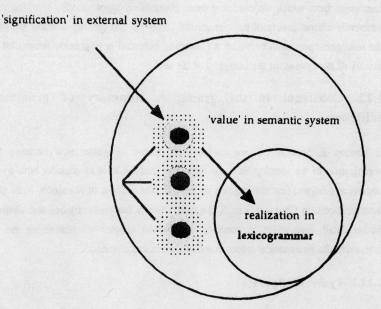

Fig. 2-18: Stratal angles on construal

Children are able to construe the semantic system because they start in situations with a material setting that is shared — cf. above, and see Hasan (1985b: 25 ff.) on Malinowski's contribution to this insight. As they build up their ideation base, they can begin to construe categories internal to the system out of existing ideational values; and they can begin to move into the abstract domains of a purely symbolic world, where the significations of semantic categories are abstract categories in social and socio-semiotic systems. But precisely because these abstract categories are construed as meanings, they can still be built up, negotiated and validated in collaboration with other members of the meaning group. The move from the realm of concrete phenomena to the various realms of abstract phenomena is made possible through the homogenizing power of meaning.

The semantic categories are themselves construed by means of **realization**; they are constructed within the grammar and the lexis of a language. If we model the ideation base as a semantic space, we are foregrounding one aspect of the construction of meaning in language, namely the way in which lexicogrammar construes our experience of the world in the guise of multidimensional matrices or grids. This is an important feature of language as a semiotic system, an inevitable consequence of the principle of arbitrariness: since the forms of expression are arbitrary, they impose discontinuity on the content. We have to decide about any given instance whether it is singular or plural, temporal or causal, possible, probable or certain; whether it is a *bus* or a *van*, *smiling* or *grinning*, *cloudy*, *misty* or *foggy*. But the semantic categories themselves (seen from above, as it were) are much more fluid and indeterminate than their realizations in wording imply. The notion of semantic space allows us to adopt a complementary standpoint from which we can view these phenomena topologically, bringing out the inherently elastic quality of the dimensions involved, and gaining a deeper insight into the semogenic processes by which the meaning potential is ongoingly remoulded in the history of the system, of the user, and of the text.

2.12 Construal in the grammar: summary of grammatical evidence

In Chapter 1, Section 1.8, we discussed the nature of grammatical evidence for the organization in the ideation base, pointing out that we have to consider both overt and covert (cryptotypic) features and that we have to take account of reactances from all three metafunctions. In Chapters 3 to 5, we shall discuss sequences, figures and elements in further detail; meanwhile to conclude the present chapter we summarize the salient features in the grammatical organization of figures and elements.

2.12.1 Types of figure

There are four types of figure — doing & happening, sensing, saying, being & having. Broadly speaking, these are constructed in the grammar as follows:

(i) Within the **ideational** metafunction, each is realized congruently by one particular transitivity type: doing & happening ⟶ material, sensing ⟶ mental, saying ⟶ verbal, and being & having ⟶ relational. These have various reactances. such as the number and nature of participants and the unmarked present tense selection (see Table 2(10)).

(ii) Relating to the **interpersonal** metafunction: in any given register there may be typical correspondences between the type of figure and the speech function; e.g. in procedural registers, material clauses are typically imperative, relational ones indicative.

(iii) Relating to the **textual** metafunction: different types of figure are presumed in different ways and have different potential for textual prominence; e.g. only material clauses are substituted by the pro-verb *do (to/with)*.

2.12.2 Types of element

There are three types of semantic elements serving in figures — processes, participants and circumstances. Broadly speaking, these are constructed in the grammar as follows.

(i) Within the **ideational** component: they are realized by different *classes* of units:

process ↘ verbal group
participant ↘ nominal group
circumstance ↘ adverbial group; prepositional phrase

Participants tend to be inherent elements of a figure; circumstances are typically optional.

(ii) Relating to the **interpersonal** metafunction: participants can serve as Subject; circumstances and processes cannot. Furthermore, participants and circumstances can serve as WH-elements, but processes cannot (if the process is being questioned, a participant element has to be construed as a Range: *what ... do?*).

(iii) Relating to the **textual** metafunction: participants and circumstances can both readily serve as Theme (though their potentials differ); processes only rarely, other than in imperative clauses. Participants and (more restrictedly) circumstances can serve as referables identified by referring expressions, but processes cannot — as with WH-interrogation, they have to be construed as a Range together with the pro-verb *do* as Process: *do it/that* (see Halliday & Hasan, 1976: 125).

These properties are summarized in Table 2(11).

The view from grammar brings into relief a number of relevant factors relating to participants and circumstances. There are certain special subcategories of these, in the grammar, which are distinguished by the fact that they embody features of interpersonal or textual meaning:

(1) interpersonal: questioning
interrogative: *who, what, when, where, how far, how long, how, why*

(2) textual: cohesive
(i) referring, personal: *he, she, it, they;* demonstrative: *this, that, now, then, here, there, thus*
(ii) generalizing: lexical items such as *person, creature, thing, stuff, affair*

Table 2(10): Grammatical (ideational) properties of different types of figure

	material	mental	verbal	relational
role in sequence — projecting clause:		↗	↗	
nature of Medium	Actor; Goal: participant (simple or macro) ↗ nominal group; clause: non-finite	Senser: participant: conscious ↗ nominal group	Sayer: participant: symbol source ↗ nominal group	Carrier; Value: participant or projected figure; circumstance ↗ nominal group; clause (projection or expansion; finite or non-finite) adv. group; prep. phrase
nature of second participant (Agent or Range)	Actor; Range: participant ↗ nominal group	Phenomenon: participant or projected figure ↗ nominal group; clause: projection	Verbiage: participant: linguistic ↗ nominal group	[Depends on subtype] ↗ various
Attribute	√ (condition or result)			√ (if ascriptive)
Beneficiary	Recipient or Client		Receiver	[except for one special subtype]
somewhat restricted circumstances	Place-directed	Matter	Matter	
directionality: two way (√) or one way (–)		√ like/ please		
TENSE: unmarked present	present-in-present	simple present		

Table 2(11) Grammatical evidence for differentiation of elements

	process	participant	circumstance
(i) ideational TRANSITIVITY: role in figures	Process	participant roles: Agent, Medium, etc.	circumstantial roles: Cause, Location, etc.
class of unit	verbal	nominal	adverbial; prep. phrase
DEIXIS	TENSE (temporal)	DETERMINATION (reference spatial)	
MODIFICATION	grammatical items	lexical & grammatical items	lexical & grammatical items
INDIVIDUATION		√ Proper names as well as class names	(except for circumstantial things)
(ii) interpersonal MOOD: WH-SELECTION Wh/	(except if construed as Range: do what &c)	√ who, what, which	√ when, where, how long, how far, how, why ...
MOOD: Subject/		√	
(iii) textual THEME: Theme/	(very rarely, except for imperative clauses)	√	√
REFERENCE	(except it construed as Range: do it &c)	√ he/she, it, this, that, ... [Note range of subtypes]	√ (but more limited:) now, then, here, there, thus, ...

These are significant in their own right because they are critical to the construction of discourse: the textual ones provide internal cohesion, while the interpersonal ones construe dialogic speech roles. They have a further significance in that they reveal by reactance the major subclasses within the general classes of participant and circumstance, as shown in Table 2(12).

Table 2(12): Grammatical evidence for differentiation of participants and circumstances

			interpers.	textual	
			WH-TYPE	REFERENCE	LEXICAL COHESION: general noun
participant	conscious		who?	s/he/ thet	person, fellow, chap
	non-	animal	what?	it/ they	animal, creature, beast
	conscious	institution			
		object			thing, object
		substance			stuff
		abstraction			matter, affair, business
circum- stance	time		when?	now/ then	
	place		where?	here/ there	
	distance		how far?		
	duration		how long?		
	manner		how?	thus, this way	
	cause		why?		

These special subcategories have the effect of construing other elements as "referable" — that is, of enabling them to retain their semiotic identity for subsequent access and hence as it were authenticating them (e.g. *Don't give me any more of that peanut butter! I can't stand the stuff.*). This applies primarily, though not exclusively, to participants (cf. Webber, 1987, on reference to phenomena other than things). At the same time it allows us to recognize not only participants of the 'simple' type (cf. Plate 5) but also the 'larger' elements known as macro- and meta-phenomena. Macro-phenomena are figures downranked to function as ordinary elements; meta-phenomena are figures projected as elements of a second order (see Chapter 3, Section 3.3 below). Halliday & Hasan (1976), where reference to macro-phenomena is called extended reference, and reference to meta-phenomena is called reference to facts, cite ambiguities which bring out the difference among elements of these various kinds:

(i) extended reference — to macro-phenomenon:

```
They broke a Chinese vase.
(i) That was valuable. (phenomenon: thing — the vase)
(ii) That was careless. (macro-phenomenon — the act of their breaking of the
vase)
```

(ii) reference to 'fact' — to meta-phenomenon

It rained day and night for two weeks. The basement flooded and everything was under water.

(i) It spoilt our calculations. (meta-phenomenon (fact) — the fact that it rained so much upset our predictions)

(ii) It spoilt our calculations. (macro-phenomenon — the act of raining destroyed physical records)

Note how this relates to the shift of perspective from figure to participant (cf. Section 2.11.3 [3]): a figure such as 'catch + mouse' becomes referable as a macro-phenomenon (*Your cat's caught a mouse — It's never done that before*), and by the same token can enter into participant-based construal through the system of modification (Table 2(11)): *(cats are) creatures that catch mice.*

This brings to an end our overview of the general ideational potential of the semantic system. In the next four chapters we shall fill out further details of the resources of the ideation base. We begin by mapping out the resources for construing experience in the congruent mode:

sequences are discussed in Chapter 3;

figures are dealt with in Chapter 4; and

elements are described in Chapter 5.

In Chapter 6, we explore the metaphorical mode of construing experience interpreting this mode as a reconstrual of the model construed in the congruent mode. Rounding off this part of the book, we then sketch the outlines of the ideation base of Chinese and raise the issue of variability across languages in how they construe experience.

3. Sequences

We introduced sequences in Chapter 2, Section 2.2 above. Here we shall characterize them in more detail, increasing the delicacy of the account to cover both the types of sequence and their mode of organization.

A sequence constitutes a model of how figures can be *related*. One prominent form of this relationship, which has been foregrounded in various guises in science and logic, is that of cause & effect, whereby experience is given a causal interpretation. But that is only one among many such possible relationships, which taken together can be said to constitute the logic of natural language.

3.1 Natural logic of sequences and propositional logic

Sequences might be said to constitute the 'natural logic' equivalent of propositional logic — that is, the *evolved* system for reasoning about relations of cause, conditionality, etc. from which propositional logic has been derived by *design*. Thus we have parallel series such as:

propositional logic	natural logic
p & q	p and q
p ∨ q	p or q
p → q	p so q; if p then q

But, as has often been pointed out, the two are not translation equivalents; for example, material implication (p → q) applies even when the rendering in ordinary language seems odd, and disjunction in logic is either inclusive or exclusive whereas natural disjunction is non-committal. Since propositional logic is a designed system, its relations are codified and defined (typically in truth-functional terms[1]). In contrast, sequential relations have evolved. A certain type of relation will have a core — the prototypical representatives of that type; but there will also be more peripheral representatives and 'grey areas' where one type shades into another.

There is another important difference between propositional logic and the natural logic of sequences. While there is only a very small handful of truth-functional connectives in propositional logic (conjunction, disjunction [exclusive or non-exclusive], implication), there is a very wide range of sequential relations in language — all the more specific varieties of projecting and expanding. A summary of these is given in Table 3(1).

---

[1] Propositional logic is interpersonally invariable. Unlike natural logic, it is only concerned with statements, or rather — since language is concerned with validity rather than truth — with the philosophical version of what are statements in natural language.

Table 3(1): The types of natural and propositional logic

natural logic of sequences			propositional logic
projection	say		--
	think[2]		--
expansion	reiterate (elaboration)		--
	add (extension)	addition	conjunction
		alternation	disjunction
		replacement	--
	qualify (enhancement)	time	--
		space	--
		cause-condition	
		reason	--
		purpose	--
		concession	--
		condition	implication
		manner	--
		...	

Both the difference in scope and the difference in 'definability' can be explained in functional terms. Sequences have evolved in the interpretation of human experience in general; consequently, they have to be flexible and powerful enough to cope with a large amount of variation, and the implicit 'definition' of each relation (i.e., its location in the semantic system along various dimensions) is the evolving distillation of innumerable instances where it is invoked (for a revealing account of how sequences may construe rationality in everyday talk, see Hasan, 1992). In contrast, the truth-functional connectives of propositional logic have been designed for a very restricted purpose — the kind of deductive reasoning western philosophy came to focus on — and their definitions are fixed by reference to values of "true" and "false" (by means of truth tables).

In a restricted register, such as those of weather forecasts and recipes (see Chapter 8 below), it may be possible to define sequential relations more precisely; but that is only because these registers are special cases, rather in the same way that the applications of propositional logic are special cases.

One might try to characterize sequences by reference to propositional logic; this would give some indication of what type of knowledge representation system is embodied in

---

[2] Projecting figures of the 'think' type — 'know', 'believe', 'want' — have been represented outside standard logic within intensional logic.

this domain of ideational semantics. However, such a characterization would be likely to distort our understanding of sequences, because sequences cover and organize a considerably larger domain of the ideational semantic space than propositional logic attempts to do.

3.2 Expansion and projection

Instead of referring to formal logic, let us ask what kind of construal of experience is embodied in semantic sequences. Throughout the semantic construal of human experience, there is a differentiation between two orders of reality: between the everyday reality of our material existence on the one hand and on the other hand the second-order reality that is brought into existence only by the system of language. This is a contrast between semiotic phenomena, those of meanings and wordings, and the first-order phenomena that constitute our material environment. (Note that the linguistic processes themselves, as apprehended by our senses, are part of the first-order reality; second-order reality is formed of the meanings and the wordings that these processes bring into being.)

This differentiation is embodied in relations of sequence in the following way. Either a sequential relation **expands** one figure by adding another one to it, the two still remaining at the same phenomenal level; or the sequential relation **projects** one of the two figures onto the plane of second-order, semiotic phenomena, so that it enters the realm of **metaphenomena** (meanings or wordings). This is the distinction between expansion and projection that we introduced briefly in Chapter 2, Section 2.2. For example, expansion: *highs will be mid-80s to mid-90s ——> but parts of Texas could reach the 100s;* projection: *the forecast predicts ——> "parts of Texas could reach the 100s".* We can explore this distinction through the conventions of comic strips. Expansions are typically represented pictorially by means of consecutive frames — 'x then y', 'x so y', 'x meanwhile y', and so on (the relationship is sometimes spelt out in writing, e.g. *Meanwhile ...*). We can even identify the three different kinds of expansion, those of elaborating, extending, and enhancing. When further detail is given in a picture of a magnifying glass, this is elaboration; where two frames are joined to form a continuous picture, this suggests extension; otherwise, consecutive frames display a relation of enhancement. But in all cases the representation is pictorial throughout. In contrast, projections involve two modes: the projecting figure is represented pictorially as the symbol source, but the projected figure is represented linguistically and this second-order reality is typically framed within a 'balloon'. (There are two types of balloon; see further below.) The two types of relation can be shown as in Figure 3-1.

We could say that the world view that is constructed in this way is (quite reasonably, from our point of view) focussed on humans, with human consciousness occupying a privileged place. Thus typically only humans can project into second-order reality. However, since human consciousness is the locus of semiotic activity, it has the power of interpreting as metaphenomenon that which is manifested by some other, non-conscious symbolic source. Thus while "sensing" (that is, semiotic activity that is unmanifested, like thinking) does require a human senser, saying can be ascribed to a non-human as well as to a human sayer (cf. *he thinks* —> *the moon is a balloon* vs. *he says/ the book says* —>*the moon is a balloon*). Figure 3-2 shows the relationship between the two orders of metaphenomena and the presence of consciousness in the act of projection.

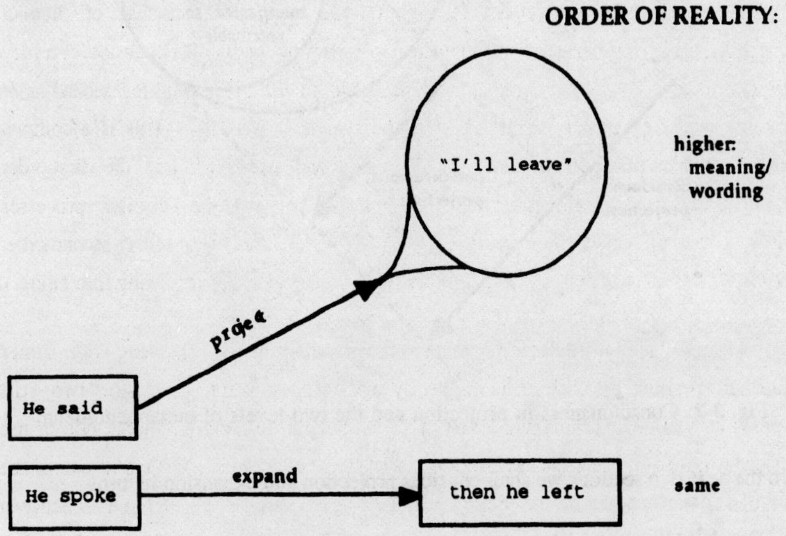

ORDER OF REALITY:

"I'll leave"

higher:
meaning/
wording

project

He said

He spoke   expand   then he left   same

Fig. 3-1: The two basic types of sequence

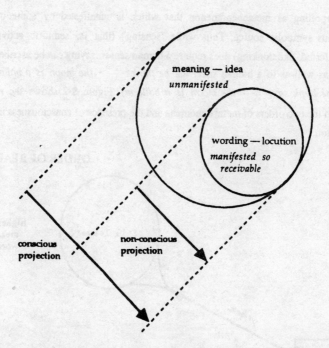

Fig. 3-2: Consciousness in projection and the two levels of metaphenomena

In the next two sections we shall consider projection and expansion in turn.

3.3 Projection

3.3.1 Two levels of projected content: ideas and locutions

We have suggested that the relation of projection sets up one figure on a different plane of reality — we refer to this as the second-order or semiotic level. This second-order level of reality is the **content plane** of a semiotic system (cf. our characterization of the linguistic system in Chapter 1, Section 1.2 above). That is to say, the projected figure is projected in the form of 'content': see Figure 3-3.

SYMBOLIC "REALITY":

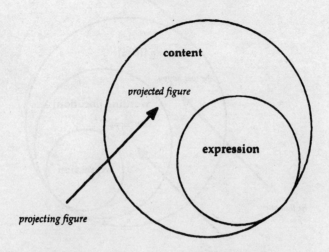

Fig. 3-3: A figure construed as content by projection

We have seen that the content plane is stratified into two levels — semantics (the level of meanings) and lexicogrammar (the level of wordings). Consequently, we would expect projections to be located at either or both of these levels, and this is indeed what happens: a projected figure is either a meaning or a wording: see Figure 3-4.

In (i) the 'content' of his thinking is the meaning. It remains internal to his consciousness and unrealized, i.e. unworded. In (ii) the 'content' of his saying is the wording. It has been externalized, realized as a wording. We will refer to these in the context of projection as (i) **ideas** and (ii) **locutions**. The contrast between these two statuses of projected figures is typically reflected in the shape of balloons in comic strip projections: see Figure 3-5.

SYMBOLIC "REALITY":

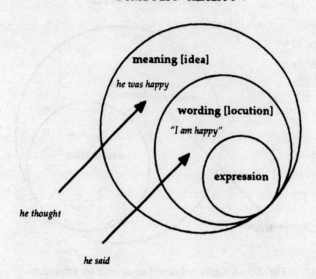

Fig. 3-4: Projection at the two levels of content

Fig. 3-5: Indication of projection in comic strips

Let us look more closely at these two modes of projecting, in both of which the projecting figure represents symbolic processing, the processing that brings the other figure into symbolic existence. Either the projection takes the prototypical form of semiosis: it is presented as verbal, shared, an exchange or joint construction of meanings (e.g. *Harriet said* 'me feed cat?'); or it is fashioned into a derived semiotic form, unshared, interiorized, and without any meaning being exchanged (e.g. *Harriet thought* 'me feed cat?'). In the first, the projecting figure is one of saying; the projected is referred to as **locution**. In the second, the projecting figure is one of sensing; the projected is referred to as **idea**. Ideas are projections which are sensed, locutions are projections which are said.

But there is another variable intersecting with the above. We pointed out in Chapter 2, Section 2.2 that whenever two figures are related in a sequence, they may be either equal or unequal in semantic weight. We illustrated this interdependency system with reference to expansion; but it applies also to projection. The projecting and the projected figures may have equal status in the sequence: this relation is that of **quoting**, as in *Harriet said/ thought "Shall I feed the cat?"*. Or they may have unequal status: this relation is that of **reporting**, as in (*Harriet asked/ wondered*) *whether she should feed the cat*. We can relate this to the fact that projection is the creating of a second-order reality. In reporting, the status of the two parts is unequal — the projected figure is *dependent on* the projecting: hence the projected figure is clearly construed as belonging to a different, second-order plane of reality — a reality that is made of meaning, as it were. In quoting, on the other hand, the two have equal status as *independent* figures; the projected figure is thus projected *as if* it was still part of the same first-order reality.

There are two consequences of this. The first is that, in quoting, the form of wording is still that of the first-order realm of experience: *"Shall I feed the cat?"* — taken by itself, there is nothing about this to show it is a projection. In reporting, on the other hand, the form of wording is clearly marked as being of the second order: *whether she should feed the cat* has lost its first-order semantic features — and hence has to be projected by words that specify its particular speech function: *asked/ wondered,* not *said/ thought.*

The second consequence is that although the two variables, locution/ idea and quoting/ reporting, can combine in either of the two possible alignments, there is a natural default condition, which is that locution goes with quoting and idea goes with reporting, as shown in Figure 3-6. The reason for this is clear: where the first-order phenomenon is one of saying (prototypically shared semiosis), the projected figure can be presented as if it was also of the same order: *Harriet said + "Shall I feed the cat?"* (reversible as *"Shall I feed the cat?" + said Harriet*). Where the first-order phenomenon is one of sensing (unshared semiosis), the projected figure has no counterpart on the first-order plane of experience and cannot be naturally presented as if it had; so, *Harriet wondered + whether she should feed the cat.* But there is always the possibility of semogenic extension by cross-coupling; so we also find the corresponding marked alignments: locution/ report *Harriet asked + whether she should feed the cat,* and idea/ quote *Harriet wondered + "Shall*

I feed the cat?" — the latter being again reversible. See Halliday (1985: Chapter 7) and Nesbitt & Plum (1988).

projecting: type	projected: status	
	quoted	reported
locution	√	
idea		√

Fig. 3-6: Default alignments (projection)

Projections of ideas have played a special role in the extension of standard logic within intensional logic (or, more restrictedly for knowing and believing, within epistemic logic) to allow for reasoning in this domain. One of the features of the projection of ideas that has received special attention in logically-oriented approaches to meaning is its "referential opacity". If a speaker knows that Henry is the king, and construes somebody else's belief as *Thomas thinks Henry is a nice man,* the referring expression *Henry* cannot be replaced by *the king* although the speaker knows they have the same referent: 'Thomas thinks the king is a nice man' cannot be inferred from 'Thomas thinks Henry is a nice man' since the identity of Henry and the king has not been established in the projected world of Thomas's consciousness.

The projection of ideas has also played an important role in hearer modelling in AI and computational linguistics. From a systemic-functional point of view, hearer modelling corresponds to one aspect of the interaction base: the interactants in a dialogue have to be able to assess and model the way their experiences diverge. This is one measure of the overall interpersonal distance between them. In hearer modelling, this tends to be construed ideationally by means of cognitive projection, where the projected idea is represented as a separate partition or space within the overall knowledge (see e.g. Allen, 1987: Ch. 15; Kobsa & Wahlster, 1989; Ballim & Wilks, 1991): 'the speaker believes ——> the hearer knows ——> ...'. Such models may involve long projecting sequences (often called "nested beliefs"), as in the example in Figure 3-7 — 'α I believe ——> 'β that you believe ——> 'γ that I believe ——> 'δ it's boiling'.

In general, there is no temporal constraint between the projected and the projecting figures: the projected figure may be past, present or future relative to the projecting one. The dimension affected by projection order of reality, not time. However, there is a major dichotomy between two types of projection which does have temporal implications. To explore it, we have to look briefly at a fundamental interpersonal category, that of mood.

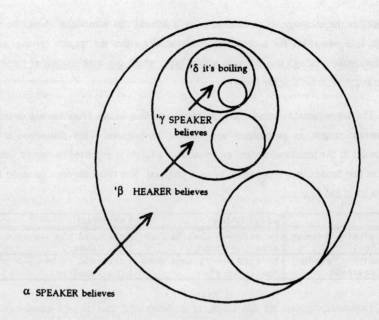

Fig. 3-7: Series of cognitive projections

3.3.2 Propositions and proposals

Interpersonal semantics is centrally concerned with varieties of symbolic exchange (Halliday, 1984b, 1985: Ch. 4). Here, as in other places in the meaning base, the system is organized in such a way that it creates a difference between non-symbolic reality and symbolic reality, between phenomena and metaphenomena. The "commodity" that is being exchanged in interpersonal dialogue is either semiotic or material: it is either one that is construed by language itself — **information** — or it is one that exists independently of language — **goods & services**. In the first case, language *constitutes* the exchange; in the second, it *facilitates* the exchange of a non-linguistic commodity. For example:

	information — proposition	goods & services — proposal
giving	statement *I've done the laundry.*	offer *I can do the laundry.*
demanding	question *Have you done the laundry?*	command *Do the laundry!*

Information is either given or demanded; in either case it is encoded as a **proposition**.[3] Similarly, goods & services are either given or demanded, but the linguistic act is a mediating one, specifying the (typically non-linguistic) action that

---

[3] The term *proposition* is not used here in its sense in logic, but in contrast with *proposal* (see immediately below).

embodies the exchange, as an offer to do or a demand that something should be done. This is a **proposal** for a deed, one that commits either the speaker (giving) or the addressee (demanding); together with a third type, which is a combination of these two, viz. suggestion: *Let's do the laundry.*

The interpersonal system for dialogic interaction thus creates a fundamental distinction between 'content' as proposition and 'content' as proposal. This distinction is then reflected in the ideational system of projection: a figure is projected in one or other of these two modes, as a proposition or as a proposal. The two categories combine freely with ideas and locutions:

	proposition	proposal
content: meaning (idea)	he said —> that he had done the laundry	she told him —> to do the laundry
content: wording (locution)	he said —> "I have done the laundry"	she said to him —> "do the laundry!"

Projected proposals are non-actual, or uninstantiated: that is, the occurrence of a projected proposal is always future in relation to the figure that projects it. In contrast, propositions are actual, or instantiated: that is, the occurrence of a proposition is located in actual time (which may be past, present or future).

Grammatically the distinction between propositions and proposals is constructed as follows. When the projection is reported, propositions are realized by finite bound clauses, i.e. clauses that select for primary tense or modality; and proposals are realized by irrealis (infinitival) non-finite bound clauses — taking the contrasting examples from above: *(he said) that he had done the laundry : (she told him) to do the laundry.* When the projection is quoted, propositions are realized by indicative clauses, i.e. clauses that select for primary tense or modality; and proposals are realized by imperative clauses — taking the contrasting examples from above: *(he said) "I have done the laundry" : (she said to him) "do the laundry".* These realizational patterns are summarized below:

	proposition ⬂	proposal ⬂
reporting ⬂	bound: finite *(he said/ thought) that he had done the laundry* *(she asked/ wondered) whether he had done the laundry*	bound: non-finite: irrealis *(she told him) to do the laundry/* *(she wanted) him to do the laundry*
quoting ⬂	free: indicative *(he said) "I have done the laundry"* *(she said/ asked) "have you done the laundry?"*	free: imperative *(she said to him) "do the laundry!"*

As was said above, in quoting, where the projected clause retains its mood, the general verb *say* can be used whatever speech function is being projected. In reporting, on the other hand, the projected clause is no longer specified for mood; its speech function is signalled by the verb in the projecting clause (*asked, ordered,* etc.). This gives the projected element more of an ideational status (cf. its treatment in traditional grammar as "object" of the projecting verb), and opens up the way to a series of agnate expressions such as (*the king ordered*) *"Execute him!" / that he should be executed / him to be executed / him executed / his execution.*

There is thus a parallel between reported propositions/ proposals and quoted ones. But with offers (proposals: giving goods-&-services) there is a difference in respect of realization. Offers, in English, are not grammaticalized in the mood system; that is, while the other categories, statements, questions and commands, have corresponding mood categories in the grammar (declarative, interrogative and imperative), offers do not. They may be realized by any of the mood categories; for example:

> declarative: `I can do the laundry.`
> interrogative: `Shall I do the laundry?`
> imperative: `Let me do the laundry!`

Significantly, the indicative clauses realizing offers are modulated; they select for an imperative modality of readiness or obligation (see e.g. Halliday, 1985: Section 10.4). Quoted offers naturally retain the property of being variously realized in the mood system:

> declarative: `She said: "I can do the laundry."`
> interrogative: `She said: "Shall I do the laundry?"`
> imperative: `She said: "Let me do the laundry!"`

However, reported offers can always be realized in the same way as reported commands — as in the case of reported propositions, the distinction in orientation between giving and demanding is realized by the projecting clause; for example:

> command: `she told him ——> to do the laundry`
> offer: `she offered (promised; threatened) ——> to do the laundry`

The category of reported proposal is thus realized generally as a perfective non-finite clause when it is reported.

We saw that quoted offers may be realized by modulated indicative clauses. This would seem to be an exception to the generalization that indicative clauses realize propositions. However, it is a principled one: the type of indicative clause involved is precisely the type that lies closer in the interpersonal clause grammar to imperative clauses — modulated indicative clauses, i.e. those with an imperative modality. As can be expected, this is then also a possible realization of commands; it is a metaphorical strategy for

expanding the meaning potential, typically to vary the tenor between speaker and listener.
For example:

> she told him: "Do the laundry!"; "You should do the laundry."
> she asked him: "Could you do the laundry?"

Commands can be reported in the same way:

> she told him ——> to do the laundry.
> she told him ——> he should do the laundry.
> she asked him ——> whether he could do the laundry.

To sum up the distinctions discussed so far. In a projecting sequence, a figure of
thinking or saying projects another figure as an idea or a locution, either of which may be
a proposition or a proposal: see Figure 3-8.

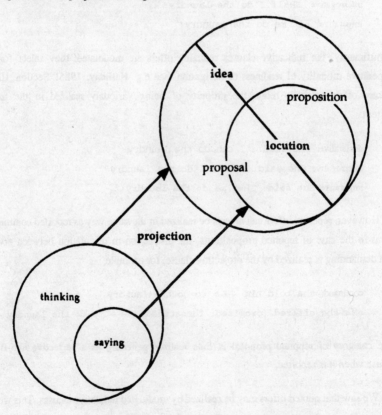

Fig. 3-8: The possibilities of projecting sequences

We can now turn to the other primary type of sequence — expansion.

3.4 Expansion

Expansion is a highly generalized type of relation, whereby one figure is joined logico-semantically to another figure by a relator to form a sequence of the same order of reality. It will be easier to characterize expansion at the next step in delicacy, in terms of its immediate subtypes: elaborate (reiterate), extend (add), and enhance (qualify):

(i) **elaboration** is a (partial) identity relation between figures: one is identified with another with a difference in perspective (*it matters a lot; it plays an important role*) or one is included under another as an example (*it plays an important role; e.g., it provides the infrastructure*). These are clearly related to one another: identity is the limiting case of inclusion and inclusion is partial identity.

(ii) **extension** is an additive relation between figures: a sequence is made bigger by the addition of another figure. This may involve pure addition ('and': *he is too young and he doesn't speak the language*) or addition with an adversative feature ('and yet': *he speaks the language but he is too young*). As a variant of addition, we also have alternation (*he is too young or else he is just immature*).

(iii) **enhancement** is a circumstantial or qualifying relation between figures: it is, in a sense, extension plus a circumstantial feature — 'and' + time ('and then', 'and at the same time', etc.), 'and' + manner ('and in the same way', 'and likewise'), 'and' + cause ('and therefore', etc.), etc.: *it is autumn, so the leaves are turning brown.*

Expansion can be thought of as construing another dimension of experience, so that superimposed, as it were, on the construal of a figure — a basic fragment of experience in the form of a **quantum of change** (event, action, behaviour &c.) — is the construal of a nexus between two figures, such that one such fragment is non-randomly (i.e. meaningfully) cumulated with another.

From one standpoint the limiting case of expansion would be accumulation in a temporal sequence (hence our general term "sequence" for the product of this construal): '*a* happens, then *x* happens'. This gives value to *a* as the temporal circumstance of *x*. From this we could derive a wide range of more complex enhancing relations: variations on the simple temporal sequence ('after, before, at the same time, immediately after, &c.) and further circumstances such as cause, condition, concession, and their subcategories. We shall not try to enumerate these here; they are familiar as categories at the level of lexicogrammar (see Halliday, 1985: Ch. 7; Matthiessen, 1995b: Ch. 3). These are 'enhancements', multiplying one figure by another, as it were. But figures may also be added to one another, making them part of the same story without assigning any kind of logical priority to either: 'x as well as/ instead of/ in contradistinction to a '. We have referred to these as extensions. And there is the third type of accumulation where the logical relation is that of 'equals': 'x is the same figure as a'. Here at this end the limiting case is a simple repetition; this may be further elaborated in such a way that one figure is reworded as another, or else further clarified or brought out by an example.

There is no sharp line between a figure and a sequence of figures: a **quantum of experience** is not defined before it is construed, and the grammar rather sets up a *cline from sequence to simple figure*. (This is, in fact, a variable across languages; we shall return to this point from a cross-linguistic point of view in Chapter 6.) For example:

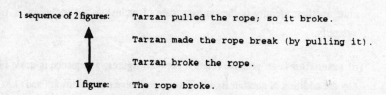

1 sequence of 2 figures:	`Tarzan pulled the rope; so it broke.`
	`Tarzan made the rope break (by pulling it).`
	`Tarzan broke the rope.`
1 figure:	`The rope broke.`

The following passage of spontaneous conversation exemplifies the principal categories of expansion (note than it also contains one example of projection):

levels	of	nesting	in	sequence	figures in sequence
x_β	1	1	1		[1] if you go into a bank
			$=_2$		[2] if you walked through to Barclays for instance
		$+_2$	1		[3] and said
			"$_2$		[4] will you look after my investments
	$+_2$				[5] or even if you went off to Hambros or one of the famous banks of that nature
α	1	α			[6] they would every year value your securities
		x_β			[7] as we do of course
	$+_2$	1			[8] but they would charge you
		$=_2$			[9] they'd send you a bill for a percentage of what they were worth

KEY: parataxis [equal]: 1, 2; hypotaxis [unequal]: α, β; elaboration: =; extension: +; enhancement: x. (Taken from Svartvik & Quirk, 1980: 430.)

Relations of expansion are typically realized in the grammar by conjunctions or conjunctive expressions linking a pair of clauses, either paratactically or hypotactically (e.g. *that is, in other words; and, but, or, also, besides; so, yet, then, when, if, because, unless*). Some of these may realize more than one category; for example, *but* may be adversative 'and yet' (extending), or concessive 'and in spite of this' (enhancing); *while* may be additive 'and in addition' (extending), or temporal 'and at the same time' (enhancing); *or* may be alternative 'or else' (extending: alternatives in the external world, like *take it or leave it*), or restating 'in other words' (elaborating: alternatives in the world 'internal' to the discourse, like *they are reduced to the smallest size, or micro-miniaturized.*). Overlaps in realization of this kind show that the primary categories we have set up do in fact shade into one another; in particular, extending in some sense occupies a space intermediate between elaborating and enhancing, and shares a fuzzy borderline with each (cf. Chapter 2, Section 2.11.1 and Chapter 13, Section 13.3).

Finally, the distinction between expansion and projection is less determinate than we have suggested. The logico-semantic relation of condition, which is prototypically construed as a form of enhancement, could also be construed as a kind of projection; and this is also brought out in the grammar. Conditions specify a potential and actualizable but non-actual situation. This potential situation can also be set up through projection:

```
If the power supply fails, what's the best thing to do?
Supposing the power supply fails, what's the best thing to do?
Say the power supply fails, what's the best thing to do?
```

Words such as *supposing* and *assuming* are verbs of projection which have come to function as conjunctions in conditional figures; while other words such as *imagine* and *say* retain more of their projecting force. Sometimes even variants of the same word have come to differ a little in their location on this cline: for example, *suppose* and *assume* seem closer to projection than their corresponding participial variants. This is an uncertain region in which a figure hangs in the air, so to speak, suspended between the hypothetical material plane and the semiotic one.

3.5 The relational character of sequences

In the overview, we introduced two distinct types of structure — the relational organization of sequences, and the configurational organization of figures (see Chapter 2, Sections 2.1, 2.2 & 2.3). In contrast to figures, sequences are not constructional units. We can specify the range of projecting and expanding relations available for further developing a sequence, but we cannot specify where a sequence has to come to an end — that is, we cannot specify a sequence as a unit whole with a conventional configuration of parts. Thus if we have expanded one figure we can always repeat the operation:

```
A then B
A then B then C
A then B then C then D ...
```

In contrast, a figure is a unit with a finite number of elements:

```
B follows A
```

Hence a sequence can be indefinitely complex, whereas a figure cannot. For instance, consider the sequence from the culinary domain (Highton & Highton,[4] p. 156) shown in Figure 3-9.

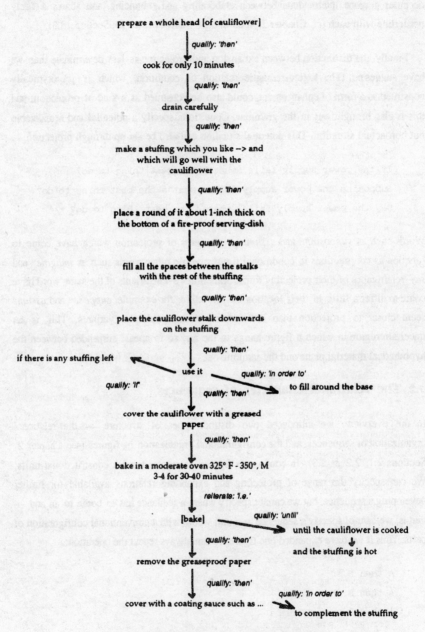

Fig. 3-9: Sequence of culinary operations

---

[4] N.B. Highton & R.B. Highton. 1964. The Home Book of Vegetarian Cookery. London Faber and Faber.

This sequence is expanded step by step: one 'operational' figure is qualified by another, which is in turn qualified by another, and so on. As the example illustrates, there may be internal **nesting**. That is, a sequential relation may relate not only to a figure but also to a sequence of figures. The sequence of culinary operations in Figure 3-9 is worded in the text as follows:

> Prepare a whole head **and** cook for only 10 minutes. Drain carefully. Make a stuffing (see section on Stuffings) which you like, **and** which will go well with cauliflower. Place a round of it about 1-inch thick on the bottom of a fire-proof serving-dish. Fill all the spaces between the stalks with the rest of the stuffing **and** place the cauliflower stalk downwards on the stuffing, **if** there is any stuffing left use it to fill in around the base.
>
> Cover the cauliflower with a greased paper **and** bake in a moderate oven 325° F. - 350° F., M3-4 for 30-40 minutes. That is, **until** the cauliflower is cooked and the stuffing is hot. Remove the greaseproof paper **and** cover with a coating sauce to complement the stuffing, such as: ...

The example illustrates a common type of sequence used to encode experience with operations — a **procedure**. The relations in a procedure are typically expansions: (i) additive: addition and alternation; (ii) qualifying: temporal and causal conditions. A procedure, like any sequence, is potentially infinite. The only reason the procedure above stops is that the cauliflower surprise is ready to serve. The procedure does not end because a unit boundary has been reached; on the contrary, because the structure is relational, the procedure could be developed indefinitely.

One important type of procedure is the algorithm of computational specifications. Here is an example of a pre-computational algorithm for searching a tree, breadth-first, construed linguistically as a procedural text (Barr & Feigenbaum, 1981: 56-7).

> 1. Put the start node on a list, OPEN, of unexpanded nodes.
>
> 2. Remove the first node, n, from OPEN.
>
> 3. Expand node n — generating all its immediate successors **and**, for each successor m, **if** m represents a set of more than one subproblem, generating successors of m corresponding to the individual subproblems. Attach, to each newly generated node, a pointer back to its immediate successor. Place all the new nodes that do not yet have descendants at the end of OPEN.

4. **If** no successors were generated in (3), **then**

    a. Label node *n* unsolvable.

    b. **If** the unsolvability of *n* makes any of its ancestors unsolvable, label these ancestors unsolvable.

    c. **If** the start node is labeled unsolvable, exit with failure.

    d. Remove from OPEN any nodes with an unsolvable ancestor.

5. **Otherwise**, **if** any terminal nodes were generated in (3), then

    a. Label these terminal nodes solved.

    b. **If** the solution of these terminal nodes makes any of their ancestors solved, label these ancestors solved.

    c. **If** the start node is labeled solved, exit with success.

    d. Remove from OPEN any nodes that are labeled solved or that have a solved ancestor.

6. Go to (2).

The default relation 'and then' is left implicit in this text; conditioning ('if; if not') is made explicit. Algorithms are often displayed by means of both verbal instructions and a simple diagrammatic semiotic, the flow chart.

Thus sequences are formed by binary logico-semantic relations which may relate either single figures or sequences of figures. Certain relations may impose constraints on the phenomena being related; for example, a projecting relation can only obtain when the first figure is one of sensing or saying. But the range of different logico-semantic relations is highly varied, so that constraints tend to be specific to particular subtypes.

3.6 Sequences and text

Sequences impose a certain order on our experience in terms of the relations that connect happening with another. Hence sequences can be used to store information about the world in the form of organized text — 'this is how to change tyres on your car', 'this is how to make cauliflower surprise', etc.. Such texts often fall into a clearly recognizable text type, such as procedures, proofs, explanations, and episodic narratives. Not all texts are as highly regulated as these; but it is usually possible to make some prediction about the kinds of sequence, and the complexity to which sequences extend, in most of our culturally recognized modes of discourse.

Texts and sequences are of the same order of abstraction; both are semantic phenomena. A text is a piece of language that is functional in context. It draws on the ideational meaning base but it involves the full metafunctional spectrum; i.e. there are interpersonal and textual contributions as well. Since text draws on the ideational meaning base, sequences are one principle for organizing text. For example, the culinary procedure for making cauliflower surprise constitutes one text. Many text types are heavily influenced by patterns in the meaning base — they can be seen as 'macro-figures', i.e. as expansions of figures by means of logico-semantic relations. This is not to say that the relationship between organization in the meaning base and discoursal organization is always one-to-one even when a text is organized according to an ideational sequence. In particular, a text may leave to be inferred certain steps that would be specified in the sequence in the meaning base (e.g. to make explicit the inferential processes involved).

As already noted, text organization also draws on the interaction base; and there are certain parallels with the ideation base with respect to sequences. The interaction base certainly has text forming resources that are uniquely interpersonal. In particular, it has the resources for the collaborative exchanges that are embodied in the notion of interaction — for producing dialogue jointly by means of coordinated moves alternating between the interlocutors (see e.g., Bateman, 1985; Berry, 1981; Halliday, 1984b; Martin, 1992). But these interpersonal moves may also form sequences of moves in a way that is similar to the formation of sequences of figures in the ideation base. Typical examples involve motivating condition ('I invite you to accept x, if you want x'; for example: *If you're thirsty, there's beer in the fridge*) and evidence ('I think, infer/ you should believe x because y'; for example: *John's in Germany because I just talked to him*).

Certain text types are heavily influenced by such interpersonally oriented sequences.[5] This is the case with persuasive text as in the following advertisement:

[1] To get to the top you have to go to the right school.

[2] The first thing we do with all new pilots, no matter how qualified, is send them back to school. [3] They must pass advanced and rigorous regular checks before they can fly with us. [4] Exacting standards. [5] Another reason why we're Australia's leading airline.

[6] Australian Airlines

[7] "You should see us now."

---

[5] In terms of Rhetorical Structure Theory (Mann & Thompson, 1987; Mann, Matthiessen & Thompson, 1992), the relations here include enablement, motivation, and evidence — interpersonally oriented relations (see Mann & Matthiessen, 1991).

Here the nuclear passage in the advertisement is [7] — getting the reader to feel inclined to see Australian Airlines; but to achieve this, [1] through [5] are also included. They stand in an interpersonally oriented reason relationship to [7] — a motivation relationship. (There are also ideationally oriented sequence relations, of course; for example, [3] is internally organized as a temporal sequence — *they must pass advanced and rigorous regular checks*   ——> *before they can fly with us.*)

We can generalize as follows: the logical resources for forming sequences have evolved in the environment of ideational meaning as sequences of figures. But these highly generalized resources can then also be applied in an interpersonal environment to form interactional sequences. (We should note here, however, that evidence from language development studies suggests that the logical-semantic relations are first construed in interpersonal contexts: see Phillips, 1985, 1986; Halliday, 1993a; and Part V below.) In producing a text, we may use either or both, depending on the nature of the text: see Figure 3-10 and see also further Chapter 9 below on the role of the text base in organizing text.

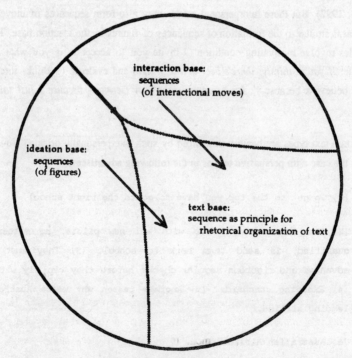

Fig. 3-10: Support in the organization of text from ideationally and interpersonally oriented sequences

3.7 Sequences and grammar

As we noted in Chapter 1, Section 1.5, semantics and grammar evolve together (in all three senses of semohistory we discussed). In the present context that means that sequences and clause complexes evolve together. The basic principle is that a sequence is realized by a clause complex. But the two may become dissociated from one another.

(i) On the one hand, a sequence may extend beyond a single clause complex, as the culinary sequence in Section 3.5 above clearly shows. That is, the general potential is simultaneously semantic and grammatical; but in the creation of this particular text, this potential may be taken up semantically to create a sequence that is more extensive than the clause complexes realizing it. Here is a very simple example of a sequence for making 'new potatoes with lemon' (Highton & Highton, p. 185), which is realized by two clause complexes:

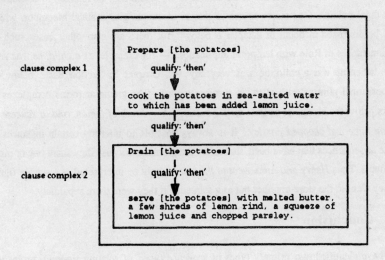

The text reads as follows:

> Prepare and cook the potatoes in sea-salted water to which has been added lemon juice. Drain and serve with melted butter, a few shreds of lemon rind, a squeeze of lemon juice and chopped parsley.

The sequence has been grouped into two clause complexes in the grammar. However, this grouping is by no means arbitrary; it serves to indicate the two major phases of the preparation of new potatoes with lemon. In other words, once sequence and clause complex have become partly disassociated so that one sequence does not automatically imply one clause complex, the decision how to associate them in realization becomes a meaningful, significant choice. (The significance may vary from one register to another; but the principle that the choice is meaningful is quite general.)

(ii) On the other hand, a clause complex may in principle correspond to a figure rather than a sequence. This happens through grammatical metaphor of an interpersonal kind (see Halliday, 1985: Section 10.4): an interpersonal modality that would be realized congruently as a modal auxiliary (*can, may, will* &c) or a modal adjunct (*perhaps, probably* &c) is 'upgraded' to the status of a projecting clause in a clause complex; for example:

```
I don't suppose || there's very much    'there is probably not'

I think || I might have walked out too from all the accounts
'I probably might have'
```

(iii) In addition, one or more of the figures in the clause may be realized by something 'less than' a clause. One major source of this is ideational grammatical metaphor, which will be discussed in detail in Chapter 6 below. But there are also other cases such as circumstances of Role with temporal implications — for example: *as a child, he was very shy* 'when he was a child, he was very shy' (cf. Chapter 8, Section 8.2.2 below on prepositional phrases with *with* in weather reports). The grammar forms complexes at ranks below the clause, of course: *melted butter, a few shreds of lemon rind, a squeeze of lemon juice and chopped parsley.* It is always possible to interpret certain instances of these as sequences that have been 'shrunk' by the grammar because they share one or more elements. Thus *Henry and Anne went to the store* might be interpreted as a simple figure if they went to the store together but as a sequence if they went there separately.

3.8 Conclusion

We have identified two primary types of sequence (ways of relating figures), projection and expansion; and with both of these the figures that are related may be either equal or unequal in status. To say that these relations are between figures means in principle that they hold between figures as a whole; that is, given a pair of related figures the domain of the expansion or projection relation between them is each of the figures in its entirety. But in some instances, some subdomain may be particularly implicated. This is perhaps especially true with elaborating sequences — the grammar of hypotactic elaborating clause complexes tells us as much: the elaborating dependent clause includes a relative reference expression (if the clause is finite) and the clause is placed immediately after the domain that is being elaborated, whether that is the whole clause (*Mary could never feel comfortable with him, which was perfectly understandable*) or some element within the clause (*Mary, who was very sensitive, could never feel comfortable with him*).

The limiting case is that where what is being expanded is not a figure but an element of a figure, in which case instead of a sequence of figures we get a sequence of elements, realized by group or phrase complexes. Thus instead of *Schank conceived of scripts and Abelson conceived of scripts as a solution to this problem,* a sequence of figures where there are two processes of conception, we get *Schank and Abelson conceived of scripts as a solution to this problem,* a single figure with a sequence of elements (serving as Senser of a single process). Putting this in terms of the grammar, the sequential relationships remain constant, but the rank at which the complex occurs depends on the domain being related: see Figure 3-11.

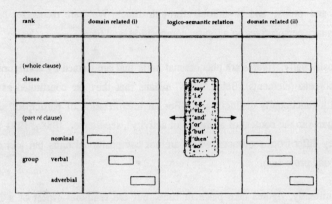

Fig. 3-11: Different domains of logico-semantic relations

One question that arises here is the extent to which the semantics and the grammar are in phase with one another. It is conceivable that a semantic sequence of figures could be realized in the grammar by a single clause with complexes at group/word rank — i.e., the sequencing is downranked in course of realization. One argument in favour of exploring this possibility is that it would be possible to sort out the potential ambiguity of examples such as *Henry and Anne went to the movies* — grammatically, we have a group complex (*Henry and Anne*), but semantically, it could be either a sequence of figures (on the reading 'separately': 'Henry went to the movies and Anne went to the movies') or a sequence of elements (on the reading 'together': 'Henry and Anne went to the movies'). This was, of course, an area investigated in terms of transformational grammar with different deep structures posited for the readings 'separately' and 'together'. It is clear that there are grammatical group complexes which cannot be expanded semantically as sequences of figures; for example, *Henry and Anne chatted* is not likely to be a grammatical compression of 'Henry chatted and Anne chatted'; rather, it is agnate with *Henry chatted with Anne.* In such cases the problem of ambiguity does not arise.

Sequences at lower ranks than that of figures retain the logical mode of realization in the grammar. Expansion and projection thus flow throughout the system, forming sequences. This is in fact an instance of a general principle: expansion and projection are **trans-phenomenal categories** in the sense that they are manifested over the system as a whole — not merely in different logical environments across ranks but also experientially. For example, projection manifested within a sequence: *Brutus said Caesar was ambitious;* projection manifested within a simple figure: *According to Brutus, Caesar was ambitious.* This feature is particularly exploited when the system is expanded through grammatical metaphor: see Chapter 6 below.

4. Figures

4.1 Two perspectives on figures

As we expressed it in the last section, a figure is a basic fragment of experience that embodies one quantum of change. As such, it is like a little drama — it is a constellation of actors and props; and it unfolds through time. We can recognize here two complementary perspectives on a figure: composition, and time.

Compositionally, figures are phenomenal units that are formed by configurations of other phenomena (elements). Being "units" means that they are constituted as organic wholes with functionally distinct parts. (For an interpretation of participant and other roles in figures in the context of a "theory of activity", see Steiner, 1988a, 1991.) In this respect they differ from sequences, which are not compositional units but loci of serial expansion and projection.

Concomitantly, figures take place in time; but the temporal aspect of a figure is typically construed in association with one particular element, the process. We shall therefore deal with this aspect of figures under the heading of process, in the context of our discussion of elements (see Chapter 5, Section 5.4 below). For the remainder of this chapter we concentrate on the compositional aspect of figures.

There are two interlocking aspects of the configuration of a figure:

(i) the domain of experience to which the figure belongs; and

(ii) the nature of the interaction among its participants.

To put this another way: as a theory of experience, the semantic system of figures embodies two subtheories: one concerning different domains of experience and one concerning the ways in which participating phenomena can interact. We deal with the first of these in Section 4.2 and with the second in Section 4.3.

4.2 Composition: domains of experience

4.2.1 Four primary domains

The system of figures construes experience as falling into four broadly conceived domains of goings-on: doing (including happening) , sensing, saying and being (including having) . Each type of figure has its own set of participant roles: see Table 4(1).

4.2.1.1 Symbolic processing: sensing and saying

Projecting sequences differentiate rather sharply between figures of sensing and saying on the one hand and figures of doing and being on the other by selecting figures of sensing and saying as the ones that have the special power of setting up other figures as second-order, semiotic reality. That is, projecting sequences construe figures of sensing and saying on two levels, the level of sensing/ saying itself and the level of the content of sensing/ saying. As we put it in Chapter 3, the projecting figure represents symbolic processing, processing that brings another figure into symbolic existence. Figures of symbolic processing involve the symbolic process itself (thinking, saying, etc.) and a participant engaged in the symbolic processing, as in 'Symbolizer:' *she* + 'Process:' *said/ thought ——> that he had left*. The projected symbolic content is either a proposition (*she said/ thought ——>he had left*) or a proposal (*she asked him ——> to leave; she wanted ——> him to leave*).

Table 4(1): Types of figure and participant roles

		Process			projection
doing	Actor		Range		
	she	*is playing*	*the piano*		
	Actor		Goal		
	she	*is polishing*	*the piano*		
	Actor		Goal	Recipient	
	she	*is giving*	*a book*	*to her brother*	
	Actor		Goal	Client	
	she	*is building*	*a house*	*for her brother*	
sensing	Senser		Phenomenon		
	she	*knows*	*his father*		
	Senser				
	she	*knows*			*that his father has arrived*
saying	Sayer		Verbiage	Receiver	
	she	*says*	*a few words*	*to her brother*	
	Sayer			Receiver	
	she	*says*		*to her brother*	*that his father has arrived*
being & having	Carrier		Attribute		
	she	*is*	*a lawyer*		
	Token		Value		
	she	*is*	*his lawyer*		

"Symbolic processing" is a generalization across sensing and saying that foregrounds the fact that they can both project. But sensing and saying differ in the level of projection: sensing projects interior content, ideas; saying projects exterior content, locutions. The level of the projected content determines the typical status of the projected content: locutions may be either quoted or reported, with quoting being favoured in many types of discourse; in contrast ideas are typically reported and only rarely quoted. That is, ideas are construed as being further removed that locuations from experience that is shared.

Projection thus construes a distinction between interior symbolic processing (sensing) and exterior symbolic processing (saying). The distinction between 'interior' and 'exterior' is reinforced by the internal organization of figures of sensing and saying.

(i) Sensing and saying construe the "Symbolizer" along different lines. The interior Symbolizer of sensing is construed as a participant engaged in conscious processing; hence it is endowed with consciousness by virtue of serving in a figure of sensing. Thus in an example such as *the thermometer thinks it is 35 degrees* , the Symbolizer has to be interpreted as if it was a conscious being.

The "Symbolizer" of a figure of saying often is a conscious speaker. However since saying is exterior rather than interior symbolic processing, the Symbolizer of saying, unlike that of sensing, is not restricted to human consciousness; it may also be any kind of symbol source, a 'semiotic thing' such as institutions, documents and instruments of measurement (see Halliday, 1985: 129-30). Thus alongside examples such as

```
In the hospital's newsletter, he tells of one patient who stopped
a two-week-long bout.
```

we also find

```
The British medical journal The Lancet recently reported a
study at Oxford University's John Radcliffe Hospital.
```

And while *the thermometer thinks it is 35 degrees* requires a metaphorical reading, *the thermometer says it is 35 degrees* does not.

We recognize the difference between a Symbolizer of sensing and a Symbolizer of saying by calling them **Senser** and **Sayer**, respectively.

(ii) Figures of saying construe the addressee of exterior symbolic processing in the form of a participant, the Receiver, as in *She told/ asked/ commanded him ...; She said to him/ asked of him ....* In contrast, interior symbolic processing cannot be addressed; figures of sensing cannot be configured with a Receiver.

Here there is a subtle difference between sensing and saying in their grammatical realization by verbal and mental clauses that project reports. In the verbal case, the Receiver is a grammatical constituent of the verbal clause, as in *she told him ——>to leave*. Being a constituent participant, it can serve as Subject in the verbal clause: *he was told (by her) ——> to leave*. However, although the mental case, e.g. *she wanted him to leave*, looks similar, it is not, since mental clauses do not have a Receiver. The element *him* is a constituent of the reported clause: *she wanted ——> him to leave*. Consequently, it cannot serve as Subject in the reporting mental clause; we cannot get *He was wanted (by her) to leave*. The difference also shows up clearly when the projected clause is in the passive voice; contrast the incongruence of *she told the car to be washed* with the acceptability of *she wanted the car to be washed*. The analysis shows the difference: *she told the car* ——> *to be washed* (where *the car* gets interpreted as Receiver) : *she wanted* ——> *the car to be washed.* [1]

(iii) Directionality. Saying is construed as proceeding from Sayer to Receiver (*she asked/ told/ commanded him* — 'she addressed him'). In contrast, sensing embodies two complementary perspectives: either the Senser's involvement in the sensing ranges over the Phenomenon or the Phenomenon is construed as impacting on the Senser's consciousness (*she likes the design : the design pleases her*).

The domain outside this conscious-semiotic centre of the ideational universe is then quintessentially either active (doing) or inert (being): see Figure 4-1.

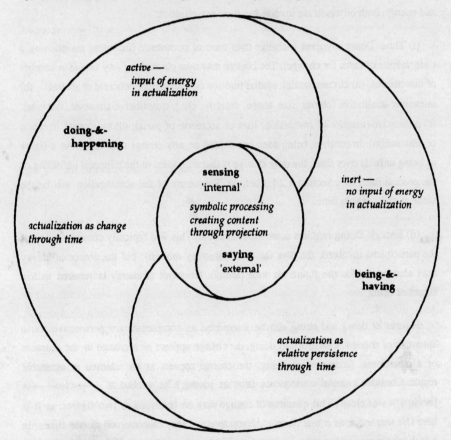

Fig. 4-1: The basic types of figure seen as different domains of experience

---

[1] As always, there are departures from the general principle. For instance, while *she asked/ told/ persuaded/ implored/ encouraged/ promised/ threatened the car to be washed* is incongruent, *she ordered the car to be washed* is perfectly fine, which suggests the mental model of the constituency boundary between the projecting and the projected clause — *he ordered* ——> *the car to be washed.* This gets support from the fact that *the car was ordered to be washed* is odd.

There is of course a great deal of indeterminacy here, including such borderline cases as those where sensing and saying are construed as forms of action (and therefore cannot project), e.g. watching, listening, chatting, speaking. These properties reflect the borderline location of such processes in the overall semantic space. We shall return to these borderline cases below.

4.2.1.2 Doing and being

Doing and **being** do not preclude the involvement of a conscious participant; but they do not require it — and hence do not have the effect of *endowing* a participant with human-like consciousness. They can be differentiated in terms of two parameters, time and energy, both of which are involved in their actualization.

(i) Time. Doing involves a change over time of occurrence (including maintaining a state in spite of force for change). The change may take place along any one of a number of dimensions: (a) circumstantial: spatial (motion or disposition, concrete or abstract); (b) intensive: qualitative (colour, size, shape, solidity, etc.), quantitative (increase, decrease); (c) possessive (transfer of ownership, loss or accretion of parts); (d) existential (creation or destruction). In contrast, being does not depend on any change over time. As a figure of being unfolds over time, the only change is that embodied in the temporal unfolding of the process itself (see Section 4.2.1.3 below). The nature of the actualization will be the same at any point in time.

(ii) Energy. Doing requires some input to occur. This will typically come from one of the participants involved, the doer (as with voluntary motion); but the source of energy may also be outside the figure (as with falling). No input of energy is required with a figure of being.

Figures of doing and being can be interpreted as complementary perspectives on a 'quantum of change'. Construed as doing, the change appears as a change in the thusness of a participant. Construed as being, the change appears as an achieved or attainable result. Consider a causal consequence such as [doing:] 'he washed it' ——<so>——> [being:] 'it was clean'. This quantum of change may be construed as two figures, as it is here (*He washed it, so it was clean.*). Alternatively, it may be construed as one figure, in which case it may adopt either point of view. If construed as doing, *he washed it clean*, the figure is elaborated with a result. If construed as being, *he made it (be) clean,* the figure is enhanced with an agentive Attributor. The wording *he cleaned it* embodies both perspectives in a single process. See Figure 4-2.

This complementarity between doing and being is most clearly brought out by the ergative model of figures, which will be discussed below in Section 4.3 (see 4.3.2

"Generalized model", esp. Figure 4-11). It is not confined to those figures where the 'being' is of the intensive (qualitative/ quantitative) type; we also find pairs such as

```
(circumstantial) I put it on the shelf/ it's on the shelf

                 they covered the floor with a carpet/ the
                 carpet covers the floor.

(possessive)     she's given him a new car/ he has a new car
```

These more delicate types are presented in Section 4.2.3 below. Here we should note finally that the category of doing includes events, so the figure is one of 'doing & happening'; while the category of being includes (i) being in some circumstantial relation, and also (ii) having, itself a special case of (i).

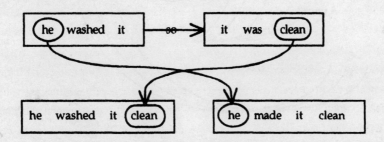

Fig. 4-2: Agency and resultative attribution

4.2.1.3 Temporal unfolding

Whatever the mode of occurrence of any figure, it will always unfold in time. This temporal unfolding is construed as an inherent property of the process itself, realized grammatically as tense and aspect; it thus serves to validate the distinction between process and participant. Whereas on the one hand in its manifestation as process, the figure unfolds in time, in its manifestation as participant, on the other hand, it persists through time — whether or not the participant undergoes a change of state. The limiting case is a creative or destructive process, such as writing or erasing a symbol, through which a participant comes into being or ceases to exist. Figure 4-3 illustrates this process/ participant complementarity.

The complementarity can also be seen in the different kinds of deixis (relation to the here & now) associated with processes on the one hand and participants on the other. A process is made finite — it is pinned down in time, with point of reference in the act of speaking. A participant is made determinate, being held in a location within a referential space. This same distinction also appears in the temporal unfolding of a text, where participants have the potential to persist as discourse referents, but processes are excluded, unless they are turned into honorary participants through the use of grammatical metaphor (see Chapter 6 below).

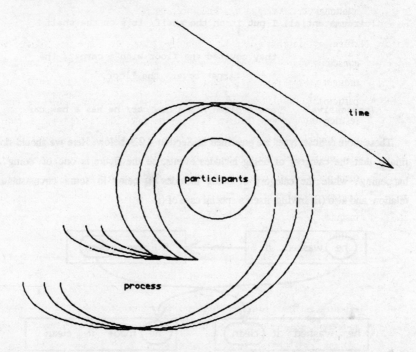

Fig. 4-3: The complementarity of participants and processes in the temporal unfolding of figures

4.2.2 Grammatical realization

We have characterized the distinctions among the different types of figure in semantic terms. Let us now relate them to the grammar of TRANSITIVITY — the ideational grammar of the clause where the semantics of figures is construed (cf. the summary in Chpater 2, Section 2.12.1 above). The different semantic types, sensing, saying, doing & happening and being & having are realized in the grammar of transitivity as shown in Figure 4-4 (cf. Halliday, 1985: Chapter 5). Thus doing & happening are realized as material clauses, sensing as mental ones, saying as verbal ones, and being (at, etc.) & having as relational clauses. The different process types are not signalled overtly in the grammar; they are covert or cryptotypic categories and emerge only when we consider their reactances (cf. Chapter 1, Section 1.8), shown in italics in Figure 4-4. The grammatical reactances for the figure types include:

> **Directionality of process:** many mental processes are typically bidirectional, appearing in two opposite configurations (*I like it/ it pleases me;* cf. *detest/ revolt; fear/ frighten; remember/ remind, notice/ strike*). It is thus possible to construe conscious processing either as the Phenomenon impinging on the

Senser's consciousness (*the music pleases him*) or as the Senser's consciousness having the Phenomenon as its domain (*he likes the music*). Neither material nor relational clauses display this dual directionality.

Nature of participants: In a mental clause, the Senser is endowed with consciousness — *s/he thought the moon was a balloon* but not normally *it thought the moon was a balloon*. This constraint does not apply to any of the participants in material or relational clauses. While the Senser is heavily restricted in this way, the other mental participant, the Phenomenon, is entirely unrestricted: it can be not only phenomenal (*she remembered the old house*) but also macro-phenomenal (act: *she remembered him coming down the stairs*) or meta-phenomenal (fact: *she remembered that they had been happy in the old house*). Participants in a material process cannot be meta-phenomenal. For instance, while it is possible to demolish not only concrete things such as buildings but also abstract things such as ideas and arguments (*she demolished the house/ their ideas/ his argument*), it is not possible to demolish "meta-things" (we do not find *she demolished that the earth was flat*).

Unfolding in time: In material clauses, the unmarked present tense is present-in-present (*he is mowing the lawn; I'm doing the job*), whereas with the other process types it is the simple present (mental: *she believes he's mowing the lawn;* relational: *he has a lawn mower; I'm busy*);

Participation: Material clauses have a special pro-verb, *do (to/ with),* as in *what he did to the lawn was mow it.* This does not occur in mental clauses: *what he did to the story was believe it;* nor in relational ones: *what he did to the lawn-mower was have it .*

Projection: Mental and verbal clauses are distinct from material and relational clauses in that the former can project ideas and locutions (quote or report; see Chapter 3 above). These represent the 'content' of sensing and saying, as in *David thought ——> the moon was a balloon,* where the relation of projection is represented by an arrow. Verbal clauses are distinct from mental clauses in that the Sayer is not necessarily an entity endowed with consciousness; and in verbal clauses there may be a further participant, the Receiver, which is not found in a mental clause.

As with all systems in language, any given instance will be more or less **prototypical**; and there may be subtypes lying intermediately at the borderline of the primary types. The grammar construes the **non-discreteness** of our experience by creating borderline cases and blends. One such area is that of behavioural processes (Halliday, 1985: 128-9): "processes of physiological and psychological behaviour, like breathing, dreaming, smiling, coughing". These can be interpreted as a subtype of material processes or as a borderline category between material and mental. They include conscious processing construed as active behaviour (watching, listening, pondering, meditating) rather than as passive sensing (seeing, hearing, believing). Like the Senser in a mental clause, the 'Behaver' in a behavioural one is endowed with consciousness; whereas in other respects behavioural clauses are more like material ones. Like material clauses (but unlike mental ones), behavioural clauses can be probed with *do: What are you doing? — I'm meditating* but not *I'm believing*. Furthermore, behavioural clauses normally do not project, or project only in highly restricted ways (contrast mental: cognitive *David believed* ——> *the moon was a balloon* with behavioural: *David was meditating* ——> *the moon was a balloon*);[2] nor can they accept a 'fact' serving as Phenomenon (mental: *David saw that the others had already left* but not behavioural: *David watched that the others had already left*). In these respects, behavioural processes are essentially part of the material world rather than the mental one. Many of them are in fact further removed from mental processes, being physiological rather than psychological in orientation.

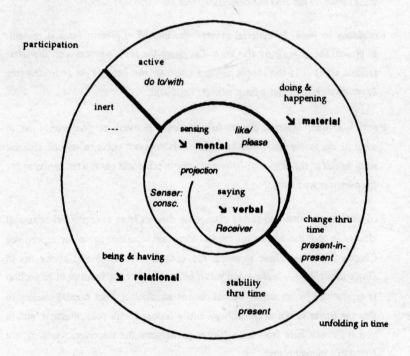

Fig. 4-4: The process types in the clause grammar

---

[2] For the special case of quoting by a behavioural process, as in *"You're late again"*, *she frowned* , cf. the discussion of saying in Section 4.3.

Such borderline cases, in which the pattern of reactances does not conform exactly to that of a major type, are typical of grammatical systems in general. Figure 4-5 represents the overall semantic space construed by figures, taking account of some of the areas of indeterminacy. Some of these will be followed up in the next section; for further discussion, see Martin & Matthiessen (1991).

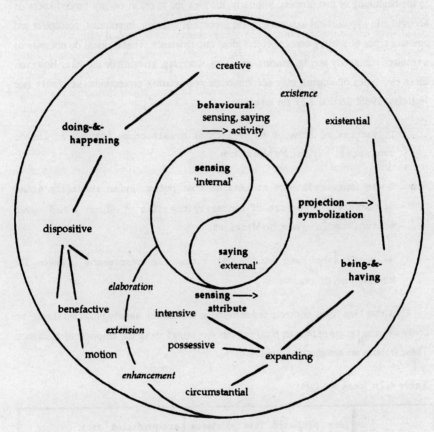

Fig. 4-5: The overall semantic space of figures with principal areas of indeterminacy and complementarity

4.2.3 Further delicacy

4.2.3.1 Types of sensing

We have presented the distinction among figures as a primary cut in delicacy. To illustrate how the delicacy of the analysis can be increased, we will discuss figures of sensing. Here projection turns out to be a major characteristic distinguishing between different types. Sensing projects ideas into existence; the projection may take place either through cognition or through desideration, for example (from Pinter, *The Birthday Party*):

```
I just thought ----> I'd tell you that I appreciate it.
```

```
I think ———> I'll give it up.

They want ———> me to crawl down on my bended knees.
```

Thus the idea 'I'll give it up' is **created** by the process of thinking; it does not exist prior to the beginning of that process. Similarly, the idea 'me to crawl on my bended knees' is brought into hypothetical existence by the process of wanting. In contrast, perceptive and emotive types of sensing cannot project ideas into existence. That is, ideas do not arise as a result of somebody seeing, hearing, rejoicing, worrying, grieving or the like. However, these two types of sensing may accommodate **pre-existing** projections, i.e. **facts** (see Halliday, 1985: Section 7.5); for instance:

```
It assures me ⟦that I am as I think myself to be, that I am fixed,
concrete⟧.   (Pinter, No Man's Land)

I was impressed, more or less at that point, by an intuition ⟦that
he possessed a measure of sincerity the like of which I had never
encountered⟧.  (Pinter, No Man's Land)

We heard ⟦that you kindly let rooms for gentlemen⟧.  (Pinter, The
Birthday Party)
```

Thus 'that I am fixed, concrete' is construed as something already projected (hence we could add *assures me of the fact that*) and this fact brings about the emotion of assurance. These features are summarized in Table 4(2).

Table 4(2): Ideas and facts

	idea projected into existence	pre-projected fact
cognitive & desiderative	*they thought —> the earth was flat* *they wanted —> the earth to be flat* Cognitive processing and desiderative processing create ideas	
emotive & perceptive	— ~~but perceptive processing and emotive processing don't;~~ —	— they are activated by facts. *they rejoiced (at the fact) that the earth was flat :* *(the fact) that the earth was flat pleased them* *they heard (the news) that the earth was flat*

The grammar thus draws a fairly clear line between cognition & desideration on the one hand and perception & emotion on the other. The former can create worlds of ideas, the latter cannot — at least, according to the theory of consciousness embodied in the grammar of English. Now, this difference with respect to the ability to project is one of a set of properties that collectively serve to differentiate perception, cognition, desideration and emotion as the major subtypes of sensing. These properties are summarized in Table 4(3).

Table 4(3): Distinctions among subtypes of sensing

	perceptive	cognitive	desiderative	emotive
(1) project ideas	--	√: propositions *He believes —> she has left : It strikes him —> that she has left*	√: proposals *He wants —> her to leave*	--
(2) metaphenomenal Phenomenon	√: *I hear (the rumour), see (evidence) that she has left :* --	--*	--	√: *He rejoices (at the fact) that she has left : It pleases him that she has left*
(3) as modality	--	√: modalization *I think : perhaps I know : certainly*	√: modulation *I insist : must I want : should*	--
(4) verbal causation	--	√: propositions *I tell you : you know I remind you :you remember I teach you : you learn*	√: proposals *I persuade you : you want*	--
(5) directionality: reversal	rare *perceive : strike, assail sb's senses*	some *believe : convince forget : escape recall : remind*	--	√ *like : please grieve : sadden fear : frighten*
(6) construed as active behaviour in behavioural clause	√ *see : watch, look (at) hear : listen (to) taste : taste ...*	√ *think : ponder, meditate,*	--	-- (Only as symbol of emotion: *giggle, laugh, cry, smile, frown*)
(7) phase (momentary, inceptive, etc.)	√ *see : glimpse, sight, spot*	√ *know : discover, realize, learn, conclude, deduce, establish, figure out; remember, recall, recollect; forget*	--	-- (no systematic lexicalized distinctions?)

(8) agnate ascriptive relational process	√ *look, sound, smell, feel (seem, appear)*	---	---	---
(9) construed as Attribute in ascriptive relational clause	--	some *know : certain, aware* *doubt : doubtful*	some *want : willing - keen, eager; unwilling*	√ *delight in : delightful* *like : fond (of)* *fear : afraid*
(10) scalable	--	some *suspect, guess - believe, think - know*	some *want - need*	√ *alarm - frighten, scare - terrify, horrify;* *interest - intrigue;* *upset - devastate* also intensification by Degree: *greatly, deeply + upset, enjoy*
(11) reification	bounded — count *sight(s), view(s), perception(s), sensation(s)*	bounded — count *thought(s), belief(s), memory(ies)* unbounded - mass *knowledge, realization,*	bounded — count *plan(s), wish(es), intention(s), hope(s)*	-- unbounded - mass *anger, fear, frustration, happiness, horror, joy, sadness*

We will comment on the properties very briefly one by one.

(1) Projection of ideas. While both cognition and desideration project ideas, they project ideas of different kinds (see Section 4.2 above). Cognition projects propositions — ideas about information that may or may not be valid: *he believed/ imagined/ dreamt ——> that the earth was flat.* In contrast, desideration projects proposals — ideas about action that has not been actualized but whose actualization is subject to desire: *he wanted/ intended/ hoped for ——> her to leave.* Projection is the critical link between sensing and saying; cf. property (4).

(2) Phenomenality. A process of sensing may range over or be caused by a metaphenomenon, i.e. by a pre-projected fact serving as Phenomenon, as in *(the fact) that she is late worries me.* The two types of sensing that can involve a Phenomenon of this metaphenomenal type are the ones that cannot project, namely perception and emotion. That is, while perception and emotion cannot create ideas, they can 'react to' facts. In this respect, they are like certain relational clauses such as *(the fact) that she is late is a worry/ worrying* — cf. (8) below.

(3) Metaphor for modality. Both cognition and desideration can come to serve as metaphors for the interpersonal system of modality — for modalization and modulation respectively — alongside congruent realizations such as modal auxiliaries and adverbs (Halliday, 1985: Section 10.4). That is, a number of processes of cognition can stand for probabilities — *I think : probably, I suppose : perhaps;* and a number of processes of desideration can stand for inclinations and obligations — *I want : should, I insist : must.* For instance:

> `I think` that in a `sense` `you've` had to `compromise`, `haven't` `you?`
> (CEC 387) 'in a sense you've probably had to compromise, haven't you'

Neither perceptive nor emotive sensing can serve as metaphors for modalities.[3]

(4) Verbal causation. Both cognition and desideration may be brought about through verbal action: *I have told you that : you know that :: I have persuaded you to : you intend to.* There are no related verbal types causing perception and emotion.

(5) Directionality. Processes of emotion are typically bidirectional. They can be construed either as the emotion ranging over the Phenomenon or as the Phenomenon causing the emotion — as in *I like Mozart's music* (the 'like' type) : *Mozart's music pleases me* (the 'please' type); cf. Figure 4-4 above. Here the grammar of English construes a complementarity between two conflicting interpretations of emotional processes, with opposing angles on whether we are in control of our emotions, as if neither one by itself constitutes a rounded construction of experience. Processes of desideration are not bidirectional; here there is no 'please' type, only the 'like' type. Here the grammar upholds the view that we are in control of our desires. Cognitive and perceptive processes may be bidirectional but favour the 'like' type — perception almost exclusively so; 'please' type perception such as *the noise assailed my ears* seems quite marginal.

(6) Construal as behaviour. Sensing is not construed in the grammar as activity. But, as already noted above, certain types of conscious process may be construed

---

[3] Emotion is related to interpersonal attitude — *I rejoice that she's returned : she has, happily, returned.* Unlike modality, attitude is not an assessment of the validity of a clause (grammatically it is not a Mood Adjunct). Rather, it is a comment on the information presented in a clause.

not only as sensing but also alternatively as a kind of doing — as behaviour (as if active sensing). For instance:

Stanley (urgently): **Look** --
McCann: Don't **touch** me.
Stanley: **Look. Listen** a minute. (Pinter, The Birthday Party)

Anna: **Listen**. What silence. Is it always as silent?
Deeley: It's quite silent here, yes. Normally. You can **hear** the
sea sometimes if you **listen** very carefully. (Pinter, Old Times)

Here *look, touch, listen* are verbs in behavioural clauses rather than mental ones; they are construed as activities controlled by an active Behaver. The difference is suggested quite clearly in the last example — *You can **hear** the sea sometimes if you **listen** very carefully*. All the modes of perception may be construed either as behaviour or as sensing. One significant grammatical difference is that present behaviour would normally be reported as present-in-present (the present progressive) — *What are you doing? I'm watching the last whales of August.* — but present sensing would not — *I (can) see the whales in the distance.*[4] Another one is that only sensing can involve a Phenomenon of the metaphenomenal kind. As long as the 'phenomenon' is of the same order of existence as ordinary things, there is no problem with either process type; we can both see and watch macro-phenomena: *I saw/ watched the last whales leave the bay.* But while we can say *I saw that he had already eaten* we cannot say *I watched that he had already eaten*, which includes a metaphenomenon. This is the borderline between the mental and material domains of experience. There are some behavioural processes that are agnate to cognitive ones (pondering, puzzling, meditating) but none that are agnate to desiderative or emotive ones. (Behavioural processes of giggling, laughing, crying, smiling and the like are outward manifestations of emotions; but they are not active variants of inert emotive processing such as rejoicing, grieving, and fearing.)

(7) **Phase**. The different types of sensing have somewhat different potentials for unfolding in time. With perception and cognition we have various categories of duration, inception, and the like: e.g. (perception) *glimpse, sight, spot* as well as *see;* (cognition) *discover, realize, remember* as well as *know*. But similar distinctions do not seem to obtain with desiderative and emotive processes.

(8) **Agnate ascriptive process**. Processes of perception are unique among the different types of sensing in that they are agnate to a set of relational processes of

---

[4] Notice also the difference with respect to ability: there is little to choose between *I can see birds in the sky* and *I see birds in the sky*, but *I can be watching birds in the sky* and *I am watching birds in the sky* are quite distinct — in fact the former would most probably be interpreted as usuality 'I sometimes watch ...'.

ascription, those which ascribe an Attribute in terms of the way in which it presents itself to our sense, as in *Madam, you'll look like a tulip.*

(9) **Construal as Attribute of ascription**. With many processes of emotion, there is an alternative construal of the emotion as a quality that can be ascribed as an Attribute to a Carrier in a relational clause; and this alternative exists for both the 'like' type and the 'please' type. Thus *I'm afraid of snakes* is an ascriptive alternative to the mental *I fear snakes;* similarly, in the other direction, *snakes are scary* and *snakes scare me.* This relational type of alternative exists for some cognitive and desiderative processes, but it is much more productive with emotive ones. Analogous attributes in the domain of perception seem always to involve potentiality (*visible, audible*); cf. footnote 4 above.

(10) **Scalability**. Related to the possibility of construing emotion as an Attribute is the possibility of scaling or intensifying emotive processes: many qualities can be intensified. We find sets of processes differentiated essentially according to degree of intensity — *scare : terrify, horrify* ; and emotive processes can be intensified by means of adverbs of degree such as *much, greatly, deeply.* These options are also open to some cognitive and desiderative processes, although not to perceptive ones; but intensification is an essentially emotive characteristic.

(11) **Reification**. Finally, when the different types of sensing are construed metaphorically as things, they are reified in different ways. Perception, cognition and desideration are reified as bounded, i.e. countable things, such as *sight(s), thought(s), plan(s),* whereas emotions are reified as unbounded things, i.e. masses, such as *anger, fear, frustration.* [5] That is, emotion is construed as boundless — like physical resources such as water, air, iron and oil (cf. Halliday, 1990). Indeed, one can see from Lakoff & Kövecses's (1987) discussion of the cognitive model of anger in American English that a number of the metaphors for anger construe it as concrete mass (e.g. as a fluid contained in the body: *He was filled with anger, She couldn't contain her joy, She was brimming with rage*). In being construed as unbounded mass, emotions are again more like qualities (cf. the unbounded *strength, height, heaviness, redness*).

As always in language, the picture that emerges from a consideration of a multiplicity of properties is far from simple; it is multifaceted. But it is possible to bring out certain salient features of the system of sensing as suggested in Figure 4-6. Emotion seems to be closer to quality-ascription than to a prototypical process; it arises from, but does not create, projections. In contrast, perception is essentially closer to behavioural processes. Cognition and desideration are different from both in that they can project (i.e., bring the

---

[5] A few processes of cognition are also unbounded, e.g. *knowledge, realization, understanding.*

content of consciousness into existence), can stand for modalities, and are not in general like either behaviour or ascription; they may be interpreted as the most central classes of sensing. Cognition is arguably closer to perception than desideration is — there are certain cross-overs like *see* in the sense of 'understand' alongside its basic sense of visual perception, and both can be construed in an active mode as processes of behaviour.

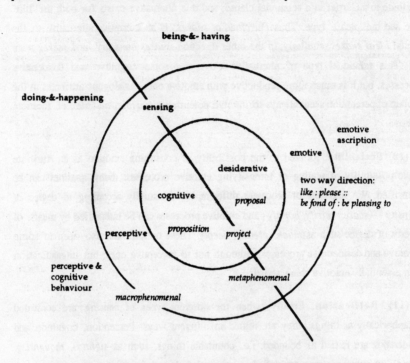

Fig. 4-6: The orientations of the different types of sensing

4.2.3.2 Types of being & having

Figures of being & having construe relations between participants. They construe the same overall range of relations as expanding sequences, and the basic subtypes also correspond to the subcategories of expansion, viz. elaboration, extension, and enhancement. Once we recognize that the semantic system construes phenomena according to trans-phenomenal (fractal) principles (see Chapter 3, Section 3.8 and above; see also Chapter 5, Section 5.6 below), it will seem natural that figures of being & having construe relations in such a way that they resonate with the semantic types manifested in expanding sequences. They do not construe an arbitrarily different theory of relations.

In a figure of being & having, one participant may thus elaborate, extend, or enhance another one. (i) One participant **elaborates** another one along the dimensions of delicacy, realization, or instantiation. In other words, the elaboration sets up a relationship either of generality (delicacy), of abstraction (realization), or of token to type (instantiation): see Table 4(4). There is another variable whereby elaboration involves either identity or membership along the dimension in question. (We saw in Chapter 2, Section 2.11.2 how in building up the grammar of ascription, Stephen started with instantiation and then moved on to include delicacy.)

Table 4(4): The elaboration of amphibians

	identity — identifying: Token + Process + Value	membership — ascriptive: Carrier + Process + Attribute
delicacy (hyponymy)	*frogs, toads and salamanders are* ('constitute') *the amphibians* : *the amphibians are* ('are constituted by') *frogs, toads, and salamanders*	*frogs are amphibians* *(amphibious)*
realization	*groda is* ('means') *'frog'* : *'frog' is* ('is meant by') *groda*	
instantiation		*This (specimen) is a frog*

Elaborating figures can thus be used to construe hyponymic taxonomies. In other words, they are, among other things, a theory of the systemic organization of the meaning potential itself; and, by virtue of this fact, they can be used to elaborate it further. For example:

> The fuels of the body **are** carbohydrates, fats and proteins. *These are taken in the diet. They are found mainly in cereal grains, vegetable oils, meat, fish and dairy products.* Carbohydrates **are** the principal source of energy in most diets. [...] Fats **make up** the second largest source of energy in most diets. [...]

(ii) One participant **extends** another in a relation of composition, possession or association. As with elaboration, there is also the intersecting variable of identity or membership: see Table 4(5).

Extending figures can thus be used to construe meronymic taxonomies. In other words, they are (among other things) a theory of constituency, semantic composition, and other meronymic relations in language; so they can be used to create further relationships of the same kind. For example, the following paragraph establishes a meronymic taxonomy for sentences in Hawaiian:

> Sentences are sequences bordered by periods, question marks, or exclamation points. In Hawaiian they can be thought of as simple, verbless, or complex. The most common simple sentence **consists of** verb phrase ± noun phrase(s). Verb phrases **contain** verbs as their heads; verbs are defined on the basis of potential occurrence with the particles marking aspect, especially *ua* (perfective aspect). Noun phrases **contain** nouns or substitutes for nouns; these are names of persons or places, or are defined on

the basis of potential occurrence after the article `ka/ ke`
(definite), or the preposition *ma* 'at'. (Samuel H. Elbert & Mary
Kawena Pukui, 1979, Hawaiian Grammar, Honolulu, The University Press of Hawaii, p.
39.)

Table 4(5): Types of extension

	identity — identifying: Token + Process + Value	membership — ascriptive: Carrier + Process + Attribute
composition (meronymy)	The sports centre comprises (consists of) four buildings : Four buildings make up the sports centre.	The sports centre has (includes) a health clinic
possession	The students own all the equipment : All the equipment is owned by the students (is the students')	The students have lockers
association	The training features videos of leading athletes : Videos of leading athletes are featured by (feature in, accompany) the training	The training involves a lot of hard work

Elaboration and extension are agnate, one with the other; they offer alternative modes
of construal, often with very little apparent difference. Thus we may find both

(1) Elaborating 'Man' is +male, +adult & + human :

'Man' is a male, adult & human being

(2) Extending 'Man' consists of +male, +adult & + human :

'Man' has the features +male, +adult & +human

But if we technicalize these alternatives, they do constitute significantly different
approaches to the interpretation of meaning — cf. Chapter 1, Sections 1.9.6 and 1.9.4
above. In this book and elsewhere in systemic-functional work, elaborating
interpretations tend to be taken further than in many other approaches: this means
emphasizing realization, delicacy, and identities across metafunctions to supplement the
traditional emphasis on constituency and composition.

(iii) One participant **enhances** another along a circumstantial dimension of time,
space, cause, condition and the like. Table 4(6) illustrates the categories of time and
cause.

Table 4(6): Types of enhancement

	identity — identifying: Token + Process + Value	membership — ascriptive: Carrier + Process + Attribute
time	Severe floods followed the rain : The rain was followed by severe floods	Severe floods ensued
cause	Heavy rain caused floods : Floods were caused by heavy rain	Severe floods resulted

Thus enhancing figures may be used to construe arrangements or orderings in space or time, such as chronologies, maps or structures. For example, the following extract from an account of the structure of skeletal muscles construes locations through enhancing figures:

> The fibrous connective tissue proteins within the tendons **continue** in an irregular arrangement **around** the muscle to form a sheath known as the epimysium (epi = above; my = muscle). Connective tissue from this outer sheath **extends into** the body of the muscle, subdividing it into columns, or fascicles (e.g., the "strings" in stringy meat). Each of these fascicles **is** thus **surrounded** by its own connective tissue sheath, known as the perimysium (peri = around). (Stuart Ira Fox, 1984, Human Physiology, Dubuque, Iowa, Wm. C. Brown Publishers.)

Enhancing figures construing temporal and causal ordering play an important role in constructing knowledge in a metaphorical mode, as the following example illustrates (see further Chapter 6 below):

> The divergence of impulses from the spinal cord to the ganglia, and the convergence of impulses within the ganglia, usually **results in** the mass activation of almost all of the postganglionic fibers. (op cit.)

4.2.3.3 Types of doing & happening

Throughout the history of the study of language, in all the major traditions, grammarians and philosophers have focussed primarily on figures of doing. Certain subtypes have been fairly well explored: usually those having some special structural feature, such as figures involving transfer of possession ('giving') where there is an additional participant role (Beneficiary, recognized in traditional grammar as indirect or dative object). And figures of doing in their very simplest form (*John ran, Mary threw the ball*) have remained for more than two millennia as the foundation of the theory of transitivity. But there has been little attempt at a systematic treatment of the total range of material clauses with their intersecting features and subtypes.

Here we shall refer to three major distinctions that have traditionally been recognized; and then take one further step based one our earlier observation (Section 4.2.1.3) bringing together figures of doing and being. The subtypes that have been generally recognized in grammar are (1) **intransitive/ transitive**; (2) within intransitive, **action/ event**; and (3) within transitive, **effectum/ affectum**. The first is the distinction between doings that involve only a doer (intransitive: *John ran*) and those that also involve something 'done to' (transitive: *Mary threw the ball*); realized respectively as Actor + Process, Actor + Process + Goal. The second is that between an intentional act by an animate (typically human) being (*John ran*) and an unintentional action or inanimate event (*John fell; rain fell*). We shall discuss both of these further in the section that immediately follows (Section 4.3). The third is the distinction between a Goal that 'exists' prior to the doing of the deed (affectum: *Mary threw the ball*) and one that is brought into existence by the doing (effectum: *Jack built a house*). We shall use this distinction, referred to as **dispositive/ creative**, to explain figures of doing in terms of their outcome in other figures.

As pointed out earlier, doing is a process of change involving time and energy. Such change implies an outcome; the outcome may be of various kinds, but it is always such that it can be construed as another figure. We can therefore examine what kind of figure emerges as the outcome of the one under investigation. (1) If the process is creative, the outcome is that some entity comes into existence: such a figure may be construed as a doing with effectum, as in *he baked a cake;* but it may be simply a creative happening such as *icicles formed*. In either case the outcoming figure is one of being (more specifically, existing):

he baked a cake	outcome: 'there exists a cake'
icicles formed	outcome: 'there exist icicles'

(2) If the process is dispositive, the outcome is more variable; it may be either (i) a figure of doing (more specifically, doing [to]/ happening), or (ii) a figure of being (more specifically, being [at]/ having):

(i) *the cat chased the mouse*	outcome: 'the mouse ran'
(ii) *the boys mended the roof*	outcome: 'the roof was whole'
John gave his sister a violin	outcome: 'John's sister had a violin'

We have seen that figures of being, other than the existential, may be elaborative (intensive), extending (possessive) or enhancing (circumstantial). This enables us to recognized further subcategories of doing according to the nature of the figure being brought about: see Table 4(7).

Table 4(7): Subtypes of figures of doing according to outcome

subtypes of figures of doing (classified according to outcome)			examples		outcome
			happening	doing (to/with)	
being &having	existential		tomatoes are growing	John's growing tomatoes	'there + be + tomatoes'
	expanding	elaborating	the rat died	the cat killed the rat	'rat + be + dead'
		extending	Jenny's received an award	they've given Jenny an award	'Jenny + have + award'
		enhancing	he moved to Canberra	the government moved him to Canberra	'he + be in + Canberra'
doing & happening			the kite flew	Bobby flew the kite	'kite + fly'

Notice that in some cases the outcome is embodied in the clause by which the figure is realized; for example in middle variants of the doing & happening type (the outcome of *John ran* is 'John + run'), and in clause with resultative elements (Attribute, Role) such as *I'll boil the eggs hard* (outcome: 'eggs + be + hard'), *Let's appoint Fred timekeeper* (outcome: 'Fred + be + timekeeper').

4.3 Composition: two models of participation

So far we have explored figures in terms of how they categorize experience into particular types or domains, showing how this typology extends in delicacy. The next step is to specify what modes of participant interaction the semantic system of figures engenders. There are two models of participation-in-process embodied in the semantic system of English —

(i) One is particularistic: it diversifies our experience of participant interaction into four domains — doing, sensing, saying and being.

(ii) The other is generalized: it unifies our experience of participant interaction across the different domains.

The system thus strikes a balance in the construal of figures between unity and diversity — between differentiating one aspect of experience from another and generalizing over the whole. These constitute distinct but complementary perspectives: see Figure 4-7.

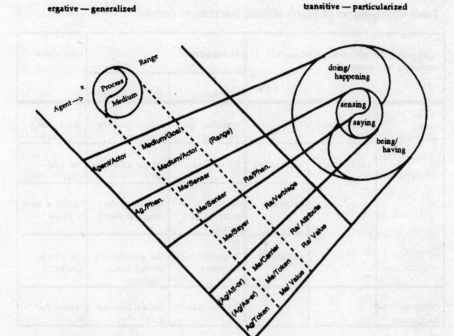

Fig. 4-7: Particularistic and generalized interpretation of figures

4.3.1 Particularistic model

In what we are calling its "particularist" modelling the grammar is *categorizing* experience for us (or we are categorizing experience through our grammar) by construing a small number of different types of figure, differentiated according to what kind of process is taking place and what kinds of participant are involved — in what relationships to each other and to the process.

What is the principle on which the grammar categorizes experience? In the most general terms, as we have seen, the principle is that all phenomena can be interpreted as falling within a small number of broad experiential domains:

those happening "inside", within the realm of our own consciousness;

those happening "outside", in the perceptual world that lies around us;

those that are not kinds of happening at all, but rather kinds of being and of relating to something else.

We have referred to these as, respectively:

(1) figures of **sensing** — or, more inclusively (since 'languaging' is treated as a distinct phenomenal realm), (1) figures of **sensing** and

(2) figures of **saying**;

(3) figures of **doing** — or, more explicitly (since the word 'doing' might suggest intentionality), figures of **doing & happening**;

(4) figures of **being** — or, more accurately (since 'having' is construed as a kind of relative 'being'), figures of **being & having**.

Each of these types of figure has its own special character, as revealed by the way it is organized in the lexicogrammar. We are not attempting to spell out here the grammatical features by which they are differentiated (for a general account of process types in the grammar, see Halliday, 1985: Chapter 5; Matthiessen, 1995b: Chapter 4; Davidse, 1991; 1992a,b,c; 1996a,b). But we shall characterize them briefly in semantic terms with reference to the forms of participation involved.

(1) Figures of sensing. Here there is one participant, the Senser, who is construed as a conscious being engaged in "inert" conscious processing ("sensing", as distinct from conscious processing as a form of active behaviour). This may involve another participant, the Phenomenon, which enters into the consciousness of the Senser (or is brought into (mental) existence by the Senser's conscious processing). Alternatively, the Senser's conscious processing may project another figure within the same sequence.

(2) Figures of saying. Here one participant, the Sayer, is involved as the originator of a process of symbolic (semiotic) activity, or "saying". There may be another participant, the Receiver, whose role is that of 'decoding' what is said. What is said may itself be construed as a further participant, the Verbiage; or else it may be projected as another figure within the same sequence. Finally, there may be a participant functioning as Target of the saying process.

(3) Figures of doing. Here there is one participant, the Actor, that performs the process in question; and this process may then impact upon another participant, the Goal (or may result in bringing the Goal into (material) existence). Other participants that may be present are the Beneficiary, the one that derives "benefit" from the process; and the Scope, the one that defines the domain over which the process extends.

(4) Figures of being. In the limiting case, there is only one participant, the Existent; but generally there are two participants, the one being related by the process to the other. They may be being related by ascription, as Attribute to Carrier; or by identification, a rather complex relationship involving two pairs of participant roles: Identifier and Identified, and Token and Value. These latter intersect with each other, so there are two

possible role combinations: (i) Identified/ Token and Identifier/ Value; (ii) Identifier/ Token and Identified/ Value.

The grammar places different constraints on these participant roles, in terms of what categories of element are typically associated with them, how they relate to the process itself, and so on. What concerns us here, however, is the particular categorization of experience that underlies each of these types of figure.

Sensing is clearly modelled as a process of human consciousness, with the Senser as a human being — so much so that merely coming to occupy that role is sufficient to endow the participant in question with human-like consciousness. The Phenomenon, on the other hand, is given a somewhat ambivalent status: in one of its guises (as in *Do you like those colours?*) it seems to be just a part of the environment; but in its other guise (as in *Do those colours please you?*) it seems to be playing a more active role.

Why does it give this impression? Partly no doubt because of the agnate form *Are you pleased by those colours?* where the Phenomenon *those colours* is brought in indirectly, like an instrument or means. But this is part of a larger syndrome whereby, on the one hand, there are other related 'sensing' figures like *How do those colours strike you?*, where the verb *strike* suggests a fairly violent kind of action; and on the other hand the prototypical form of a 'doing' figure seems quite analogous to these, as in *Were those boys hitting you?* (with *those boys* as Actor, *you* as Goal).

The 'doing' figure is based prototypically on a schema we might refer to as "action and impact". There is always an Actor, the participant that performs the Process; and in an example such as *the boys were jumping*, the Process stops there — that is all there is to it. But in examples such as *the boys were throwing stones*, or *the stones hit the wall*, the Actor's performance of the Process extends beyond, so as to 'impact' on another participant — this is the one known as the Goal (see Figure 4-8). In the typical case (the "active voice", in grammatical terminology), the clause unfolds iconically, reflecting the movement of the impact from Actor to Goal.[6] And, as we saw above, the latter may then be followed by representation of the outcome of the impact — a resultative Attribute (*he knocked it flat*), a circumstance of Role (*he cut it into cubes*), or a circumstance of Location (*he threw it into the corner*).

---

[6] This iconicity is, however, easily overridden by the textual metafunction, which has its own mode of iconic realization (see e.g. Halliday, 1979a; Matthiessen, 1988a; 1990b; 1992).

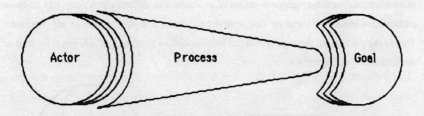

Fig. 4-8: Actor impacting Goal through Process of doing

In figures of saying, the Sayer is the symbolic source: prototypically human, but not necessarily so (e.g. *the instructions tell you to switch it off first*). The Process is symbolic; but here too there is a subtype of figures of saying that imparts a similar sense of action and impact, those where the Sayer 'does something to' another participant by means of a verbal process, as in *Don't blame the messenger, Everybody praised her courage*. We refer to this participant as the Target; and again we may note a partial analogy with figures of doing (though only partial — for example, such figures cannot take a resultative Attribute or other representation of the outcome).[7]

But these "impacting" figures of sensing and saying are only submotifs within these two overall types. The general motif of figures of sensing is 'conscious processing'; that of figures of saying is 'symbolic processing'. And in figures of being, where we might characterize the general motif as 'relational ordering', there is no trace of a submotif of impacting at all. What we find, if we try to take in the picture as a whole, is a kind of focussed model in which the essentially human processes of consciousness, and the prototypically human processes of symbolic action, constitute the experiential centre; while the two other types of figure, that of doing on the one hand and of being on the other, lie on opposite sides of this centre: the one (doing) lying towards the pole of the concrete, with the experience construed as 'this impacts on that', the other (being) lying towards the pole of the abstract, with the experience construed as 'this is related to that'.

This is one model construed by the ideation base. At the same time, it also construes a contrasting, complementary model in which all figures are treated as alike. This is the topic of the following section.

4.3.2 Generalized model

The particularistic model, then, comprises a set of submodels: (i) impacting, (ii) conscious processing, (iii) symbolic processing, (iv) relational ordering. The model that

---

[7] In the idiomatic expression *praised her sky high, sky high* is a circumstance of Manner; cf. *praised her highly* (not *praised her high*).

generalizes across these various domains of experience is different from any one of these particular submodels. It sets up one central participant that is common to all processes. This is the participant through which the process comes to be actualized. We refer to it as the Medium: see Figure 4-9.

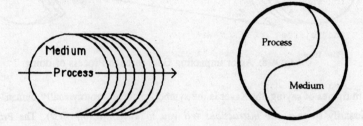

Fig. 4-9: The medium of the unfolding process

Medium and Process form the **nucleus** of the whole figure (see further Section 4.4 below) — that part of the figure which is essential to the complementarity of unfolding and persisting (cf. Figure 4-3 above). The participant functioning as Medium may be affected in various different ways, depending on the particular domain — the 'trace' may by physical, mental, and so on; but the status of Medium generalizes across these domains.

The model thus construes a nuclear figure consisting of a process unfolding through the medium of a participant. This then makes it possible to construe a further variable: namely, the causal origin of this unfolding. The Medium's actualization of the Process may be construed as being brought about by a further participant — the Agent: see Figure 4-10. If the figure is construed with an Agent, it is **other-agentive**; if it is construed without an Agent, it is **self-agentive**.

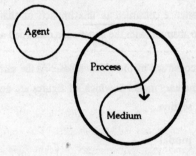

Fig. 4-10: Actualization of Medium + Process caused externally by Agent

For example:

```
Several alternatives have developed :
We have developed several alternatives (Agent: we)
```

```
The door opened :
Catherine opened the door (Agent: Catherine)

The scones should cool on a wire rack :
You should cool the scones on a wire rack (Agent: you)

She rejoiced (at the news):
The news delighted her (Agent: the news)

The batter will be very heavy :
This amount will make the batter very heavy (Agent: this amount)
```

Semantically, the **Medium** is the participant through which the process is actualized. It is in the combination of Medium + Process that we find the complementarity we spoke of earlier: between the temporal unfolding (the Process) and the atemporal persistence (the Medium). This close bonding of Medium and Process is manifested in a number of ways.

(i) Of all the participants, the Medium is the most restricted in terms of the range of phenomena that may function in that role. We can see this in relation to the general types of figure:

type of figure	range of phenomena functioning as Medium
doing	phenomenon (of any kind — but not metaphenomenon, i.e. not fact)
sensing	conscious being
saying	symbol source
being	phenomenon (of any kind, *including* metaphenomenon)

We can also see this in relation to more delicately specified subtypes such as:

type of figure	range of phenomena functioning as Medium
shine	heavenly body
ache	body part
decant	wine
neigh	horse
dress	salad

In other words, whatever the type of figure, the participant that is most closely bonded with the Process is the one that takes on the generalized role of Medium; it is this that is in a relation of mutual expectancy with the Process. This is not to say that only horses can neigh, but rather than anything that neighs is thereby endowed with horse-hood.

(ii) In the **taxonomy** of figures, the nature of the Medium is more criterial than that of any other participant or circumstance. For instance, if we consider processes such as 'strew, spill, pour, sprinkle', it is the Medium, not the Agent, which enables us to differentiate among them (cf. Hasan, 1987) (cf. sprinkle + salt, spill/ pour + water, coffee; strew + flowers); similarly with 'bend, straighten, flatten; melt, freeze, evaporate, condense; crack, break, shatter' and so on.

(iii) The **manner of performance** of a process may vary, in which case it is the Medium by which it is typically determined. This may be a major variation in the mode of actualization, for example 'open + door, open + account, open + eye' where the process is respectively mechanical, verbal, or physiological; or simply a minor difference in the means that is employed, e.g. 'brush + teeth, brush + clothes'. Some examples:

	Process + Medium
'control access'	open/ close + door
	open/ close + eyes
	open/ close + account
'(de)stabilize structure'	stand up/ collapse + building
	stand up/ collapse + argument
'suspend above ground'	hang + prisoner
	hang + painting
'disrupt integrity'	break + glass
	break + equipment
'remove extraneous matter'	brush + teeth
	brush + clothes
'travel by mounted conveyance'	ride + horse
	ride + bicycle

In many cases, the difference in the manner of performance is the basis of a lexically codified (cf. Chapter 1, Section 1.6 above) taxonomic distinction; for example:

	Process + Medium
'remove protective cover'	skin + rabbit
	peel + fruit
	unwrap + parcel
'grow towards fulfilment'	grow up + child
	ripen + fruit
	age + wine
	mature + policy

These are some of the ways in which the close bonding of Medium with Process is made manifest in the grammar of the clause, such that the two together constitute what we have referred to as the clause nucleus. Semantically, the nucleus construes the centre of gravity of a figure, the focal point around which the system of figures is organized. When we describe the Medium as "actualizing" the Process, we are really saying that the unfolding is constituted by the fusion of the two together — there can be no Process without an element through which this process is translated from the virtual to the actual.

In the grammar therefore the Medium appears as an obligatory element — the only element that has this status in the clause. This does not mean that we will find a nominal reflex of the Medium made explicit in the syntagm of every clause; there are various ways in which the Medium may be present as a cryptotypic feature rather than as an overt form. Nevertheless its presence is required in some guise or other; and this distinguishes the Medium from all other participants in the figure. We shall go on to consider certain of these other participants in Section 4.4 below.

As Figure 4-7 above shows, the generalized participant roles of Medium and Agent correspond to different sets of roles in the particularistic model — one or more for each type of figure. For example, in a figure of saying the Medium corresponds to the Sayer, whereas in a figure of sensing it corresponds to the Senser. We summarize the correspondences in Table 4(8), where the generalized participant roles are represented in columns. These include one role, that of Range, which we will refer to below.

Table 4(8): Correspondences between participant roles in the (i) generalized and (ii) particularistic models

(ii)		(i)			
		Agent	Medium	Range	
doing	happening		Actor	Scope	The river is overflowing its banks
			Actor		Lakes are forming
	doing (to/with)	Actor	Goal		The river is forming lakes
		Initiator	Actor		The river is making lakes form
		Initiator	Actor	Scope	The rain's making the river overflow its banks
sensing	'liking'		Senser	Phenomenon	The cat likes mice
	'pleasing'	Phenomenon	Senser		Mice please the cat
saying			Sayer	Verbiage	He's telling the cat a story
being	existential		Existent		There were heavy showers
		Creator	Existent		The cold front brought heavy showers
	ascriptive		Carrier	Attribute	The cat's hungry
		Attributor	Carrier	Attribute	The thought of mice makes the cat hungry
	identifying		Token	Value	The cat is our hungriest family member
		Assigner	Token	Value	The thought of mice makes the cat our hungriest family member

In addition to Medium and Agent, we can recognize two more generalized participant roles, viz. those of **Range and Beneficiary**. The Range role is quite pervasive, as indicated in Figure 4-7 and Table 4(8) above; it can occur in all types of figure that are construed as self-agentive, and also in certain figures of being that are construed as other-agentive. The Range construes the range or domain of the actualization of the Process, with reference to taxonomic scope (as in *play : play tennis/ volley ball*), spatial scope (as in *climb : climb mountains/ hills*), etc.: see further Section 4.4.2 (2) below.

The Beneficiary role is more restricted: it occurs in certain subtypes of figures of doing as Recipient (e.g. *they awarded her the Pulitzer Prize : they awarded the Pulitzer Prize to her*) or Client (e.g. *she designed them a vacation home : she designed a vacation home for them*), in figures of saying as Receiver (e.g. *they told her a story : they told a story to her*) and in a couple of subtypes of figures of being (e.g. *he made her a good husband*).

Figure 4-11 summarizes the generalized participant roles in diagrammatic form. It shows Process and Medium as a complementarity — the Process is actualized through the Medium; and it represents the other participants as external to this nucleus, indicating the type of role relationship that obtains (x enhancing, + extending and = elaborating: see further Section 4.5 below).

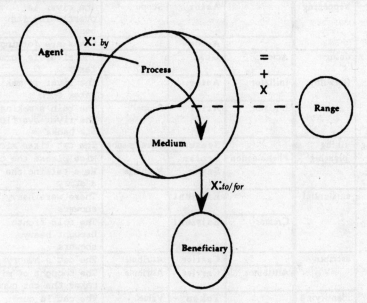

Fig. 4-11: The generalized participant roles

The two models of participation that we have described in this section thus differ in degree of generality. The particularistic model construes figures into a small number of distinct types, sensing, saying, doing and being, with different participants in each; while the generalized model construes figures as all being alike, having a Process that is actualized through a Medium. These two models embody complementary perspectives on participation, the one **transitive**, the other **ergative**.[*] Note that there is no *necessary* tie-up between the switch of perspective and the degree of generality: it is a feature of English that the generalized model is construed in ergative terms.

---

[*] For further discussion of the transitivity/ ergativity complementarity in the domain of material clauses, see Davidse (1992c).

4.3.3 Complementarity of doing and being

A good place to illustrate the complementarity of the two models of participation is in the area of doing and being. Here the two models also bring out the complementarity of doing and being as modes of construing a quantum of change in the flow of events. Let us begin by returning to the examples in Table 4(7) above. Here figures of doing are (tentatively) differentiated in terms of their outcome: this takes the form either of being or of doing. We shall focus on the "elaborating" row.

The final stage in the flow of events that constituted the rat's life can be construed as Process: 'end life' + Medium: 'rat'; that is, some process concerning the termination of life is actualized through the rat. This may further be construed as having an external cause: Process: 'end life' + Medium: 'rat' + Agent: 'cat'. Finally, the scope of the Process may be construed within that element itself or as a separate element, the Range: Process: 'die' or Process: 'happen/ do' + Range: 'dead/ death'. Thus the generalized model allows for the following possibilities:

Agent	Process	Medium	Range	
	'happen: die'	'rat'		*the rat died*
	'happen'	'rat'	'death'	— [*the rat did a death*]; but cf. *the rat underwent/ feigned death*
	'happen'	'rat'	'dead'	*the rat fell dead*
'cat'	'do: die'	'rat'		*the cat killed the rat*
'cat'	'do'	'rat'	'dead'	— [*the cat did the rat dead*]; but cf. *the cat struck the rat dead*
	'be: dead'	'rat'		—
	'be'	'rat'	'dead'	*the rat was dead*
'cat'	'be'	'rat'	'dead'	— [*the cat made the rat dead*]; but cf. *the cat made the rat sad*

As the table illustrates, the generalized model allows for a range of ways of construing the termination of the rat's life, where the rat is always construed as Medium and the termination is construed as Process or as Process + Range; but not all the possibilities are lexicalized, so there are certain 'gaps'. These gaps seem to be systematic. The transition from life to death is construed in two phases: (i) as happening/ coming into being and (ii) as the outcome of happening/ being. (i) The first phase can always be construed as Process (the process of dying); more restrictedly, it can instead be construed as Process + Range. Consequently, the Range is 'optional'. (ii) The second phase must always be construed as Process (the process of being) + Range; it cannot be construed as Process alone. Consequently, the Range is 'obligatory'. In either phases, the 'Medium + Process' nucleus can be construed as being self-engendered or as being other-engendered, with an additional participant — the Agent. The difference is that the first phase makes explicit how the Agent engenders the actualization of Process through Medium, whereas in the second phase only the relation of engendering is specified.[9]

The two phases of course correspond to two of the modes of construing change in the particularistic model: the first phase corresponds to the construal of change as doing, the second phase corresponds to the construal of change as being. Looked at in terms of this model, the change can be construed as doing: the cat does something, which extends to impact the rat: Actor: 'cat' + Process: 'strike' + Goal: 'rat'. The outcome may be specified as an optional Attribute: Actor: 'cat' + Process: 'strike' + Goal: 'rat' + Attribute: 'dead'. Alternatively, the change can be construed as being: the rat is something: Carrier: 'rat' + Process: 'be' + Attribute: 'dead', which may be represented as initiated by the cat: Attributor: 'cat' + Process: 'be' + Carrier: 'rat' + Attribute: 'dead'.

Figure 4-12 brings the two models together to show (i) how they complement one another, the generalized one showing how doing and being are based on the same configuration of Agent + Medium + Range and the particularistic one showing how doing and being are different configurations of roles; and (ii) how doing and being serve as complementary perspectives on a quantum of change, construing it either as happening/ coming into being or as outcome of happening/ being.

Doing and being thus focus on different phases of a quantum of change; but either can be extended in the direction of the other to indicate (with 'being') the source of change or (with 'doing') the outcome of change. When this happens, the wordings that realize a figure of doing and a figure of being may come to resemble one another. For example, take the two wordings *he drove his car hot* and *he drove his friends crazy*. They *could* both be interpreted as Agent + Process + Medium + Range to show them as related to *his car drove hot* and *his friends were crazy* respectively. But at the same time they are differentiated as doing versus being: Actor + Process + Goal + Attribute versus Attributor + Process + Carrier + Attribute. This shows that they are related respectively to *he drove his car* (without the Attribute) and to *his friends were crazy* (without the Attributor; but not to *he drove his friends*); and explains why we get *his car drove hot* but not *his friends drove crazy*, and why *his car drove hot* is agnate with *his car ran hot* (and *his car moved, rolled, travelled*) as another kind of happening but *his friends were crazy* is agnate with *his friends seemed crazy* as another kind of being.

In the simple constructed examples used above, we contrasted doing: happening with pure being; but being also includes 'coming into being', i.e. 'becoming'. In such cases

---

[9] In the case of 'dead' as Range, the wording is not very acceptable; but in many cases it is the regular option: *the rain made it very wet, the luggage made it quite heavy, the discount made it very cheap; the news made him very sad, this experience made her very wise.*

doing and being both construe change leading up to an outcome, but they use different models: Process and Process + Range respectively. For example:

The lava	cools	and	[it]	becomes	very hard.	It	becomes	igneous rock.
Actor/ Medium	Process		Carrier/ Medium	Process	Attribute/ Range	Carrier/ Medium	Process	Att./ Range
part.: thing	process		part.: thing	process	participant: quality	part.: thing	process	part.: thing

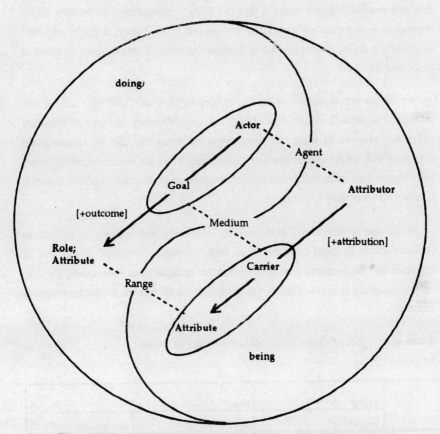

Fig. 4-12: Doing and being as complementary perspectives on change

Here the first transition in the state of the lava is represented as doing: happening — Medium/ Actor: 'lava' + Process: 'cool'. Coolness is construed as a process; consequently, it is something that is unfolding and which cannot readily be intensified. In contrast, the second transition is construed as being: becoming — Medium/ Carrier: 'lava' + Process: 'become' + Range/ Attribute: 'very hard'. Coolness is construed as a quality rather than as a process; consequently, it is something which can come into being — which can be attained. The second transition is more closely related to the third: 'it becomes very hard : igneous rock'. However, the two options in construing coolness, as process and as quality, are very close,[10] which is shown by a parallel text associated with an accompanying picture of a volcano:

The magma	cools and hardens	and			becomes	igneous rock.
Actor/ Medium	Process				Process	Attribute/ Range
participant: thing	additive sequence of processes				part.: thing	processs

Here the transition in hardness is construed as a process within a figure of doing rather than as a process + quality within a figure of being. Consequently, the hardness is not represented as an intensified "destination" coming into being. Further it can be construed as part of a complex process of cooling-&-hardening within a single figure, as indicated in the analysis above.

We started our discussion with the 'elaborating' row of Table 4(7) and all our subsequent examples have also been elaborating, i.e. elaborating outcomes of doing and elaborating relations of being. However, doing and being can also be compared and contrasted with respect to extension and enhancement. There are various interesting issues here; but we shall confine ourselves to an observation about the place where the boundary is drawn between doing and being.

In the case of elaboration, both 'coming into being' and 'causing to be' can be construed either as forms of doing or as forms of being. However, in the case of extension and enhancement, there is no comparable multiplicity of perspectives: they can only be construed as forms of doing. Table 4(9) sets out the patterns for the three types of expansion.

Table 4(9): Types of expansion in relation to doing vs. being

[a]

	doing	being	
	happening	phasal: inceptive	non-phasal
elab.	the lava hardened	the lava became hard	the lava was hard
ext.	Jenny got an award		Jenny has an award
enh.	Jenny moved to Canberra		Jenny was in Canberra
	happening/ coming into being		being

---

[10] That is, they are very close in the semantic space of figures: this is a good example of a case where the topological perspective discussed above in Chapter 2, Section 2.11 is helpful since 'doing: happening' and 'being: becoming' seem to be typologically quite distinct.

[b]

	doing	being	
	doing to/with	assigned	non-assigned
elab.	the pressure hardened the lava	the pressure made the lava hard	the lava was hard
ext.	they gave Jenny an award		Jenny has an award
enh.	they moved Jenny to Canberra		Jenny was in Canberra
	doing/ making be		being

To round off this discussion of complementarity, let us reproduce the short text from which we cited the lava example above. This text illustrates some of the main points made in this section. We present this text twice, first showing the distinction between clauses realizing figures of doing and clauses realizing figures of being[11] and then showing the distinction between clauses realizing self-agentive figures and clauses realizing other-agentive figures. These two versions of the text are followed by the diagram that elaborates the text. Note that where one clause contains another that is rankshifted the features of both will be shown.

(i) Particularistic model: **doing/** being

The rocks that cover the surface of the earth are called the earth's crust. Most of the crust is made of igneous rock. Igneous means **[made by heat]**.

Inside the earth it is very hot — hot enough **[to melt rock]**. The melted rock is called magma.

Sometimes the magma pushes through cracks in the crust. **When magma comes to the surface** it is called lava. **The lava cools** and becomes very hard. It becomes igneous rock.

(ii) Generalized model: *self-agentive/* other-agentive

The rocks **[that cover the surface of the earth]** are called the earth's crust. *Most of the crust is made of igneous rock. Igneous means [made by heat]*.

[11] For another illustration of this distinction in discourse, see the "duck" text in Chapter 11, Section 11.3.1 below.

Inside the earth it is very hot — hot enough <u>to melt rock</u>. <u>The melted rock is called magma</u>.

Sometimes the magma pushes through cracks in the crust. When magma comes to the surface <u>it is called lava</u>. The lava cools and becomes very hard. It becomes igneous rock.

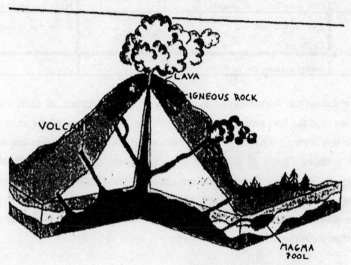

LAVA
IGNEOUS ROCK
VOLCA
MAGMA POOL

POOLS OF MAGMA SOMETIMES FORM BENEATH THE EARTH'S SURFACE. THE MAGMA COOLS AND HARDENS AND BECOMES IGNEOUS ROCK

Commentary: (i) Particularistic model: doing/ being. Figures of doing and being complement one another in the construction of geological knowledge. Figures of being construe geological conditions ('rocks cover [= are all over] the surface', 'the crust is made of [= is] igneous rock' etc.) and technical categories of geology ('igneous means [= is] made by heat', 'the melted rock is called [= is] magma', etc.). Figures of doing construe geological activities ('magma comes to the surface', 'the lava cools', etc.). (ii) Generalized model: self-agentive/ other-agentive. The geological conditions and activities are construed as spontaneously engendered — with the exception of 'to melt rock' and 'made by heat': there are essentially no causes external to the Process + Medium nucleus of figures. In contrast, figures representing technical categories are construed as other-agentive ('it is called lava', 'the melted rock is called magma').

The short text above has been extracted from a book for children on collecting rocks. In academic discourses in geology, the generalized model of participation seems to play an important role: geological activities are construed on the model of Process + Medium, either as happening spontaneously or as being brought about by an external cause. This model seems much more relevant than the impact model where an Actor initiates a process, which may then extend to affect (impact) another participant, the Goal. For example, the configuration 'form' + 'limestone' is construed first as self-agentive and then as other-agentive:

> **Limestone can form** in many ways as shown in Table 4-4. Most limestone probably originates from organisms that remove calcium carbonate from sea water. The remains of these animals may accumulate **to form the limestone** directly, or they may be broken and redeposited.

4.4 Degree of participation

4.4.1 Construing out participants

A figure embodies both analysis and synthesis of our experience of the world: an analysis into component parts, and a synthesis of these parts into a configuration. That is, process, participants and circumstances are separated out analytically and are thus given independent phenomenal statuses. This is a creative act of construal. The world is not seamless and amorphous; it is highly variable in the way it presents itself to us as experience — in its perceptual salience, physical impact and material & psychological benefit. But it is not "given" to us as an established order; we have to construe it. Not surprisingly, there is a great deal of variation in the way that different languages do this. To cite just one example, the phenomenon of precipitation from clouds is typically construed in Italian as a figure with a process alone *piove* 'rains', in Akan as figure with process + one participant *nsuo retø* 'water + fall', and in one local variety of Cantonese as a figure with process + two participants *tin lok sui* 'sky + drop + water'.

What is relevant to us here, however, is that there is also considerable variation within one and the same language. Thus in English we have sets of agnate expressions such as the following:

> it started to rain : the rain started
> there's a wind : it's windy : the wind's blowing
> there was a fog : it was foggy

Such variation is not restricted to the weather; cf.

> I fear the consequences : I'm afraid of the consequences : the consequences scare me
> he rejoiced : he felt happy
> the shades darkened the room : the shades made the room dark
> she was limping : she was walking with a limp

As the examples illustrate, there are numerous points at which the system allows for alternative semanticizations of the flux of experience. These may differ in the extent to which the 'quantum' of experience is analysed into separate components. There is a cline from unanalysed and continuous to analysed and discrete; from example, from 'it's raining' (one phenomenon) to 'the sky's dropping water' (a configuration of three phenomena): see Figure 4-13.

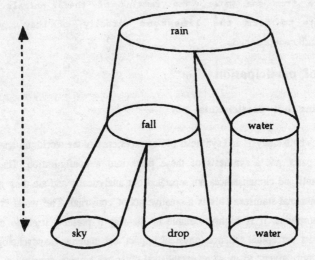

Fig. 4-13: Cline from compositionally unanalysed to analysed experience

While there is potential for variation, however, the variation is not arbitrary or random. The semantic system embodies certain general principles which guide the choice of one or other pattern of construal. These include:[12]

> process: (a) whether the process is non-actualized ('irrealis') or actualized ('realis'); (b) how the process unfolds in time (its eventuation profile);

> participants & circumstances: (a) whether they are (i) general class, (ii) non-specific representatives of a class or (iii) specific representatives; (b) how far, and in what ways, they are involved in the process.

We shall take the notion of degree of participanthood as an example of the general principle that the phenomena of experience may be construed as having more, or less, independent status within the semantic system.

---

[12] Cf. Hopper & Thompson (1980) on degrees of transitivity and Taylor (1989) on categorization in general.

4.4.2 Degrees of participanthood

We are using the term **participanthood** to suggest that the status of participant in the grammar is not absolute, but rather is a matter of degree. Among the various functional roles that the grammar construes as participants, we will discuss here two that are at opposite ends of the scale: Goal, which is has a clear status as prototypical participant, and Range, whose status as participant is much less clearly established.

(1) **Goal**. As we have seen, the Goal in the particularistic model corresponds to the Medium in the generalized model, wherever the figure is one of doing to or doing with. The Goal is impacted in some way by its participation in the Process; the "impact" either (i) brings a participant into existence or else (ii) manipulates one that already exists.

```
(i) Prepare the sauce according to your favourite recipe
(ii) Fry the aubergines for 5-10 minutes
Skin the tomatoes
Heat the olive oil
Boil the eggs hard
Beat all the items together
Shape the lentil purée into cakes
```

If the Goal is something that already exists, the result of the Process is to bring about some change — in its location, make-up, temperature, shape, &c.; and the result may be construed as a separate element, with the function Attribute (*hard*) or Role (*into cakes*).

These examples highlight the participant status of the Goal, showing the senses in which the Goal can be said to be impacted. There is no such impacting in the case of the Range (see (2) below). There is a further contrast between Goal and Range in the degree of individuation that is typical of each. In the examples above, what is impacted is a specific representative of a class, or specific set of representatives; and this is typical of the degree of individuation of the Goal. Compare in this respect the contrast between *move the piano*, where *the piano* is Goal, and *play the piano*, where *the piano* is Range:

```
move the piano Process + Goal: specific representative of class
play the piano Process + Range: general class of instrument
```

Representatives of a class can be impacted (regardless of whether they are specific or non-specific at the point in the discourse at which they occur); but it is harder to impact the general class itself. Consequently, if the Goal is a general class rather than a set of specifiable representatives, it has a lower degree of participanthood. This appears iconically in the grammar in the limiting case of a clause where the Goal is simply that class of phenomenon that can serve as Goal of that particular type of figure: the grammar allows us to select 'goal-intransitive', which means that the Goal is simply not specified — for example:[13]

```
he drinks __ heavily [alcohol]
he eats __ all the time [food]
they've gone to the hills to hunt __ [game]
he buys and sells __ [any commodity]
```

Such examples are typically either habitual (the process unfolds repeatedly) or durational (the process unfolds over time): this generalization across time correlates with the generalization across potential participants — both are ways of generalizing from experience. In some special cases the generalization of the Goal across a class of entities is shown by treating it as a mass, dispensing with the plural marker:

```
They often shoot duck during the winter months.
```

Such a Goal may even be incorporated into the Process, as in *he is baby-sitting* (and even *who's baby-sitting me this evening?*); this is a restricted option with figures realized as ranking clauses, but not uncommon where the figure is used to qualify an element and is realized by a pre-modifying clause, e.g. *a fun-loving colleague, a wood-burning stove.*

(2) Range. Like other participants **Range** is realized grammatically by a nominal group, but it does not participate in the process operationally: it does not bring about or act out the process, nor is it affected by it materially or mentally. It specifies the domain over which the process is actualized. For instance, if a process of walking ranges over Manhattan, it can be represented as Process + Range: *They walked the streets of Manhattan.* There are three respects in which the Range is not a prototypical participant: (I) its relationship to the Process, (II) its degree of individuation, (III) its interpersonal potential.

(I) Relationship to the Process. The Range is not some entity that is impacted by the Process; it either (i) expands the Process, or (ii) is projected by it.

---

[13] Here, because of its generality, the Goal is predictable experientially. The Goal may of course be predictable textually, which is the reverse case: so specific at that point in the discourse that it can be anaphorically presumed. Typically in such cases an explicit pronoun is used to refer back; but it can be omitted in certain registers, especially instructional ones such as recipes: *when all the pancakes are made, garnish the dish and serve __ with cheese and egg sauce.*

(i) Where the relationship is one of expansion, this take one of two forms: the Range either (a) elaborates the Process in an objectified form, or (b) enhances it by delimiting its scope.[14]

(i.a) In the first case, where the relation is **elaborating**, the Range simply **restates** the Process or else further **specifies** it in terms of its class, quality or quantity.[15] Here, we often find related pairs of 'Process : Process + Range'; the latter may involve nominalizing the process (a form of grammatical metaphor). Examples:

Process   **Process + Range**

(1) doing

```
sing                                 sing a song
play well                            play a good game
play twice                           play two games
—                                    play tennis
err                                  make a mistake
clean regularly                      do the regular cleaning
```

(2) saying

```
ask                                  ask a question
ask politely           ask a polite question
—                                    tell a story
```

(3) being

```
matter                               be important
suffice                              be sufficient
attend                               be attentive
--                                   be content
```

In type (3), being (more particularly, ascriptive being), the Range is the Attribute that is ascribed. This construction, Process + Range/ Attribute, is much more common that the agnate form with Process only (that is, 'be + important' is the preferred model rather than 'matter'). The Process just embodies the category meaning of ascriptive being — 'be a member of' — and the Range carries the specific information about the experiential class. It is interesting to note that the ranged construction sorts out the ambiguity of the

---

[14] The Range elaborates the Process, whereas the circumstantial element Role (see below) elaborates a participant in its particular participation in the process.

[15] This restatement may involve nominalizing the process itself, as some of the examples given below do.

simple present tense between habitual (doing) and occupational (being): *she dances/ does a dance every night , she dances/ is a dancer (by profession).*

(i.b) In the second case, where the relation is **enhancing**, the Range specifies some entity that delimits the scope of the Process; here, therefore, there is often an agnate form where the scope is construed as a circumstantial element. For example:

Process + Range	Process + circumstantial element

(1) doing

```
cross the street         cross over the street
climb the mountain        climb up the mountain
enter an agreement        enter into an agreement
```

(2) being

```
be a witness      act as a witness
become a prince             turn into a prince
```

(ii) Where the relation is one of **projection**, the Range represents the subject matter (either as a general term, e.g. *issue, matter,* or as the specific domain of the Process, e.g. *politics, your holiday*). As with enhancement, there is often an agnate circumstantial form.

Process + Range	Process + circumstantial element

(1) saying

```
discuss the issue        talk about the issue
talk politics            talk about politics
describe your holiday    write about your holiday
```

(2) sensing

```
ponder the problem       think about the problem
investigate the crime    find out about the crime
```

Type (ii) is like type (i.b) in that in both types the agnate expression takes the form of a circumstantial element (grammatically, a prepositional phrase). But in the projected type the circumstance is one of Matter, whereas in the enhancing type it is typically one of Extent or Location. This corresponds in process type to the distinction between saying and sensing on the one hand and doing and being on the other.

(II) Degree of individuation. We shall see below (Chapter 5) that participants are located at some point along a scale of individuation, ranging from most generalized (e.g., *diamonds are forever*) to most individuated (e.g., *Elizabeth's diamonds were stolen*).

The Range element tends towards the generalized end of the scale. This is especially the case with those of the elaborating type (i.a above), where the Range usually represents a general class; and it is always the case if the figure is one of being, with Range as Attribute. For example:

```
Peter plays tennis (cf. is a tennis-player)
Peter plays the piano (cf. is a pianist)
His opinion is not important (cf. does not matter)
```

As a corollary to this, when some element that has functioned as Range is carried through the discourse, being picked up either by a lexical repetition or by a pronominal reference, it is more likely to be being picked up as a class, rather than as individuated:

```
Sharon plays tennis at the same time every other day .... Tennis
is a wonderful game, but tennis-players tend to be very obsessive.

Peter spends a lot of time at the piano ... It is a difficult
instrument.
```

Hence a form of reference such as the following is somewhat improbable:

```
Peter used to play the piano; but he sold it.
```

(III) Interpersonal potential. The Range element is not very likely to function as Subject in the clause: that is, to be entrusted with the interpersonal function of carrying the burden of the argument (cf. Chapter 1, Section 1.4). This means that passive clauses with Range as Subject are very much rarer than those where Subject is Goal; and where they do occur, the participant that is functioning as Medium (Actor, Senser or Sayer) also tends to be of a generalized kind. Thus *tennis is played by everyone* is not uncommon, whereas *tennis is played by Sharon* is a highly marked construction.

Again, the category of Range/ Attribute provides the limiting case. An Attribute can never serve as Subject in the clause.

We have summarized the features of two participant roles, Goal and Range, which vary considerably in their degree of participanthood, lying as it were at the two ends of this continuum. We saw earlier that the Medium is the element that is most closely bonded to the Process, the two together forming the nucleus of the figure. Thus the highest degree of participanthood is that of whichever element, in each particular type of figure, is conflated with the generalized function of Medium; in the case of a figure of doing, this is the Goal, the element that is impacted (moved, changed, created or destroyed) by the Process.

At the other end of the cline are those elements whose status as participant is highly precarious, those which conflate with the generalized function of Range. These, as we have seen, are closely agnate to other types of figure, either those consisting of Process alone or those with Process + circumstantial element. We can thus extend the continuum further, outside the status of participant altogether, into the realm of circumstances. In the next subsection we discuss the circumstantial roles; and we can order these also in terms of their degree of involvement in the process (Section 4.5 below).

4.5 Degree of involvement; circumstantial roles

As we have already noted (cf. Chapter 2, Section 2.3), a figure consists of a **process**, **participants** involved in the process, and associated or attendant **circumstances**. Of these, the process can be seen as the organizational centre — the element that reflects the relative arrangements of the other parts in the configuration. These other parts (participants and circumstances) are more or less closely involved in the actualization of the process. Broadly speaking, participants are directly involved in the process; circumstances are more peripherally attendant on it.

The different **degrees of involvement** are reflected in the way the figure, and its elements, are realized in the grammar of the clause. A participant is realized as a nominal group, and is typically placed next before or next after the verbal group realizing the process. Circumstances typically occur further away from the process, and are of two distinct types. Type 1, simple circumstance, represents a quality; this type is realized as an adverbial group, and will be discussed under elements below (Chapter 5, Section 5.5). Type 2, macro circumstance, is realized as a prepositional phrase, which in turn consists of preposition + nominal group. The nominal group, as we have seen, construes an entity — something that could function directly as a participant. Here however the entity is functioning only as a circumstantial element in the process: a location, or an instrument, or an accompanying entity, or so on (e.g. *don't walk on the grass, I washed it with sugar soap, she came with her children*); it enters into the clause by courtesy of the preposition, only indirectly so to speak.

What is the status of these "macro circumstances"? They are really reduced or minor figures, functioning as elements inside other figures. The preposition is a kind of mini-verb; the line between circumstances and figures is a very fuzzy one, and we often find agnate expressions where one is a prepositional phrase and the other a non-finite clause: cf. *I washed it using sugar soap, she came accompanied by her children*. The entity that occurs inside the macro circumstance is therefore already entering into a relationship with a reduced form of a process; its participation in the main process is thus mediated and oblique. We can thus contrast the different statuses of two entities where one is a direct participant and the other enters in circumstantially; e.g. *this dictionary was published in two volumes,* where *this dictionary* is Goal while *two volumes* enters into the publishing process indirectly in a circumstance of Role.

Sometimes some entity can be construed in a figure either as a participant or as (an element in) a circumstance; in that case, construing it as participant means that it is being treated as more directly involved. Compare pairs of examples such as:

entity as participant :   entity as circumstance:

(1) doing

```
shoot the pianist :          shoot at the pianist
grab somebody :              grab at somebody
paint the wall :             spread paint on the wall
buy mother a present :       buy a present for mother
```

(2) sensing

```
guess the answer :           guess at the answer
find something out :         find out about something
```

The pianist is more likely to escape unscathed as a circumstance than as a participant; likewise, the answer seems more inpenetrable if guessed at than if guessed.

The difference in the degree of involvement is also reflected in the extent to which an element is available for a critical role in the interpersonal metafunction. Prototypically, as we have noted, participants can be assigned the status of Subject, being made to carry the burden of the argument, whereas circumstances cannot (cf. Halliday, 1985: Ch. 5). This distinction is however being obscured in Modern English, where although the prepositional phrase as a whole cannot function as Subject, the nominal group inside a prepositional phrase often can; e.g. *the grass shouldn't be walked on.*

The "degree of involvement", in the sense of how deeply some element is involved in actualizing the process that is construed by the figure, can thus be represented as a cline: the difference appears not only between participants and circumstances as a whole, but also within each of these primary categories, so that there is a continuum from one to the other along this scale.

At the same time, and cutting across this cline of involvement, we find that — like the participants themselves — the circumstantial elements fall into distinct types according to their relationship to the Process + Medium nucleus. These types correspond to the four transphenomenal categories of logico-semantic relations that are now familiar: the circumstance is either a circumstance of projection or a circumstance of expansion and, if the latter, then either elaborating, extending or enhancing. If we combine the degree of involvement with the logico-semantic categories, we can represent the elements of a figure in the form of a helix (Figure 4-14).

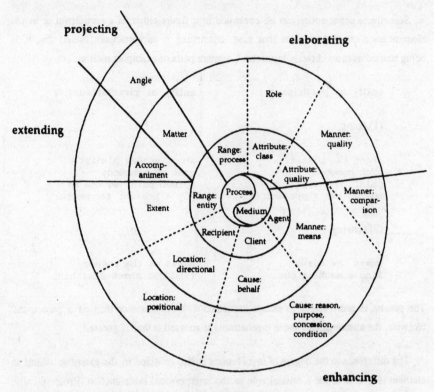

Fig. 4-14: The spectrum of circumstances according to the different types of expansion and projection

Notes to Figure 4-14

(i) Accompaniment. The circumstance of Accompaniment does not correspond to any one particular participant role. Rather, it corresponds to an extending of the participant itself, by addition or variation: *John came with Mary* is agnate to *both John and Mary came; Mary came without John* is agnate to *Mary but not John came; Mary came instead of John* is agnate to *not John but Mary came.* Grammatically, the analogous type of participant is one represented by a nominal group complex.

(ii) Manner: comparison. This category lies on the borderline of elaborating and extending: compare *he spoke like an expert* 'in the manner of', *he spoke as an expert* 'in the role of'. The analogous participant is that of Attribute in an ascriptive clause as in *he was/ seemed an expert,* which is construed as elaborating; but the analogous sequence is an enhancing clause complex *he spoke as if he was an expert.*

(iii) Angle. This type of circumstance relates to projection rather than expansion, and specifically to the projecting not the projected component. Hence there is no agnate participant; instead, the Angle corresponds to the *process* of saying (grammatically, the projecting verbal clause in a 'locution' nexus) or the *process* of sensing (grammatically, the projecting mental clause in an 'idea' nexus). Thus *according to the newspaper* corresponds to *the newspaper says;* and *to her students* corresponds to *her students think.*

The examples in Table 4(10) illustrate both the different degrees and the different kinds of involvement of elements falling outside the Process + Medium nucleus.

Table 4(10): Expansion and projection and types of participant/ circumstance

	participant	circumstance: inner	circumstance: outer
elab.	Attribute: quality they lived happy	Manner: quality they lived happily	
	Attribute: class he died a hero; he became a miser	Role he died as a hero; he turned into a miser	
	Range: process he did/ sang a song		
enh.	Range: entity she'll swim the river Range: measure she'll swim a mile	Extent: entity she'll swim across the river Extent: measure she'll swim for a mile	
	Agent he opened the door : the door was opened by him	Manner: means the door was opened by/ with a key	
	Client he cooked her a dinner : a dinner for her	Cause: behalf he accepted the invitation on her behalf/ for her	Cause: reason &c he accepted the invitation because of her
	Recipient he sent her an invitation : an invitation to her Receiver she told him a story : a story to him	Location: directional he sent a parcel to NY he postponed the meeting until 4	Location: positional in LA, he sent a parcel in the morning, he postponed the meeting
ext.	complexes: she and her aunt are travelling	Accompaniment she is travelling with her aunt	
proj.	 Range: entity the board discussed the financial situation	 Matter the board talked about the financial situation	Angle according to the board, the financial situation ...

What this brings out is that there are a small number of very general domains within this overall semantic space, which may be construed in different ways according to the status they are assigned within the figure. For example, there is one area that is concerned with the spatial orientation of the process. Construed as an outer circumstance, this appears as the position within which the process unfolds; construed as an inner circumstance, it means the direction towards which the process is oriented; construed as a participant, it shows up as receiver or recipient in the process. Thus this general motif is manifested in a form which corresponds to its ecological niche at that location. Note that the boundaries do not exactly coincide across the different bands of the helix; in any case, they are fuzzy, and they tend to become more fuzzy with increasing distance from the centre. Our characterization here is inevitably somewhat overdeterminate. The outer circumstances, in turn, are typically agnate to clauses (e.g. *while he was in LA, he sent a parcel*); thus we could construe the same general relationships over again in the form of a sequence — grammatically, as one nexus in a clause complex.

5. Elements

5.1 The primary types of element

Elements serve as component parts of figures. Three primary types of element may be differentiated according to the generalized categories of configurational roles: process, participant, and circumstance. In addition to these three, we need to recognize a fourth category of element, the relator; this is the element which forms figures into sequences.

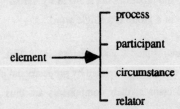

The congruent (prototypical) grammatical realizations of these types of element in English are as follows:

process	↘	verbal group
participant	↘	nominal group
circumstance	↘	adverbial group; prepositional phrase
relator	↘	conjunction group

These phenomena are "elemental" in relation to figures (just as chemical elements such as H and O are elemental in relation to compounds such as H_2O, CO_2). But the elements themselves may be internally complex, as in the following examples of processes and participants:

```
processes:

verbal group            verbal group complex

will have boiled         cool and store
had been going to chop   is continuing to fail to meet

participants:

nominal group            nominal group complex

a shallow tin            lunch or dinner
invaluable advice        some boneless chicken pieces and a few
a tasteless vegetable    rashers of bacon
powdered white sugar
thin slices of lemon
ballpoint pen remover
```

However, there is a significant difference between elements and figures in the nature of their internal organization. While figures consist of phenomena that are ontologically of different types — participants, processes and circumstances, the components of an element belong in principle to the same type. That is, the components of a participant are themselves potential participants, and the components of a process are themselves potential processes. Grammatically speaking, participants are realized by nominal groups, which are groups of nouns; and processes are realized by verbal groups, which are groups of verbs. The limiting case of a group is a single word.

The situation with circumstances and relators is a little more complicated. (i) Circumstances of the "macro" type are realized by prepositional phrases, which as we have seen are like miniaturized clauses; their components are thus of different types — a (minor) process plus a participant. Circumstances of the simple type, on the other hand, are realized by adverbial groups; these are groups of adverbs, like *more soundly, not so very fast,* with the single adverb again as the limiting case. (ii) Relators are typically realized by conjunctions, like *and, so, if, that, because, however;* these can form groups, such as *as if, and yet,* but conjunctions are more often expanded by adverbs (*just because, even if*). In addition there are numerous other types of relator: prepositional phrases (*in addition, in the event (that), for fear that*), nominal groups remaining from earlier prepositional phrases ([*at*] *the moment (that),* [*on*] *the day* (*that*)), and various expressions involving non-finite verbs (*supposing (that), provided* (*that*)). The relator construes a logico-semantic relation between the clauses in a clause nexus (realizing a sequence), but it is itself an element in the structure of one or other of the two clauses concerned; e.g. *if you have some ink fish preserved in oil, add a few slices at the same time as the halibut* (Elizabeth David, Italian Food).

5.2 Similarities and differences between participants and processes

Being elements, participants and processes occupy roles in figures; but whereas processes only serve in the single role of Process, participants (as we have seen) range over a much wider experiential spectrum — the direct participant roles of Actor, Goal, Senser, Phenomenon, and so on, and also the indirect participant roles within circumstances such as Location and Cause. Thus, seen from the point of view of figures, participants are construed as being experientially more complex, in the sense that they can take on a variety of configurational roles: see Figure 5-1. This difference between participants and processes is also reflected in differences in their internal organizations, as we shall suggest below.

In our discussion of figures, we pointed out that participants and processes form a temporal complementarity: participants persist, whereas processes unfold, through time. (For a functional-typological comparison of nouns and verbs, stated in terms of prototypes, see Hopper & Thompson,1985.)This complementarity is reflected both in the similarities and in the differences between the two.

figure:

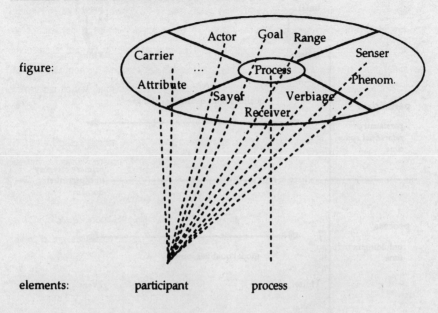

elements: participant   process

Fig. 5-1: The plurifunctionality of participants

(i) Both types of element begin with a location in the 'here & now': they construct a path from the spatio-temporal moment defined instantially by the interaction base — the 'here & now' of the act of speaking — to a primary category of ideational phenomena: see Figure 5-2. For example:

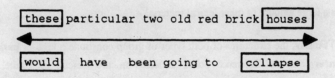

In other words, both types of group include **deixis**. But the deixis is of two different kinds: nominal deixis (such as near/ remote) and verbal deixis (such as past/ present/ future), structurally realized as Deictic and Finite respectively. What this suggests is that, since processes occur in time — their mode of existence is temporal — that is how they are tied to the speech situation; whereas participants exist in some kind of referential space, which may be grounded concretely in the speech interaction (*this* = 'near me'; *that* = 'away from me') but may also be a more abstract, discoursal space. The latter is the space where we 'record' discourse referents as we work our way through a text (*this* = 'about to be mentioned (by me)'; *that* = 'mentioned earlier').

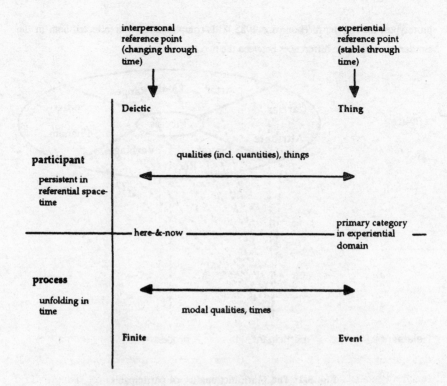

Fig. 5-2: Comparison of nominal and verbal group structures

(ii) Secondly, both types of group include a specification of a primary **experiential category** — Thing in the nominal group and Event in the verbal group. But in the simple verbal group, this is the only semantic category that is lexicalized — other categories are represented grammatically by auxiliaries; whereas in the nominal group, there is a large amount of other lexical material.

(iii) Finally, the structures of both types of group constitute a kind of **path between the interpersonal** reference point, reflected in the Deictic or Finite, **and the experiential** one, reflected in the Thing or Event. But in the case of the verbal group, the path is made up of one or more temporal relations: past/ present/ future in relation to a moment in some dimension of time construed between 'now' and the time of the occurrence of the event; for example, see Figure 5-3. In the nominal group, on the other hand, the path from Deictic to Thing is not a chain in time — altough it does reflect time in another way. The path goes through qualities of various kinds, beginning with qualities that are textual and transitory (unstable in time) and moving towards increasing permanence (time-stability) and experiential complexity.

Nominal groups have, in fact, far greater potential than verbal groups for creating experientially complex categories; and this reflects a fundamental difference between participants and processes. The nominal group has the potential for intersecting any number of qualities in the representation of a participant; and this makes it possible for the taxonomic ordering of participants to be considerably more elaborated than that of processes.

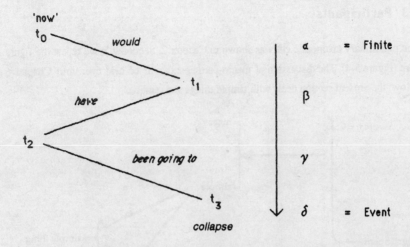

Fig. 5-3: The temporal path in the verbal group from Finite to Event

Both the difference in temporal permanence and the difference in experiential complexity are reflected logogenetically. Participants tend to persist in the unfolding of a text; and since they do, they can accrue various qualities. In contrast, processes cannot persist in text: unlike the deictic system of the nominal group, the deictic system of the verbal group, the tense system, is not a system for tracking textual instances of processes as a text unfolds. To achieve persistence in text, processes have to be reconstrued metaphorically as participants (see Chapter 6). When processes are construed as if they were participants, they can be established and maintained as referents in a text; hence under these conditions they also can accrue various qualities.

A different kind of parallelism between participants and processes, having to do with how they are manifested over space-time, has been suggested by other grammarians (see e.g. Quirk et al, 1985). Taking the traditional distinction between 'mass' nouns and 'count' nouns (explained as a contrast between things that are unbounded and things that are bounded and discrete), they have mapped this distinction onto that between 'states' and 'non-states', in the realm of processes. It then becomes possible to recognize further similarities, e.g. between plurality in the realm of participants and repeated or iterated occurrence in the realm of processes. Such analogies may serve as the basis for metaphorical reconstrual (cf. Chapter 6 below); for example: *they have demolished many buildings : many demolitions have taken place : : he knew a great deal : he had a great deal of knowledge; the ball bounced again and again : the repeated bouncing of the ball :: the train stops three times : the three stops of the train.* Jackendoff (1991) presents a recent treatment of some aspects of the same issue. We shall not pursue the point further here; it needs to be explored in terms of the transphenomenal types of logico-semantic relation that we have already referred to in various places — in particular the question of how participants and processes are elaborated and extended in space-time.

5.3 Participants

The preliminary taxonomic cut was shown in Chapter 2, Section 2.5; we repeat the figure here (Figure 5-4). The discussion of macro-participants will be held over until Chapter 6 below; the present section deals with simple things and qualities.

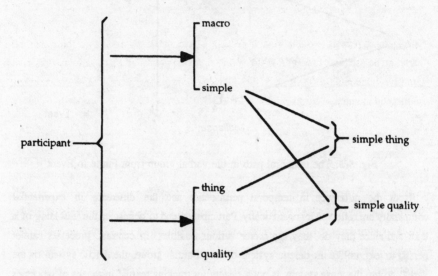

Fig. 5-4: First step in taxonomy of participants

We have already set up the general theory of participants, defining them in relation to ascriptive processes of being, being at, and having, in a process-participant configuration. There are three elements in such a configuration: the Process, intensive, possessive or circumstantial; the Attribute, which is being ascribed by one or other of these processes; and the Carrier. It is the role of Carrier which defines the concept of a participant. A participant, according to this theory, is that which may have assigned to it, in the discourse, properties, parts or circumstantial features. For example:

(a) properties (Process of 'being')

```
some dishes are very tolerant
the grain looks orange and full
a kitchen should be a cheerful place
the swede is more nutritious than the turnip
```

(b) parts (Process of 'having')

```
it has branching stems covered with a green succulent flesh
```

```
spinach has a decided flavour which some people dislike
they have a pleasant fresh flavour
```

(c) circumstantial features (Process of 'being at')

```
this plant is like chicory
these mangoes are from Mexico
the seeds will be inside long coffee-coloured pods
this effect might be because of over-heating
```

This analysis reveals two important aspects of a participant: (i) that it is a thing that can 'carry' or be ascribed attributes, and (ii) that the ascription may be of different kinds — intensive (elaborating), possessive (extending), circumstantial (enhancing). We comment on these in the next two paragraphs.

(i) Experientially, there is a 'carrier' — the Thing — and there are 'attributes' — Epithets and other modifiers. However, participants are construed not only experientially but also logically, which means that the Thing (typically) serves as a Head that can be modified by successive attributes and that this modifying relation is inherently ascriptive. There is thus no equivalent, in the nominal group, of the Process in an ascriptive figure; this is construed instead as the logical relation of modification, indefinitely repeatable. For instance, corresponding to the figure *the swede is nutritious* we have the participant *the nutritious swede,* which, unlike the figure with its experiential, multivariate organization (Carrier + Process + Attribute), can be logically expanded through further modification: *the tasty tolerant orange nutritious swede.* That is, participants are construed as things that can accrue attributes.

(ii) There is the same range of types of ascription as are found in ascriptive figures, and these, as we have seen in Chapter 3, Section 3.2.3.2, can be interpreted in terms of the different categories of expansion. These are exemplified in the following table (see below for discussion of the structural roles):

expansion [of Thing]	Deictic	Epithet	Classifier	Thing	Qualifier
elaboration (intensive)	these these a	**nutritious** **cheerful**	**Mexican**	swedes mangoes kitchen	
extension (possessive)	my aunt's the the		table	teapot stems leg	of the leek
enhancement (circumstantial)	these some a	chicory-like	18th c	vases mangoes plant	from Mexico

The table illustrates how participants are interpretable as expansions of things — they are things, with added qualities. It also shows how things can be construed into highly elaborate taxonomies (e.g. *this extremely desirable two-storey double-brick executive residence*) which are categorized by ascriptive figures of these different types — elaborating, extending and enhancing. The Thing in these examples corresponds to the Carrier of the agnate figure of ascription: *these nutritious swedes : these swedes are nutritious :: these vases from the 18th century : these vases are from the 18th century :: my aunt's teapot : the teapot is my aunt's/ belongs to my aunt.* Note that with extension, there may be a reversal of the Carrier-Attribute correspondence: the Thing may correspond most naturally to the Attribute, as in *my aunt has a teapot : the leek has a stem.*

The theoretical principle that a participant can be defined as the potential carrier of an attribute holds for participants of all kinds. We need however to make one proviso: namely, that more or less any figure can be construed metaphorically "as if" it was a participant. This is a central feature of grammatical metaphor, discussed in detail in Chapter 6 below. An example would be *Our earlier encounter with this species [had led us to believe that ...]* where 'encounter' is semantically a process: cf. *We had encountered this species earlier [and as a consequence we believed that ...].* If 'encounter' is construed congruently in the grammar as a process, it cannot enter into an ascriptive figure. But once it is metaphorized into a participant, it can: *our earlier encounter with this species had been almost disastrous.* This in fact is one of the discursive contexts favouring this type of grammatical metaphor, and hence serves indirectly as a further illustration of the general principle we have outlined.

5.3.1 Things and qualities

Grammatically speaking, (simple) participants are realized by nominal groups, which are made up of both things and qualities. In terms of the structure of the nominal group, the cut-off point between things and qualities is between the Classifier and the Thing: see Figure 5-5.

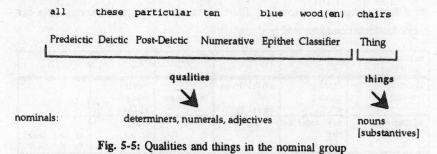

Fig. 5-5: Qualities and things in the nominal group

Semantically, Classifiers are qualities of the 'class' type (cf. Table 5(4) in Section 5.3.3.3 below): they are like things and may be derived from things, but unlike things they do not have independent existence — they cannot be established in referential space and re-identified in running discourse. So for example although a 'passenger' is undoubtedly a thing, in *a passenger train,* where *passenger* functions as Classifier, it is being construed as a quality; hence it cannot be picked up by anaphoric reference — we cannot say *this is a passenger train; they must have valid tickets*. (Contrast *this train is for passengers; they must have valid tickets*, where *passengers* is functioning as Thing.) Grammatically, Classifiers are realized by 'substantives' or by 'adjectives' (cf. Section 5.3.3.1 below), and this indeterminacy in grammatical class is symbolic of their status as qualities which are like things.

This distribution of qualities and things across the nominal group indicates two related points:

(i) things are more time-stable than qualities; and

(ii) things are more experientially complex than qualities.

This second point has been brought out in discussions of the question by scholars writing from very different points of departure:

Boole's (1854: 27) *The Laws of Thought*:

Appellative or descriptive signs, expressing either the name of a thing, or circumstance belonging to it. To this class we may obviously refer the substantive proper or common, and the adjective. These may indeed be regarded as differing only in this respect, that the former expresses the substantive existence of the individual thing or things to which it refers; the latter implies that existence. If we attach to the adjective the universally understood subject "being" or "thing", it becomes virtually a substantive, and may for all essential purposes of reasoning be replaced by the substantive.

Paul (1909: 251):

Das Adj. bezeichnet eine einfache oder als einfach vorgestellte Eigenschaft, das Subst. schliesst einen Komplex von Eigenschaften in sich.

Jespersen (1924: 75):

Apart from "abstracts," then, I find the solution of our problem in the view that on the whole substantives are more special than adjectives, they are applicable to fewer objects than adjectives, in the parlance of logicians, the extension of a substantive is less, and its intension is greater than that of an adjective. The adjective indicates and singles out one quality, one distinguishing mark, but each substantive suggests, to whoever understands it, many distinguishing features by which he recognizes the person or thing in question.

Although Jespersen rejects 'substance' as the characteristic property of substantives, he finds an "element of truth" in it (1924: 79-80):

... I am inclined to lay more stress on the greater complexity of qualities denoted by substantives, as against the singling out of one quality in the case of an adjective. This complexity is so essential that only in rare cases will it be possible by heaping adjective upon adjective to arrive at a complete definition of the notion evoked by the naming of a substantive: there will always, as Bertelsen remarks, remain an undefinable x, a kernel which may be thought of as "bearer" of the qualities which we may have specified. This again is what underlies the old definition by means of "substance." which is thus seen to contain one element of truth though not the whole truth. If one wants a metaphorical figure, substantives may be compared to crystallisations of qualities which in adjectives are found only in the liquid state.

But this difference in experiential complexity is in turn related to the first of our two points, in that whatever is being construed as stable, as having persistence through time, is essentially a construct, an assemblage of different qualities, that (to borrow Jespersen's metaphor) can be crystallized only as an organic whole. The nominal group embodies this essential association between complexity and permanence.

Qualities tend to be experientially simple, specifying values along a single dimension or scale such as age, size, weight, loudness, colour, according to either scalar or binary distinctions (e.g. scalar: 'large' — 'small', 'tall' — 'short'; binary: 'male' — 'female', 'dead' — 'alive'). Things, on the other hand, tend to be experientially more complex than qualities. They are often definable in terms of an elaborate taxonomy where several dimensions (parameters) are needed to distinguish them (cf. Section 5.3.2.5 and the example of clothing in Figure 5-8). Consider for example the scale of size. The various qualities named by *large, big, giant, small, tiny,* and so on indicate a region on the scale, but do not specify the "substance" of whatever it is that size is being ascribed to. If we look for objects that are characterized in terms of size, we will find e.g. *a giant, a morsel,* and *a mini.* These, however, involve far more than the single dimension of size. A giant is 'any imaginary being of human form but of superhuman size and strength'. A morsel is 'a small bite or portion of food'. A mini is usually understood as 'a small car capable of holding a normal complement of passengers'. Small objects are typically objects of some particular kind, e.g. droplet, booklet, and kitchenette.

Even with qualities that form binary and taxonomic oppositions rather than scalar ones, there seem to be differences in experiential complexity between adjective (quality) and noun (thing) pairs. A standard example of this contrast between qualities and things involves the two dimensions of maturity and sex: see Figure 5-6. Taxonomically organized qualities are often named by denominal adjectives, but they are still experientially simpler than the corresponding nouns. Consider e.g. nationality, philosophical persuasion, and biological kind: as qualities, these are classes and therefore closest to things, but their extension is still greater than that of the things that correspond to them: see Table 5(1).

Table 5(1): Taxonomic things and qualities

Example	gloss	meaning as thing	meaning as quality
Albanian	'of Albania'	'human: citizen'	(any thing) 'originating in Abania'
Aristotelian	'of Aristotle'	'human: philosopher'	(any thing) 'reminiscent of Aristotle'
canine	'of dog'	'animal: dog'	(anything) 'doglike'

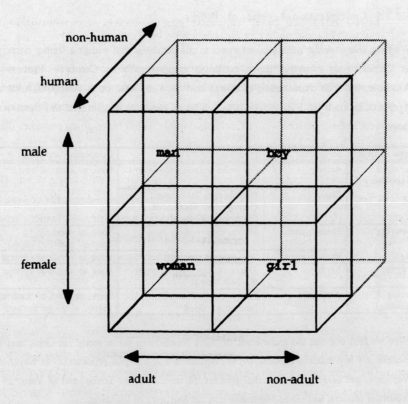

Fig. 5-6: Complex objects in terms of simple qualities

Thus *an Albanian* always means 'a human citizen of Albania', whereas the adjective *Albanian* could refer to any of a large number of concrete or abstract entities: *Albanian wine, Albanian literature, Albanian economy*.

5.3.2 Things

We have observed that things tend to be relatively stable in space and time, and relatively complex in their semantic make-up and in their interrelationships; and that these special characteristics of things are construed linguistically in various ways. By comparison with other elements, things tend to stand out (i) by their varied roles as elements in figures, (ii) by the overall weight and discursive force of their primary categorization of experience, (iii) by their tendency to be elaborated into numerous micro-categories, (iv) by their complex internal organization, and (v) by their highly systematic relationship one with another. In this section we explore these characteristics a little further. In the next chapter, we will take account of a sixth characteristic of things, their power to function as model for other realms of experience.

5.3.2.1 Configurational roles of things

We were able to define a thing by reference to one particular role within a figure: namely, as Carrier in an ascriptive figure construed grammatically as Carrier + Process + Attribute. But it is characteristic of things that they can take on a variety of roles in figures of all kinds (cf. Figure 5-1). Here is a set of examples to illustrate this functional range:

type of figure	participant role	example	perspective on book
doing & happening	Actor	*The book is losing its cover*	book as material object
	Goal	*They burned 1000 books* *They printed 1000 books* *She bound the book*	
sensing	Phenomenon	*She remembered the book*	book as semiotic content/ material object
	Phenomenon	*She enjoyed the book*	book as semiotic content
saying	Sayer	*The book says that winter is the best time to visit*	book as semiotic content
being & having	Attribute	*This is a very heavy/ interesting book*	books as class of material object/ semiotic content

Here we find one and the same class of thing functioning (a) as Actor, as Goal, and as Beneficiary in a material process; (b) as Phenomenon in a mental process; (c) as Sayer, as Verbiage, and as Target in a verbal process; (d) as Carrier, as Token, and as Value in a relational process, and (e) as Minirange in a circumstance of Location.

Even if we generalize across these configurational types in ergative terms, these examples still cover the full participant spectrum: the 'book' occurs as Medium, as Agent, as Beneficiary and as Range. There is thus a marked contrast between things and all other elements. A quality enters into a figure only as Attribute; a process only as Process; and a circumstance only in some particular circumstantial role. Other than this, the only functional environment for qualities, processes and circumstances is that where they form parts of things — that is, grammatically, where they enter into the structure of the nominal group.

	in figure (clause)	in participant (nom. gp.)
quality	*your hands are cold*	*your cold hands*
process	*a star is falling*	*a falling star*
circumstance (loc)	*the cat sat on the roof*	*the cat on the roof*
circumstance (matter)	*the story concerns two cities*	*a tale of two cities*

The fact that these other elements can themselves enter into the specification of a thing is another indication of the relative complexity of things.

5.3.2.2 Weight and discursive force of primary categorization

The major classes of thing recognized in our school grammars have traditionally been presented as a list of category meanings of the word class 'noun': something like "persons, other living beings, objects, institutions, and abstractions". We will start with this categorization, modifying it to take account of the point made in Chapter 4, Section 4.2, to the effect that the primary distinction within figures is that between conscious processing and other forms of experience (cf. Figure 4-1): the key participant in a conscious process, the Senser, is restricted to things that are construed as being endowed with consciousness, so we take conscious/ non-conscious as the primary distinction. It is also helpful, in the case of English, to make an initial distinction between objects, which are treated as bounded, and substances, which are not. This gives us an initial categorization in the form 'conscious/ non-conscious: animals/ institutions/ objects/ substances/ abstractions'.

The most prominent reflex of the conscious/ non-conscious distinction in English is that it is built into the system of **pronouns**:

| personal | conscious | *he/ she* | non-conscious | *it* |
| interrogative | conscious | *who* | non-conscious | *what* |

This distinction is all-pervasive, since third-person pronouns provide one of the main resources for constructing discourse through anaphora. The boundary between conscious and non-conscious, of course, is fluid and negotiable: different systems, and different speakers (or the same speaker on different occasions), may draw it in different places. But the guiding principle is that 'conscious' means prototypically adult human and may be extended outwards (a) to babies, (b) to pets, and (c) to higher animals — as well as by rhetorical strategies of various kinds.

The further categories introduced above are distinguished in the grammar by the class of **general nouns**, which are used discursively to refer to instances of the category in question:[1]

conscious (human):	*person, people, man, woman, child, boy, girl;* and numerous terms of endearment and abuse
animal:	*creature, animal*
institution:	*place, show, set-up*
object:	*thing, object*
substance:	*stuff*

---

[1] General nouns are used anaphorically and are typically unstressed: see Halliday & Hasan (1976: 274 ff). For example: *I don't know who that cat belongs to. But I've often seen the creature around.*

abstraction: *business, affair, matter; move, event; fact*

These primary categories of things represent an ordering of the phenomena of experience. This ordering has to do with their inherent potential for bringing about change: that is, their ability to initiate processes and to affect other participants.

One way of exploring this is by noting which participant roles each category of participant is typically associated with. The critical roles, in this respect, are those of Senser, Sayer and Actor, operating respectively in figures of sensing, saying and doing & happening. When we investigate these, however, we find that the overall categorization of phenomena that is revealed in this way displays a further dimension of complexity: at the highest level, all phenomena are distributed into two broad experiential realms, the material and the semiotic. This suggests that we should further modify the schema of primary categorization by splitting it into these two realms as shown in Figure 5-7. This figure also splits the categories of object and abstraction between the two realms.

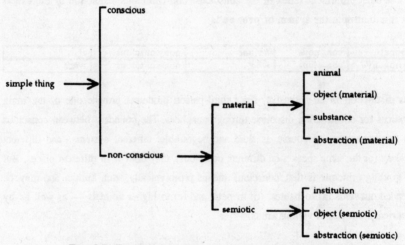

Fig. 5-7: The first few steps in the taxonomy of simple things

We give a brief description of each of these categories in turn.

conscious (prototypically adult human)

> typifying roles: active participant in figure of sensing [Senser, e.g. *do you think so?*], of saying [Sayer, e.g. *the teacher said ...*] and of doing [Actor: middle, e.g. *Pat skipped*, or effective, e.g. *Chris held the rope*].

> pronoun *he/she/they* (also *I/you*); general noun *person* etc.; number category: count (singular/ plural).

has potential for voluntary action [material: doing, including doing to another participant; verbal (semiotic): saying] and conscious processing of all kinds [mental: sensing, including feeling, thinking, intending as well as perceiving].

animal

typifying role: active participant in figure of doing [Actor, typically middle, e.g. *birds fly*].

pronoun *it/they;* general noun *creature;* number category: count (singular/ plural).

has potential for self-initiated action and movement [processes in which animal occurs as Actor are (unconscious but) voluntary; and may also be effective, e.g. *... was bitten by a snake*]; also for perception [Senser in process of seeing & hearing].

object (material)

typifying role: impacted participant in figure of doing [Goal, e.g. *build a house, pick up sticks*].

pronoun *it/ them;* general noun *thing;* number category: count (singular/ plural).

has extension in space, bounded so participates in figures as unit whole; if acting, then in figure of happening [Actor in involuntary process, e.g. *the button fell off*].

substance

typifying role: thing as part of circumstance [Range in prepositional phrase, especially Location, e.g. *on the ground*], rather than having direct role as participant in figure.

pronoun *it;* general noun *stuff;* number category: mass.

has extension in space, but unbounded; can be manipulated and measured; if participant in figure, is typically being distributed [Goal, e.g. *cut the string, keep rain out*].

abstraction (material)

typifying role: as Phenomenon in figure of sensing [e.g. *estimate the depth*], as participant in figure of being [Carrier in ascriptive figure, e.g. *the colours were too bright;* Value in identifying figure, e.g. *the score was 2 -1*].

pronoun *it;* general noun: none; number category: mass.

has no extension in space and is unbounded; typically some parameter of a material quality or process.

institution

typifying roles: active participant in figure of saying [Sayer, e.g. *the ministry announced* ...], of doing [Actor, e.g. *the school is closing down*]; also of sensing, typically thinking and intending [Senser, e.g. *the class decided that* ...].

pronoun *it ~ they;* general noun *people, place, set-up* etc.; number category: count (singular).[2]

has potential for voluntary action, typically semiotic with authority of a collective [verbal process of ordering, mental process of deciding or judging]; also material [material processes, middle and effective].

object (semiotic)

typifying role: scope-defining participant in figure of saying [Range in verbal process, e.g. *read the notice, tell me a story*]; also active participant [Sayer, e.g. *the book says* ..., *the regulations require* ...].

pronoun *it/them, they;* general noun (none); number category: count (singular/ plural).

may also exist as material object, e.g. *book, clock;* has potential for being symbol source [hence Sayer in projecting clause].

abstraction (semiotic)

typifying role: scope-defining participant in figure of sensing or saying [Range in mental process, e.g. *find out more information;* in verbal process, e.g. *tell the truth*]; also participant in figures of being & having [e.g. possessed Attribute, *have you any evidence*].

pronoun *it;* general noun: some attitudinally loaded ones such as *nonsense* [non-attitudinal ones for some, e.g. *idea, fact*]; number category: mass.

---

[2] Institutions of course do appear in the plural — although relatively infrequently: the plural pronoun *they* typically refers to a single institution.

unbounded semiotic substance; may be qualified by projection [as Thing + Qualifier in nominal group, e.g. *the knowledge that they had failed*]; no material existence.

As is to be expected with a very general schematic framework of this kind, the categories outlined above are not at all sharply defined. Their boundaries are indeterminate, and we will expect to find things of mixed, overlapping and intermediate kinds at every step along the cline. Among the more prominent of these intermediate categories we can recognize three as follow.

(i) Natural forces (tides, hurricanes, etc.); instruments (as extended body parts); powered artefacts (locomotives, industrial machines, etc.): intermediate between animals and material objects. These are typically active (including effective action, moving other objects), but non-volitional; hence when the Actor is of this category, the process does not admit phases that construe intentionality (e.g. *the hammer tried to force the lock*).

(ii) Human collectives: intermediate between conscious beings and institutions. These can function as Senser in figures of sensing of all kinds, including those embodying desideration; but they accept either singular or plural pronouns, and if singular pronominalize with *it* (e.g. *the family says it is united/ the family say they are united*).

(iii) Discrete semiotic abstractions: intermediate between semiotic objects and (non-discrete) semiotic abstractions. These include non-personalized 'facts' and 'cases', mental entities like 'thoughts' and 'fears', and speech functions 'questions' and 'orders'; they are bounded, cannot function as Sayer but can accept a projection as Qualifier (e.g., *the order to retreat, her anxiety that she might be disqualified*).

In Table 5(2) we have included these intermediate categories.

The general picture we are suggesting, then, is that it is in the category of **thing** that the grammar captures to the greatest measure the complexity of the elemental phenomena of human experience. Put together with the different types of **figure**, which construe the complexity of goings-on upon the broad foundational categories of doing, sensing, saying and being, the different types of **participant** we have sketched in here foreground the dual nature of experience as being at once both material and semiotic — a world that is constituted out of the interaction between entities and meanings. On each of these dimensions there is a progression from things that are most like to things that are least like ourselves. The grammar imposes a categorization that is compromising, fluid, indeterminate and constantly in process of change, along with changes in the human condition and in the interaction of humans with their environment. Yet it is also strong enough to bear and carry forward this wealth of often conflicting experience, and transmit it over and over again from one generation of human beings to the next.

Table 5(2): Ordering of things according to different criteria

			(i) role potential in figure:			(ii) internal organization of participant:		
			Senser:	Sayer:	Actor (in effect- ive):	pron:	general noun:	number:
								count/ mass
conscious			√	√	√	s/he/ they	person &c	count
non- conscious	mater- ial realm	animal			√	it/ they	creature, animal	count
		natural force			√	it/ they	—	count
		object (material)				it/ they	thing, object	count
		substance				it	stuff	mass
		abstraction (material)				it	—	mass
	sem- iotic realm	human collectives	√	√	√	it~they/ they	—	count
		institution	√	√	√	it~they/ they	place, show, set- up	count
		objects (semiotic)		√		it/ they	—	count
		abstraction (discrete)				it/ they	(see note)	count
		abstraction (non- discrete)				it	—	mass

5.3.2.3 Elaboration of things into micro categories

What we have suggested in the last section is that the grammar, in its role as a theory of human experience, categorizes those phenomena that it construes as participants by locating them in a spectrum based on a scale of distance from the human — at one end humans themselves, and things most similar to (i.e. categorizable as) humans, at the other end things that are farthest away from being human: concrete substances in the material world and abstract "substances" in the semiotic world. By reference to the grammar of the clause on the one hand, and of the nominal group on the other, certain broad categories are set up such that some things will fall squarely into one category, while others will lie on the borderline, showing certain features of one category and certain features of another, or finding themselves equally at home in both.

But there is no limit to the differentiation that may be drawn between one class of things and another; each of these very broad categories comprises numerous micro-categories within which (as a glance at Roget's Thesaurus quickly reveals) relatively small sets of closely related things are grouped together. We naturally think of these as being semantic groupings, for which we can find general labels by moving a little way up in the taxonomy: parts of the body, household appliances, edible grains, spectator sports, emotional disorders, and so on, and so on. Such groupings are most readily presented as lists of words and word compounds; but they are not simply lexical, they are lexicogrammatical, displaying some characteristic combination of grammatical properties or preferences.

Here we shall do no more than refer to a small selection of such micro-domains, making a brief comment about each with regard to its special characteristics and its place in the overall spectrum. For a further account of the organization of one such domain, see Section 5.3.2.5 below.

Professional associates: *doctor, dentist, hairdresser, lawyer, teacher, butcher*

General category: 'conscious'.

Particular features: may be "possessed" by clients (*my doctor, Jane's music teacher* — on model of kin: *my daughter, Fred's first cousin*); formerly masculine, gender now (redesigned as) common (*he/she*); membership very variable: *butcher* etc. probably leaving this class with change in shopping practices.

Domestic pets: *cats, dogs*

General category: between 'conscious' and 'animal'.

Particular features: alternation between *he/she* and *it;* general nouns as 'animal' (*she's a stupid creature*); individuated by proper names, with attitudinal variants; addressed as if conscious (*what do you want?*); expanded in talking to children (*pussy-cat, puppy-dog*).

Small human collectives: *family, household, class* (at school)

General category: between 'conscious' and 'institution'.

Particular features: common number (as institution: *the class is ~are writing a report*); can be Senser (*the family seemed to think that ...*); pronominalized as *it ~ they*, not *he/she*, but self-referenced as *we* and addressed either as *you* or in third person (*Do you eat together?/ Does ~ do the household eat together?*).

Musical instruments: *piano, cello, flute, drum*

General category: 'object (material)'

Particular features: represented as general class with definite article (*play the flute, study the cello*); alternate between Range and Goal (*play the piano/ shift the piano*); performer construed as derivative in *-ist* or *-er* (*pianist, flautist, drummer*).

Two-pronged implements: *scissors, pliers, tweezers, tongs, shears, clippers*

General category: 'object (material)'

Particular features: inherent plural (hence pronominalized as *they: the scissors/ they are in the drawer*); counted as *a pair of ...* (*two pairs of shears*, not *two shears*), but not referred to as *both* (contrast *a pair of shoes, both shoes*).

Drinks: *coffee, beer, whisky*

General category: 'substance'

Particular features: whereas in general a substance, if counted, means 'a kind of' (*these soils are less fertile*), the counted form of this category may mean either 'a kind of' (*I like this coffee*) or 'a measure of' (*Would you like a beer? Two coffees please!*).

Types of enhancement: *reason, time, place, way*

General category: between 'semiotic object' and 'abstraction'

Particular features: countable, though typically occurring in singular; are names for major circumstantial classes (*reason : why; time : when; place : where; way : how*); can be qualified by relative clause (without the need for a circumstantial marker: *did you see the way [that] they glared at us?*), varying with clause having corresponding relative adverb (*did you see how they glared at us?*), and sometimes both together (*do you know the reason why they glared at us?*).

Nuisances: *nuisance, mess, disaster, shambles*

General category: 'abstraction'

Particular features: formed as countable (*a nuisance*) but largely restricted to singular indefinite (forms such as *nuisances, the nuisance, your nuisance* are rare and outside this category); typically exclamative and/or ascriptive (*that's a mess; what a mess*), and accompanied by interpersonal Epithets (*a horrible shambles, an utter disaster*).

5.3.2.4 Internal structure of things

We have referred above to the syntagmatic potential of the nominal group: how the grammar builds up the representation of a thing, expanding outwards by modification. For example:

					bike
				touring	*bike*
			reinforced	*touring*	*bike*
		tenspeed	*reinforced*	*touring*	*bike*
	European	*tenspeed*	*reinforced*	*touring*	*bike*
latest	*European*	*tenspeed*	*reinforced*	*touring*	*bike*

The expansion proceeds by adding qualities; these qualities, as we have seen, are typically ordered in English from right to left according to the degree of systemicity, with the most systemic (most permanent, least particularized) at the right, the most instantial (least permanent, most particularized) at the left. Broadly speaking these are distributed by the grammar into distinct functions as Classifier, Epithet, Numerative, and Deictic (for the different types of quality these represent, see Section 5.3.3 below).

This syntagmatic resource serves prototypically to construe things into strict taxonomies, based on the principle of hyponymy (see Chapter 2, Section 2.11.3 above). Thus a *touring bike* is *a kind of bike*, a *reinforced touring bike* is *a kind of touring bike*, and so on. Since *touring* is a Classifier, this means that it is one of a defined set: perhaps *touring/ racing/ mountain/ exercise/ trail*. Epithets do not assign classes, but they specify a particular dimension of taxonomic space: e.g. source 'European/ American/ Japanese ... .

One type of classification is meronymic (part-whole), where the thing is classified by the whole of which it forms a part, e.g. *bicycle wheel* 'wheel (that forms part) of a bicycle'. These are often indeterminate in meaning: if definite, they tend to be strictly meronymic (*somebody stole my bicycle wheel*), whereas if indefinite, they are often classifying by type (*the kids were playing with a bicycle wheel* 'wheel for/ from a bicycle').

5.3.2.5 Systematic relationships among things

The expanded form of the nominal group makes explicit the systematic taxonomic relationship which links one thing with another: it is clear that (theoretically at least) a *touring bike* is a kind of bike, a *bicycle wheel* is a kind of wheel. It is always possible, of course, to expand in a metaphorical way, as with *cart wheel* (in *turning cart wheels*) and *catherine wheel* (a kind of firework); these are not, strictly speaking, kinds of *wheel*, so we have to recognize either that these fall outside the taxonomic organization or that the taxonomy itself is being extended metaphorically. But this does not affect the general principle at work; indeed, it is the taxonomic principle which makes such divergence possible.

But we also have to recognize that there is a systematic relationship among a set of terms such as *bicycle, tandem, scooter, car, van, truck* and *bus*. Here the form of wording gives no clue to any such relationship; all we have is an inventory of different words. Yet these also form some kind of a taxonomic set: they are all wheeled vehicles. We can have taxonomies of things without using the syntagmatic resources of the nominal group, simply by the device of naming — the organizing principle is not syntagmatic but paradigmatic.

But there is a difference. The paradigmatic strategy, that of inventing new names, typically construes sets of things which are systemically related but not in a relationship of strict taxonomy. This resource is typically associated with **feature networks**: that is, networks made up of systems of features, such that each lexical item (as the name of a thing) realizes a certain combination of these features selected from different systems within the network — a particular clustering of values of systemic variables.

Figure 5-8 gives an example from an everyday commonsense domain, that of clothing. Obviously a set such as this does not form a strict taxonomy; and this has certain consequences. The division into things of this particular semantic space is highly variable, both synchronically (regional and social dialect, and even idiolect) and diachronically. Thus what were previously non-occurring combinations may come to occur (e.g. *pantyhose*, covering both extremities and torso of lower body), systems may shift their entry conditions (e.g. *trousers* previously had 'male' as an entry condition), and so on. Table 5(3) shows how each clothing item realizes a selection of features from related systemic sets.

Furthermore, although the characterization is essentially experiential, this kind of network may easily be intruded by interpersonal systems. There is trace of this here in the opposition of 'casual' and 'formal'; but probably the most widespread of all such interpersonal systems is that of 'desirable'/ 'undesirable', often referred to as an opposition of "purr"/ "snarl". Such systems are much more readily admitted into domains of things which are not governed by strict taxonomy. There is a host of humorous examples associated with the person system, such as *I have views/ you have opinions/ he or she has prejudices.*

This resource, the construal of systematically related lexico-semantic sets, illustrates well the principle of "lexis as most delicate grammar" (Halliday, 1961; Hasan, 1987; Matthiessen, 1991b; Cross, 1993). We have discussed above the principle that categories in the experiential grammar are ordered in delicacy, so that starting from the very general types of process that are construed into figures, we can differentiate both processes and participants into finer and finer subcategories, until we reach the degree of differentiation that is associated with the choice of words (lexical items). Note that it is not (usually) the lexical items themselves that figure as terms of the systems in the network. Rather, the systems are systems of features, and the lexical items come in as the synthetic realization of particular feature combinations. Thus lexis (vocabulary) is part of a unified lexicogrammar; there is no need to postulate a separate "lexicon" as a pre-existing entity on which the grammar is made to operate.

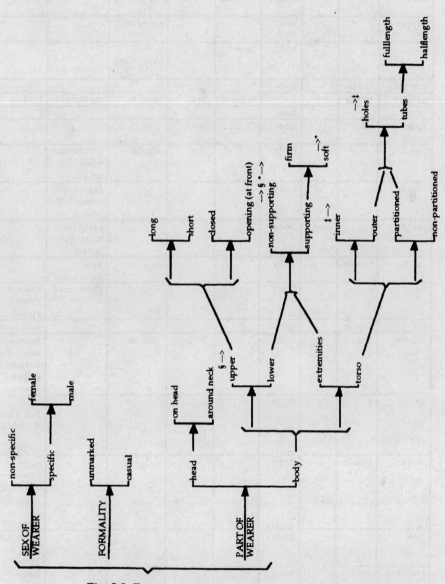

Fig. 5-8: Feature network for some items of clothing

Table 5(3): Items of clothing defined by intersections from feature network

thing ↘ lexical item	sex	form-ality	part					
shoe			body	lower &	extrem.	supporting : firm		
slipper			body	"	"	supporting : soft		
sock			body	"	"	non-supporting [soft]		
stocking	female		body	"	"	"		
panties	female		body	lower &	torso	inner &	partitioned	[holes]
briefs			body	"	"	"	"	["]
under-pants	male		body	"	"	"	"	["]
trousers			body	"	"	outer &	partitioned: tubes: full-length	
shorts			body	"	"	"	partitioned: tubes: half-length	
jeans		casual	body	"	"	"	partitioned: tubes: full-length	
skirt	female		body	"	"	outer &	non-partitioned	
vest			body	upper &	torso	inner &	partitioned:	holes & short & closed
bra	female		body	"	"	"	"	holes
blouse	female		body	"	"	outer &	"	holes ~ tubes: f~h & short & closed ~ opening
shirt			body	"	"	"	"	tubes: f ~ h & short & closed ~ opening
dress	female		body	"	"	"	"	holes ~ tubes: f ~ h & long & closed ~ opening
coat			body	"	"	"	"	tubes: f & long & opening
jacket			body	"	"	"	"	tubes: f (~ h) & short & opening
cloak			body	"	"	"	non-partitioned	long ~ short & opening
jumper	female		body	"	"	"	partitioned	tubes: f ~ h & short & closed

pullover	male		body	"	"	"	"	holes ~ tubes: fulllength & short & opening
sweater			body	"	"	"	"	holes ~ tubes: fulllength & short & opening
cardigan			body	"	"	"	"	tubes: fulllength & short & opening
waistcoat			body	"	"	"	"	holes & short & opening
glove			body	"	extrem.	[non-supporting:] [soft]		
cap	(male)	casual	head	on head				
hat			head	on head				
scarf			head	round neck				

'partitioned & upper' = 'having sleeves' (or 'sleeveless')

'partitioned & lower' = 'having legs' (or 'legholes')

'f' = 'full-length'

'h' = 'half-length'

optional alternative features: X~Y

features assigned by default: [X]

'unmarked' formality, 'non-specific' sex: not shown

It will be clear that both these strategies, the expansion of word to group and the accumulation of contrasting words, are strategies for assigning qualities to things: we can gloss a *slipper*, for example, as a *soft supporting garment worn by either sex at the lower extremities of the body*. In general the qualities involved will come from the same semantic domains in either case; and there is often fluctuation between the two strategies within the language — we sometimes talk of *slippers* and sometimes of *soft shoes*. Compare Chapter 7 below, where we point out that there are many realms of things which are construed in English as different words but in Chinese as syntagmatic constructs: e.g. bicycle 'self-propelled wheeler', car 'gas wheeler', lorry 'goods wheeler' all as explicit subcategories of 'wheeled-vehicle'. And although we have presented the two strategies as discrete, there are of course intermediate modes of construing that form a continuum between the two: noun-compounding (more syntagmatic) and morphological derivation (more paradigmatic). So we find compounds such as *pushbike, motorbike;* and derivational series like *cycle : bicycle, monocycle, tricycle.* It is not difficult to invent new categories if we need them such as *bikelet* or *megabike*. Note also the morphological strategy for deriving casual terms from formal ones: *bicycle > bike* (cf. *omnibus > bus*).

The sort of strict taxonomy that is typically associated with related series of nominal groups is often a feature of special registers of the language; compare our examples from the domains of cooking and weather in Chapter 8 below. The limiting cases of such taxonomies are those found in the specialized technical registers of science and technology (cf. Halliday & Martin, 1993); these include some which are partially or even wholly designed in a conscious exploitation of the grammatical resources involved. The "things" that are construed in this way include the more abstracts concepts of a scientific theory, the virtual objects that are postulated to explain the more arcane phenomena that impinge on human experience.

5.3.2.6 Recurrent semantic principles

In the various categories of thing we find a manifestation of the same very general semantic principles that we have established before, the principles of **projection** and **expansion**. Certain categories of thing have grammatical properties that relate them to one or the other: see Figure 5-9.

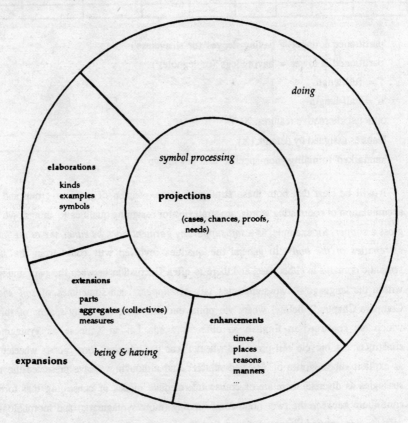

Fig. 5-9: Projections and expansions construed as things

(i) Projections as things

Things of this category are the names of types of projection; in the taxonomy of things, they are **semiotic abstractions,** some discrete and some non-discrete, and as a grammatical class they are referred to under the heading of **fact nouns.** They are grammatically distinct because they can function as Thing in a nominal group with a fact clause as Qualifier, e.g. *the notion that pigs can fly* (see Halliday, 1985: Section 7.5). Such clauses have the property that they can stand alone as participants in a figure, e.g. *that pigs can fly is an intriguing notion.*

Things of this type fall into four subcategories, defined by their interaction with modality: cases, chance, proofs and needs. **Cases** represent simple facts; **chances** represent facts to which some degree of modalization is attached; **proofs** are demonstrations of facts. The fourth category, that of **needs,** are facts accompanied by modulation, that is, where the projection is that of a proposal rather than a proposition.

type of projection	subtype	modality	lexical items realizing Thing
proposition	case	— (simple fact) 'it is the case that'	*accident, case, fact, grounds, idea, lesson, news, notion, observation, point, principle, rule,*
	chance	modalization 'it may be the case that'	*ability, certainty, chance, hypothesis, likelihood, impossibility, possibility, probability, theory*
	proof	caused modalization 'this makes it certain that'	*confirmation, demonstration, disproof, evidence, implication, indication, proof,*
proposal	need	modulation	*duty, expectation, necessity, need, obligation, onus, requirement, rule,*

Things of this type have an important role in discourse, because they function anaphorically to refer to (and at the same time to classify) previous sections of text interpreted as projection. For example:

> [Graham's] simulated atmosphere evolved in much the same way as the real atmosphere had — the temperature rose, and evaporation and rainfall over the tropical ocean increased closely matching actual records.

> Based on **these findings,** Graham concludes that the increases in sea surface temperatures could well have caused the intensification of the hydrological cycle, explaining the warming.
> (New Scientist, 4 February 1995)

(ii) Expansions as things

Certain categories of thing denote an element which is an expansion of something else, either elaborating it ('kind of', 'instance of', or 'symbol of'), extending it ('part of', 'amount of', 'collection of', or 'extension of'), or enhancing it ('time of', 'place of', 'cause of', 'manner of'). The following are some typical examples:

type of expansion	subtype	lexical items realizing Thing
elaboration	symbol	*picture, drawing, portrait, painting, photo*
	kind	*type, sort, kind, mode, species, genus, brand, model*
	instance	*example, illustration, instance*
extension	part	*part, element, portion, top, bottom, side; arm, leg, trunk*
	amount	*unit, cup, glass, jar*
	collection	*herd, crowd, bunch, list*
	extension	*combination, conjunction, addition, contrast*
enhancement	time	*time ([that/ when] we ran away), era, period*
	place	*place ([that/ where] we ran away)*
	cause	*reason ([that/ why] we ran away), result, cause, purpose*
	manner	*way ([that/ in which] we ran away), manner*

Those of the **elaborating** type may function in the nominal group either as Thing or as Facet. As Facet (always constructed with *of*), they serve to construe the element functioning as Thing in some particular guise or perspective; for example, *picture* in *this will give you a general picture of the situation*, *kind* in *a jet cat is a kind of passenger vessel*, *example* in *there were no examples of successful integration*. As Thing, they are participants in their own right, either 'objects' (e.g. *is that picture for sale*) or 'abstractions' (e.g. *Darwin showed how species first evolved*).

Similarly, those of the **extending** type may also function in either of these two grammatical roles. As Facet, they specify some quantity (either by container, e.g. *a jar of jam*, or by division, e.g. *a piece of cake*), some aggregate (e.g. *a crowd of onlookers*), some aspect or component (e.g. *the other side of the argument, the top of the mountain, the trunk of the tree*), or something added or substituted (e.g. *an extension of your ideas, the latest addition to the family, an alternative to this proposal*). As Thing, again, they are participants, typically concrete objects (e.g. *a glass jar, the top* [= lid] *of the canister, build an extension on the property*).

Things of the **enhancing** type have already been cited as a micro category in the preceding Section 5.3.2.5. They construe one or other of the general logical semantic relations of cause, manner, time and place. As Facet, they specify some circumstance of an element functioning as Thing: *the cause/ result/ purpose of the breakdown, the manner of the breakdown, the time/ occasion of the breakdown, the place/ location of the breakdown;* cf. also *the circumstances of the breakdown*. As Thing, they give the logico-semantic relation itself the status of participant; here the usual words are *reason, way, time, place,* and the phenomenon becomes a figure realized by a qualifying clause: *the reason/ way/ time/ place we broke down.* These are closest to the borderline with projections: we may have either expansion *the reason for which we broke down,* or projection *(the reason) why we broke down.* Those with 'reason' and 'way' often enter into an identifying relation with some other figure; for example, *the reason we broke down was that/ because the engine overheated.*

Since things of these various kinds are the names of semantic relationships, it is not surprising that their status is somewhat ambivalent. Consider an expression such as *a volume of poetry:* this may be *volume* as Thing, qualified as being concerned with poetry, e.g. *she picked up an old volume of poetry from the shelf,* or Facet (extending: amount), e.g. *she has just published a new volume of poetry.* The latter example shows up the nature of the ambivalence: the quality 'new' is presumably a quality of the poetry (cf. *I'd like a strong cup of tea*). Similarly we have the ambivalent relationship between parts and wholes (the basis of synecdoche), and between symbols and what they represent, regarding which to construe as the participant in particular figure. In general, the uncertainty that arises is whether the expansion is to be construed as an independent thing or as a facet of something other than itself. This uncertainty is sometimes foregrounded under pressure from the textual metafunction: as Theme, for example, do we say *the end of that story you're never going to hear!* or *that story you're never going to hear the end of!* ?

As with names of projections, names of expansions often serve a role in creating cohesion in discourse: e.g. *Instances such as these ..., Another way of approaching the situation ..., That aspect hadn't occurred to me.* Such expressions construe preceding figures and sequences as participants in their turn, and so enable the speaker or writer to make explicit the organization of the discourse itself.

5.3.3 Qualities

The discussion of 'facets' illustrates the difference between things and qualities of things; it also illustrates the indeterminacy of the distinction. Let us begin our discussion of qualities by relating them to things.

5.3.3.1 The status of qualities

In Section 5.3.1, we discussed the complementary contributions made by qualities and things in the construal of participants. We showed that qualities and things differ in two related respects, temporal stability and experiential complexity: things tend to persist through time and to represent intersections of many dimensions, whereas qualities tend to be less stable through time and tend to represent values on single dimensions. Qualities thus construe values on dimensions such as size (e.g., 'big/ small'), weight ('heavy/ light'), and shape ('round'/ 'square'/ 'rectangular'/ 'oval' ...).

These values may be of three kinds, according to the type of contrast they set up: (i) binary, e.g. ('dead'/ 'alive'); (ii) scalar, e.g. ('happy/ 'sad'); (iii) taxonomic, e.g. 'wooden'/ 'plastic'/ 'stone'/ ... . Of the three, the most complex, experientially, are the taxonomic qualities; for example, the taxonomy of materials (whether a folk taxonomy or one that is more scientifically informed) is based on a variety of different features, such as (in a folk taxonomy) its appearance, its texture, its range of functions, its relative value in different contexts, and the like. Taxonomic qualities are thus the closest to things; they are often realized as denominal adjectives, or even as nouns, and they tend to function as Classifier rather than Epithet (i.e. they sort things into classes rather than describing them).

Since qualities are assigned to things, they are construed with things as their frame of reference: in the first instance, a quality characterizes a thing relative to other things in the same (primary) class. Thus a *thick book* is not a 'thick thing'; rather, it is a 'thick book' as opposed to a 'slim book': the scale of 'thick' to 'slim' is relative to book and a *thick book* would be much thicker than a *thick envelope*. This characteristic is particularly noticeable with scalar qualities, which have received particular attention in semantic studies; but it is also, in principle, a feature of taxonomic adjectives — even those construing complex classes. For example, the criteria for assigning 'wooden' to a 'spoon', a 'house' and a 'carriage' are fairly different in terms of the actual material make-up of these things.

As a category, qualities lie somewhere along a cline between things and processes, and their status varies considerably among different languages. In English, qualities belong more closely with things, since they contribute primarily to the construction of participants: grammatically, English favours construing a quality as Epithet in a nominal group, and the class of adjective is clearly related to that of noun. (By contrast, in Chinese, where qualities are typically construed clausally, as Attribute, rather than nominally, as Epithet, the adjective is equally clearly related to the verb.) Here English is similar to Latin, where in the traditional grammars a general class "noun" was classified into "noun substantive" and "noun adjective":

participant	↘	noun
thing	↘	noun substantive
quality	↘	noun adjective

As an example, consider the following from R.R. (1641), based on Lily's grammar:

A Noun is a part of speech, which signifies a thing, without any difference of time or person. A Noun is the name of a thing that may be seen, felt, heard, or understood: as, the name of my hand in Latine is *Manus,* the name of hous is *Domus,* the name of goodnesse is *Bonitas.* Of Nouns, some be Substantives, and some be Adjectives.

A Noun Substantive, is that which standeth by himself, and requireth not another word to be joyned with him, to declare his signification: as, *Homo,* a man. And it is declined with one article: as, *hic Magister,* a master: or else with two at the most: as *hic & haec Parens,* a father or mother. ...

An Adjective is that, which in speech needeth a Substantive to cleave unto ... A Noun Adjective is that which cannot stand by himself, in reason or signification, but requireth to be joyned with another word. ...

A Verb is a part of speach declined with Mood and Tense, and betokeneth doing; as, *Amo,* I love: or suffring; as, *Amor,* I am loved: or being; as, *Sum,* I am.

Here, nouns and verbs are distinguished as primary classes, whereas substantives and adjectives are distinguished only as secondary classes. (It is important to keep the degree of delicacy (primary, secondary, etc.) in mind when interpreting statements to the effect that a particular language has only nouns and verbs, but no adjectives.) More recently, it has often been asserted that adjectives are really stative verbs, or "stative predicates". This is the position in predicate logic, where both qualities and processes are simply predicates — but so also are things. It complicates the description of English grammar; but it is a reminder of the intermediate status of qualities as elements of figures.

We said that both things and qualities are construed as participants. This does not mean that they are different kinds of participant. Rather, it means that within the structure of a participant, they serve different kinds of role.

Typically, a quality combines with a thing to make up a participant in a figure: *a dry plate,* where the quality 'dry' is Epithet in the nominal group. The only context in which a quality serves on its own in a participant role is as Attribute; here it stands in intensive relation to a participant, either (i) in a figure of being, where the participant is Medium/ Carrier (i.e. its sole function is to have the quality ascribed to it) or (ii) in a figure of doing, where the participant is Medium/ Actor or Medium/ Goal and quality results from the doing; for example:

```
being:          The plate's dry —I've made the plate dry
doing:          I've wiped the plate dry
```

Note that, in the doing figure, where *I* is Actor, the Attribute could be omitted: *I've wiped the plate;* in the being figure it cannot, since the process itself is one of ascription and the other participant, if present, is merely the ascriber.

The Attribute is not a prototypical participant. We have already noted that as it stands it cannot function interpersonally as Subject. On the other hand, it can easily be instated as a participant by adding the noun or the noun substitute *one(s)* to the nominal group which realizes it: *this is a dry plate, this is a dry one.* The fact that the thing can be instated as the Head of a nominal group serving as Attribute illustrates the point already made: the quality does not construe a separate class of thing, it presumes this class from the environment. Thus *this is heavy* means that it is heavy relatively to whatever class of thing it has been assigned to; compare *the truck was very heavy/ a very heavy one* (i.e. 'heavy for a truck') with *the chair was very heavy/ a very heavy one* (i.e. 'heavy for a chair'). Hence it is not possible to re-instate the thing where the Attribute occurs as resultative in a process of doing: we do not say *I've wiped it a dry plate* or *I've wiped the plate a dry one*.

Thus in its typical construal, as Epithet or as Attribute, a quality is clearly "participant-like"; we might also note that realized as an adjective in superlative form it does appear as a participant (*these are the driest, pass me the driest; the smallest will fall through the holes*). But there are also environments where a quality resembles a process or a circumstance.

(i) Some qualities can be construed as processes of doing; here for example there is an agnate form *I've dried the plate,* with 'dry' worded as a verb. In these cases, the quality is not repeated as an Attribute — we do not usually say *I've dried the plate dry;* it may however reappear in an intensified form, e.g. *I've dried it very dry.* Very many qualities may be construed as verbs in this way.

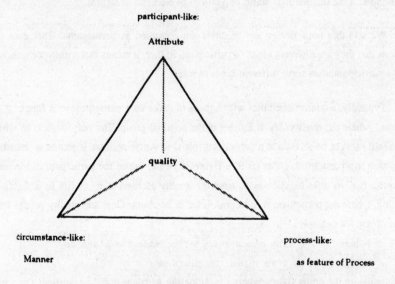

Fig. 5-11: The intermediate status of qualities

(ii) Some qualities may occur as depictive (as opposed to resultative) Attribute in a figure of doing & happening; in such instances the quality is very close to a circumstance of manner, as is shown by agnate pairs such as the following:

```
quality as Attribute:              quality as Manner:
she came home cheerful             she came home cheerfully
he walked in drunk                 he walked in drunkenly
```

As always with such closely agnate expressions, while they are semantically related they are not synonymous; we could even imagine a figure such as *he walked in drunk quite soberly*. But they make the point that a quality, when attached to the figure as an Attribute (rather than to a participant as in *the drunken man walked in/ the man who walked in was drunk*), is construed as being more like a circumstance. The fact that manner circumstances are typically realized by adverbs that are simply derived from (and in some cases identical with) adjectives is a further symptom of the way a quality may resemble a circumstance.

Figure 5-11 above summarizes the multivalent status of quality.

5.3.3.2 Types of quality

We suggested in Sections 5.2-3 above that the nominal group is organized as a move along two semantic dimensions: the elements become increasingly stable in time, and increasingly complex in their taxonomy of features. Lexicogrammatically, this corresponds to a move from grammatical items (determiners, determinative adjectives such as *usual, same, typical,* cardinal and ordinal numerals) to lexical items (adjectives [in general], and nouns); that is, a move from closed systems to open sets. The former are taxonomically simple (although they are notoriously difficult to interpret in lexical glosses); they include specific/ non-specific; personal/ demonstrative; near/ far; total/ partial &c (see Halliday, 1976: 131-5, for the systems). In contrast, elements at the latter end tend to be construed in complex taxonomies; see for example the multiple taxonomy involved in the lexical construal of clothing (Section 5.3.2.5 above). That is, greater experiential complexity is handled by means of greater taxonomic complexity. The semantic movement in the nominal group is summarized in Figure 5-12. Qualities lie at differences places along these various dimensions; hence they vary in their potential for taking on roles in different types of figure.[3] Table 5(4) suggests a very tentative classification.

Qualities can be distinguished according to the transphenomenal types of projection and expansion. Qualities of projection and qualities of expansion differ in a number of respects. Most fundamentally, they differ in their patterns of agnation. Qualities of projection are agnate with processes in figures of sensing; for example, *happy* in *the happy child* (or *the child is happy*) is agnate with *rejoice* in *the child rejoices*. In contrast, qualities of expansion display patterns of agnation within figures of being & having, with variation according to subtype (see below). This fundamental difference explains other differences; for example, qualities of projection tend to occur in agnate pairs

---

[3] Thompson (1988) offers a complementary account of 'adjectives' based on their use in discourse.

of the 'like' and 'please' type that we find with figures of sensing (e.g. *afraid/ scary, suspicious/ suspect, bored/ boring*), whereas qualities of expansion do not. We will review qualities of projection first and then turn to qualities of expansion.

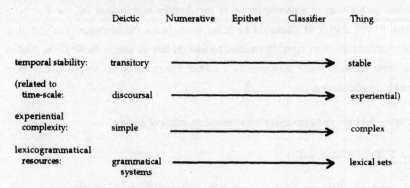

Fig. 5-12: Clines in the construal and realization of participants

(i) **Qualities of projection** are all scalar and they are, as we just noted, agnate with processes of sensing in figures of sensing; they are often realized by participial verb forms used as adjectives. The thing they are assigned to, as Attribute or as Epithet, is agnate either with the Senser (the 'like' type, realized by v-*en* if verbal in origin: *happy, sad, angry, afraid, frightened, certain, sure*) or with the Phenomenon (the 'please' type, realized by v-*ing* if verbal in origin: *sad(dening), tragic, irritating, scary, certain*). From this it follows that when they are agnate with the Senser, they are ascribed to conscious beings (as in *an angry child/ boss/ cat*), whereas when they are agnate with the Phenomenon, they can be ascribed not only to things but also to metathings, i.e. to projections (as in *it's sad(dening)/ tragic/ irritating/ scary/ certain that they ignore world opinion*). In the former case, these qualities may be 'transferred' to tokens of the senser's sensing, as in *an angry face/ look/ letter/ reaction*. As we have seen, sensing is agnate with modality and, in the case of emotive sensing, with attitude. Similarly, qualities of projection extend to include modalities and attitudes; when the thing (or metathing) they are assigned to is agnate with the Phenomenon, these qualities are construed as objective, impersonal ones: *it is certain/ likely/ possible that the moon's a balloon.* (Contrast: *I'm certain the moon's a balloon.*) With qualities of usuality, this is the only possible orientation. Qualities of projection are unlikely or impossible as the Attribute of figures of doing (thus it is hard to interpret *she polished it certain* [contrast *she polished it clean*] and while we can say *he drove her mad* [caused figure of being] and *he drove the car hot* [figure of doing with Attribute], we cannot say *he drove the car mad*).

(ii) **Qualities of expansion** cannot normally be assigned to metathings. They expand the thing they are related to by elaboration, extension or enhancement. These different subtypes display different patterns of agnation, but as Epithet (or Classifier) + Thing configurations they are all agnate with figures of being & having.

Table 5(4): Tentative classification of qualities

qualities of:					taxonomic type	agnate figure Epithet (Classif.)	Thing	examples
proj.	(as sensing:)	(as assessment:)				figure of sensing: Process	Senser/Phen.	
	emotive	attitude (evaluation)			scalar	rejoice, grieve		happy, sad; delightful, tragic; good, bad
	cognitive	probability			scalar	suppose, believe, know		doubtful, sure; likely, certain
	desiderative	modulation			scalar	like, want, desire		willing, keen; desirable, necessary
	——	usuality			scalar	——		usual, common
exp.						figure of being:		
	elaboration	attribution	class	national. material etc.	taxonomic	Attribute	Carrier	Thai, Burmese; plastic, wooden; ...
			status	life; sex; marital; etc.	binary			alive, dead; female, male; single, married; ...
			sense-measure	visual: colour & shape	taxonomic			red, blue, pink; round, oval, square
				weight; texture; age; etc.	scalar			heavy, light; rough, smooth; old, young; ...
			prop-ensity	(behav. qual.)	scalar [dynamic]			skilful, naughty
			quantity	inexact	scalar			few, many
				exact	taxonomic			one, two, three
		identity			scalar	Process: be, resemble	Carrier, Token	same, similar, analogous, different
	extension				taxonomic	Process: accompany, replace, be instead of		additional, alternative, contrasting
	enhance-ment	temporal			taxonomic	Process: be before, after, at		previous, preceding, subsequent
		spatial			taxonomic	be above, within, ourside		interior, external, anterior, posterior
		causal						consequent, resultant; conditional; contingent

The most prototypical qualities are those of **elaboration**, subtype **attribution**: they stand in a purely intensive relation to the thing they are assigned to, being construed as inherent qualities. They are typically scalar, but certain types are taxonomic or binary. As Epithets (or Classifiers) they are agnate with the Attribute of a figure of being. Many of them can serve as the Attribute of a figure of doing (as in *he squashed it flat, she painted it blue*) and are related to the outcome of such figures (cf. *she heated/ widened/ enlarged it : it was hot/ wide/ large*). The limiting case of qualities of attribution are quantities; they are assigned to a thing as a discoursal instance rather than as a general experiential class. Consequently, they do not serve as Epithets; they have a special role, that of Numerative (as in *two/ many brave volunteers*).

Qualities of elaboration, subtype **identity** are not inherent properties, but rather are comparative. Thus the standard of comparison can always be construed: *their car is the same/ similar/ different* : *their car is the same as/ similar to/ different from ours;* and they are agnate with processes: *their car is/ resembles/ differs from ours.* The line between elaboration: identity and enhancement: manner: comparison is a fuzzy one; and processual agnates such as *their car resembles ours* are within the domain of enhancement.

Qualities of **extension** resemble those of 'elaboration: identity' in that they construe a relation between the thing they are assigned to and some other thing. The relation typically obtains between the thing as a discoursal instance rather than the thing as a general experiential class. Thus *an alternative solution* is a solution that can replace the one we have just been talking about. Consequently, properties of extension tend to serve as deictic elements (Post-Deictic) rather than as Epithets: they indicate how an instance (or instances) of the general class of the thing they are assigned to is selected from that class: *we need an additional two volunteers* means 'two further instances of the general class of volunteer'. Like other properties serving as Post-Deictic, they may precede the Numerative (*additional ^ two*); but they may also follow, with no strong contrast in meaning: *we need two additional volunteers.*

Qualities of **enhancement** also resemble those of 'elaboration: identity' and those of extension in that they construe a relation between the thing they are assigned to and another thing. This is brought out by the fact that they are agnate with processes relating participants circumstantially: *subsequent : be (come) after, preceding : be (come) before/ precede, interior : be within, exterior : be outside,* as in *previous occasions : occasions coming before this one, interior design : design of what is within a house.* This relation is typically a temporal or spatial one involving the thing as a discoursal instance rather than the thing as a general experiential class. Consequently, like qualities of extension, qualities of enhancement tend to serve as deictic elements (Post-Deictic) rather than as Epithets; as Post-Deictics, they come before Numeratives in the structure of the nominal group: *the preceding/ subsequent two meetings.* Here they relate a specific referent, recoverable in the current situation: *the subsequent two meetings : the two meetings that followed this one.* But the spatial qualities can also, being taxonomic, serve to subclassify the thing they are assigned to: *interior monologue, external pipes.* Here they relate to a general class of thing, inferrable from the experiential system: *interior monologue : monologue that is within a person, external pipes : pipes that are outside a house.*

5.4 Processes

Much of what we have to say about processes as elements of figures has already been brought into the discussion, either under "figures" (Chapter 4) or in the section on elements in general (Sections 5.1 and 5.2). This was inevitable (i) because a figure is the semantic construction of a process, having the structural element Process (realized as verbal group) at its core, and (ii) because in understanding the concept of participant we are naturally led to contrast participants with processes.

Let us summarize the essential points. The key to the construal of experience is the perception of change; the grammar construes a quantum of change as a figure (typically one clause) and sorts out figures in the first instance into those of consciousness (sensing and saying), those of the material world (doing & happening) and those of logical relations (being & having). The central element of a figure is the process; 'things' are construed as entities participating in processes, having different roles, of which one is 'that participant in which the process is actualized' (if there is 'flying', there has to be something that flies or is flown: *birds fly, people fly kites*); hence the grammatical nucleus of the clause is the configuration of Process with Medium.

While participants are located in referential space, processes are located in time. The verbal group realizing a process constructs a "moment" in time beginning with the 'now' (the time of speaking) leading up to a categorization of the Event; this is analogous to the way the nominal group, realizing a participant, constructs a "body" in space beginning with the 'here' and leading up to a categorization of the Thing. But while the Thing is enmeshed in a elaborate taxonomy of things, the Event is taxonomically rather simple and its complexity lies in the construal of time itself. Hence the verbal group is lexically sparse — typically the Event is the only lexicalized part; whereas nominal groups can be lexically extremely dense (cf. Figures 5-2 and 5-3 above).

Thus from the point of view of the figure, a process is the central element, forming a nucleus around which participants and circumstantial elements are organized into a meaningful pattern (Figure 4-13). From the point of view of its own internal organization, a process is the construal of 'eventing' — a phenomenon perceived as having extension in time. In the rest of this section we shall look briefly at the parameters along which time is construed, with special reference as throughout to English.

5.4.1 Making sense of time

It is not easy to construe experience of time, and different languages vary considerably in the way they do it: there are differences from one language to another, and differences within the same language over the course of time. Like everything else we are exploring here, the grammar's model of time has been evolving unconsciously in the context of human survival; it is part of the selective and collective wisdom that the species has accumulated in the understanding of its relationship to its environment and in the interaction of its members one with another. And again like everything else in the construal of experience it is the product of continual compromise, whereby divergent and often conflicting aspects of experience are adjusted and accommodated in such a way that all of them have some place in the total picture.

In transforming experience of time into meaning, human communities have evolved a number of basic parameters. We can identify four of these that are relevant in the present context:

(1) the temporal **staging** of a process: it may be beginning, taking place or ending.

(underlying concept: a process occupies a certain measure of time)

(2) the temporal **perspective** on a process: we may frame it in or out of temporal focus. This takes many different guises in different languages, and even within the same language; such as (a) in focus: ongoing, out of focus: terminated; (b) in focus: significant in itself, out of focus: significant for what follows; (c) in focus: actualized, out of focus: visualized. (It is the last of these that is relevant to English.)

(underlying concept: a process relates to the flow of experience as a whole, including other processes)

(3) the temporal **profile** of a process: it is either unbounded or bounded.

(underlying concept: a process has the potential for being extended in time)

(4) the temporal **location** of a process: it can be related to 'now' as past, present or future.

(underlying concept: a process takes place within a linear flow or current of time)

Each of these variables differs from all the others; but at the same time, each is related to all the others, so that there are certain patterns of association among them. For example, a process that is unbounded (e.g. *travel*) is more likely than one that is bounded (e.g. *arrive*) to be put under temporal focus (e.g. *while travelling* is more likely than *while arriving*); a process located in the future is more likely to be beginning than ending (e.g. *it will start warming up* is more common than *it will finish warming up*). Some combinations may be more or less excluded: for example, a process that is beginning can vary in its perspective (e.g. *the sun started to shine/ started shining*), whereas one that is ending is always actualized (e.g. *the sun stopped shining;* but not *the sun stopped to shine*). Thus, in any given language, (i) one or other parameter may be given prominence, (ii) two or more parameters may be combined into a single semantic system, (iii) any parameter may be construed either more grammatically or more lexically, and (iv) a number of features that are not strictly temporal may be incorporated into the picture, both ideational ones like attempting/ succeeding and interpersonal ones like the speaker's angle on the process — judgement of its likelihood, desirability, and so on.

When these parameters are grammaticized, they are referred to respectively as (1) phase, (2) aspect, (3) aktionsart, (4) tense.

5.4.2 Patterns of time in English

English foregrounds location in the flow of time (tense), and construes this not only as past/ present/ future relative to 'now' [*they paid me/ they pay me/ they will pay me*], but also as past/ present/ future relative to some moment that is relative to now [*they are going to pay me* (future in present), *they've been paying me* (present in past in present)], with the possibility of up to five shifts of reference point, as in

        They said they'd been going to've been paying me all this time ...

(present in past in future in past in past). This system is fully grammaticized, and is unusual in that it construes location in time as a logical relation rather than as an experiential taxonomy; it thus becomes a form of serial time reference. The tense categories also combine with time adverbs such as *already, just, soon* [*they'd already paid me, they've just paid me, they soon paid me*]. Interestingly, the deictic time reference (that appealing to 'now') can be switched off; either there is no deixis (the clause is non-finite, e.g. *not having paid me yet, ...*) or the deixis takes the form of modality (speaker's angle on the process, e.g. *they should have paid me*).

By comparison with temporal location, temporal perspective (aspect) is relatively backgrounded in English. (Some 20th century grammarians have interpreted the serial location as a kind of aspect, with "present in ..." as continuous, "past in ..." as perfect; but the earlier description as we have presented it here accounts more richly for the semantic patterning.) The temporal perspective takes over, however, when there is no *deictic* location (the clause is non-finite); in such cases, instead of making reference to 'now' the process is construed as either actualized, as in *(on) reaching the gallery, turn left*, or visualized, e.g. *to reach the gallery, turn left*. Sometimes the difference in meaning is very slight (e.g. *a way of doing it/ the way to do it*); but it is always there. (We will see in Chapter 7 that in Chinese, while temporal location is relatively backgrounded, temporal perspective is foregrounded — though the shift of focus is of a different kind from that in English.)

Temporal staging is explicit and lexicalized, with a basic system of categories as shown in Figure 5-13; for example (this was the continuation of the five-term tense example above)

```
... but the money kept on not coming through
```

The combination of staging with perspective has already been referred to; note in this connection sequences such as

```
started doing        went on doing        stopped doing
started to do        went on to do        stopped to do
```

where the move in staging creates an increasing semantic distance between the two perspectives. Staging also extends to other categories that are not strictly temporal, which the grammar however construes as analogous: especially conation (*tries to do/ succeeds in doing*), and appearance (*seems to be/ turns out to be*).

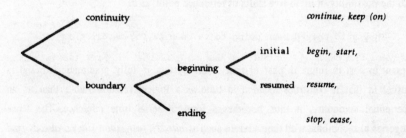

Fig. 5-13: Different types of phase

The temporal profile, of unbounded/ bounded, is not an independent option available to processes in general. Boundedness is a feature which may accrue to certain classes of process, typically processes of doing: contrast for example unbounded *use* with bounded *use up* (*use some salt — but don't use it up!*). It is on the borderline of lexis and grammar: the verb is extended by *up* or some other adverb of the locative-directional class (*drink up, eat up, load up, pour out, melt down, fly away*). The boundedness is not in fact temporally defined; its degree — and often its exact nature — is specific to the kind of process concerned, and may depend on the total figure and on the context; e.g.

```
pour out the water        'until the bowl is empty/ until everyone has a drink'
write up the results      'in a publishable form'
```

But there is a clear proportionality involved, which allows us to treat this as a systemic feature of a significant subset of processes in English.

Obviously, choices made in all these parameters relate to the figure as a whole (at least; they may have implications for longer stretches of discourse). The major process types — the primary categories of sensing, saying, doing & happening, being & having — tend to have inherently different temporal characteristics, affecting all aspects of the way time is construed: in terms of what temporal categories are possible, what the relative probabilities are, and what the different choices mean (note for example the total lack of proportionality in pairs such as *I go : I'm going ≠ I know : I'm knowing*). Part of the meaning of any fragment of experience is its potentiality for being variably construed in time.

From an ideational point of view, the temporality of processes is their salient characteristic. As we saw, there are no semantic or grammatical systems for construing processes into elaborate taxonomies, as there are for construing things. Apart from considerations of time we have also shown that processes can be classified according to their potential for serving in figures of different types (see Chapter 4 above). We shall raise again the question of differentiating between processes and figures when we consider alternative treatments in Chapter 11, Section 11.3.2 below.

5.5 Circumstances

We noted in Chapter 4, Section 4.5 that circumstantial elements can be realized grammatically either as adverbial groups or as prepositional phrases. These represent circumstances of two different types.

Type (1) are qualities ("simple circumstances" in Chapter 2, Section 2.8) — but construed not as qualities of a particular participant but as qualities of a figure as a whole; for example, *steadily, extremely loudly, perfectly* in *it rained steadily all night, they were shouting extremely loudly, it suits your complexion perfectly*. Typically such adverbs are derived in the grammar from adjectives, with the added suffix *-ly;* a few have special forms, like *well* (from *good*), and sometimes the same form is both adjective and adverb, e.g. *fast* in *a fast car, she drives fast*.

The usual function is as circumstance of Manner, with the meaning 'in such a way'. 'to such a degree'; and if the manner of doing determines the quality of the outcome there may be very little difference between a circumstance of this kind and a resultative Attribute: cf. *don't chop the parsley too fine/ too finely*. There are some adverbial expressions realizing other types of circumstance, e.g. *everywhere* (Location: space), *recently* (Location: time); as well as others which might be interpreted differently because of the nature of the quality itself, e.g. *pointlessly* 'in a pointless manner' or 'for no good reason' (Cause).

Sometimes the Manner element is a quality of the process itself, rather than the manner in which it unfolds, for example *he was falsely accused/ wrongly dismissed;* these tend to be bonded rather closely to the Process element in the clause. (The adverbial form also functions as a quality of a quality, like *frostily, superficially* in *a frostily polite receptionist, what he says is superficially correct;* here it is not a circumstantial element but is part of the Epithet in the nominal group.)

Finally, some adverbial groups are interpersonal in function — the speaker's comment on the figure, like *sensibly* in *sensibly, they didn't argue* 'I consider their behaviour sensible' (contrast *they didn't argue sensibly* 'in a sensible manner'). These lie outside the ideational structure of the clause: they are not serving as qualities in the figure realized by the clause, but rather derive from features within the interaction base.

Type (2), those circumstantial elements that are realized by prepositional phrases, are rather more complex, since they include another element — a participant — in their makeup ("macro circumstances" in Chapter 2, Section 2.8): e.g. *the table, my knowledge, peace and quiet* in *right under the table, without my knowledge, for the sake of peace and quiet.* In such cases the element realized by the nominal group is still functioning as a participant in the process — but indirectly, being implicated only through the mediation of a preposition. That this is possible is because the preposition itself constitutes a subsidiary kind of 'process'; one that does not function as Process in the main figure but is nevertheless related systematically to the spectrum of process types — mainly, though not exclusively, to processes of being.

In Chapter 4, Section 4.5, above we tried to suggest how the circumstantial elements were related to **participants**. There, we were looking at them as oblique "cases", from the point of view of their function in the larger figure. Two points emerged: one, that participants and circumstances taken together formed a cline, rather than being separated by a clear boundary; the second, that some of the circumstantial elements could be 'paired off' with participants, being seen as a more oblique manifestation of a similar role. We were able to incorporate these two points in a helical form of presentation in Figure 4-13.

We are now looking at these same circumstantial elements from a complementary standpoint, from the point of view of their own internal composition. As we remarked, a prepositional phrase represents a figure in miniature, with a structure analogous to one component of a figure — closest, perhaps, to Process + Range (so we refer to the participant in the circumstantial phrase as a "Minirange"). This means that, shifting our perspective, we can also suggest how the circumstantial elements are related to different **figures**. Table 5(5) combines the two perspectives, showing their relationship both to participants and to figures. We referred to the cline from participants to circumstances as the "degree of involvement" in the actualization of the process. This degree of involvement ranged from the closest, the Medium, which is part of the nucleus of the figure, to those that appear most remote, circumstances such as Matter (e.g. *concerning your request*) and Angle (e.g. *in my own opinion*). Somewhere in the middle was an area of overlap, where participants and circumstances are very closely akin. The two overlap because there are some functions which can be construed either as a form of participant in the process or as a circumstance attendant on it.

Table 5(5): Agnation between participants, circumstances and figures

	contracted to participant	circumstance	Type	expanded to figure
elab.	**Epithet** in n.gp. *heavy [rain]*	**Manner: quality** *[it rained] heavily*	1 (simple)	being: intensive & ascriptive — **Attribute** *[the rain was] heavy*
	Thing in (n.gp. in) n.gp. complex *[I,] your lawyer [am speaking]*	**Role** *[I'm speaking] as your lawyer*	2 (macro)	being: intensive & identifying — **Value**
ext.	**Thing** in (n.gp. in) n.gp. complex *[she] and her friends [departed]*	**Accompaniment** *[she departed] with her friends*		being: possessive & ascriptive — **Attribute** *[departing] she had her friends*
				being: circumstantial & identifying — **Token** *[departing] she was accompanied by her friends*
enh.	**Agent** *the cloth [cleaned it]*	**Manner: means** *[I cleaned it] with the cloth*		doing — **Goal** *[to clean it], [I] used the cloth*
	Client *[she brought] the children [presents]*	**Cause: behalf** *[she brought presents] for the children's party*		being: circumstantial & ascriptive — **Attribute** *[she brought presents] which were for the children's party*
		Cause: reason, purpose, condition, concession *[they left home] because of the fire*		being: circumstantial & ascriptive *[they left home and] [it] was because of fire*
	Recipient *[I sent] Joan [the message]*	**Location: directional** *[I sent the message] to Joan's place*		doing: — **Range** *[I sent the message] which reached Joan' ('s place)*
		Location: positional *[I parked the car] outside the gate*		being: circumstantial & ascriptive — **Attribute/ Location** *[I parked the car and] [it] was outside the gate*
	Range: entity *[ice covered] the pond* ———	**Extent** *[ice was] all over the pond* *[they walked] for an hour*		being: circumstantial & identifying — **Value** *[ice] covered the pond* *[their walk] lasted an hour* ascr. — Attr.
	Range: entity	**Extent**		doing — **Range**

	[she sailed/ crossed] the Pacific	[she sailed] across the Pacific	[sailing] [she] crossed the Pacific
	Verbiage [they have described] the experiment	**Matter** [they have written] about the experiment	saying — **Verbiage** [they] have described the experiment
			being: circumstantial & ascriptive — **Attribute** [they have written something/ that ..] which concerns the experiment
proj.		**Matter** [they have written] about the experiment	saying — **projected figure** [they have written] that/ how they experimented
		Angle according to the paper [it's Wednesday]	saying — **Sayer** the paper says [that it's Wednesday]
		Angle in their opinion [it's Tuesday]	sensing — **Senser** they consider [that it's Tuesday]

The grammar does draw a line between the two: participant as nominal group, circumstance as prepositional phrase. But because of the continuous nature of the distinction, we find three kinds of mixed categories: (i) participants that may look like circumstances (being introduced by prepositions); (ii) circumstances that may look like participants (being introduced without prepositions); and (iii) pairs where one is circumstance, the other participant, but with very little difference in their meaning. These are illustrated in turn.

(i) Participants introduced by prepositions:

(Recipient)   give milk **to the cat**   cf. give **the cat** milk
(Range)   play all night **at poker**   cf. play **poker** all night
(Actor)   **a bus** ran over them   cf. they were run over **by a bus**

(ii) Circumstantial elements introduced without prepositions:

(Extent)   she jogs **30 minutes**   cf. she jogs **for 30 minutes**
(Location)   we're meeting **next Sunday** cf. we're meeting **on next Sunday**

That those in (i) are being construed primarily as participants, whereas those in (ii) are being construed primarily as circumstances, is shown by a variety of other grammatical factors; to give just one example, the question equivalent to (i) is *who?* or *what?* (*who did you give milk to?*, not *where did you give milk?*), whereas the question equivalent to those in (ii) is *how long?*, *when?* (*when are we meeting?*, not *what are we meeting on?*).

By the same token, in (iii) we have two different elements, one participant and one circumstance, but with hardly any difference between the two:

(iii) Participant/ circumstance pairs with little difference in meaning:

```
(Range) cross the canal  (Location) cross over the canal [cross what?]
                                                         [cross where?]
(Client) bring the children presents  (Cause) bring presents for the
                                              children
[bring who presents?]                 [why bring presents?]
```

Coming back now to the distinction between type (1) circumstances, those realized by adverbial groups, and type (2), those realized by prepositional phrases: as typically happens in language (since grammar abhors determinacy), we find a crossing between the two types. This happens mainly in one direction: there are prepositional phrases which construe qualities of figures, and hence function as circumstances of Manner; for example *in a hurry, without proper care* (cf. *hurriedly, carelessly*). Typically these may also appear as qualities of participants, as in *he was in a hurry* (realized as Attribute in a clause), *a man in a hurry* (Qualifier in a nominal group — not Epithet, since English does not like phrases and clauses before the Thing). These usually involve some kind of metaphor, either (as here) grammatical metaphor, where a quality or process is made to look like a participant (see the next chapter), or lexical metaphor (metaphor in its traditional sense) as in *they left the matter up in the air*. Less commonly, we find a cross-over in the other direction; an example would be the adverb *microscopically* where this has the sense of 'using a microscope' (*we examined the tissue microscopically*).

It is interesting to note how this two-faced character of circumstances — that they are on the one hand like participants and on the other hand like figures — is reflected in their treatment in languages other than English. In the way they are construed in the grammar, in a language such as Finnish, where what corresponds to the English preposition is often a "case" in the nominal group, they appear to be (relatively to English) closer to participants; while in a language such as Chinese, where what corresponds to the English preposition is typically a class of verb, they appear (again, relatively to English) closer to figures. But they typically seem to have a status that lies somewhere intermediate between the two.

But even within one language, however they are construed grammatically, the status of circumstantial elements is variable. In English, those that are nearer the centre of our helix are more like participants, as shown by the examples above; while those that are on the periphery are more like figures. We can give some examples of agnate pairs of this kind.

circumstance		figure
Role	*as a child (he couldn't tell the difference)*	*when he was a child (he couldn't tell the difference)*
Accompaniment	*without enough money (he was unable to complete his education)*	*not having enough money / since he hadn't got enough money (he was unable to complete his education)*
Cause: condition	*in case of fire (call 9000)*	*if there's a fire (call 9000)*

5.6 Major motifs in the ideation base

The ideation base construes experience as a vast, multidimensional and highly elastic semantic space. We have only been able to survey a small fraction of this space. But we have adopted the perspective that we believe most clearly reveals the principles on which the ideation base is organized, highlighting the least delicate end of the system so as to produce a map of the system as a whole rather than detailed maps of isolated regions. This means that, as seen from below, we have approached the ideation base from the grammatical pole of lexicogrammar rather than from the lexical pole.

In addition to setting out the main dimensions and systems of ideational meaning, we have tried with this approach to bring out a small number of very general motifs that run throughout the grammar's construal of experience.

The first of these motifs is that of **meaning as expansion**: the way regions of semantic space are opened up and defined by the three vectors of elaboration, extension and enhancement — elaborating a region that is already as it were staked out, extending the regions boundaries to take in more, and enhancing the region's potential by enrichment from its environment.

The second motif is that of **meaning by projection**: the way new dimensions of semantic space are created by the orders of human consciousness, sensing and saying — by projecting into existence another order of reality, one that is constituted by language itself.

These two motifs together have made it possible for human beings to transform experience into meaning, taking the experience of meaning itself — the "inner" processes of consciousness — as the central figures, and those with the ability to mean — prototypically humans themselves — as the central participants. These then serve as the point of reference for construing "outer" experience, the complementary experiences of the processes of doing and of being. Figure 5-14 shows the two motifs manifested in the environments of sequences, figures and elements.

Fractal types:

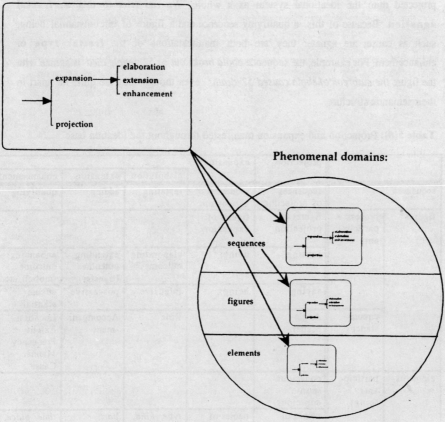

Fig. 5-14: Two fundamental semantic motifs

Since projection and expansion operate across the various categories of phenomena, we referred to them as **transphenomenal categories** in Chapter 3, Section 3.8 above. As transphenomenal categories, they are meaning types that are in some sense "meta" to the organization of the ideation base: they are principles of construing our experience of the world that generate identical patterns of semantic organization which are of variable magnitude and which occur in variable semantic environments. Such patterns therefore constitute **fractal types**. Projection and expansion are manifested at three levels of organization: as sequences, as figures and as elements. Table 5(6) presents a partial summary of the cases we have discussed in Chapters 3 through 5.

Sequences, figures and elements, and their subclasses, constitute different environments within the ideation base. If we construe some phenomenon of experience as a **sequence** of **qualification**, we give it a location in the overall ideational system that is quite distinct from the location it would be assigned if it was construed as a **figure** of **circumstantial cause**. These two types are thus not particularly close agnates in the system. However, the fractal types constitute an additional order of agnation that is projected onto the ideational system as a whole. We can refer to this as **fractal agnation**. Because of this, a qualifying sequence and a figure of circumstantial being, such as cause, are agnate: they are both manifestations of the **fractal type** of enhancement. For example, the sequence *ebola broke out so 52 people died* is agnate with the figure *the outbreak of ebola caused 52 deaths* even though they are quite far apart in their semantic structure.

Table 5(6): Projection and expansion manifested throughout the ideation base

		projection	expansion		
				elaboration	extension	enhancement
sequences		sequences of projection	sequences of expansion:	restating	adding	qualifying
figures	process + participants	figures of projection	figures of expansion:			
		sensing	doing:	elaborating outcome	extending outcome (transfer)	enhancing outcome (motion etc.)
		saying	being:	intensive	possessive	circumstantial
	circumstances	Angle Matter		Role	Accompaniment	Location Extent Frequency Manner Cause
elements	participants: things	conscious/ (non-conscious)				
		names of projections (*fact, idea, possibility, chance* etc.)	names of expansions:	*type, kind, example* etc.	*part, element; unit* etc.	*time, place, way* etc.
	participants: qualities	qualities of projection (*attitude, probability, modulation*)	qualities of expansion:	attribution, identity	addition, alternation, contrast	temporal, spatial, causal

The fractal types of projection and expansion are also a primary resource by which the semantic system creates new meanings: we illustrated this **auto-genetic potential** in Chapter 2, Section 2.11 above. The ideation base thus itself embodies, auto-genetically, the principles on which it is organized and enabled to develop further; such that the primary systems of ideational meaning then serve as a grid within which more delicate categories are construed. Here we have foregrounded especially the motif of elaborating, with particular reference to its manifestation in the identifying and ascriptive figures of being. We have tried to show how elaboration makes it possible to "import" extra-linguistic experience into the meaning base by actively construing it (as in 'that [thing there] is a circle'); and also to "transport" meanings internally from one region of the ideation base in order to construe new meanings in another (as in 'balance means you hold it on your fingers and it does not go'). The extension of meaning in delicacy — not merely generalizing across different types but construing such types into dimensional and open-ended taxonomies — is a function of the elaborating potential, exploiting the basic dimensions of the system itself.

There are other "transphenomenal" motifs, often related to these, which are more specific in their scope; for example, the foregrounding of perceptual space, and of the concrete having extension in space, so that these serve as models for construing more abstract, non-spatial realms; and, more specifically, the spatial construction of the human body as an orientational framework.

Thus our concept of "construing experience through meaning" refers to the construal in human consciousness of an ideational system in which such motifs play a critical part. Expansion and projection are, as we put it earlier, fractal principles; they generate organization within many environments in the ideation base, at different strata and at different ranks within one stratum. These environments are thus related to one another through the local manifestations of these different motifs; and this opens up the system's potential for *alternative* construals of experience: for example, the types of expansion create new meaning potential through "figures of speech" (see Figure 5-15). Specifically each type of expansion contributes one figurative mode, as in the following examples:

			Example
elaboration — intensive	restatement: a resemblance is construed between A and B so that A can be restated in terms of B	metaphor	INTENSITY ==> LOCATION IN VERTICAL SPACE, e.g. He loved her very much ==> He loved her deeply
extension — possessive	meronymy: a part-whole relationship is construed between M and N so that so that part M can stand for the whole N	synecdoche	BODY ==> BODY PART, e.g. She has many people to feed ==> She has many mouths to feed
enhancement — circumstantial	a circumstantial relationship is construed between O and P so that circumstance O can stand for that which it is circumstantial to, P	metonymy	OPERATION ==> MANNER OF OPERATION, e.g. Think! ==> Use your brains!

In these examples the figures of speech are largely lexical; but the principle they illustrate — that because of the "play" that occurs between different strata the system has the potential for construing figurative meanings — extends throughout the grammar, as we shall see in the next chapter. What this means is, that whatever is construed can also be reconstrued, giving yet another dimension to the topology of semantic space.

The ideation base as we have presented it so far, with its framework of sequences, figures and elements, serves well enough for construing the experience of daily life, and for organizing and exchanging commonsense knowledge. But it proves inadequate to meet the semiotic demands of advanced technology and theoretical science. In the construction of scientific knowledge, the system needs to invoke the power of metaphor on a more global scale.

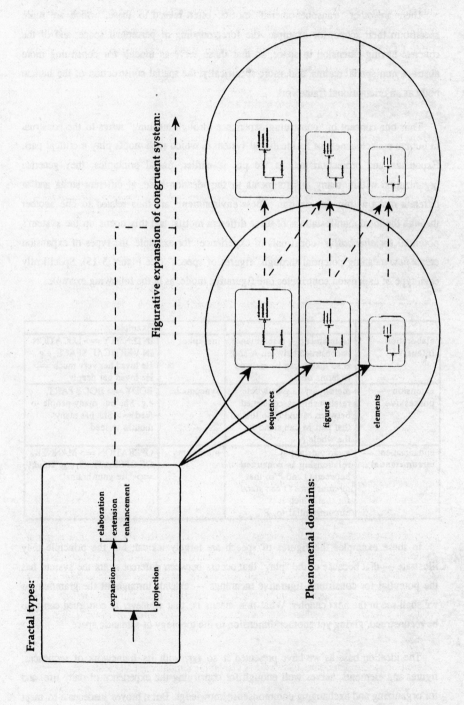

Fig. 5-15: Figurative expansion of the ideation base

6. Grammatical metaphor

In Chapter 2, we presented an overview of the meaning base. In this overview, we assumed that phenomena were construed in a 'congruent' form, and the details were then discussed in Chapters 3 (sequences), 4 (figures) and 5 (elements). To conclude this summary account of the meaning base of English, we shall consider how these resources may be expanded, through the deployment of grammatical metaphor (see also Halliday, 1985: Ch, 10; in press a, b; Halliday & Martin, 1993; Matthiessen, 1995b: Sections 1.4.3, 2.3.2, 3.1.6.1 and 4.12; Ravelli, 1985, 1988).

6.1 Congruent and metaphorical variants

We have seen that sequences, figures, and elements are congruently realized in the grammar as follows:

	clause complex	clause	group
sequence	√		
figure		√	
element			√

But these resources may be expanded by taking up further options in realization; for example, sequences may alternatively be realized by clauses and even groups. This is what we refer to as grammatical metaphor. Grammatical metaphor expands the semantic potential of the system.

Suppose that in the course of a text we came across the following portion of wording:

> Smith et al. have shown that if one takes alcohol one's brain
> rapidly becomes dull. Alcohol's rapid dulling effect on the brain
> has also been observed by other researchers in the field.

What is the semantic relationship here between *if one takes alcohol one's brain becomes dull* and *alcohol's rapid dulling effect on the brain*?

Grammatically, of course, the two have different status in rank: the former is a clause complex, hypotactic with rising dependency $^{x}\beta \wedge \alpha$, whereas the latter is a nominal group, structure Deictic ^ Epithet ^ Classifier ^ Thing ^ Qualifier. If each is functioning in its unmarked role in the realization of a semantic unit, then the first represents a sequence, the second represents an element. We can also find a third variant that would represent a figure, intermediate between the two; e.g. *the effect of alcohol is a rapid dulling of the brain.*

Here are some other pairs of wordings displaying similarly agnate relationships:

```
strength was needed to meet      it had to be strong because
driver safety requirements in    the driver needed to be safe
the event of missile impact      if it was impacted by a
                                 missile


he also credits his former big   he also believes he was
size with much of his career     successful in his career
success                mainly because he was formerly
                       big


some animals rely on their       some animals are able to
great speed to escape from       escape from danger by moving
danger                           very fast
```

In each pair of examples the grammatical status varies between clause and clause complex; and it would not be difficult also to construct a third variant which is a nominal group, e.g. *the strength needed to ..., his crediting of ..., the reliance of some animals on ...* . This would then function as an element in some other figure; for example, *the strength needed to meet driver safety requirements in the event of missile impact was provided by the use of specially toughened glass.*

In order to get a sense of the grammatical relationship between the members of pairs such as these, let us model one such pair — using a simpler example — in terms of a systemic-functional grammar (but taking account only of the ideational metafunction): see Figure 6-1.

If we take as our startingpoint the wording *the cast acted brilliantly so the audience applauded for a long time* and derive from it the agnate wording *the cast's brilliant acting drew lengthy applause from the audience*, we find the rewordings as set out in Table 6(1).

Let us summarize some of these in a prose commentary. (i) The verbs *acted* and *applauded*, each functioning as Event in a verbal group functioning as Process, each in a different clause, have been replaced by verb *acting*, noun *applause*, each functioning as Thing in a nominal group, the two nominal groups functioning respectively as Actor and Goal in the same clause. (ii) The conjunction *so*, functioning as logical-semantic relation between two clauses, has been replaced by the verb *drew* functioning as Event in a verbal group functioning as Process in a single clause; thus:

... acted ... so ... applauded => ... acting drew ... applause

(iii) The adverb *brilliantly*, functioning as Quality in an adverbial group functioning as Manner in clause (1), has been replaced by the adjective *brilliant*, functioning as Epithet in nominal group (1); while the expression *for a long time* (in origin a prepositional phrase but now codified as a single item) functioning as Duration in clause (2) has been replaced by an adjective *lengthy* functioning as Epithet in nominal group (2).

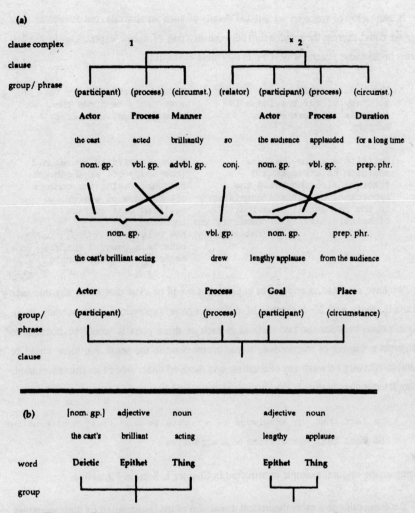

Fig. 6-1: Correspondence between congruent and metaphorical wordings

Table 6(1): Congruent wording and metaphorical rewording

	congruent					metaphorical			
	word class	function in group/phrase	group/phrase class	function in clause		word class	function in group/phrase	group/phrase class	function in clause
'cast'	noun	Thing	nom.gp.	Actor	=>	nom.gp. (poss.) rankshifted	Deictic	nom.gp.	Actor
'act'	verb	Event	vbl.gp.	Process	=>	verb (parti-cipial)	Thing		
'brilliant'	adverb	Quality	advbl. gp.	Manner	=>	adjective	Epithet		
'so'	conjunct-ion	——	——	——>	=>	verb	Event	vbl.gp.	Process
'audience'	noun	Thing	nom.gp.	Actor	=>	nom.gp rankshifted	Range	prep. phr.	Place
'applaud'	verb	Event	vbl.gp.	Process	=>	noun	Thing	nom.gp.	Goal
'long time'			prep. phrase	Duration	=>	adjective	Epithet		

It takes a lot of space to set out the details of such an analysis; but it will be clear that we could express the relationship between any pair of agnate expressions in explicit terms in the same general way. To cite two more examples:

```
The truest confirmation of the        If we act effectively this
accuracy of our knowledge is           most truly confirms that we
the effectiveness of our               know [things] accurately.
actions.
```

```
Griffith's energy balance              Because Griffith approached
approach to strength and               [the study of] strength and
fracture also suggested the            fracture [using the concept
importance of surface chemistry        of] balance of energy, we
in the mechanical behaviour            realized that surface
of brittle materials. chemistry was    important in
              [determining] how brittle
                                       materials behaved [under]
                                       mechanical [conditions].
```

We have set these examples out in pairs; but it will be clear that given any one such example, there will be a number of different agnate expressions corresponding to it. Furthermore, between the two variants in each of these pairs it would be possible to construct a number of intermediate steps: intermediate in the sense that there would be minimal distance between any one variant and those on either side of it. Thus an example of an intermediate variant in the first pair above would be

```
The fact that our knowledge is accurate is most truly confirmed by
the fact that our actions are effective.
```

Compare the original example constructed in Chapter 1, Section 1.2, above.

Before coming to a more theoretical discussion of the issues raised by these examples, let us note two related general properties that they display. One is that at some point in the set of rewordings there is typically a shift on the grammatical rank scale: from clause complex to clause, and/or from clause to nominal group. A generalized form of such a shift would be:

(clause complex) *a* happens, so *x* happens

(clause)   happening *a* causes happening *x*

(nominal group)   the cause of happening *x* by happening *a*

The second point is that, if we plot the shift in this direction (i.e. 'downwards' on the rank scale), there is typically some loss of information. We can attest this if we reword in the reverse order: we are often uncertain how to construct the higher rank variant. For example: for *the truest confirmation of the accuracy of our knowledge is the effectiveness of our actions*, should we reword as *if we act effectively this confirms that we know things accurately* or as *how effectively we act confirms how accurately we know things*? Other examples:

Increased responsiveness may be reflected in feeding behaviour.	The way [the creature] behaves when it feeds shows that it has become more responsive. —or:
	Because [the creature] has become more responsive it behaves in a different way when it feeds.
Higher productivity means more supporting services.	If more goods are produced, more supporting services will be provided. —or:
	More goods cannot be produced unless more supporting services are provided.

Here the ambiguity is mainly in the verb. When a logical relationship of this kind is realized as a verb, then one or both of two ambiguities may arise: (i) the relationship may be one of cause or proof, either 'x is the result of a' or 'x is the outward sign of a'; (ii) the relationship may go in either direction, either 'a causes x' or 'a is caused by x'. But while this is one major source of indeterminacy it is by no means the only one. An example such as the next shows the extent to which information may be lost when a clause complex is replaced by a clause, or a clause by a nominal group:

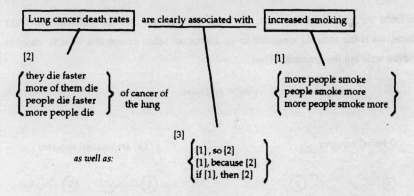

In other words, a nominal group (such as *lung cancer death rates*) is less explicit than the corresponding clause (*how fast people die when they have lung cancer, how many people die of lung cancer,* &c.), so one such group will correspond to many clauses; and a clause (such as *higher productivity means more supporting services*) is less explicit than the corresponding clause complex (*in order to produce more, you need ...* or *if you produce more, you will get ...*&c.), so one such clause will correspond to many clause complexes. The principle would seem to be that, where the members of a pair of agnate wordings differ in **rank**, the wording that is **lower** in rank will contain less information.

This suggests that the pattern displayed in the (constructed) example at the beginning of this section, in which the lower rank wording occurs as a repetition of the wording at a higher rank (where information has previously been made explicit), may be a typical context for these more condensed variants. This leads into the general theoretical issue of what the semantic status of such agnate sets actually is.

6.2 The nature of grammatical metaphor

We refer to this phenomenon under the general rubric of **grammatical metaphor** (following Halliday, 1985). The relationship among a set of agnates such as those just illustrated is a relationship of metaphor; but it is grammatical, not lexical as metaphor is in its classical sense. In order to make this clear, let us reverse the direction from which metaphor is traditionally approached.

6.2.1 Lexical and grammatical metaphor

The traditional approach to metaphor is to look at it 'from below' and ask what does a certain expression mean. For example the lexical metaphor *flood* means either, literally, an inundation of water or, metaphorically, an intense emotion as in *she felt a flood of relief*. But we could look 'from above' and ask how is intense emotion expressed. Then we would say it is expressed either, literally, as *she felt very relieved*, or, metaphorically, as *she felt a flood of relief*.

Once we look from above in this way, we can see that the phenomenon under discussion is the same as metaphor in its traditional sense except that what is varied is not the lexis but the grammar. Thus:

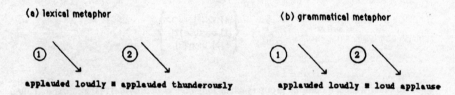

Here in (a) the lexico-semantic domain of 'volume' has been mapped onto the lexico-semantic domain of 'meteorological commotion'; while in (b) the grammatico-semantic domain of 'figures' has been mapped onto the grammatico-semantic domain of 'participants'. The metaphoric principle is the same in both cases; they differ only in generality.

Lexical and grammatical metaphor are not two different phenomena; they are both aspects of the same general metaphorical strategy by which we expand our semantic resources for construing experience. The main distinction between them is one of delicacy. Grammatical metaphor involves the reconstrual of one domain in terms of another domain, where both are of a very general kind; for example:

congruent domain	metaphorical domain
sequences	figures
figures	elements: participants
elements: participants: qualities, processes	elements: participants: things

Lexical metaphor also involves the reconstrual of one domain in terms of another domain; but these domains are more delicate in the overall semantic system. For example:

congruent domain	metaphorical domain
participant: thing: abstraction ... bright + idea	participant: thing: concrete object ... brainwave
participant: thing: abstraction ... fanciful, unrealistic + idea	participant: thing: abstraction ... pipedream
participant: thing: collective: human ... congregation in the charge of religious official	participant: thing: collective: animal: ... flock

There are two other characteristics of lexical metaphors which are also central to metaphor in its grammatical sense. The first is syntagmatic: lexical metaphors tend to occur in regular clusters, which we shall refer to here as "syndromes"; for example, the metaphor *congregation ==> flock* forms a syndrome together with *religious official ==> shepherd, group of believers ==> fold* and so on. The second is paradigmatic: lexical metaphors typically involve a shift towards the concrete, a move in the direction of "objectifying" ('making like an object', not 'making objective'), as the same examples show.[1] For these properties of grammatical metaphor, see Sections 6.4 and 6.5 below.

More than half a century ago, Whorf (1956: 145-6) provided a revealing account of the metaphorical construction of the domains of duration, intensity, and tendency in English and other standard languages of Europe:

---

[1] Because of the vastness of lexis, we do not yet have a general description of lexical metaphorical syndromes or of the location of metaphorical domains within the overall ideation base. But it is possible to discern that a central resource for metaphor is human bodily experience; and that the human body itself, concrete phenomena located in space-time, and features of daily social life are the most favoured metaphorical motifs. Renton (1990: 513-514) lists 37 such motifs, which account for 87 % of the 4215 metaphorical items in his dictionary of metaphor. The most common are human body (23%), animals (9%), sport (4%), food & drink (4%), war & military (4%), buildings (4%), geography (4%), clothes (3%), nautical (3%), religion & biblical (3%), transport (2%), plants (2%), meteorology (2%), science & medicine (2%), colours (2%), commerce (2%), manufacture (1%), and the remaining types 1% or less. The descriptive challenge is to systematize the domains of lexical metaphor, as Lakoff & Johnson (1980) and researchers building on their framework have started to do.

To fit discourse to manifold actual situations, all languages need to express durations, intensities, and tendencies. It is characteristic of SAE and perhaps many other language types to express them metaphorically. The metaphors are those of spatial extension, i.e. of size, number (plurality), position, shape, and motion. We express duration by 'long, short, great, much, quick, slow,' etc.; intensity by 'large, great, much, heavy, light, high, low, sharp, faint,' etc.; tendency by 'more, increase, grow, turn, get, approach, go, come, rise, fall, stop, smooth, even, rapid, slow'; and so on through an almost inexhaustible list of metaphors that we hardly recognize as such, since they are virtually the only linguistic media available. The nonmetaphorical terms in this field, like 'early, late, soon, lasting, intense, very, tending,' are a mere handful quite inadequate to the needs.

It is quite clear how this condition "fits in". It is part of our whole scheme of OBJECTIFYING — imaginatively spatializing qualities and potentials that are quite nonspatial (so far as any spatially perceptive senses can tell us). Noun-meaning (with us) proceeds from physical bodies to referents of far other sorts. Since physical bodies and their outlines in PERCEIVED SPACE are denoted by size and shape terms and reckoned by cardinal numbers and plurals, these patterns of denotation and reckoning extend to the symbols of nonspatial meanings, and so suggest an IMAGINARY SPACE. Physical shapes 'move, stop, rise, sink, approach,' etc. in perceived space; why not these other referents in their imaginary space? This has gone so far that we can hardly refer to the simplest nonspatial situation without constant resort to physical metaphors. I "grasp" the "thread" of another's arguments, but if its "level" is "over my head" my attention may "wander" and "lose touch" with the "drift" of it, so that when he "comes" to his "point" we differ "widely," our "views" being indeed so "far apart" that the "things" he says "appear" "much" too arbitrary, or even "a lot" of nonsense!

As Whorf's examples illustrate, lexical metaphors have grammatical implications: they occur at a lexical degree of delicacy in the overall system, but precisely because grammar and lexis form a continuum related by delicacy, lexical domains are in fact more delicate elaborations of grammatical ones. So for example, if understanding is construed metaphorically as grasping, it follows that a high degree of understanding can be also construed according to the same material model: understand very well ==> grasp firmly, as in *she grasped the principles firmly.* Similarly, if intensity is construed metaphorically in terms of location or movement in abstract space, this lexical reconstrual also has grammatical consequences, e.g. in terms of circumstantial elements within metaphorical figures: *prices fell sharply, prices rose to a new high, costs hit the ceiling,* and so on.

Thus in many instances, not unexpectedly, lexical and grammatical metaphor go together. What we are most likely to be told, after the performance, is that *the audience gave thunderous applause.* In *she felt a flood of relief* there is not only the lexical metaphor of *flood* but also the grammatical metaphor of *a flood of relief* where intensity is represented as a Thing and the emotion as its Qualifier, contrasting with *very relieved,* with intensity brought in as Submodifier *very* to the Epithet *relieved.* Similarly, in the example of grammatical metaphor *increased responsiveness may be reflected in feeding behaviour* there was also the lexical metaphor *reflected.* But they are not automatically associated, and in most instances of grammatical metaphor, if we reword in a less metaphorical direction, we can retain the same lexical items, merely changing their word class (often with morphological variation, e.g. *we act effectively / the effectiveness of our actions*).

6.2.2 Semogenetic priority of the congruent mode

Usually, as we have seen, we are confronted not just with a pair of wordings but with a larger set; and the first question that arises is whether there is any priority among these different wordings: why do we regard one or the other as being non-metaphorical, or at least less metaphorical than the rest? We would not, in considering grammatical metaphor, maintain a simple dichotomy between 'literal' and 'metaphorical'; rather, we would propose that there is a continuum whose poles are 'least metaphorical' and 'most metaphorical'. The immediate evidence for this is historical, in the sense of the three axes of semohistory referred to in Chapter 1, Section 1.5.3 above.

If we view a set of metaphorically agnate wordings synoptically, any member of such a set appears metaphorical by reference to all the others. Given *the announcement [was made] of his probable resignation* and *he announced that he would probably resign* there is no reason to say that either is the less metaphorical. But if we view them dynamically, taking account of their relation in time, then in all three histories the same one precedes: *he announced that he would probably resign comes before the announcement of his probable resignation*. It evolved earlier in the language (phylogenesis); it is learnt earlier by children (ontogenesis); and it typically comes earlier in the text (logogenesis). We have also seen that there is a *derivational* priority because of the loss of information: given *she announced that she was accepting* we can derive *the announcement of her acceptance*, but given *the announcement of her acceptance* we do not know who made the announcement, she or someone else ('they'); whether she had accepted, was accepting or would accept; or whether it was a case not of her accepting but of her being accepted — twelve possible rewordings in all. On all these grounds we have to acknowledge that the metaphorical relationship is not a symmetrical one: there is a definite directionality to it, such that one end of the continuum is metaphorical and the other is what we shall call **congruent**. Thus given the pair

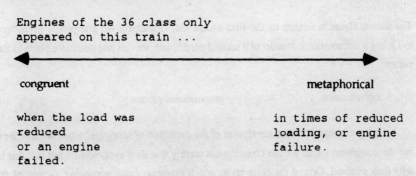

```
Engines of the 36 class only
appeared on this train ...
```

congruent   metaphorical

```
when the load was              in times of reduced
reduced                        loading, or engine
or an engine                   failure.
failed.
```

we shall locate the two with respect to each other on a metaphor scale as above. The expression *engine failure* evolved after the expression *the engine failed* in the evolution of industrial discourse; to explain *in times of engine failure* to a child you gloss it as *whenever an engine failed* (as one of the authors had to do to his 7-year-old son); the text would be likely to progress from *loads were reduced, engines failed* to *reduced loading, engine failure* rather than the other way round. And when we derive one from the other, we find ambiguity in one direction only: *reduced loading* might be agnate to *loads were reduced, had been reduced* or *were lighter than usual, engine failure* might be agnate to *an engine failed, the engine failed* or *engines failed*, and to ... *failed* or *had failed* in each case.

6.2.3 Location of grammatical metaphor in the content system

Let us now interpret a prototypical instance of grammatical metaphor in terms of our semantic model. Consider the example in the second sentence of the following:

> The atomic nucleus absorbs and emits energy in quanta, or discrete
> units. Each absorption marks its transition to a state of higher
> energy and each emission marks its transition to a state of lower
> energy.

We will focus simply on *each absorption marks its transition (to ...)*. A more congruent variant of this would be *each time (whenever) it absorbs [energy], it changes/ moves to ...* . Semantically we have a sequence consisting of two figures with a logical relationship between them. The first figure consists of two participants, 'the atomic nucleus' and 'energy', related to a process, 'absorbs'. In the congruent form the pattern of realization is as follows:

sequence ↘	clause complex	
figure	↘	clause
process	↘	verbal group
participant	↘	nominal group
logical relation	↘	conjunction

The second figure is similar to the first except that (assuming we interpret it as 'moves to') it has a circumstance instead of a second participant; we can add one more piece to the pattern:

circumstance	↘	prepositional phrase

Looking at these from the standpoint of the evolution of language, when we say they are the congruent forms we are claiming not merely that they evolved first but that this is *why* they evolved. One of the contexts in which grammar came into being — one of its metafunctions — was that of construing human experience; and, as we have seen, the model that emerged was one which construed the continuum of goings-on into taxonomies: taxonomies of parts (meronymic) and taxonomies of kinds (hyponymic). The central construct was that of the 'figure'; figures could be further constructed into 'sequences' and also deconstructed into 'elements'. How did the grammar construe this hierarchy of phenomena? — as clauses, clause complexes, and elements in the structure of the clause:

sequence ↘   clause complex

figure   ↘   clause

element   ↘   element of clause structure

The elements making up a figure were of three kinds: a process, participants in that process, and circumstantial features. How did the grammar construe this classification? — as verbs, nouns, and other things:

process   ↘   verb (expanding to verbal group)

participant   ↘   noun (expanding to nominal group)

circumstance   ↘   (others)

The circumstance could be either some quality of the process or some participant that was indirectly involved:

circumstance (quality)   ↘   adverb (expanding to adverbial group)

circumstance (indirect   ↘   prepositional phrase

      participant)   (preposition (= minor verb) + nom. gp.)

This pattern of construal was described above, in Chapters 3, 4, and 5; we now draw on it to model grammatical metaphor. What was described above was the congruent pattern: 'congruent' in the sense that is the way language evolved. Of course, what we are recognizing here as two distinct constructions, the semantic and the grammatical, never had or could have had any existence the one prior to the other; they are our analytic representation of the overall semioticizing of experience — how experience is construed into meaning. If the congruent pattern had been the only form of construal, we would probably not have needed to think of semantics and grammar as two separate strata: they would be merely two facets of the content plane, interpreted on the one hand as function and on the other as form.

Why then in our present interpretation have we to recognize two parts, one a lexicogrammar and one a semantics? Because the system continued to evolve beyond that point, enriching itself (i.e. engendering a richer model of experience) by forcing apart the two 'facets' of the sign so that each could take on a new partner — sequences could be realized by other things than clause complexes, processes could be realized by other things than verbs, and so on. We described this step briefly in the introduction, depicting it as the dissociation of the two halves of the Chinese representation of the sign (see Chapter 1, Section 1.5.4).

It is this step that gives rise to grammatical metaphor. When a sequence is realized as a clause complex, or a process as a verb, this is congruent: it is the clause complex, and the verb, in the function in which it evolved. When a sequence is realized as something other than a clause complex, or a process as something other than a verb, this is metaphorical. Some other grammatical unit is supplanting them in these functions.

6.2.4 Metafunctional effect of metaphoric shift

What is the effect of this shift, in relation to the construction of experience? Suppose that a sequence is now realized not as a clause complex but as a clause; and a process not as a verb but as a noun — as in many of the examples above, but let us construct a new one for the sake of brevity: say *his defeat led to his resignation* instead of *because he had been defeated he resigned*. Are these two simply synonymous, just different ways of saying the same thing? In principle, of course, they might be; but it is well-known that idle variants are highly unstable, at least in language and probably in any semiotic system. Even if through some confluence of historical processes a set of 'free variants' does emerge, as can happen (e.g. in various types of language contact situation), it will not be long before those variants come to construe different meanings — at which point they are no longer 'free'.

It seems clear that these sets of agnate forms are not and never have been free variants; they have always been, at the very least, to some extent context-specific. For example, the metaphorical forms tend to occur more in writing, the congruent ones tend to occur more in speech. The question is not *whether* they differ but *how*, and *why*, they differ. What kind of meaning is being construed by the systemic contrast between them?

To explore this question we formulate it in terms of the metafunctions: do they differ ideationally, or interpersonally, or textually — or, of course, in any combination of these? We have already had clear evidence that they differ in **textual meaning**: e.g. *The atomic nucleus absorbs energy ... Each absorption marks its transition ...* Another such example would be *Cracks in glass can grow at speeds of less than one-trillionth of an inch per hour, ... On an atomic scale the slow growth of cracks corresponds to ...* Here the move from *absorbs* to *absorption*, from *cracks in glass can grow at speeds less than ...* to *the slow growth of cracks* has a very clear status in the rhetorical construction of the discourse. At the first occurrence, it is presented to us as new information; we had not been told it before. At the second occurrence, we already know it; it is to be taken for granted and used as the point of departure for a further item of information (*marks its transition to a state of higher energy; corresponds to the sequential rupturing of interatomic bonds at rates as low as one bond rupture per hour*). The grammatical resources whereby this pattern is constructed are the textual systems of 'theme' and 'information', which organize the discourse in terms of Theme-Rheme and Given-New (Halliday, 1967/8; 1985: Ch. 3 & 8; 1988; Fries, 1981, 1992, 1995, in press; Halliday

& Martin, 1993; Bateman & Matthiessen, 1993; Matthiessen, 1992, 1995b: Chapter 6). If the Theme of the clause (realized as the element in first position) is also explicitly located as Given, this has a very strong 'backgrounding' effect: the message is 'you already know this; now use it as stepping-off point for a further move, to something you don't know'. By the same token, the remainder of the clause (either the whole of it, or at least the culminating element) is strongly 'foregrounded'. The total construction is obviously a powerful device for reasoning and argumentation.

What is the relation of this to grammatical metaphor? The significant point is that the Theme of an English clause has to be nominal. Not that there cannot exist other kinds of Theme — adverbials, prepositional phrases or even verbs; but these construe Themes which are highly marked (verbal Themes in particular), embodying features of contrast which are not appropriate in these contexts. The only kind of grammatical entity that construes the message in precisely the way required, without special effects, is a nominal — which may be a nominal group or else a nominalized clause or clause complex.

If therefore an experiential meaning such as 'nucleus + absorb + energy', or 'crack + grow + slowly', is to be mapped on to the textual meaning of 'backgrounded as point of departure', it has to be constructed nominally, in some form such as

```
[the fact] that the nucleus absorbs energy
the absorbing of energy by the nucleus
the nucleus' absorption of energy
```

In this way it comes to constitute a textual 'package', a packed and compacted quantum of information ready to take on its role in the unfolding of the argument. Such packages are also favoured as foregroundings: the culmination of the clause, as the New information the listener/ reader is explicitly invited to attend to, often also takes the form of a metaphoric nominal, e.g. *its transition to a state of higher energy; the sequential rupturing of interatomic bonds* in the examples above. We have discussed the thematic nominal first because that is the one that is easiest to explain in its own terms; but it is likely that the whole **syndrome of features** we have been illustrating evolved together. This syndrome is made up of:

semantic unit	congruently ↘	metaphorically ↘
sequence	clause complex	clause
figure	clause	nominal group
logical relation	conjunction (relating clauses in complex)	verbal group

If we show this in terms of the table we presented at the beginning of Section 6.1, we see how the metaphorical expansion of the system fills out previously empty cells:

	clause complex	clause	group
sequence	congr.: √	metaph: √	metaph: √
figure		congr.: √	metaph: √
element			congr.: √
			metaph: √

Thus *each absorption marks its transition ...* displays four metaphorical properties: (1) sequence as clause (the whole); (2), (3) figures as nominal groups: *each absorption and its transition to ...* ; (4) logical relation as verb: *marks.* (Contrast the congruent representation given earlier.) One of the earliest writers to use this type of metaphor in English was Isaac Newton, and already in his writing the various features co-occur in this same syndrome, e.g.

```
The explosion of gunpowder arises therefore from the violent
action whereby all the Mixture ... is converted into Fume and
Vapour.
```

Here too we have (1) a sequence realized as a clause; (2), (3) figures as nominal groups: *the explosion of gunpowder, the violent action whereby ...;* (4) logical relation as verb: *arises.* The same syndrome is found in the Italian of Galileo, written some decades earlier (cf. Biagi, 1995); it may well be that English was directly influenced by Italian, since many 17th century English scientists studied and worked in Italy.

We could take the view, then, at least on the evidence presented up to this point (we shall consider a greater range of types of grammatical metaphor below), that a pair of agnate wordings related to each other as metaphorical to congruent differ in their textual meaning but are identical in their ideational meaning. This would be a plausible hypothesis, and one that might be adopted in text generation. But there are reasons for thinking that it is not, in fact, the whole story.

Let us enumerate some of these reasons here. (i) We may wonder why the backgrounding-foregrounding pattern, which itself is clearly motivated, should then depend on this tactic of nominal "packaging". Why would there not be other, equally effective ways of codifying this rhetorical structure? (ii) Secondly, we might note that the use of this kind of packaging, while it seems to have originated in the context described for it above, now extends far beyond these requirements. Most scientific writing, most bureaucratic and technocratic writing, and many other kinds of writing as well (not to mention many instances of spoken discourse), use metaphorical representations as the norm, whether or not they are demanded by the rhetorical structure of the discourse. (iii) Thirdly, we have seen that ideational meanings stand in a natural relationship to ideational wordings. It seems unlikely that this powerful principle relating the two strata of the content plane would be destroyed by the emergence of grammatical metaphor. On the contrary, it would seem that metaphor is possible precisely because the principle of conguence is still operative.

To explain these observations, we can consider the other two metafunctions — the ideational and interpersonal metafunctions. The metaphors we are considering here are in fact all shifts within the **ideational** realm — from sequence to figure, from figure to participant, and so on — and their primary effect is ideational. They constitute a resource for *reconstruing experience* along certain lines, redeploying the same categories that have evolved in the congruent mode of construing experience. Thus when experience of a quantum of change has been construed as a figure consisting of 'atomic nucleus + absorb + energy', it can be reconstrued as if it was a participant: 'absorption (+ of energy) (+ by atomic nucleus)'. Here the process element of the figure is reconstrued as a thing; and the participants involved in that process are reconstrued as qualities of that thing. Since they are qualities, they are no longer "obligatory"; like any other thing, 'absorption' need not be further specified by reference to qualities. The metaphoric shift does not mean that the natural relationship between meaning and wording is destroyed; rather, this relationship is extended further when new domains of realization are opened up to semantic categories through metaphor. The shift does however create a greater distance from the everyday experience; the metaphorical mode of construal makes it possible to recast that everyday experience, retaining only certain features from the congruent wording but adding others that it did not include.

We shall explore the ideational effect of grammatical metaphor in considerably more detail below (see in particular Sections 6.7 - 6.8). Here we only need to complete the metafunctional circuit. We have already noted that grammatical metaphor is textually significant; and we can now relate this textual significance to the ideational significance we have just mentioned. Ideationally, grammatical metaphor is a resource for reconstruing experience so that, alongside congruent configurations, we also have alternative metaphorical ones. At the same time, these different configurations map onto different textual patterns. For example, a figure maps onto a message; but a participant maps onto part of a message, so that a figure construed as if it was a participant can be given a textual status within that message.

In a similar way, phenomena in the ideation base also map onto constructs of **interpersonal** meaning. For example, a congruent figure maps onto a move in a dialogic exchange; it is enacted interpersonally as a proposition or a proposal. It follows that when phenomena are reconstrued metaphorically within the ideation base, there are also interpersonal consequences. For instance, the figure 'atomic nucleus + absorb + energy' can be enacted interpersonally as a proposition that is open to negotiation: *The atomic nucleus absorbs energy — Does it? — Yes, it does — No, it can't.* However, when this figure is reconstrued as the participant 'absorption (+ of energy) (+ by atomic nucleus)', it no longer has the potential for being enacted interpersonally as proposition;

rather, it would be taken for granted in discourse. You can't argue with *the absorption of energy by the nucleus* since it is not enacted as an arguable proposition. Such interpersonal differences can have a powerful rhetorical effect in persuasive discourse. (There is an analogous effect with respect to proposals in regulatory discourse.)

But the interpersonal significance of grammatical metaphor is likely to be felt most clearly at the macroscopic level, in the overall pattern of interpersonal relationships, and the ideological orientation, that emerge over the course of the text. We shall have more to say about this in a later section (Section 6.7.3).

6.3 How grammatical metaphor evolves: transcategorization

Some form of grammatical metaphor is found in all languages and in all uses of language. Like lexical metaphor, it is not something odd or exceptional; it is part of the inherent nature of language as a social-semiotic system, a natural process by which the meaning potential is expanded and enriched. Even in the language of small children there is *some* grammatical metaphor present almost from the start.

The phenomenon of **transcategorizing** elements would seem to be a feature of the grammar of every language. This implies two things: (i) that each etymon belongs inherently to a major class; (ii) that at least some etymons can be transferred to another class — by some grammatical means, syntactic and/or morphological. Thus in Indo-European languages there is typically a battery of derivational morphemes whereby a root can be transcategorized; for example in English,

flake noun :	(*flaky* adj. : *flakiness* noun) / *flake* verb
shake verb :	(*shaky* adj. : *shakiness* noun / *shakily* adv.) / *shake* noun
awake adj. :	*awaken* verb : *awakening* noun

These Anglo-Saxon resources were reinforced and largely overtaken as productive devices by those borrowed from Greek and Latin, e.g.

analyse verb:	(*analyst* n. / *analysis* n. / *analytic* adj. : *analytically* adv.)
nation noun:	(*national* adj. : *nationally* adv. / *nationalism* n. : *nationalist* n. : *nationalistic* adj. / *nationalize* verb)
behave verb:	*behaviour* n. : (*behavioural* adj.: *behaviourally* adv. / *behaviourist* n.)
develop verb:	*development* noun ... &c.

All these are means of shifting a lexeme from one class to another. If we now relate them to the types of element, we find that in some instances the semantic nature of the transcategorization is clear. For example, *flake* - thing: 'turn into flakes' - process; *shake* - process: *shaky* 'tending to shake' - quality, *shaker* 'that which shakes (= vessel in which dice is shaken)' - thing; *awake* - quality, *awaken* 'cause to become awake' - process; *analyse* - process, *analyst* 'one who analyses' - thing. We can gloss these in everyday terms, without recourse to technicality. In other instances, however, the nature of the change is less clear. What for example would be the semantic interpretation of *shakiness, awakening, analysis, development?* Here we find ourselves using precisely the terms of our own metalanguage in the definition: '**quality** of being shaky', '**process** of being awake, or causing to become awake', '**process** of analysing, developing'.

When this happens, it is a signal that a phenomenon of this other kind — quality, or process — is being *treated as if it was* a thing. The grammar has constructed an imaginary or fictitious object, called *shakiness,* by transcategorizing the quality *shaky;* similarly by transcategorizing the process *develop* it has created a pseudo-thing called *development.* What is the status of such fictitious objects or pseudo-things? Unlike the other elements, which *lose their original status* in being transcategorized (for example, *shaker* is no longer a process, even though it derives from *shake*), these elements do not: *shakiness* is still a quality, *development* is still a process — only they have been construed into things. They are thus a **fusion**, or '**junction**', of two semantic elemental categories: *shakiness* is a 'quality thing', *development* is a 'process thing'. All such junctional elements involve grammatical metaphor.

How do such junctional elements evolve? Probably through the extension of what are originally transcategorizing derivations. Much of the technical terminology that developed in ancient Greek was based on four nominalizing processes: (i) -της -tes, which originally meant 'one who [+ process]', as in ποιητης *poietês* 'one who makes', and then evolved further as the nominalization of a quality (e.g. μανοτης *manotês* 'porousness'); (ii) -ια -ia, originally 'that which is [+ quality]', e.g. ευθεια *euthêia* 'that which is straight - a line', likewise becoming a nominalized quality, e.g. φαντασια *phantasía* 'imagination'; (iii) –μα -ma, originally the product or goal of a process, e.g. ποιημα *poíema* 'that which is made', via an abstract product e.g. πραγμα *prâgma* 'that which is done, deed' to a nominalized process e.g. πληρωμα *pléroma* 'that which is made by filling, the sum', κινημα *kínema* 'movement (a being moved)'; (iv) –σις -sis 'an act of ... [+ process]', e.g. πραξις *prâxis* 'doing', ποιησις *poíesis* 'making; creation', becoming generalized to other processes e.g. μιμησις *mímesis* 'copying, imitation', κινησις *kínesis* 'moving, movement, motion', παραλλαξις *parállaxis* 'alternating motion, alternation'. In all these instances it seems that meaning-making by transcategorizing has evolved, through intermediate stages, into meaning-making by metaphorizing; there is no sharp line between deriving a thing from a process, as 'one who makes', 'that which is made', and construing a process as a thing 'making, creation'; with 'action of making, act of making' somewhere in between.

However these 'things' evolved, it is virtually certain that no language as we know it today is without some metaphoric shifting of this kind. But it is only under certain historical conditions that it comes to be a dominant feature of the semantic system, as it is in English today. Here is a sentence from a local newspaper sports page:

> Dorrigo cruised to an effortless win by virtue of a strong batting
> display which saw them compile 4/194 from 38 overs. (Bellingen
> Courier-Sun, 14/ii 90)

There is no obvious motivation for such a high degree of grammatical metaphor; yet it does not strike us as in any way unusual.

6.4 Types of grammatical metaphor: elemental

It seems to us necessary to identify the types of grammatical metaphor and characterize them explicitly in relation to the semantics as a whole. We therefore introduce a general distinction between metaphoric (elements or features) and others. Metaphoric elements, as we said above, are junctional in that they embody a junction of two semantic categories. In the previous chapters, 3-5, we dealt just with elements that could be assigned to a single category: process, thing, quality &c. We shall refer to these as 'ordinary' elements, and contrast them with 'junctional' elements which are those that embody grammatical metaphor. Junctional elements will always have two categories in their description, e.g. 'process thing', 'circumstantial quality', 'relator process'.

Let us now enumerate and classify the principal types of grammatical metaphor in English. Drawing on our discussion of transcategorization, we shall base our classification on metaphoric shifts from one elemental class to another. In doing so we shall treat each type as a phenomenon on its own; we should therefore give a reminder here that instances of grammatical metaphor do not typically occur in isolation. When we find grammatical metaphors in discourse, they nearly always cluster into what we are calling **syndromes** (see further Section 6.5 below); these are typical clusterings of metaphorical effects among which there is some kind of interdependence (for example, in *the government decided => the government's decision*, there is an obvious relationship between *decide => decision*, process as thing, and *the government => the government's*, participant as prossessor of the thing). Nevertheless there are two metaphorical effects here, not just one; and they have been treated separately in the taxonomy that follows.

The elemental metaphors are mappings from a congruent categorial domain to a metaphorical one. The primary types are set out and exemplified in Table 6(2) below. For example, the categorial domain of 'process' can be reconstrued metaphorically in terms of the domains of (i) thing and (ii) quality. (We have added "Ø" under "congruent domains": this signals that a metaphorical process may be added, to which there is no corresponding congruent form, as part of a syndrome in which the original congruent process has been metaphorized as a thing.)

Table 6(2): Domains of elemental metaphors

congruent:	metaphorical:			
	=> circumstance	=> process	=> quality	=> thing
quality => *unstable*				1 *instability*
process => *absorb*			3 *absorptive*	2 *absorption*
circumstance => *instead of;* *on the surface*		6 *replaces*	5 *alternative;* *superficial*	4 *replacement;* *surface*
relator* => *for/ because [b,* *for/ because a]* *so [a, so b]*	10 *because of;* *as a result*	9 *causes,* *proves;* *ensues,* *follows from*	8 *causal;* *consequent*	7 *cause,* *proof;* *result*
Ø =>		12 *occurs;* *imposes;* *does, has*		11 *phenomenon,* *fact*
thing, circumstance => *driver [be safe]* *decided [today]*	13 expansion of thing <in environment of 1 or 2> *driver [safety], driver's [safety], [safety] of the driver* *today's [decision], [decision] of today*			

*A sequence is construed congruently by the grammar as a clause nexus joined by a conjunction (cf. Chapter 3 above). A nexus may be either paratactic or hypotactic. Where the sequence is construed paratactically, the preferred order is the iconic one; thus, in the case of 'time' and 'cause', "precedent, *then* subsequent", "cause, *so* effect". The alternative causal sequence "effect, *for* cause" (as in *I strove with none, for none was worth my strife*) is rather infrequent; while the alternative temporal sequence apparently does not occur. (These relationships can of course be expressed cohesively — that is, without being construed as grammatical structures at all: *I strove with none. The reason was that ... .*) Where the sequence is construed hypotactically, either order is possible: "*after* precedent, subsequent"/ "subsequent, *after* precedent"; "*because* cause, effect"/ "effect, *because* cause". Note also "precedent, *before* subsequent"/ "*before* subsequent, precedent"; "cause, *so that* effect"/ "*so that* effect, cause" — where tying the relator to the 'effect' typically implies intentionality. For example:

[β ^ α: 'purpose'] So that they could get there in time, they broke the door down.

[α ^ β: 'purpose'] They broke the door down so that ('in order that') they could ('would be able to') get there in time.

[α ^ β: 'result'] They broke door down, so that ('with the result that') they could ('were able to') get there in time.

The reason for the disparity is that hypotaxis construes an order of its own — ordering in dependence; whereas in parataxis the only ordering is that being imposed by the grammar on the experiential phenomena themselves.

Table 6(2) shows that there are clear patterns in the metaphoric shift. For example, the 'relator' can be reconstrued metaphorically in terms of any of the other types of element; but it cannot itself be a target domain in metaphors. Such particular patterns are part of more general metaphoric motifs. We shall identify and interpret these patterns and motifs in Section 6.7 below. But first we need to consider the types of metaphoric shift in a little greated detail.

Table 6(3) gives a more detailed description of the types shown in Table 6(2) above, together with an example of each. Several of the numbered types identified in the previous table have been differentiated further into subtypes, represented by Roman numerals. The first two columns present the metaphoric shift as a grammatical phenomenon: (1) as a shift of (word) class and (2) as a shift of function (in clause, phrase or group, as appropriate). The third column gives examples of each type. The last two columns show the metaphor as a semantic relationship between types of element: (4) the domain of the congruent variant, then finally (5) that of the metaphorical variant. It should be remembered that almost every one of the metaphoric categories is immensely variable. Wherever possible, examples have been drawn from texts cited in the discussion in the present chapter; but they are just examples, and should not be read as glosses describing the category as a whole.

Table 6(3): Types of grammatical metaphor

TYPE:		Grammatical shift		Example	Semantic element	
		(1) grammatical class	(2) grammatical functions		congruent =>	metaphorical
1		adjective => noun	Epithet/ Attribute => Thing	*unstable => instability; quick(ly) => speed*	quality	thing
2		verb => noun:			process:	
	i		Event => Thing	*transform => transformation*	event	
	ii		Auxiliary => Thing	*will/ going to => prospect; can/ could => possibility, potential*	tense; modality	
	iii		Catenative => Thing	*try to => attempt; want to => desire*	phase; contingency	
3		preposition(al phrase) => noun			circumstance:	
	i	preposition	Minor Process => Thing	*with => accompaniment; to => destination*	minor process	
	ii	prepositional phrase	Location, Extent &c => Classifier	*[dust is] on the surface => surface dust*	minor process + thing	
4		conjunction => noun	Conjunctive => Thing	*so => cause, proof; if => condition*	relator	
5		verb => adjective			process:	quality

	i		Event => Epithet/ Classifier	*[poverty] increases => increasing [poverty]*	event	
	ii		Auxiliary => Epithet/ Classifier	*was/ used to => previous; must/ will => constant*	tense; modality	
	iii		Catenative => Epither/ Classifier	*begin (to) => initial*	phase; contingency	
6		preposition(al phrase) => adjective			circumstance:	
	i	preposition	Minor Process => Epithet/ Classifier	*with => accompanying*	minor process	
	ii	prepositional phrase	Location, Extent &c => Epithet/ Classifier	*[marks are] on the surface => superficial [marks]*	minor process + thing	
7		conjunction => adjective	Conjunctive => Epithet/ Classifier	*before => previous; so => resultant*	relator	
8		preposition(al phrase) => verb			circumstance:	process
	i	preposition	Minor Process => Process	*(be) about => concern; (be) instead of => replace; (go) across => traverse*	minor process	
	ii	prepositional phrase	Location, Extent &c => Process	*(put) in a box/ in house => box/ house*	minor process + thing	
9		conjunction => verb	Conjunctive => Process	*then => follow; so => cause; and => complement*	relator	
10		conjunction => preposition(al phrase)			relator	circumstance:
	i	=> preposition	Conjunctive => Minor Process	*when => in times of; because => because of*		minor process
	ii	=> prepositional phrase	Conjunctive => Location, Extent &c	*so => as a result, in consequence; if [it snows] => under/ in [snow(y)] conditions*		minor process + thing
11		+ noun	+ Thing	*[x] => the fact/ phenomenon of [x]*	(none)	thing
12		+ verb	+ Process			process
	i	+ verb		*[x] => [x] occurs/ exists; [x] => have, do [x] (e.g. impact => have an impact)*	(none)	

	ii	+ (causative &c) verb		*make [x : y] => impose [y on x]; think [x = y] => credit [x with y]*	**(agency &c)**	
	iii	+ (phasal &c) verb²		*started/ wanted [to survey] => started/ wanted [a survey]*	**(phase &c)**	
13	i	noun => (various)	Thing =>	*the government [decided] =>*	thing	expansion of thing:
			(a) Qualifier	*[decision] off by the government*		**(qualifying)**
			(b) Possessive Deictic	*the government's [decision]*		**(possessive)**
			(c) Classifier	*government(al) [decision]*		**(classifying)**
	ii	adverb => adjective	Manner => Epithet	*[decided] hastily => hasty [decision]*	circumstance	expansion of thing:
		prepositional phrase => adjective	Location, Extent &c => Epithet	*[argued] for a long time => lengthy [argument]*		**(descriptive)**
		adverb => (various)	Location, Extent &c => Possessive Deictic	*[announced] yesterday => yesterday's [announcement]*		
		prepositional phrase => (various)	Location, Extent &c => Qualifier	*[departed] for the airport => [departure] for the airport*		

Here is a typical passage of written English analysed for the types of grammatical metaphor listed in the table above (from an editorial in the *Sydney Morning Herald*):

```
The Federal Government's decision to ask the Arbitration
         13.i (b)              2.i
Commission to determine whether the BLF has engaged in
                                12.i
serious industrial misconduct, as part of its      move to
     6.ii              2.i                     13.i (b)  2.iii
deregister the BLF in certain states, is one of the weakest
actions ever taken by a government in the face of industrial
     2.i         12.i       10.i                           6.ii
thuggery.
    1
```

---

² Note that where the grammar has a simple verbal group (types 12i and 12ii), this construes a single 'process' element in the figure. Where the clause contains a verbal group complex (type 12iii), while this (congruently) still construes a single 'process' it is now somewhere along the cline towards a sequence of two figures. Thus: *the government deregistered the union —> the government moved to deregister the union —> the government moved/ acted (in order) to deregister the union.* Cf. Chapter 3, Section 3.4.

```
"Their    guerilla tactics and use of   thuggery, violence and
13.i (b)   3.ii                2.i 13.i (a)   1           1

intimidation have had a disastrous impact not only on
    2.i          12.i           13.ii    2.i

building employers but also on fellow workers in the industry."
  3.ii                                6.ii


Obviously the Government is frightened of union    reaction to
                                      13.i (c)     2.i

its     move to impose proper behaviour on unions.
13.i (b)  2.ii    12.ii  13.ii    2.i    13.i (a)
```

[The text "unpacked" according to this interpretation:]

The Federal Government have decided to ask the Arbitration
Commission to determine whether the BLF have seriously misbehaved
in the industry, as they are intending to deregister the BLF in
certain states; no government has ever acted more weakly when
people have behaved like thugs.

"Because they have used tactics like guerillas, and behaved like
thugs, been violent and intimidated people, this has disastrously
affected not only employers in building but also those who work
with them.'

Obviously the Government is frightened how the unions will react
when they begin to make them behave properly.

6.5 Syntagmatic and paradigmatic dimensions of grammatical metaphor

In Section 6.4 we identified individual types of grammatical metaphor, such as "process => thing". For analytic purposes we treated these as isolates having just the two values "congruent/ metaphorical". We now need to consider two respects in which this is an idealized, oversimplified account of what actually happens. We need to add a dimension of complexity on both syntagmatic and paradigmatic axes.

Syntagmatically, instances of grammatical metaphor typically occur not in isolation but in organic clusters or "syndromes". Paradigmatically, there will typically be other wordings intermediate between an instance of grammatical metaphor and its "most congruent" agnate variant. These two aspects of complexity are taken up in the next two subsections.

6.5.1 Syntagmatic complexity: syndromes of elemental metaphors

We noted above that the individual types of grammatical metaphor set out in Table 6(3) tend to occur not one at a time but together in syntagmatic clusters, or "syndromes". We can enumerate some of the common syndromes as follows.

(1)	2i/1 + 13i(a)	the fracture of glass/ the instability of diamond
(2)	13i(c) + 2i/1	engine failure/ union intransigence
(3)	13i(b) + 2i/1	the government's decision/ indecision (indecisiveness)
(4)	6ii + 2i/1	interatomic bonding/ industrial thuggery
(5)	13i(b) + 2i + 13i(a)	his arrest by the police
(6)	13ii + 2i + 12i	rapid bonding occurs
(7)	13ii + 2i + 13i(a)	yesterday's decision by the group
(8)	5ii + 1 + 13i(a)	the apparent innocence of the accused
(9)	1 + 13i(a) + 13i(b) + 2i	the cogency of his argument

The most pervasive of the types of grammatical metaphor listed in Table 6(3) are types 1 and 2: "quality => thing" and "process => thing". We can see here that these typically occur as elements of syndromes, such as those just illustrated; these are syndromes formed of metaphoric shifts from one class of element to another. Some of these shifts can occur indpendently, while others — those we have called type 13 — occur only under the driving force of the shift of type 1 or type 2.

These syndromes of elemental metaphors fall into three general types, not very sharply distinct but worth using as a conceptual framework. The distinction relates to the rank where the metaphoric reconstrual takes place: (I) from figure to element, (II) from sequence to figure, (III) from figure with process to figure with process as thing.

I. Figure ==> element

Here a figure is being construed metaphorically on the model of a participant: grammatically, the figure is construed not as a clause but as a nominal group. There is a shift in rank from figure to element, and concomitantly a shift in status among the elements making up the construction. The way these syndromes are construed is shown in the following displays (omitting numbers (1) to (4), since these are included in the others).

(5) *he was arrested by the police ==> his arrest by the police* 13i(b) + 2i + 13i(a)

		figure: process *arrest*	participant *he*	participant *the police*
elements:				
participant	thing	2i (process ==> thing) *arrest*		
	quality		13i(b) (thing ==> possessive expansion) *his*	13i(a) (thing ==> qualifying expansion) *by the police*
process				
circumstance				

Similarly (from above): *the union's use of thuggery*

(6) *(...) bond rapidly => rapid bonding occurs* 13ii + 2i + 12i

		figure: process *bond*	participants	circumstances *rapidly*
elements:				
participant	thing	2i (process ==> thing)*bonding*		
	quality			13ii (circumstance ==> expansion of thing: descriptive) *rapid*
process		12i (+ process) *occur*		
circumstance				

(7) *the group decided yesterday ==> yesterday's decision by the group* 13ii + 2i + 13i(a)

		figure: process *decide*	participants *the group*	circumstances *yesterday*
elements:				
participant	thing	2i (process ==> thing) *decision*		
	quality		13i(a) (thing ==> expansion of thing: qualifying) *by the group*	13ii (circumstance ==> expansion of thing: possessive) *yesterday's*
process				
circumstance				

(8) *the accused appeared to be innocent* ==> *the apparent innocence of the accused* 5iii
+ 1 + 13i(a)

elements:		figure (being):		
		process *appear*	participant *the accused*	participant (Attribute) *innocent*
participant	thing			1 (quality ==> thing) *innocence*
	quality	5iii (phase process ==> quality) *apparent*	13i(a) (thing ==> expansion of thing: qualifying) *of the accused*	
process				
circumstance				

(9) *he argues cogently* ==> *the cogency of his argument* 1 + 13i(a) + 13i(c) + 2i

elements:		figure:		
		process *argue*	participants *he*	circumstances *cogently*
participant	thing			13ii (circumstance ==> expansion of thing: descriptive), *cogent* then: 1 (quality ==> thing) *cogency*
	quality	2i (process ==> thing) *argument* then: 13i(a) (thing ==> expansion of thing: qualifying) *of argument*	13i(b) (thing => expansion of thing: possessive) *his*	
process				
circumstance				

II. Sequence ==> figure

Here the syndrome involving the shift of type 1 or 2 occurs in a more general
environment, that of construing a sequence on the model of a figure — grammatically,
the sequence is construed not as a clause complex but as a clause.

(1) *They shredded the documents before they departed for the airport* ==> *(They shredded the documents) before their departure for the airport* 10i + 13i(b) + 2i + 13ii

figures:	elements:		sequence		
			figure *(They shredded the documents)*	relator *before*	figure *they departed for the airport*
figure	participant	thing			
		quality			
	process				
	circumstance			(relator + figure ==> circumstance) *before their departure for the airport*	
				10i (relator ==> minor process) *before*	(figure ==> participant) *their departure for the airport*

(2) *They shredded the documents before they departed for the airport* ==> *Their shredding of the documents preceded their departure for the airport* 13i(b) + 2i + 13i(a) + 9 + ...

figures:	elements:		sequence		
			figure *They shredded the documents* [process + participant + participant]	relator *before*	figure *they departed for the airport* [process + participant + circumstance]
figure	participant	thing	2i (process ==> thing) *shredding*		2i (process ==> thing) *departure*
		quality	13i(b) (thing ==> expansion of thing: possessive) *their*		13i(b) (thing ==> expansion of thing: possessive) *their*
		quality	13i(a) (thing ==> expansion of thing: qualifying) *of the documents*		13ii (circumstance ==> expansion of thing: qualifying) *for the airport*
	process			9 (relator ==> process) *precede*	
	circumstance				

These examples of a 'sequence ==> figure' metaphor both involved a sequence of the **expansion** type. However, this type of metaphoric shift also occurs with **projection** sequences; for example:

    The colonel declared his innocence.

— where the congruent form would be a projection, either hypotactic or paratactic:

```
The colonel declared that he was innocent.
The colonel declared, "I am innocent".
```

(III) Figure with process ==> Figure with process as thing

The kinds of syndrome illustrated under (I) and (II) represent the main motifs in ideational metaphor (to be explored further in Section 6.7 below). But there are also syndromes of various other kinds, not clearly belonging to either of these categories. Those illustrated here are variants of the figure ==> element syndrome, where only part of the figure is reconstrued as a participant and the syndrome often involves an elemental metaphor of type 12i (+process).

(1) *They surveyed the property* ==> *(They) did a survey of the property* 12i + 2i + 13i(a)

elements:		figure		
		process *surveyed*	participant *the property*	participant *(they)*
participant	thing	2i (process => thing) *a survey*		
	quality		13i(a) (thing => expansion of thing: qualifying) *of the property*	
process		12i (+ process) *did*		
circumstance				

(2) *They started to survey the property* ==> *(They) started a survey of the property* 12iii + 2i + 13i(a)

elements:		figure		
		process *start to survey*	participant *the property*	participant *(they)*
participant	thing	2i (process ==> thing) *a survey*		
	quality		13i(a) (thing ==> expansion of thing: qualifying) *of the property*	
process		12iii (phase ==> process) *start*		
circumstance				

(3) *They discussed in the early afternoon* ==> *Their discussion took place (in the early afternoon)* 13i(b) + 2i + 12i

		figure		
elements:		process *discussed*	participant *they*	circumstance *(in the early afternoon)*
participant	thing	2i (process ==> thing) *discussion*		
	quality		13i(b) (thing ==> expansion of thing: possessive) *their*	
process		12i (+ process) *took place*		
circumstance				

6.5.2 Paradigmatic complexity: degree of metaphoricity and steps in "unpacking"

In selecting examples to illustrate typical syndromes of grammatical metaphor we chose as far as possible instances where the metaphorical derivation, or re-wording, of each element could be 'unpacked' in a single step. Thus in *the fracture of glass, fracture* has been shifted from process to participant (thing) and *glass* from participant (thing) to qualifying expansion of thing. When we reword as a clause *glass fractures* we have reached a congruent form.

Very often, however, in deriving any one element we should have to take two or more steps in the course of unpacking. For example, in *the development of our understanding*, which has the same immediate history, we can similarly unpack to *our understanding develops*. However, *our understanding* is itself a metaphorical entity consisting of a 'thing' derived from a process; and a 'possessor' derived from a participant; so it can be unpacked further to *we understand*, giving something like *[the way] we understand develops*. We then might want to consider *develops* as (be/ become) quality => process, so *[the extent to which] we understand becomes greater*, i.e. *we understand more and more*. One or two of the examples treated above involved more than one step in this way.

It would take many pages of discussion to follow through such examples discursively in any detail. Instead we will present one brief example with step-by-step unpacking of all the grammatical metaphors simultaneously, using a form of graphic display (with labelling of grammatical functions) which will give a sense of the overall metaphorical space that may be covered in a single instance of this kind: see Figure 6-2.

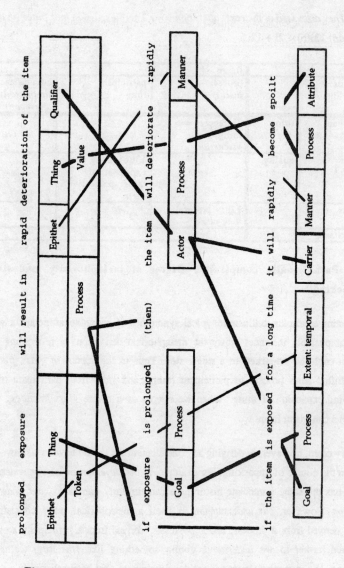

Fig. 6-2: Step by step "unpacking" of metaphorical wording

It will also (see the discussion below) bring out another equally important issue, which takes us back to the point made in Section 6.1 above: that metaphoricity is a relative matter. We can take a pair of agnate expressions and order them with respect to each other, showing that one of the two is more congruent. But if we are rewording in either direction — 'packing' or 'unpacking', to use the (lexical) metaphor that was adopted for this by the students to whom it was originally presented —, there is no clearly definable point where we say 'now we have reached the end'. Obviously we cannot go on for very long; the actual number of steps taken will in fact be extremely limited. But any sequence that is reasonably complex in its semantic patterning will be likely to show considerable elasticity at both ends of the continuum.

One interesting strategy that can be used for 'unpacking' is the following. Take a sentence that is highly metaphorical but reasonably non-technical, and reword it so that you think it would become intelligible to a 15-year-old. Then re-word it again to make it accessible to a 12-year-old; then to a 9-year-old, and then to a child of 6. (It is probably not worth trying to reduce the intervals to less than three years — or the age to less than six!) Ideally this should be done in dialogue with some member, or members, of the age group in question; but if they are not available you can construct them in your mind's eye and attempt it monologically. You may not succeed in enlightening any small children in this way; but you will gain a remarkable insight into the workings of grammatical metaphor. Here is an example from a philosophical text, unpacked step by step in this way.

> "The truest confirmation of the accuracy of our knowledge is the effectiveness of our actions."[3]

> 15 The fact that our knowledge is accurate is best confirmed by the fact that our actions are effective.

> 12 What proves that we know things accurately is the fact that we can act effectively.

> 9 The best way of telling that we know what's happening is to see that what we do is working.

> 6 You know you've got the right idea because you can do something and it works. Like watering plants: you water them, and they grow.

> 3 Look — wasn't it good that we watered that philodendron? See how well it's growing!

Let us know construct a piece of conversation that might be addressed to a three-year-old, and repack it along similar lines:

> 3 Look — it must be raining! People have got their umbrellas open.

---

[3] From Leszek Kolakowski, Main Currents of Marxism, trans. P.S. Falla (Oxford University Press, 1981). There would of course be very many ways of unpacking this particular syndrome of metaphors. We have retained the thematic ordering ('know + accurately' before 'act + effectively'), and the internal form of the logical-semantic relation ('actions prove knowledge', not 'knowledge leads to actions'). We assume that the younger versions would be part of an ongoing dialogue.

6 You can tell it's raining because people have got their umbrellas open.

9 The best way of telling that it's raining is that people's umbrellas are open.

12 What proves that it's rainy weather is the fact that the umbrellas have been extended.

15 The fact that the weather is pluvious is best confirmed by the fact that the umbrellas are extended.

"The truest confirmation of the pluviosity of the weather is the extendedness of the umbrellas."

Like lexical metaphors, so also grammatical metaphors may become codified in the language and 'take over' as the normal mode of expression. We shall refer below (Section 6.7.1) to two instances of this type in English: those like *have a look, take a step* and those like *span, cover, accompany.* There are other features of the grammar that are in origin metaphorical (many of the uses of the possessive form, such as *[he didn't approve of] my leaving home* — cf. the syndromes listed above), but whose origin is so obscured by the natural evolution of the language that all sense of their metaphoric nature has long since been lost.

The overall effect of the grammatical metaphor is that semantic relations between one element and another, and between one figure and another, become progressively less explicit as the degree of metaphoricity increases. We can illustrate this by taking a text example and relating it to more congruent and more metaphorical variants:

[i] (most congruent)

glass		*cracks*		*more quickly*	
participant a	does	process b	acc. to	circumstance c	(lineally determined by how far)

	the harder	*you*		*press*	*on it*
acc. to.	circumstance x	participant w	does	process y	to participant a

[ii]

cracks in glass		*grow*		*faster*	
participant b in a	does	process d	acc. to	circumstance c	(lineally determined by how far)

the more pressure		*is put on*	
participant **xy**	has	process **z**	done to it

[iii]

glass crack growth	*is*	*faster*
participant **abd**	has	attribute **c**

if	*greater stress*		*is applied*	
(under condition that)	participant **xy**	has	process **z**	done to it

[iv]

the rate of glass crack growth	*depends on*	*the magnitude of the applied stress*[*]
participant **c** of **abd**	is caused by	participant **x** of **zy**

[v] (most metaphorical)

glass crack growth rate	*is associated with*	*applied stress magnitude*
participant **abdc**	causes/ is caused by	participant **zyx**

Notice how the semantic information construed by the grammar in the most congruent version is gradually lost at each step in the course of metaphoric rewording.

[*]Original version *the rate of crack growth depends on the magnitude of the applied stress* (from Michalske & Bunker, 'The fracturing of glass', in *Scientific American*, December 1987).

6.6 Metaphor, transcategorization & rankshift: semogenic resources

We noted in our discussion of the grammar (Chapter 1, Section 1.4 above) that the grammars of natural languages include among their resources the potential for **rank shift**, whereby one grammatical unit functions in the place of another: typically, a clause functions in an environment whose original defining occupant is a nominal group. This is one way in which the resources of grammar have expanded as language evolved.

Rank shift is not inherently metaphorical. There is a parallel here between rank shift and **class shift**. In origin, both these could be described as metaphorical *semogenic processes*: a verb or adjective is metamorphosed into a noun (a shift of class, e.g. *strong : strength, lose : loss*), a clause is metamorphosed into a group (a shift of rank, e.g. *they went bankrupt : their bankruptcy*). But *as a synchronic relation* neither of these necessarily involves metaphor; there may be no systematic alternation such as there is between a metaphoric and a congruent form. We have already discussed non-metaphorical forms of class shift, under the heading of **transcategorization**. Similarly, in the following examples of rank shift, where a clause is rankshifted to function either as Head (1, 2) or as Qualifier (3, 4) of a nominal group, no grammatical metaphor is involved:

1. ⟦Not having a proper job⟧ made my life unbearable

(semantically) non-projected figure as participant

(grammatically) clause (as Head of nominal group) functioning (as Agent) in clause structure: "act" type

2. ⟦How they escaped⟧ was a mystery

(semantically) projected figure as participant

(grammatically) clause (as Head of nominal group) functioning (as Carrier) in clause structure: "fact" type

3. That woman ⟦(who was) sitting behind the desk⟧ reminded me of Tracy

(semantically) non-projected figure as quality

(grammatically) clause functioning as Qualifier of nominal group ("defining relative" clause)

4. The idea ⟦that anyone would visit/ of anyone visiting⟧ seems incredible

(semantically) projected figure as quality

(grammatically) clause functioning as Qualifier of nominal group

Class shift becomes metaphorical when the "shifted" term creates a **semantic junction** with the original. A good way of illustrating this is to bring together two instances of the same lexical item, used once as (non-metaphorical) transcategorization and once as grammatical metaphor. Let us return to a previous example (cf. Section 6.1 above):

many failures	are preceded by	the slow extension of existing cracks
process => thing	relator => process	process => thing

More congruently, this would be *many (pieces of glass) fail after the cracks have slowly extended,* or *often the cracks slowly extend and then the glass fails.* The congruent form is a sequence of two figures linked by a relator; in the metaphoric form, each figure becomes a participant and the relator becomes a (relational) process to which two participants subscribe — a syndrome of 2i + 9 + 2i. Here, then, *failure* is an instance of metaphorical class shift; there is a semantic junction between two features:

(1) 'process' (class meaning of verb *fail*),

(2) 'thing/ participant' (class meaning of noun *failure*).

Note that there is an asymmetry between the two — a time line, such that the feature 'thing' is as it were a reconstrual of the original feature 'process': we could gloss it as "a process reconstrued as a participant". Contrast this now with *failure* in a technical expression such as *heart failure;* in origin this was no doubt a grammatical metaphor for *the heart fails,* but the metaphorical quality has since been lost, or at least significantly weakened (the metaphor is "dead"), and *heart failure* is now the only congruent form. Likewise contrast *he regretted his failure to act,* agnate to *that he had failed to act* (or *that he had not acted*), where *failure* is a grammatical metaphor, with *he always felt that he was a failure,* where *failure* is now the congruent form and this is not a metaphorical agnate of *he always felt that he had failed.*

When we reach this point, we find that rank shift sometimes operates as an alternative to class shift of this metaphorical kind. In examples A-1 and A-2, there is metaphorical class shift:

A-1 a cow is a **ruminating** quadruped [verb: adjective; process => quality]

A-2 **your escape** was a miracle [verb: noun; process => thing]

In B-1 and B-2, on the other hand, there is rank shift but no class shift; these are the agnate congruent forms:

B-1 a cow is a quadruped **that chews the cud/ that ruminates**

B-2 it was a miracle **how/ that you got away/ you escaped**

Here 'ruminate' and 'escape' remain as process, without shifting in class. This now helps to explain the meaning of forms such as C-1 and C-2:

C-1 a cow is a **cud-chewing** quadruped

C-2 it was a miracle **you/ your getting away**

These represent a kind of semantic compromise, a means of having it both ways. The junction is now as it were symmetrical, with the time line removed, so that 'chew + cud', 'you + escape' are *simultaneously* both figures and (parts of) elements. What the grammar is construing here is an exchange of functions without shifting class; the figure takes on a special kind of clausal structure which conserves the transitivity relations.

We have shown that the typical manifestation of grammatical metaphor in discourse is as a 'syndrome' of features including both class shift and rank shift. Let us now recall two of the frequently occurring syndromes described earlier, noting where these features occur (we ignore here shifts of type 13, since these follow automatically from types 1 and 2):

(1) Their frequent dismissal of personnel does not inspire people's confidence

[class shift] 2 + 9 + 1 (process 'dismiss' as thing, relator 'cause' as process ['inspire'], quality 'confident' as thing)

[rankshift] sequence as figure

[congruent variant]

Because they frequently dismiss personnel, people are not confident [in them]

(2) Rapid bonding resulted

[class shift] 2 + 9 (process 'bond' as thing, relator 'cause' as process)

[rankshift] none (figure as figure)

[congruent variant]

As a result [the substances] rapidly bonded.[4]

Note that in (2) the other term in the relation is to be presumed from the preceding text.

These two syndromes — really variants of a single syndrome — define the type of clause that might well be considered as the favourite type of modern scientific English. The metaphorical 'things' are packaged processes or qualities that have thematic or informational value in the text, construed as Theme in the clause or New in the information unit (N-Rheme in the clause: see Fries, 1992). The metaphorical 'process' is one of the typical semantic relations that link figures into a sequence: 'cause' & 'time' are the prototypical relations in question, but in modern writing 'identity' has tended to take over as the central type — often by a further metaphorical step whereby *causes* becomes *is the cause of, results* becomes *is the result of.* At the same time, a further distinction has evolved between two kinds of logical-semantic relation: (i) a relation **'in rebus'**

---

[4] Note the distinction between *bonding occurred,* type 11ii, congruently *[the substances] bonded,* and *bonding resulted,* type 9, congruently *so [the substances] bonded.* The wording *bonding ensued* is probably also type 9, congruently *then [the substances] bonded* — although, as is often the case, the metaphorical version is somewhat less explicit, and may suggest more than one congruent unpacking. There is a similar uncertainty with *impose* in the text at the end of Section 6.4 above; we have interpreted *impose proper behaviour on* as agnate to *make ... behave properly,* but it could be unpacked as two figures, *act so that ... behave properly.*

between two experiential events, (ii) a relation **'in verbis'** between two stages in the discourse; e.g.

> (i) Political pressures brought about his downfall. Major changes ensued.

> (ii) This section illustrates the main argument. Further discussion follows.

These correspond respectively to the 'external' and 'internal' types of conjunctive relations in cohesion (Halliday & Hasan, 1976: Ch. 5; Martin, 1992: Section 4.2.3).

6.7 Interpretation of grammatical metaphor

Metaphorical syndromes exploit very general semantic resources which have always been present in the language, but have come to be foregrounded by the new demands made on the language as a result of changing historical conditions during the last half millennium. Grammatical metaphor has played a central part in the construction of new meanings through this period in our history. Let us try to interpret the broad outlines of this development.

In the semantic construction of experience, 'process' and 'participant' emerge as prototypical categories; and there is a broad agreement among different languages both about the nature of this distinction and about which particular phenomena should be assigned to which category. But as in any semiotic endeavour there are always some domains of uncertainty: are rain, wind, thunder processes or things? are fear, worry, regret processes or qualities? Examples like these prevent the categories from being too reified and rigid, and provide a kind of **gateway of analogy** through which a phenomenon can drift or be propelled from one category to another. In transcategorization some other semantic feature triggers the propulsion; e.g. dark + make/ become = *darken*, flake + like/ composed of = *flaky*. In metaphor, however, the phenomenon is reconstrued as another category; what is being exploited is the potential that arises — but only *after* the categories have first been construed as distinct; not otherwise — of *treating* every phenomenon in more ways than one. In this process the original interpretation is not supplanted; it is combined with the new one into a more complex whole.

6.7.1 Motifs in grammatical metaphor

It is possible to distinguish two **predominant motifs** in the phenomena characterized here: one major or primary and one minor or secondary one.

(i) The primary motif is clearly the drift towards 'thing'.

(ii) The secondary motif is what appears as a tendency in the opposite direction: the move from 'thing' into what might be interpreted as a manifestation of 'quality' (qualifying, possessive or classifying expansions of the 'thing').

We will consider the explanation for this secondary motif below; meanwhile, we can summarize the principle of metaphoric shift as in Figure 6-3 (cf. Table 6(2) above).

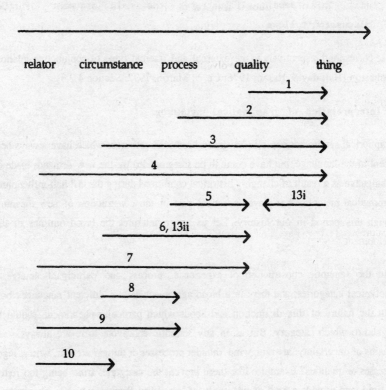

Fig. 6-3: Direction of metaphorization

We can see from this figure that the drift towards 'thinginess' is the culminating and most clearly articulated form of a shift which can be characterized in more general terms as *a shift towards the experiential* — towards that mode of construing experience that is most readily organized into paradigmatic sets and contrasts. Things are more easily taxonomized than qualities, qualities than processes, and processes more easily than circumstances or relations. Since the 'noun-ness' is being used to construe phenomena that start out as something else than a noun, metaphors will inevitably be abstract. If the surgeon *makes an incision*, instead of *cutting*, the cut is being presented as a more abstract version of the experience. This is further reinforced if, as is often the case, the metaphorical term comes from the more highly valued lexical stockpile of Latin and Greek roots.

We can explore the implications of the "drift towards thinginess" by reviewing the different types of element in terms of the potential that they embody for construing experience (cf. Chapter 5 above).

Participants are realized by **nominal groups**, which allow more or less indefinite expansion (through the univariate structure of modification). This expansion is the grammar's way of constructing taxonomies of things: grouping them into classes, assigning properties to them, quantifying them and then uniquely identifying any individual thing, or any number, set or class of things, in relation to the 'here-&-now' of the speech event. The expansion involves open sets of things and qualities, realized by lexical items; but it can also capture a circumstance, realized by a prepositional phrase, or an entire figure, realized by a clause, and put it to use as a quality in describing or identifying such a thing or set of things, e.g. *this unique 20-piece handpainted china dinner service with optional accessories never before offered for sale at such a bargain price.*

Qualities are attached to things, and so contribute to this overall expansion. They also have possibilities of expansion of their own, by submodification (at least for intensity, but sometimes along other lines as well: *very long, longest; dark blue, red hot*).

The grammatical potential of the nominal group for construing taxonomies by syntagmatic expansion was described in Chapter 5, Section 5.3.2.4 above. This grammatical potential for taxonomizing is complemented by the lexical potential of the nominal group for construing feature networks: see Chapter 5, Section 5.3.2.5 above. So by construing any phenomenon of experience as a thing, we give it the maximum potential for semantic elaboration.

Processes are realized by **verbal groups**, where, typically, the only lexical material is the verb itself, functioning as Event (material action or event, conscious or verbal process, or relation). Apart from the adverbial complement of a phrasal verb, which may serve to construct a distinct lexical item e.g. *make out* (*I can't make out the difference*), *come to* (*she'll come to in a minute*), *let on* (*don't let on about this*), &c., all contrasts made by the verbal group are grammatical ones — tense and other quasi-temporal systems, and modality. There is no lexical expansion classifying processes into taxonomies or assigning them sets of contrasting qualities.

Processes do resemble other processes, but they share different features with different others; no single line-up is dominant enough to form the basis for permanent hyponymy. For example, if we consider a small subset of the words expressing verbal processes *offer, tell, promise, threaten, recommend, warn:*

(1) *offer, promise, threaten* have the feature 'offer'; *tell, recommend, warn* have the feature 'command'

(2) *offer, tell* are neutral in orientation; *promise, threaten, recommend, warn* have the feature 'oriented to addressee'

(3) within the addressee-oriented, *promise, recommend* have the feature 'desirable', *threaten, warn* have the feature 'undesirable'.

(4) *offer, promise, recommend* take direct participant ('propose to give ... to Receiver'; 'propose that Receiver should obtain ...').

(5) *tell, warn* take circumstance of Matter 'about ...'.

Processes thus have much less potential than participants for being characterized and taxonomized. For example, with a process like *decide* we can add a circumstance to it, saying *he decided quickly* or *he decided on the spur of the moment;* but if we want to identify the occasion as unique we have to say *this decision, the previous decision, the only good decision he ever made.* We can say *his absurd decision* but not *he decided absurdly* — at least not in the same sense, since *absurdly* could only characterize the figure (how he carried out the act of deciding), not the quality of the process of deciding as such.

The **minor processes** that form circumstances (realized as prepositions in English) are even less taxonomizeable; they are intermediate between processes and relators, and only the spatial ones (spatio-temporal) display any real paradigmatic organization (*to/ from// towards/ away from; inside/ outside// into/ out of; before/ after// in front of/ behind* &c.).

Relators show the least organization of any, since they are experienced only indirectly in the form of logical relations **between** other configurations; they share some of the systematic features of minor processes, but other than that they display only the contrast between the two relative statuses they assign to these configurations, as being equal or unequal (paratactic/ hypotactic, in the grammar) — *a* then *x / x* after *a // b* so *y / y* because *b* &c. Thus a relator can be metaphorically reconstrued into any other category:

relator:	(equal) so	a happened; so x happened
	(unequal) because	x happened, because a happened

=> minor process: because of x happened because of a

=> process: cause   that a happened caused x to happen

=> quality: causal   happening a was (in a) causal (relation)
to happening x

=> thing: cause   happening a was the cause of happening x

— whereas a process can be reconstrued only as a participant (quality or thing), and a quality only as a thing.

Thus in English the more structure that is to be imposed on experience the more pressure there is to construe it in the form of things. But things are merely the end-point of the metaphoric scale, as set out in Figure 6-3. Processes, though more constrained than things, still have more semantic potential than relators: they accommodate categories of time and phase, among others, and are construed in open lexical sets, whereas relators form closed systems. So there is also a pressure there too, to metaphorize conjunctions into verbs: *then, so, because, before, therefore* becoming *follow, result, cause, anticipate, prove.* (Circumstances are something of a special case because most of them already contain participants in minor, subsidiary processes — prepositional phrases in the grammar.) But it remains true that things are the most susceptible of being classified and organized into taxonomies; hence the primary motif of grammatical metaphor is that of construing a world in the form of things.

6.7.2 Metaphoric instability of relators

Let us now look at this phenomenon of metaphoric drift from the other end, asking not what are the special properties of participants that make them the preferred destination of metaphoric movement, but what are the special properties of relators that make them the most volatile and easily displaced. It is clear that, among the various elements involved, the relators are the most unstable in terms of their susceptibility to metaphoric transformation. They are, as it were, the first to leave; and they travel farther than the rest.

We can perhaps link this property of relators to their status in the overall ideation base. Relators construe the highly generalized logico-semantic relations of expansion that join figures into sequences: elaborating, extending, enhancing (Chapter 3, Section 3.2). We have remarked already on the fact that these relationships of expansion pervade very many regions of the semantic system: they are manifested in the organization of figures of being, in the types of circumstantial element that occur within a figure, in the taxonomy of 'things', and elsewhere, as well as of course in their 'home' region of the construal of sequences, as links between one figure and another. This led us to characterize the categories of expansion as "transphenomenal" and as "fractal" (Chapter 5, Section 5.6): transphenomenal in the sense that they re-appear across the spectrum of different types of phenomena construed by the ideational system; and fractal in the sense that they serve as general principles of the construal of experience, generating identical patterns of organization of variable magnitude and in variable semantic environments.

It is these characteristics of relators that make them particularly liable to migrate: to be displaced metaphorically from their congruent status (as paratactic and hypotactic conjunctions) and to appear in other guises in other locations — as minor processes (in circumstantial elements), as processes, as qualities and as things. Thanks to this metaphoric instability, relators are able to play a central part in the re-construal of experience that is a feature of the discourse of the sciences — that makes these discourses possible, in fact, and hence provides the semiotic foundation for the construction of scientific knowledge. We return to this enquiry in Chapter 14 below.

6.7.3 Grammatical metaphor and experiential meaning

The "secondary motif" referred to in Figure 6-3 above, numbered 13i in Table 6(3), is that whereby a 'thing' (congruently construed as a noun functioning as Thing in a nominal group) is metaphorized on the model of some quality — qualifying, possessive or classifying. This represents a shift one step 'backwards' along the logical-experiential scale. It is thus contrary to the prevailing general tendency, since something that is congruently a participant on its own terms is now treated as existing only by virtue of some other participant.

This type of shift occurs only in syndromes, where it accompanies a metaphor of either type 1 or type 2. In such a syndrome, the process is reconstrued as a participant; and as a corollary the participants in that process become its 'qualities'. For example, *Griffith's energy balance approach to strength and fracture*, where the participants *strength and fracture* and *energy balance* have become 'qualities' expanding the metaphoric 'thing' *approach* — compare the more congruent *Griffith approached strength and fracture in terms of (the concept of) energy balance*. The process itself may of course already be metaphorized from something else, e.g. *replace* in

```
The Council's proposed replacement of subsidies by a loan
The Council proposed to replace subsidies by a loan
The Council proposed to lend [money] instead of subsidizing
```

This perturbation of the dominant pattern has the effect of making a participant more abstract. In *the engine failed*, *the engine* is set up as a thing. In *engine failure*, it is as it were deconstructed into a mere characteristic of some other 'thing', a way of classifying failure into its various contrasting kinds, such as *crop failure, power failure* and *heart failure.* The engine has lost its identity — it has no Deictic (note that it cannot be individuated any longer — only the failure can: *this engine failure, the earlier engine failure, any future engine failures,* etc.); and it has exchanged 'thingness' with an ephemeral process, that of failing. But it is still within the compass of a participant in the figure; grammatically, it is within the nominal group.

We can say therefore that grammatical metaphor is predominantly a 'nominalizing' tendency. But if we look at it semantically we can see that it is a shift from the logical towards the experiential: that is, making maximum use of the potential that the system has evolved for classifying experience, by turning all phenomena into the most classifiable form — or at least into a form that is *more* classifiable than that in which they have been congruently construed. We saw in discussing *have a look, make a mistake* &c. that if you make *look, mistake* into nouns you can expand them within nominal groups: *have another good long look, don't make the same silly spelling mistake again!* We now have classes of mistake (*spelling mistake*); properties, both experiential (*long look*) and interpersonal (*silly mistake*), quantities, and identities (*that same mistake, another look, three mistakes*). The same principle holds when any process is reconstrued metaphorically as a thing, as in the many examples cited throughout this section.

It should be remembered that the account we are offering here is always an interpretation of the semantics of English. (We shall refer briefly to metaphor in Chinese in Chapter 7.) In English, then, the metaphoric movement is from the logical towards the experiential and, within the experiential, from processes to things. Hence when we find, in the evolution of scientific discourse in the six centuries since Chaucer's *Treatise on the Astrolabe,* a historical progression in the favoured clause type (along the lines of the implicational scales in Figure 6-3 above):

$$a, \text{ so } x$$

$$\text{because } a, x$$

$$a \text{ causes } x$$

$$a \text{ is the cause of } x$$

we recognize this as a shift towards a more highly taxonomized way of meaning. But the *basis* for such a shift is found in the ordinary spoken language of everyday discourse. Consider the following series of examples:

```
You made three mistakes.
That was his biggest mistake.
Give it another big push.
```

```
She gave him one of her most heart-warming smiles.
Can't I have just two little bites of your cake?
That last dive was the best dive I've ever done.
```

All these are instances of grammatical metaphor, with 'mistake' (verb *err*), *push, smile, bite, dive* turned into things (nouns) and the 'process' taking the form of a lexically very general verb *give, have, do, take, make* which retains the full semantic potential of a figure (tense, modality, &c.). The effect of nominalizing these processes is to open them up to all the 'quality' potential that is associated with things: they can be classified, qualified, quantified, identified and described. This range of grammatical metaphors has become fully codified in English and is, in fact, used by children almost from the start. Another type that is also not specifically associated with learned discourse — with the registers of educational knowledge — is that of *be/ go* + minor process => process (type 8i in Table 6(3)): for example

```
her speech covered five points ('was about')
the road skirts the lake ('goes alongside')
shall I accompany you? ('go with')
this replaces the one you had before ('is instead of')
who does she resemble most? ('is like')
```

These are not in the language of a pre-school child; they are learnt as the written language of the primary school, intermediate between the commonsense language of daily life in the home and the technicalized educational discourse of the secondary school. We shall return to the difference and complementarity between commonsense and educational knowledge in Chapters 14 and 15 .

6.7.4 The significance of grammatical metaphor

We can then summarize our interpretation of grammatical metaphor as follows.

(1) There is an increase in textual meaning, since participants have the most clearly defined status as information: in particular, they can be construed (by the thematic and information systems) into a 'backgrounded + foregrounded' pattern which maximizes the information potential of the figure.

(2) There is a loss of experiential meaning, since the configurational relations are inexplicit and so are many of the semantic features of the elements (e.g. *engine failure : an engine / engines // the engine / the engines; failed / fail / will fail* &c.)

(3) There is a further loss of experiential meaning, since the categories of experience become blurred (*failure* is not most obviously felt as a 'thing', otherwise it would have been construed as such in the first place); the construction of reality becomes a

construction of unreality, detached from ordinary experience and hence inaccessible and remote.

(4) There is however a *gain* in the *potential* for experiential information, because the participant, more than any other element, can be expanded in respect of a wide range of semantic features; this enables anything construed as a *thing* to become part of an experiential taxonomy which embodies far greater generalization about the overall nature of experience. Martin (Halliday & Martin, 1993: Chapters 9 and 10) has shown that it would in fact be impossible to construct technical knowledge without grammatical metaphor of this kind.

Thus grammatical metaphor is a means of having things both ways. An element that is transcategorized loses its original status because of the nature of the semantic feature(s) with which it comes to be combined (e.g. 'like ...' is a quality; so when we say *mousy* 'like a mouse' this is *only* a quality — it has none of the thing-ness of the original mouse). A element that is metaphorized does not lose its original status. Its construction is not triggered by its being associated with any new semantic feature. If it *has* a new semantic feature this is as a result of the metaphorizing process. So *failure* is both process and thing: it is a process construed as a thing (or rather, a phenomenon construed as a process and reconstrued as a thing); its initial status as process remains, but because it has been nominalized, and the prototypical meaning of a noun is a thing, it also acquires a semantic status as something that *participates* in processes: see Figure 6-4. It has become a 'junctional' construct, combining two of the basic properties that the grammar evolved as it grew into a theory of experience.

Metaphors are dangerous, however; they have too much power, and grammatical metaphor is no different in this respect. Because it leaves the relations within a figure almost totally inexplicit, this demands that they should be in some sense already in place. In the typical rhetorical context for the highly favoured 'backgrounding' type, as we have seen, the configurational relations have been established in the preceding discourse: cf. the first example in Section 6.1 above ... *if one takes alcohol one's brain rapidly becomes dull. Alcohol's rapid dulling effect on the brain* ... Here by the time we reach the metaphor they are already in place: we know that *rapid dulling effect* means 'causes ... rapidly to become dull', not any of the other things it might mean such as 'has an effect which soon becomes dull, or blunted'. But this is an idealized example, constructed for the purpose. Usually the configurational pattern will have been built up over long stretches of the text, or (especially if it is a technical form of discourse) over a great variety of different texts — for example, a series of textbooks used in teaching a science subject throughout a school. Very often the learner has to construct the configurational relations from various sources without their being made fully explicit in any one place; and in the limiting (but by no means unusual) case they have never been made explicit at all, so that the figure has to be *construed from the metaphor* — a very difficult task indeed. So the more the extent of grammatical metaphor in a text, the more that text is loaded against the learner, and against anyone who is an outsider to the register in question. It becomes elitist discourse, in which the function of constructing knowledge goes together with the function of restricting access to that knowledge, making it impenetrable to all except those who have the means of admission to the inside, or the select group of those who are already there.

It is this other potential that grammatical metaphor has, for making meaning that is obscure, arcane and exclusive, that makes it ideal as a mode of discourse for establishing and maintaining status, prestige and hierarchy, and to establish the paternalistic authority of a technocratic elite whose message is 'this is all too hard for you to understand; so leave the decision-making to us' (see Lemke, 1990b). Even those who most exploit its potential for organizing and constructing knowledge — theoretical physicists and other specialists in the natural sciences — are now finding that they have had 'too much of a good thing' and are seeking ways of overcoming it and carrying it to less extreme manifestations. But this involves the whole consideration of language in the construal of experience, to which we return in the culminating sections of the book.

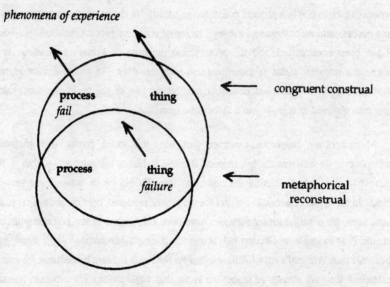

Fig. 6-4: Congruent construal and metaphorical reconstrual — junctional constructs

6.7.5 Metaphor as interpersonal reconstruction

It is many years now since Whorf first drew attention to some of the prevailing metaphors in what he referred to as "Standard Average European" languages: such things as the way cognitive processes are typically construed in terms of concrete actions and movements in physical space: e.g. *grasp, follow* = 'understand', the *line* or *direction* of an argument, and so on (cf. Section 6.2.1 above). In a well-known paper, Reddy (1979) explored this particular domain in greater depth and showed how in English the entire semantic field of saying and sensing is permeated by what he called the "conduit metaphor", according to which meaning is "contained" in thoughts or words and may be "conveyed" along some "channel" from a speaker to a listener.

Lakoff & Johnson (1980), in *Metaphors We Live By*, showed just how many of our basic conceptual schemata and reasoning strategies are shaped by their metaphorical make-up in the everyday language. To continue with this same domain: using examples such as *you're going around in circles, their argument has holes in it, if we keep going the way we're going we'll fit all our facts in*, they demonstrate that the motif of 'argument' is construed by a combination of two metaphors, the 'journey' and the 'container' (Chapter 16). Such patterns of coherence (or "frames of consistency", in Whorf's term) across metaphoric regions are typical of the "structuring of concepts" (p. 96) which determine (to quote their own use of this same metaphor) "how human beings get a handle on the concept" (p. 116) and function with it in daily life.

Although they make some reference to particular grammatical categories (e.g. "with few exceptions, ... in all the languages of the world the word or grammatical device that indicates ACCOMPANIMENT also indicates INSTRUMENTALITY" (p. 135) — *with* in English), Lakoff & Johnson's "metaphors we live by" are largely presented as lexical metaphors: that is, in terms of individual words, and sets of words that are semantically related. Sometimes however the metaphors of daily life arise rather from metaphoric movement in the grammar: for example, many of our everyday expressions for behavioural processes, like *have a bath, take a look, give a smile, do a turn*, involve construing the process (congruently a verb) in the form of a noun. Such metaphors are even less accessible to conscious reflection than the lexical ones, and so readily diffuse throughout the system and become the norm.

Since we are suggesting that grammatical metaphor is not simply an alternative realization of the same meanings, but a distinct construing of experience in which there is junction of semantic features (*have a bath, do a turn* may be "dead metaphors", but in *bring about a conclusion* there is clearly a junction between the 'process' meaning of 'conclude' and the 'thing' meaning of noun), we could expect to find this same phenomenon in lexical metaphor: that the 'literal' meaning of the transferred term would remain, in junction with the features acquired in its metaphorical environment. Just as, in *bring about a conclusion, conclusion* combines the category (word class) meanings of verb and noun, so in *get a handle on the concept, handle* combines the item (word) meanings of *handle* and *idea*. Just one instance, or a few instances, would have little or no effect; but when there is a rather massive frame of consistency whereby the same metaphor, or metaphoric syndrome, extends across a major region of semantic space this must play a significant part in our overall construction of reality. So, to cite another example from Lakoff's work, in his (1992) study of the metaphors "used to justify [the

1990] war in the [Persian] Gulf", he identifies a number of dominant motifs — he refers to these as "metaphoric systems" — such as state-as-person, fairy tale of the just war (with "self-defence" and "rescue" scenarios), ruler-for-state metonymy; war as, selectively, violent crime, competitive game or medicine — all of which he finds to have been applied in portraying Saddam Hussein as villain, Kuwait as victim, and in constructing the concept of "victory" ('the game is over'), of the "costs" of war and so on. Lakoff comments "What metaphor does is limit what we notice, highlight what we do see, and provide part of the inferential structure that we reason with".

Lakoff's conclusion is that, while we cannot avoid such an all-pervasive outbreak of metaphor, we can learn to recognize it and to understand the harmful effects it may have ("that it can kill", in his formulation); we may also be able to seek more benign forms of metaphor to replace it. Looking at such examples in our own terms, we would want to add another dimension to the interpretation, by seeing the metaphoric process as essentially a lexicogrammatical one and pointing to the grammatical element in the overall construct. This enables us to do two things. On the one hand, we can bring out a further aspect of the semantic picture by pointing to the conjunction of *category* meanings — an aspect of grammatical semantics — that is involved; and on the other hand, we can relate this particular metaphoric phenomenon to the overall semantic potential of the system — the construal of experience as a generalized ideation base. And we should stress once again that to describe the "reality" that is construed in this way as being generalized does *not* imply that it is "coherent", in the sense that it is internally consistent and unselfcontradictory. On the contrary: much of the power of metaphor derives from the tensions and contradictions set up (a) within the metaphor itself, (b) between one metaphor and another, and (c) between the metaphor and other regions of the ideation base. Thus to follow through the metaphor of war as game, we can recognize a number of other factors relevant to its interpretation: both are typically construed as behaviour + Range (*fight a battle/ war, play a game/ set ...*); each can stand as metaphor for the other (cf. the language of sports commentaries); the war-as-game metaphor conflicts with their different semantic loadings in affective clauses (e.g. *enjoy the game!*) and, even more, in impersonal existentials (*there's a war on, there was a fierce battle last night* — see below on the depersonalizing of war discourse); and so on. This is not to say that every instance of a lexical metaphor resonates powerfully throughout the grammar. But the general phenomenon of metaphor, as an inherent property of language as a stratified semiotic, is a feature of the system as a whole — of the construal of meaning in lexicogrammatical terms.

One of the instances of grammatical metaphor we will use to illustrate the principle of (lexico-)grammatical unpacking in Section 6.8.3 below was in fact taken from a military training document; so it is interesting to review it in this light. One of the features that stands out is that, with the syndrome of grammatical metaphors, all personalized participants disappear; and it is noticeable that this is not just a feature of this particular clause — there are no human participants throughout the text, with the single exception of *the enemy*, which is the nearest thing to a person that occurs. The following is a typical extract:

```
The Airland Battle Concept outlines an approach to military
operations which realizes the full potential of US forces. Two
notions — extending the battlefield and integrating conventional
nuclear chemical and electronic means — are blended to describe a
battlefield where the enemy is attacked to the full depth of his
formations. What we seek is a capability for early initiative of
offensive action by air and land forces to bring about the
conclusion of the battle on our terms. [...]

This concept does not propose new and radical ways to fight.
Rather it describes conflict in terms of an environment which
considers not only conventional systems, but also chemical,
nuclear, and electronic. It also forces consideration of this
conflict in terms of reaching the enemy's follow-on echelons.
Consideration of such a battlefield is necessary if we are to
reinforce the prospects of winning.
```

What the metaphor does is on the one hand to construct an entirely abstract world of virtual objects such as *concept, approach, capability, environment, considerations, prospects,* and *potential*; and on the other hand to set this up in stark contradiction to the highly concrete processes that begin to emerge as the metaphors are unpacked. This in turn is a kind of hyper-metaphor for modern war, in which the only "military" action taken may be the inherently benign one of keying a message into a computer — the outcome of which is that thousands of people, thousands of miles away, die a violent and wholly unmetaphorical death. Granted that this is an extreme and perhaps sensational example; but the point we are trying to make is one that is central to language itself — namely, that it is the potential for (grammatical) metaphor (itself a product of the stratified ideational resource system) that makes it possible to construe experience in terms of such complementarities and contradictions.

6.7.6 Metaphor as ideational reconstruction

We have suggested that grammatical metaphor has been central in the construction of scientific, or uncommonsense, experience. This is equally true of lexical metaphor: experience construed within various disciplinary frames depends on metaphorical syndromes that are lexicogrammatical in nature — i.e., that combine lexical and grammatical metaphorical syndromes. We will return to this point in Part V when we examine the metaphorical construction of the domain of study in mainstream cognitive science in Chapter 14. Here we will illustrate briefly with reference to the discourse of economics (recall here Whorf's account of intensity in Section 6.2.1 above). Consider the following report from the Federal Reserve Board in the U.S.:

```
Steep declines in capital spending commitments and building
permits, along with a drop in the money stock pushed the leading
composite down for the fifth time in the past 11 months to a
level of 0.5% below its high in [month] [year]. Such a
decline is highly unusual at this stage in an expansion; for
example, in the three most recent expansions, the leaders were
rising, on average, at about a 7% clip at comparable phases in
the cycle. While not signalling an outright recession, the
current protracted sluggishness of the leading indicators
appears consistent with our prognosis of sluggish real GNP
growth over the next few quarters.
```

Economics construes quantities in terms of economic things: either their location and movement in space (shown above in bold) or their size and growth/ shrinkage (shown above in bold italics). These lexicogrammatical metaphors may be further metaphorized by grammatical metaphor, as with 'decline + steeply' ==> 'steep + decline'. These metaphorical movements can then take on participant roles in other movements, as in 'steep declines ... pushed the leading composite down'. The report is highly metaphorical, as the following chain suggests: 'people were committed to spending capital less and less quickly' ==> '[people's] commitments to spending capital declined sharply' ==> 'commitments to capital spending declined sharply' ==> 'capital spending commitments declined sharply' ==> 'sharp decline in capital spending commitments'. We could imagine one step further towards the metaphorical pole: 'sharp capital spending commitment decline'!

The spatial metaphor actually makes it possible to express the domain graphically as well as verbally. The following passage illustrates how the spatial metaphor serves as the cross-over point between the two semiotic systems:[5]

```
With these considerations in mind, we can construct the marginal
cost of funds schedule shown in Figure 4.6. Region A represents
financing done by the firm from retaining earnings (RE) or
depreciation (D). There is no risk factor involved in this
```

[5] From Michael K. Evans, 1969. Macroeconomic Activity. Theory, forecasting and control. New York: Harper & Row, Publishers, p. 89.

region; the only cost of funds is the foregone interest that
could be earned by investing funds elsewhere. Thus true cost of
borrowing in region A is equal to market interest rate. Region
B *represents* financing done by borrowing from banks or bonds. The
sharp rise in the true cost of borrowing is not primarily due to
a rise in the market interest rate at which firms must borrow.
It is due instead to the imputed risk factor which occurs with
increased debt servicing. Region C *represents* financing done
through equity capital. Here again there is no imputed risk,
because the firm does not have to pay dividends. The gradual
upward slope is due to the fact that as a firm offers more and
more of its stock on the market, this will invariably depress
its price and raise the yield that is paid.

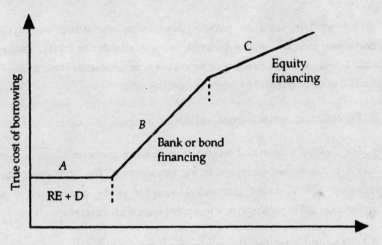

Fig. 4.6

The correlation between the two semiotics is constructed verbally by means of figures of identifying, e.g. *region A represents financing* (shown in italics). Quantities and quantitative changes are construed verbally in an abstract space, e.g. *gradual upward slope* (shown in bold); and also diagrammatically in a symbolic space.

In the construction of meaning in economics, economic things such as prices, salaries, yields, financing are quantities. At the same time, they are also elastic bodies that grow and shrink; and also 'mountaineers', climbing up and down slopes. This is at one level an impossible conjunction: things cannot be both quantities and mobile elastic bodies — but the semantic system of English makes this possible through lexicogrammatical metaphor. This proliferation of perspectives is part of the semogenic power of metaphor.

We noted above that the deployment of spatial metaphor in the construction of economic 'knowledge' serves, among other things, as an interface to another form of semiotic — that of using space symbolically in a diagrammatic representation of quantities. The same kind of principle of cross-over between semiotic modes applies to the construal of meaning in linguistics. We have relied in our own discussion on metaphors of abstract space for construing meaning — most centrally, metaphors of semantic networks and semantic space. These metaphors allow us to cross over to diagrams of symbolic space, viz. system networks (as a kind of acyclic directed graph) and topological representations. The system networks can, in turn, be restated algebraically, as in the various computational implementations of systemic accounts. The question of how to restate the topological representations so that they can be manipulated computationally remains very much more open (see Matthiessen, 1995a, on fuzzy representation).

When we now come to consider the question representing our account of (grammatical) metaphor in analytic terms, we will naturally be asking, among other things, how to represent metaphor as we ourselves metaphorically construe it — as an expansion of semantic space by means of junctions.

6.8 Representing grammatical metaphor

We have sketched a theoretical account of grammatical metaphor — an account that relates it to our overall conception of the ideation base. This still leaves open the question of how to model grammatical metaphor at the lower level of formal representation; and in particular, how to represent junctional categories.

6.8.1 Recapitulation for the purpose of representation

Let us start with a quick recapitulation of the central features of grammatical metaphor. Categories in the ideation base are realized by those categories in the ideational grammar with which they have co-evolved. These are the congruent realizations that developed first in the language, are learnt first by children and tend to occur first in a text. For instance, a sequence is realized by a clause complex, and the figures related in the sequence are realized by the clauses strung together in the clause complex: see Figure 6-5. Thus a sequence consisting of four temporally related figures such as the following:

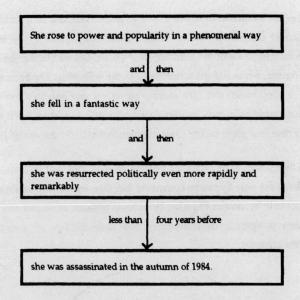

would be realized congruently by a clause complex consisting of four clauses related by enhancement, the first three paratactic and the final pair forming a hypotactic subcomplex:

1 She rose to power and popularity in a phenomenal way, *2 she fell [from power and popularity] in a fantastic way, *3α and then she was resurrected politically even more rapidly and remarkably 3*β less than four years before she was assassinated in the autumn of 1984.

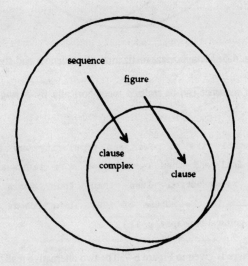

Fig. 6-5: Congruent realizations

(There are metaphors internal to the figures — e.g. phase construed as a vertical motion relative to a quality dimension (*rise to power* = 'become powerful') — but we are concerned with the realization of the sequence as a whole. Deconstructing the metaphors internal to the figures, we would get something like the following: *She became powerful and popular in a phenomenal way, she became powerless and unpopular in a fantastic way, and she was made politically powerful and popular again even more rapidly and remarkably less than four years before she was assassinated in the autumn of 1984.*)

The system then comes to be expanded through shift in rank and in class. Sequences come to be realized not only by clause complexes but also by clauses, and figures come to be realized not only by clauses but also by groups/ phrases, as shown in Figure 6-6. They are pushed downwards in complexity and rank relative to their congruent realizations in the grammar.

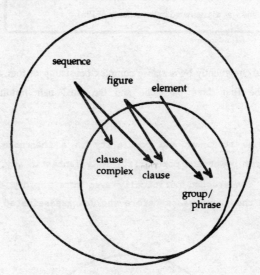

Fig. 6-6: Metaphorical realization of sequences and figures

Thus our earlier sequence can be realized metaphorically by a single circumstantial relational clause:

> Her phenomenal rise to power and popularity was followed by a fantastic fall and then by an even more rapid and remarkable political resurrection less than four years before her assassination in the autumn of 1984. (Inder Malhotra, Indira Gandhi. A personal and political biography. p. 11.)

The clause structure is given in Figure 6-7. The two alternative realizations are shown in Figure 6-8 as a shift from the congruent to the metaphorical within the lexicogrammar. Such a representation suggests that the congruent and the metaphorical are simply realizational variants. But is this kind of interpretation rich enough? At this point, let us consider the issue of representation with respect to structural configurations in text such as the one shown in Figure 6-8. We will then turn to the question of how the metaphorical expansion of the semantic system might be represented.

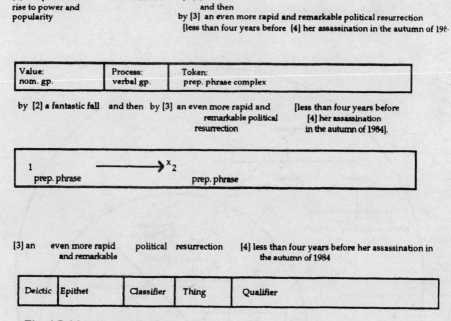

Fig. 6-7: Metaphorical realization of sequence as circumstantial relational clause

6.8.2 Representing text examples

The following are some of the factors to be taken into account when we try to represent examples of semantic structural configurations:

(i) Do we represent the text as it is (metaphorically)?

(ii) Do we represent the text in "unpacked" form (congruently)?

(iii) How far do we unpack it (move towards congruence)?

(iv) If we give two (or more) representations, what relationship do we show between them (how do we show the agnation between congruent and metaphorical)?

For example, given [*engines of the 36 class only appeared on this train*] *in times of reduced loading or engine failure:*

(i) Do we analyse *in times of reduced loading?*

(ii) Do we analyse *when the load was reduced?*

(iii) Do we unpack to *when less freight was being carried?*

(iv) Given the analyses in (i) and (ii) (and (iii) if applicable), how do we show
them to be related?

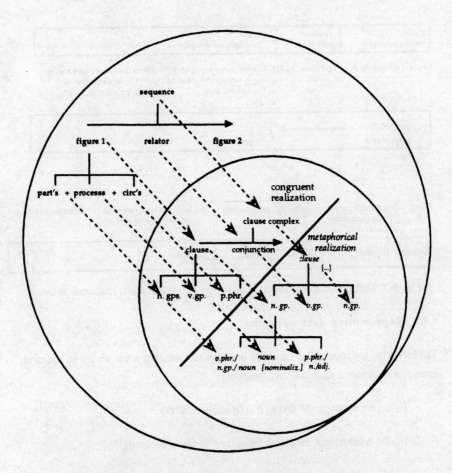

Fig. 6-8: From congruent to metaphorical realization of sequence

(i) Do we represent the text as it is (metaphorically)?

In the account of the introductory example above concerning the fall and rise of Indira
Gandhi, the burden of the representation would be placed entirely on the **inter-stratal**
relation between semantics and lexicogrammar. The metaphorical variant is introduced
merely **as a realizational variant**. In a text-generation system, this would imply
that, instead of a sequence being realized as a clause complex from the start, the

realization is 'delayed' until the grammatical domain is that of the clause rather than the clause complex, and the clausal resources of TRANSITIVITY are used to realize the sequence, as with the example in Figure 6-7. This means that the sequence is realized as a circumstantial relational clause. The first figure is realized as a nominal group serving as the Value and the remaining three figures of the sequence are grouped together as the Token, internally organized as a nominal group complex (if we treat the preposition *by* simply as a structure marker). The last figure is further downgraded as a Qualifier in the second nominal group of the complex. These realizational relations are shown in Figure 6-9.

semantics — sequence   lexicogrammar — clause

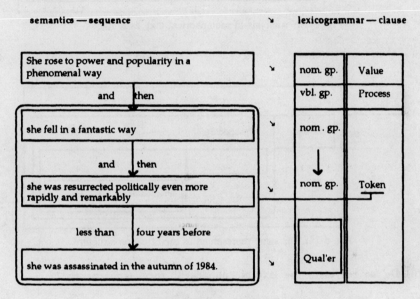

Fig. 6-9: Sequence realized by clause

Such an approach, where grammatical metaphor is a free realizational variant, could be made to work; and there may be good practical reasons for adopting it for certain purposes. However, we have shown that the metaphorical version is not simply a meaningless (i.e. synonymous) variant of some more congruent form; it is **'junctional'** — that is, it embodies semantic features deriving from its own lexicogrammatical properties. We therefore analyse it in the first instance just as it stands — see Figure 6-10 for the engine failure example. Here we have the logico-semantic relation of time 'when' (congruently construed as an expanding sequence) construed as if it was a minor process 'during'; and the figures 'load being reduced' and 'engine failing' construed as elements participating in this minor process.[6]

---

[6] We might note here that in analysing *in times of* as a preposition group we have already gone beyond analysing it strictly 'as it stands', since the Head of the nominal group construction is *times:* that is, the logico-semantic relation is 'first' construed nominally, as if it was itself a participating element (a minor process of location). We can bring this out

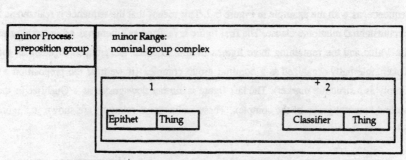

Fig. 6-10: Analysis of metaphorical text 'as it stands'

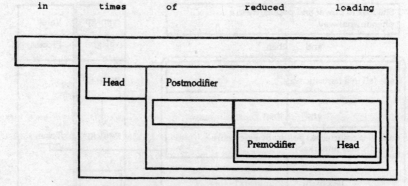

Fig. 6-11: The same represented as modification structure

(ii) Do we represent the text in "unpacked" form (congruently)?

If the metaphor can be unpacked — demetaphorized — to yield a more congruent wording such as *when(ever) the load was reduced, or an engine failed,* then we can represent the text over again in this congruent form (see Figure 6-12). Here the sequential logico-semantic relation of time is construed as a hypotactic conjunction *when* (or *whenever*), and 'being reduced' and 'failing' are construed as processes. What we are saying, with this analysis, is that *in times of* ... represents a separate figure, rather than a circumstance within a figure; and that this in turn is made up of a paratactic sequence of two figures, one ascriptive 'the load was reduced' (or possibly one of doing-&-happening, 'the load had been reduced'), the other one of doing & happening 'the engine failed'. The

---

by representing the nominal structure logically in terms of modification (see Figure 6-11). It would be possible to go one stage further and interpret *times* experientially as Thing; if we do this we are saying that it is actively metaphorical, retaining the semantic feature of participant from its realization as a noun. Usually in analysing contemporary texts we do not treat forms such as these as active metaphors (cf. facet expressions such as *in front of*), since they appear semantically and grammatically dormant. Historically all such expressions embody a nominalizing metaphor.

text as it stands is metaphorical; a more congruent construal would be as reworded here; and the analysis now reveals the difference between the two.

```
...   when the load was     reduced   or an engine   failed
```

α	x β						
	1				**+**		
		Carrier	Process: ascriptive & intensive	Attribute		Actor	Process: material
	conj.: hypo.	nom. gp.	verbal gp.	nom. gp.	conj.: para.	nom. gp.	verbal gp.

Fig. 6-12: Analysis of metaphorical text reworded in more congruent form

(iii) How far do we unpack it (move towards congruence)?

Regarding question (iii), we could continue to 'unpack' the metaphor further at one point, for example from *(when) the load was reduced* to *(when) less freight was being carried*. This does not change its status as a figure; it merely redistributes the semantic features among the elements of the figure (see Figure 6-13).

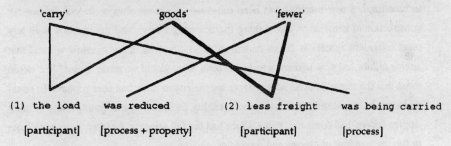

'carry'	'goods'	'fewer'
(1) the load was reduced	(2) less freight	was being carried
[participant] [process + property]	[participant]	[process]

Fig. 6-13: Further unpacking of first figure in paratactic expansion

The argument against taking this further step is that it introduces another element of metaphor. In (1), the bracketing is ((carry + goods): **fewer**), and this construes the message congruently with 'the goods carried' as point of departure (*the load* as Subject/ Theme) and 'fewer' in culminative position; whereas in (2) the bracketing is ((goods + fewer): **carry**), which distributes the information in a rather less congruent form, having 'carry' instead of 'fewer' in the position typically associated with the 'news'. In other words, the cost of removing the experiential metaphor is to introduce a new textual metaphor; this provides an important insight into why experiential metaphors evolve in the first place, namely in order to get the texture right (cf. Section 6.3 above; Halliday, in press a, b), but is also a useful criterion for stopping short in the process of unpacking. Of course, this is a feature that applies only to certain classes of example, not to all; but it is typical of the sort of consideration that would be relevant to answering the third of our four questions.

(iv) How do we show the agnation between congruent and metaphorical?

Coming now to the fourth question: how do we show the analyses under (i) and (ii) to be related? There are really two distinct parts to this question. One is: do we need two separate phases in our representation? And the second is: if we *do* need both, do we need a third phase whereby the two are shown to be related? The first raises the issue of metaphorical junction. In our interpretation, the text as it stands, with the grammatical metaphor left in, embodies semantic junction: it is not just a variant form, identical in meaning with its congruent agnate — it also incorporates semantic features from the categories that its own form would congruently construe. Thus *engine failure* is not synonymous with *engines fail;* it is *both* a figure consisting of participant ('engine') and process ('fail') *and* an element (participant) consisting of thing ('failure') + classifier ('engine'). In other words, we need both analyses in order to represent it adequately.

This will always be true whenever the metaphor can be unpacked to yield a plausible more congruent form. And this is what distinguishes a grammatical metaphor from a technical term. Almost all technical terms start out as grammatical metaphors; but they are grammatical metaphors which can no longer be unpacked. When a wording becomes technicalized, a new meaning has been construed — almost always, in our present-day construction of knowledge, a new thing (participating entity); and the junction with any more congruent agnates is (more or less quickly) dissolved. If for example we said that *engine failure* had now become a technical term, what would we mean by this? We would mean that the semantic bond with a figure *an/ the engine fails* had been ruptured (it could no longer be 'unpacked'); and that a new meaning, an abstract participating entity or thing 'engine failure' had come into being which had the full semantic freedom — to participate in figures, to admit of classes and properties, and the like.

But let us return to grammatical metaphor that has not become technicalized and retains its character as semantic junction. Here we might want not merely to retain the two phases of representation, that of the metaphorical wording as it stands and that of the congruent wording as it is unpacked, but also to build in some representation of the agnate relationship between them. This can be done with some kind of composite representation as in Figure 6-14 (and cf. Figures 6-1, 6-2 above). (Such diagrams are considerably more effective if they can be colour-coded.)

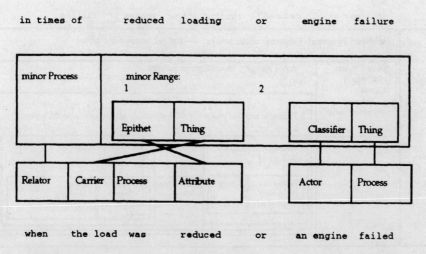

Fig. 6-14: Composite representation of metaphorical and congruent wordings

The alternative is to try to conflate the two into a single representational phase. It is difficult to do this without making the result far too complicated; but an attempt is made in Figure 6-15. What this does is set up distinct junctional categories based on the types of grammatical metaphor shown in Table 6(3) above. This kind of approach is perhaps the one to be developed further, since it brings out more clearly the potential of grammatical metaphor as a semogenic resource. But we shall not attempt to pursue it further here.

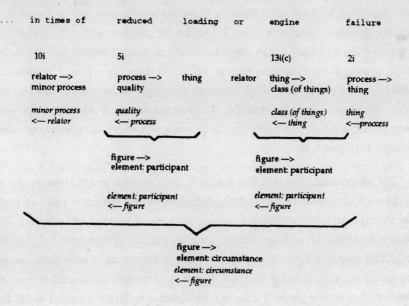

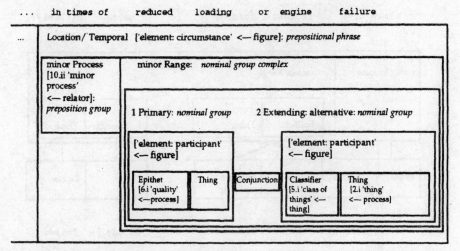

Fig. 6-15: Single phase representation of text with metaphorical wording

6.8.3 Grammatical metaphor as elaborating relation between semantic configurations

The type of representation used in Figure 6-14 (and also in the representation of the 'prolonged exposure' example in Section 6.5 above) shows metaphor as a correspondence between two semantic configurations. The correspondence that is construed through grammatical metaphor is an **elaborating relationship**: an identity is set up between two patterns, a sequence and a figure, a figure and a participant, and so on. In this identity, the metaphorical term is the 'Token' and the congruent term is the 'Value' (cf. Figure 6-4 above): 'engine failure' stands for (means, represents) 'engines fail'. This is the 'core' meaning of the elaborating relation; but it also covers the senses of 'summarize', 'distil' — the metaphor may 'distil' congruent meanings that have accumulated in the text. The identity holds between the two configurations as a whole; but, as our representations indicate, the components of the configurations are also mapped one on to another: see Figure 6-16.

The metaphorical relation is thus similar to **inter-stratal realization** in that it construes a token-value type of relation. Here, however, the relation is **intra-stratal**: the identity holds between different meanings, not between meanings and wordings. The metaphor consists in relating different semantic domains of experience (cf. Section 6.2.1): the domain of figures is construed in terms of the domain of participants, and so on (just as in a familiar lexical metaphor the domain of intensity is construed in terms of the domain of vertical space). It is the fact that metaphor multiplies meanings within the semantic system that opens up the possibility of metaphorical chains, with one congruent starting-point and another highly metaphorical end-point (A''' stands for A'' stands for A' stands for A; e.g. 'engine failure' stands for 'the failing of an engine' stands for 'an engine failed'). The semantic system is being expanded along the dimension of the metaphorical token-value relation; but the expansion is still within the semantic system itself.

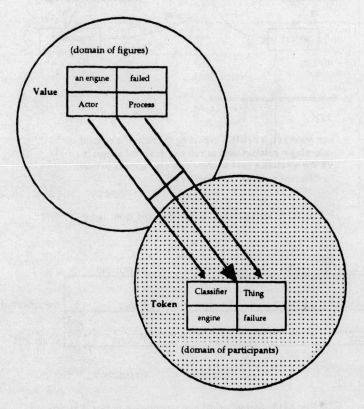

Fig. 6-16: Metaphorical Token representing congruent Value

Another possible form of representation would be in terms of the VIEW relation introduced by Jacobs (1987) to handle metaphorical pairs. Jacobs suggests that the relationship between pairs such as *Ali punched Frazier* and *Ali gave Frazier a punch* can be handled at the level of conceptual structure by means of a metaphorical relation of VIEW set up between the two types of process. The VIEW represents the metaphor of action as transfer-event, in Jacobs' terms: see Figure 6-17. According to this representation, an action is viewed as a transfer-event and the object of the action as the recipient of the transfer. The VIEW relation reflects the same type of correspondence that is embodied in the box diagram interpretation of a grammatical metaphor used in Halliday (1985); cf. Figure 6-14 above. For instance, the metaphorical example *Ali gave Frazier a punch* can be diagrammed as in Figure 6-18. Note that the metaphorical function of *a punch* is modelled not on that of Goal but on that of Range — in traditional terms, it is a "cognate object" rather than a "direct object" (Halliday, 1985: Section 5.6).

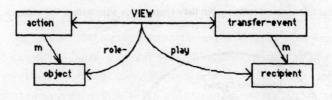

KEY:

m = manifest, a relation indicating the role of a concept
role-play = relation used to roles of different concepts
VIEW = a relation used to show correspondences between
    different concepts and their roles

Fig. 6-17: Metaphorical VIEW adapted from Jacobs (1987)

Ali	gave	Frazier	a punch	
Actor	Process	Recipient	Range	metaphorical
Actor		Goal	Process	congruent

'Ali   (ii) Frazier   (i) punched'

Fig. 6-18: Metaphorical correspondence in box diagram

For most types of metaphor, it is important to take account of the fact that the metaphor represents more than one construction of goings-on; the metaphor adds a further perspective on the phenomenon being represented, without displacing the perspective that is congruent. Thus, *Ali gave Frazier a punch* is like *Ali gave Frazier a rose;* but it is also unlike it, precisely because of its metaphorical status: it evokes a non-metaphorical agnate *Ali punched Frazier*. There are also grammatical distinctions between the two; for instance, there is no systematic proportion

```
Ali gave Frazier a rose : Ali gave a rose to Frazier  ::
Ali gave Frazier a punch : Ali gave a punch to Frazier
```

The grammatical metaphor will typically show features of the congruent perspective as well as features of the metaphorical one.

The approach outlined by Jacobs may account for certain types of grammatical metaphor. However, it leaves a number of issues still to be addressed. (i) The VIEW relation represents the correspondence between two concepts and their roles, but it does not adequately represent the meaning of the metaphorical view. For instance, what does it mean to view an 'action' as a 'transfer-event'? (ii) Secondly, it does not take account of the conditions under which the metaphorical view is chosen over the congruent one. For instance, with an example such as 'Ali gave Frazier a punch', the crucial factor is probably not that it is being viewed as a transfer-event; rather, a more complex twofold "remeaning" has taken place. The process 'punched' is being represented as a participant 'a punch': it thus takes on the experiential status of a thing — it is objectified, and so can be disposed of (like a gift); and by the same token, it takes on the textual potential whereby it can appear in culminative position in the clause — the unmarked locus of new information. But it does not thereby lose its experiential standing as a process.

As far as representing text instances of grammatical metaphor is concerned, the two forms of representation that we have used in our own discussion in this section — the composite box diagram above, and the arrow-field diagram (Figure 6-8 in Section 6.8.1) — could be seen as variants of Jacobs' view approach. But they do perhaps constitute a third type, since they show the construction of metaphorical space; or rather, the metaphorical construction of space, the way the grammatical metaphor adds a further dimension of depth to semantic construal of experience. The box diagram shows this in synoptic form, presenting each element in the grammatical structure as semantically complex. The arrow-field diagram shows it in dynamic form, the motifs of the congruent wording being tracked through one by one to their metaphorical values.

As we presented these, they both portrayed a simple binary relation between two forms of wording, one metaphorical the other congruent. But we have pointed out more than once that the metaphorical dimension in grammar is in reality a cline. There are often numerous intermediate steps between the "most congruent" and the "most metaphorical" wordings; indeed it is the scale of metaphoricity that is reasonably clearly defined, not its end points. Given two agnate wordings that are positioned along this scale, we seldom have any difficulty in locating them relative to each other: we know which of the two is the more metaphorical one. But we hard put to it to specify a point at either end where we feel we could go no further.

It is not difficult to embody these intermediate steps in a form of representation such as the following in Fig. 6-19. This does not incorporate any new features; it merely combines the direction of derivation with the functional labelling. What it does, however, is to model the history of the particular instance, showing what semantic features it has, as it were, picked up along the way. It would be possible to explore many other modes of visual presentation; there is no single ideal form, and the approach will vary according to the purpose of the teacher or researcher. Any picture that brings out the two properties of elasticity and directionality would meet the basic requirements.

Value	=	Token		early			early					
What we seek	is		a capability for	early	initiative of	offensive action		by air and land forces	to bring about	the conclusion of	battle	on our terms
we seek		air and land forces	should be capable of		initiating	acting offensively	early		in order to	conclude	battling	in our favour
we want		air and land forces	to be able to		start	attacking	early		so as to	finish	fighting	on top
we want		airmen and soldiers	must be able to		attack		early ?= first		so as to		win	

metaphorical → congruent

|| [[what | we | seek]] | is | a capability [for [early initiative [of [offensive action [by
[air and land forces]] [[to bring about |
the conclusion [of [battle]] [on [our terms]]]]]]]] ||

Fig. 6-19: From metaphorical to congruent with intermediate steps

6.8.4 The representation of metaphor in the system

We have considered how metaphorical examples might be represented as semantic configurations related to congruent configurations, very likely with several intermediate steps. We now have to take one step further and explore how semantic **types** can be represented as metaphorically related to congruent types within the overall semantic system. Such a representation has to meet the kinds of ideational and textual demands that we have already considered in our representation of examples:

(i) ideational: the representation has to show that metaphor constitutes an expansion of the semantic system. The expansion is an elaborating one, creating chains of token-value relations; and it increases the semantic potential for construing experience.

(ii) textual: the representation has to make it possible to show how metaphorical and congruent variants are given different values in the text base — in the textual semantics.

These considerations suggest to us that metaphor is best construed as an opening up of a new dimension of the semantic system that allows the whole system to be elaborated by itself along a token-value chain. In other words, what we identified as a simplified way of dealing with grammatical metaphor in the relation between semantics and lexicogrammar in Figure 6-8 we can now recognize as a dimension internal to the semantic system. Figure 6-20 shows this opening up of a metaphorical dimension within the semantic system.

This diagrammatic sketch is also intended to show that metaphor involves a mapping from one ideational domain to another, construing a value-token relation between the two (cf. Figure 6-16 above). For instance, the whole semantic domain of sequences may be mapped onto the domain of figures. The token domain may in turn be the value in a further metaphorical move, such as the move from figures to participants. The metaphorical expansion thus can thus involve multiple planes. As we noted above in Section 6.7, the general tendency in the metaphorical move away from the congruent is away from the logical towards the experiential; and within the experiential towards the domain of participants in figures of being & having. We shall return at the end to a related aspect of this move — a move from commonsense or folk models of our experience towards uncommonsense or scientific ones — and illustrate it from the field of cognitive science with respect to the construal of 'the mind' (see Chapter 14). The proliferation of ideational meaning through metaphor thus also means that a person gains access to a wider repertoire of communicative roles.

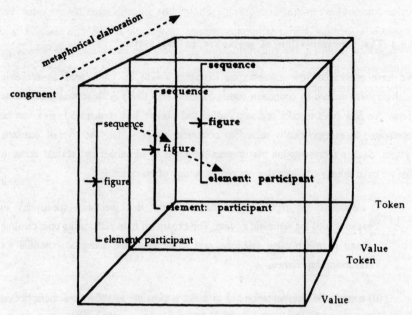

Fig. 6-20: Metaphorical elaboration of the semantic system

Each 'plane' has the same kind of interface to the textual metafunction. In choosing whether to construe some phenomenon as a sequence of figures or as a sequence reconstrued as a figure, we can thus also compare the implications for the textual presentation of these alternative ideational articulations as quanta of information.

Each plane also has the same realizational potential in the lexicogrammar. Thus if the domain of sequences is construed metaphorically within the domain of figures, the realizational domain in the grammar will automatically be that of the metaphor: it will be the domain of clauses rather than that of clause complexes.

The diagram in Figure 6-20 illustrates global mappings between sequences and figures, and between figures and participants. We also need to take account of local mappings: some more delicate type of figure must be able to be represented by some more delicate type of participant. Thus figures of quality ascription will typically be represented by participants with the quality rather than the process reified as the thing: 'her speech was brilliant' ==> 'the brilliance of her speech'.

Our representational sketch is just that — a sketch. Many details have to be filled in; and the representation has to be made fully explicit. There is one further consideration we have not mentioned yet that we believe is part of the key to a general solution of the representational problem. The whole metaphorical elaboration is made possible by a *fractal pattern* that runs through the whole system. We have suggested that the metaphorical elaboration is a token-value relation; but in order for it to be a token-value relation within the semantic system, it has to be natural in the sense that the token and value domains have to be similar enough to allow the token to stand for the value. For instance, a sequence has to be similar enough to a figure to allow it to stand as a metaphorical token for this congruent value. The principle behind this similarity is the fractal pattern of projection/ expansion that we met throughout the semantic system of sequences, figures, and elements in Chapters 3, 4, and 5 above and that was summarized in Section 5.6.

That is, while grammatical metaphor constitutes a move from one "phenomenal domain" to another — from sequence to figure, and from figure to element, this move is made possible because the fractal types engender continuity across these domains: the metaphorical move from one phenomenal domain to another takes place within one and the same transphenomenal domain. For example, the metaphorical shift from *he added and smiled* to *he added with a smile* is a shift from the phenomenal domain of sequence to the phenomenal domain of figure (accompanied by the shift from figure *and smiled* to element *with a smile*); but the transphenomenal domain of 'extension' remains constant: the extending sequence *he added and smiled* is metaphorically agnate with the figure *he added with a smile* with an extending circumstance.

The detailed example of 'cause' as a grammatical motif given in Appendix 3 of Halliday (1994) can be interpreted along these lines: 'cause' is a transphenomenal type within the more general type of 'enhancement'. It is manifested within sequences, figures and elements, so like other transphenomenal types it engenders transphenomenal relations of agnation involving grammatical metaphor (cf. the schematic example on p. 267 above); for example:

> [sequence (congruent):]
>
> she died, **because** she didn't know the rules
>
> [figure (metaphorical):]
>
> she died **through** ignorance of the rules
>
> her death was **due to** ignorance of the rules
>
> her death **was caused by** ignorance of the rules
>
> ignorance of the rules was the **cause** of her death
>
> [element (metaphorical):] her death **due to** ignorance of the rules (was reported in the paper)

In conclusion, we will give one set of examples for each transphenomenal type: see Table 6(4). (For further examples, see Matthiessen, 1995b: 163-8.)

Table 6(4): Transphenomenal agnation

	projection	expansion		
		elaboration	extension	enhancement
sequence	He ordered that the chief be dismissed	The treaty was concluded, which was important	He added and smiled	Matthew sloped off to chat with Kate
figure	He ordered the dismissal of the chief.	The conclusion of the treaty was important	He added with a smile	Matthew sloped off for a chat with Kate

7. Comparison with Chinese

In our descriptive account so far we have focussed almost entirely on English; but having established a fairly comprehensive (though not very delicate) map of the resources of English ideational semantics, we should now be able to compare and contrast with other languages. Here we shall provide a very brief sketch of Chinese ideational semantics against the background of our previous account of English; and in Section 7.8 below, we shall conclude with a few remarks about typological variation across languages in general. Comparative description of this kind is important not only for theoretical reasons but also in relation to tasks in natural language processing such as machine translation and multilingual text generation and understanding.

7.1 Historical background

In the perspective of world languages as a whole, Chinese and English share many common features in their histories. Both are languages that have been associated with a long period of settlement. In their modern form, both have been shaped by the extended period over which their speakers were first and foremost agricultural producers, living in villages, staying most of the time in one place, and very gradually developing on the one hand the technology and on the other hand the forms of social organization that went with their agricultural life style. Both languages were written down; some members of the community learnt to make meaning in the written mode, by reading and writing, while others did not. And both languages engendered forms of verbal art and other highly valued discourse such as religious texts, which were on the one hand codified in writing and on the other hand also committed to memory. In all these respects Chinese and English have much more in common, in their historical conditions, than either has with languages that developed outside the Eurasian culture band (or with many that developed within it, such as the languages of the Caucasus).

There are also some far-reaching differences. The two belong, obviously, to different ends of that cultural continuum, and were located within very different material environments. In particular, English emerged out of the westward movement from the centre of the continent, while Chinese evolved in the migration towards the east; the trek to the west, into and across Europe, was much more uneven, sporadic, and disruptive than the relatively steady and homogeneous eastward movement (only relatively steady, of course, but significantly more so than the shifts of population into Europe). More importantly, perhaps, while Chinese was always at the centre of the eastern cultural sphere, English — at least for the time during which it has had a distinct history — has mostly been at the periphery. In that respect, English has evolved under conditions more like those of Japanese. The populations of Britain and Japan were both regularly overrun from outside: Britain by Celts, Romans, Anglo-Saxons and Norsemen/ Normans; Japan by Austronesians, Altaic peoples and Chinese, each following the previous arrivals within some five to seven centuries; their modes of production and social structures, including the structures of feudalism, were evolved with frequent intrusions from outside. The time depth was fairly similar (even the present hereditary monarchies in Japan and Britain probably originated in the same century). Similarly, the Japanese and English languages were first written down at roughly the same time — each in a script that was imported from another language (in the case of English, a distantly related language; in the case of Japanese, a language that was not related at all, namely Chinese).

Both Japanese and English evolved through various perturbations and discontinuities, and probably both were equally creolized in the process (whereas Chinese remained very largely unmixed). Japanese borrowed its learned vocabulary from (ultimately classical) Chinese, English from (ultimately classical) Latin; both languages of learning came in more than one wave, and both were mediated through spoken languages descended from these classical tongues (early forms of Northern (Mandarin) and Central (Wu) Chinese; Norman and other early forms of French). In the modern forms of English and Japanese, the relative frequency, the functions and the domains of the borrowed vocabulary are remarkably similar. The effect, in both, has been to develop two co-existent phonological systems, which are only partly homogenized, and are kept apart (more or less clearly) by their different representation in the script (in English, the spellings of Graeco-Romance and Anglo-Saxon words follow distinct conventions; in Japanese, words of Chinese origin are written in kanji, those of Japanese origin in a mixture of kanji and kana). There is an interesting reversal at this point: in English, the learned words tend to be long and morphologically complex, the native words short and simple, whereas in Japanese it is the other way round.

Both English and Japanese have been heavily technologized, as their countries became, in turn, the 'workshop of the world' — Britain in the nineteenth century, followed by America after two world wars; and now Japan. Chinese technology led the world for about two thousand years, till about 1500; its technical forms of discourse were then comparable to those of late medieval Latin. But there was no effective development of scientific discourse in Chinese till the beginning of the twentieth century. Now, 100 years later, scientific Chinese is strikingly similar to scientific English, partly because it has borrowed some of the semantic styles, through translation, and partly because scientific registers tend to call for the same kind of organization anyway. But there are no *word* borrowings in Chinese, or hardly any; unlike English and Japanese, both of which are 'borrowing' languages, Chinese creates new word meanings by 'calquing' — constructing new forms out of its own lexical stock by compounding, often on the model of some outside source. All three are now 'Pacific Rim' languages, with English in the United States, Canada, Singapore, Australia and New Zealand and Chinese not only in mainland China, Hong Kong (soon to be part of mainland China), Taiwan and Singapore, but also wherever there are overseas Chinese communities; Japanese remains, up to now, relatively unexported. And all three are major languages of information, likely to be the centre of information technology, from word processing to machine translation, for as far as we can see into the future (but it would be rash to predict beyond about twenty-five years).

Following this thumbnail sketch of the historical context, we shall attempt to make a few points suggesting how Chinese would be represented, by comparison with English, in terms of the model we have outlined.

7.2 Some general features compared

It goes without saying that Chinese shares with English all those properties which are the properties of human language as such. But despite the many assertions that are made about "language universals", these are from being clearly defined — largely because, in our view, they have usually been sought at rather too concrete a level. We shall not attempt to explore this issue here. In what follows we shall simply present certain features in respect of which Chinese may be contrasted with English, in its construal of ideational meaning; beginning with a few general observations and then proceeding to some more specific points of comparison (cf. Halliday, 1956; 1959).

(i) As we pointed out right at the start, one property of language which is universal is the stratal organization of the content plane into semantics and lexicogrammar, with the lexicogrammatical stratum forming a continuum: at one pole are the most "grammatical" features, closed systems of just two or three terms, mutually defining along a single dimension and with very general meanings and contexts of use; at the other pole are the most lexical features, open sets of an indefinite number of items, taxonomically arranged along various dimensions and with highly specific meanings and contexts of use.

In most cases, the two languages locate the various semantic domains at roughly equivalent points along the lexicogrammatical continuum. Thus, in both, polarity, person and nominal deixis are clearly grammatical, while the vast thesaurus of experiential categories of processes, things and qualities are clearly lexical. But there are one or two significant disparities. For example, Chinese treats the "phase" of a process more grammatically than English: there is in the Chinese verbal group a network of systems of completive phase and directional phase realized by a large but closed set of "post-verbs" (postpositive verbs), e.g.:

completive: --断 *duàn* 'apart, into two pieces'

折 *zhé*	break	折断 *zhéduàn*	break in two
剪 *jiǎn*	cut (with scissors)	剪断 *jiǎnduàn*	cut in two
切 *qiē*	cut (with knife)	切断 *qiēduàn*	cut in two
砍 *kǎn*	chop (e.g. tree)	砍断 *kǎnduàn*	chop down
摔 *shuāi*	fall (of person)	摔断 *shuāiduàn*	break (limb) by falling

directional: --出 *chū* 'exit' (often in compound 出来 *chūlái* 'come out', 出去 *chūqù* 'go out')

看 *kàn*	look	看出来 *kànchūlái*	make out by looking
走 *zǒu*	walk	走出 *zǒuchū*	walk out
分 *fēn*	separate	分出 *fēnchū*	distinguish
赶 *gǎn*	chase, drive	赶出 *gǎnchū*	drive out

On the other hand, "tense" (linear time) in Chinese is considerably less grammaticalized than in English, being construed through definite and indefinite time adverbs like 'already', 'soon', 'yesterday', 'last year'; and there is no necessary representation of linear time in the clause (see next point).

(ii) In English, while lexicalized meanings are optional, grammaticalized meanings are typically obligatory in their functional environments. For example, the English nominal group *the train* is entirely neutral as between 'passenger' and 'goods', and among 'electric', 'steam' and 'diesel', because these meanings are construed lexically; but it is explicitly 'singular' (and therefore 'not plural'), and it is explicitly marked as 'definite — identity known', because number and deixis are construed grammatically. Thus *train* does not normally occur as a nominal group by itself; the deixis is always specified (note that the plural *trains is* selecting explicitly in the deictic system).

In Chinese, on the other hand, not only lexicalized meanings but also many of those that are construed grammatically have this characteristic of being optional. So 火车 *huǒchē* 'train' is neutral not only as regards consciousness of cargo and type of fuel but also as regards both number and deixis. It regularly occurs as a nominal group by itself, and may be equivalent to English 'a train', 'trains', 'the train' or 'the trains'. (Number is obligatory in Chinese only in the personal pronouns; deixis not at all.) Similarly, aspect in Chinese, while — unlike tense — it is fully grammaticalized, includes a "neutral" (unmarked) term in which neither perfective nor imperfective is selected.

(iii) Thirdly, and related to the last point, if we look at Chinese from the point of view of English, it appears that in its lexicogrammar as a whole there is some tendency for avoiding unnecessary specificity. As we have seen, grammatical systems tend to have unmarked, neutral terms; the neutral term "opts out" from choosing in the system — either because the systemic choice will be irrelevant in the given context, or because, while it is not irrelevant, the meaning is construed elsewhere (in the text or in the situation). Likewise lexically, at least in construing participants, it is typical for Chinese to use a general term where the more specific one, even if relevant, is rendered unnecessary by the context. We can illustrate both of these from a single example: imagine parent and child standing at a bus stop, and the bus arriving in front of them. The English speaking parent says *Hurry up and get on the bus!* The Chinese speaking parent says

你快上车吧！ *Nǐ kuài shàng chē ba!* 'you + quickly + go up + wheeled vehicle [+ mood particle]'. English specifies **both** (grammatically) the deixis — that the bus is identifiable (in this case by the situation; they may also have been talking about it) — **and** (lexically) the type of vehicle. Chinese specifies neither; there is no need for a deictic (such as 那个 *nàge* 'that'), and no need to specify that the vehicle is a bus (公共汽车 *gōnggòng qìchē*) as distinct from a train (火车 *huǒchē*) or a horse drawn cart (马车 *mǎchē*). It would seem a little odd to bring in any further detail!

(iv) Fourthly, while in technical and other elaborated forms of Chinese the nominalizing tendency of grammatical metaphor is every bit as prominent a feature as it is in English, it perhaps does not penetrate as deeply into everyday discourse. To give a simple example: in English, a typical, and entirely colloquial, answer to an enquiry about some commodity in a shop or market would be *they come in all sizes*. The more likely answer in Chinese would be 大的小的都有 *dàde xiǎode dōu yǒu* 'there are both big ones and little ones'. This is not from any lack of the relevant abstract terms such as 'size'; in some cases Chinese is more endowed with these than English is, because Chinese distinguishes between two different senses of such terms: between size meaning 'how big?' (as in *I need to know the size*) and size meaning 'the fact that ... is big' (as in *I'm impressed by the size*). But there are numerous kinds of expression like these where the more nominalized form has not taken over in the encounters of daily life.

All these points will be illustrated in more specific contexts in the course of the next few sections.

7.3 Sequences

Sequences, figures and elements are distinguished, and related to each other, in Chinese as they are in English, with the same congruent realizations in the grammar:

sequence ↘	clause complex
figure ↘	clause
element ↘	element of clause structure

The degree of overall indeterminacy is about the same as that in English.

In the written language, the clause complex is codified as a sentence. In spoken Chinese (Mandarin), as in English, decisions have to be take about where clause complexes begin and end; in both languages it is necessary to recognize some grammatical structure even where it is not explicitly marked by conjunction. Semantically, the same range of logical relations is involved in constructing sequences; the relationship within any one nexus may be one of expansion or projection, and may be either equal or unequal (paratactic or hypotactic, in the grammar). The main differences are found in the grammar itself: in expansion, in Chinese, (i) the unmarked paratactic extending relation, 'and', is typically not marked by any conjunction; (ii) in a hypotactic nexus the dependent clause almost always precedes the one on which it depends, and (iii) the dependency relation is signalled obligatorily in the primary clause and optionally in the dependent one, instead of the other way round as in English. Where the dependent clause is marked, the conjunction may occur in various places (at the beginning, following the Subject, or at the end), or even in two and (with an effort) all three,[1] instead of being just confined to the beginning of the clause. Thus the pattern of preferences in construing dependent sequences in Chinese is as follows:

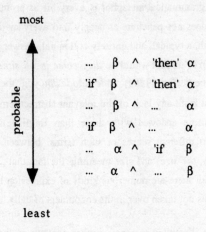

In projection, the same distinction is made between ideas and sayings, and between direct (paratactic) and indirect (hypotactic) modes of projecting them. Since there is no system of tense in Chinese, there is no tense sequence; but the shift of deixis takes place in the same way as in English (cf. e.g. 明天 *míngtiān* 'tomorrow', 第二天 *dì'èr tiān* 'the next day', as well as of course the shift of pronouns and demonstratives), and there are minor adjustments for mood, for example between direct and projected questions.

The (paradigmatic) range of different logical relations through which figures are construed into sequences is very much the same in Chinese as in English; and, as a corollary to this, the (syntagmatic) extent of the sequences is very similar. It should be remembered, of course, that our concern here is with those registers which are likely to be encountered in information processing — automatic documentation and retrieval, text generation and parsing, machine translation and the like. Not all of these are technical registers; but they are all to some extent multinational, and so permeable to semantic influences from one to another. In these registers, in translating between Chinese and

---

[1] One of the authors noted, in conversation, the clause 假如他如果还不赞成的话 *jiǎrú tā rúguǒ hái bù zànchéng de huà* 'If he still doesn't agree', in which the meaning 'if' is expressed three times over (假如 *jiǎrú*, 如果 *rúguǒ*, 的话 *de huà*)

English it is possible to match the sequences syntagmatically one to one: what works as a construction of figures in the one language will also work in the other.

As regards the individual clause nexus, two points arise from the fact that in Chinese the grammar constructs dependency relations by marking the primary rather than the dependent clause. One is that there is more indeterminacy between parataxis and hypotaxis than in English (unless one construes as hypotactic only those instances where the *dependent* clause is marked as such, which is contrary to one's sense of their proportionalities as agnate sets).[2] The other is that some English figures have to be reconstructed in order to go into Chinese, particularly the notorious 'unless' and 'until': the Chinese parallel to '*a* not until/ unless *x* ' is '(if/ when) *x* only then *a* '. There is thus a subsystem of relators 就 *jiù* 'then'/ 才 *cái* 'only then' which has no direct parallel in English: 你答应我就告诉你 *nǐ dāying wǒ jiù gàosù nǐ* 'I'll tell you if you promise', 你答应我才告诉你 *nǐ dāying wǒ cái gàosù nǐ* 'I won't tell you unless you promise'.

7.4 Figures

Figures are also clearly comparable between the two languages. Like that of English, the figure in Chinese is typically a configuration of a process with one, two or three participants (even meteorological processes require one: 'rain' is construed as a thing, which 'falls') and optional circumstantial elements. The main differences in the way figures are constructed are the following.

(1) The overall construction of **process types** is the same as in English: there are processes of doing, sensing, saying, and being, accommodating the same participant types and participant roles. In processes of doing, the transitivity potential is also very similar, with two-participant processes typically constructed ergatively: 车子开（了）： 我开车子 *chēzi kāi (le): wǒ kāi chēzi* 'the car drives : I drive the car'. Sensings however are not normally construed as action *by* some phenomenon *on* the conscious being; there is no regular configuration of the type 'it pleases me', 'it reminds me'. Analogous patterns are construed analytically with a semantic feature of causative:

使我高兴 *shǐ wǒ gāoxìng* 'makes me happy, pleases me'

使我想到 *shǐ wǒ xiǎngdào* 'makes me think of, reminds me'

---

[2] That is, if a nexus of two clauses neither of which is marked for dependency is always taken as paratactic. But one of the strong arguments for recognizing the system of 'taxis' (hypotaxis/ parataxis) in Chinese is precisely that a nexus with both clauses unmarked in most likely to be interpreted as b ^ a (cf. the diagram above). Thus x 高 *gāo*, y 低 *dī* ('x high, y low') could mean either (paratactic) 'x is high and y is low' or (hypotactic) 'when x is high, y is low'. (The third interpretation, 'x is high when y is low', is almost though not quite impossible.)

(2) As in English, the **process** is the category of experience that is located in *time*. In English, time is construed grammatically as tense: as a flow, with a more or less extended 'present' forming a moving but impermeable barrier between 'past' and 'future'; and each instance of a process is located somewhere in the flow. In Chinese, time is construed grammatically as aspect: and specifically as an opposition of unfolding versus culminating; and each instance of a process *may*   be given a value in this opposition, either 'significant as unfolding — in its own right' or as 'significant as culminating — perhaps by virtue of its consequences'. For example:

(i) 我看着报 *wǒ kànzhe bào* 'I (am, was) reading the newspaper' (imperfective)

(ii.a) 我看了报 *wǒ kànle bào* 'when I (have, had) read the newspaper' (perfective 1)

(ii.b) 我看报了 *wǒ kàn bào le* 'I (have, had) read the newspaper' (perfective 2)

There is a further difference, however, in that the system of aspect accommodates an unmarked option:

(iii) 我看报 *wǒ kàn bào* 'I + read+ newspaper' (unmarked)

So whereas in English each process in a figure (provided the figure is arguable — grammatically, one where the clause is finite) must be located somewhere in the construction of tense, in Chinese the process may simply be left as neutral, without being assigned to either category of aspect.

It might be suggested that the last type, though formally unmarked, actually represented a third marked term in the system — as happens in English where formally unmarked terms of positive and singular are just as marked semantically as the formally marked alternatives (thus singular excludes plural as categorically as plural excludes singular). This is certainly true of some categories in Chinese, e.g. positive polarity. But with aspect this is not the case. Neutral aspect, as in 我看报 *wǒ kàn bào*, does not exclude the meanings of the other terms; it is simply not selecting in the perfective/ imperfective system.

(3) **Qualities** in Chinese include within themselves the 'be' (the relation of ascription); hence ascriptive figures (e.g. 'I am busy') are construed as two elements ('I + be busy' 我忙 *wǒ máng*). Syntactically therefore they belong to the class of verbal elements rather than the class of nominal elements — i.e. in Chinese "adjectives" are verbs, whereas in English they are a kind of noun. As in English, ascriptive figures are located in time (but by aspect, of course; e.g. 胖了 *pàng le* 'culminate in being fat, get fat'). Qualities can be used to construct participants (e.g. 胖人 *pàng rén* 'a fat man'), but, relative to English, this is much less favoured. Where English prefers to introduce qualities in a nominal group, as Epithet + Thing *fat man*, Chinese prefers to introduce qualities in a clause, as Carrier + Attribute 'man is-fat'. Thus while an English speaker

will say *That's a very fat man,* a Chinese speaker will say 那个人很胖 *Nàge rén hěn pàng* 'that man (is) very fat'. If the quality is to be construed in a nominal group in Chinese, there is a tendency for it first to be constructed into a figure and then deconstructed again in a form of rankshift: 很胖的人 *hěn pàng de rén* 'a man who is very fat'. In a simple sequence of quality + thing the quality is often a means of assigning to a class: e.g. 慢车 *màn chē* 'slow (= stopping) train'.

Figures such as 'she has long hair', 'I have a headache' are construed ascriptively (predicatively): 她头发长 *tā tóufà cháng* 'she + hair + be long', 我头疼 *wǒ tóu téng* 'I + head + be painful'. Note that for both Chinese and English the problem with such constructions is to make the person rather than the part of the body thematic (which in both languages means making the person the first element in a clausal figure). English achieves this by constructing the quality 'into' the participant and ascribing this to the person by possession 'I + have + a headache/ a sore throat'; Chinese does it by detaching the person as a syntactic 'absolute' located at the beginning of the clause and constructing the quality predicatively '[as for] me + head + aches/ throat + is sore'. The English construction is mildly metaphorical. (On Theme in Chinese, see Fang, McDonald & Cheng, 1995; on the grammar of pain, see Halliday, in press c.)

(4) The accommodation of **elements in a figure** is very similar to that of English; as mentioned above, processes may have one, two or three participants, and the distribution is closely parallel. As in English, **'indirect' elements** are introduced circumstantially, with a 'mini-process' locating them with respect to the main process. In Chinese, such circumstantials retain more of a 'process' flavour (see below, however, for their internal construction); the Chinese equivalents of English prepositions are clearly verbs and can construct figures on their own (e.g. 到 *dào* 'reach; to': 他到北京去 *tā dào Běijīng qù* 'he's going to Peking'; 他到了北京 *tā dàole Běijīng* '(when) he has reached Peking'). Thus the interpolation of such circumstances as downranked figures is relatively more foregrounded in Chinese.

7.5 Elements

But it is in the construction of elements that Chinese and English differ most — although even here the similarities are more striking than the differences. There is no morphological variation or marking in Chinese; but the primary categories of participant and process are clearly construed in the forms of word classes — nouns and verbs — by the syntax, both the syntax of the group and the syntax of the clause. The nominal and verbal groups are again rather similar to those in English.

7.5.1 Nominal groups

The **nominal group** is constructed out of much the same materials, arranged more or less in the same order, but with two significant differences. (1) A thing, with or without associated quality, may stand by itself: 树 *shù* 'tree, the tree(s)', 皮袄 *pí'ǎo* 'fur jacket(s)'; if however it is *either* identified (made definite) (other than by possession) *or* quantified (or both), it typically also gets assigned to a measure-type, either collective, partitive, quantitative or individuative, e.g.

(a) 三杯茶 *sān bēi chá* three cups of tea

(b) 那块草地 *nà kuài cǎodì* that (piece of) lawn

(c) 这两包衣服 *zhè liǎngbāo yīfu* these two parcels of clothing

(d) 一所房子 *yī suǒ fángzi*   one (individuated) house

一棵树 *yī kē shù* one (individuated) tree

The last has no equivalent in English; these are the unit- or measure-words of Chinese, which are sometimes called 'noun classifiers' because they group things into classes — according to a mixture of criteria based on shape (long, flat &c.), natural class (birds and mammals, trees &c.) and functional domain (books, letters, living quarters &c.). Now, unlike English, where the grammar makes a categorial distinction between objects (bounded) and substances (unbounded), in Chinese 'things' are not *inherently* construed into these two types; that is to say, there is no clear opposition of count/ mass in the grammar. However, this distinction is in fact construed cryptotypically (in Mandarin, though not in Cantonese), because corresponding to type (d), the individuating measure words (and corresponding only to this set), is an unmarked term 个 *gè* (the original of the pidgin *piece, piecee*) which in certain contexts replaces the specific individuating term. Hence the 'entity' is anything that can be measured as 个 *gè* and the set of things that are defined in this way is similar to the set of things which are construed as count in English.

(2) In the syntactic construction of the Chinese nominal group the Thing comes last; hence while English distributes qualities on either side of the Thing (simple ones before, macro-qualities after), Chinese lines them all up in front. This has a minor effect, perhaps, in making a sharper distinction between two kinds of quality — roughly, simple versus macro — in English than in Chinese; but it becomes significant in the Chinese construction of complex taxonomies, and we shall return to it below.

7.5.2 Verbal groups

The **verbal group** is also not unlike that of English, with a lexical verb and various closed classes of 'auxiliaries'; there are no tense forms, of course, but there are modal forms forming a system of modality, codified grammatically although not to the same degree as in English. But there is one major difference in the semantic construction of processes.

Given that a process takes place in time, there will be some sense in which it has a beginning, a middle and an end. These may be observable as distinct constituents, if it is a process having duration; even if it is instantaneous, however, they represent possible facets, points of view from which it can be considered. In English, the meaning of a process typically *includes its completion:* if I 'cut' a piece of string, I cut it in two. To construe a process as non-completed, English uses conative or inceptive phase: 'try to cut it', 'start to cut it'. In Chinese the meaning of a process *does not imply its completion;* if it *is* to be construed as completed this is made explicit by a second verb marking completive phase, either resultative or directional. Thus 'cut' 剪 *jiǎn*, 'cut in two' 剪断 *jiǎnduàn;* 来 *lái* 'come', 来到 *láidào* 'come so as to arrive, reach'. In English no such systematic distinction is made; there are a few processes that require completion, such as 'seek', but there the distinction is lexicalized, *look for/ find.* In Chinese it is codified grammatically; there is a small set of seven directionals and a larger set of 60 - 80 resultatives, some of which are specialized to just one or two processes. This system is of course related to the temporal category of aspect: a process + completive is typically culminative in aspect. See Figure 7-1.

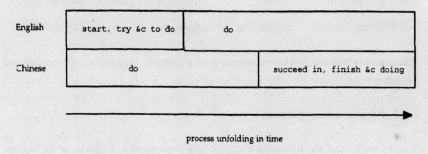

process unfolding in time

Fig. 7-1: Process as 'phased' in English and Chinese

It is difficult to exemplify cryptogrammatic features of this kind because they depend on myriads of small semantic encounters none of which by itself is likely to be particularly striking. And it is impossible to investigate them experimentally, because conscious reflection distorts the semantic process: what speakers say they would say is very different from what they really do say. But we could contrast the following two wordings, both taken from spontaneous dialogue:

I tried to phone Sam but didn't get him; he was out.

我	刚才	给	他	打	电话,	打不通。
Wǒ	gāngcái	gěi	tā	dǎ	diànhuà,	dǎbùtōng
I	just now	to	him	call	phone	call-not-through

(I tried to telephone him just now but couldn't get through.)

It would be possible in English to say *I phoned Sam but didn't get him,* but it is less likely — and on the occasion recorded above, the speaker had actually started to say that but then corrected herself: *I phoned — I tried to phone Sam, ...* In Chinese it is very unlikely that anyone would say 'I tried to phone him' (我试试给他打电话 *wǒ shìshì gěi tā dǎ diànhuà* would mean something like 'I tried out the experiment of phoning him'). Thus whereas in English the inceptive/ conative contrasts with an unmarked phase which is (by implication) completive, in Chinese the completive contrasts with an unmarked phase which is (by implication) inceptive/ conative.

There is the further consequence that the negation of a process in Chinese may be construed in four different ways:

	aspect	phase	
不剪 *bù jiǎn*	neutral	neutral	not + cut
没剪 *méi jiǎn*	culminative	neutral	not yet + cut
剪不断 *jiǎn bù duàn*	neutral	completive	cannot + cut (through)
没剪断 *méi jiǎnduàn*	culminative	completive	not yet + succeed + cut

This contrasts with the English construction of polarity in association with primary and secondary tense.

7.5.3 Prepositional phrases

We said earlier that circumstantial elements were constructed in Chinese, as in English, by associating a participant with an ancillary or minor process -- one that is not however available for constructing an entire figure, since it accepts only the one participant. In English, this type of circumstance is the prepositional phrase, and the class of prepositions is largely distinct from that of lexical verbs, although some prepositions are clearly non-finite forms of verbs in origin (e.g. *concerning, during*). In Chinese these 'minor processes' are related more explicitly to figures, since all words of the class of "pre-verb" (prepositive verb, analogous to prepositions) are words which function also as full processes. We should add one further point about these circumstantial elements: that the relation by which they are 'attached' to the figure as a whole is often construed not just by the minor process but by the minor process plus a generalized ('thing' that is a) **facet** of the participant in question. The model for these is of course a locative, e.g.:

zài   huāyuán   lǐ   在花园里   'in the garden'

at   garden   inside

but other, more abstract locations (including temporals) are construed in the same way:

zài   bàozhǐ   shàng   在报纸上   'in the newspaper'

at newspaper top

zài zhè zhǒng qíngxíng zhīxià 在这种情形之下'under these circumstances'

at this kind (of) circumstances bottom

Thus the relation constituting the minor process is at is were deconstructed into a 'relation' (typically 'at', 'to', 'from', 'around', 'along') and a 'facet' (back, front, top, bottom, left, right, inside, outside, before, after, middle).

These 'facet' nouns form an exception to the principle that the lexicalized 'thing' is the final component of the nominal group, since they follow it in every case. On the other hand they can in turn be construed as Head, by having the 'thing' made to modify them with a 的 *de* 'of': 书柜的前面 *shūguì de qiánmiàn* 'in front of the bookcase'. They thus have the same kind of intermediate status that nouns like 'front' (cf. *in front of* vs. *in/from the front of*) have in English. There is a sense in which, in Chinese

circumstantial 'pre-verb' (relation) : full verb

::

circumstantial 'post-noun' (facet) : full noun

— both as it were representing the ***relational*** rather than the ***substantive*** aspect of processes and things. In English the proportion is lacking because prepositions are less clearly related to verbs.

We can now return to the construction of processes and of things, as the major classes of elements. We have already seen that the nominal and verbal groups in Chinese are in significant respects similar to those of English. We now need to note an important difference between them in the way they construe experience.

7.6 Processes and things

We saw that, in English, things were much more richly taxonomized than processes. One of the principles behind grammatical metaphor was that, by reconstituting processes as things, we are able to construct them systematically into classes — and hence, ultimately, into the technical abstractions of a scientific theory. Processes are much less constructible into taxonomies; they lack the necessary stability through time.

This distinction appears considerably heightened in Chinese, in various respects. (1) Processes are construed as very specific: we may note, for example, twelve verbs corresponding to 'cut', twenty or more corresponding to 'carry', and so on:

切 qiē	cut
剁 duò	cut (meat), chop up
剪 jiǎn	cut with scissors
割 gē	cut (grain), mow
裁 cái	cut (cloth)
削 xiāo	cut (skin off fruit), pare
修 xiū	cut (nails, small branches), trim, prune
裂 liè	cut (logs), split
劈 pī	cut (firewood chips), chop
砍 kǎn	cut (tree), chop
拆 chāi	cut (paper), slit
剌 lá	cut (skin, flesh), slash, gash
刮 guā	cut (flesh), nick
解 jiě	cut off, sever

拿 ná	take, bring, fetch, hold, carry
抱 bào	in both arms, against body
怀 huái	in the crook of one arm
捧 pěng	in cupped hands
挑 tiāo	on pole across both shoulders
担 dàn	on pole across one shoulder
抬 tái	supported from underneath
提 tí	by handle
扛 káng	on one person's shoulder
扛 gāng	on two people's shoulders
端 duān	in hands with arms outstretched
夹 jiā	under arm
含 hán	inside mouth
叼 diāo	protruding from mouth
顶 dǐng	on head
背 bēi	on back
带 dài	(take) along with

拿 ná and 切 qiē are the most general terms, typically used in abstract and metaphoric senses; but they are not strictly superordinates — and in concrete contexts the preferred choice is the specific one. This contrasts not merely with English (which prefers general verbs) but also, more importantly, with the way **things** are construed in Chinese. While processes are construed as specifically as possible, things are construed as generally as possible. The way this works is as follows.

Things are typically construed in sets consisting of a superordinate plus a group of hyponyms, the relationship being explicitly signalled in the structure of the words themselves: the hyponym is a compound, formed of the superordinate preceded by another lexical element. For example,

笔 *bǐ*	writing implement
铅笔 *qiānbǐ*	pencil (lead —)
毛笔 *máobǐ*	brush (hair —)
墨水笔 *mòshuǐbǐ*	pen (ink-water —)
&c	

车 *chē*	wheeled vehicle
电车 *diànchē*	tram (electric —)
火车 *huǒchē*	train (fire —)
自行车 *zìxíngchē*	bicycle (self-go —)
马车 *mǎchē*	horse cart (horse —)
汽车 *qìchē*	car (automobile) (gas —)
&c	

机 *jī*	in 机器 *jīqì* 'machine'
打字机 *dǎzìjī*	typewriter (strike-character —)
计算机 *jìsuànjī*	computer (calculate —)
飞机 *fēijī*	aeroplane (fly —)
织布机 *zhībùjī*	loom (weave-cloth —)
割草机 *gēcǎojī*	lawnmower (cut-grass —)
洗衣机 *xǐyījī*	washing machine (wash-clothes —)
印刷机 *yìnshuājī*	printing press (print —)
照相机 *zhàoxiàngjī*	camera (photograph —)
&c	

Thus the taxonomic organization is made fully explicit in the naming: a 铅笔 *qiānbǐ* is a kind of 笔 *bǐ*, a 火车 *huǒchē* is a kind of 车 *chē*, and so on. This happens sporadically in English, for example with (some of) the names of fishes, trees and birds; but it is by no means regular — and it can be tricksy: a *shoetree,* for example, is *not* a kind of tree (the word *shoetree* is not a hyponym of *tree*), nor is a *foxglove* a kind of *glove,* or a *sauceboat* a kind of *boat.* In Chinese there are very few such metaphorical compounds; moreover, large parts of the everyday noun stock are constructed in this way, in the form of explicit taxonomies. These can sometimes be extended to three or even more levels.

Furthermore, in contrast to processes, where the principle is 'be as specific as you can', in referring to things the principle is 'be only as specific as you need'. So when asking your friend to pass you your pencil, which both of you can see in front of you, you do not specify what kind of a 笔 *bǐ* (writing implement) it is; you say 我那个笔请你递过来 *wǒ nàgè bǐ qǐng nǐ dìguòlái* 'please pass my 笔 *bǐ* across' — or more likely just 笔 *bǐ*. Thus, in discourse, things are construed at the most general level that their naming and the context permits.

What this means is that the dichotomy of experience into processes and things is rather more explicitly semanticized in Chinese than in English. While in both languages the same lexeme may often be either noun or verb, the two are clearly distinct in the syntax; in Chinese, in addition, there are some systematic differences in the semogenic principles by which processes and things are constructed. One interesting consequence of this is that while **processes** tend to be differently named from one dialect to the next, **things** usually have the same names throughout the whole of China (with different pronunciations, of course; but the same lexemes). More important for our present purposes, however, is the significance for grammatical metaphor.

7.7 Grammatical metaphor

We will limit these brief comments to grammatical metaphor in its more scientific and technical aspects. As in English, so in Chinese technical terms are typically nouns; and we have seen how the typical structures of the everyday nominal vocabulary lend themselves to the creation of technical taxonomies. Sets of abstract and theoretical terms are readily constructed on this model, using entirely Chinese lexical resources; and the taxonomic relationships among them are fully transparent. Compare the Chinese and English terms in a set such as the following:

率 *lü*	rate
频率 *pínlü* ('repeat —')	frequency
速率 *sùlü* ('fast —')	speed
音率 *yīnlü* ('sound —')	musical pitch
呼吸率 *hūxīlü* (breathe —)	respiration rate
周转率 *zhōuzhuǎnlü* ('turn-over —')	turnover
折射率 *zhéshèlü* ('refract —')	index of refraction

Thus the semiotic transition from commonsense knowledge and experience on the one hand to educational experience and the technical knowledge of the disciplines on the other may appear somewhat less abrupt in Chinese than in English.

Many such creations are, of course, metaphorical in the sense in which we used the term with respect to English. We have not undertaken a systematic survey of types of grammatical metaphor in Chinese; but from a study of scientific writing in various fields we have the impression that the range of types of metaphor is not very different (Halliday & Martin, 1993: Chapter 7). The prevailing tendency is to reconstrue other phenomena as things, which means — as in English — that whole figures are reconstrued as qualities of those things.

Again as in English, the nominal group in Chinese stretches to accommodate this kind of reconstruction. But its resources are somewhat different. On the one hand, as we have seen, the Head of the nominal group always comes at the end, an instance of the very dominant principle in Chinese whereby modification is regressive — all modifiers precede what they modify. So everything that is construed as a quality has to precede the thing to which it is assigned.

This can lead to considerable syntactic ambiguity — rather more, in fact, than in English, because in English such meanings can be construed as prepositional phrases and clauses coming *after* the Head. In Chinese, too, both circumstances and figures can become qualities of a thing, represented as phrases and clauses in the nominal group; but these always come *before* the Head, along with the 'ordinary' qualities that are construed as single words. So for example in the following clause everything up to 断块 *duàn kuài* 'fragment' forms a single nominal group, in which 断块 *duàn kuài* is the Head noun.

由	断层	面	倾斜	相向		的	两	条
yóu	duàncéng	miàn	qīngxié	xiāngxiàng		de	liǎng	tiáo
from	fault	plane	inclined	towards (face to face)	**		two	

正	断层	组成	两	断层	中间	相对
zhèng	duàncéng	zǔchéng,	liǎng	duàncéng	zhōngjiān	xiāngduì
straight	fault	formed	two	faults	between	relatively

陷落	的	断块	[叫	"地堑"	或	断陷盆地]
xiànluò	de	duànkuài	[jiào	dìqiàn	huò	duànxiàn péndì]
depressed	**	fragment	[is called	"graben"	or	"depression trough"]

** Note: The structure marker 的 *de* signals that what precedes it modifies (is dependent on) what follows.

We have referred above to how information is lost, in English, when figures are metaphorically construed as single elements: between, say, *how many people die because their lungs develop cancer* and *lung cancer death rates*. In Chinese there is even greater loss of information, for two reasons: first, because more items (words, phrases and clauses) are strung together (since all precede the Head), and so the number of possible bracketings is higher; and secondly, because most of the semantic relations among down-ranked elements within the nominal group are left implicit in Chinese, whereas in English at least some are preserved. We can compare the above Chinese example with its English translation:

```
A relatively lowered fragment between two faults,
formed by two straight faults whose planes are
inclined towards each other, [is called a "graben" or
"depression trough"]
```

The reader has to supply rather more of the linking structure in the Chinese than in a typical English equivalent.

On the whole, however, the scope of grammatical metaphor in technical and other formal written varieties of modern Chinese is about the same as it is in English. As far as its effect on the construction of meaning is concerned, grammatical metaphor in the form of nominalization (turning processes and qualities into things) engenders considerable syntactic complexity and ambiguity, perhaps more in Chinese than in English; at the same time, the construction of technical vocabulary and technical taxonomies is rather more accessible in Chinese than it is in English. Overall, however, as far as technical discourse is concerned the two languages are not excessively different in their creation of meanings; and this has implications for any kind of shared information processing, such as multilingual text generation, in which both English and Chinese are involved.

7.8 The meaning base: concluding remarks

Chinese and English share many common features in the construction of the ideation base. Thus, if we consider how they construe happenings as '**quanta of experience**', the two languages are to a large extent congruent: Chinese sequences tend to correspond to English sequences, and Chinese figures to English figures. At the same time, both languages allow a comparable degree of elasticity at this point in the system, whereby one and the same happening in the phenomenal world may be construed either as a sequence or as a figure — or as something indeterminate between the two. In English, we may say either *she mended it* ‖ *by using string* or *she mended it with string*, construing the means either as a full process in a separate figure or as a minor one in the form of a circumstance. In Chinese, on the other hand, these two overlap, so that 她用绳子来修理 *tā yòng shéngzi lái xiūlǐ* could be interpreted either way.

One major source of this kind of elasticity is the manifestation of the very general semantic types of projection & expansion throughout the ideation base. In English, as we have shown, we find them manifested both logically as relations and experientially as elements within figures:

[i] logical manifestation:

> as relations between figures in the construal of sequences (realized by clause complexes);

> as relations between processes in the construal of figures (realized by verbal group complexes);

[ii] experiential manifestation:

> as circumstances within figures (realized by prepositional phrases or adverbial groups);

> as circumstantial processes within figures of being & having (realized by relational clauses);

> as non-nuclear participants within figures, i.e., participants other than Medium — Agent, Beneficiary, Range (realized by nominal groups with or without a preposition).

This elasticity of construal is further increased through grammatical metaphor, which also relies on the manifestation of projection & expansion within participants (realized by the different types of modification in nominal groups). We have illustrated the range of options throughout the system at various points, and a schematic example will be enough here:

[i] logical

> A happened, so B happened;

> A caused B to happen;

[ii] experiential

> A happened causing B/ B happened because of A;

> A happening caused B happening

> A affected B ['cause-happened']

with additional metaphorical variants:

B happened because of the happening of A

the happening of A caused the happening of B

the happening of A was the cause of the happening of B

As we have shown in the context of grammatical metaphor, the choice among alternative construals is made on the basis of both ideational and textual factors. These factors 'conspire' together so that different strategies are favoured in different registers: the congruent form (sequences) in casual speech, the metaphoric form (figures of being & having) in elaborated forms of writing.

Where there is variation of this kind within one language, we may expect to find typological variation across different languages. Consider for example the construal of a speech event. Here English favours a single figure with a configuration of Sayer + Process + Receiver: *A said to B*. Chinese favours an intermediate, borderline type: (Mandarin) *A duì* 对 *B shuō* 说 [A facing B said], (Cantonese) *A wa béi* 话俾 *B tèng* 听 [A said giving B to hear]. In Trique, a language spoken in Mexico, a speech event is construed as a sequence of two figures (Longacre, 1985: 262-3), as in *Gatah Juan* ——> *guni Maria*, which we can gloss adhocly as Process ['said'] + Sayer ——> Process ['heard'] + Senser. Akan, a language spoken in West Africa, is in a loose sense intermediate between the English model and the Trique model: a speech event is construed as one figure, but to bring in a 'receiver', the Process is construed as a sequence of processes (realized by a 'serial-verb construction' within a simple clause), as in *ka* ——> *kyerɛ* 'tell: say + show' (e.g., *ɔkāa asɛm kyerɛɛ Kofi*. 'Process α: he: say + Verbiage: something + Process β: show + Receiver: Kofi', i.e. 'he told Kofi something'). In general, Akan tends to construe the equivalent of English beneficiaries on this model; and it also construes causal, temporal, and spatial enhancements along these lines by means of sequences of processes.

Such examples illustrate the kind of typological variation in the construal of quanta of experience that we suggested above, but they are only fragments: we need more comparative studies based on comprehensive accounts of particular languages. Pawley (1987) notes the general lack of typological studies in this area outside of lexis, and contributes an important investigation of differences between Kalam, a language of Papua New Guinea, and English in construing experience of change ("encoding events", in Pawley's terms). Kalam and English may, he suggests, "indicate the outer limits of variation among languages in resources and conventions encoding event-like phenomena"; "Kalam may be as different from English as any language on earth" (p. 335).

The Kalam clause usually construes what Pawley calls a "simple event" (a "conceptual event which comprises a single action, unrepeated", typically "within the space of a few seconds or less"), represented minimally as a Process. This Process is realized by a single inflected verb (showing "subject" reference and various other categories such as tense/aspect and mood) or by a series of verbs — "up to five or six bare verbs plus one inflected verb". The class of verb is different from that of Chinese or English in one critical respect: the set of verb stems is closed, with about 90 members, and out of these fewer than 30 make up 90% of all instances in text.[3] These few verb stems all have "very broad or abstract meanings", which are naturally fairly ineffable in English; examples include *d-* 'control, constrain, get, hold, touch ...', *g-* 'do, act, make, work, occur, happen, ...', *md-* 'exist, be alive, dwell, stay, remain, ...', *mŋ* 'perceive, sense, be aware'. More specific meanings are achieved not by an increase in experiential delicacy in the taxonomy of processes realized by verbs, but by complexing verbs or clauses.

Both Kalam and English can construe the following roles within one clause: Process (realized as verb), "actor/ agent, patient", "time and beneficiary" (p. 353). However, English can expand the clause nucleus considerably further. For example, the happening construed as one figure in English realized by the simple clause *The man threw a stick over the fence into the garden* (Actor: 'the man' + Process: 'threw' + Goal: 'a stick' + Location: 'over the fence into the garden') would be construed as three figures realized by three clauses in Kalam (p. 354; our adhoc functional interpretation):

B	mon- day	d	yokek	waty	at	amb	wog-mgan	yowp
man	stick	hold	he-displaced-different subject	fence	above	it-went	garden-inside	it-fell
Actor	Goal	Process		Location		Process	Location	Process

In English, the path of motion could also be construed as a sequence (realized by a clause complex), as in *The man threw the stick, so it went over the fence and then fell into the garden.* This is not only ideationally different but also textually, allowing for an unmarked mapping of the ideational meanings onto three information units instead of only one.

Pawley identifies the following enhancing relations as points of contrast between English and Kalam. English may construe them within a single clause; Kalam construes them by means of separate clauses: instrument, direction, location/ source, cause, beneficiary (pp. 354-5). Pawley summarizes the differences as follows (p. 356):

---

[3] Having a fairly small stock of verbs is a feature of "a good number of Papuan languages" according to Foley (1986), who discusses "verbal semantics" in Kalam and other Papuan languages.

... clauses do rather different jobs in the two languages. English clause structure is a syntactic Procrustean Bed into which a wide range of diverse conceptual structures are squeezed. For example, unlike Kalam, English allows several conceptual situations/ events to be fused into a single clause. This result is largely achieved by reducing certain situations/ events to the status of peripheral or backgrounded elements in the clause, expressed as arguments of the verb. [...] ... verbs do rather different jobs in the two languages. In the case of English, it is convenient to speak of a division of labor between full verbs, which do lexical-referential work, and grammatical functors (auxiliaries, prepositions, etc.) which do grammatical work. In Kalam verbs do both kinds of work, but always as full verbs. But Kalam is more restrictive than English in the amount of information it allows to be compressed into a verb stem, and the kinds of case relations which may be associated with a single verb.

It is perhaps possible to interpret the kind of variation across languages we have just discussed with reference to Trique, Akan, and Kalam as variation in the division of labour between the two modes of the ideational metafunction, the experiential and the logical. In construing some flux of experience, Chinese and English have considerable *experiential* resources for construing figures as configurations of a nucleus (Process + Medium), plus up to 2 additional participants, and a range of different circumstantial elements; with large stocks of verbs organized into fairly extensive taxonomies. In writing, Chinese and English experientialize experience even further through grammatical metaphor (see Figure 6-3 in Chapter 6, Section 6.7.1). Other languages, such as Kalam, may foreground the *logical* mode of construal over the experiential mode, with considerable logical resources for construing sequences of processes and sequences of figures.

In general, wherever there is indeterminacy within a language, we may expect to find this reflected in typological variation. Let us briefly cite three further examples. (1) We saw that in the experiential grammar of the English clause there was a complementarity of perspective between the transitive and the ergative: processes may be construed either as 'one participant is doing something, which may or may not extend to another participant that it is being done to', or as 'one participant is involved in something, which may or may not be brought about by another participant that is the agent of it'. Probably all languages display this transitive/ ergative complementarity in their transitivity systems; but at the same time it appears at different depths and in different proportions. (2) Secondly, we referred to projection as something that overlaps the 'boundary' between interpersonal and ideational metafunctional space; in English it is typically construed ideationally, though with a close relationship to the interpersonal systems of modality and mood. Other languages locate projection rather differently in relation to this boundary, sometimes foregrounding its interpersonal aspects, for example through a special category of 'reporting' mood. (3) Some process types tend to lie on the borderline between major categories, forming mixed and overlapping categories; typical of these are the behavioural and existential processes in English. It is likely that equivalent types of process will be liable to greater typological variation than those that fall squarely within the core categories of material, mental, and relational. (See Chapter 13, Section 13.4 below for a note on the kinds of indeterminacy in language.)

We are not attempting to take up such typological issues here. But we do want to stress the extent of the variation that is possible in the construal of experience among different human groups; and it is helpful to consider languages that are culturally very disparate, and remote from well-researched languages like Chinese and English. There can be striking variation also in the semantic construction of elements. In the Reefs - Santa Cruz family of languages (Äyiwo; Nanggo, Löndä, South-western Santa Cruz) in the south-western Pacific, there is a highly complex classification of phenomena involving individual lexical items, often with very specialized semantic ranges, which combine (i) with each other, and (ii) with verbal or nominal affixes, including three cross-cutting noun classes and a large inventory of verbal categories, to produce complex words whose meaning is often (from our point of view) entirely opaque and unpredictable (see Wurm, 1987). The following example of derivatives from a noun base illustrates this point:

-modyi indicates the concept of the right hand and strength. It also occurs only with noun class prefixes, such as *lo-* acquisition through labour and effort class prefix, resulting in *lo-modyi* "small adze" (something used for acquiring something else through labour and effort by one's strong right hand"); *mo-* extending far class prefix, resulting in *mo-modyi* "small outrigger canoe" ("something that goes afar when using one's strong right hand for paddling"); *oyä-* mangrove class, resulting in *oya-modyi* "a type of mangrove with very strong wood". (Wurm, 1987: 445-6)

The phenomena of human experience are held in tension by so many intersecting analogical lines that, while all of us have the same brains and live on the surface of the same planet, such diverse ways of semiotic mapping are not only possible but inevitable.

~*~*~*~

This brief excursion into Chinese and other languages concludes our survey and discussion of the meaning base. In this part, we have only hinted at the question of what role the meaning base plays in text processing. We shall now explore this issue further in Part III. Then we shall turn to another issue we have not discussed in this part, viz. how our approach resembles and differs from other approaches, both theoretically and descriptively. This will be the topic of Part IV.

Part III:

The meaning base as a resource in language processing systems

We shall now explore how the meaning base we sketched above in Part II can serve as a resource in language processing systems, in particular in text generation systems. We shall start with the question of how specific 'domains' can be modelled, given the general meaning base outlined above. We shall then move on to the role of the meaning base in the global architecture of a text generation system.

8. Building an ideation base

8.1 General

In any given language processing task, there will be one or more domains to be modelled as part of our general taxonomy. To illustrate how the taxonomy is used, we have selected the following two specific domains:

    (a) meteorological: the ideational meanings of weather reports (Section 8.2)

    (b) culinary: the ideational meanings of recipes (Section 8.3)

First we need to say a few words about extending the meaning base to cover such specific domains. There are two central points — (i) the relationship between context and language, and (ii) the relationship between the general model presented in Part II and specific domains such as the meteorological and culinary ones.

8.1.1 Field and ideation base

Just as the semantic system is functionally diversified (into the ideational, interpersonal and textual metafunctions), so the context in which language is 'embedded' is also diversified. The context encompasses both the **field** of activity and subject matter with which the text is concerned ('what's going on, and what is it about?') and the **tenor** of the relationship between the interactants, between speaker and listener, in terms of social roles in general and those created through language in particular ('who are taking part?'). The field is thus the culturally recognized repertoires of social practices and concerns, and the tenor the culturally recognized repertoires of role relationships and interactive patterns. Now, both these contextual variables are, in some sense, independent of language, even though they are constituted in language and the other semiotic systems of a culture. That is, they concern realities that exist alongside the reality created by language itself, semiotic reality. However, there is a third contextual variable that is specifically concerned with the part language is playing in any given context — the symbolic **mode**, how the linguistic resources are deployed. This covers both the medium (spoken, written, and various subtypes such as written in order to be spoken) and the rhetorical function — persuasive, didactic, informative, etc..

Together, field, tenor and mode define the 'ecological matrix' in which particular types of text are processed: there is a systematic relationship between such matrices (particular combinations of field, tenor and mode values) and particular types of text. We can see this clearly with actual **instances** of text — for example, an individual recipe or weather forecast; but these are instances of general classes, to be characterized in terms of the systemic **potential** that is instantiated in them. That is, there is a correlation not only between a contextual matrix and a given instance of a recipe but also between that matrix and the linguistic potential that is deployed in recipes in general. This latter correlation is known as a functional variety or **register** of the general systemic potential. This much has been known for a long time — the notion of functional dialect was worked out by the Prague School in the 1930s (see e.g. Havránek, 1932, and Vachek, 1964), and systemic register theory has its roots in Firth's (e.g., 1957) work on restricted languages. The concept of register is also recognized in computational linguistics under the heading of **sublanguage**, particularly in work on machine translation (see e.g. Kittredge & Lehrberger, 1982; Kittredge, 1987). However, we can take one further step, as systemic theory did in the 1970s (see Halliday, 1978a), and recognize that the co-variation between context and language is not undifferentiated — it is differentiated according to the functional diversification of each of the two strata: the variables of context correlate respectively with the metafunctions of the language, field with ideational, tenor with interpersonal, and mode with textual. These pairs are mutually predictive. Thus of the three contextual variables it is **field** that is implicated in variation within our ideational meaning base.

From this point of view, field can be characterized as the deployment and organization of the ideation base. As we have already implied, there are two aspects to this category. In most contexts, there is both a first order field and a second order field — the first order field is the social activity being pursued (e.g., instructing somebody in how to prepare a dish, predicting tomorrow's weather, informing somebody about yellow-pages information over the phone) and the second order field is the 'subject matter' the activity is concerned with (e.g., the ingredients and methods of cooking, meteorology, construction businesses, international travel). So for instance, in a context where a telephone operator provides a caller with information there is (i) the social activity of exchanging information as a service and (ii) the area of information, e.g. copying & printing services.

And both these guide the way the ideation base is deployed. Fields vary in both these respects; and a full account of field would include a *typology* of the possible first and second order values that occur in a culture. Such a typology would show how closely various fields are related — how they form families. So given three different fields, 1, 2, and 3, the typology will show three different ways of deploying the ideation base. Each field is projected onto one variety of the ideation base: that is, it can be thought of as activating some portion of the total semantic resources — see Figure 8-1. This projection of field onto the ideation base involves both the particular domain and the general types under which this domain is classified.

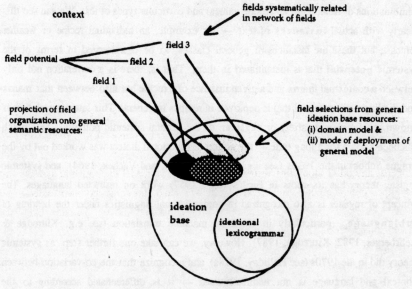

Fig. 8-1: Types of field within context projected as organization onto the ideation base

A given field is thus constituted as a principled selection of types from within the ideation base; this is so to speak its semantic image projected from context. If the field is defined in relatively broad terms, it may activate most of the general part of the ideation base; but a more restricted field may call on only one particular part of it. In such cases, it may be useful to reduce the whole ideation base to only those parts that are implicated for the particular field; that is, to set up a field-specific ideational semantics. (More generally, this might be a context-specific semantics, including interpersonal and textual as well as ideational meanings).[1] However, the price of this would be to isolate such a field from others to which it is related.

---

[1] The latter option was explored in Halliday (1973) and used as the basis for the SLANG generator developed by Patten (1988) — see also Matthiessen (1990a) and Matthiessen & Bateman (1991) for discussion relative to text generation, and Caffarel (1990, 1992) for discussion pertaining to the semantic system or systems of tense in French.

8.1.2 Domain models and the general model

As we have said, the semantic correlate of a contextual field is a **domain**. When we model the ideational semantics of a particular field, we create a **domain model**. What is the relation of this to the general model outlined in Part II?

Domain models are **variants** of the general model. A particular domain model specifies which of the semantic systems in the overall model are activated in a particular contextual field: the ideational meanings that are "at risk" (Halliday, 1978a; cf. O'Donnell, 1990). Each field thus has its own **semantic profile**, which can be seen against the background of the overall semantic potential. For instance, in the culinary field of recipes (cf. Section 8.3 below), the domain model occupies a fairly narrow band within the overall model of figures of doing and being, including various particular subtypes such as cutting, being crisp. If we then switch our point of vantage, the overall model appears as a generalization across the full range of such field-specific varieties.

The relationship which links the domain models with the general model is **instantiation**. Instantiation relates the **system** to the **instance**, at any given stratum; thus, at the semantic stratum, instantiation is as shown in Figure 8-2. We can choose to model at any point along this instantiation cline. If we model the semantic system, we have the "general model" outlined in Part II. We could choose, at the other extreme, to model a particular instance: the semantics of just one text. But we are more likely to model some intermediate region, a semantic space that is less than the overall meaning potential of the language, but greater than that occupied by any single text. In other words, we expect typically to be modelling a **domain**.

A domain is located somewhere between the system and the instance. Hence it can be looked at from either end. Seen from the 'system' end, a domain is regular and repeated patterning in the way the potential is deployed, over the course of time. Seen from the 'instance' end, it is generalization across particular instances of text.

Instances do not usually repeat each other word for word; there is some variation, for example between one cooking recipe and another. It is this variation that constructs the domain. With each instance of the field, the overall meaning potential is instantiated in slightly varying ways; this variation both confirms the earlier patterns and nudges them along some novel path.

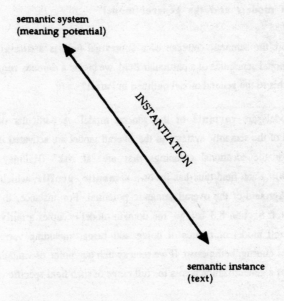

semantic system
(meaning potential)

INSTANTIATION

semantic instance
(text)

Fig. 8-2: The cline of instantiation at the semantic stratum

Thus when we model a domain, we are still defining a meaning **potential**, a semantic space in which meanings are constantly being realigned and new meanings created. In other words, we are describing a **register**; or, more accurately, a region of registerial variation (sometimes called 'diatypic' variation to suggest the analogy with dialectal variation). Register is systematic variation within the overall meaning potential; from this point of view, a domain is a region of registerial variation corresponding to the contextual variable of field — the meaning potential determined by, and determining, 'what's going on'.

Figure 8-3 represents the location of registerial domains within the ideation base along the dimensions of instantiation and variation. The overall semantic potential is diversified into registerial varieties that emerge as patterns of instantiation. In the figure, we have had to show the registerial domains as discrete locations within the semiotic space of instantiation & variation. This is, of course, only a convenient representational fiction. (i) On the one hand, registerial domains form families within which there is variation, such as the family of culinary procedures, which encompasses a variety of different kinds of recipes, or the more extended family of procedures for creating artefacts. (ii) On the other hand, the variation is multidimensional.

Since domains are instantiations of the overall ideational potential, any properties associated with types in this potential are also present in the domains. Thus 'cooking' in the recipe domain carries with it whatever information is associated with 'cooking' in the ideational potential — in particular, information concerning the participant roles and the nature of the phenomena that take on these roles. At the same time, it is likely that further constraints will be attached that are specific to a given domain. For instance, 'cooking' in recipes may be distinguished from 'cooking' in the overall ideational potential (i) in that it has to have an Agent, and (ii) this Agent is restricted to being the addressee.

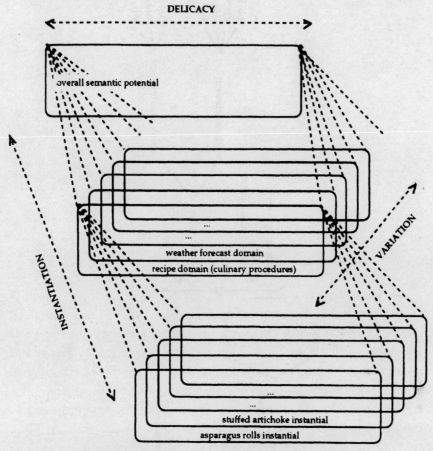

Fig. 8-3: Domain models in relation to the overall model

The diagram in Figure 8-3 shows that delicacy is distinct from instantiation. Delicacy is the degree of detail, or specificity, to which the description is taken. A contextual field may be specified to varying degrees of delicacy, e.g. see Figure 8-4. We may compare the category of 'semantic field' in the field theory associated with the name of Trier; these are lexicosemantic (that is, the contrasts in meaning are those realized by lexical choices), which indicates that they are located towards the more delicate end of the content continuum. Our domain models are likely to occupy more of a middle ground; for most purposes, we will be more inclined to model, say, 'team & ball games', than either 'recreation' at the very general extreme or 'hockey' at the very specific. Such a domain is general enough to cover a reasonably expansive semantic space, both instantially (large number of instances) and potentially (capable of engendering further meanings), while still being specific enough to allow us to construe particular semantic features (types of figure, elements, etc.).

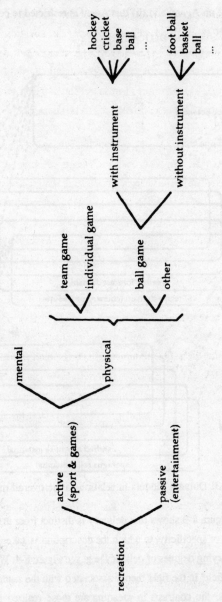

Fig. 8-4: Example of delicacy in field

Thus in selecting the degree of delicacy of the field description we are locating ourselves in the semiotic space defined by instantiation and variation. Any properties associated with less delicate categories are inherited by those that are more delicate. For instance, 'simmering' is a kind of 'cooking', both of which are culinary phenomena; but 'cooking' is also, via some intermediate steps, a kind of 'dispositive doing'. Consequently, simmering will inherit the participant roles of (i) Actor, (ii) Goal, and (iii) resultative

Attribute (the construal of the resulting change affecting the Goal); and, like figures in general, it can cooccur with a number of circumstantial roles such as Manner, Time, and Duration. These properties do not have to be specified over again for simmering. For instance, Highton & Highton (1964) define *simmering* as 'cooking very slowly in water which is just below boiling point'. This suggests that it can be modelled as a subtype of 'cooking' where the Manner is restricted to 'very slowly in water just below boiling point'. At the same time, 'simmering' will inherit from 'cooking' the value restriction on the Goal: that is, only that which can be cooked can be simmered.

It is important perhaps to make quite explicit the distinction among the three concepts of realization, instantiation, and delicacy, since each of these is a distinct scale of abstraction. It is easiest to describe them in terms of metalanguage dynamics: what we are doing when we move along these different scales. (1) **Realization** is the relation of one stratum to other strata (in any stratified system, with language as prototypical); when we shift attention from semantics 'upwards' into context or 'downwards' to lexicogrammar and phonology/ graphology, we are moving in realization. We can do this at any degree of delicacy, from most general to most specific; and we can do it at any point along the instantiation scale, from system to text. (2) **Instantiation** is the relation between the system and the instance. When we shift attention along this scale, we are moving between the potential that is embodied in any stratum and the deployment of that potential in instances on the same stratum (between the climate and the weather, to use the analogy from our illustration below). Again, this move can be made at any degree of delicacy. (3) **Delicacy** is the relation between the most general features and the most specific. When we shift attention from, say, 'recreation' to 'hockey' at the level (stratum) of context, or from 'syllable' to 'long open nasal syllable' to /pã:/ in phonology, we are moving in delicacy. Again, we can do this at any point along the instantiation scale.

It is common in natural language processing to approach the problem of modelling in a philosophical mode: one reasons about what the domain is or could be like, perhaps starting with some central 'concepts'. But a more powerful alternative is to derive a tentative sketch of the domain model and its relationship to the general model through lexicogrammatical analysis of a corpus of texts in the appropriate register, e.g. a corpus of weather forecasts or a corpus of recipes. This is in fact how we have approached the culinary and meteorological domains: exploring the lexicogrammatical patterns in sample texts and relating them to the semantic system.

We now pass to the illustration of these two domain models, meteorological and culinary.

8.2 The language of the weather

8.2.1 Introduction

A considerable amount of discourse, in English, and no doubt in every language, is
concerned with the weather. As far as English is concerned this ranges from casual
greetings and observations that fall within what Malinowski (e.g., 1923) called 'phatic
communion' — communing with people by 'phasis', i.e. togetherness through talk — to
theories of climate formulated at a highly technical and abstract level in scientific papers
and reports.

The terms *climate* and *weather* are related to each other as *langue* to *parole*: as the
system of language is to its instantiation in text. Weather is the instantiation of climate;
climate is the system 'behind' the weather. As with language, there is, of course, only one
set of phenomena here not two; when we refer to climate we are construing general
principles and tendencies that 'explain' the multidimensional microvariation that is what
we actually have to live with when gardening or planning an outing — and what farmers
and sailors have had to struggle with wherever, as a result of settlement, weather became
the dominant factor in shaping the human condition. This variation is represented in
countless folk sayings both old and new, staid and humorous, many of which are attempts
at predicting what will come next, e.g.

         Red sky at night is the shepherd's delight.
         Red sky in the morning is the shepherd's warning.

Some suggest the futility of making any predictions at all, a point of view naturally
voiced by the Irish:

         If you can see the hills it's going to rain. If you can't see the
         hills, it's raining.

In colonial days the British who had served in India used to explain what it was like to
live there by saying

         In England we have no climate — only weather. In India they have
         no weather — only climate.

And now that we are less 'at the mercy of the weather' than our ancestors used to be we
can afford to take a more positive view of variation:

         If you don't like the weather, just wait five minutes.

Not surprisingly, the weather is a good domain for applying chaos theory, from the most sophisticated to the most popular level. The sheer number of different variables, and the immense variation in scale across which any one of them has to be observed and measured, ensures that there are no simple linearities relating weather to features of climate; just as in acoustics, where minor fluctuations in the phasing of different variables produce what appear as totally different wave shapes (causing major problems for automatic speech recognition), so in the weather small perturbations in the timing of different components cause local weather patterns to vary in apparently unpredictable ways. Thus predicting weather is rather like predicting text: one can make certain predictions about what people are going to say or write with a certain probability of being right — a probability that is significantly greater than chance, but not great enough to be easily used in (for example) parsing programs, because of the great number of variables that play a part in conditioning choices in the text. Similarly, predicting the weather appeared to have reached a similar level of probability, but then to have struck a plateau from which it proved immensely difficult to proceed any higher. We understand that what finally enabled the forecasting to move beyond this level of success was a shift in the relative perspective that is given to chaos and order: instead of saying 'the *unmarked* state of a system is one of order; our task is to see through the apparent chaos behind which the order is hidden', if you say rather 'the *unmarked* state of a system is one of chaos; our task is to impose some kind of order upon it' you open the way to improving the accuracy of your predictions about one level up (say, from around 0.7 to around 0.8, which would be very significant in a number of practical contexts). Since linguistic patterns are very clearly fractal, with patterns repeated not merely across differences of scale but also across differences of level of realization (stratum), it seems possible that a similar shift in our thinking will be helpful in text forecasting also. (The starting point in linguistics is however very different from that in physical science, the received wisdom in linguistics being that no prediction is possible at all. We should stress, perhaps, that we do not subscribe to this view.)

Wignell, Martin & Eggins (1990) have shown that in a high school geography text book which they analysed in lexicogrammatical terms (using systemic grammar) one of the critical steps that the learner had to take was that of constructing from the text a taxonomy of climate. This taxonomy was both compositional (meronymic — *parts* of climate) and hyponymic (*kinds* of climate), yielding a structure that is summarized in Figure 8-5. It was not set out in the form of tables or diagrams; but it could be recovered from the text, and Wignell et al. showed what discourse-semantic patterns (types of process and so on) were characteristically built up in the grammar in the course of presenting the information on the basis of which this taxonomy could be construed. Given that, as part of mastering scientific knowledge in the course of education, the learner has to construct such taxonomies, we can interpret this task as the learner's construction of **meanings** — which in turn are construed in specific lexicogrammatical forms. The general principles behind this meaning-making or semogenic approach to learning, and more specifically to learning science, will be found in the work of Lemke (1984; 1990a). Lemke's 'thematic systems' are the systems of meanings that the pupils are required (by the teacher, text book, syllabus and educational ideology) to build up into their ideational meaning base. In this process, the children are simultaneously working at both ends of the instantiation cline, constructing both system and text. They have to build up the systems of 'geographical meanings' (such as the two taxonomies shown above) from the written and spoken texts they engage with; and these systems are their potential for creating their own geography texts.

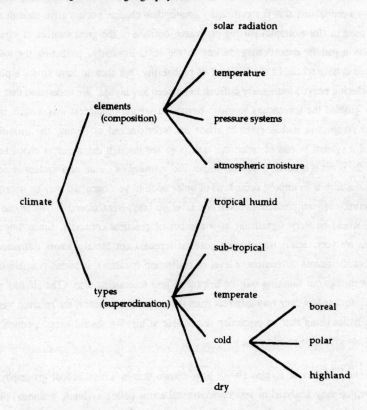

Fig. 8-5: Geographical taxonomy of climate (meronymic & hyponymic)

Here we are focussing not on the language of the geography text book, or of climatic theory as scientific construct, but on another register having to do with the weather: namely the language of weather forecasting. We have used as our sources those weather forecasts that are presented in print in a special section of a daily newspaper; the specimens that we used for detailed analysis were taken from the Chicago Tribune and the New York Times, but we have not limited ourselves exclusively to the forms of text employed in these two organs. We use our outline of the meaning base, as presented in Part II, to characterize the construction of ideational meanings in this register, in illustration of the principles of this approach as they would apply to a form of discourse that is semi-specialized and semi-technical. Since much of the text that needs to be processed in information systems of various kinds is of roughly this degree of specialization and technicality it seemed an appropriate choice for purposes of illustration. It is not a 'closed' register, i.e. one in which the set of possible messages can be listed; but neither is it a random sample of the English language. Anyone having mastered English beyond a certain degree of proficiency could construct the text from the situation or, equally, construct the situation from the text. Here is a typical sentence:

> Tonight will be cloudy, with a chance of rain or thunderstorms.
> (NYT)

There is little doubt about the source of an instance such as this.

One final introductory point concerns **grammatical metaphor**. This register is not highly metaphorical; but it does contain instances of grammatical metaphor, e.g. *in the wake of recent storminess*. These are part of the language of weather forecasting and have to be treated as such — storminess is construed as a participant (thing) and thus enters into the paradigmatic construction of phenomena as systems or sets of things. Weather is one of the domains of experience that is particularly problematic in this respect; we referred above to the example of rain as indeterminately process or thing, with neither appearing as obviously the more congruent form. In the overall semantics of weather forecasting, it is not so much the metaphorical nature of particular instances that is significant; what is of interest is whether, and if so how far, grammatical metaphor is systematically involved in construing this aspect of experience into information — into a commodity that can be stored, disseminated, withheld, used for policy-making and planning, and so on.

Let us first attempt to describe the context of weather forecasting informally in terms of field, tenor and mode: its 'contextual configuration' as defined by Hasan in Halliday & Hasan (1985/9).

I. Field

Keeping people informed: disseminating information by mass media: print: newspaper: daily.

State of natural environment: natural phenomena: weather — present conditions and prognostications for immediate future (0-2 days), specifying locality (varying focus, from district to world, with emphasis on 'region').

Special features: (1) explanations of events; (2) warnings of disaster; (3) information for special interest groups: those engaged in agriculture and gardening, boating and fishing, aviation, sport.

II. Tenor

Expert to laity, but with only moderate distance.

Expert standpoint: impersonal, with acknowledgment of uncertainty; attitude to subject-matter neutral.

Audience: interested general public, plus some groups of special concern (whose actions may be affected by the information).

Monologue.

III. Mode

Written: print: prose format.

Rhetorical mode: informative; semi-technical.

Accompanied by other visual modes: maps, with special (technical) symbols.

Day-to-day continuity, with date and place of origin specified.

Since we are concerned here with the ideation base, the relevant aspects of the situation are mainly those specified under 'field'. If we are *generating* texts, a description of the field will show which areas of ideational meaning are likely to be activated, and which options within those areas foregrounded. In other words, it will point to semantic features incorporated in the domain model. If we are *parsing*, we shall be able to construct the field from the meanings that are foregrounded in the text; and as the field emerges (or if it is known beforehand) it can be used to guide the parsing, for instance by ranking alternative interpretations and by managing the complexity of the parsing process.

For example: in the sample of texts used for this study, two thirds of all finite clauses had finite verbal operator *will*, and another 30% had finite verbal or some other form of modality: *could, is/ are likely* &c. Semantically, these represent future time and probability, which in turn are meanings we expect to find in a context of prognostication and prediction — and from which, therefore, we are able to construe such a context. Note that what is significant is not that there are one or two odd instances of future time reference, but that future has taken over as the norm; globally (across contexts) it is a highly marked choice of time reference (cf. Halliday & James, 1993), but locally in this context it has become the unmarked option (see further Chapter 13, Section 13.3 below).

In what follows we shall summarize the main features of weather forecasting texts in terms of the semantic model we sketched in Part II — recognizing sequences (Section 8.2.2), figures (Section 8.2.3) and elements (Section 8.2.4). Since this is not a quantitative study we have included features from other weather forecast texts which were not included in the original sample. The aim is to show how discourse in a specific register can be related to, and derived from, the meaning potential of the linguistic system as a whole.

8.2.2 Sequences

The meanings that are construed as sequences in weather forecasting texts are fairly restricted ones. There is very little projection (none in the sample studied), and within expansion only the logical relation of extending is exploited to any extent, though there is a certain amount of elaborating as well (no enhancing, apparently; cf. below on causality in the *figures*).

Extending relations, in turn, are either additive or adversative (contrastive). The additive nexus joins two related figures either on an equal basis with *and:*

> The chance of showers will end by Sunday night, and winds will shift to north (CT)

> Skies are expected to clear Wednesday, and afternoon highs will approach 70 (CT)

or unequally, the second being non-finite:

> Winds will shift to north, pushing ('and this will push') lows into the low 50s (CT)

> Tonight will be cloudy, with ('and there will be') a chance of rain or thunderstorms (NYT)

An additive nexus can then be extended further, like the following with one unequal and one equal:

> Warmer temperatures are likely Thursday, with ('and there will be') partly cloudy skies and highs ('will be') in the mid- to upper 70s. (CT)

No sequence of more than three figures occurred in the sample, and very few sequences consisted of more than two (i.e. a single nexus).

Adversative nexuses contrasted two figures, always in terms of either place ('here rain, elsewhere dry') or time ('morning sunny, afternoon cloudy'); they could be equal or unequal, in varying degrees. Note that in the first example the sequence containing the adversative relation is construed in the grammar not as a clause complex, but as a cohesive tie between complexes:

> High pressure will keep skies sunny and dry from New England south
> to Maryland. However, the Virginias and Carolinas will be hot &
> humid ... (CT)

> Skies will be sunny tomorrow morning, but will become increasingly
> cloudy during the afternoon. (NYT)

> Skies will be clear to partly cloudy over the rest of California,
> though widely scattered thunderstorms could develop in southern
> sections. (CT)

> The heatwave in the Southeast will weaken slightly, although
> northern Florida will remain hot. (CT)

> Morning skies will be partly cloudy today, becoming ('but will
> become') partly sunny by afternoon. (NYT)

— by which time, of course, they will no longer be morning skies. Less common is a
third type of extending, the subtractive:

> The rest of the south will be mostly dry and sunny, with only
> ('except that there will be') isolated showers in Florida. (CT)

Elaborating nexuses are less common than extending, and seem to be always unequal:

> High temperatures will be 70s to low 80s, warmest in the
> Carolinas. (CT)

The second figure adds specificity to the first. The following might also be
elaborating, though it is probably to be reinterpreted as temporal, 'while at the same
time':

> Skies will be partly sunny in Alabama and Georgia as scattered
> thunderstorms diminish later in the day. (CT)

We could derive from these the general principles that, given any two figures, (1) if
they represent different but related weather features staying constant in one location (time
and place), they form an additive nexus; (2) if they represent the same weather features
varying across different locations (time or place), they form an adversative nexus; and
perhaps (3) if they represent the same weather features varying across locations where the
second location is part of the first, they form a subtractive nexus. One instance *not*
covered by these principles is

```
Highs will be mostly 70s and 80s; a few 60s are likely near the
Canadian border, and parts of the southern plains will reach the
90s. (CT)
```

— where the second nexus would be expected to be adversative; the reason it is additive is that the last two figures are alike in both being exceptions (subtractive) to the first.

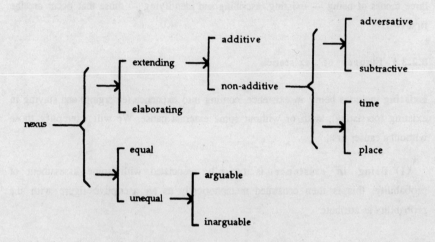

Fig. 8-6: Meteorological sequences

Any such nexus may assign equal or unequal status to the figures; where it is unequal, the sequence seems to be typically descending (grammatically, the dependent clause follows). It is difficult to find a general principle governing the choice of status, but in the adversative there is perhaps a prosody of evaluation here: if the second condition is felt to be 'worse' (less desirable) than the first, the adversative relation is more likely to be equal, because of the somewhat negative connotation of an explicit 'but'. Thus compare:

```
Morning skies will be partly cloudy today, becoming partly sunny
by afternoon. (NYT)
```

```
Skies will be sunny tomorrow morning, but will become increasingly
cloudy during the afternoon. (NYT)
```

In New York, at least, sunny skies are to be preferred over cloudy ones.

We can represent the postulated semantic options for sequences in a network as shown in Figure 8-6 above. We have included the distinction, within the unequal, between those where the second, minor figure is arguable and those where it is inarguable (grammatically, finite versus non-finite hypotactic clause), although in the main sample the only clear example of a finite dependent clause is *skies will be partly sunny ... as thunderstorms diminish* (adversatives with *although, though* are hardly dependent). It seems likely that the distinction will be significant in the register as a whole.

8.2.3 Figures

All figures in the sample are figures of being; there is no doing, sensing or saying. Of the three modes of being — existing, ascribing and identifying — those that occur are the first two.

8.2.3.1 Figures of 'existence'

Existing includes being in existence, coming into existence (emerging) and staying in existing (persisting); with or without some external cause. We will exemplify those without a causer first.

(1) **Being in existence** is typically associated with some assessment of probability; this is then construed metaphorically as an ascriptive figure with the probability as attribute:

> rain is forecast today for the Middle Atlantic States and the
> Missouri Valley (NYT)
> clouds and showers are likely in Idaho and parts of Montana (CT)
> rain is likely in the Ohio River Valley and Kentucky (CT)
> scattered showers are also expected in the Carolinas (NYT)

(Note that some such examples are, however, still ascriptive in their congruent mode; e.g. *clear skies are forecast for tonight, high temperatures are expected,* where the sense is 'skies will be clear', 'temperature will be high'. See Section 8.2.3.2 below.)

It seems that figures of 'being in existence' without attached probability occur mainly in nonfinite clauses; e.g.

> with only isolated showers in Florida (CT)

(For the subregister where 'figures' consist of one element only, such as *Variable cloudiness,* see below, the final paragraph of the present section.) The simple existential *there will be ...* is not generally favoured, although related formulations sometimes occur with the sense of 'there is a warning', e.g.

> an air pollution advisory is also in effect for Cook and Lake
> Counties until 4 PM Saturday (CT)

(2) **Coming into existence**, on the other hand, is commonly asserted either with or without probabilities attached, e.g.

```
showers and thunderstorms will gather over the northern Rockies
(CT)
widely scattered showers will develop in the Balkans (CT)
scattered showers may develop (CT)
```

Verbs such as *gather* and *develop* typically realize figures of doing; here, however, they represent figures of being, in a metaphorical syndrome in which the weather processes are construed as participants, e.g. *showers*. These examples are different from congruent figures of doing, such as *birds will gather over the northern Rockies,* in both aspects of the participant-process configuration: (i) *showers, thunderstorms,* and other such metaphorical participants are not like Actors such as *birds* that are involved in figures of doing; and (ii) the processes of *gathering, developing,* etc. are metaphoric expressions of phase — they are inceptive, with the sense of 'beginning to be', whereas there is no inceptive feature in such processes in figures of doing.

Since it is entirely possible to create a semantic proportion of the kind:

modality \ phase \	(1) be in existence	(2) come into existence
(a) absolute	*rain will occur*	*rain will develop*
(b) probable	*rain may occur*	*rain may develop*

it is not obvious why type (1a) should be disfavoured, as it seems to be — although possibly it is felt to be more absolute than (2a) on the grounds that the inceptive phase already has a slight prosody of uncertainty about it.

(3) **Staying in existence** and (4) **ceasing to exist** should also be included as options (e.g. *rain will/ may persist; rain will/ may cease*), although much rarer in the sample studied.

What are the 'things' that are being said to 'exist', in a weather forecast? Typically they are forms of precipitation: rain, snow, showers &c. Sometimes, by a further grammatical metaphor, it is the probability that is said to exist, e.g.:

```
with (= 'there being') a chance of rain or thunderstorms (NYT)
the chance of showers will end by Sunday night (CT)
```

— the latter suggesting that an opportunity is about to be missed!

Existing may be construed as the effect of some **external cause**, with or without a probability being attached. Typical 'causes' are weather systems, fronts, and high or low measurements of pressure:

```
a warm front may bring scattered showers or thunderstorms to the
northern Tennessee Valley (CT)
a separate weather system will bring thunderstorms to the eastern
Dakotas and Minnesota in the morning and into the Great Lakes
later in the day (CT)
low pressure will produce scattered showers from the Pacific (CT)
a cool front stalled in the Carolinas may set off scattered
afternoon thunderstorms (CT)
```

There is a systemic relation between *produce* in this context, as 'causing to be', and *produce* as 'doing' with a doer involved; analogous to that which we saw with *develop* and *gather* above (as 'beginning to be' and as 'doing'). These provide interesting illustrations of the complementarity of 'being' and 'doing', which we discussed in Chapter 4, Section 4.3.3 above.

8.2.3.2 Figures of 'ascription' (attribution)

Ascribing ('being' in the sense of carrying an attribute), like existing, distinguishes a neutral phase 'be' and marked phases of becoming, staying or ceasing to be. The carrier of the attribute may be (a) a feature (a component thing or quality) of the weather, e.g. skies, temperatures, storms, or (b) a time or place; and again, some external cause may be involved.

(a) **Carrier as weather feature.** Those where the carrier is a weather feature typically consist of a configuration of this feature with a relational process 'be', an attribute, and a circumstance of time or place:

```
skies will be clear tonight (NYT)
some storms could be heavy with hail and strong winds (CT)
skies will be mostly sunny over the southern plains (CT)
high temperatures will be in the middle 70s[2] (NYT)
lows will be near 60 degrees (NYT)
```

---

[2] Note that *high* in this example is a *class* of temperature not a *property* — the meaning is 'the top temperature in the 24 hour period'; cf. *highs, lows*.

(i) Sometimes the circumstance of time is construed as a class of the weather feature in question, e.g.

> ```
> morning skies will be partly cloudy today (NYT)
> afternoon highs will range from 50s and 60s in the northern
> Rockies to 100s in Arizona deserts (CT)
> afternoon highs will approach 70 (CT)
> ```

In the last of these the process is metaphoric for 'be' + minor process (type 8.i in Chapter 6, Table 6(3)): congruently *will be near 70*.

(ii) Secondly, the attribute itself may be a circumstance of place, of the 'extent' type; the feature 'extent' is also present in the process:

> ```
> rain will be scattered across the central lake region (NYT)
> rain showers will be scattered from New England to the Virginias
> today (NYT)
> showers will also extend from Montana, across northern Idaho, to
> Washington (NYT)
> ```

There are also odd occurrences of a related figure in which the place is not being *ascribed* to the weather feature as its attribute but rather set up as something to be *defined by* it, e.g.

> ```
> sunny skies will dominate most of the region
> ```

Grammatically such examples are identifying clauses, as shown by the fact that they select for voice — although here the sense of the agnate passive clause *most of the region will be dominated by sunny skies* suggests that *dominate* should be interpreted as an ascriptive, i.e. as 'prevail' + circumstance of extent 'over most of the region', rather than as 'prevail over' + 'most of the region'.

(iii) Thirdly, while there were no examples of *become* in the texts under study, a figure such as

> ```
> skies will become cloudy in the late afternoon
> ```

would presumably be a possible sentence in a weather forecast. There are however many instances where an attribute is transcategorized as a process of becoming, e.g.

> ```
> the heat in the Southeast will weaken slightly ('become weaker')
> (CT)
> ```

```
scattered thunderstorms will diminish ('become less') later in the
day (CT)
skies are expected to clear ('become clear') Wednesday (CT)
winds will shift to north ('become northerly') (CT)
```

In the last example, *shift* is relational not material; the sense is 'change so as to become northerly', not 'move to the north' (cf. *the sand dunes shifted to the north*).

(iv) Fourthly, the configuration may include an **extrinsic cause**, as in the following example with *keep* ('cause to remain'):

```
high pressure will keep skies sunny and dry from New England south
to Maryland (CT)
```

(b) **Carrier as time/place.** Those where the carrier is a time or place form configurations consisting simply of this feature with 'be' plus attribute:

```
the Plains States will be sunny, warm and dry (NYT)
tonight will be mostly fair (NYT)
most of the South West will be clear to partly cloudy and dry (CT)
northern Florida will remain hot (CT)
```

Occasionally this relationship is construed as a process of acquiring, with the acquired possession as Range, as in:[3]

```
some areas could get 1-3 inches of rain (CT)
```

We saw above that some existential figures are construed metaphorically as ascriptive: namely those where a probability is represented in the form of an ascribed quality, as in:

```
rain is likely in the Ohio River Valley and Kentucky (CT)
scattered showers are also expected in the Carolinas (NYT)
widely scattered showers and storms are possible in the northern
Tennessee Valley (CT)
```

These are congruently existential: 'there may be rain', 'there may be scattered showers' (not 'showers may be scattered'). Similarly in an ascriptive figure the probability may be

---

[3] Such instances are on the borderline of being and doing: the verb *get* suggests a process of doing, with *obtain* and *acquire* as agnates (cf. Halliday, 1985: 125), but here on the other hand the more likely agnate seems to be a process of being with *have*. Cf. again Chapter 4, Section 4.3.3 above.

mapped onto an ascribed quality; the attribute is then construed as a quality of the 'carrier' participant (Epithet + Thing construing Carrier + Attribute); e.g.

```
warmer temperatures are likely Thursday (CT)
clear skies are forecast for tonight (NYT)
high temperatures in the 100s are forecast for Texas and the
Southwest (NYT)
```

These are ascriptive: the congruent sense is 'temperatures may be warmer', 'skies may be clear'. The relationship is diagrammed in Figure 8-7.

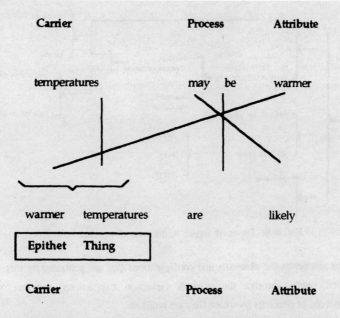

Fig. 8-7: Modalized ascription reconstrued as ascription of modality

Some instances seem indeterminate, e.g.

```
heavy to severe thunderstorms are possible in Colorado and
northern sections of Utah and Nevada during the afternoon (CT)
```

— either 'there may be heavy to severe thunderstorms' or 'thunderstorms may be heavy to severe'.

The carrier may be a metaphoric nominalization of a process or property as thing:

```
variable cloudiness is expected tomorrow (NYT)
gradual clearing is expected tonight (NYT)
```

8.2.3.3 Summary of figures

Our network of figures would then be as shown in Figure 8-8. This may be too constrained, in not generating caused ascriptives with location as carrier, e.g. *will keep tomorrow fine;* but no instances of this type were found. On the other hand it may be too generous, in allowing for all phases with all types of existence and ascription, whereas only a subset were found to be represented in the texts studied; here however there seems no clear reason for excluding the remaining combinations (e.g. *rain will persist; a cool front will reduce temperatures*). It would also be possible to treat as a systematic option the mapping of probability on to attribute or existent: see Figure 8-9.

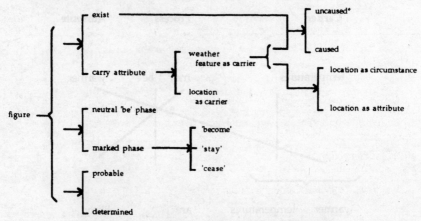

Fig. 8-8: Types of figure in domain of weather forecasts

Let us enumerate the elements and configurations that are generated by this network. We specify paths through the network (selection expressions) together with the configurations of elements by which they are realized:

(1) 'Existing' figures

exist: uncaused

Existent + Be1 (+ Place) (+ Time)

exist: cause

Agent + Be2 + Existent (+ Place) (+ Time)

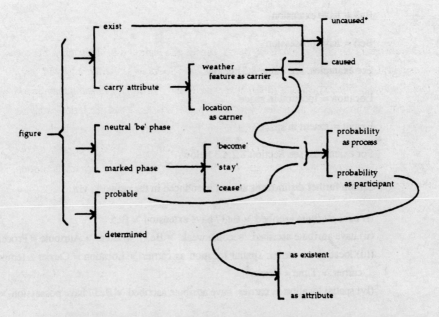

Fig. 8-9: Types of figure, including construal of probability

(2) 'Ascribing' figures

ascribe: weather as Carrier: uncaused

Carrier + Be3 + Attribute (+ Location) (+ Extent) (+ Time)
Carrier + Be5 + Extent (+ Location) (+ Time)
Carrier + [Attribute = Process] (+ Time)

ascribe: weather as Carrier: caused

Agent + Be4 + Attribute (+ Location) (+ Extent) (+ Time)

ascribe: location as Carrier: uncaused*

[Carrier = Location] + Be3 + Attribute (+ Time)
[Carrier = Time] + Be3 + Attribute (+ Location) (+ Extent)
[Carrier = Location] + Be6 + Attribute

Notes:

(1)

Be1 = 'exist, come to exist, continue to exist, cease to exist'

Be2 = 'cause to exist'

Be3 = 'have attribute ascribed'

Be4 = 'cause to have attribute ascribed'

Be5 = 'have extension'

Be6 = 'have possession'

For examples, see Table 8(3) below.

Location = 'location in space'

Extent = 'extent in space'

For examples, see Section 8.2.4.3 below.

(2) Certain further distinctions are not introduced in the network, viz.:

(i) have attribute ascribed ↘ Be3 / have extension ↘ Be5

(ii) have attribute ascribed: 'become weak' ↘ Be3 / 'weaken' ↘ Attribute = Process

(iii) location as carrier: spatial location as carrier ↘ Location = Carrier / temporal location as carrier ↘ Time = Carrier

(iv) spatial location as carrier: have attribute ascribed ↘ Be3 / have possession ↘ Be6

(3) Features of time and place are not included in the network; in principle, any selection expression may be accompanied by either or both of these.

Tables 8(1) and 8(2) display the features in the network (rows) and show how they are realized as the presence of functions or constraints on functions (columns).

Finally, we note transcategorizations and junctions, showing the type of element involved:

Transcategorizations	Attribute => Being	process (*weaken, diminish, end, increase, clear*)
Junctions	Probability = Attribute	participant: quality
	Probability = Existent	participant: thing
	Time = Carrier	participant: thing
	Attribute = Existent	participant: thing

~*~*~*~

Table 8(1): Features of 'existing' figures

			Be	Agent	Existent	Attribute	Place	Time
exist			Be		Existent: participant: (quality:) thing		(Place)	(Time)
	uncaused		Be1: process, 'exist' (be/ come to be/ stay being)					
	caused		Be2: process, 'cause to exist' (bring, produce, set off)	Agent				
	probable					Probability = Attribute		
	determined							
	neutral phase be		Be1: be					
	marked phase	become	Be1: gather, develop					
		stay	Be1: persist					
		cease						

There is one sub-register within the "weather" register where the figures appear to be constructed not as configurations but as single elements; for example

```
Saturday: Mostly sunny; highs 78 to 83.

Saturday night: Clear; lows 58-63.

Sunday: Increasing cloudiness, chance of thundershowers
north; highs 80s. (CT)
```

However, when they are scrutinized more closely such figures turn out to be identical in their semantic construction with some of those in the primary register. What is different is the type of grammatical structure through which they are realized. Those just cited are in telegraphic form (cf. Halliday, 1985: Appendix 2), and it is not difficult to match them with their expanded agnates:

```
Saturday: Mostly sunny;          Saturday will be mostly sunny.
Sunday: Increasing cloudiness,   Cloudiness will increase
                                     Sunday,
chance of thunderstorms north;   with a chance of thunderstorms
                                     in the north.
highs 80s.                       High temperatures will be in
                                     the 80s.
```

Semantically however they do not need any special provision.

Table 8(2): Features of 'ascribing' figures

			Process: Be	Agent	Carrier	Attribute	Location (location in space)	Extent (extent in space)	Time
ascribe			Be		Carrier	Attribute	(Location)	(Extent)	(Time)
	weather feature as carrier								
	location as carrier				Carrier = Location OR Carrier = Time		Location		Time
	uncaused		Be3:						
	caused		Be4: process, 'causing to have ascribed'	Causer					
	probable	probability as process	Be: modalized						
		probability as attribute				Probability = Attribute			
	determined								
	neutral phase be		Be3: be						
	marked phase	become	Be3: become, turn, shift						
		stay	Be3: remain, stay						
		cease							

8.2.4 Elements

The elements occurring in the weather forecast texts can be specified according to their potential functions within the figures just described. In the most general terms, they can be categorized as processes, participants, and circumstances:

(1) processes: existing, having ascribed, extending, possessing (= Be 1-6 above)

(2) participants: precipitation, and other weather phenomena; weather systems;
                      temperature and pressure; times and places; probabilities

(3) circumstances: locations & extents in time & space (= Place 1-2 above)

We will consider each of these in turn.

8.2.4.1 Processes

All the processes in these texts are types of being: existing (including causing to exist), having some attribute (including causing to have some attribute), or having some extension or possession. These are shown together with examples in Table 8(3).

Table 8(3): Processes: types of 'being'

FUNCTION IN FIGURE	TYPE	EXAMPLES
Be 1	exist:	be
	: come to be	gather, develop
	: keep being	persist
Be2	cause to exist	bring, produce, set off
Be3	be ... (= have attribute ascribed)	be, range, approach
	become ...	become, turn, shift
	keep ...	remain, stay
Attribute => Process	become ...	weaken, diminish, end, increase, clear
Be4	cause to be ... (= have attribute ascribed)	make, keep
Be5	be ... (= have extension)	extend, be scattered, dominate
Be6	be ... (= have possession)	have, get

In addition, processes may have attached to them an expression of probability: *may, could, should,* etc.. (Probability may also be construed metaphorically as a participant serving as Existent or Attribute.)

8.2.4.2 Participants

Participants of the subtype 'thing' include various types of precipitation; skies, wind, frost and cloud; conditions; temperature, pressure; weather system, front; particular times and places. They also include two sets of qualities construed as things: names of weather conditions, and names of probabilities. These are differentiated (i) according to which functional roles they take on in figures and (ii) according to which qualities are ascribed to them. Table 8(4) shows which types of participant take on which functions in a figure. We have separated out a function of Possession (e.g. *showers,* in *some parts will have showers*) from that of Attribute, of which it is a subtype, because in this register such "possessed" Attributes pattern more like Existents than like Attributes of other types.

Table 8(4): Participants according to roles in figures

TYPE OF PARTICIPANT:		FUNCTION IN FIGURE:			
		1. Existent or Attribute	2. Carrier	3. Agent	4. Attribute
things	precipitation	√	√		
	other: wind, frost, cloud	√	√		
	quality: quality of expansion: cloudiness, storminess	√ Attribute = Existent			⇓ (see below)
	quality: quality of projection (chance, possibility, likelihood)	√ Probability = Existent			⇓ (see below)
	temperatures		√		
	skies		√		
	conditions		√		
	places		√ Location = Carrier		
	times		√ Time = Carrier		
	front			√	
	weather system			√	
	pressure			√	
qualities (not construed as things)					√

We can now group the things into sets according to their functional roles: (1) Existent or Possession, (2) Carrier, (3) Agent, (4) Attribute; and specify the various qualities that are assigned to the members of each set.

(1) Existent or Possession

Table 8(5) shows the qualities ascribed to participants functioning as Existent or Possession.

Table 8(5): Qualities ascribed to things as Existent or Possession

TYPE OF PARTICIPANT				time - frequency			space - extent		intensity		light/ strong/ gale force/ moderate	severe/ light/ moderate	space-location high/ low
				occasional	persistent	variable	scattered	isolated	heavy	light			
precipitation	rain	showers	showers	✓	✓		✓		✓	✓			
			rain showers	✓			✓		✓				
			thundershowers	✓			✓		✓				
		storms	storms	✓			✓		✓				
			thunderstorms	✓	✓		✓	✓	✓				
		rain	rain	✓					✓	✓			
			drizzle	✓					–				
	other	hail	hail	✓			✓	✓	✓				
			hailstorms	✓	✓		✓		✓				
		sleet		✓	✓				✓	✓			
		snow	snow	✓			✓	✓	✓	✓			
			snowshowers	✓			✓		✓	✓			
			snowstorms	✓					✓				
other			winds			✓					✓		
			frost									✓	
			clouds										✓

(2) Carrier

All the types of 'thing' that function as Existent or Possession can also function as Carrier in a figure of ascription; see Table 8(5) for the qualities assigned to these. In addition, as Carrier we find *temperatures* (classified as *high/ low*; also *highs*), *skies* (classified as *morning, afternoon, evening* or *night*) and *conditions*.

There are also circumstantial elements in this function: Location as Carrier and Time as Carrier.

Location = Carrier

[any expression of location, e.g. *the Plains States, the northern plateau region, Texas, inland, the northern half of the country, the Carolinas, the Rockies, the metropolitan area, the Northwest, the Mexican border,* &c&c]

Time = Carrier

today; this morning, this afternoon, this evening, tonight
tomorrow; tomorrow morning/ afternoon/ evening/ night
mornings, afternoons, evenings, nights
the morning hours, the early/ middle/ later part of the day

(3) Agent

The 'things' that function as Agent in figures of existence and ascription are *front, weather system* and *pressure;* the qualities that are assigned to these have to do with degree or with position and movement:

TYPE OF THING:	TYPE OF QUALITY:			
	temperature		space	intensity
front	warm, cool, cold	occluded	stationary, moving	
weather system			separate, departing	
pressure				high, low

(4) Attribute

All the types of quality that can occur as Epithet with the things functioning as Existent or Possession (see Table 8(5)) can also occur as Attribute in a figure of ascription (e.g. *heavy showers/ showers will be heavy*), though some are less likely in this latter function (e.g. *occasional*). In addition, other qualities occur as Attribute in configuration with a specific Carrier; these are shown in Table 8(6).

8.2.4.3 Circumstances

Circumstances are almost exclusively spatio-temporal — locations and extents in space-time; the only others are a small number of circumstances of manner. Those occurring in our sample can be listed as follows.

1. Place 1: location

> in (on)/ to/ from/ near [+ place expression]
> north/ south/ east/ west of [+ place expression]

2. Place 2: extent

> over/ across [+ place expression]
> as far as [+ place expression]
> from [+ place expression] to [+ place expression]
> generally

3. Time

> today, this morning, this afternoon, this evening, tonight
> tomorrow, tomorrow morning/ afternoon/ evening/ night
> during/ in + the day/ morning/ afternoon/ evening/ night
> during/ in + the morning hours
> during/ in + the early/ middle/ later part of the day

4. Manner

> slightly, gradually

8.2.5 Commentary on weather forecasting domain

What we have set out to do in this section is to use our general semantic characterization of the ideation base to construct a semantic representation of the ideational band within a particular register of English — a "domain", that of weather forecasts as printed in the daily press. The examples were drawn from a small collection of such texts; but the sample was used as a means of entry to show what were the typical meaning formations within this register, not as a corpus covering the entire range of possibilities. So both the networks and the constructional categories go beyond what was present in the sample. The words used to exemplify the elements were taken from the sample texts, but it should not be difficult to assign other words to the appropriate categories when extending the coverage beyond what we have been able to include here (cf. Figure 8-3).

Table 8(6): Other Attributes combining with specific Carriers

Carrier	Attribute						
	of expansion: elaborating						of projection
	temperature	humidity	[sky]	[wind]	space	intensity	probability; expectation; prediction
temperatures	hot, warm, mild, cool, cold, [all + er] freezing; high, low [+ er]; in the low/ mid/ upper [decile, e.g. 50s]						
conditions, locations, times	hot, warm, mild, cool, cold	dry, humid	cloudy	stormy			
skies			(partly/ mainly/ mostly +) clear, sunny, cloudy, overcast				
front, weather system					stationary, stalled, moving		
pressure						high, low	
...							Probability = Attribute likely/ probably, possible; expected, forecast, projected, predicted

In texts of any register, unless it is totally closed and listable, there will always be maverick instances which are more or less outside the range of typical forms. Here for example we found [most of the region will be sunny and dry] in the wake of recent storminess and [a departing weather system] may still exert enough influence to [produce showers in the Pacific Northwest]; neither in the wake of nor exert enough influence to have been included in our coverage. They could be. On the other hand, the patterns they represent have little generality in this register, so the pay off would be rather small. In generating weather forecasts one could do without them, and not much would be lost if one failed to interpret them in parsing. We have concentrated on patterns which are typical, frequent and productive. (We have also ignored those passages which refer to the weather in the past. But the same principles applying to tomorrow will be ... will also apply to yesterday was ... .)

A description of this kind can be taken over by the **grammar** and turned into text. Here we have not attempted to take it the whole way (see further Chapter 9 below); the specification of future time reference in the process, for example, would be taken into the grammar as a **preselection** of tense: future, which in turn would be realized as *will* + the verb representing the process. We have indicated some of the wordings, both lexical and grammatical, in order to make our account clear; but these are not necessarily — in fact not usually — the only output forms. For example, we have specified *clear skies are expected* and *skies should become clear,* because these are construed differently *in the semantics:* they are agnate but they are not synonymous. On the other hand we have not described *skies are expected to clear* as something separate from *skies should become clear;* not because we regard them as completely identical in meaning, but because the distinction is a more delicate one and we consider it would be out of place in the present context. The choice between the two would be left to the grammar.

There are two important principles at work. (i) One is that of delicacy. In a paradigmatic model such as the present one, both the lexicogrammar and the semantics accommodate variable delicacy: two agnate constructions may be both 'the same' and 'different' according to the delicacy of the focus adopted. (ii) Secondly, although we are presenting the semantics as input (in the case of a text generation system), the assumption being that the grammar then does what it is told, our metatheoretic position is that the construction of meaning is *both* a discourse-semantic *and* a lexicogrammatical process, so that the particular way in which this is modelled in any designed information processing system (e.g. a text generation system) is an artefact of that system, reflecting on the one hand the state of the technology (hardware and software) and on the other hand the aims of its designers and the level of their understanding of the language and language variety they are working with.

In the present instance, the system might be that of Penman, in which the text generation is driven by the grammar, but at every choice point there is a 'chooser' which consults the meaning base for instructions on which way to go. Or one might adopt, instead of a 'chooser', a principle that we might call a 'charger', whereby the text is generated in the semantics which then 'charges' the grammar with the task of realizing the sequences, figures and elements that have been construed. In both these models (see further Chapter 9 below), some discretion will be left to the grammar. Partly this is for metafunctional reasons; we should recall here that our present semantics is ideational only — we are describing only the 'ideation' base, not the interaction base and the text base, and these also provide input to the grammar. But even with this input there will still be underdetermination; the grammar will never be exhaustively controlled 'from above'. It would take us beyond our present scope to try to discuss principles for selection within the grammar itself — default choices, favouring or avoiding repetition, and the like. What we do want to stress is that an information system needs to be flexible enough to allow for various ways of modelling the relationship between the semantics and the grammar (including *mixtures* of various ways); and that this is likely to be more readily achieved if the level 'above' the grammar is construed as a meaning base — that is, in terms of linguistic concepts derived from the grammar itself — than if it is construed in the form of knowledge that in some sense 'exists' independently of the language that encodes it.

Furthermore, the meaning base in turn can be related to a further level of environment, the **context of situation** (cf. Steiner, 1988a). We have given only a very general sketch of the situation type from which these weather forecast texts derive. But the same point could be made here too: we may model the relationship in one direction or the other, but text and context are construed together. There is an important variable here, of course, that we have already referred to as the cline from 'language in reflection' to 'language in action'. In situations of the 'language in action' kind, where the discourse is a relatively minor component of the total activity, the grammar and semantics are obviously less constructive of the whole than in a 'reflection' context such as the present one. In weather forecasting, while the weather itself is not constituted of language, the activity of forecasting is; the entire situation is built up out of black marks on large white pieces of paper towards which is directed the attention of some human consciousness. Out of this is construed a particular context or situation-type; since the semantics is specific to that situation, the reader knows where he is, construes the situation in the particular instantial form ('oh — so it's going to rain this afternoon'), and perhaps varies his actions in accordance with this construction.

How is the non-discursive component — the weather — made to impact on the discourse? In the old days, I went out and sniffed the air; there was no institutionalized register of weather forecasting, only some bodily activities, physical and conscious, forming part of the total continuum of existence. Now, we may envisage something more along these lines: that the weather satellites record pressures, temperatures, air movements and so on and transmit a large number of measurements with indication of their place and time of origin. The weather has now become **information**; but in numerical, not yet discursive form. Using guiding principles derived from some representation of the situation, the system construes these measurements into meanings, in the form of sequences, figures and elements. The knowledge that the system needs in order to take this step is itself represented in this form: that is, in the form of meanings, such as 'low pressure will produce rain', which, although they may be considerably more complex, are constructed out of the same resources. The resulting semantic formations are then construed by the lexicogrammar into wordings, and output in the form of text.

The system may also be designed to produce output in the form of other, non-discursive graphic modes, most typically maps. One of the interesting questions to be explored is how far these other modes of meaning can be built into the same overall model, and at what points — for example, as alternative 'wordings' of a given semantic construction. In this particular register it seems that much of what it put out in the form of a map *could* be interpreted in this way; that, for example, isotherms on the map and clauses such as *high temperatures will range from 60s in the northern Rockies to 100s in Arizona* could be construed as alternative realizations of the same semantic figure, or sequence of figures. Many visual semiotic systems are 'paraphrastic' in this sense, although certainly not all.

Finally we should note that not all discourse about the weather, even if it is printed under the same rubric in the same newspaper, falls within the register described above. Here is a much more heteroglossic meteorological text:

```
South in 6th day of deadly heat


From Chicago Tribune wires


ATLANTA — Churches offered air-conditioned refuge for poor people,
Alabama provided fans to poultry farmers and some merchants ran
out of ice Thursday as Southerners baked and crops wilted under a
killer heat wave for a sixth straight day.

But forecasters promised that relief from the 100-degree-plus
temperatures was just a few days away.
```

Characterized in terms of the general domains of experience construed by figures, weather forecasts fall within being & having — and this is one respect in which they differ from the last text quoted above (e.g. *forecasters promised ...*). This does not mean that they are completely static — there are phases of being (coming to be, etc.); nor that there is no sense of causation — fronts, weather systems, and pressures can serve as Agent. However, the basic motif is one of states of being without any external causes; put in terms of scale, a weather forecast construes a **macro-being** — the meteorological state of the environment — consisting of a number of atomic micro-beings which move in and out of existence of their own accord. The domain construed in recipes, which we turn to now, is at another pole of figures — one of doing, where a human acts to impact on the world (within the confines of the kitchen).

8.3. The language of recipes

Having satisfied ourselves that today's skies will be sunny, we can worry about today's food. We need a plan, a recipe. Breakfast seems the natural place to start —

```
1. Put nutritious Kellogg's Sultana Bran into a clean bowl.
2. Pour fresh milk.
3. Ready to serve.
4. Eat and enjoy Kellogg's Sultana Bran.
```

A recipe is a kind of procedural text — a sequence of operations for arriving at some well-defined end result, such as an assembled piece of furniture, a smoothly running car, a well-kept garden or a dish (e.g. Martin, 1985: 5-6; Longacre, 1974, 1976). The notion of procedure can be taken as a summary gloss of the domain; it is a **macro-operation**, consisting of a number of atomic **micro-operations**. It is dominated by procedures (algorithms, figures of doing) that lead to some specific goal: the dominant cause is purposive. An agent or agents try to produce, assemble, repair, etc..

From the interpersonal point of view, the notion of procedure can also be taken as a gloss on the interaction between the writer and the reader; it is a macro-proposal, consisting of a number of instructions or directions to the reader.

8.3.1 The specific domain of a recipe

Before interpreting the culinary field in terms of our general taxonomy, we will present it first in terms of its own register-specific organization. In a recipe, we find representations of the cook, food items (including both dishes and their ingredient parts: *the butter, the onion, the stock* ...)), utensils (*with a knife, ...*) and other tools, time units (*20-30 minutes, ...*), culinary happenings that occur without the cook's intervention, culinary operations where the cook acts on food items; and culinary ascriptions where a food item is assigned to a class of dish or to a state of consistency, colour, etc. (*tender, brown, ...*). There is also a component of judgement, either personal, the cook's preference, or impersonal, the desirability or necessity of an act. Consider the following example:[4]

> Hungarian Potatoes
>
> [ingredients]
>
> Melt the butter in a saucepan and add the onion; cook gently until soft. Add the stock and the purée. Bring to the boil and add the potato cut into 1/2 - 3/4 inch dice. Add seasoning and paprika, cover and cook gently until tender, about 20-30 minutes. Taste and adjust the seasoning if necessary. Serve with garnish. (H & H, p. 192)
>
> Roast Artichokes
>
> Place some oil or vegetable/ nut fat in a roasting-tin and heat to about 400° F. Place peeled artichokes in tins and roast until

---

[4] For our examples, we use N.B. Highton & R.B. Highton, 1964, The Home Book of Vegetarian Cookery. London: Faber and Faber [H & H].

cooked. They will become discoloured but the flavour is very good. You may prefer to roast them around a nut or similar savoury. If they are roasted in their skins, the skins are uneatable as they become bitter but the flesh is good. (H & H, p. 138)

Artichoke Chips

Peel artichokes, cut into thin slices and place immediately in acidulated water — leave there for 20-30 minutes and then pat dry with a clean absorbent cloth (a clean drying-up cloth is good but should be cleaned after use). Fry immediately in deep fat or oil. Serve at once. (H & H, p. 138)

Asparagus Rolls

Prepare some small rolls (from your favourite bread recipe) well cooked and crusty, remove from the oven and slice off the tops. Scoop out the inside and fill with asparagus tips and mousseline sauce. Replace the lids of the rolls and warm in the oven for 10-15 minutes. This is a good savoury, either for the beginning or end of a meal, or as a supper dish. (H & H, p. 139)

As far as figures are concerned, there are some states of culinary being — *until tender, until cooked, but the flavour is very good.* Here an Attribute of some material quality is ascribed to an ingredient or whole dish serving as Carrier. (There is also a minor type with a modality as Attribute and a typically implicit figure as Carrier — *if necessary.*) However, operations changing the state of what is being prepared tend to dominate — *then pat dry with a clean absorbent cloth, cook gently, leave there for 20-30 minutes.* Here the Medium is food, an ingredient or the emerging dish, and the Agent is the cook. The result of the change may be construed as an Attribute characterizing the Medium — *then pat dry, cut into thin slices;* or the Attribute may construe a condition of the Medium — *Serve hot* (not illustrated in the recipes quoted above). The likely circumstances are Place (*in tins, in the oven*), Manner-quality (*gently*), Manner-means (either equipment: *with a clean absorbent cloth*, or ingredient: *with asparagus tips and mousseline sauce*), Duration (*for 20-30 minutes*). The groupings of the classes just mentioned and illustrated are shown in Figure 8-10. It also shows the value restrictions on Medium and Agent as examples of such restrictions in the culinary domain.

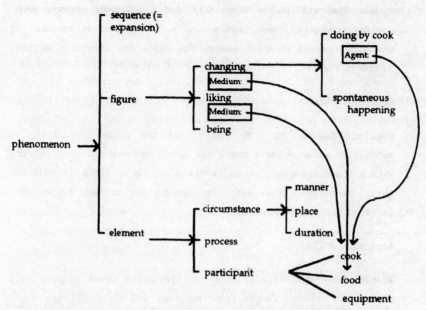

Fig. 8-10: Taxonomy specific to the culinary domain (in recipes)

Interestingly, the culinary domain seems to be largely congruent in recipes; there is very little grammatical metaphor, if any. If we consider recipes written for children where grammatical metaphor is likely to be avoided (cf. Chapter 6, Section 6.8), we find that they are quite similar to adult recipes in this respect; they are also congruent — for example:

```
Grilled Cheese and Tomato Sandwich

Preheat broiler.

On a piece of Whole-Wheat Bread (page 51), spread slices of any
cheese you like. Sprinkle a little dill weed, salt, and onion
powder on the cheese. Place slices of tomato on top of the cheese
and cover with another piece of bread.

Put sandwich in the broiler, 2-3 inches from the flames or coil.
Watch carefully and toast until bread turns golden brown and
cheese begins to melt. Turn sandwich over and repeat process.
```
(Sharon Cadwallader, Cooking Adventures for Kids. Boston: Houghton Mifflin Company.)

There may be differences in the sophistication of the dish and type of instructions (controlling behaviour, e.g., *Watch carefully*); but there is no perceptible difference in the degree of metaphor between the recipes for kids exemplified here and adult recipes — both types are quite congruent. In this respect, they contrast with texts concerned with scientific exposition for children and for adults.

The domain-specific taxonomy in Figure 8-10 can be contrasted with other domain-specific taxonomies (cf. Section 8.2 above); we will return to this comparison. The point is that the domain taxonomy above is incomplete in relation to the overall ideational potential and that it foregrounds certain distinctions. We will now turn to its relationship to the general taxonomy.

8.3.2 Relation to general taxonomy: overview

How does our domain-specific taxonomy differ from the general one presented in Part II? We shall approach this question from the point of view of the breadth of the culinary taxonomy, its depth, its partialness, and its favoured types. Obviously, the culinary taxonomy differs from the general one in terms of breadth; there are general categories we simply do not find in the culinary taxonomy. For example, among the figures, there are no figures of saying at all. But, more important than the breadth per se is the nature of the categories we do not find. For example, there are no metathings — no facts, ideas, or locutions. Things are not meta-; they are predominantly concrete objects.

The narrowed scope in the culinary taxonomy also means that very general categories such as 'doing', 'being', and 'object' can be given correspondingly narrower interpretations. For example, in this register, 'being' means 'intensive & ascriptive being', since there are no other subtypes; and 'object' means 'concrete object', since there are no abstract ones. Similarly, 'doing' means 'concrete doing'. The restricted extension of subtypes is illustrated in Figure 8-11 for figures of being.

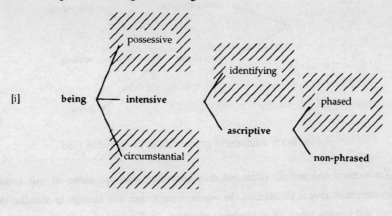

Fig. 8-11: Restricted extension of subtypes of being

As we can see from the illustration above, another aspect of the narrowed breadth is that the taxonomy is telescoped or truncated in intermediate delicacy. Thus 'being' can be differentiated as 'be' and 'make' without the intermediate steps 'intensive', 'ascriptive', 'non-phased', and 'real'. (There is a price to be paid for this reduction, of course, since information about 'be' in the paradigm of figures of being is lost.) Similarly, we can go from 'object' to 'cook' in one step; since there is only one kind of person, it is not necessary to include intermediate steps in a taxonomy of persons.

There is another important consequence of the absence of certain subtypes: not surprisingly, it affects the organization of the (field-specific) taxonomy. In the general case, agency and process type are parallel, but in the culinary taxonomy distinctions in agency are only evident in figures of doing; sensing and being are both middle (that is, no agency feature can be present). As a result, two field-specific alternatives seem justified, one with process type as the primary distinction and the other with agency as the primary distinction: see Figure 8-12.

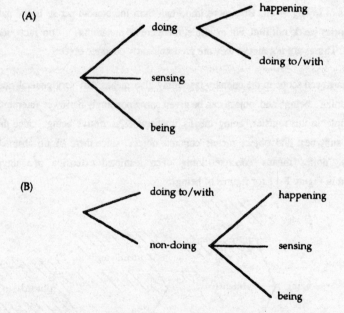

Fig. 8-12: Alternative organizations in restricted field

Taxonomies (A) and (B) differ but they constitute *partial* views of our general taxonomy: they give a glimpse of the whole system, but not enough to indicate that agency and process types are independent variables. Both models look as if sensing and being & having processes cannot be effected.

In (A), processes are of the physical world (= culinary world; the physical universe = the kitchen), of the world of consciousness (= preference/desire), of the world of being (= membership); and if they are of the physical world, then either spontaneous (happening) or brought about by an agent (doing to/with).

In (B), processes are either caused physical (= culinary) operations or else spontaneous, in which case they occur in the world of physical (= culinary) reality, consciousness, or abstract relations.

In either case, the notion of **agency** is quite narrow. While, in the overall ideational potential, agents of processes can be metathings as well as things and, within things, abstractions as well as physical objects, tools, animals, persons, and natural forces, the culinary notion of agent is *restricted* ('value restricted') to be a person, more specifically, a(n apprentice) cook: see Figure 8-13.

So, for example, tools do not as a rule figure as agents in the register of recipes, only as means, enabling the occurrence of the process:

[Means:] With a sharp knife, [Agent] 'you' cut ...

cf. the general case:

The knife cut my hand [BUT, Highton & Highton, p. 54: The point of the knife must pierce the centre of the grapefruit on each insertion]

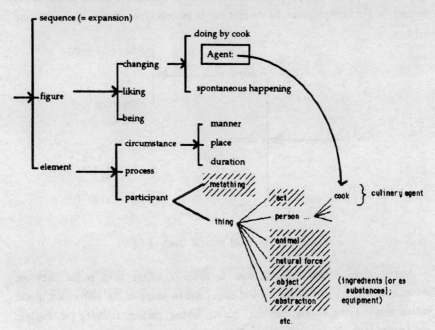

Fig. 8-13: The culinary notion of agent

But the notion of agency in the culinary world is narrow not only in terms of the spectrum of possible Agents, but also in terms of the directness and nature of the Agent's **involvement** in the process. While in the general case, agency is not inherently intentional (volitional), here it is: 'doing to/with' means 'doing to/with intentionally'. This is reinforced by the range of interpersonal options: volitional Agent = addressee responsible for carrying out instruction. — The Agent of chopping, frying, adding, mixing, mashing, &c. brings about the occurrence of these processes intentionally and is, moreover, assigned the responsibility by the writer of the recipe. (The writer and the reader are far apart in time & space; a written recipe is very different in this respect from spoken instructions where joint participation is possible, as in *let's* 'you + I'.)

Related to the intentionality of the Agent is the directness of its participation in the process; in the culinary world we have a kind of 'hands-on' agency. In contrast, agency in general can be quite indirect — for example: *we dress our dancers in white*.

When we compared the breadth of the culinary taxonomy with that of the general one, we saw that there are certain semantic types missing — e.g. figures of saying and metathings. But among those that are present, there may be considerable variation in frequency: some types are **marginal** — they are almost missing, while other types are **favoured** and predominate throughout the text. We can see this difference both in the number of subtypes in the registerial domain and in the number of tokens in the recipes themselves. For example, consider the first cuts in process types, shown again in Figure 8-14.

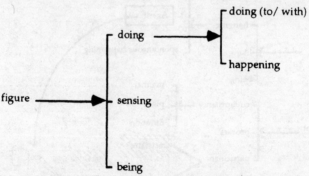

Fig. 8-14: The most general types of figure

Among these, doings dominate both in terms of tokens in a recipe (they are instantiated in every step in the method stage) and in terms of the elaboration of the subtaxonomy: frying, baking, mashing, mixing, adding, peeling, scooping out, rinsing, etc. applied to the various ingredients. There are very few tokens of figures of sensing, and their subtaxonomy is not elaborated (the only subtype is that of 'liking'). Figures of being are more common, but their subtaxonomy is not elaborated. We can summarize these facts graphically as in Figure 8-15.

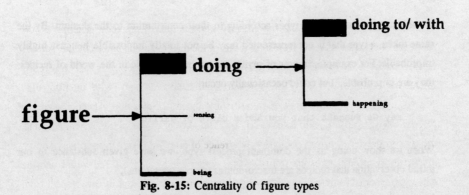

Fig. 8-15: Centrality of figure types

Table 8(7): Types of phenomena in culinary domain

TYPE					EXAMPLE
figures	doing	doing (to/with)			chopping, mashing, adding, removing ...
		happening			simmering, boiling ...
	sensing	perceiving			
		thinking			
		desiring			wanting, liking
		feeling			
	saying				
	being	intensive			being, making
		possessive			
		circumstantial			
	non-projected				
	projected (fact// idea/ locution)				
elements	participants	things	conscious		'cook'
			non-conscious	animals	
				objects [material]	onion, leek, fillet, cutlet ...
				substances	stock, flower, ham ...
				abstractions [material]	temperature, colour ...
				institutions	
				objects [semiotic]	
				abstractions [semiotic]	
		qualities	of projection		
			of expansion	sense-measure	brown, hot ...
	circumstances				in an oven, on a plate, for 30 minutes

The diagram serves to correct the earlier categorial picture by bringing out the relative prominence of the different types (see further Chapter 13, Section 13.3 below on the probabilistic interpretation of the system). By introducing the concept of probability, we are able to order the different types according to their contribution to the domain. By the same token, a type that is not represented may be not totally impossible but just highly improbable. For example, figures of saying are not inconceivable in the world of recipes; they are improbable, but could occasionally occur:

```
may we suggest that you add a clove of garlic ...
```

When we show doing as the dominant process type, we have given substance to our initial observation that recipes are macro-doings (macro-operations).

Among the simple things, material objects dominate. There is only one kind of person, the cook; this is a world with only one Agent. There are virtually no abstractions (e.g. 'flavour', 'colour', 'temperature'), only concrete material objects and substances. There are few qualities and circumstances. Qualities are either "material" (object qualities: texture, colour, and consistency) or "modal" (act qualities: necessity and desirability).

Table 8(7) above presents a rough summary of the observations made so far about restrictions on the general taxonomy.

Having presented this general overview, we can now discuss the culinary field in some more detail. Sequences will serve as our starting point.

8.3.3 Sequences in the culinary domain

In the semantic system in general, sequences are either projections or expansions; but in the culinary domain only expansions occur.[5] Expansions are themselves fairly restricted. The favourite type is temporal enhancement with equal figures, which construes (sub)procedures as sequences of culinary operations. Enhancements may also be unequal, expressing either temporal limit or condition, in which case the conditioning figure is essentially restricted to being a non-operation, i.e. a culinary happening, a sensing or a being.

Examples:

Elaboration:

This vegetable is not very popular; ——> *it has a distinctive sweetish flavour, and like brussels sprouts and celery, it is the better for having been frosted.*

---

[5] There are occasional instances which could be interpreted as projection within the Process of a figure (cf. Halliday, 1985: Ch. 7 Additional, Section 6). They serve to indicate a possible alternative that may be preferred, e.g. *may prefer to roast* in the example *You may prefer to roast them around a nut or similar savoury.*

Extension:

— adversative: *They will become discoloured* ——> *but the flavour is very good.*

Enhancements:

— temporal: succession & equal: *Replace the lids* ——>*and* ['then'] *warm in the oven for 10-15 minutes.*

— temporal: point & unequal: *When the pan and fat are hot,* <——*pour in the egg mixture, stir slowly with a fork ...*

— temporal: limit & unequal:

    qualitative limit: *roast* ——> *until cooked; cook gently* ——> *until the bottom is set and light brown; cook* ——> *until nearly tender but not brown.*

    happening limit: (i) 'until' *place in a hot oven 375° F. - 425° F.* ——>*until simmering well; heat* ——>*until the oil is just smoking.* (ii) 'before' *add 2-3 tablespoons of cooked sweet corn to the egg mixture* — —> *before cooking.*

— causal-conditional & unequal:

    qualitative limit: *If the pastry tends to brown too much on top,* <—— *cover with a greased paper.*

    preference limit: *toss the artichokes in butter, chopped parsley and seasoning* ——>*if so desired; if you prefer not to mix proteins,* <—— *plain soufflés flavoured with vegetables can easily be made.*

— causal-purposive & unequal: *stir slowly with a fork* ——>*to allow the liquid to run on to the bottom and set; the omelette should be cooked as quickly as possible* ——> *so that the egg does not become tough and leathery.*

8.3.4 Figures in the culinary domain

The dominant type of culinary figure is an operation by the cook on a food item, potentially with a means and a duration — it is a type of **doing to/with** (as opposed to happening). The Means is some kind of equipment and the duration is a quantified unit of time. The roles of this figure serve to differentiate a number of different kinds of objects, viz. [person:] cook (filling the Agent/Actor role), [concrete:] food item (Medium/Goal), [concrete:] equipment (Means), and [abstract:] time-unit (Duration). The interdependence between the figure taxonomy and the element taxonomy is a specific example of what was observed to be a quite general tendency above in Part II. The diagrammatic representation is given in Figure 8-16 below.

Examples of lexicogrammatically represented subtypes of this culinary operation include:

```
wash and peel artichokes
cook the washed apricots for 5-10 minutes
with a knife make a cut
mash the potatoes with a potato-masher
add the tomatoes with a little seasoning
garnish with plenty of onion rings
```

This culinary operation gives us a sense of what the culinary world is like. There is one Agent in control of the world, the cook;[6] he or she only participates in an operation as the agent. In other words, the cook is always the doer, never the done to or with. Similarly, there is only one kind of Medium, food items. These two kinds of things are thus sharply distinct from the point of view of what participant roles they take on. There are two other classes of things, items of equipment and time-units. The former are almost always the Means in a process rather than serving a participant role; they never compete with the cook for the Agent role, as tools and instruments may do in other registers. Time-units in the world of food preparation never serve as participants in a figure; they are only involved indirectly as circumstances of Duration.

Now, it is perfectly possible to conceive of a world where the cook is not in sole control of culinary processes; but this would not be the world of recipes (it may be more

---

[6] On occasion, an implement may serve as Agent, as in *the point of the knife must pierce the centre of the grapefruit on each insertion.* This is agnate with *You must pierce the centre of the grapefruit with the point of the knife on each insertion,* with the cook as Agent and the implement as Manner-means.

like   the   real   world   of   the   kitchen!).

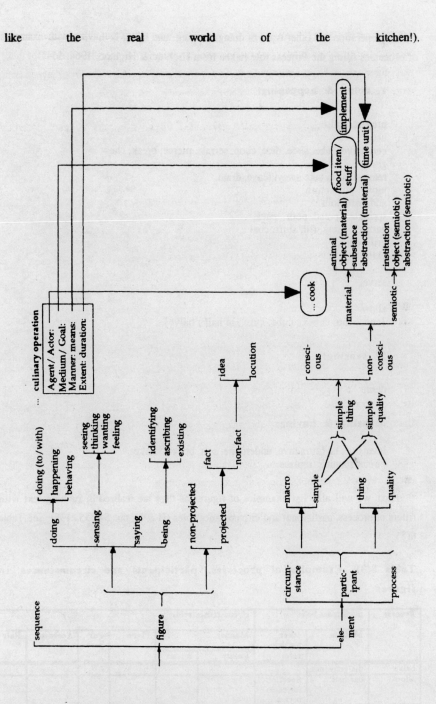

Fig. 8-16: Network showing typical culinary operation

Although culinary operations dominate, there are figures of other kinds also: culinary happenings, liking/wanting, and ascriptions. To give a sense of the range of possible figures, we list the total set of primary types below, including both the subtypes of culinary operation and other types of doing, sensing, and being & having with examples of processes filling the Process role (taken from Highton & Highton, 1964: 55-7).

1. doing & happening:

prepare, finish,
use,
cut, halve, cube, slice, dice, chop, serrate, pierce, break, chew
grate,
remove, free, take away, leave, drain,
move, put, return,
add, mix, join
sprinkle, spread, pour, pack,
garnish, dress, fill, stuff, coat
grill, cook,
chill,

serve,

allow
{cut ... into cubes : cube; cut ... in half : halve}

2. sensing:

desire

3. being & having:

intensive: be (attractive, underdone, soft, better), make
circumstantial: replace

Next, we will also list examples of figures as they are realized in running text with fillers of process, participant and circumstance roles (H & H, pp. 54, 55, 138): see Table 8(8).

Table 8(8): Examples of processes, participants and circumstances in figures

Process	participant roles		circumstance roles					
	Medium	other particip. roles	Manner		Place	Pur- pose	Accomp.	Role
			quality	means				
halve	the grapefruit							
allow	one half	Benef.: for each person						
remove	pips							
cut	[the grapefruit]			a grapefr uit-knife	around the centre			
remove	it							
move	knife		up and down with a sawing motion					
free	each section							
remove	the skin							

sprinkle	grapefruit				with a little brown sugar			
add	kirsch							
chill	grapefruit							
put	a half cherry				in the centre			
chill	the melon							
cut	[the melon]							into wedge shapes
remove	the seeds							
serve	[the melon]						with powdered or chopped ginger and brown sugar	
may be used	lemon wedges							
to replace	the ginger							
serve	[the melon]				on cold plates			
wash and peel	artichokes							
place	[artichokes]				in a boiling white stock		with a squeeze of lemon juice and some fried onions	
add	herbs or a bouquet garni							
place	[dish]				in a hot oven ...			
until simmering	[it]		well					
reduce	heat				to 300°F.-350°F.			
remove	bouquet garni							
drain	the artichokes							
toss	the artichokes				in butter, ...			
drain	the artichokes							
keep	[the artichokes]	Range: warm						
use	the stock					for a sauce		
cover	the artichokes			with it				
serve	[the dish]				in the casserole			

Culinary happenings are processes that involve food items as mediums; they go on in time without the cook's intervention, primarily *cooking, boiling, simmering, evaporating, smoking,* and *coming away.* In recipes they are temporally or causally related as conditions on processes that are controlled by the cook; e.g.

```
... until (it) has evaporated
... if (they) come away
... until (it) begins to smoke
... until the mixture comes away from the sides
... so that (it) does not boil
```

Sensings are mainly of the desire type, more particularly 'liking', with the cook as the Senser and some kind or aspect of a dish as the Phenomenon. They are related to culinary operations in conditional enhancing sequences, and can serve to condition an alternative method:

```
... if you want a more substantial stuffing
... if you would like a mere hint instead
(the rings can be egg-and-breadcrumbed) if you prefer
```

Figures of **being & having** are ascriptive, either ascribing a quality to an ingredient, an act or a dish, or assigning a dish to a particular class.

```
... but the flavour is very good
... until (they) are brown
... until the pastry is smooth and pliable
```

8.3.5 Simple things in the culinary domain

Simple things can be differentiated according to the roles they may play in figures, as we have already seen in Figure 8-16 above. Thus we have:

role type	role	filler
participant roles	Agent/ Actor	cook
	Medium/ Goal *or* Actor	food
	Range/ Attribute	class [of dish]
circumstantial roles	Manner-means (of doing)	item of equipment (i.e. implement)
	Manner-means (of doing)	speed, degree, etc.
	Duration (of doing)	time

These correspondences indicate how the culinary world is constrained in terms of the nature of participants and circumstances; in terms of who can be expected to do what to whom, and how. When we check whether humans and non-humans can participate as Medium and/or Agent in figures of doing, these constraints are brought out quite clearly: see Table 8(9).

This concludes our illustration of domain models and their relation to the meaning base we presented in Part II. Adding such domain models is a necessary step towards having a functional text processing system. But their importance goes beyond their role in text generation and parsing. On the one hand, it is likely that in most task-oriented descriptions of language, whether in natural language processing or in other fields such as education, language disorders, legal practice and the like, domains of this intermediate scope will typically be the most relevant; while on the other hand, in our view, the modelling of specific domains of ideational meaning is an essential component of our theoretical understanding of the nature of human cognition.

Table 8(9): Figures of doing, showing types of Agent and Medium found in culinary domain (italicized)

		Medium	
		non-human	human
effective:	human	*chop the onions*	
Agent		they built the house	they cured him
	non-human		
		it broke the wall	the arrow pierced him
middle		*until it begins to smoke*	
		it collapsed	they danced

9. Using the ideation base in text processing

In this chapter we shall go outside the ideation base and locate it in relation to other parts of a model of the linguistic system as a resource for meaning in context. We shall look at the kind of generation system that seems technically manageable at the present stage of development.

9.1 Organization of a generation system

9.1.1 Relationship to a client system

The need to present information in the form of text (or indeed in the form of graphs, tables, maps, etc.) usually arises in a computational system that was not developed for the purposes of generating text in the first place. Most typically, this is a database system or an expert system; we can call it the **client system** since it will engage the services of, and define the required output of, the generation system to be developed:[1] see the Figure 9-1 below. The client system will provide some 'raw' information source — the data base of a data base system (e.g., containing information about the weather) or the reasoning of an expert system (in some form, e.g. as the rules of the system and traces of the execution of these rules).

The central 'module' to be built is the model of the linguistic system itself; this is where the ideation base is located. In addition, we shall need to construct a model of the context in which the linguistic system and the client system are embedded. The context will serve to co-ordinate the client system and the linguistic system and it will support the generation process.

To accommodate the client system, we have to undertake both contextual modelling and linguistic modelling. The need for text and the raw information source have to be interpreted in this context in terms of field, tenor and mode (see Chapter 8, Section 8.1.1 above). Furthermore, the raw information source has to be construed in terms of a domain model capable of being verbalized. That is, whatever the demands on the information source are in the client system, they do not include the demands placed on it by a linguistic generator; it has to be transformed from a data base to a meaning base.[2] Once

---

[1] Or if such a generation system already exists, the task is to slot the client system into its context and to 'customize' the generation system to allow it to interact with the client system.

[2] We assume that the client system has not been conceived of, and modelled as, a language-based system. However, it follows from our approach that we would see them as language-based. Thus reasoning in the expert system would be modelled as semantic processes, which would make it possible to build in more of the power of language in an explicit way: see Halliday (1995). This is also the approach being developed by Michio Sugeno and his researchers under the heading of **intelligent computing**.

information from the database has been transformed into meaning, it can be **fused** with the meanings of the ideation base, more specifically the meanings of the relevant domain model (cf. Sugeno, 1993; Kobayashi, 1995). This transformation involves classifying the objects and relations of the data base within a domain model and then locating this domain model on the cline of instantiation relative to the overall ideation base as described in Chapter 8, Section 8.1.2 above (see Figure 8-3). The transformation may also involve adding temporal features where these are not part of the information encoded in the data base.

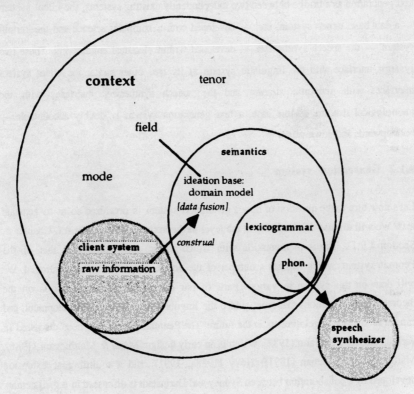

Fig. 9-1: A text-generation system embedded in context together with a client system providing the raw information source

The development of the overall generation system will thus include 'growing' a linguistic component as well as revising and expanding what has been imported from the client system into its ideation base. This expansion will thus take place stratally within the semantics and metafunctionally within the ideational metafunction. In addition, the generation system will have to include subsystems that are not likely to have any seeds in the client system — the lower strata of lexicogrammar and phonology (graphology), of course, but also the non-ideational parts of the overall meaning base — the interaction base and the text base at the semantic stratum. The system will have to have a model of how to interact with its addressee (the interaction base, relating to tenor within context) and also a model of how to present ideational and interpersonal meanings as text in context (the text base, relating to mode).

If the task is to produce *spoken* text, the text generator has to be linked up with a speech synthesizer through an interface, as shown in Figure 9-1 above. We can then see text generation as a bridge between two independently existing systems, the client system — a data base, expert system, etc. — developed within computer science and the 'output system' — the speech synthesizer — developed within electrical engineering. These two systems interface with the linguistic system at its two outer strata: the client system interfaces with semantic stratum and the speech synthesizer interfaces with the phonological stratum. In this case, a text generation system is doubly accountable — both upwards and downwards.

9.1.2 Generation system

Let's now turn to the question of how a generation system is organized so as to generate text. We will discuss this basically at the level of theoretical specification (cf. Chapter 1, Section 1.9.1). The implementation with which we are most familiar is that of the Penman system, which realizes a number of the design properties to be mentioned. We will draw on this system in various parts of our discussion; but our focus is on the theoretical considerations that have guided the linguistic aspects of its development, and can serve to guide developments in the future. The Penman system has been discussed in various places, e.g. Mann (1982), which is an early design; Mann & Matthiessen (1985), Matthiessen & Bateman (1991); Hovy (1988a, 1991); and a multilingual extension developed by a collaboration between Sydney and Darmstadt is discussed in e.g. Bateman, Matthiessen, Nanri & Zeng (1991), Matthiessen, Nanri & Zeng (1991), and Bateman, Matthiessen & Zeng (forthc.). Other current systemic text-generation systems are COMMUNAL, developed by Robin Fawcett and his team (see e.g. Fawcett (1988b) and Fawcett, Tucker & Lin (1992), and Fawcett (1981) for an early model of systemic generation), KPML (Komet-Penman multilingual), as a develpment of Penman together with the Komet system, developed by Bateman (1996) and his team (see also Teich, 1995; Teich & Bateman, 1994); MULTEX, a multilingual systemic generator developed by Zeng (e.g. 1993, 1996) as an alternative to the multilingual version of Penman within the multilingual project at Macquarie University in Sydney, and O'Donnell's (1994) WAG system for sentence analysis and generation.

A text-generation system can be modelled in terms of the overall theoretical framework we sketched in Chapter 8, Section 8.1. Most fundamentally, it can be modelled as **stratified** resources extended along the cline of **instantiation** from overall potential to particular instance: see Figure 8-3 above.

9.1.2.1 Stratification of resources

Let us first review the stratal organization of the resources. The resources are stratified into context and language; language is in turn stratified into semantics, lexicogrammar and phonology/ graphology (see Chapter 1, Section 1.2, Figure 1-1); and as we shall see, the processes of instantiation are guided by this stratification. Stratification simplifies the global organization of a generation system since it introduces the strata as more local organizational domains; it is a way of managing complexity. For instance, instead of one large unwieldy semanticogrammatical system, there are two strata — semantics and lexicogrammar.

At the same time, this stratal organization means that it is crucial to specify the realizational relations between strata — **inter-stratal realization**. In systemic theory, this relationship is stated in terms of the organization of the higher stratum — for a simple reason: a higher stratum provides a more comprehensive environment than a lower one (as our stratal figures with concentric circles suggest). For instance, a certain semantic feature such as 'probability' may be dispersed in realization throughout various regions of the grammar (*I think; in my opinion; probably; will*). More specifically, inter-stratal realization is specified by means of **inter-stratal preselection**: contextual features are realized by preselection within the semantic system, semantic features are realized by preselection within the lexicogrammatical system, and lexicogrammatical features are realized by preselection within the phonological/ graphological system. This type of preselection may take different forms between different stratal boundaries, but the principle is quite general.

[1] **Context**. Context is the 'semiotic environment' of language (and other socio-semiotic systems such as image systems [maps, diagrams, etc.]); its systems specify what demands may be placed on language and what role it may play in responding to those demands. There are three sets of contextual systems — field, tenor and mode; we gave an example of a fragment from field in Figure 8-4 above. Recurrent combinations of (ranges of) field, tenor and mode values define regions within the overall system of the context of culture. In most cases, text generation will take place within such a contextual region —

within a range of field, tenor and mode values. For example, weather forecasts are generated within the contextual region characterized in Chapter 8, Section 8.2.1 above.

[1/2] **Realization of context in semantics.** Such contextual regions evolve together with special functional varieties of the language or "registers". These are, in the first instance, registerial subsystems of the *semantic* system. A register is a semantic region within the overall semantic space. It is made up of contributions from all three metafunctions: a domain within the ideation base and similar regions within the interpersonal and textual parts of the overall semantic space. Our specifications of the meteorological and culinary domains constitute the ideational aspects of the registers of weather forecasting and recipes.

A given contextual specification of field, tenor and mode is thus realized by "preselecting" a register within the semantic system; Figure 8-1 above shows ideational domains being preselected by different fields.[3] This contextual preselection within the semantics narrows down the overall potential to a registerial subpotential; a field specification narrows down the ideational potential from that of the overall ideation base to that of a domain model.

[2] **Semantics — meaning base.** The semantic system, or "meaning base", thus consists of the three familiar metafunctional contributions, first introduced in Chapter 1, Section 1.3: the ideation base, the part of the meaning base that we have focussed on, but also the other two bases, the interaction base and the text base. All three bases are extended along the cline of instantiation from potential to instance. As we have seen (Chapter 8), the ideation base includes both the most general ideational meaning potential and a repertoire of domain models located along the cline of instantiation midway between potential and instance and associated with particular ranges of values within field. Let us say a few more words about (i) the interaction base and (ii) the text base. Table 9(1) summarizes those aspects of the three bases to be discussed.

(i) **The interaction base** provides the resources for enacting social roles and relations as meaning, (prototypically) in dialogue. The interaction base includes the strategies for adopting and assigning speech roles, for giving and demanding assessments, and the like. The locus of these strategies is a unit of interaction or **move**. A move is

---

[3] If we introduce time, we can think of the context as activating the register: cf. O'Donnell, 1990, on the notion of activation.

typically mapped onto a figure from the ideation base: a speaker construes a quantum of experience as a figure and enacts this figure as a move in dialogue, either as a proposition or as a proposal. This mapping between figure and move is a central feature of the way we jointly construct and negotiate experience.

Table 9(1): The metafunctional diversification of the meaning base

	ideation base	text base	interaction base
upwards: context	field	mode	tenor
mode of meaning	construing (experience)	creating (ideational and interpersonal meanings) as information	enacting (social roles & relations)
semantic units	sequence		
	figure [quantum of change]	**message** [quantum of information]	**move** [quantum of interaction]
	element		
register variant	domain models		exchange relationships

The interaction base extends along the cline of instantiation. (1) At the potential end of the cline of instantiation, the interpersonal strategies that have the move as their domain are defined by all the options persons have in exchanging meanings with one another, adopting speech roles of giving/ demanding information or goods-&-services and assigning complementary roles of accepting or giving on demand to the addressee. These constitute all the patterns of interaction within a culture. (2) Midway between potential and instance, sets of such strategies cluster within ranges of tenor values. Such a cluster is the interpersonal analogue of a domain in the ideation base: it is a region within the overall interpersonal space of meaning, selected according to tenor, just as a domain is a region within the overall ideational space of meaning, selected according to field. The options in interpersonal meaning that make up the cluster together enact a tenor relationship, such as that between a client and a server (unequal in power, low in familiarity, neutral in affect) where the client initiates demands for goods-&-services and information about them and the server responds, such as that between two friends (equal in power, high in familiarity, positive in affect) where the interpersonal options are wide-ranging, or such as that between the writer of a weather report and the readers (unequal in expertise, no familiarity, neutral in affect) where the writer gives information and the readers accept. We might call such a cluster an **exchange relationship** to foreground that it is semantic (i.e. constituted in meaning through exchanges of meaning) and that it is interpersonal (rather than one-sidedly personal). To indicate that it is analogous to a domain model, we might have called it an exchange or interaction "model"; but we have avoided that term because it suggests a construal of something and construal is the ideational mode of meaning — it is more like a protocol than like a model.

A particular domain model within the ideation base correlates with a particular exchange relationship within the interaction base and together they form the ideational and interpersonal aspects of a register. An exchange relationship thus has ideational implications: it involves the exchange of some ideational meanings rather than others and it embodies a division of labour between the interactants in the exchange relationship. For example, in a service encounter in a local shop (cf. Halliday & Hasan, 1985; Ventola, 1987), the customer may demand goods and information about goods within the relevant domain and the server supplies these on demand and demands goods (payment) in return; and this involves the general domain of business transaction and the particular domain of the business (e.g. hardware). An exchange relationship thus gives interpersonal values to meanings within the domain model it is associated with. For example, as we have seen, the ideation base embodies both congruent and metaphorical construals of experience; and these variants will be selected partly according to differences in interpersonal distance along dimensions such as age and expertise (cf. Chapter 6, Section 6.5.2 above).

The **text base** is oriented towards the ideation base and the interaction base. It provides the resources for constructing meanings from these two bases as information of a kind that can be shared as text. An ideational figure and an interpersonal move are constructed as information in the form of a **message**. Such a message is related to the preceding discourse and differentiates informational statuses in terms of thematicity and newsworthiness. From the speaker's point of view, the text base is a resource for developing a text, message by message, and for guiding the listener in his/ her interpretation of the text; and from the listener's point of view, it is a resource for constructing such an interpretation (for building up an instantial system; see below). We shall return to the text base and its relationship to the ideation base in some more detail below, in Section 9.3.

[2/3] **Realization of semantics in lexicogrammar.** Semantic features are realized by lexicogrammatical ones; we have illustrated this relationship within the ideational metafunction at various points in our discussion (e.g. sequence ⩾ clause complex; figure of doing ⩾ material clause). The realizational relationship between semantics and lexicogrammar is one of preselection: semantic features such as 'sequence', 'figure', and 'doing' are **realized** in lexicogrammar by means of prespecification of lexicogrammatical information, most centrally preselection of lexicogrammatical features.

For instance, 'doing' is realized by the preselection of the clause feature 'material', which means that the clause that realizes a figure of doing is constrained to be a material clause. This type of approach was adopted by Patten (1988) in his generator SLANG, and has also been developed for the multilingual version of Penman at Macquarie University (see Zeng, 1996). Here the realization of semantics in lexicogrammar is modelled as a direct one. However, researchers in text generation have developed an alternative way of modelling the realization of semantics in lexicogrammar (see Matthiessen, 1990a, for a comparison of the two approaches).[4]

In this approach, realization is mediated by an interface between semantics and lexicogrammar. Semantic features such as 'sequence', 'figure', and 'doing' are first expressed as specifications of various fields of information in a **local plan** for a clause (complex). For, instance, 'doing' would be expressed as a particular type-specification for the local plan field FIGURE (e.g., FIGURE = x/ doing, meaning the value is the instantial figure 'x' of type doing). This local plan specification then supports the computation of responses to inquiries presented by a special interface between the lexicogrammar and the semantics, the chooser-&-inquiry interface. This approach was developed for the Penman generator (e.g., Mann, 1983a,b; Matthiessen, 1988b; Matthiessen & Bateman, 1991: Section 6.4).

These alternatives are contrasted diagrammatically in Figure 9-2. While direct realization clearly is simpler in that it does not involve the addition of an interstratal interface, mediated realization makes it easier to co-ordinate and integrate information from various sources (ideational, interpersonal and textual). In particular, during that phase of the development of the Penman system when the semantic environment of the lexicogrammar was still being designed and specified, the mediated approach provided a detailed set of demands for information to be accommodated within the semantic resources. In our example in Section 9.2 below, we shall use mediated realization since it will be most familiar from discussions of the Penman system.

---

[4] Other mechanisms have also been used, for instance relations that can be interpreted as inter-stratal pairings (Jacobs, 1985), semantic conditions on rule application (as in augmented phrase structure grammar), unification of semantic and grammatical representations (McKeown, 1982).

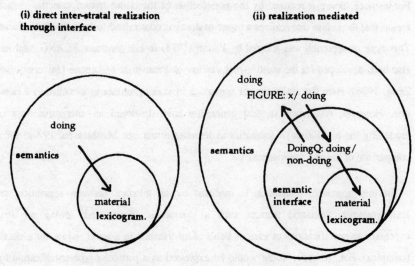

(i) direct inter-stratal realization through interface

(ii) realization mediated

Fig. 9-2: Direct and mediated inter-stratal realization

[3] Lexicogrammar is the resource for construing meaning as wording. It is organized as a set of system networks representing options in wording. Systemic options may have realization statements associated with them; these statements specify how the options are realized in wording (structure & grammatical/ lexical items). Figure 9-3 shows a simplified version of the ideational and interpersonal systems of the clause.

The lexicogrammatical system networks are distributed by metafunction (ideational: experiential & logical — interpersonal — textual) and by rank (clause — group/ phrase — word — morpheme) and extend in delicacy from grammar to lexis.[5] As we have noted,

---

[5] In systemic functional theory, lexis is thus interpreted as most delicate or specific grammar (on the implications of this perspective for text generation, see Matthiessen, 1991b, and Cross, 1991, 1992, 1993). Grammar comprises syntax and morphology; there is no stratal boundary between the two, but merely a move down the rank scale: "syntax" is simply the grammar of clauses and groups/ phrases and morphology is the grammar of words and morphemes. Systemic functional grammatical theory can be seen as part of a (typological) family of grammars that have been used in computational linguistics for various tasks. Winograd (1983) calls this family 'feature and function' grammars since most members rely heavily on (declarative) representations involving both features and functions. Another salient characteristic is the clear separation of grammatical representations as declarative data structures and grammatical processes, with unification as a central operation (see Shieber, 1986, on unification based grammars and Kasper, 1988, on the inter-translatability of Systemic Functional Grammar and Kay's, e.g. 1979, 1985, Functional Unification Grammar). Other members include Lexical Functional Grammar, Functional Unification Grammar, Generalized Phrase Structure Grammar, and Head-Driven Phrase Structure Grammar (HPSG). HPSG as developed by Pollard & Sag (1987, 1993) is of particular comparative interest, since it includes typing of feature structures and organization of types into subsumption lattices: this means that the paradigmatic organization of grammar is foregrounded more explicitly than in previous approaches within the generative tradition. Systemic Functional Grammar is

the ideation base is realized by the ideational resources: sequences and figures are realized at clause rank by clause complexes and (simple) clauses respectively; and elements are realized at group/ phrase rank. In a similar way, interpersonal meanings are realized by interpersonal features in the lexicogrammar, and textual meanings by textual ones. The grammar unifies the different metafunctional contributions; for example, a figure, a move and a message are unified in their realization as a clause. It achieves this unification by realizing combinations of ideational, interpersonal and textual features in the same wording. For example, the wording *well unfortunately they must have missed the train* is a realizational unification of a figure (of doing & happening), a move (of giving information, assessed as certain and undesirable) and a message.

The wordings that are constructed by the lexicogrammatical system are in turn realized in one or other of the two expression strata, phonology or graphology. Figure 9-4 represents the stratal organization of the resources, diversified into field, tenor and mode (within context) and into ideational, interpersonal and textual (within the content strata of language). As we have noted, these resources are extended along the cline of instantiation from potential (language in context of culture) via subpotentials (registers in situation types) to instances (texts in contexts of situation). Figure 9-4 shows the stratified resources as being extendable along the cline of instantiation. Let us now map out the overall semiotic space defined by stratification and instantiation, and then discuss how the processes of instantiation move through this space. Table 9(2) represents the intersection of instantiation and stratification, providing a schematic map of the overall semiotic space (the table has been adapted from a fuller version presented in Halliday, 1995). We have shown the ideational 'slice' of the overall picture in bold italics. (We have left the phonological cells unspecified since phonology falls outside the scope of our discussion of the ideation base in text generation; but the cline of instantiation is equally important at this lowest stratum of language.)

---

unique in organizing features into choice networks, as the central organizing principle, and in being multifunctional; the combination of these properties make it particularly suited to text generation.

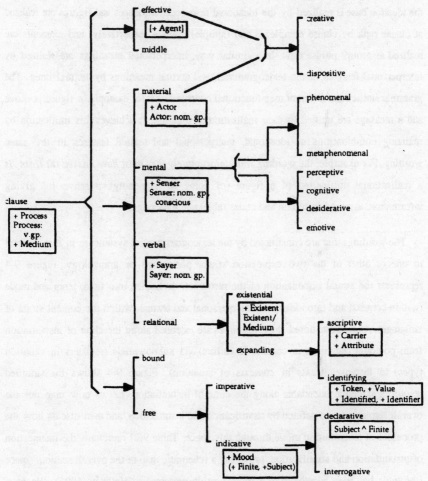

Fig. 9-3: Fragment of the clause grammar

9.1.2.2 Processes of instantiation

To the model summarized in Table 9(2), we can now add processes of instantiation: in generation, they have to *move from potential to instance* (from system to text); and in analysis, they have to *move from instance to potential* (from text to system). These processes are explicitly located in time; they unfold in time, so the model has to specify how they are sequenced relative to one another. (As we will suggest below, in generation, options and realizations tend to be instantiated first at higher strata and later at lower strata; but there is no strict temporal linearity.)

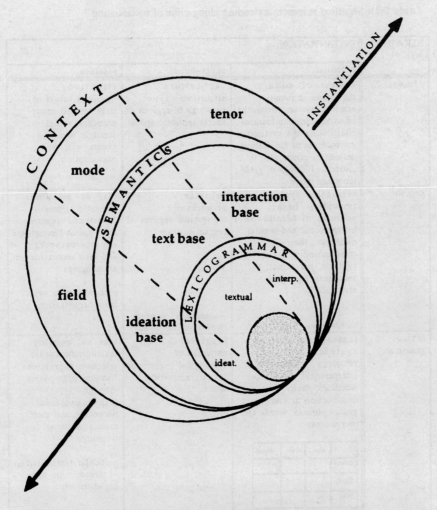

Fig. 9-4: The stratal and metafunctional 'address' of the ideation base in the overall resources

In generation, instantiation can in principle be initiated at any point along the cline of instantiation. This is precisely the significance of the fact that instantiation is a cline. Most likely a given generation task can be addressed in terms of an existing registerial system, so instantiation can be initiated midway along the cline of instantiation. That is, it is not necessary to select options from within the overall meaning potential, but only from within a much more restricted registerial subpotential (cf. Patten, 1988, on the significance of this restriction in a problem-solving approach to text generation). Generation may also operate further down the cline of instantiation, with more local subpotential within a registerial potential.

Table 9(2): Stratified resources extending along cline of instantiation

STRATIFIC-ATION:	INSTANTIATION:		
	potential	subpotential	instance
context	**context of culture:** the culture as social-semiotic system: networks of social semiotic features constituting the systems-&-processes of the culture; defined as potential clusters of values of *field*, tenor and mode	**"subculture"/ situation type:** networks of regions of social-semiotic space	**situation:** instantial values of field, tenor & mode; particular social semiotic situation events, with their organization
semantics	**semantic system (meaning base):** networks of *ideational*, interpersonal and textual meanings; their construction as texts, subtexts, parasemes, sequences, figures & elements — *ideation base*	**register:** networks of topological regions of semantic space — *domain models* (*within ideation base*)	**text as meaning:** semantic selection expressions (features from passes through the semantic networks), and their representation as meanings particular texts, with their organization
lexico-grammar	**lexicogrammatical system:** networks of *ideational*, interpersonal and textual wordings; their construction as clauses, groups/phrases, words and morphemes | ideat.	interp.	textual
clause			
group			
word			
morph.					**[register:]** networks of typological regions of lexicogrammatical space	**text as wording:** lexicogrammatical selection expressions (features from passes through lexicogrammatical networks), and their manifestation as wordings particular texts, spoken or written, with their organization
phonology			

A text is generated within the **logogenetic time-frame** (see Chapter 1, Section 1.5.3 above). In fact, generation is a logogenetic process: it creates meaning in the course of instantiation as the text unfolds — see Figure 9-5. If we look at logogenesis from the point of view of the system (rather than from the point of view of each instance), we can see that logogenesis builds up a version of the system that is particular to the text being generated (cf. Butt, 1983, on "semantic drift" in unfolding text and Butt, 1987, on "latent patterning"): the speaker/ writer uses this changing system as a resource in creating the text; and the listener/ reader has to reconstruct something like that system in the process of interpreting the text — with the changing system as a resource for the process of interpretation. We can call this an **instantial system** (see Matthiessen, 1993c). For example, in the course of logogenesis, a recipe is built up as a series of ordered loops through the system of sequences, whereas an encyclopaedic entry may be built up as a systemic taxonomy, developed step by step in delicacy. An instantial system may fall entirely within the registerial system it instantiates; in other words, the meanings created within it may all have been created before. However, it may also create new meanings — new to the speaker and/or listener. In either case, the instantial system is built up successively by the generation process; but as it is developed, it in turn becomes a resource for further instantiation. We will illustrate this process in some detail below.

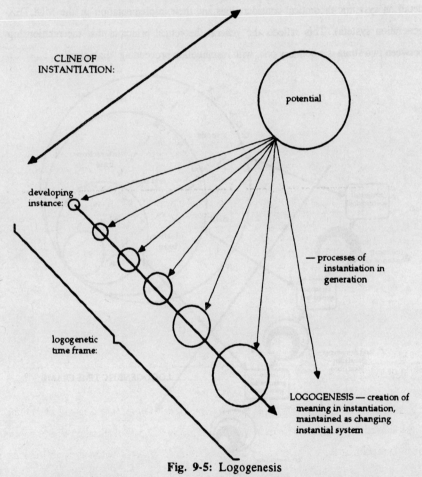

Fig. 9-5: Logogenesis

We had indicated how the process of instantiation relates to the cline of instantiation. How does this process relate to the other global dimension of organization shown in Figure 9-4 and set out in Table 9(2) above — i.e. the dimension of stratification? The strata are ordered in symbolic abstraction, but they are not ordered in instantiation time.

The process of instantiation can shunt up and down the stratal hierarchy. However, the general tendency in instantiation is one of **stratal descent**: see Figure 9-6. First systemic features are instantiated (selected) at the highest stratum and their associated realization statements are also instantiated (executed). Then the instantial specifications at this stratum are realized at the stratum below. Within this overall stratal descent, there is interleaving: higher-stratal systems need not be fully instantiated until lower-stratal ones have been instantiated. This means that selections at higher strata can be made in the logogenetic environment of preceding selections at lower strata (see Zeng, 1996, for more detail on systemic theoretical considerations and their implementation in the MULTEX generation system). This reflects the general theoretical principle that the relationship between two strata is a solidary one, with instantiation proceeding "dialogically".

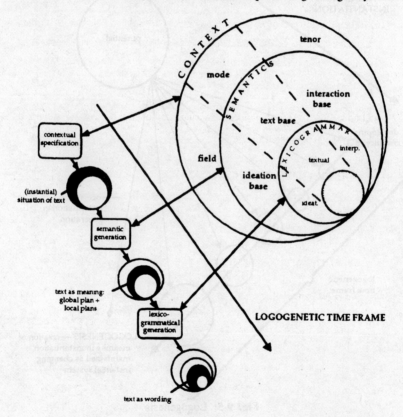

Fig. 9-6: Organization of system into resources and processes

For present purposes, it will be helpful to differentiate three major phases in the process of generation, viz. (i) situational specification, where the text to be generated is 'situated' in an instantial context specified (up to a point) in terms of field, tenor and mode, (ii) semantic generation, where the text as a whole is planned globally and more local text plans are 'spawned' [text as meaning], and (iii) lexicogrammatical generation, where the semantic plans are realized in lexicogrammatical wordings [text as wording].

The two approaches to the mapping between semantics and lexicogrammar mentioned above, direct and mediated realization, have different implications for the realization of local semantic plans.

> (i) If the realization is direct, the process will essentially be a backward chaining traversal of the lexicogrammatical system network: preselections specify delicate lexicogrammatical features and the main task of the generation process is to infer the paths that lead to these features and to execute any structural realization statements on that path.

> (ii) If the realization is mediated, the process will essentially be one of forward chaining traversal of the lexicogrammatical system network, with activation of the chooser of each system for consultating the local plan to obtain the semantic information needed to make the choice.

We will now illustrate how a generation system may operate by looking at these three major phases in the generation process.

9.2 An example from recipe generation

As our illustrative generation task, we shall take the following recipe for Almond and Apricot Stuffing (Highton & Highton, p. 127):

ALMOND AND APRICOT STUFFING

[Ingredients:]

            1 oz. butter or suenut
            2 large chopped onions
            4 oz. coarsely grated or chopped almonds
            6 fresh or about 12 soaked apricots, diced
            finely
            1 tablespoon chopped fresh herbs
            Grated zest and juice of 1/2 lemon
            Sea salt and brown sugar to taste

[Preparation:] (1) Melt the fat and (2) fry the onions (3) until slightly brown, (4) add the almonds and (5) continue

cooking for 3-5 minutes. (6) Remove from the heat and (7) add
the remainder of the ingredients.

[Use:] (8) This makes a very good stuffing for cucumbers.

[Variation:] (9)If you want a more substantial stuffing
(10) add a little mashed potato and [Alternative use:] (11)
use for stuffing marrows.

9.2.1 Contextual specification

The recipe generator has the **contextual resources** to plan and organize a recipe,
giving it the *text structure* indicated in bold face in the text above: Ingredients ^
Preparation ^ Use ^ Variation ^ Alternative use. This structure is projected from the
context of situation. The text is largely organized on the model of the food preparation
activity itself, or, more generally, on the model of purposeful behaviour aimed at solving
a problem. The problem is the making of the dish. The text starts out by specifying the
preconditions for solving the problem (Ingredients). It then specifies a step by step
algorithm for the purpose (the steps in Preparation). This algorithm is an abstract or
summary of the fully detailed procedures represented in the culinary domain. For example,
the text reads *Melt the fat and fry the onions until slightly brown*, leaving out the
specification of where the fat is melted, the step of placing the onions in the frying pan
with the melted fat, and so on, since an adult reader can be expected to 'fill in' these steps
and specifications. Once the basic algorithm has been introduced, a variation of it can be
given (Variation). In addition, there is a specification of the use of the dish created by the
method (and then again of the alternative use of the version of the dish created by the
alternative method). There is no strong general reason why Use should follow Preparation
in the recipe, since it is not part of or dependent on the procedure; and in many recipes it
precedes Ingredients.

The generic structure potential is diagrammed below (we have used Hasan's,
conventions first (Hasan, 1978; Hasan in Halliday & Hasan, 1985): optionality is
indicated by parentheses and sequence by ^; and then restated as simple transition network
(cf. McKeown, 1985), fixing the placement of Use at the end): see Figure 9-7.

- **Preparation** is the only obligatory element of structure, which is the
  sequence of directions taking the reader through the steps of making a
  particular dish. Depending on various factors, one or more additional
  elements may be present.

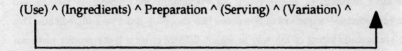

Fig. 9-7: Generic structure of recipe

- **Use** may occur either at the beginning of the recipe or at the end. It is a specification of how the dish can be used, e.g. as a starter or as the main dish.

- **The Ingredients** element specifies the ingredients used in the Preparation phase; it is usually just a list. Mention of ingredients in the Preparation phase of the recipe may satisfy the need to specify them, in which case there is no Ingredients element.

- **Serving** specifies how the dish is to be served - hot, immediately, garnished with parsley, etc.

- Finally, **Variations** may be present to give alternative methods of preparation and/or substitute ingredients. Alternative methods or ingredients may also be introduced during Preparation or Serving by means of an alternative complex (Serve with onion or brown sauce or a green vegetable; Serve immediately with tomato or herb sauce), in which case there is no need for a separate Variations element.

9.2.2 Semantic generation

The contextual specification guides the process of semantic generation, which instantiates information from the ideation base: the generic elements shown above are indexed into the meaning base. (See Hasan, 1984b, for a detailed discussion of the semantic realization of generic elements from the contextual specification.) Since procedures in general and recipes in particular are ideationally oriented (in contrast to persuasive texts such as advertisements, which are interpersonally oriented), each generic element corresponds to one or more sequences of certain types. So Preparation, for example, is indexed into culinary sequences — sequences of operations like chopping and frying ingredients. This is the syntagmatic aspect of the way in which different context types project particular organizations onto the ideation base.

Those features of the ideation base that are instantiated in this text are set out informally in Figure 9-8. The diagram specifies (i) the sequence into which the text is organized, and (ii) the figures comprising each sequence. We have included in square brackets the full specification of the participants that are ingredients in the recipe together with some other implicit information in angle brackets. This is obviously still only a partial specification: the categories are labelled in rather general terms (i.e., they are not very delicate); and it is likely there are additional operations to be performed in the kitchen that get left out in the actual text because they are 'obvious' to an (adult) reader: before you can melt the fat, you have to light the stove, etc.. — as well as other pieces of information such as where the fat is melted.

While the structure of a recipe essentially follows the organization of a culinary sequence, there seem to be two kinds of perturbations in the way the information is presented in the discourse:

(i) all the referents which are of the type 'ingredient' are extracted and presented first as Ingredients. They are then picked up later by means of anaphoric reference. (Note that this presupposes familiarity with the domain taxonomy; for example: *1 oz. butter or suenut* —> *the fat.*) Some cookery books do not present the referents as a separate generic element but may print them in a special font for easy identification.

(ii) the alternative method need not be presented as Variation at the point at which it constitutes a variation on the main method, but may be separated by Use: Procedure ^ Use ^ Variation.

This is one simple illustration of the need to separate the organization of the text, which is likely to reflect considerations arising from all three metafunctions and all three contextual variables, from the organization of figures into sequences in the ideation base.

Both domain specifications and rhetorical specifications are part of the local plans that guide micro-generation. They are thus available as sources of information for responding to inquiries in the 'chooser and inquiry' interface between the grammar and the semantics.

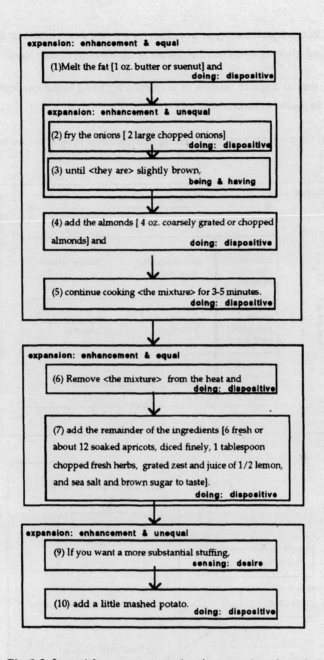

Fig. 9-8: Instantial sequence supporting the generation of a recipe

Let's assume that the **information in the local plan** for Unit (1) has three metafunctional regions (ideation base, interaction base, text base), as shown in Figure 9-9:

(i) there is a particular figure of melting in a frying pan, executed by the cook and operating on the fat (from the list of ingredients) [ideation base];

(ii) there is a speech function of instruction assigning modal responsibility to the reader [interaction base], and

(iii) the process is specified as having thematic status in the plan [text base].

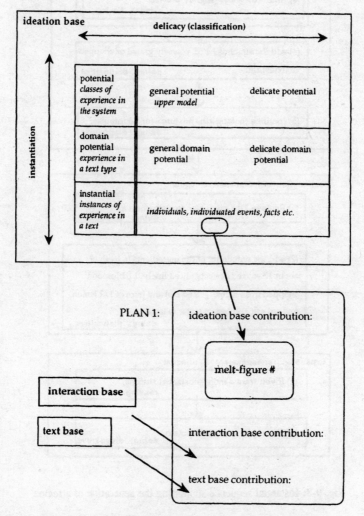

The metafunctional fields in the local plan for unit (1) are as follows:[6]

---

[6] In the Penman system, local plans are specified in a special notation, SPL ('sentence plan language'), described in e.g. Kasper (1989); we have used a similar form.

PLAN 1:

figure: melting-figure1
  process: melting 1
  actor: 'you'
  goal: fat 1
  time: t1

move: (speech function:) instruction 1
  speaker: system
  addressee: 'you'
  speaking-time: 'now'

message:
  theme: melting1
  recoverable (identifiable): fat1

The ideational part of the local plan has been drawn from the instantial ideation base (as indicated in Figure 9-9), where the procedure for making the stuffing is stored as a sequence of figures constituting a particular culinary procedure — diagrammatically, see Figure 9-10.

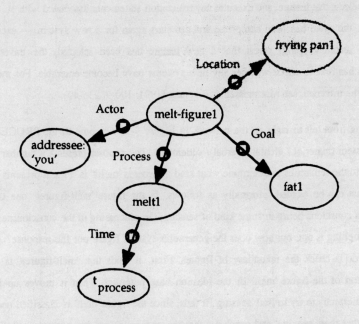

Fig. 9-10: First step in Preparation, the figure of melting

The location of the melting can be assumed to be part of the ideation base; but it is not instantiated in the text since it is predictable, given that the reader is assumed to be familiar with processes of melting, frying, heating, and so on.

9.2.3 Lexicogrammatical generation

The **grammar** provides the recipe generator with the resources to represent the information in the figure above grammatically *and* to integrate it with interpersonal and textual considerations. The grammatical fragment we need for our illustration was given in Figure 9-3 above.

Since lexicogrammatical choice in the Penman system is guided by choosers (see Section 9.1.2 above), the traversal of the system network is essentially forward chaining — from least delicate to most delicate (left to right in graphic representations of the system network). If there are simultaneous systems available for entry, each one has to be entered — ideally in parallel (see Tung, Matthiessen & Sondheimer, 1988) but in current practice in sequence. For any enterable system (i.e., a system whose entry condition has been satisfied), the traversal algorithm activates the system's chooser, steps through the chooser-decision tree until a selection of one of the system's output features has been reached, selects that feature, and executes any realization statements associated with it. At this point, the cycle has been completed and can start again for a new system — except for some record keeping: given that a new feature has been selected, the traversal algorithm has first to check whether any new systems have become enterable. For more detail on the traversal, see Matthiessen & Bateman (1991: 100-9, 236-40).

Moving from left to right in the network in Figure 9-3, we come to the PROCESS TYPE system (material / mental / verbal / relational). The chooser presents a number of inquiries to the semantics to determine what kind of process 'melt#' is. First it presents an inquiry that can be worded informally as follows: Is the figure 'melt-figure#' one that involves a conscious being in some kind of sensing; i.e. processing in the consciousness? Clearly, melting is not, but how does the generation system figure out the response? All it has to do is check the taxonomy of figures. First, it finds that 'melt-figure#' is an instantiation of the figure 'melt' in the ideation base potential. Then it moves up the delicacy hierarchy to try to find 'sensing'. It fails, since the figure 'melt' is classified under 'doing' rather than 'sensing' and concludes that the answer is "no, it's not sensing". The taxonomic information used is diagrammed in Figure 9-11.

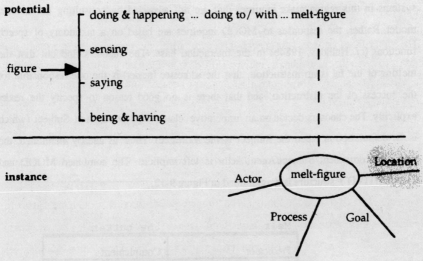

Fig. 9-11: 'melt' in the process taxonomy

After the negative response, the chooser proceeds to ask the next inquiry: Is the figure 'melt-figure#' a saying, i.e. a symbolic one involving a Sayer and potentially a Receiver? Again, the response is a negative one, since the figure 'melt' is not classified under 'saying' in the taxonomy. The chooser then asks a similar kind of question to establish whether 'melt-figure #' is a being & having figure, finds out that it is not, and finally asks: Is the figure 'melt-figure #' a doing one involving an Actor? Since 'melt' is classified under 'doing' in the model, the response is in the affirmative and the chooser acts on it by choosing the grammatical feature 'material'. As a result, there is potentially an Actor present in the TRANSITIVITY structure of the clause (represented by [+Actor] in the network); it would be present if the MOOD component of the grammar inserted a Subject (in an operative clause), but there are good interpersonal reasons for leaving the Subject implicit, namely that in questions and commands the unmarked interpretation is 'you'.

The chooser of the AGENCY system (effective / middle) asks a couple of inquiries and chooses the grammatical feature 'effective'. As a result, the function Agent is potentially present and, if present, conflated with Actor. In a material clause, there is a Goal, which is conflated with Medium. The choices of the features 'effective' and 'material' satisfy the entry condition to the system DOING TYPE (creative / dispositive) and the traversal of the TRANSITIVITY part of the network continues.

At the same time (in principle, although in the current model the traversal is sequential), the MOOD part of the clause network is explored. The choosers of the systems in this region make inquiries that are not answered by consulting the domain model. Rather, the responses to MOOD inquiries are based on a taxonomy of speech functions (cf. Halliday, 1984b) in the interaction base. The choosers find out that the melting of the fat is an instruction, that the addressee (reader) is the one responsible for the success of the instruction, and that there is no good reason to specify the reader explicitly. The choosers decide on an 'imperative' clause with an implicit Subject (which is the default option when the Subject is the addressee). Thus, as already mentioned, the potential constituent Subject/Agent/Actor is left implicit. The combined MOOD and TRANSITIVITY structure is diagrammed in Figure 9-12.

Melt	the butter
Predicator	Complement
Process	Medium/ Goal
[verbal group: nonfinite]	[nominal group]

Fig. 9-12: MOOD and TRANSITIVITY structures combined

Predicator/ Process is then developed as a non-finite verbal group and Complement/ Medium/ Goal as a nominal group.

Let's now consider the generation of two further units, Unit (8) and Unit (9).

Unit (8)

To express unit (8), the generator has to make a different set of TRANSITIVITY and MOOD selections. The choosers discover that the process to be represented is a relation rather than a culinary operation such as melting: the dish is to be represented as belonging to a certain class of stuffings, viz. stuffings for cucumbers; the features 'relational & middle' are chosen, and then 'ascriptive'. The resulting TRANSITIVITY structure is Attribuend/Medium (*this*) Process (*makes*) Attribute/Range (*a good stuffing for cucumbers*). At the same time, the generator is informing rather than instructing the reader; and the chooser of the system INDICATIVE TYPE ('declarative / interrogative') discovers the current speech function is a statement and chooses 'declarative'. As a result Subject is ordered before Finite. The combined TRANSITIVITY and MOOD structure is shown in Figure 9-13.

This	makes	a good stuffing for cucumbers

Subject	Finite/ Predicator	Complement
Medium/ Carrier	Process	Range/ Attribute
	[verbal group: finite: present]	[nominal group]

Fig. 9-13: Combined TRANSITIVITY and MOOD structure for (8)

Unit (9)

As a final example from this text, let's consider unit (9) from the Variation stage of the recipe. The figure of wanting is classified under 'sensing' with 'reaction' as one of the intermediate classes. Based on this taxonomy, the grammatical features 'mental' and 'reactive' are chosen. The entry condition to the system PHENOMENON TYPE ('phenomenal / metaphenomenal') is satisfied and its chooser determines what the nature of the Phenomenon participant is; it asks the environment whether the Phenomenon desired, a stuffing of more substance, is a metaphenomenon (an idea, fact, or saying) or an ordinary phenomenon. When the taxonomy is consulted, it is found that stuffings are things rather than metaphenomena and the grammatical feature 'phenomenal' is chosen. As a result, the function Phenomenon is preselected to be a nominal group rather than a clause. In terms of speech function, the generator is hypothesizing rather than stating or instructing and the grammatical feature 'dependent' is chosen.

From an experiential point of view, the Preparation part of the recipe is a macro-process, more particularly a macro-operation (dispositive doing): an ordered series of operations on food items. From an interpersonal point of view, it is a macro-proposal, more specifically a macro-instruction: an ordered series of instructions to the reader.

In the generation examples we have discussed in this section, we have focussed on the use of ideation base information and made a few observations about the interaction base and interpersonal clause generation. However, we have said very little about the text base apart from noting that it also contributes to local plans. The reason is that we wanted to explore, in a separate step, the way in which the text base relies on the ideation base in a text processing system. We are also moving to territory where less work has been done in NLP and our discussion will be more exploratory.

9.3 Ideation base supporting text base

The textual metafunction differs from the ideational one in a number of fundamental respects — its mode of syntagmatic progression is wave-like, with periodic prominence; it is inherently dynamic in that it organizes text as process; and it is a second-order mode of meaning. Here we shall focus on the last property (mentioned in Chapter 1, Section 1.3) since this leads into the question of what the nature of the text base is and how it might be modelled given current techniques (see Matthiessen, 1992, from which the discussion here is drawn; see also Matthiessen, 1995c; Matthiessen & Bateman, 1991: 219-230; Bateman & Matthiessen, 1993).

9.3.1 Second order nature of textual metafunction

The textual metafunction is second-order in the sense that it is concerned with **semiotic** reality: that is, reality in the form of meaning. This dimension of reality is itself constructed by other two metafunctions: the ideational, which **construes a natural** reality, and the interpersonal, which **enacts an intersubjective** reality. (Cf. Chapter 1, Section 1.3, and Figure 1-4 for diagrammatic interpretation). The function of the textual metafunction is thus an enabling one with respect to the rest; it takes over the semiotic resources brought into being by the other two metafunctions and as it were operationalizes them:

> All the categories under this third heading [i.e., mode, MAKH & CM] are second-order categories, in that they are defined by reference to language and depend for their existence on the prior phenomenon of text. It is in this sense that the textual component in the semantic system was said to have an 'enabling' function vis-à-vis the other two: it is only through the encoding of semiotic interaction as text that the ideational and interpersonal components of meaning can become operational in an environment. (Halliday, 1978b: 145)

This second-order, enabling nature of the textual metafunction is seen both at the level of context, where **mode** (the functions assigned to language in the situation) is second-order in relation to **field** and **tenor** (the ongoing social processes and interactant roles), and at the levels of content — the semantics and the lexicogrammar, where the systems of THEME and INFORMATION, and the various types of cohesion, are second-order in relation to ideational and interpersonal systems of TRANSITIVITY, MOOD, and the rest. See Matthiessen (1992) for a general discussion of the textual metafunction.

One manifestation of the second-order nature of the textual metafunction that is important for our purposes is grammatical metaphor (cf. Chapter 6 above). Grammatical metaphor is a 'second-order' use of the grammatical resources: one grammatical feature or set of features is used as a metaphor for another feature or set of features; and, since features are realized by structures, one grammatical structure comes to stand for another — with the semantic effects discussed in Chapter 6. For instance, an identifying clause may be used to represent a non-identifying one, thereby providing an alternative construal of that other clause as a configuration of Identified + Process + Identifier. Thus, the clause *you want this* may be reconfigured as an identifying clause by nominalizing 'the thing that you want', *what you want,* and identifying it with *this,* either as *what you want is this* or as *this is what you want:*

```
        and I said "I am not competent to do it and I wouldn't have
    my name on the title page to do it" and I said "I'm bloody sure
    that Hilary and Gavin aren't competent to do it either" and I
    said "if this is what you want, I would put maximum pressure
    upon somebody like Derek Brainback to do it" but I said ...
    (Svartvik & Quirk, 1980: 802-3)
```

The two versions of the clause are related in Figure 9-14.

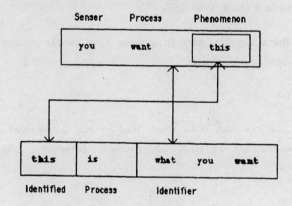

Fig. 9-14: Clause construed as identifying clause (1) — THEME
IDENTIFICATION

The motivation behind the identifying metaphor is actually textual: the alternative configuration in the identifying clause constitutes a textual alternative for distributing information in the clause, in which the message is structured as an equation between two terms. This system is known as THEME IDENTIFICATION. What is significant here is that the textual organization is realized by the second-order resource of grammatical metaphor. That is, the grammar is as it were turned back on itself: it reconstrues itself with a particular effect in the discourse, as diagrammed in Figure 9-15. We can see, then, that experiential grammatical metaphor is a strategy for creating a 'carrier' of textual meanings, as noted in Chapter 6.

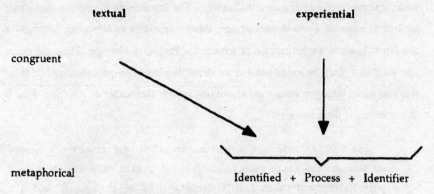

Fig. 9-15: Textual organization carried by experiential metaphor

A related textual system is that of THEME PREDICATION (the so-called "cleft construction" of formal grammar), which similarly employs the identifying type of clause to achieve a particular balance of meaning in the discourse.[7] We again give one example taken from Svartvik & Quirk (1980: 255):

    A: There's a lot more in grammar than people notice. People
    always notice the lexis.

    B: Yes.

    A: Lots has been done about that -- but I mean you can only
    get so far and so much fun out of 'pavement', 'sidewalk',
    etcetera.

    B: Mm.

    A: It's the grammar where the fun is.

    B: //1 Yes // 4 it's the grammar which is interesting //

---

[7] Both these systems, THEME IDENTIFICATION and THEME PREDICATION, assign exclusive identity to the identified term of the equation. They differ, however, in the kind of prominence this identity carries with it: in THEME IDENTIFICATION, in which the original figure is restructured, the effect is one of second-order (semiotic) prominence, whereas in THEME PREDICATION, where the figure is not restructured, but one element within it is explicitly predicated, the effect is that of assigning first-order (natural or inter-subjective) prominence to the predicated element.

Here 'the thing which is interesting' is identified as grammar rather than lexis; the relationship between *the grammar is interesting* and *it's the grammar which is interesting* is shown in Figure 9-16.

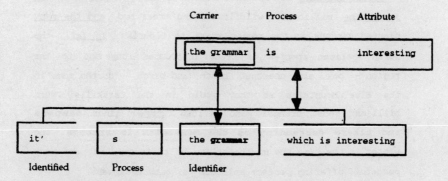

Fig. 9-16: Clause construed as identifying clause (2) — THEME PREDICATION

9.3.2 Grammatical metaphor as second-order semantic resource

These two clause systems, THEME IDENTIFICATION and THEME PREDICATION, are components of the overall system of THEME in English grammar. They produce structures in which identifying relational processes are used to reconstrue figures as equations (the two together are referred to as "thematic equatives" in Halliday, 1985: 41-4). But ideational grammatical metaphors typically have a discourse function of this kind; they are as it were pressed into service by the textual metafunction, to provide **alternative groupings of quanta of information.** Here are two further examples of this deployment of ideational metaphors.

(1) Metaphorical mental clauses of perception, such as *the fifth day saw them at the summit* (cf. Halliday, 1985: 324-5), may serve to create two quanta of information, Senser (Theme) + Phenomenon (New); consider the following example:

[Theme underlined in ranking clauses, paragraph 2; seasonal Themes in italics; relevant culmination of the New in bold.]

One of Australia's most majestic mountain ranges is one of Sydney's most popular year-round playgrounds. The Blue Mountains to the west of the city have beckoned Sydneysiders to its resorts since the last century, but only after World War I have the pleasures of the Blue Mountains been developed to attract foreign visitors as well. The main town in the mountains is Katoomba, 104 km (62 mi) west of Sydney.

Spring and fall are the most beautiful times of year here. *In springtime*, millions of wildflowers and trees bud, and the many planned gardens in the region start to flourish. *In fall*, the North American species of trees introduced long ago to the region -- oak, elm, chestnut, beech, and birch -- do the same in the Blue Mountains as they would in the Catskills: turn brilliant reds, oranges, and yellows. *Summer* finds **campers and hikers descending on the mountains in throngs**, and *winter* is the time the mountains are at their quietest and most peaceful, offering perfect solitude for city escapees.

If you're looking for a swinging resort, the Blue Mountains may not be for you. ... (Fodor's Sydney, p. 115)

Here the metaphorical clause *summer finds campers and hikers descending on the mountains in throngs* is textually motivated in terms of both THEME and INFORMATION. From the point of view of THEME, it provides *summer* as the unmarked Theme of the clause — one instalment in the seasonal method of development. From the point of view of INFORMATION, it groups *campers and hikers descending on the mountains in throngs* as one quantum of information (the Phenomenon of the metaphorical mental clause); contrast the congruent version, which has the same Theme (marked) but a different culmination of the New: *In summer, campers and hikers descend on the mountains in throngs.*

(2) In the second type to be exemplified, a clause or clause complex is nominalized as a Medium participant in a clause whose Process simply means 'happen' (i.e., existence of a process: *happen, occur, take place; begin, continue, stop*). The Medium constitutes a thematic quantum of information, as in the following example:

[Information involved in progression in italics; relevant culmination of New in bold.]

The speed of light, and of all electromagnetic waves, was given as a constant by Maxwell's equations, and this speed and the existence of the waves themselves was independent of any outside effect. However, Einstein realized that if an observer was travelling alongside a light wave at the same speed as the

light wave, *the wave would essentially disappear*, *as no wave*
peaks or troughs would pass by the observer. But *the*
disappearance of light waves because of the motion of an
observer should not happen **according to Maxwell**, so Einstein
concluded that either Maxwell's equations were wrong or that no
observer could move at the speed of light. He preferred the
latter explanation for a particular reason. (M. Shallis, On time: An
investigation into scientific knowledge and human experience, p. 38.)

Here the metaphorical clause makes it possible to summarize the preceding clause
complex *the wave would essentially disappear, as no wave peaks or troughs would pass*
by the observer as a thematic nominalized participant, *the disappearance of light waves*
because of the motion of an observer.

9.3.3 Text base stated in terms of ideation base

The principle of the deployment of ideational metaphor by the textual component,
illustrated in Figure 9-15, also applies to the bases of the semantic stratum. The text base
both sets up information states within figures (presents them as messages organized
around quanta of information) and guides the movement from one figure to another. In the
former capacity, the text base can be interpreted as **patterns stated over** the ideation
base. That is, the representation of ideational meaning in the ideation base constitutes the
first order of representation in terms of which second-order, textual meaning can be
specified.

We have seen that ideational meanings are represented as a large network of nodes
linked by various kinds of relations (such as hyponymy and participant relations). When a
text is produced, certain nodes in this network are selected for presentation (cf. Sigurd,
1977). As an example, Figure 9-17 presents a semantic network of the information
contained in a biographical note, the short biography of Joseph Conrad in the Penguin
edition of Nostromo (for a discussion of the representation and generation of this text in
Chinese, see Bateman, Matthiessen & Zeng, forthc; for the representation of texts as
networks of meaning, see de Beaugrande, 1980, in press.).

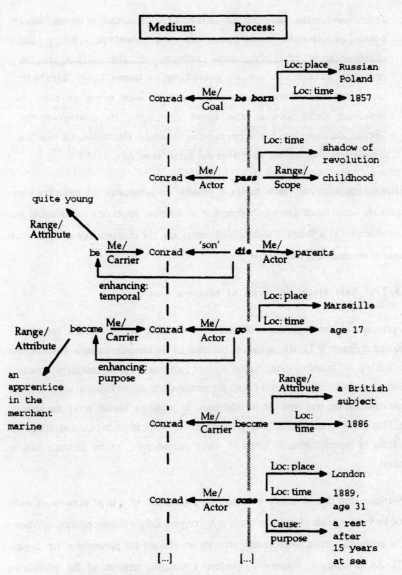

Fig. 9-17: Example of informal ideational semantic network

We have drawn this network as a succession of figures, with processes (be born, pass, be, etc.) as nodes accompanied by participant roles (Medium, Range) and circumstantial roles (Time, Place, Destination, etc.). We have only included information that is present in the source text;[8] any actual semantic network would include a good deal of information

---

[8] The text presents instantial meanings concerning Conrad; we have not represented the semantic systemic potential that these meanings instantiate. This potential would include, among other things, a hyponymic taxonomy.

that is not presented in any particular text: producing a text means selecting from the information given in the network (just as with our recipe example earlier in Chapter 8). We have organized the diagram in such a way that it is fairly easy to see how one can read it as a text. The vertical axis represents process time, from 1857 onwards. Processes on the same horizontal line are related by some type of logico-semantic relation within a clause complex in the text. The actual Conrad biography reads as follows (clauses not diagrammed in Figure 9-17 are in italics; ideational Themes are underlined and will be discussed presently); note that this is only one possible 'textual rendering' of the ideational meanings represented in Figure 9-17:

> Joseph Conrad (originally Konrad Korzeniowski) was born in Russian Poland in 1857, and __ passed his childhood in the shadow of revolution. His parents died when he was quite young. At the age of seventeen he went to Marseille to become an apprentice in the merchant marine. *This began a long period of adventure at sea, Conrad having his share of hardship, shipwreck, and other accidents.*
>
> He became a British subject in 1886. In 1889, at the age of thirty-one, he came to London for a rest after fifteen years at sea. *On this short London holiday, he began writing a sea novel, which, after surviving subsequent jungle travel, shipwreck on the Congo, and a railway cloakroom in Berlin, came into the hands of Edward Garnett and through him to a London publisher. The book was 'Almayer's Folly', __ destined to be the first of a long series of novels and stories, __ mostly inspired by his experiences of life at sea, which have placed him in the front rank of English literature. He died in 1924.*

Once the semantic network has been defined, it is then possible to state textual patterns over the network, such as those imposed on it by grammatical metaphor (cf. again Figure 9-15). One way of representing such patterns is to **partition** the network — to divide the network into domains or spaces consisting of collections of related nodes and links (see Hendrix, 1978; 1979).[9] Partitioned semantic networks are characterized succinctly in Bundy (1986: 110) as follows:

---

[9] Alternatively, we can define *processes* in terms of the semantic network — processes for

Means of enhancing the organizational and expressive power of **semantic nets** through the grouping of nodes and links, associated with Hendrix. Nodes and links may figure in one or more **'spaces'**, which may themselves be bundled into higher-level **'vistas'**, which can be exploited autonomously and structured hierarchically. The effective encoding of logical statements involving **connectives** and **quantifiers** was an important motivation for partitioning, but the partitioning mechanisms involved are sufficiently well-founded, general and powerful to support the dynamic representation of a wide range of language and world knowledge.

As noted in this characterization, such partitions have been used to represent various kinds of information; of particular interest here is the use of partitioned spaces to represent textual states of prominence. Grosz (1978) presents the idea of representing focus as a partitioned space in a semantic network — what she calls a **focus space**. A focus space "contains those items that are in the focus of attention of the dialog participants during a particular part of the dialog" (op cit., p. 233). Since focus is really only one kind of textual status of prominence, we need to generalize Grosz's original proposal: textual states of prominence in general can be modelled as partitioned spaces in a semantic network. Against the background of this, it is now possible to suggest very briefly how information in the text base can be modelled:

(i) The second-order character of textual information is captured by defining it in terms of the already existing semantic network in the ideation base (the first-order representation, such as the fragment shown in Figure 9-17). This is clearly only a first approximation: as we showed in Chapter 6 and noted again here, the textual metafunction may in fact motivate ideational metaphor as a means of 'carrying' textual organization.

(ii) Textual prominences constituting textual statuses can then be modelled as partitioned textual spaces of the semantic network. As already noted, this is a generalization of Grosz's notion of focus spaces to include thematic spaces, new spaces, identifiability spaces and so on. This is also only a first approximation: textual prominence is a matter of degree and we need to think of a textual space not as a clearly bounded region but rather as a central region, the peak of prominence, from which one can move to more peripheral regions, the troughs of non-prominence. Such gradience is necessary not only to deal with degrees of thematicity and newsworthiness but also to handle

---

moving through it and 'linearizing' it as text; textual states such as Theme could then be modelled by making the process visit nodes in the network in a certain sequence (cf. Sowa, 1983b). For a general discussion of the representation of textual and interpersonal meaning in a lattice, see Parker-Rhodes (1978).

identifiability by 'bridging' (cf. Clark, 1975; for example, bridging from a centrally identifiable whole to more peripherally identifiable parts).[10]

The use of textual spaces defined on an ideational semantic network in the ideation base can be illustrated by adding thematic spaces to Figure 9-17 above: see Figure 9-18. With the exception of Conrad's parents, the thematic spaces are either Conrad or a time.

Thematic spaces in an ideational semantic network can be seen as a model of the systemic understanding of Theme and method of development articulated by Martin, where "field" corresponds to what has been discussed here in terms of ideational semantic networks in the ideation base:

> Method of development ... establishes an angle on the field. This angle will be sensitive to a text's generic structure where this is realised in stages. Method of development is the lens through which a field is constructed; of all the experiential meanings available in a given field, it will pick on just a few, and weave them through Theme time and again to ground the text — to give interlocutors something to hang onto, something to come back to — an orientation, a perspective, a point of view, a perch, a purchase. (Halliday & Martin, 1993)

The speaker thus selects 'thematic spaces' as points of entry into larger regions of the ideational semantic network. From the listener's point of view, these thematic spaces constitute indications of where to integrate the new information being presented in the text — cf. Reinhart (1982). If we think of the listener's processing of a text as being partly a matter of expanding his or her current semantic network with new information, the thematic spaces guide him/her to appropriate expansion points.

In the Conrad biography, there are essentially two competing types of node to be partitioned into thematic spaces: (i) Conrad himself and (ii) significant times in his life. (Conrad's works come in as another type of Theme in the second half of the text not diagrammed in Figures 9-17 and 9-18.) The writer has resolved the conflict by alternating between these two candidates; in the segment shown in Figure 9-18, temporal Themes are selected when there is a transition in Conrad's life associated with Conrad's move to a new destination (Marseille, London). (One could, of course, write the text in such a way that times consistently fall within the thematic spaces: compare the different thematic versions of texts provided in Fries, 1981, and Martin, 1992.) Here Conrad remains the Subject of

---

[10] Grosz (1978: 273) operates with both explicit focus and implicit focus. When a physical object in the semantic network is in explicit focus, its subparts are in implicit focus.

the clause. But even when Conrad is thematic, the discoursal movement through the semantic network is still essentially a chronological one (with certain elaborating excursions realized in dependent clauses).

Thematic space: 'Conrad'   'time'

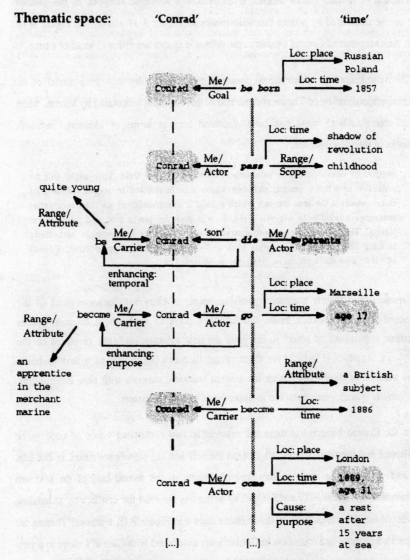

Fig. 9-18: Semantic network partitioned into textual spaces

So far we have hinted at the possibility of taking a 'snapshot' of textual information by partitioning a semantic network into textual spaces representing peaks of textual prominence[11] (crudely, since the spaces are discretely bounded regions at this stage). This

---

[11] Since at this stage the spaces are discretely bounded regions, the effect of partitioning is

still leaves us with the task of modelling the guided **transitions** between different
textual states (again not unrelated to organization in the ideation base: cf. Chapter 3,
Sections 3.4 and 3.6 above; we shall return briefly to this point in our last summary
example). To do this, to deal with what Grosz (1978: 233) called the dynamic requirement
on focus representation, we can use one of the mechanisms developed in computational
linguistics for dealing with 'discourse history'. Grosz used the computational notion of a
stack to model transitions or shifts from one focus space to another; see Figure 9-19.[12]
As a discourse develops, focus spaces are stacked one on top of another so that the most
recent is always on top of the stack. The stack itself can thus be used a record of
progression through discourse time. Now, the stack is always manipulated from the top:
if a new focus space is to be added to the stack, it is pushed onto the top of the stack; and
if an old one is to be removed, it is popped off the top of the stack.

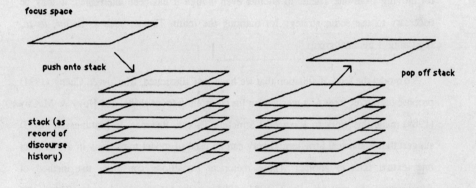

Fig. 9-19: The stack as a model of successive textual states

For instance, the succession of thematic spaces might include from bottom to top: 'at
the age of seventeen', 'in 1889, at the age of thirty-one', 'on this short London holiday'.
While the account based on the stack mechanism is a very explicit model of how textual
states of prominence might get manipulated in the development of discourse, it is very
clear from a functional-linguistic point of view that the stack is too simple a record of
discourse history. In particular, it represents a discourse as a flat structure; it does not

---

to make prominence appear as categorical feature. A more theoretically informed
representation would show prominence as a gradient (cf. Pattabhiraman's, 1992,
modelling of salience).

[12] As an ordering principle, the stack means 'last first out'; this contrasts with the queue,
where the principle is 'first in first out'. For a discussion of the stack in the modelling of
exchange, see O'Donnell (1990).

represent the kind of hierarchic constituency organization or internal interdependency nesting that various approaches to discourse have revealed: see for example Fox (1987) on reference and rhetorical organization (modelled in terms of Rhetorical Structure Theory). A typical guide-book text would illustrate the issue with respect to Theme: while the global principle of development is a spatial one (say, that of the walking tour) and is constructed in spatial Themes, this type of text often changes locally to other principles, such as the temporal one reflected in *As the battle ended, the last six cadets are said to have wrapped themselves in the Mexican flag and __ jumped from the hill to their deaths rather than surrender to the U.S. forces,* which occurs on a walking tour of a park in Mexico City. After this temporal detour, the text returns to the spatial development, where it left off: see Figure 9-19. This is quite typical of Theme selection in discourse (cf. suspended exchanges in conversations). There is no problem with returning to the earlier principle for moving from one Theme to another even though it has been interrupted; it may be necessary to use some strategy for marking the return Theme, such as *as for, as to, regarding* + nominal group.

To model the kind of situation that we have just illustrated, McCoy & Cheng (1991) propose hierarchic trees as a mechanism for controlling focus shifts, and Hovy & McCoy (1989) relate this work to Rhetorical Structure Theory. Bateman & Matthiessen (1993) suggest that Rhetorical Structure Theory can be used to model transitions in a text from one textual state to another. These rhetorical transitions constitute the method of development of a text (see Fries, 1981, 1995 for the relationship between Theme and method of development). The Conrad biography illustrates this principle, but in a slightly complex way: the main type of transition is temporal sequence, which means that thematic spaces are likely to included reference to time, and that shifts from one space to another will occur along with the sequence in time; but sequence often also involves a constant participant (Conrad in this text), which is then also a likely thematic candidate.

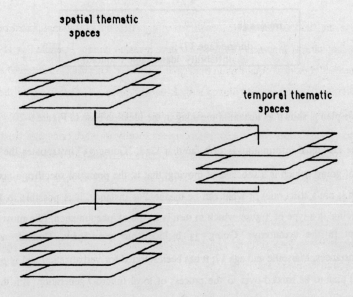

Fig. 9-19: Detour through temporal stack, with return to spatial one

9.3.4 Summary example of text base

We can now use an example to summarize what we have said about the text base in relation to the ideation base. Assume the generation system is at the point at which it will generate the first clause in the clause complex *At the age of seventeen he went to Marseille to become an apprentice in the merchant marine.* The local plan includes the following information:

Plan 5/ going

> **figure:** going-Marseille-figure
> : actor (Conrad/ person)
> : process (going/ happening
>   : time ty < tx)
> : destination (Marseille/ place)
> : time (17/ age)

> **move:** speech function (going-act/ statement)

```
message:
    :theme (age 17)
    : identifiability  identifiable (Conrad)
```

This plan is shown as instantial meaning in the ideation base in Figure 9-20.

The ideational information is of a familiar kind. "Going 23" instantiates the general class of going, which is a subclass of moving; that is, the potential specifies a taxonomy (which is not a strict one) of what can be meant. For instance, it is possible to find out that 'going' is a type of 'figure' which in turn is a type of 'phenomenon' (the most general concept in the taxonomy). Going 23 includes one participant, Conrad, and two circumstances, Marseille and age 17; it has been selected for verbalization and is *part* of a local plan to be handed over to the process of local (micro-) generation. But that local plan also contains textual (and interpersonal) information, viz. that the Theme has been planned to be 'age 17'. This is a specification of a textual partition in the ideation base, representing (as we have seen) a textual state of information. It can be motivated by reference to the other major phenomenon the text base has to deal with — textual transitions. As we suggested already in Chapter 3, Section 3.4 (cf. also Figure 3-10), the relational organization of text (the rhetorical transitions) that the text base manages may be supported by sequences in the ideation base. This is likely to happen both in narrative text (such as the biography discussed in this section) and in procedural text (such as the recipes discussed earlier). In any case, at that point in the global text plan where there is a local plan covering the clause complex *At the age of seventeen* he went to Marseille to *become an apprentice in the merchant marine* , a purposive relation is introduced within the sequence; but that sequence is itself in a relation of temporal succession to an earlier sequence: see Figure 9-21. That is, the going to Marseille expands the previous text in terms of temporal succession; and there is every reason to select a Theme that indicates the point of temporal expansion — Conrad's age (realized as *at the age of seventeen* in initial position in the clause).

It is clear, then, that the ideation base supports the text base: textual information can be stated as patterns over the text base — partitions, and moves between partitions. At the same time, it is also very clear that the way the ideation base is organized — the various configurations that have evolved — must have been shaped by textual pressure. So, for instance, given that a relationship could be construed either as 'that boy's hair is green' or 'that boy has green hair', the preference in English for the construal where the whole is

Carrier and the part is Attribute can be understood in textual terms: it means that the whole can serve as Theme. We have already seen that the textual metafunction is a powerful part of the explanation of ideational metaphor: ideational meaning is reconstrued in such a way that it suits textual organization when meanings are being distributed in text. This is an area where the evolved system of English and designed systems such as logics differ sharply: the latter are not designed to construe textual differences and instead place a high value on canonical forms.

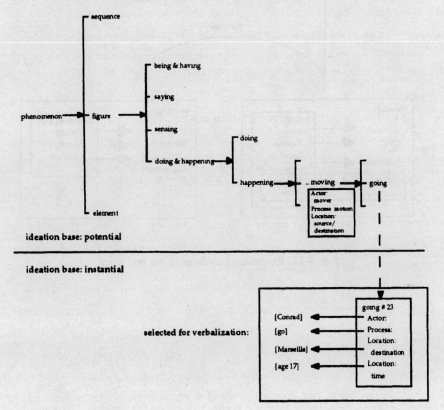

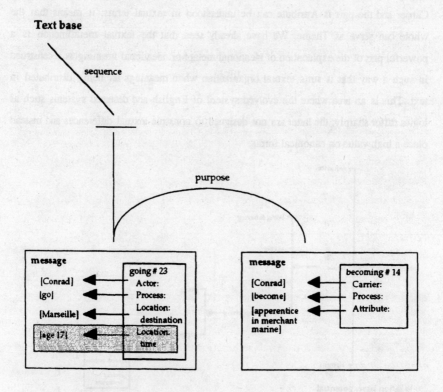

Fig. 9-21: Rhetorical transitions in the text plans

Part IV:

Theoretical and descriptive alternatives

10. Alternative approaches to meaning

We began our book with some general observations about the approach we have adopted
— seeing knowledge as meaning, approaching it through the grammar, taking account of
different kinds of semo-histories, and so on (Part I). We then introduced the ideational
meaning base and discussed the different kinds of phenomena in some detail (Part II). We
then went on to show how domain models are located within the ideation base and how a
language processing system can draw upon these ideational resources (Part III). We are
now in a position to compare and contrast our approach with alternatives — both
theoretical alternatives and global descriptive ones (this chapter) and alternatives in details
of description (Chapters 11 and 12).

10.1 Logico-philosophical vs. rhetorical-ethnographic orientations

It is impossible to offer anything more than the barest outline of the historical
background to work on the ideation base. We can identify two main traditions in Western
thinking about meaning (see Halliday, 1977):

> (i) one oriented towards logic and philosophy, with language seen as a system of
> rules;

> (ii) one oriented towards rhetoric and ethnography, with language seen as resource.

It is typically the logical-philosophical tradition that provides the background for work on
knowledge representation and proposals for the knowledge base. Since the 50s, a link has
been forged between this tradition and cognitivism under the general rubric of **cognitive
science**. However, although it is less often referred to, the rhetorical-ethnographic
tradition is equally relevant to work on the modelling and representation of knowledge —
for example, in recent times, the work on folk taxonomy carried out by anthropologists
and anthropological linguists (often in the framework of ethnoscience) and the work on
intellectualization in the Prague School framework are central to understanding the
organization of the ideation base. Our own work here falls mainly within the second
tradition — but we have taken account of the first tradition, and the general intellectual
environment in which versions of our meaning base are being used also derives primarily
from the first tradition. Indeed, the two traditions can in many respects be seen as

complementary, as contributing different aspects of the overall picture. Our own foundation, however, is functional, as noted in Part I.

Mainstream work in psycholinguistics, e.g. Miller & Johnson-Laird (1976), is in general located within the logico-philosophical tradition. Two other distinctive contributions to the study of meaning within linguistics, those of Lamb (1964, 1992) and of Wierzbicka (1980, 1988), derive in more or less equal measure from both the major intellectual movements we have referred to.

The two orientations towards meaning thus differ externally in what disciplines they recognize as models. These external differences are asscociated with **internal differences** as well.

(i) First, the orientations differ with respect to where they **locate meaning** in relation to the stratal interpretation of language:

(a) intra-stratal: meaning is seen as **immanent** — something that is constructed in, and so is part of, language itself. The immanent interpretation of meaning is characteristic of the rhetorical-ethnographic orientation, including our own approach.

(b) extra-stratal: meaning is seen as **transcendent** — something that lies outside the limits of language. The transcendent interpretation of meaning is characteristic of the logico-philosophical orientation.

Many traditional notions of meaning are of the second kind — meaning as reference, meaning as idea or concept, meaning as image. These notions have in common that they are 'external' conceptions of meaning; instead of accounting for meaning in terms of a stratum within language, they interpret it in terms of some system outside of language, either the 'real world' or another semiotic system such as that of imagery. The modern split within the "transcendent" view is between what Barwise (1988: 23) calls the **world-oriented** tradition and the **mind-oriented** tradition, which he interprets as public vs. private accounts of meaning:

> The world oriented tradition in semantics, from Tarski on, has focussed on the public aspect of meaning by trying to identify the meaning of a sentence or text with its truth conditions, the conditions on the actual world that are needed to insure its truth (Davidson 1967 and Montague 1974). The psychological tradition, by contrast, has focussed on the private aspect by trying to identify meaning with an intrinsically meaningful mental representation (Fodor 1975 or Jackendoff 1983 e.g.).

The world-oriented tradition interprets meaning by reference to (models of) the world; for example, the meaning of a proper noun would be an individual in the world, whereas the meaning of an intransitive verb such as *run* would be a set of individuals (e.g. the set of individuals engaged in the act of running). The mind-oriented tradition interprets meaning by reference to the mind; typically semantics is interpreted as that part of the cognitive system that can be "verbalized".

(ii) Secondly, the approaches differ with respect to what they take as the **basic unit of meaning**. In the logico-philosophical orientation, the basic unit tends to be determined "from below", from grammar: since sentences are seen as encoding propositions, the basic unit of semantics is the proposition (as in propositional calculus).[1] In contrast, in the rhetorical-ethnographic orientation, the basic unit tends to be determined "from above", from context: since language is seen as functioning in context, the basic unit of semantic is the text (see Halliday & Hasan, 1976; Halliday, 1978a). So in the logico-philosophical orientation, semantics means in the first instance propositional semantics,[2] whereas in the other orientation it means text or discourse semantics. (We have not attempted to extend our present coverage to include the semantics of discourse; see Martin, 1992, for a comprehensive model of discourse semantics in systemic functional terms. A rich meaning-oriented approach to text linguistics will be found in de Beaugrande, 1980, and in a new framework in de Beaugrande, in press.)

(iii) The two orientations differ in the **metafunctional scope** of their models of semantics. In the logico-philosophical orientation, meaning is closely associated with representation, reference, denotation, extension or 'aboutness', so the metafunctional scope is restricted to the ideational metafunction: semantics means ideational semantics. In the rhetorical-ethnographic orientation, meaning is closely associated with rhetorical concerns, so the metafunctional scope involves all three metafunctions: semantics means ideational, interpersonal and textual semantics; it is multifunctional. If interpersonal and textual meanings are dealt with by logico-philosophical accounts (they are often outside their scope), they are handled under the heading of pragmatics rather than the heading of semantics. For example, speech act theory was developed as a logico-philosophical interpretation of speech function (or rather of its ideational construal) and has come to be included within pragmatics.

(iv) Finally, we can note that the two orientations differ in what kind of **semantic organization** they focus on. In the logico-philosophical orientation scholars have focussed on syntagmatic organization: they have been concerned with semantic structure — including principles relating to structure such as those of compositionality and

---

[1] Note that *proposition* has a different sense here from *proposition* in our interpersonal semantics, where it contrasts with *proposal*.

[2] This is changing to some extent, e.g. with the formal semantic work by Hans Kamp and his followers. In computational linguistics it was necessary to model discourse patterns from a fairly early stage, so approaches to discourse semantics originating in the logico-philosophical tradition began to show up in the 1970s.

semantic decomposition. For example, in their analysis of the senses of "words", they have tended to analyse these as being composed of semantic components, semantic markers, semantic primitives or the like (following Katz & Fodor, 1963, in the generative tradition). In the rhetorical-ethnographic orientation scholars have focussed on both paradigmatic and syntagmatic organization, often foregrounding the paradigmatic: they have been concerned with the semantic system, with the meaning potential — including principles of taxonomy and the metafunctional simultaneity of systems. For example, scholars in "ethnoscience" have studied folk taxonomies of animals, plants, diseases and the like (cf. Chapter 2, Section 2.11.3 above); and systemic-functional scholars have tried to map out semantic systems such as those of speech function and conjunction. Another example is our own work on the ideation base presented here.

The two different orientations are summarized with the internal differences we have just reviewed in Figure 10-1. We now turn to the two variants within the logico-philosophical tradition, the "world-oriented" one of formal semantics (Section 10.2) and the "mind-oriented" one of cognitive semantics (Section 10.3).

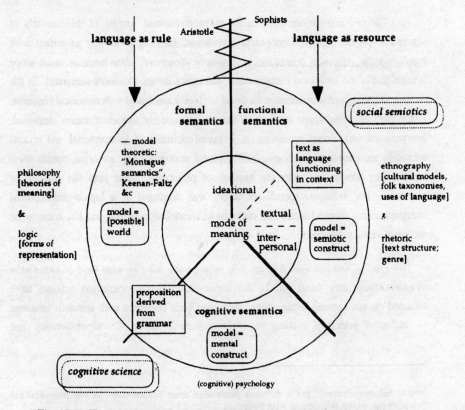

Fig. 10-1: The manifestation of the two traditions in the study of meaning

10.2 Formal semantics

Relevant discussions primarily illuminating **the logical-philosophical tradition** include Kneale & Kneale (1962) on the history of logic; Large (1985), Knowlson (1975), Slaughter (1986), Salmon (1966; 1979) on the history of 'artificial languages' and taxonomy in the period of early Western science; Sowa (1983a, 1991), Brachman (1979) and Brachman & Levesque (1985) on modern knowledge representation in AI, with notes on precursors; Eco et al (1988) on different contemporary views of the status of meaning and cognition; Bursill-Hall (1971) on medieval theories of meaning. Here we are merely noting some particularly important developments. These are charted in Figure 10-2.

The development of logic is of interest in itself in the present context as a tradition of 'semiotic design' whereby logical systems were developed out of the resources that have evolved in language. This design of logical systems was carried out to meet certain restricted purposes having to do with reasoning; but once such systems had been developed, philosophers and linguists turned them back on language and used them as systems for representing and theorizing meaning. In the present century, when formal semantics was developed for underpinning logical systems, this was then taken as a model for work on the semantics of natural languages.

As we have shown, natural language includes a "natural logic" (Chapter 3); and in the discourses of philosophy this was gradually transformed into models of logic and reasoning. Such philsophical models were first constituted in language, but later developed into the designed systems of symbolic logic. Leibniz had a vision of an "algebra of thought" for correct reasoning. He took note of the work by Wilkins and others on "artificial languages"; but these were concerned in the first instance with taxonomic organization (within the domain of the experiential mode of meaning), whereas Leibniz' primary concern was with reasoning (within the domain of the logical mode of meaning). His own work was left unfinished, but symbolic logic can be seen as a continuation of his attempt to design a special semiotics for reasoning with. In the 19th century, de Morgan codified the "laws of reasoning" (modus ponens, etc.); and subsequently Boole (1854) formulated an algebra of the relations of conjunction and disjunction and of negation, "Boolean algebra", which he thought of as constituting the "laws of thought". In 1879, Frege published his "Begriffsschrift", subtitled "eine der Arithmetischen nachgebildete Formelsprache des reinen Denkens". Frege's work laid the foundation for predicate logic, and for modern symbolic or mathematical logic in general. One of his contributions to the emergence of formal semantics was his distinction between *Sinn* and *Bedeutung* (Frege, 1892), translated into English as *sense* and *reference*. This distinction was later developed by Carnap as the contrast between intension and extension, and is part of the foundation of semantics of the model-theoretic kind.

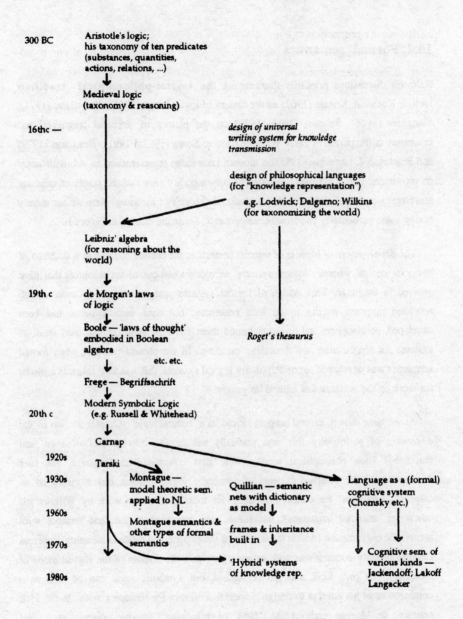

Fig. 10-2: Development of approaches to meaning

In the 20th century, as the scope of logical systems grew, it became possible to use them as a representational resource in the description of meaning in language: cf. Chapter 1, Section 1.9.2 above. In the 1930s, Alfred Tarski developed the truth conditional approach to semantics for the designed semiotic system of predicate logic. He criticized the current correspondence theory of truth, according to which a proposition is true if it corresponds to a fact (proposed e.g. by Russell and Wittgenstein but in fact going back to Aristotle), adopting another version whereby truth is defined in terms of **truth**

conditions:[3] a proposition is true if and only if it refers to an actual state of affairs in the world. The example that is usually cited is: *snow is white* [proposition] is true if and only if snow is white [state of affairs in the world]. In this way, states of affairs came to be represented as models of the world, and the 'meaning' of the constructs of logic as either extensions in these models or as truth values. For example, the extension of a constant is an individual, the extension of one-place predicate is a set of individuals. The semantics of logical systems was thus stated in terms of **model theory**. This approach to meaning is **objectivist**: (extensional) meanings are phenomena existing in the world. There are no meaners construing meanings, and there is no perceptual system mediating between semiotic expressions and their extensions. Truth is a matter of correspondence, not (as it is in everyday discourse) a question of consensus among people.

In the 1950s and 1960s, the philosopher Richard Montague took the semantics of designed logics as a model for describing the meaning of natural language: "having worked with formal languages of increasing complexity, he came to realize that by having a lexicon of English words and a list of structural operations consisting of English constructions, English itself could be regarded as one of these formal languages" (Thomason in his introduction to Montague, 1974: 16). Bach (1989: 8) calls this "Montague's Thesis": "natural languages can be described as interpreted formal systems". That is, a natural, evolved language such as English was treated as if it was a formal, designed "language" such as predicate logic. In order for it to be treated in this way, it had to be disambiguated, so that its expressions would be unambigous just as those of formal logic are. But Montague himself did not see this approach as a *metaphorical* treatment of English. In a paper entitled "English as a formal language", he writes:

> I reject the contention that an important theoretical difference exists between formal and natural languages. ... I regard the construction of a theory of truth — or rather, the more general notion of truth under an arbitrary interpretation — as the basic goal of serious syntax and semantics; and the developments emanating from the Massachusetts Institute of Technology offer little promise towards that end. ... I shall accordingly present a precise treatment, culminating in a theory of truth, of a formal language that I believe may be reasonably regarded as a fragment of ordinary English. ... The treatment given here will be found to resemble the usual syntax and model theory (or semantics) of the predicate calculus [footnote: The model theory of the predicate calculus is of course due to Alfred Tarski].

Formal semantics, or "Montague semantics" as the approach has also come to be called, was taken up in linguistics by e.g. Dowty et al (1981), Bach (1989), Cann (1993), Partee (1975), and carried further by Keenan & Faltz (1985). In philosophy, Barwise & Perry (1983) introduced new ideas into formal semantics in the form of their "situation semantics". For a recent critique of formal semantics, see Bickhart & Campbell (1992).

---

[3] Haack (1978: 99) calls Tarski's theory of truth a **semantic theory**; on the question whether it is a correspondence theory, see pp. 112-114.

In its relation to syntax, the formal approach to semantics is compositional, being formulated in terms of syntagmatic organization: the meaning of larger syntagmatic units such as sentences is built up as functions of smaller units such as nouns and verbs. This semantic composition is in tandem with the syntax, so what becomes important is the nature of the syntactic rules themselves, not just the result of their application. Montague used a form of categorial grammar in formalizing the rules of syntax for this purpose.

In modelling meaning, formal semantics models it as both extensional and intensional: extensional meaning is cast in terms of sets of entities in a model of some world, and intensional meaning is the relation between a linguistic expression and its extension in any possible world. Formal semantics has thus been concerned with how semantic representations can be related to some extra-linguistic world model. Dowty et al (1981: 5) emphasize the relationship between language and the world in their introductory characterization of truth conditional semantics:

> "... truth conditional semantics, in contrast to other approaches mentioned [including Katz & Fodor, Jackendoff, and generative semantics, MAKH & CM], is based squarely on the assumption that the proper business of semantics is to specify how language connects with the world — in other words, to explicate the inherent "aboutness" of language."

This is, of course, an ideational orientation: the focus here is on representational meaning only. One central method has been to build models of the world in set theoretic terms, and to relate these to linguistic expressions — the model theoretic approach mentioned above.

The model theoretic approach to meaning is a transcendent one: meanings are located in the world outside of language. This is seen as a strength by the proponents of the model theoretic approach. Dowty et al (1981) criticize various other theories of meaning for ignoring the "inherent aboutness of language", its relationship to the real world:

> Any theory which ignores this central property, it is argued, cannot be an adequate theory of natural language. Examples would be theories which, in effect, give the meaning of a sentence by translating it into another language, such as a system of semantic markers or some sort of formal logic, where this language is not further interpreted by specifying its connection to the world. The approach of Katz and his co-workers seems to be of this sort (Katz and Fodor, 1963; Katz & Postal, 1964), as is that of Jackendoff (1972) and of the framework of Generative Semantics (Lakoff, 1972; McCawley, 1973; Postal, 1970).

It would seem that formal semantics is quite far from the concerns of cognitive science; but formal semantics is often carried out within the broad program that cognitive scientists adopt. Writing from a cognitive standpoint, Johnson-Laird (1983) assesses model-theoretic semantics as follows:

> The power of model-theoretic semantics resides in its explicit and rigorous approach to the composition of meanings. ... Some idealizations definitely complicate the 'ecumenical' use of model-theoretic semantics as a guide to psychological semantics. One such idealization is the mapping of language to model without any reference to the human mind, and this omission gives rise to certain intractable difficulties with the

semantics of sentences about *beliefs* and other such propositional attitudes. These
difficulties are readily resolved within the framework of mental models. (p. 180)

... model-theoretic semantics should specify what is computed in understanding a
sentence, and psychological semantics should specify how it is computed. (p. 167)

Johnson-Laird's own psychological approach is one based on **mental models**. In
contrast to this approach, Jackendoff (1983: Ch. 2), working within cognitive semantics,
argues that the account of 'aboutness' in formal semantics is simplistic:

> ... I will take issue with the naive (and nearly universally accepted) answer that the
> information language conveys is about the real world. (p. 24) ... If indeed the world as
> experienced owes so much to mental processes of organization, it is crucial for a
> psychological theory to distinguish carefully between the source of environmental
> input and the world as experienced. For convenience, I will call the former the *real world*
> and the latter the *projected world* (*experience world* or *phenomenal world* would also be
> appropriate). (p. 28) ... It should now be clear why we must take issue with the naive
> position that the information conveyed by language is about the real world. We have
> conscious access only to the projected world — the world as unconsciously organized
> by the mind; and we can talk about things only insofar as they have achieved mental
> representation through these processes of organization. Hence *the information
> conveyed by language must be about the projected world.* We must explain the naive
> position as a consequence of our being constituted to treat the projected world as reality.
>
> According to this view, the real world plays only an indirect role in language: it serves
> as one kind of fodder for the organizing processes that give rise to the projected world.
> If this is the case, we must question the centrality to natural language semantics of the
> notions of truth and reference as traditionally conceived. Truth is generally regarded as a
> relationship between a certain subset of sentences (the true ones) and the real world;
> reference is regarded as a relationship between expressions in a language and things in
> the real world that these expressions refer to. Having rejected the direct connection of
> the real world to language, we should not take these notions as starting points for a
> theory of meaning. Thus an approach such as that of Davidson (1970), which attempts
> to explicate natural language semantics in terms of Tarskian recursive theory of truth, is
> antithetical to our own inquiry. (pp. 29-30)

The projected world in Jackendoff's account is the result of creative acts of perception:
it is constructed as a model of sensory input, but with the significant addition of
information from the perceptual system itself. Writing from a different orientation within
cognitive semantics (see below), Lakoff (e.g. 1988) is also very critical of what he calls
"objectivist metaphysics" (metaphysical realism). He presents a detailed critique of this
position, also noting the problem that arises if meanings are located in the world:

> To view meaning as residing only in the relationship between symbols and external
> reality is to make the implicit claim that neither color categories, nor any other
> secondary category, should exist as meaningful cognitive categories. Yet color
> categories are real categories of the mind. They are meaningful, they are used in reason,
> and their meaning must be accounted for. But the mechanism of objectivist cognition
> cannot be changed to accommodate them without giving up on the symbolic category of
> meaning. But to do that is to abandon the heart of the objectivist program. (p. 132)

We also have emphasized that reality is not something that is given to us; we have to
construct an interpretation of it — or, as we prefer to put it, we have to **construe** our
experience. Interpretation is a semiotic process, and our interpretation takes into
account not only the concrete natural world but also the socio-cultural realm that is

brought into existence as a semiotic construct (see Hasan, 1984a, for discussion, with reference to Whorf). The constructive power of meaning is perhaps most easily observable in scientific and technical fields where the resources of language are used in metaphorical ways; for example, the technical concept of financial markets is constructed largely by means of the notion of spatial movement (see also Chapter 6, Section 6.7.4 above):

> With exports **falling** to their **lowest** **level** in a year, the trade deficit **widened** sharply relative to the average **shortfall** in the first quarter. The fact that export demand in April **stands** **at** a 16% annual rate **below** the first quarter average underscores the combination of adverse currency effects and **sluggish** activity abroad. Import demand **rose** fractionally, with all of the gain reflecting an **upturn** in the energy area.

But in everyday language also we can see the process of interpretation at work; here too quantity and intensity are constructed metaphorically, by means of spatial resources.

10.3 Cognitive semantics

Cognitive semantics has emerged out of the generative tradition in the last ten to fifteen years. It is a natural development of the general cognitivist research program that began in the 1950s with the birth of cognitive science, Artificial Intelligence, and Chomsky's cognitively oriented linguistics.

10.3.1 Two approaches within cognitive semantics

Those adopting the cognitive approach to semantics share certain assumptions about semantic organization as part of conceptual organization, and tend to reject formal, Montague-style semantics, as indicated by the passages from Jackendoff and Lakoff quoted above. However, they seem to fall into two groupings, which can be conveniently described in terms of the US coastline.

(i) On the East Coast, Jackendoff (e.g., 1983), drawing on his earlier work on interpretive semantics (Jackendoff, 1972), has developed a generativist type of cognitive semantics,[4] which he calls **conceptual semantics**. This is integrated with a number of aspects of modern generative theory, e.g. the X-bar syntactic subtheory. Jackendoff puts

---

[4] Jackendoff calls his approach conceptual semantics and Lakoff calls his cognitive semantics. We use the term cognitive semantics as the generic term for cognitively oriented approaches to semantics.

forward a conceptual ontology and suggestions for conceptual structure that we shall return to in Section 10.3.2 below. This version of cognitive semantics is arguably the more closely associated with the logical and philosophical tradition (cf. Jackendoff, 1988: 81-2).

(ii) On the West Coast, a number of linguists have developed a "cognitive" alternative to generative linguistics. Some of them (e.g., Lakoff, Langacker) come from a generative background (Lakoff's starting point was generative semantics), but have made a radical departure from this tradition. They have widened the scope of study relative to the generativist research agenda so as to include metaphor as a prominent feature (Lakoff & Johnson, 1980, and other subsequent writings, such as Lakoff, 1987, 1988) and a detailed theoretical model of the relationship of language to cognition and perception (Langacker, 1987). A few have also oriented their work towards discourse (notably Chafe, e.g. 1979; 1987; cf. also Tomlin's, 1987a, discussion of the linguistic reflection of cognitive events). This version of cognitive semantics is arguably more closely associated with the rhetorical and ethnographic tradition (perhaps not so much in terms of its roots, but in terms of where it is headed); cognitive anthropology, with its interest in folk taxonomy and more recently in cultural models, provides a meeting point between the two.

Various aspects of the West Coast work in cognitive semantics are relevant to the organization of the ideation base; for example, the work on metaphorical systems already mentioned, Talmy's (e.g. 1985) work on lexicalization, and Chafe's (1970) early work on the organization of meaning. We shall return to a brief discussion of Chafe's typology of 'semantic verbs' in Chapter 12, Section 12.3.2 below.

10.3.2 Jackendoff's conceptual semantics

Jackendoff (1983) presents a major study of semantics and cognition from a generativist point of view. As part of that study, he presents an ontology of conceptual types that are linguistically motivated. While his purpose is theoretical rather than descriptive, and the ontology is not very extensive, it has become a frame of reference for work in this area; it will be useful to characterize this ontology briefly and compare it with the organization of our ideation base.

Jackendoff sees semantic organization as part of conceptual organization — that part which can be verbalized; this is a position that distinguishes him from a number of other generativists. He identifies two possible positions on the relationship between semantic organization and conceptual organization (1983: Section 1.7; interpreted by us in Figure 10-3):

(1) "conceptual structure could be a further level beyond semantic structure, related to it by a rule component, often called *pragmatics,* that specifies the relation of linguistic meaning to discourse and to extralinguistic setting."

(2) "semantic structures could be simply a subset of conceptual structures — just those conceptual structures that happen to be verbally expressible."

(1) Conceptual organization as separate level   (2) Semantic organization as verbalized
                                                                  subpart of conceptual organization

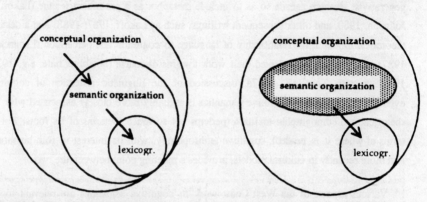

Fig. 10-3: Two possibles relationships between conceptual and semantic organization

Jackendoff and a number of others now prefer the second position. It is also shared by e.g. Langacker (1987), representing cognitive semantics from the other US coastline:

> Meaning is a mental phenomenon that must eventually be described with reference to cognitive processing. I therefore side with Chafe (1970, p. 74-76) by adopting a "conceptual" or "ideational" view of meaning ... I assume it is possible at least in theory (if not yet in practice) to describe in a principled, coherent, and explicit manner the internal structure of such phenomena as thoughts, concepts, perceptions, images and mental experience in general. The term **conceptual structure** will be applied indiscriminately to any such entity, whether linguistic or nonlinguistic. A semantic structure is then defined as a conceptual structure that functions as the semantic pole of a linguistic expression. Hence semantic structures are regarded as conceptualizations shaped for symbolic purposes according to the dictates of linguistic convention. (pp. 97-8)

From our standpoint, this appears as a transcendent interpretation of meaning: we on the other hand prefer an immanent approach to meaning, where "conceptual organization" is interpreted as meaning that is created by various semiotic systems, among which language is the primary one (see Chapter 1, Section 1.1 above). We shall review the implications of this approach below; see also Chapter 14 on construing "the mind". Jackendoff presents evidence suggesting that there are interesting correspondences between the conceptual categories that are expressed linguistically and the categories that have to be posited in an account of vision, derived from studies of perception. This is complementary to recent systemic research investigating semiotic systems other than language, such as visual art and diagrams (Kress & van Leeuwen, 1990, 1996; O'Toole, 1989, 1992, 1994).

Jackendoff takes seriously the relation between conceptual organization and syntactic organization; this might be challenged from a classical formalist point of view, but from a functional point of view it is quite natural (cf. Chapter 1, Section 1.1). In particular, he identifies correspondences between syntactic classes (i.e., categories in generative terms) and conceptual ones. Such correspondence is in fact a major source of evidence for the conceptual ontology. In particular, Jackendoff uses wh-items and non-interrogative reference items to support the ontology; he recognizes things, amounts, places, directions, manners, events and actions. For instance, both things and places have to be recognized because English has both the forms *what did you buy?* and *where is my coat?* The ontology is tabulated in Table 10(1) below together with the grammatical evidence for each type. The left-most column provides a rough translation into our ideation base ontology.

Table 10(1): Jackendoff's (1983) ontology

the ideation base ontology	Jackendoff's ontological category		
element: participant	thing	*what* (did you buy?)	
	amount	*how long* (was the fish?)	*this, that, yay long*
element: circumstance	place	*where* (is my coat?)	*here & there*
	direction	*where* (did they go?)	*thataway*
	manner	*how* (did you cook the eggs?)	*thus, so, this way*
element: process	event	*what happened* (next?)	*that ... happen*
	action	*what* (did you) *do?*	*do it*

Jackendoff contrasts his ontology with that of "standard first-order logic", and makes the important point that the ontological classes of logic are vastly underdifferentiated from a linguistic point of view — that this type of logic is not an adequate theory of the semantic structure of natural language (but cf. Chapter 1, Section 1.9.2 above, where we raised the issue of the status of logic as a system of representation). Compared to this type of logic, Jackendoff's ontology is much more highly differentiated. However, it is not very rich compared to what we believe is needed in an account of the ideation base. The classes recognized are roughly a list of semantic correlates of word classes at primary or secondary delicacy (such as one finds in traditional grammars). The list is not exhaustive, it does not include any significant paradigmatic organization (i.e., it contains no organization showing how types are arranged into a subsumption lattice) and some of the most revealing distinctions of the ideational semantics of English are absent — e.g. the distinction between phenomena and metaphenomena, the recognition of the role played by projection, and the expansion of the system through grammatical metaphor.

These are general observations. Since Jackendoff relies on reference as a source of evidence for the ontological distinctions, he might in fact have taken note of the semantically crucial phenomena of 'extended reference' (the move to 'macro') and reference to fact (the move to 'meta') discussed in Halliday & Hasan (1976) — cf. Chapter 2, Section 2.11.3.2.

Returning to Barwise's contrast between the mind-oriented view of meaning and the world-oriented view discussed in Section 10.1, we can note Barwise's general argument against the mind-oriented view:

> ... representational mental states have meaning in exactly the same way that sentences and texts have meaning, and saying what one means is a complicated matter. This makes attempts to explicate linguistic meaning in terms of mental representations an evasion of the main issue: How do meaningful representations of all kinds, sentences and states, mean what they do? (Barwise, 1988: 38)

We acknowledge this problem, but we believe the solution lies in a socio-semiotic view of meaning such as the one we are presenting here. Jackendoff views information about the projected world in conceptual terms; hence reality construction is seen as a process taking place within the consciousness of the individual. Our own view, that the projected world is a semantic construction, foregrounds the interpersonal perspective: meaning is construed in collaboration. Meanings are **exchanged**; and the "projected world" is constantly calibrated against the interpersonal negotiation of meaning. This means that **consensus** and **conflict** take over much of the domain that is usually conceptualized in terms of truth and falsehood (cf. Eggins, 1990). The semantic system (as part of the linguistic system) is **shared**; it is part of our social being. Thus while our view that the ideational semantic system construes human experience is similar to what Lakoff (1987; 1988) calls the position of "experientialist cognition" (the position he has himself espoused, in contrast with what he calls "objectivist cognition"), it differs in that for us construing experience is an intersubjective process. It is at once both **semiotic** (the construction of meaning) and **social** (as in Peter Berger's "social construction of reality": cf. Berger & Luckmann, 1966, Wuthnow et al, 1984). It is the intersection of these two perspectives that characterizes the **social semiotic** we are attempting to present in this book (cf. Lemke, 1995; Thibault, 1993).

10.3.3 Fawcett's cognitive model of an interactive mind

Within systemic-functional linguistics, Fawcett (e.g. 1980) has pioneered a "cognitive model of an interactive mind". There are many fundamental similarities with the approach we are taking here, e.g. in construing an experiential system of process configuration within the content plane. However, there are two related differences of particular interest in the context of our present discussion:

(i) in Fawcett's model, there is only one system-structure cycle within the content plane: systems are interpreted as the semantics, linked through a "realisation component" to [content] form, which includes items and syntax, the latter being modelled structurally but not systemically;

(ii) in Fawcett's model, the semantics is separate from the "knowledge of the universe", with the latter as a "component" outside the linguistic system including "long term memory" and "short term sort of knowledge".

With respect to (i), in our model there are two system-structure cycles, one in the semantics and one in the lexicogrammar. Terms in semantic systems are realized in semantic structures; and semantic systems and structures are in turn realized in lexicogrammatical ones. As we saw in Chapter 6 in particular, grammatical metaphor is a central reason in our account for treating axis and stratification as independent dimensions, so that we have both semantic systems and structures and lexicogrammatical systems and structures. Since we allow for a stratification of content systems into semantics and lexicogrammar, we are in a stronger position to construe knowledge in terms of meaning. That is, the semantics can become more powerful and extensive if the lexicogrammar includes systems. It follows then with respect to (ii) that for us "knowledge of the universe" is construed as meaning rather than as knowledge. This meaning is in the first instance created in language; but we have noted that meaning is created in other semiotic systems as well, both other social-semiotic systems and other semiotic systems such as perception (cf. Chapter 15 below). Our account gives language more of a central integrative role in the overall system. It is the one semiotic system which is able to construe meanings from semiotic systems in general.

Fawcett's model, although in certain ways closer to mainstream cognitive science than ours, is also a systemic-functional model. In other words it is within the same general theoretical framework as that within which our own work is located.

10.4 Work on meaning in NLP

The work we have discussed so far has its roots in linguistics, philosophy, or anthropology. Some of it has made contact with natural language processing (NLP); for example, Rosner & Johnson (1992) contains contributions on Montague semantics in computational linguistics, and Lamb's work has been computationally oriented from the start. However, there is also a considerable body of linguistic work that is more internal to NLP, and to certain aspects of AI. Arguably most of this work in the area of semantics has been concerned with issues of representation — consider, for example, the collection of articles in Brachman & Levesque's (1985) reader in knowledge representation, and that in the more recent volume edited by Sowa (1991). Schank's work from the 1970s onwards is an exception: he and his associates have been concerned not only with forms of representation (scripts, conceptual dependency) but also with an ontology of primitive acts and states (with emphasis on the former) out of which word senses can be built. We shall discuss this work briefly in Section 10.4.1 below.

In the last decade or so, interest in comprehensive ontologies has grown, and the work on the Penman "upper model" can be seen as an early and continuing move in this direction; cf. also Klose et al's (1992) work on the LILOG project. Other NLP research has usually been lexically oriented and thus complementary to our own work. This includes research on the semantic organization of a dictionary as embodied in its defining vocabulary, e.g. Amsler (1981); the thesaurus-like organization of 'concepts' in the "Concept Dictionary" of the Japan Electronic Dictionary Research Institute (e.g. Technical Report 009, 1988); the WordNet system of Princeton University, developed to reveal lexical semantic relations for an extensive set of lexical items (see Miller & Fellbaum, 1991); the Lexicon Project at MIT, by B. Levin and others (cf. Levin, 1993); research by Okada and associates at Kyushu Institute of Technology (e.g. Nakamura & Okada, 1991); and Hobbs' (e.g. 1984, 1987) Tacitus project, where the aim was to derive a naive world view from careful and detailed study of word senses. One approach with roots in both linguistics and computational linguistics is Dahlgren's (1988) naive semantics, which includes an ontology (see Section 10.4.2 below).

10.4.1 Schank's conceptual dependency

Schank's basic approach was developed in the 1970s (Schank, 1972; Schank & Abelson, 1977) and has been tested and refined since then in numerous systems and accounts (Schank, 1982; Schank & Kass, 1988). The current approach includes (i) an account of macro-organization (scripts and, later also, memory organization packages), and (ii) an account of micro-organization (primitive acts and states entering into conceptual dependency (CD) relations).

Micro-semantic organization is handled by CD, which was the first part of the model to be developed, and is characterized by Schank and Kass (1988: 182) as "a theory about the representation of the meaning of sentences". CD adheres to a number of principles: the representation should be canonical (only one representation for sentences with identical meaning), unambiguous (a given CD structure should have only one meaning), and explicit (grammatically implicit information should be made explicit). Further, CD representation is intended to be "language free" — an early motivation for this was the need for a "language free" representation in machine translation work.

CD is very much a theory built on what we interpret as the extending subtype of expansion (see Chapter 3, Section 3.4 above) — it is a decompositional, syntagmatically oriented theory, and in this respect it is similar to Jackendoff's theory discussed in Chapter 4, Section 4.1. Schank & Kass (1988: 184) use a metaphor of matter:

> The basic propositional molecules of CD are called conceptualizations. A conceptualization can represent either an action or a state. Conceptualizations consist of a main predicate and some number of case-slots. For action conceptualizations the main predicate is one of the primitive actions (called ACTs). For state conceptualizations it is one of the primitive states. Each slot can be filled by either a symbol or another conceptualization. Action conceptualizations have an actor, object, direction and sometimes an instrument case. The instrument is another action, which was performed in order to accomplish the main action. State conceptualizations specify an object and the value (along some arbitrary scale) of some state the object is in.

The distinction between actions and states is familiar; we meet it in many approaches in one form or another. Composition in CD is clearly not rank-based: relationship between different (non-primitive) actions is shown in terms of decomposition rather than systemic agnation. ACTS correspond to our figures, with the exception that their complexity (i.e. their potential for expansion) is interpreted in terms of extensions in composition rather than in terms of elaboration in delicacy. This means that ACTS often consist of other acts, whereas figures only do so only under restricted conditions (e.g. as the Phenomenon of a figure of sensing, for example *the eagle landing* in *Can you see the eagle landing?*). Let us consider an example provided by Schank & Kass (1988: 186); we have indicated ACTS in bold:

English: *Mary gave John her car*

CD: (**ATRANS** (ACTOR (PERSON (NAME MARY)))
        (OBJECT (PHYS-OBJECT (TYPE CAR)))
        (DIRECTION (FROM (PERSON (NAME (MARY))))
              (TO (PERSON (NAME (JOHN))))))

English: *Mary read "Fine Dining in New Haven"*

CD: (**MTRANS** (ACTOR (MARY))
        (OBJECT (INFORMATION)
        (DIRECTION (FROM (BOOK (NAME "Fine Dining ...")))
              (TO (CP (PART-OF (MARY)))))
        (INSTRUMENT
           (**ATTEND**
              (ACTOR (MARY))
              (OBJECT (EYES (PART-OF (MARY))))
              (DIRECTION
                  (TO (BOOK (NAME "Fine Dining ...")))))))))

The first example corresponds to a figure of doing and, since 'giving' is quite general in the typology of acts of transfer, it is represented by the simple ACT **ATRANS** ("the transfer of an abstract relationship such as possession, ownership, or control"). The Recipient role is treated as the 'destination' of DIRECTION. The second example corresponds to a figure of sensing. The top-level ACT is **MTRANS** ("the transfer of information between animals or within an animal"). The roles are the same as for **ATRANS** except that there is also an INSTRUMENT role filled by another conceptualization whose ACT is ATTEND ("the action of attending or focussing a sense organ towards a stimulus"). So the interpretation is roughly 'Mary transfers information mentally from "Fine Dining ..." to part of her by directing her eyes to "Fine Dining ..." '. It is intriguing that this analysis of 'read' treats it as a form of expansion — specifically an enhancing sequence.

ATRANS, MTRANS, and ATTEND are drawn from a set of eleven primitive acts. We list them here grouped according to our primary differentiation among figures; the grouping is based on our interpretation of the definitions and examples given by Schank & Kass (1988: 184-5): see Table 10(2).

Table 10(2): Schank's primitive acts and our types of figure

subdomain of figure in the ideation base	primitive act
doing	ATRANS
	PTRANS
	PROPEL
	MOVE
	GRASP
	INGEST
	EXPEL
sensing (or as behaviour)	MTRANS
	MBUILD
	ATTEND
saying (but also other)	SPEAK
being & having	(primitive states such as JOY, ANGER, HEALTH, ...)*

* It seems that states correspond to figures of being & having of the ascriptive intensive type.

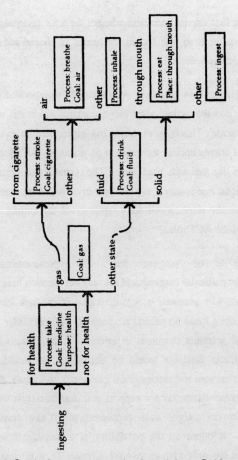

Fig. 10-4: Lexical system network adapted from Goldman (1974)

We see how Schank's Conceptual Dependency can be used to differentiate among non-primitive acts if we consider an example from Goldman's (1974) account of lexical differentiation and choice in his BABEL system. Goldman differentiates among word senses in a discrimination network by using ACTS, and restrictions on the fillers of their roles. Thus, for example, given a conceptual representation 'henry + ingest + beer' (where INGEST is one of the primitive ACTS from the listed quoted above), the lexical network will allow us to select 'drink' for 'ingest', since 'beer' is liquid.

In generation, BABEL is presented with a conceptual structure. As BABEL traverses the discrimination net, it checks this conceptual structure against defining characteristics each time it comes to a node in the net. The outcome is the selection of a word sense. Goldman developed fifteen discrimination nets for BABEL. We have adapted one of them freely and present it here as a system network with value restrictions on roles; it covers some processes of ingesting: see Figure 10-4 above. (We have maintained the binary splits of Goldman's discrimination network and also its arrangement as a strict taxonomy.) The discriminations are based on the reason for ingesting and the nature of what is ingested. The first inquiry ascertains whether the actor undertakes the ingesting to improve his or her health; if so, the feature 'for health' is chosen and the lexical item is *take* (as in *take cough medicine*).

The example illustrates how primitive ACTS can be incorporated into a typology of (non-primitive) acts; and shows that, when they are interpreted in this way, the 'primitive' seems to mean 'indelicate'. This is an **elaborating** rather than an **extending** notion of primitiveness; but it leaves unclear the relation of primitive ACTS to other ACTS in conceptual structures like that with 'read' above. The systemic interpretation given in 10-4 raises various questions. For instance, can the 'primitive' ACTS be organized systemically themselves? What are the implications for a typology of the entities (objects, etc.) that can serve as fillers of the ACT roles?

CD is intended to be "language free". CD representations cannot support grammaticalization in particular languages in the way our ideation base does. Thus (i) CD theory cannot explain why grammar is organized as it is (perhaps less of concern in AI than in linguistics), since it has no natural relationship with particular grammars; and (ii) it cannot show how grammar construes experience — the contribution made by the grammar of a particular language would be neutralized, as would, presumably, the difference between congruent and metaphorical construals. All other things being equal, the fact that CD representations do not support grammaticalization would seem to be a serious drawback. One could argue, as the proponents of CD have done, that this is in fact part of its virtue — it opens up the possibility of a language neutral representation. However, that is not the only path to take (cf. Chapter 7): it is possible to construct a multilingual ideation base that is an assemblage of perspectives from different languages (Bateman, Matthiessen & Zeng, forthc.; Zeng, 1996).

CD was the first part to be developed of a more extensive account. While the domain of CD was the sentence, Schank & Abelson (1977) proposed a form of organization that we can recognize as being based on context of situation — their **script**, "essentially a pre-packaged inference chain relating to a specific routine situation" (Schank & Kass, 1988: 190). The script that has become most famous is the restaurant script — roughly a sequence of conceptualizations. Scripts can be used to support processes in text generation and understanding. In systemic theory and in Firthian system-structure theory, there has been comparable work on the organization of situation types into stages: first the pioneering work by Mitchell (1957), and later the work by Hasan (1978; 1984b), followed up in various studies, and applied to text generation by Cross (1991). One difference is that in the systemic work situation types were always seen as part of a family or typology of contexts of situation, variable according to field, tenor and mode (see Martin, 1992). Schank (1982) introduced a new concept, that of Memory Organization Packages (MOPs) as successor to the earlier scripts; these are linked to one another in an abstraction hierarchy, and they are also organized into 'scenes' such that one scene may be shared across several MOPs. This strongly suggests a rank-like organization projected onto the ideation base, in the form of an ascending sequence of acts/ conceptualizations, scenes, MOPs and sequences of MOPs. A script might be interpreted as a conventionalized sequence projected onto the ideation base from a particular context of situation.

10.4.2 Dahlgren's naive semantics

Dahlgren (1988) and colleagues have developed a valuable, fairly extensive account of semantic organization comparable to our ideation base, one of whose purposes is to support text processing in a computational system. Dahlgren calls the approach **naive semantics**, because it is intended to model "the detailed naive theory associated with words" (p. 28) — that is, in contrast to our approach through the clause, based on cryptogrammar, the move into the system in naive semantics is through words. (Since it is concerned with word senses, its task is obviously not to support the grammaticalization of ideation base information; rather it is to be used for inference based on word senses in text understanding.) It is proposed as an alternative to theories based on primitives of meaning, and draws on prototype theory instead. It is intended to reflect both linguistic and psychological evidence.

Concepts are organized into an ontological hierarchy — called ontological rather than taxonomic because naive semantics is a realist theory. Each node in the hierarchy may have generic knowledge associated with it (p. 33). This knowledge is organized according to types of feature such as age, colour, sex, location, has part; for noun concepts there are 54 such features in all, distinguished into "typical features" and "inherent features" (p. 59). So, for instance, *office,* in the sense of a work place, is characterized as follows (p. 60):

```
{PLACE
        <typical:> {haspart (*, chairs),
        haspart (*, desks),
        haspart (*, typewriters),
        location (downtown)},

        <inherent:> {haspart (*, doors),
        haspart (*, windows),
        location (building)}}
```

That is, to use an identifying clause: an office is a place (typically) with chairs, desks, and typewriters located in downtown and (inherently) with doors and windows in a building. It is construed as a participant with extending ('with') and enhancing ('in') roles: the features are comparable to the roles we have used in characterizing types in the ideation base. However, the roles we posit are grammatically motivated — they are construed in the grammar as those 'features' associated with participants, figures, and so on. Dahlgren identifies a rich but quite restricted set of features — 54 for nouns (as already noted; p. 74) and another, smaller, set for relational types (location, time, cause, enablement, p. 99). The former fall within the domain of participant and, as we would predict, we find e.g. features corresponding to different kinds of Epithet — colour, size, age, etc.. The latter fall within the domain of figures and, as we would predict, we find features concerned with enhancing (circumstantial) roles — location, time, cause, enablement, consequence, sequel, manner, and purpose. This is a useful confirmation of the value of approaching the semantics of verbs from figures, construed in the grammar as clauses as we have done.[5]

Now, even if the set of features is not arbitrarily large, the possible number of combinations of sets of features associated with nodes in the ontology is, of course, very extensive. Dahlgren demonstrates that the combinations are constrained through kind types (for nouns) and relational types (for verbs). She characterizes these "correlational constraints" as "commonsense reflections of the actual world" (p. 69): "kind types are types of kind terms with predictable feature types in their descriptions". For instance, the type ENTITY from the noun ontology has the feature types 'haspart' and 'partof' associated with it, and the more delicate type PHYSICAL adds 'color', 'size', and 'texture'. From the point of view of our ideation base, these then are types with associated realization statements; and one central reason for recognizing them as types in the system network is precisely the 'features' they have associated with them. More delicate types simply inherit the 'features' from less delicate types.

The typology of entities proposed is set out in Figure 10-5 (based on Dahlgren, 1988: Chapters 2 and 4). The nominal kind types in this ontology are the following (p. 74): entity, sentient, living, animal, physical, social, role, person, propositional, artefact, and institution.

The relational subontology reflects Vendler's (1967) typology, which we shall present and comment on in Chapter 12, Section 12.2; it adds the distinctions 'mental/ emotional/ nonmental' and (for events) 'goal/ nongoal'. The evidence for these is partly psychological; but there is not enough detailed discussion of the individual types, or linguistic evidence for the distinctions, to enable us to compare the overall typology with our own.

---

[5] It would be helpful to be able to review the full set of features used in Naive Semantics and interpret them systematically in terms of our ideation base. But most of the features are only listed, and it is difficult to read off their meaning with enough certainty to support the interpretation.

10.5 Stratal perspectives on meaning

To conclude this brief survey of alternative approaches to meaning, let us raise the question of how the system of meaning, the semantic system, relates to other systems within and outside language. Given our stratal interpretation of the semantic system as an interlevel, we can characterize the perspectives on meaning that may be taken by a semantic theory along the following lines:

(i) **intra-stratal (internal organization of semantics):** a theory of meaning may focus on the organization of meaning itself using some framework for describing sense relations — e.g. the paradigmatic organization of the meaning potential, as in our present work; the dimensions of semantic agnation, as in (classical) componential analysis; the syntagmatic decomposition of senses, as in Katz & Fodor's theory, in interpretive semantics and in generative semantics.

(ii) **inter-stratal:** a theory may focus on the stratal interfaces of the semantic stratum — how meaning relates upwards to context (according to our approach) and how it relates downwards to lexicogrammar:

(ii.1) **inter-stratal: upwards (semantics in relation to context):** the question of how meaning relates upwards to context is foregrounded in rhetorical-ethnographic approaches rather than in logical-philosophical ones. We discussed the contextual perspective on meaning in Chapters 8 and 9 (see e.g. Figure 8-1), focussing on the relationship between differences in contextual settings of field, tenor and mode, and on registerial variation in meaning.

(ii.2) **inter-stratal: downwards (semantics in relation to lexicogrammar):** the interface between semantics and lexicogrammar is internal to language and has received far more attention in studies of meaning from all standpoints than has the interface between semantics and context. In the logical-philosophical approach, within generative linguistics, interpretive semantics has focussed on the question of how semantic representations can be derived from below, from syntactic ones; and an important aspect of the debate in the late 60s and early 70s was precisely concerned with the directionality of inter-stratal mappings and the nature of the inter-stratal boundary. One key question that emerged, particularly in the 1970s and early 1980s, was whether syntax is autonomous or not. In the standard Chomskyan theory it was; but this was rejected by Montague and those who were influenced by his idea of building syntactic and semantic specifications "in tandem" (as in the successive developments of GPSG and HPSG). Within the rhetorical-ethnographic approach, we have taken the position that not only is lexicogrammar not autonomous, but it is natural in relation to semantics: our approach to the ideation base rests on this theoretical assumption (cf. Chapter 1, Section 1.2 above). This is what explains the further possibility of grammatical metaphor, opened up at the interface between semantics and lexicogrammar.

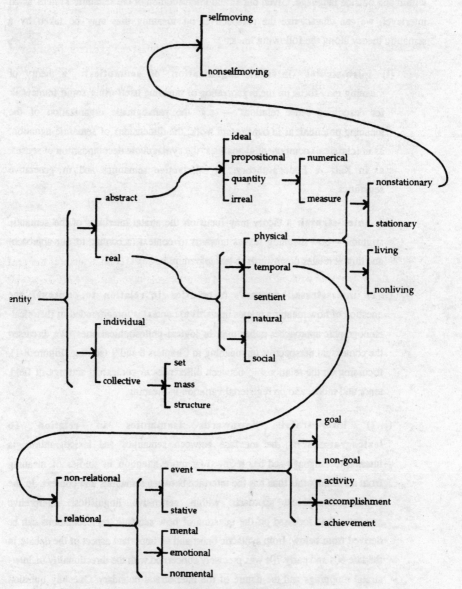

Fig. 10-5: Dahlgren's typology of entities

(iii) **extra-stratal (relation between language and non-semiotic systems):** the theory may focus on how language in general and semantics in particular relate to systems of other kinds, i.e. to non-semiotic systems. We have already discussed the way in which this focus has been built into transcendent approaches to meaning, where meaning is 'exported' into the realms of the material world or the mind.

The stratal perspectives on meaning are represented in Figure 10-6. We are not suggesting that a given theory deals only with one of the three areas of stratal concern. Interpretive semantics is clearly concerned both with the mapping between syntax and semantics and with the internal organization of meaning in terms of decomposition (as in Jackendoff, 1972). Looked at from the standpoint of a stratal interpretation of language, these different approaches are not so much mutually exclusive alternatives — as they have often been thought to be — as complementary perspectives on meaning: they focus on different aspects of the stratum of semantics — its internal organization or its interfaces to other systems, linguistic, conceptual or physical. This is not to say, of course, that they could all be put together into one internally consistent theory of meaning! For example, it is hard to reconcile a model-theoretic approach with an experientialist cognitive one or with our own immanent approach. However, this does not mean that, from our standpoint, it does not make sense to model the steps that relate semiotic systems to material ones. It does; but the relationship has to be modelled in such a way that we can show how people as biological organisms and socio-semiotic persons interact with their material environment. We leave these issues here; but we shall return to them in the final part of this book. After problematizing the construction of "the mind" in Chapter 14, we shall discuss how the semantic system relates to other systems in Chapter 15, Section 15.1.

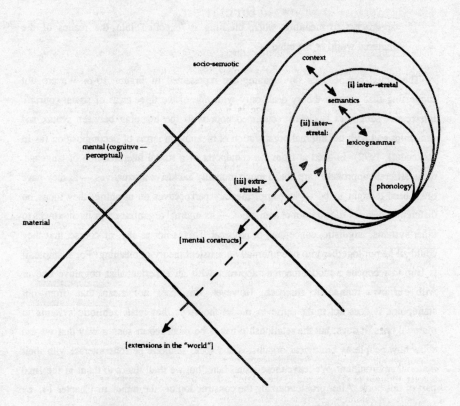

Fig. 10-6: Approaches to different aspects of semantics

11. Distortion and transformation

In the preceding chapter, we compared alternative interpretations of the semantic system in terms of how it is located relative to a global model of language (and of whatever is conceived of as its environment). But if the task is to build a knowledge base, then the question arises to what extent language is involved at all. The interpretation of the ideational semantics of English could obviously be different from what we have proposed here. Leaving aside approaches to meaning that do not proceed from linguistic interpretation (cf. Chapter 10, Section 10.1 above), there are others that contrast with ours but are still grounded in language, with reference points either in linguistics or in philosophy. Others again fall somewhere in between a linguistically motivated model and a model supported on other grounds: for example, theories of deep cases in case grammar (e.g. instruments and beneficiaries) and theories with semantic terms derived from predicate logic. The latter can lead to the argument that, since predicate logic is being used to represent the semantic structure of English, this structure must be like that of predicate logic; that is, they can lead to arguing not from the object language but from the metalanguage. We shall begin by examining briefly the possible frames of reference that have been adopted in work on ontologies and on ontological categories (Section 11.1). We then turn to the notion that language cannot be trusted as a frame of reference because it 'distorts' thought or reality, and to the related notion that syntax cannot be trusted because it 'distorts' semantics (Section 11.2). Finally, we discuss the typological status of qualities, as an illustrative example of the tendency to interpret one class of phenomenon on the model of another (Section 11.3).

11.1 Frames of reference

In Figure 10-6 above we summarized different perspectives on meaning — intra-stratal, inter-stratal and extra-stratal ones. If we set ourselves the task of creating an ontology for a "knowledge base", each of these perspectives might serve as a frame of reference. (There are others as well, to be mentioned below.)

From our standpoint, the choice of frames of reference follows from our conception of the "knowledge base" as a "meaning base" (see Chapter 1, Section 1.1 above), where our conception of meaning is immanent (see Chapter 10, Section 10.1 above). Throughout our discussion of the organization of the meaning base, we have made reference both to intra-stratal considerations (such as patterns of agnation and the transphenomenal types that emerged in the course of our exploration) and to inter-stratal considerations. With respect to the latter, we have foregrounded considerations 'from below', from the stratum of lexicogrammar (see Chapter 1, Section 1.2 and Chapter 2, Section 2.2). There were two main reasons for this: on the one hand, the meaning base has to be realized in worded texts and the statements of realization will be simpler if the resources of wording are part of the picture from the start; on the other hand, the relationship between meaning and wording, between the system of semantics and that of lexicogrammar, is a natural one:

they are both strata of the content. Although it has not been part of the central argument about particular distinctions in the meaning base, we have also referred to the relationship between semantics and context (Chapter 8, Section 8.1 and Chapter 9, Section 9.1). Just as the meaning base has to be accountable lexicogrammatically, it also has to be accountable contextually. In our discussion, we emphasized register or functional variation as one of the keys to the relationship between semantics and context.

If a different standpoint is adopted, the frame of reference may be an extra-semantic one: either because the approach to meaning is transcendent rather than immanent or because the object of modelling is taken to be knowledge rather than meaning. Work on participant roles and circumstance roles in figures, cast in terms of "case relations" or "deep cases", provides a good example of contrasting frames of reference. Starosta (1988: 115-7) contrasts two approaches to such roles:

> Case relations (CRs) are syntactic-semantic relations obtaining between (non-predicate) nouns and their regents, which can be verbs, prepositions, or other nouns. CRs include the kind of intuitive categories characterized in traditional and modern generative grammar by terms such as 'Agent', 'Patient', etc. Their function is mediating between overt grammatical configurations (word order, case inflections, etc.) and semantic role concepts and scope phenomena, and facilitating discourse cohesion in languages such as Dyirbal.

> Case grammar in the Fillmorean tradition is based on a not necessarily linguistic intuition about actions or processes or states, participants in those actions, processes, and states, and the roles played by the obligatory or optionally present participants in these actions, processes and states. These roles are the 'case relations' or 'deep cases' in classical case grammars and many computational applications, and the 'thematic relations' in the Chomskyan tradition, which is based on Gruber's work (Gruber, 1965). In practice, such roles are established without any necessary connection with language at all: one simply envisions a kind of silent movie of an action, for example a person loading hay onto a wagon with a pitchfork, identifies the elements necessary for such an action to take place (someone to do the loading, something to be loaded, someplace to load onto or into, and something to load with) and assigns a 'case relation' (or 'thematic relation') to each one. Then the case relations in any sentence referring to that situation must correspond to the previously established silent movie roles. Because this determination is independent of the particular way in which the action is described linguistically, case relations in this approach are constant across sentences and across languages.

> The situation-oriented procedure is reflected in the use of paraphrase to identify case relations in both the Fillmorean case grammar and the Gruberian thematic relations traditions: two sentences are paraphrases if they have the same truth values, which is a more precise way of saying that they characterize the same external situations. ... In effect, what this practice amounts to is constructing a typology of situations, which is independent of language, so that case relations are necessarily universal: ...

As Starosta describes them, the considerations brought to bear on "case relations" are thus derived from an extra-semantic perspective. In contrast, Starosta's own approach is language-based (op cit., p. 119):

> The lexicase approach to case relations differs from the usual Fillmorean case relations and Chomskyan thematic relation analyses in that its definitions are stated not in terms of external situations directly, but rather in terms of sentence-specific PERSPECTIVES of those situations ... Thus if two different sentences refer to the same situation but portray if from different viewpoints, they may contain quite different arrays of case relations. ... the redefinition of case roles in terms of perspective rather than situation

results in a dramatic increase in the language-specific and cross-typological explanatory power of the theory, as reflected in the large number of generalizations that can be stated assuming this sort of definition but not assuming a Fillmorean situational one.

Our own approach is also language-based: participant roles and circumstance roles in the figures are based on intra-semantic considerations (e.g. the transphenomenal types of projection and expansion) and on inter-stratal considerations from below, from lexicogrammar. The original systemic work on transitivity roles in the clause (Halliday, 1967/8), which appeared at about the same time as Fillmore's (1968) *Case for Case,* had the language-based frame of reference advocated by Starosta.[1] For further discussion of the issues involved from a systemic point of view, see Martin (1996 a, b). We will compare and contrast certain proposals in this area in Chapter 12 below.

Similar considerations to those just exemplified with respect to "case relations" apply to all areas of the organization of a "knowledge base". In a discussion of a particular ontology for a knowledge base (*Wissensbasis*), the LILOG ontology, Lang (1992, in Klose et al, 1992) differentiates between ontological types that have a conceptual base and ontological types that have a linguistic base:

Wenn eine Sorte nicht bloß ein etikettierter Knoten in der Verbansstruktur sein soll, sondern legitimiertes Element einer Wissensbasis, die (i) außersprachliches Alltagswissen repräsentiert und zwar so, daß sie (ii) über (deutsche) Texte zugreifbar ist und (deutsche) Texte aus ihr generierbar sein sollen, dann stellt sich die keineswegs nur sophistische Frage (F):

(F) Ist die gegebene Sorte X

(a) eine konzeptuelle (d.h. sprachunabhängige) Kategorie, deren Bezug zu sprachlichen Einheiten zwar regulär, aber prinzipiell arbiträr ist und auch einzelsprachlich variiert,

oder

(b) verdankt die Sorte X ihre Aufnahme in die Ontologie dem Vorhandensein unter häufigen Okkurenz eines gleichnamigen Ausdrucks in den (deutschen) Texten, d.h. in der Textbasis, die der Ontologie-Konstruktion als Ausgangsmaterial zugrunde liegt?

As examples of conceptually based types he cites 'Entität', 'Zustand', 'Ereignis', and 'Situation'.

From our standpoint, types motivated in terms of Lang's category (b) clearly belong to the ideation base; and they are motivated intra-stratally and inter-stratally. Types motivated in terms of category (a) would (by definition) be extra-semantic. Consequently they would fall outside the ideation base. However, if we reconstrue knowledge as meaning, it follows that we cannot simply refer such types to an extra-semantic conceptual system (as could be done in a cognitive approach to semantics; cf. Chapter 10, Section 10.3 above): we would have to explore the possibility that these types are construed as meaning by some semiotic system other than language. We shall return to the relationship between language and other semiotic systems in Chapter 15, Section 15.1. Here let us just reiterate our view that all of experience is construed as meaning. Language is the primary semiotic system for transforming experience into meaning; and it is the only semiotic system whose meaning base can serve to transform meanings construed in other systems (including perceptual ones) and thus integrate our experience from all its various sources (cf. Sugeno's 1993 application of the notion of data fusion).

It might be objected that this view leaves no room for scientific or metaphysical models — for example, that we do not allow for the possibility that science has advanced our understanding of the world. This objection would be misplaced: such models are construed in the ideation base as domain models within the overall meaning potential (cf. Chapter 8, Section 8.1). We shall return to the question of different models in Chapter 14.

11.2 The motif of distortion

Attempts to create an ontology without reference to language in general, or without reference to lexicogrammar in particular, seem to derive from the belief, familiar in the history of Western thinking, that language comes between us and a 'real' or scientific understanding of the world, that it somehow somehow distorts our awareness of reality. There are two somewhat distinct versions of this belief. The first is the notion that language distorts reality — or, as a variant of this, that language distorts our thinking (which includes our thinking about reality). This is **extra-linguistic** deception: language is deceiving us by the way it represents something else. The second is the notion that syntax distorts semantics. This is **intra-linguistic** deception: language is deceiving us by the way one part of it represents another part. We will say a little about each of these in turn.

11.2.1 The notion that language distorts (our thinking about) reality

The view that language distorts the picture of reality, and that there is a mismatch between language and thought, is reflected the opposition of "deep" and "surface" as these figured in a prominent approach to text generation. In this model, "deep generation" is concerned with thinking what to say (the thoughts "behind" the words) and "surface generation" with how to say it (see e.g. McKeown & Swartout, 1987). This view was discussed many years ago by Whorf, in terms which are still relevant today; Whorf refers to it as the "natural logic" view:

> According to natural logic, the fact that every person has talked fluently since infancy makes every man his own authority on the process by which he formulates and communicates. He has merely to consult a common substratum of logic or reason which he and everyone else are supposed to possess. Natural logic says that talking is merely an incidental process concerned with communication, not with formulation of ideas. Talking, or the use of language, is supposed only to "express" what is essentially already formulated nonlinguistically. Formulation is an independent process, called thought or thinking, and is supposed to be largely indifferent to the nature of particular languages. Languages have grammars, which are assumed to be merely norms of conventional and social correctness, but the use of language is supposed to be guided not so much by them as by correct, rational, or intelligent THINKING.

> Thought, in this view, does not depend on grammar but on laws of logic or reason which are supposed to be the same for all observers of the universe — to represent a rationale in the universe that can be "found" independently by all intelligent observers, whether they speak Chinese or Choctaw. In our own culture, the formulations of mathematics and of formal logic have acquired the reputation of dealing with this order of things: i.e., with the realm and laws of pure thought. Natural logic holds that different languages are essentially parallel methods for expressing this one-and-the-same rationale of thought and, hence, differ really in but minor ways which may seem important only because they are seen at close range. It holds that mathematics, symbolic logic, philosophy, and so on are systems contrasted with language which deal directly with this realm of thought, not that they are themselves specialized extensions of language. (Whorf, 1956: 207-8)

After characterising the position of 'natural logic' in this way, Whorf (op cit.: 211) goes on to identify two problems with it:

> Natural logic contains two fallacies: First, it does not see that the phenomena of a language are to its own speakers largely of a background character and so are outside the critical consciousness and control of the speaker who is expounding natural logic. Hence, when anyone, as a natural logician, is talking about reason, logic, and the laws of correct thinking, he is apt to be simply marching in step with purely grammatical facts that have somewhat of a background character in his own language or family of languages but are by no means universal in all languages and in no sense a common substratum of reason.

> Second, natural logic confuses agreement about subject matter, attained through use of language, with knowledge of the linguistic processes by which agreement is attained: i.e., with the province of the despised (and to its notion superfluous) grammarian.

This belief in the distorting effect of language was propounded by the early European humanists, who held that medieval scholars had focussed too strongly on language, whereas the real task of the scientist was to see through the verbal disguise and penetrate to the reality underneath (for example, Francis Bacon's well-known warnings against the seductive power of natural language). Natural languages were considered to be inadequate vehicles for the new scientific knowledge; hence it was necessary to construct artificial languages to record, transmit and extend it. These artificial languages would, it was thought, be more in harmony with the objective world of experience.

This same attitude continues to prevail in the ways people talk about language in our own time. It dominated much of the early work on machine translation in the 1950s and

1960s; the task of the analysis was seen to be that of stripping the underlying ideas of their linguistic disguise (Firth, 1956, referred scathingly to current formulations according to which language was a "clothing" for "naked ideas"). When the "interlingua" model was proposed, many of those working in the field regarded it not as a construction of meaning that would be a compromise among different linguistic systems but as a language-free representation of concepts and conceptual structures (cf. Schank's conceptual dependency in Chapter 10, Section 10.4.1 above), very much in the 17th century tradition.

The same view of language as distortion is frequently to be met with when language is contained within a model of communication, where a common motif is that language is a vehicle for lying, or at least for concealing the truth. One might surmise that, if language is defined in communicational terms, as a means of transmitting information — especially if this is combined with a semantics based on considerations of truth — then this is how it is likely to appear.

11.2.2 The notion that lexicogrammar [syntax] distorts semantics

The view that syntax distorts semantics implies that the relation of grammar to meaning is indirect and arbitrary. This view became tenable in modern linguistics, where meaning was either excluded from its scope altogether, as among structuralist linguists in the U.S., or, with Chomsky, kept at a distance by the metaphor of deep and surface structure in the syntax, only the former being semantically responsible. This paved the way for a number of analyses on the model of 'surface x is really deep y'. We find suggestions such as the following: adjectives are really verbs (e.g. Chafe, 1970), nouns are really verbs (cf. Bach, 1968), pronouns are really articles (Postal, 1966), negation is really a [higher] verb, tense is really a [higher] verb (cf. Huddleston, 1969), auxiliaries are really full verbs, verbal group complexes are really reductions of embedded clauses, moods are really separate clauses of saying, and so on.

For example, Bach (1968) argued that the distinction between nouns, verbs and adjectives is a superficial one and that nouns are really something else:

> Grammars of English traditionally maintain a sharp division between nouns, verbs, and adjectives. It is my purpose here to demonstrate that the differences between these 'parts of speech' exist only on a relatively superficial level and that the fundamental dichotomy underlying the distinctions is of quite a different sort. By saying 'sentences' rather than 'English sentences', I intend to suggest that the deep structures of sentences in different languages are identical; that is, I am subscribing to the idea of a universal set of base rules. (p. 91)

> To summarize, I have argued on the basis of many pieces of evidence that it is reasonable to suppose that all nouns come from relative clauses based on the predicate nominal constituent. ... I have tried to show that the distinctions between such parts of speech as nouns, adjectives, and verbs have no direct representation as such in the base, but are results of transformational developments in one or another language. ... The base component here looks in some ways very much like the logical systems familiar from the work of modern logicians like Rudolf Carnap, Hans Reichenbach, and others. In particular such systems do not have any subdivision of 'lexical items' into nouns,

verbs, and adjectives. Much more basic is the distinction between variables, names, and general 'predicates' ... It should not be surprising that a system of universal base rules should turn out to be very close to such systems, which are after all the result of analyzing the most basic conceptual relationships that exist in natural languages. Such a system expresses directly the idea that it is possible to convey any conceptual content in any language, even though the particular lexical items available will vary widely from one language to another — a direct denial of the Humboldt-Sapir-Whorf hypothesis in its strongest form. (pp. 121-2)

Such analyses were often supported by universalist arguments such as "negation is a verb in certain languages, so it is reasonable to claim that it is really a verb in all". As the quote from Bach illustrates, they tended to make deep structure, the 'real' structure, look like predicate logic. Surface structure came out looking like a (transformationally) twisted version of logical structures. But predicate logic had been derived from one particular area of the grammar, a simplified version of the experiential aspect of the clause; it could be used as an idealized model of certain types of figure, for the purpose of explicit rule-based reasoning, but it was not intended to be a tool for analysing the entire semantic structure of a natural language.[2] This view has largely been abandoned and the notion of a semantically irresponsible surface structure is no longer generally held.

In rejecting both these views of language as distortion, we are not propounding an alternative version according to which language is a perfect match. What is wrong with all such conceptions is that they misconstrue the nature of a semiotic system — the fundamental relation of **realization** to which we are always having to return. A semiotic system is not some kind of outer garment which may either reveal or conceal what is beneath. Rather, it is a transformation of experience into meanings, and each stratum within the system is construed by, and construes, all the rest. A "language", in this sense, may be artificially constructed or engineered, like a scientific theory or a logic; but all such semiotics are ultimately related to natural language, and natural language is still an accomplice in their overall construction of reality.

But whether or not it is engineered in this way, natural language will continue to evolve. The artificial languages of the 17th century were never actually used; but this did not mean that the forms of natural language persisted without change. On the contrary,

---

[2] In terms of our model of a stratified metalanguage (see Chapter 1, Section 1.9.1 above), we can see that taking the categories of predicate logic (or any other logical systems) to be linguistic ones constitutes a stratal slippage: categories from the level of representation in the metalanguage are imported into the theoretical account of the object language.

new registers were always evolving, some of them as part of the ongoing reconstruction of experience in the form of systematic knowledge and experimental science.

11.3 The status of qualities: an illustration

We shall not attempt to document the views referred to above in any greater detail. But it seems important to take them into account as part of the overall picture; not just because such views, in their turn, distort the nature of language, but also because they can obstruct progress in particular language-based activities — for example, the practice of "intelligent computing", which is computing carried out entirely in natural language (Sugeno, 1993). In the remainder of this chapter, we will illustrate these notions by considering just one of the types of element that make up a figure, namely qualities, and showing how the way in which these are described can be influenced by such thinking. This will refer mainly to the idea of intra-linguistic distortion — a mismatch between syntax and semantics; but one can often recognize an implication that behind this lies a distortion of reality. In Chapter 12, when we come to look at a number of different descriptions that stand as alternatives to our own, we will also find certain traces of this general perspective on language.

The problem of classifying qualities is often approached grammatically as a question of word classification: are adjectives funny verbs, funny nouns, or a completely distinct word class? All three questions have been asked, and all three answered in the affirmative. The questions themselves reflect one of the biases of traditional grammar: it is based on words. Our approach to these questions is a functional one, which does not start with word classes taken out of context; so here we will begin our enquiry with the clause. Semantically, the relevant question is how a figure is organized in English. This allows us to look at qualities 'from above', keeping their semantic environment in view.

11.3.1 Some significant transitivity types

There are two transitivity types that will be significant for arguments concerning the location of qualities in relation to other semantic classes: (1) middle material clauses, and (2) middle relational clauses. These types were described in Chapters 2 and 4; they are distinguished in terms of both process type and agency. Some culinary examples are:

```
middle material (happening):

Add the mushrooms, washed and chopped, and cook until all the
liquid from the mushrooms [Medium/Actor] has evaporated [Process]
```

middle relational (ascriptive):

Use a little stock or apple juice, *if the stuffing*
[Medium/Carrier] *is* [Process] *too firm* [Range/Attribute].

This [Medium/Carrier] *makes* [Process] *a good stuffing for a whole
cabbage* [Range/Attribute].

They [Medium/Carrier] *will become* [Process] *discoloured*
[Range/Attribute],

but the flavour [Medium/Carrier] *is* [Process] *very good*
[Range/Attribute].

These two types realize figures of (i) doing & happening and (ii) being & having
respectively. Let us review their structures and discuss their distinct discourse
contributions.

(1) The **material clause** above represents a happening in which the Medium (all the
liquid from the mushrooms) participates; the happening is a change from liquid to gaseous
state. The clause indicates that the cooking should continue as long as the liquid keeps
evaporating. We can represent the semantic structure that is construed in this way by
Figure 11-1.

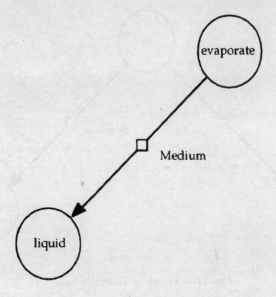

Fig. 11-1: Figure of happening

In recipes, material clauses form the backbone of the procedure. This is something these texts have in common with narratives: here is a traditional tale that is moved forward by material clauses alone.

```
Jack and Jill went up the hill to fetch a pail of water. Jack fell
down and broke his crown, and Jill came tumbling after. Up Jack
got and home he trot as fast as he could caper; went to bed to
mend his head with vinegar and brown paper.
```

Material processes lend themselves naturally to sequential ordering in time; this is much less a feature of other process types.

(2) The **relational clauses** above represent descriptions in which the Medium is related to a quality or a class. More generally, the Medium is related as a member of a set, which is defined either by a quality or by a class. The relation is a composite of the participants (the Carrier and the Attribute) and the nuclear relation. The nuclear relation is not necessarily a state; it can be either a being ('be' and 'make' in the examples above) or a becoming ('become' above), both of which are located in time, as are processes in general. But its participants are static things; the Carrier is an individual or class, and the Attribute is a lasting quality or a wider class. The Attribute of the relation of becoming applies to the Carrier in the final state of the becoming; it is a resultative Attribute. We can represent the semantic structure of the last relational clause as in Figure 11-2.

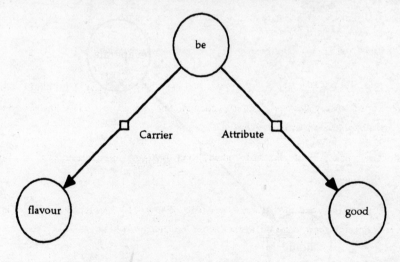

Fig. 11-2: Figure of ascriptive being

Descriptions and characterizations draw heavily on the grammatical resources of transitivity to represent relational processes. Consider for example the following entry for "duck" in The New International Encyclopaedia:

DUCK. (...) The ducks <u>are</u> a large and well-defined group of birds of the order Anseres and the family Anatidae. They <u>are</u> <u>distinguished</u> from the swans and geese by <u>having</u> the tarsi scutellate in front, and the sexes <u>are</u> unlike in color; and they <u>are separated</u> from the mergansers by the shape of the bill, which <u>is</u> broad and flattened .

The term "duck" <u>is</u> generally restricted to <u>designate</u> the female, while "drake" <u>is</u> the term applied to the male.

The ducks <u>are</u> largely animal feeders (insects, snails, frogs, fish, etc.), although some species <u>are</u> noted for their fondness for wild celery and other vegetables.

The legs <u>are</u> short and placed far back, so that ducks **move** with difficulty on land, and with the characteristic gait <u>known as</u> a waddle, but they <u>are</u> splendid swimmers, and <u>are</u> noted for their powers of **diving and swimming** under water.

The neck <u>is</u> short as compared with geese or swans. There <u>is</u> a peculiar anatomical feature of the windpipe, <u>consisting</u> of a large dilatation of the trachea on each side at its bifurcation.

The tongue <u>is</u> large and fleshy and very sensitive.

The plumage <u>is</u> remarkably thick, soft, and compact.

The wings <u>are</u> stiff, strong, and pointed, <u>giving</u> the power of rapid and vigorous flight, though the speed of wild ducks has probably been exaggerated.

The tail <u>is</u> of variable shape and <u>made up</u> of usually 14 or 16 feathers.

The oil gland <u>is</u> always present and well developed, with two openings, and <u>crowned</u> with a tuft of feathers.

The ducks **have been** easily **tamed**, and many breeds <u>are</u> known which will be considered later by themselves. (...)

Here the ducks are ascribed to classes (group of a particular order, animal feeders, swimmers, etc.); distinguishing subparts are specified, and the various parts of a duck (legs, plumage, etc.) are characterized in terms of their qualitative attributes. Note that the text is itself organized as a series of elaborating relations (constituency, attribution, etc.).

The functional differentiation between material clauses and relational ones becomes very clear when we look at texts that draw on both: they make different kinds of contribution to the creation of the text. For example, in a procedural text such as a recipe, material clauses serve to express the steps in the procedure to be followed. In contrast, relational clauses occur at a different stage in the text, the stage concerned with the use of the dish that is the outcome of this procedure (cf. Chapter 9, Section 9.2.1 above):

SWEET CORN STUFFING.

[Ingredients: ...]

[Procedure :] **Melt** the butter and cook the onion in it without browning. **Strip** the cobs and add the sweet corn to the onion. **Cook** for a further 2-3 minutes. **Remove** from the heat and add the remainder of the ingredients.

[Use:] This makes a good stuffing for tomatoes.

Other examples of 'Use':

These are lovely when fresh but after a day or two they should be warmed through before being eaten. They are very pleasant served with soup or salad.

Young beetroots are very good on their own.

This dish is very attractive in appearance.

11.3.2 Three different transitivity interpretations

The previous discussion shows the importance of recognizing material and relational clauses as distinct types having complementary roles in the discourse. In our interpretation, neither type is accorded priority. There are, however, descriptions in which one of the two is interpreted on the model of the other. Middle material clauses have served as a model for interpreting middle relational (ascriptive) clauses; likewise middle relational clauses have served as a model for interpreting material clauses. For the purposes of our discussion, we can identify three different positions.

[i] According to the first position, a material nuclear process is interpreted as if it was a participant in a relational process. This gives a logical analysis of the form "Subject 'be' Predicate": *Socrates ran* is analysed as "Subject: 'Socrates' 'be'

Predicate: 'running'". In terms of grammatical classes, a verb is a copula plus an adjective.

[ii] The second position is the reverse of the first in terms of the distribution of the nuclear process and participants. A relational process is interpreted on the model of a material one; the attribute (participant) is interpreted as if it was a nuclear process. Thus, to continue with the same artificial examples, *Socrates was white* is analysed as 'Socrates whited'. The copula is not interpreted as representing a process but is thought to be only a "bearer" of tense, person, and number.

[iii] The third position accepts both the material process model and the relational process model without trying to interpret one in terms of the other. According to this model, *Socrates was white* is not primarily like *Socrates ran* but is more directly related to *Socrates was a philosopher* and, by an additional step, to *Socrates was the teacher of Plato*. In this model, nuclear processes are verbs and participants are nominals (substantival or adjectival).

The three positions are summarized diagrammatically in Figure 11-3.

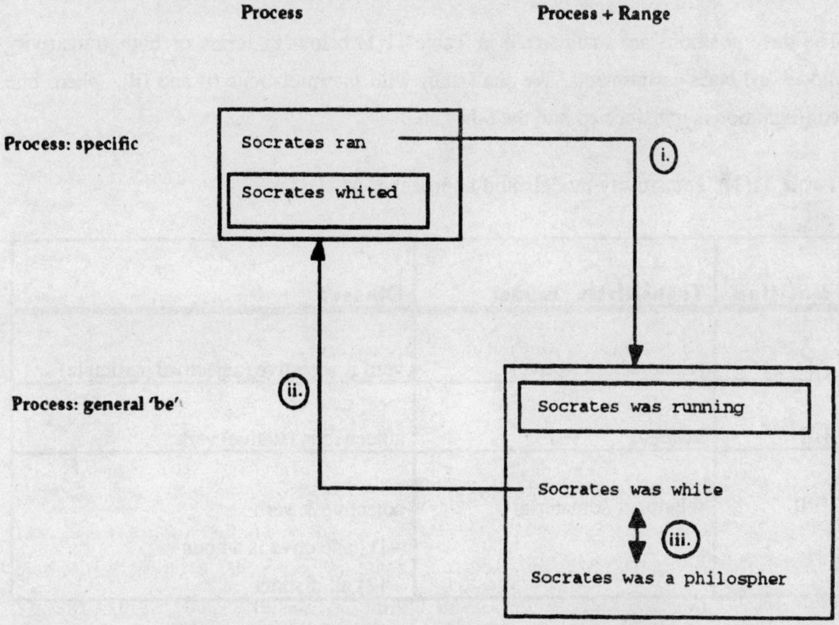

Fig. 11-3: Transitivity models — three positions

The three approaches have different consequences for word class assignments. According to the first approach, verbs are really adjectives (their true shape is revealed in the adjectival participle), while the second approach assumes that adjectives are really verbs; they just happen to be superficially defective (in English) in that they cannot be inflected. The third approach aligns adjectives with 'substantives', but it still allows for two possibilities. They can either be treated as independent classes or they can be grouped together as nouns. The alternatives are summarized in Figure 11-4.

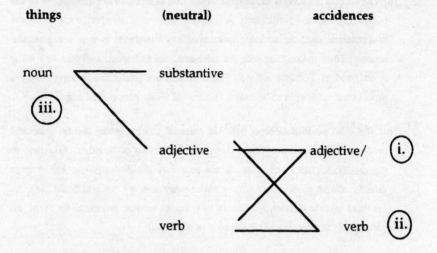

Fig. 11-4: The alternative models in terms of class assignments

The three positions are summarized in Table 11(1) below in terms of both transitivity model and class assignments. We shall start with interpretations (i) and (ii), where one configuration is transformed into the other one.

Table 11(1): Transitivity models and approaches to classes

Position	Transitivity model	Classes
[i]	relational (ascriptive)	verb is adjective (adjectival participle)
[ii]	material	adjective is (stative) verb
[iii]	relational & material	adjective & verb [1] adjective is a noun [2] all distinct

11.3.3 The transforming interpretations: adjectives & verbs vs. nouns

The first two positions identified above transform one configuration into another so that the first can be interpreted on the model of the second. Similarly, there is transformation of the classes: adjectives are really verbs or verbs are really adjectives.

Both transforming interpretations can be seen as attempts to find a *canonical logical form*, either Subject - Copula - Predicate or Subject - Predicate, rather than have to operate with different forms. These two logical structurings correspond to relational and material models respectively:

material   **relational**

Subject - Predicate   Subject - Copula - Predicate
Actor   Process   Carrier   Process   Attribute

11.3.3.1 Subject - Copula - Predicate (relational model)

As we have seen, of the two approaches that group adjectives and verbs together, one is based on the model of an ascriptive relational clause: *Socrates was white*. Interpreted according to this model, the verb in *Socrates ran* is really a copula plus an adjective, 'Socrates was running' (on the possibility of the expansion, cf. Aristotle [On Interpretation]). This kind of approach was pursued in logic and philosophical grammar in the Middle Ages (cf. Padley, 1985: 374; Kneale & Kneale, 1962: 206-7, on Abelard); we also find it in the Port-Royal philosophical grammarians, and in Wilkins' (1668) work. As late as 1924, Jespersen could note "Logicians are fond of analysing all sentences into the three elements, subject, copula, and predicate" and observed that linguists "must find this analysis unsatisfactory". It seems that they do; the approach probably does not have any adherents any longer (except perhaps as an analysis of the so-called progressive aspect and the passive voice on a relational model; cf. Langacker, 1978). It might be argued that the copula is semantically motivated as the locus of (primary) tense or modality and polarity. However, this is an interpersonal function, not an ideational one: in the grammar of the English clause, there is indeed an element which serves as the locus of these categories, viz. the Finite, which is separate, or separable, from the Predicator, and combines with another interpersonal function, the Subject, to form the Mood element of the clause (as in [Subject:] *they* [Finite:] *will* [Predicator:] *come*, [TagFinite:] *won't* [TagSubject:] *they?*: see Halliday (1985: Ch. 4). This element is present in the verbal group anyway; there is no need to invent an artificial copula to serve its functions.

While the medieval Subject + Copula + Predicate analysis is no longer favoured, it is no more far-fetched than the opposite position which interprets relational processes on the model of material processes. Relationally interpreted, *Aristotle runs/ jogs /swims (well)* means that Aristotle is a member of the set of running/ jogging/ swimming entities; and this is close enough to *Aristotle is a (good) runner/ jogger/ swimmer*. But notice how we have arrived at this apparent correspondence between the material model and the relational model. We have taken one special case of the material type, where the occurrence of the material process is not a specific instance but rather a potential that depends on the actor's ability (it relates specifically to the simple present tense, whereas in material clauses the unmarked present tense is the present-in-present *Aristotle is running*). It is this 'behaviour potential' that can be taken as the basis for ascribing the Behaver to a class, using the relational model. (Cf. the pairs *Socrates speaks Greek/ Socrates can speak Greek* [verbal] and *Socrates is a speaker of Greek* [relational]; and *the door opens easily* 'can easily be opened' [material] and *the door is easy* ⟦*to open*⟧ 'is an easy one to open' [relational].) However, if we turn to cases where the occurrence of the material process is a specific instance, as in *Jack is running up the hill*, there is no obvious relational alternative. Similarly, repeated occurrences that constitute habits, as in *Socrates swims twice a week*, cannot be represented relationally (except by assigning Socrates to the class of bi-weekly swimmers: *Socrates is a bi-weekly swimmer*).

The correspondences are brought out in texts or segments of texts that describe classes, i.e. that are essentially relational. Consider the following excerpts from our duck text and from a geology text. (Agnate variants of the original are given in italics.)

Relational	**Material**
The ducks <u>are</u> largely animal feeders (insects, snails, frogs, fish, etc.), [...]	*The ducks <u>feed</u> largely on animals ....*
The legs <u>are</u> short and placed far back,	so that ducks <u>move</u> with difficulty on land, and with the characteristic gait known as a waddle,
but they <u>are</u> splendid swimmers, [...]	*but they <u>swim</u> splendidly,* *[...]*
The tongue is large and fleshy and very sensitive.	
The plumage is remarkably thick, soft, and compact.	
[...]	
The ducks are easy to tame or *The ducks are easily tameable*	The ducks <u>have been</u> easily <u>tamed</u>, [...]
Rivers are agents of erosion, transportation, and deposition.	That is, they carve their own valleys and carry the eroded material downstream, where it is either deposited by the river or delivered into a lake or ocean.

Rivers are the most important agents
in transporting the products of
erosion: they drain glaciers, and, even in their
                                  infrequent times of flowage on deserts,
                                  they probably are able to carry more
                                  material than the wind can.

(R.J. Foster, Physical Geology, p. 149)

In the geology text, the writer specifies a restatement relation ('that is', ':') between the relational and material models, which is possible since the text deals with generic classes of rivers, etc.. Table 11(2) sums up the difference between material and relational processes depending on the type of occurrence.

Table 11(2): Transitivity and potentiality of occurrence

PROCESS TYPE	TYPE OF OCCURRENCE		
	potential	habitual instantiation	instance
material	Socrates swims well	Socrates swims in the morning	Socrates swam across the river; Socrates is swimming
relational	Socrates is a good swimmer	Socrates is a matutinal swimmer	

11.3.3.2 Subject - Predicate (middle material model)

In modern predicate logic, a different view is taken, whereby nouns, adjectives, and verbs are all predicates. The second approach we mentioned above brings two of these, adjectives and verbs, together as a single class of verbs. Here the model is that of as a material clause, exemplified by *Socrates ran* ('run (Socrates)'). According to this model, *Socrates was white* is really *Socrates whited:* 'white (Socrates)'. In this view, the adjective is a surface class, and the need for a copula to carry tense, number, and person is also a property of surface structure.

One example of this approach is Chafe (1970). Chafe treats adjectives and prepositions as "semantic verbs". He comments on his position in relation to the traditional analysis (pp. 159-160):

It runs counter to traditions based on the study of surface structure to consider *in* a verb root, as in fact it does to consider *wide* a verb root, as we did earlier. In the surface structure of English and many other languages, *in* is traditionally regarded as a preposition and *wide* as an adjective. Both are typically preceded by forms of *be*, which plays the surface role of verb: *The knife is in the box, The road is wide.* This *be*, however, is surely not the *semantic* verb root in such sentences. Its function is to carry the tense and other inflectional units originally attached to roots like *in* and *wide* because the latter, as surface items in English, are incapable of being so inflected. In addition, we find in English surface phrases like *the knife in the box* and *the wide road* where *be* is not present and *in* and *be* appear to be outside the context of verbs altogether. As many readers may realize, however, phrases like these are readily explainable on the basis of semantic structures in which *in* and *wide* again are verb roots. ... It is significant to observe that there are languages in which such items do appear in surface structures in the form of verbs, not prepositions or adjectives.

In another context, Chafe (1987: 34) restates his position as follows:

> One clear type of word *sequence* that may express a single new concept is the construction that consists of a copula followed by either an adjective, a prepositional phrase, or a noun phrase. Examples from this narrative include "is funny" (1), "was interesting" (38), "was at Wesleyan" (19), or "was still a men's school" (20). In many such cases one can imagine the concept in question being expressed by a single word in some other language, where it has become institutionalized.

There are three arguments given by Chafe in favour of this position:

1. "*be* ... is surely not the *semantic* verb root in such sentences. Its function is to carry the tense and other inflectional units" ... "what I hope is a non-controversial case of a single quality being expressed by a word sequence"

2. "we find in English surface phrases like *the knife in the box* and *the wide road* where *be* is not present and *in* and *be* appear to be outside the context of verbs altogether"

3. "It is significant to observe that there are languages in which such items do appear in surface structures in the form of verbs, not prepositions or adjectives."

The first point (1) is not an argument, of course, and may not be intended as one. It is merely an assumption, that *be* is not a semantic verb (a process, in our terms); as such it is just an alternative to the assumption that *be* represents a process.

It is not unusual for philosophers, and even for linguists, to claim of items that are very general in meaning that they have no meaning at all but are mere structural place-holders, prop-words, or dummies; this has been the fate of words such as *it*, *there*, *one*, *be*, and *do* in English. In relation to *be*, it is pertinent to observe that *be* is only the most general member of an ascriptive set that includes also *seem*, *appear*, *look*, *sound*, *taste*, *feel; weigh*, *measure*, *number; become*, *turn*, *fall*, and *grow*. These can be contrasted with *be* as in the following made-up examples, where the contrast is between real (*be*) and apparent (*seem*) ascription:

```
He's very nice. - No, he only seems nice.
She seems very nice. - She is very nice.
```

Such words may also occur as more specific variants of *be;* e.g. weighing is a specific mode of being and *weigh* is used to indicate 'be + in weight':

```
It's five pounds. / It weighs five pounds.
```

It does not make sense to exclude the most general member of this set from having relational meaning simply because its meaning is general. It contrasts with more specific members, just as e.g. *do* contrasts with a number of more specific verbs that serve in material clauses.

Chafe's second point (2) argues from the structure of the nominal group for a particular interpretation of clause structure. If this argument is to have any force, we must be able to show that the following relational proportion holds: wide : road [in 'the wide road'] :: wide : road [in 'the road is wide']. In other words, *wide* and *road* must be related functionally in comparable ways. We do not think they are: rather, in the nominal group they are related non-contrastively as modifier to modified, but in the clause they are related as participant 1 (Attribute) to participant 2 (Carrier), through a process which embodies a contrast with other possible relationships.

Furthermore, the fact that an item *may* be absent in environment x, and *is always* absent in environment y, does not mean that it is meaningless if it is present in environment x. For example, *for* as a marker of duration may be absent, as in *we worked seven hours,* but it does not follow that *for* does not mark duration when it is present.

Table 11(3): Transitivity models and transformations

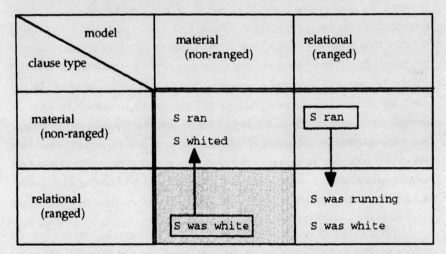

model / clause type	material (non-ranged)	relational (ranged)
material (non-ranged)	S ran S whited	[S ran]
relational (ranged)	[S was white]	S was running S was white

Chafe's third argument (3) may again not really be intended as an argument but rather as an observation about the plausibility of the analysis, based on languages other than English. In any case, it is not directly applicable to English, unless we do adopt the assumption that all languages categorize our experience in the same way. But this assumption is not justified. As we saw in our brief characterization of Chinese (Chapter 7 above), there is a difference between Chinese and English precisely at this point in the system, in that qualities in Chinese are realized by a class that is more like a type of verb than the English adjectival realization. But this difference in class assignment is not an argument in favour of English really being like Chinese in the construal of qualities. Rather, it is an indication that qualities are ontologically unstable across languages (cf. Chapter 5, Section 5.3.3).

To summarize the discussion so far, we have identified the following transformational interpretations in the paradigm of material and relational clauses: see Table 11(3) above.

11.3.3.3 Filling out the paradigm

We have set this out as a paradigm with two associated variables — (i) PROCESS TYPE (relational/ material) and (ii) RANGING (the possible addition of a Range participant, ranged/ non-ranged). The table makes it appear that material and non-ranged are always associated, and that relational and ranged are always associated. These are the unmarked combinations; but ranging and process type are, in fact, independent variables, and in English the remainder of the paradigm is filled out. Consequently, the transformational interpretations raise a problem.

Many non-ranged material processes can be construed as ranged, with the nuclear process as the range participant: *do* [Process] + *a dance* [Range] instead of *dance* [Process]. The ranged clause is one of a small set of very general Processes: *do, make, take, have, give*. So where position 1 in Section 11.3.1.2 above postulated a hypothetical or virtual form *Aristotle* ['Subject'] *was* [copula] *dancing* ['Predicate'], with a relational process 'be', English has evolved an actual clause type *Aristotle* [Medium] *did* [Process] *a dance* [Range], with a material process 'do' (cf. the discussion in Chapter 4, Section 4.4.2 and Chapter 6). The two processes 'be' and 'do' are comparable in terms of generality; both are very general. But they are clearly distinct in the same way as material and relational processes in general are distinct, as is shown by the unmarked tense selection in each case, for example *Aristotle is dancing / Aristotle is doing a dance*, by contrast with *Aristotle is wise* (see Chapter 2, Section 2.11.3.1 and Chapter 4, Section 4.2.2 on the tense selection).

Similarly, although ascriptive relational processes are typically ranged, with the quality ascribed to the Carrier as the Attribute/Range, we find ascriptive non-ranged processes as well. For example, if we start with *The problem is* [Process] *(very) important* [Range/Attribute] *(to me)*, we can relate this to *The problem matters* [Process]*(a great deal) (to me)*. In a sense, the Attribute is incorporated into the Process 'matter' in the same way as the Means is incorporated into a verb such as *hammer*. This class of ascriptive processes includes *matter, count* (as in *your past achievements don't count), suffice* and *figure*, and also an evaluative set, such as *stink, suck, drip, reek*. But in English this is the marked way of ascribing a quality to a thing, and these processes are clearly not material, as is shown by the unmarked tense selection, for example: *it doesn't matter* 'it is not important' rather than *it's not mattering,* thus parallel to *it's not important* rather than *it's not being important.*

The paradigm is summarized in 11(4) below.

Table 11(4): The paradigm — a wider focus

	non-ranged	ranged
material	A. danced	A. did a dance
relational	A.'s ideas mattered	A.'s ideas were important

Thus both the approaches discussed in this section are problematic. Let us now look in more detail at the third position.

11.3.4 The non-transformed relational interpretation

The third approach, which does not involve any transformations of transitivity patterns, maintains the alignment of ascriptive clauses with relational clauses in general rather than moving them into the material domain. Furthermore, it unifies the notion of participant, since Attributes are interpreted as participants rather than as processes. We will explore these two consequences in turn.

11.3.4.1 The intensive relation: ascription and identification

Let us return to the paradigm of relational processes, starting with three examples. Under our interpretation they are all brought together as intensive relational processes:

> (1a) This is very savoury   ——
> (1b) This is a good savoury   ——
> (2) This is the best savoury   The best savoury is this

Examples (1a and 1b) are ascriptive intensive relations. They represent a relation of inclusion: the referent is included in the class of savoury things.

Example (2) above is an equative intensive relation; it is a relation of identity, where 'this' is identified as 'the best savoury'. The identification can be reversed: *The best savoury is this.* Identity and inclusion are two versions of the intensive relation: identity is the limiting case of inclusion and inclusion is partial identity. Thus while *habits are complicated acts* represents a relation of inclusion — 'habits belong to the class of complicated acts', the following definition is an identity; the specification 'complicated acts' has been qualified so that it describes a one-member class:

```
Habits are complicated acts which, when learned, become automatic
through constant repetition. Habits may be good or bad. Good
habits are useful, for they make us more efficient by saving time
and energy. (Kraus, Concepts in Modern Biology, p. 193)
```

Being an identity, it is reversible — *Habits are complicated acts which, when learned, become automatic through constant repetition : Complicated acts which, when learned, become automatic through constant repetition are habits.* In contrast, *Habits are complicated acts* is not reversible. The similarity between identity and ascription is indicated by the fact that both can be expressed by *be, remain* or *become;* the difference between them by the fact that they belong to different sets: see Figure 11-5.

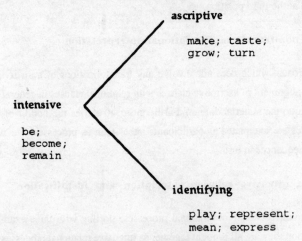

ascriptive
```
make; taste;
grow; turn
```

intensive
```
be;
become;
remain
```

identifying
```
play; represent;
mean; express
```

Fig. 11-5: The markers of intensive relations

Here is an example where an equative is followed by an ascriptive intensive relation; the first identifies a particle and the second characterizes it:

```
To complete our understanding of natural radiation, it is
necessary to consider another particle. This particle is the
neutron, and it is particularly interesting because of its central
role in atomic and nuclear bombs. (R.J. Foster, Physical Geology)
```

Another relational type is (generalized) possession, an important subtype of which is the part-whole relation. If a quality is represented as if it was an abstract thing, it can be possessed; people can have beauty, virtue, and grace. The potential paraphrase relationship between examples like *She has great beauty* and *She is very beautiful* points to the closeness between having and being. The two typically go together in descriptions, of course. In the first example below the two are in a restatement relation:

```
Minerals are crystalline  substructures; that is, they have an
orderly internal structure (arrangement of atoms). ...
```

```
Protons are heavy and have a positive electrical charge. ...

In addition, an atom may have neutrons in its nucleus. Neutrons
have a mass slightly slightly lighter than that of a proton plus
an electron, and are electrically neutral.
```

(R.J. Foster, Physical Geology)

To sum up, when ascription is given an interpretation in its own right, it has the following relational neighbours: see Table 11(5).

Table 11(5): Part of the relational paradigm

	middle	effective
possessive	This has a good savour	
intensive	This is a good savoury	This is the best savoury
	This is very savoury	This is the most savoury

We will now turn to the second consequence, the implications for the contrast between participants and processes.

11.3.4.2 Participants (nouns: substantives & adjectives) vs. processes (verbs)

If the material model is used to interpret ascriptive processes, like the one represented by the clause *This is very savoury*, the notion of process will be widened to include a realization like *savoury* and the notion of participant will be narrowed to exclude it (Position [ii]). In contrast, with our own interpretation participant is a more general notion that includes the realization of qualities: see Figure 11-6.

With the unified notion of participant, the class realizations of participants and processes in the semantics are as follows:

semantics   grammar (class)

participant: nominal group;
                                   noun = substantive / adjective
process: verbal group

That is, a participant is realized by a nominal group and a process is realized by a verbal group. The significance of this generalization is that exceptions to it are always metaphorical. In particular, it is only when a process is being construed as if it was a participant that it will be realized in nominal form (see Chapter 6).

position [iii]:   position [ii]:

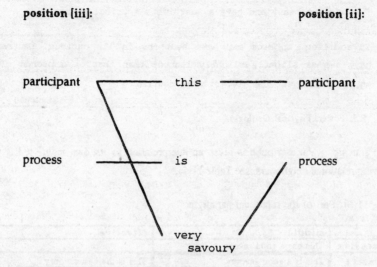

Fig. 11-6: Non-transforming [iii] vs. transforming, material model [ii] — notions of participant

We have seen that where the process is of a material type, there is often an agnate form, originating as a grammatical metaphor, whereby the happening is construed as the Range participant configured with a generalized Process such as *do, make*. Where the process is material, the metaphor involves no change in process type.

We can contrast this with the situation in a mental clause. Here, in the metaphorical version, the sensing is construed as the Range/ Attribute of an possessive ascriptive relational process, with a generalized ascriptive verb such as *have*. There is thus a shift in process type from mental to relational. Examples are shown in Table 11(6) below.

Table 11(6): Representation of process — congruent & metaphorical

		congruent process	metaphorical process as participant (Range)
		[verbal group]	[nominal group]
[i]	material	He danced	He **did** a dance
[ii]	mental	He hated dogs	
	relational		He **had** a hatred of dogs

As always in the case of grammatical metaphor, we need the metaphorical representation as well as the congruent one to account for the organization of the metaphor. For example, the Qualifier in the attributive nominal group of *he had a hatred of dogs* corresponds to the Phenomenon of the congruent version: see Figure 11-7.

He   had   a   hatred   of dogs

metaphorical	Carrier	Process	Attribute		
			Deictic	Thing	Qualifier
congruent	Senser			Process	Phenomenon
	He			hated	dogs

Fig. 11-7: Metaphorical and congruent representations

It seems therefore that there is no real advantage, theoretical or descriptive, in analysing the grammatical realizations of qualities as if they were something other than what they seem. On the contrary: not only does this complicate the description, but more importantly it fails to bring out systematic patterns of agnation. This is a small indication of something we believe to be a general principle: if you treat language as distortion, you end up by distorting language.

12. Figures and processes

A characteristic of work on grammatical semantics, where this is based on linguistics or on natural language philosophy, is to move in at the lower ranks of the grammar rather than the higher ones and to start with classes rather than with functions. This is a continuation of the method of traditional grammar, which (because it originated with the study of observable features in language, cf. Halliday, 1984a) was *word*-oriented and leant heavily on word classes in its descriptive statements, as we noted in Chapter 10, Section 10.1. We find this tendency in discussions of word classes and their semantic values — the issue of the proper interpretation of adjectives, the exploration of various verb types, and so on.

It would take too long to contrast every aspect of our lattice with other proposals, either existing or conceivable ones, so we shall only highlight a few key areas. In doing this, we have to keep in mind that we are dealing with a semantic *system* and not with a collection of unrelated items. Consequently, it is of little value to argue about an isolated node in the system; we have to operate with a broader focus. For example, if we recognize figures of **saying** (usually overlooked as a distinct type), this goes together with certain other features: with the distinction between phenomena and metaphenomena, and between ideas and sayings, with the organization of projections as sequences rather than as figures, with the identification of symbol sources as a kind of participant, and with the recognition of circumstances of matter. In other words, we have to consider **syndromes** of features that occupy a region of semantic space.

In this chapter we shall be concerned with alternative approaches to a typology of configurational phenomena — of figures, as composites of processes, participants, and circumstances. Various classifications have been proposed not only in linguistics but also in philosophy and sociology. What we are looking for are the distinctions that are systematic in English semantics, rather than incidental distinctions or distinctions that follow automatically from others.

12.1 Criteria for process typology

In Chapter 5, Section 5.4, we discussed two perspectives on a process: a process is both an organizer of participants and an event that is instantiable in time. These two perspectives lead to different criteria for establishing process typologies. For example, *will have left* is the Process part of *they will have left the house by now,* where it organizes the participants *they* and *the house;* but it also has internal organization as an event *will —> have —> left:* see Figure 12-1.

The two perspectives are associated with different grammatical units, the clause (for the participant organizing perspective) and the verbal group (for the temporal instantiation). The difference between the two perspectives has been obscured for two reasons. In the first place, syntacticians have continued to tend to fail to recognize the unity of the verbal group, favouring instead a Predicate-based constituent, the Verb Phrase, with the Auxiliary then detached within it or located outside it altogether; furthermore, parts of the verbal group complex have been exported to a higher node (e.g. *seem, continue*). In the second place, the preference for immediate constituency rather than rank-based models of constituency effectively masks the generalizations that can be made about any one rank.

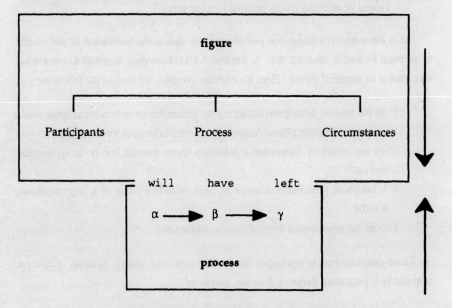

Fig. 12-1: The two perspectives on a process

(i) In the participant-organizing perspective (see Chapter 5, Section 5.3), it is the nature of the participants involved in the process that determines the different process types. Relevant variables include the following:

1. Is some participant created, brought into existence, by the process?
2. Is some participant restricted to conscious being?
3. Can some participant be a metathing as well as a thing?
4. Is the process directed towards some participant?
5. Does the process benefit some participant?
6. Does the process occur spontaneously or does it need an input of energy?
7. Does the process affect some participant materially or does it impinge on its consciousness?
8. Is the process symmetric?
9. Is the process reflexive?

Questions such as these lead to typologies with terms like action, transaction, happening, sensing, saying, relation, existential, ambient, and so on. In the typology presented here as part of the ideation base, there are two very general considerations:

1. process type: what kind of reality does the figure or process configuration pertain to (the material world, the world of consciousness, the world of symbolization, the world of abstract relations)?

2. agency: is the occurrence of the process (in conjunction with the medium) caused by an entity that is external to it (an agent)?

(ii) In the temporal instantiation perspective, the issue is the occurrence of the process as an event located in time (cf. Ch. 5, Section 5.4.1): how does it unfold through time, and what is its temporal profile? Here the relevant variables are such as the following:

1. Is the process homogeneous during its occurrence or does it decompose into a sequence of distinct phases (stages); is it a mini-tableau or a mini-drama?

2. Is the period of occurrence a relatively short interval, or is it an extended interval?

3. Is the whole period of occurrence in view or only a phase of it (e.g. beginning or end)?

4. Does the process tend to occur once or repeatedly?

These questions lead to typologies that include terms like stative, dynamic, perfective, imperfective, punctiliar, iterative, durative, and so on.

The distinction most commonly drawn here is based on **change**. Is there change over time or not; i.e. is there a change in the course of the occurrence of the process? The most common dichotomy is state vs. non-state (with terminological oppositions such as stative/dynamic); this has been favoured both by philosophers (see e.g. Nordenfelt, 1977, and his references) and by linguists (see e.g. Quirk et al, 1985 and their references). States and non-states have different temporal profiles. States are homogeneous; any time we check a process whose occurrence is a state, it will be the same. Non-states, or changes, are not homogeneous; during the course of the occurrence of a process something will have changed, for example the spatial location of a participant (as with processes of movement) or parts of a participant, or some other attribute of a participant (e.g. possession or location in a 'quality space' such as colour or temperature).

As we have seen, the two perspectives represent two different kinds of profile. One is the configuration of process, participants, and circumstances — the transitivity profile; and the other is the occurrence or unfolding of an event through time — the temporal profile.

The two perspectives are not unrelated, of course. As we shall see, the specification of an element of transitivity structure may determine the temporal profile: the created Goal that constitutes the completion of the performance of the process (as in *Mr. Blandings built a house*), a Range that constitutes its finite scope (*They sang two Hungarian folk songs*), a destination that gives its spatio-temporal endpoint (*He walked to the store*), a resultative Attribute that constitutes the (qualitative) endstate (*He was shot dead*), and so on. But the mere presence of such an element is not sufficient to determine the temporal profile; it is also influenced by the 'boundedness' of the elements: are they in infinite supply or not — a definite number of units, or an indefinite number? In general, then, the temporal profile is determined by other factors such as the presence, and the boundedness in quantity, of participants and circumstances.

We shall start by looking at one particular temporal typology of processes that a number of researchers have based their work on, Vendler's (1967) activity / accomplishment / achievement / state typology; this involves consideration of both perspectives, but we shall intersect it with our process types in order to compare the two. Then, we explore a typology based on control (intentionality, volitionality, etc.), and look at proposals using this distinction together with the distinction between states and non-states (events: activities, accomplishment, achievements).

12.2   Temporal   profile: activities,   accomplishments, achievements, and states

There have been numerous treatments of temporal categories such as aspect, "lexical aspect" (Aktionsart) and phase, and various typologies have been proposed. Vendler's (1967) classic philosophical discussion does not represent the most recent work, but it has been used in a number of later studies (cf. Verkuyl, 1972, Dowty, 1979, Nordenfelt, 1977, Platzack, 1979, Foley & Van Valin 1984, Dahlgren, 1988) and will serve as a starting point for a comparison, together with other proposals based on Vendler's ideas.[1] Vendler focuses "primarily upon the time schemata presupposed by various verbs", while recognizing that other factors such as "the presence or absence of an object ... also enter the picture".

Vendler recognizes two groups of verbs based on whether they "possess continuous tenses" or not.[2]

(1) **Group 1.** Verbs from the first group can be used to answer the question "What are you doing?". They fall into two "species", activities and accomplishments. **Activities** are homogeneous through time (drawing, running, eating, etc.), whereas **accomplishments** work up towards a climax

---

[1] For a systemic functional treatment of "Aktionsarten", see Steiner (1991: Section 3.10).

[2] Vendler's characterization in terms of 'continuous tense' in fact breaks down: his achievements (see below) may also go with secondary present ('continuous present').

(drawing a circle, running a mile, eating a steak, etc.). Platzack (1979) calls them unbounded processes (activities) and bounded processes (accomplishments), in order to bring out the character of the temporal profile.

(2) Group 2. Verbs in the second group can be used to answer the question "Do you [verb: know/love ...]". Vendler distinguishes two subtypes, achievements and states, which are called punctual events and states in Platzack's (1979) terms. **Achievements** include a short (or instantaneous) transition to an endstate, e.g. reaching a peak, spotting, and realizing. **States** involve no change: thinking that, knowing, having, etc..

The four types and their temporal characteristics as discussed by Vendler are given in Table 12(1).

Table 12(1): Vendler's four event types

Type		Admit "continuous" tense	Temporal profile	Example
events	activities (unbounded)	yes	homogeneous	running, pushing a cart
	accomplishments (bounded)	yes	climax	running a mile, drawing a circle
	achievements (punctual)	no	occur at single moment	reaching the top, winning a race
states		no	last for a period of time	having, believing

Platzack (op cit.) uses three dimensions to distinguish Vendler's four event types, viz. change vs. no change, bounded vs. unbounded (in time), and duration vs. no duration. If we try to tabulate these as independent dimensions, we find that there are certain dependencies. 'No change' (state) implies duration and unbounded, for example. Using graphic representations from Schneider (1977: 33) cited in Platzack, we can summarize the parametric analysis of the four event types as in Table 12(2).

The dependencies that emerge from the table suggest the systemic arrangement of Platzack's three parameters shown in Figure 12-2 as one possible systemic interpretation. Dahlgren (1988: 85) arrives at a similar arrangement, represented in the form of a decision tree (her Figure 10).

Table 12(2): Parametric and graphic analysis of Vendler's event types

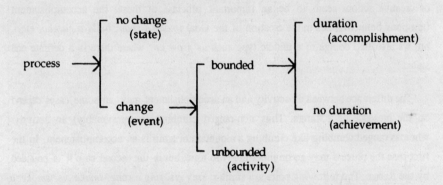

no change		change			
	state e	**activity** e		unbounded
		accomplish- ment e	**achievement** e	bounded
no duration	duration		no duration	

Fig. 12-2: Systemic organization of the temporal parameters

Having presented Vendler's temporally based taxonomy of events, we can now intersect it with the typology of figures we introduced earlier, viz. doing (& happening), sensing, saying, and being & having. Using only examples given by Vendler, we find the correspondences as in Table 12(3).

According to this table, **activities** are always processes in figures of doing. Processes of motion, either middle or effective, form an important subclass (*walk, run, push,* etc.), unless there is a single destination (*fly to Nairobi, walk home,* etc.). We also find a behavioural process like *think about* (Vendler's example) and we might add other behaviourals such as *ponder, listen to, watch, look at,* and *smile;* but behavioural processes with a delimited range would not presumably be classified as activities, because they are bounded: *watch the film Brief Encounter.*

Table 12(3): Vendler's event types and the typology of figures

	doing	sensing	saying	being & having
activities	run, walk, swim, push/ pull sth, think about			
accomplish- ments	paint a picture, make a chair, grow up			
achievements	reach a peak, win a race, die, start	recognize, realize, spot		
states	[habits, e.g.: he smokes]	desire, want, like, dislike, love, hate, know, believe, think that		have, possess, dominate, rule

Accomplishments are similarly always processes in figures of doing. Resultative or creative actions seem to be an important subclass of these: the accomplishment (temporal bounding) lies in the creation of the Goal (*make a chair, build a gazebo*, etc.), but we also find doings of a middle type such as *grow up* where there is a definite end state.

The difference between an activity and an accomplishment may in some cases depend on the presence of a Range. Thus non-ranged climbing is (presumably) an activity, whereas ranged climbing like climbing a mountain or a hill is an accomplishment. In the first case the process may go on indefinitely in time, but in the second case it is bounded by the Range. The following pairs are similar: *sing* vs. *sing a song*, *smoke* vs. *smoke a cigar*, *play* vs. *play a game of tennis*, and *run* vs. *run a mile* (Vendler's example). However, what is important is clearly not just the presence of a Range, but rather the nature of the Range: is it a unit or a set of units? For example, contrast *play a game of tennis* (an accomplishment: a particular quantity of playing) with *play tennis* (an activity: a particular kind of playing activity).

The same is also true of a Goal created by the process: if it is a single unit, we have an accomplishment, as in *Henry is making a chair;* but if we have an indefinite number of units, we have an activity, as in *Henry makes chairs for a living*. If the Goal is a mass, the interpretation seems to depend on whether the mass is conventionally produced in finite units or not; contrast *make tea* (an accomplishment) with *make gold* (a never-ending activity?).

Again, the presence or absence of a resultative Attribute may determine whether an effective material process is an activity or an accomplishment. Thus, beating somebody may be an activity (as in *He kept beating him*), but beating somebody dead is an accomplishment (*He beat him dead*).

In a similar way, it seems that the presence or absence of a circumstantial element may determine whether the process in a figure of doing is interpreted as an activity or an accomplishment. For example, contrast *walk* (an activity) with *walk to the market* (an accomplishment; the spatial destination correlates with a temporal bound).

Further, if the process is expanded the interpretation may change from activity to achievement. Thus while *running* is an activity, *stop running* is presumably an achievement — just as stopping is.

Vendler's **achievements** are transitional: accomplishments occur over a stretch of time, while achievements are more instantaneous. According to the examples in the table, the transition can be either one of doing (*die, win a race*) or one of sensing (*recognize, realize, spot*). In the doing type, the achievement may lie in the Range specified for the Process. Thus *die* is an achievement; the nature of the achievement may be specified, as in *die the death of a hero*.

To judge from Vendler's examples, **states** are either processes in figures of sensing (*desire, like, hate, know, believe*) or processes in figures of being & having (*have, possess*). However, *Do you smoke?* is a question about a state, according to Vendler (contrasting with the activity in *Are you smoking?*); it would appear, therefore, that habits of doing are states. If we expand the process in a figure of sensing or being & having, we may no longer have a state. For example, *she has stopped loving him* is presumably an achievement. And what about: *I'm beginning to believe that he knew all along; I'm understanding the problem better and better; I'm liking this album more and more* (said by a DJ playing it repeatedly)?

When we take the four types of figure as our starting point, we see that processes in figures of **doing** can be activities, accomplishments, or achievements, and, in a habitual interpretation (and perhaps also in so-called eternal truths), states. Processes in figures of **sensing** can be achievements or, predominantly, states. (There are sensing activities (*ponder, listen, watch, smell*, etc.), but we interpret these as behavioural rather than as inert sensing.)

There are no processes in figures of **saying** exemplified in the table of comparison above. When we intersect such processes with the various event types, we find examples of all classes: saying states, saying achievements, saying accomplishments, and saying activities. Examples like *the sign says that visitors have to take off their shoes* and *the law states unambiguously that this is a felony* would appear to be states. Sayings that can be interpreted as causative sensings such as *remind sb that* 'cause to remember' and *convince sb that* 'cause to believe' seem to be achievements. Next, ranged figures of saying where the Range specifies a genre or speech-functional 'unit' of verbalization are accomplishments: *tell (sb) a story, ask a question*, etc.. Finally, there are saying activities: *speak* and *talk*.

Processes in figures of **being & having**, finally, are states, according to the examples in the table. However, we have to add inchoatives — *become, grow, turn*, etc. — and they seem to be accomplishments, *become an adult, grow dark, turn sour*, etc. (Range: result of change); or activities, *become larger, grow heavier*, etc. (Range: unbounded). (Incidentally, notice the difference between doing *widen, grow, expand*, etc., which presumably are activities, since there is no end state, and being & having *become wide, big, large*, etc., which would be accomplishments.)

The result of our brief exploration of the intersection of Vendler's typology of processes with our typology of figures is summarized in Table 12(4).

We can draw some conclusions from our comparison of Vendler's event taxonomy and our typology of figures. First, Vendler presents his distinctions as pertaining to verbs; but, as we have seen, the configuration and nature of participants and circumstances are just as important as the verb realizing the nuclear Process of a figure (cf. Ehrich, 1987), particularly in deciding whether a process is an activity, an accomplishment, or an achievement.

Second, the correlations are not particularly systematic. For example: *sing* (activity), *sing a ditty* (accomplishment), *sing folk songs* (activity), *sing a ditty every evening* (habitual accomplishment => state). In some sense, the particular type of event is an *automatic consequence* of the particular configuration of the process and the nature of its participants and circumstances.

The distinction between state and non-state (event) seems more stable in relation to our process types than the subtypes of event (activities, accomplishments, and achievements). We can state the relations as implications: see Figure 12-3.

These correlations are perhaps not surprising. Given that there are two aspects to a process — configurational (the composition of a figure into process, participants, and circumstances) and temporal (its profile in time) — processes without participants (meteorological ones) have to involve change in order to be construed as processes at all (consequently they are always events); likewise one-participant processes, with existentials as the limiting case. Conversely, in order for a state to be construed as a process, it has to rate high as a participant organizer; it has to be interpreted as a relation between two participants.

Table 12(4): Elaborated table of correspondences

	doing	**sensing**	**saying**	**being & having**
activities	run, walk, swim, push/ pull sth, *ponder*	*ponder*	speak, talk, chat	be [naughty/ difficult]
accomplish- ments	paint a picture, make a chair, grow up		tell a story, ask a question	become, grow, go
achievements	reach a peak, win a race, die, start	recognize, realize, spot	convince, remind	turn, fall
states	[habits, e.g.: he smokes]	desire, want, like, dislike, love, hate, know, believe, think that	say, ask, tell	have, possess, dominate, rule

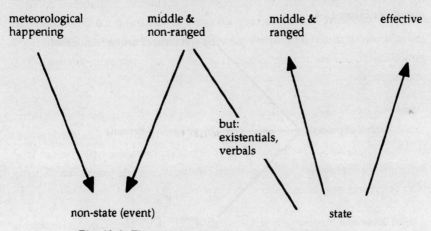

Fig. 12-3: Figure and stativity — implicational relations

As noted earlier, Vendler's typology has formed the basis of various other frameworks. We will return in Section 12.4 below to Dowty's (1979) development of Vendler's typology, and the use Foley & Van Valin (1984) make of Dowty's work in their typology events.

Our general conclusion is that as a systemic specification of the potential of processes — of the options that are open in their construal — Vendler's typology is essentially epiphenomenal. The temporal profile of a process is an interpretation that results from various factors that *are* systemic, such as the configurational profile of the figure in which the process serves, the nature and quantity of participants involved in it, and the phase of the process itself; but it does not define an area of semantic potential.

12.3 Control (and stativity)

We have been considering a typology of processes based on temporal distinctions. Next, we turn to typologies that incorporate a notion of control. These are concerned with the nature of participation and process in the figure as a whole, rather than the Process element alone. But such typologies often embody both control and stativity: the general question is whether one of the participants involved in a process controls the occurrence of it or not. The control parameter has been used to distinguish pairs of participant roles such as the following:

control	no control
agent	patient
actor	undergoer
agent	force

There are different possible kinds of control, and scholars vary in the way they use the notion: see Figure 12-4.

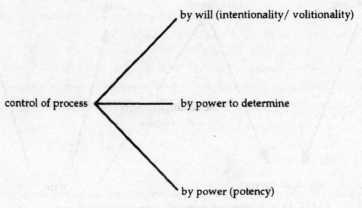

Fig. 12-4: Types of control

We can see the difference among these notions of control in the classification of 'natural force' agents: Chafe (1970) argues that they are potent entities and hence agents (in his sense), while Dik (1978) treats them as forces rather than agents, and Nordenfelt (1977) also takes them to be non-agentive (specifically, non-intentional): see Figure 12-5.

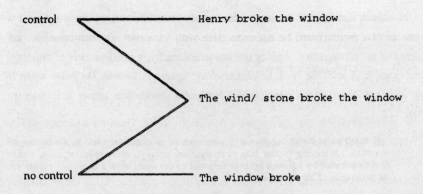

Fig. 12-5: Breaking and control

This difference in the treatment of natural forces suggests that control by will is a stronger and more restrictive notion of control than control by power. We will consider these three notions of control, each in turn:

1. **Intentionality:** Nordenfelt's (1977) notion of control, which is defined by intentionality.

2. **Potency:** Chafe's (1970) notion of control, which is restricted to nonstates, where an action is carried out by a potent doer.

3. **Power to determine:** Dik's (1978) more generalized notion of control, which is applicable to states as well as actions ("a state of affairs is controlled if one of the entities involved in it, the controller, has the power to determine whether or not the state will obtain.").

12.3.1 Intentionality

Nordenfelt (1977) proposes a philosophical account of episodes drawing on G. von Wright and D. Dowty. It is "concerned with episodes in the world and not with words or any other linguistic elements" (p. 41). However, the "limits and contents of the episodes will be determined by ordinary English sentences. Thus, *John runs* signifies an episode; so do *the wind breaks the window* and *Peter kills John by shooting him with a gun*". It is not clear that these two positions are compatible: it would seem that they build an ambivalence into the foundation of the account, between accounting for (physical) action etc. (a philosophical construal of action) and accounting for the construal of action etc. in English (a philosophical construal of the construal of action in English). But this kind of ambivalence seems to us to characterize a good deal of philosophically oriented work on categories such as action and intention.

Nordenfelt distinguishes states, processes, and events (the coming about either of a state or of a process); and he intersects these with 'causative' vs. 'non-causative' and 'agentive' vs. 'non-agentive'. Agency is really intentionality; it is independent of causality. For example, *A holds the book* is 'causative' and 'agentive', whereas *The pillar supports the bridge* is 'causative' and 'non-agentive'. Nordenfelt characterizes agency as follows (p. 54):

> ... [I shall] adopt the strong notion of action which is completely tied to the notion of *intention*. According to this line of thought an action is an episode, which is either directly intended by a human agent or believed by the agent to be a necessary means for the realisation of an intention of his.

To the extent that intentionality enters into the semantic system of a language, it could in principle be construed ideationally as some aspect of the overall system of figures or be enacted interpersonally as a modality of inclination. If it is construed ideationally, it could in principle be a global property of a figure as a whole or a local property of the process or a participant.

In English, intentionality can be enacted within the interpersonal system of imperative modality (modulation) in the form of inclination, as in *he won't be ordered around* ('refuses to be'). It is independent of ideational agency; inclination is oriented towards the Subject, i.e. the modally responsible element of the clause, rather than (say) the Actor or Agent (as our passive example illustrates).

Intentionality can be construed in the clause as circumstances of Manner ('according to plan', e.g. *he found the book by chance; he turned left by mistake; he turned left intentionally*) and as verbal group complexes of projection or enhancement realizing the Process (e.g., *she intended to leave at 4; she happened to be in the neighbourhood*). It may also be a factor in certain lexical contrasts within delicate process types; but we have no evidence that intentionality is a primary variable in the semantic system of figures and its grammatical construal in transitivity. Rather, whether an example is read as construing something as intentional or non-intentional will depend on a variety of factors, such as the consciousness of the most active participant. Thus all Nordenfelt's examples contrasting 'agentive' and 'non-agentive' in his summary (p. 57) involve A (presumably a person) contrasting with non-persons (either inanimate objects and forces or lower animates), e.g. *A keeps water running : The pump keeps the water running :: A shuts the door : The wind breaks the window :: A starts the engine : The germs initiate the deterioration of the organism :: A lets the door close : The window breaks.*

12.3.2 Potency (Chafe)

Chafe (1970) draws a basic distinction between states (e.g. *The wood is dry*) and non-states. Non-states involve either one participant undergoing the process (a "process" component involving a patient, e.g. *The wood dried; Henry died*), or one participant in control of the process as a doer (an action component done by an agent, e.g. *The boy sang*). The main probe Chafe uses to differentiate processes from actions is "What did N do?" (action) vs. "What happened to N?" (process):

> What happened to the wood? *It dried.*
> What did the boy do? *He sang.*

In examples like these, "process" (in Chafe's sense) and "action" can be interpreted as subtypes of middle figures of doing, and "Patient" and "Agent" as further differentiation of our Actor: see Figure 12-6.

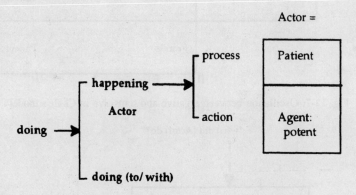

Fig. 12-6: Two types of Actor according to potency

Both "What happened to the butter?" and "What did Henry do?" can be answered by *Henry melted the butter:* a process can be carried out by an Agent; and it can combine with an action to give an "action process": *Henry* (Agent) *melted the butter* (Patient). In Chafe's analysis, there is an oscillation between an ergative interpretation and a transitive interpretation, with "Agent" used in both middle and effective as in a transitive model, but with a grouping of Process and Patient in the effective as in an ergative model: see Figure 12-7. In contrast, our interpretation (based on Halliday, 1967/8; 1985) accommodates both the transitive (Actor + Process [+Goal]) and the ergative model (Process + Medium [+Agent]) as complementary perspectives: see Figure 12-8.

Chafe's notion of agent comes closer to our notion of actor (a transitive function) than to our notion of agent (an ergative function); but it is more restricted than our actor, since our actor may also correspond to Chafe's patient. The agent of an action is "a thing which has the *power* to do something, a thing which has a force of its own, which is self-

motivated"; agents are "largely animate beings" but also include e.g. *heat, wind, ship.*[3]
Chafe characterizes these things as 'potent'.

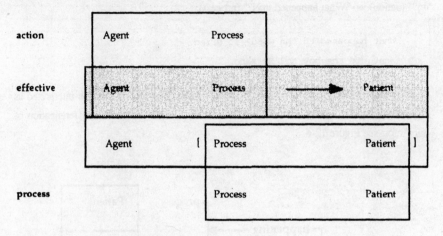

Fig. 12-7: Oscillation between ergative and transitive in Chafe's model

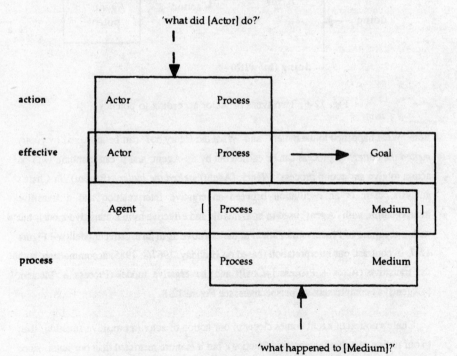

Fig. 12-8: Representing both transitive and ergative models

---

[3] Contrast Dik's (1978) treatment (discussed below) where *The wind opened the door* is interpreted as an uncontrolled process rather than a controlled action. For Dik, control is not only power but power to determine.

It would seem that Chafe's paradigm is incomplete; we can find action-actions and action-states in addition to action-processes. Compare:

	non-action	action
process	The butter melted	The sun melted the butter
action	The soldiers marched/ ate	The officer marched/ fed the soldiers
state	We were warm	The sun kept us warm

Chafe links his notion of control to a typology of things ("semantic nouns"); agents are things which are potent and typically animate:

figure type:	participant role:	thing filler:
action	agent	potent
		(animate / inanimate:
		heat, wind, ship, ...)

(Note that this model treats potency as a property that is *inherent* in a certain class of things: inherent ability to act.) This correlation between figure type and thing type contrasts with our correlation between (i) figure & participant type (the senser of a sensing) and (ii) consciousness (inherent ability to sense):

figure type:	participant role:	thing filler:
sensing Senser	conscious being	

contrast:

saying	Sayer	symbol source

The question arises: should we add a category of potent (ability to act) to our general taxonomy and integrate it with the distinction based on consciousness (ability to sense)? The notion of consciousness is very clearly reflected in the grammar: in addition to the value restrictions just mentioned, we find it reflected in pronominal choices (he/she vs. it; who vs. which/that; etc.). Further, metaphorical Sensers are quite clearly discernible: *My car dislikes inexperienced drivers.* But is potency equally clearly defined? Let us consider first whether or not all agents are potent, starting with figures of doing.

Are all Actors potent? Obviously, the answer depends on how we define potency. If the figure is middle, it can be interpreted fairly narrowly, since the agent of an action is in opposition to the patient of a process (in Chafe's sense): y in (y process) can be either agent or patient. However, if the figure is effective, Chafe's paradigm only allows for one alternative: x in x (y process) can only be agent. Since an agent is supposed to be potent, it seems we have to allow for a fairly wide interpretation of the notion of potency.

Although, according to Chafe, most agents are animate as well as potent, he notes (p. 109) that "there seem to be some nouns ... which are not animate but which may nevertheless occur as agents"; his examples are:

```
The heat melted the butter
The wind opened the door
The ship destroyed the pier
```

(Note the emergence of potency in the following sequence: *John* (Actor / Patient) *fell and [he]* (Actor / Agent) *hit the rock* (Patient), where John's falling impacts on the rock.) However, in addition to persons, animals, natural forces, and self-propelled objects like ships, we find tools, abstractions & conditions, and events as agents. It is important to draw examples from fairly abstract fields to counter-balance the concrete examples given by Chafe (breaking dishes, drying wood, melting butter, opening doors, destroying piers, etc.). Here are some examples, beginning with three that are constructed as illustration:

```
Lack of sleep killed him in the end

The key opened the door

Circumstances scattered the family

those proposals which do not affect the basic structure of the
Constitution and those which do (Quadrant, Sept. 86)

Quantitative proposals set fixed limits on fiscal aggregates. (op
cit.)

Politically committed art took over one wing of the modernist
movement. (David Harvey, The condition of postmodernity, p. 33)

The myth either had to redeem us from 'the formless universe of
contingency' or, more programmatically, to provide the impetus for
a new project for human endeavour. (op cit., p. 31)

When the sense of progress is checked by depression or
recession, by war or social disruption, ... (op cit., p. 202)

The new systems of transportation and communication ...
tightened the skein of internationalism ... (op cit., 278)

Through these mechanisms capitalism creates its own distinctive
historical geography. (op cit., p. 343)
```

All these examples have Agents of doing (effective: Actor/Agent). Some of them extend the notion of Agent from concrete doing to abstract doing, but they would presumably still be action-processes in Chafe's model. Our own notion of Agent is not confined to doings; it extends to the other process types as well (see Chapter 3, Section 3.3). There are Agents of sensing (phenomena impinging on a Senser's consciousness) and Agents of being & having, as well as Agents of doing. When we move from figures of doing to the other types (which Chafe does not do, of course, since his Agent is restricted to actions), there are many cases where the notion of potency seems very hard to apply:

> Brilliance in other people scares me (Agent of sensing = Phenomenon)

> The fact that you lied didn't surprise me at all (Agent of sensing = Phenomenon)

> The solution to our problem is this: (Agent of being & having = Token)

> Anne's my sister-in-law (Agent of being & having = Token)

> The schedule kept us busy (Agent of being & having = Attributor)

We can either opt for a very wide interpretation of "potent" or allow for the possibility of non-potent Agents; the latter would extend the "action" paradigm even further. Table 12(5) summarizes possible Agents, clearly potent or possibly non-potent, in the environment of Chafe's different process types.

Table 12(5): Extending the paradigm to non-potent agents

first participant =		outer participant =	
		[Agent: potent]	[Agent: ? potent]
state		The wood is dry [Patient]	The sun made/ kept the wood dry	The lack of rain kept the wood dry
non-state	process	Henry died The wood dried [Patient]	They killed Henry They dried the wood	The lack of medicine/ Greed killed Henry
	action	Henry sang The soldiers marched [Agent: potent]	(They made him sing) He marched the soldiers	

Chafe's typology has since been adopted by Cook (e.g. 1977), who retains all of Chafe's distinctions. Cook tabulates those we have already discussed (state vs. nonstate: process/ action/ action-process) against another set of his own (basic vs. nonbasic: experiential/ benefactive/ locative). We can represent this systemically as in Figure 12-9.

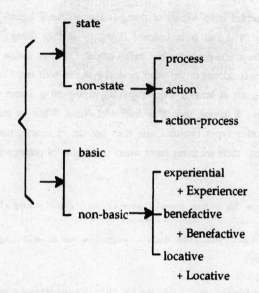

Fig. 12-9: Systemic representation of the Chafe/Cook typology

The option 'nonbasic' means the addition of a further participant, a Benefactive, Experiencer, or Locative, as shown in Table 12(6) together with the basic types.

Table 12(6): The Chafe/Cook typology and process types (material unless otherwise marked)

	basic	**benefactive** **+ Ben**	**locative** **+ Loc**	**experiential** **+ Exp**
state	Os Proc *broken, dry, dead, tight* [relational]	Ben Obj Proc *have (got), own* [relational]	Obj Loc Proc *(be) in, be (on)* [relational]	Exp Obj Proc *know, like, want* [mental]
process	Obj Proc *break, die, dry, tighten*	Ben Obj Proc *find, lose, win*	Obj Loc Proc *come, go, move*	Exp Obj Proc *feel, hear, see* [mental]
action	Ag Proc *dance, laugh, play, sing*	Ag Ben Proc *arm, bribe, help, supply*	Ag Loc Proc *come, go, run, walk*	Ag Exp Proc *frighten, please* [mental] *ask, question* [verbal]
action--process	Ag Obj Proc *break, dry, kill, tighten*	Ag Ben Obj Proc *buy, give, sell, accept*	Ag Obj Loc Proc *bring, place, put, take*	Ag Exp Obj Proc *ask, say, tell, speak* [verbal]

12.3.3 Power to determine (Dik)

Like Chafe (1970), Dik (1978) uses the parameters of control and stativity (dynamicity) to make the most general distinctions in the typology of figures (or states of affairs, to use his term). One difference is that Dik intersects the two parameters so that there are controlled states in his typology rather than only controlled processes ("action processes" in Chafe's terms); in all, there are four basic types of state of affairs: actions, positions, processes, and states. They are tabulated in Table 12(7) with a simple example of each type.

Table 12(7): Dik's basic types of state of affairs

	controlled	uncontrolled
dynamic	action John ran away	process John fell down
static	position John stayed motionless	state Roses are red

Each type of state of affairs, action, process, etc., can have one or more arguments. For example, John ran away, John read a book, John gave Peter a book, John sent a book to London, and John took a book from the shelf are all actions.

Dik (op cit.: 35) argues that the two parameters "enable us to define a number of selection restrictions pertaining to nuclear predications taken as a whole in a simple way". The examples he gives are (i) orders and requests, and promises, (ii) Manner, Beneficiary (Behalf in our terms), and Instrument (a kind of Means in our terms). These fall into two groups; the first is concerned with MOOD and the second with CIRCUMSTANCES. According to Dik, their distributions correlate with the distinction between controlled and not controlled as shown in Table 12(8).

We comment on each of these two groups in turn.

(i) **Mood** is an interpersonal system rather than an experiential one. What is at issue in the direct speech imperatives is whether a participant can function as Subject or not; according to Dik's claim, it can only be the Subject if the state of affairs is controlled. However, we would suggest that there are two different notions here. The first is the experiential notion of a participant's control of (the execution of) a process, while the second is the interpersonal notion of modal responsibility (see Halliday, 1985: Ch. 4).

Thus, in an imperative clause the Subject is the participant that is made responsible for the command. In examples such as

```
Fall asleep, will you.
Don't be stupid; be intelligent instead!
```

(neither of which is at all problematic) one participant is given modal responsibility, even though the participant assigned this responsibility may not normally be thought of as being in control of the process from an experiential point of view. Such examples are possible precisely because modal responsibility and "control" are metafunctionally distinct variables; there is merely an unmarked association between them. Thus the main constraint is an interpersonal one: the modally responsible participant, the Subject, of an imperative clause has to be an interactant — the speaker, the addressee or the combination of the two: *Be quiet; go to sleep! Be patient! Be guided by your parents! Don't be scared! Don't get mad, get even!* are all clauses with an implicit addressee Subject, assigned the responsibility of making the command a success, regardless of the participant role.

Table 12(8): States of affairs and "selection restrictions"; shaded areas ruled out by Dik's typology

	MOOD		CIRCUMSTANTIATION	
	orders & requests	promises	behalf	instrument
+ control	John, come here!		John cut down the tree for my sake	John cut down the tree with an axe
	Bill ordered John to be polite	John promised Bill to be polite	John remained in the hotel for my sake	John kept himself in balance with a counter-weight
- control	John, fall asleep!		The tree fell down for my sake	The tree fell down with an axe
	Bill ordered John to be intelligent	John promised Bill to be intelligent	The tree was red for my sake	John knew the answer with his intelligence

(ii) The second set of considerations have to do with **circumstances**. It is important to note that Dik has chosen to focus on circumstances rather than on participants: given that participants are more nuclear to (more directly involved in) a process than circumstances, one would expect them to rank higher in their influence on the typology of figures than the less central circumstances. Since we have taken participant organization as the starting point for our figure typology, our typology and Dik's notion of control may complement each other: see Figure 12-10. Moreover, if we take the more nuclear part of a figure as the primary basis for a typology, it is clear which elements have to be considered — the Process and the participants involved in it. If we take circumstances as a primary basis, we have to decide which circumstances should be considered. Why the ones selected by Dik and not, for example, Matter? If we select Matter as a central criterion, the parameter of projection would be more important than that of control since it seems only figures that can project (essentially sensing and saying) can have a circumstance of Matter.[4]

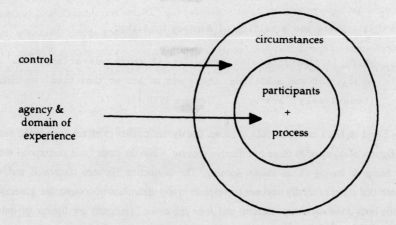

Fig. 12-10: Parameters and nuclearity

Agent is related to Means (see Halliday, 1985: 139) and it seems reasonable that the presence of the Means depends on the control exercised by the Agent. But what about Behalf: does it really depend on the control of an explicit Agent controlling the process? Consider for example:

The door was ajar for the sake of the cat.

The air-conditioning was off for our sake.

Dik characterizes the distribution of various types of Manner (-quality) in terms of dynamicity as well as control. He suggests that states (-control, -dynamic) are not compatible with Manner (-quality), while other actions, positions, and processes are compatible with various subtypes. But consider the following example of the state of

---

[4] This is borne out by text counts. For example, in a roughly 90,000 word sample from Time magazine, circumstances of Matter marked by *about* occur with 'sensing' and 'saying' and not with doing and being except where being involves a mental Attribute.

existence, taken from a discussion about the existence of acts (our bolding of the expression of manner):[5]

> Short arguments for their existence ['the existence of acts', MAKH & CM]
> are easy enough to come by. Here is one I rather like.
>
> (1) Sirhan killed Kennedy
>
> is true; and surely it is equivalent to
>
> (1') There was a killing of Kennedy by Sirhan,
>
> which is therefore also true. But if there was at any time an
> entity that was a killing, there was an act at that time. So there
> (**tenselessly**) are acts. (Thomson, 1977: 13)

Based on Dik's examples only, it seems that dynamic states of affairs correspond either to figures of doing or to those of effective sensing, while the static ones correspond either to being & having or to middle sensing. The distinction between controlled and not controlled states of affairs does not correspond to any distinction of comparable generality. Thus both *John ran away* (action) and *John fell down* (process) are figures of doing. Similarly, both *John remained in the hotel* (position) and *The substance is red* (state) are figures of being & having.

On the other hand, if we take our own types of figure as point of departure, in this survey of his typology, certain other discrepancies appear. First, Dik does not give any examples of figures of **saying**. Secondly, **doings** are all dynamic, and **being & having** figures are all static. Thirdly, as far as **sensing** is concerned, there are a few examples of middle **sensing** figures, which are states; and there is one example of an effective sensing, *The dog frightened John*, which is interpreted as a process (in Dik's sense). Sensings do not form a homogeneous class in Dik's typology; nor does he accept Experiencer (cf. Senser) and Experienced (cf. Phenomenon) as functions (1978: 41-43):

> ... experiences are conceptualized within the model of non-experiences, and different
> analogies are operative both within and across languages. There is no single underlying
> semantic representation of experiences, and no special functions need to be assigned to
> the Experiencer and the Experienced. That some experience is involved will result from
> the interpretation of the meaning of the predicate, and of the properties of the terms
> related by the predicate.[6]

---

[5] Notice how the argument hinges on the metaphorical reconstrual of (1) as (1')!

[6] Incidentally, we may note that this last observation could be applied to the distinction between controlled and uncontrolled (e.g. action vs. process).

The different expressions of experiences cited by Dik are

Example	Dik's type	Our type
John was afraid of the dog	state	being & having: intensive
John had a great fear of the dog	state	being & having: possessive
The dog frightened John	process	sensing

The first two examples are figures of being & having, in our terms; further, they are metaphorical versions of *John feared the dog* (cf. Chapter 6, Sections 6.8 and Chapter 11, Section 11.3 above). Since they are metaphorical, they do not constitute arguments against recognizing a congruent representation of a class of mental processes — any more than an example like *Henry began his walk* is an argument against recognizing *Henry* [Actor] *began to walk* [Process] as a figure of doing. Grammatical metaphors do reorganize experience; that is one reason why they are identified as metaphors, rather than simply being incorporated into the congruent options. Since they are sensings of the affective type, the first two examples have in common with their congruent equivalents the possibility of a **fact** as Phenomenon: *John feared that the others had lost their way, John was afraid that the others had lost their way* ['because of the (possible) fact that'], *John had a great fear the others had lost their way*. (All in the senses of 'was distressed by the (possible) fact that'.)

In the third example, *The dog frightened John,* the experience is represented "as if some Force works on the experiencer". In our view, this is not an argument against the interpretation of the example as a figure of sensing; rather, it simply reflects the ergative interpretation of it with *the dog* as Agent, comparable to Dik's Force in this particular case, and *John* as Medium. In other words, in our model both interpretations of the example are captured simultaneously: *The dog* [Agent/Phenomenon] *frightened* [Process] *John* [Medium/Senser]. The ergative interpretation brings out its agnate relation to examples like *The wind* [Agent/Actor] *opened* [Process]*the door* [Medium/Goal]; the transitive interpretation preserves its relation to *John* [Medium/Senser] *feared* [Process]*the dog* [Range/Phenomenon], as does the identity of *John* as Medium in both *John feared the dog* and *The dog frightened John.* In other words, a figure of sensing, configured as Senser + Process + Phenomenon, can be represented either as the Phenomenon impinging on the Senser's mental processing (effective: Phenomenon as Agent) or as the Senser's mental processing ranging over the Phenomenon (middle: Phenomenon as Range) — see Chapter 4, Section 4.3.2.3.1 above. This kind of a reversal of perspective on the figure (like/please, fear/frighten, believe/convince, etc.) is a special feature of sensing and one important reason for recognizing it as a distinct type. (This is also true of the metaphorical variant; cf. *John was afraid of the dog : The dog was scary [to John].*)

The sensing example discussed by Dik, *The dog frightened John,* is phenomenal rather than metaphenomenal. Consequently, it does not illustrate one of the other reasons for recognizing sensing as a distinct type: as we have seen (reference as above), a figure of sensing may combine with a metaphenomenon or fact (*It frightened/surprised/pleased John that there was no reply to his letter.*) They are, of course, quite different from figures of doing in this respect. For example, while metaphenomena can please and frighten conscious beings (sensing), they cannot open doors (doing).

Table 12(9) shows the comparison of Dik's typology of states of affairs with our typology of figures.

Table 12(9): Dik's typology and the process types

	doing	sensing	saying	being & having
action	John ran away			
process	John fell down	The dog frightened John [effective]		
position				John stayed motionless
state		John saw a beautiful bird [middle]		Roses are red

As the table shows clearly, Dik's account does not embody any generalizations about figures of sensing; it takes no account of projection, reversibility, the wide range of possible entities serving as Phenomenon, or the constraint on the Senser requiring it to be conscious. It also fails to recognize saying as a distinct type, where again projection is a major consideration. Dik's account thus does not recognize what, according to our interpretation, the grammar construes as the symbolic centre of the universe. Being & having is split between positions and states; and examples such as *John became the leader; the milk turned sour* would presumably be categorized as process. Since being & having is fragmented, the generalization that the different types of expansion (elaboration, extension, and enhancement) are manifested as different subtypes of being & having — intensive, possessive, and circumstantial — would be difficult to make. Yet such generalizations are needed to explain the nucleus of these figures (process + participants) and the role they play in sequences, especially those involving projection.

12.4 Foley & Van Valin

12.4.1 Two sets of semantic roles according to specificity/ subsumption

Foley & Van Valin (1984: Ch. 2) characterize their approach to transitivity within 'Role and Reference Grammar' as follows:

> One of the most fundamental problems in the analysis of clause structure is the characterization of predicates and the semantic relations which obtain between them and their arguments. ... In this chapter we will develop a system for capturing the semantic role structure of the clause. This system is based on an opposition between the notions of actor and undergoer, on the one hand, and a program of lexical decomposition of predicates into a set of primitive predicates and operators, on the other.

As the quote indicates, they propose two sets of semantic roles:

macro-roles: These are "generalized semantic relations between a predicate and its argument": **actor, undergoer.**

token-specific semantic relations: Verbs are decomposed into predicates, general operators (DO, BECOME) and connectives (CAUSE); and token-specific semantic relations (thematic relations) are assigned according to this semantic representation of verbs: **agent, effector, locative, theme, patient**.

It seems to us that there are two advances here over 'classical' case grammar:

(i) macro-roles are introduced, making a number of generalizations possible, in particular in the 'inter-face' to syntactic functions, for example in the statement of voice (Actor vs. Undergoer as Subject)

(ii) specific 'case roles' are identified on a more principled basis, with reference to verb classification.

But, interpreted in systemic terms, the relationship between the two sets of roles, macro-roles and token-specific semantic relations, is one of delicacy. This does not capture the systemic insight that a transitivity system in one language may embody complementary perspectives (e.g., ergative + transitive); and that different languages use different transitivity models (contrast English and Tagalog). The differences between RRG and the systemic-functional account of grammar (SFG) in this respect can be tabulated as follows.

Relationship between two sets of roles:	RRG	SFG
difference of perspective	(None)	ergative model and transitive model
difference of delicacy	macro-roles and token-specific semantic relations	generalized ergative roles and specific transitive roles

In contrast to the descriptive transitivity categories used in SFG, the RRG categories are universal in the etic sense (p. 28):

> These constructs have the same status as Jakobsonian distinctive features; languages employ different sets of them in a variety of ways, but they provide the basis for a unified description of aspects of phonological systems. Thus the concepts to be developed in this chapter should be considered etic categories out of which the analyst constructs emic analyses of the verb systems of particular languages.

12.4.2 Macro-roles

The macro-roles, actor and undergoer, are characterized as follows (p. 29):

> **actor**: "the argument of a predicate which expresses the participant which performs, effects, instigates, or controls the situation denoted by the predicate"

> **undergoer**: "the argument which expresses the participant which does not perform, initiate, or control any situation but rather is affected by it in some way"

Foley and Van Valin give the following introductory example:

```
The hunter shot the bear          The bear was shot by the hunter
Actor           Undergoer          Undergoer          Actor
```

The example illustrates that Actor and Undergoer may be mapped onto "syntactic subject" and "syntactic object" in different ways. Foley & Van Valin point out that this is true also of "single-argument predicates":

```
John ran down the street          The janitor suddenly became ill
Actor                              Undergoer

Mary swam for an hour              The door opened
Actor                              Undergoer

The boy went to the store         Fritz was very unhappy
Actor                              Undergoer
```

Since they are *generalized* roles, Actor and Undergoer are not equivalent to case roles or thematic relations. Both Actor and Undergoer can range over a number of more

specific case roles. Foley and Van Valin give the following examples to illustrate this
point:

```
Colin killed the taipan        Phil threw the ball to the umpire
Actor/                                          Undergoer/
Agent                                           Theme

The rock shattered the mirror   The avalanche crushed the cottage
Actor/                                          Undergoer/
Instrument                                      Patient

The lawyer received a telegram  The arrow hit the target
Actor/                                          Undergoer/
Recipient, Goal                                 Locative

The dog senses the earthquake   The mugger robbed Fred of $ 50.00
Actor/                                          Undergoer/
Experiencer                                     Source

The sun emits radiation         The announcer presented Mary
Actor/                                          Undergoer/
Source                                          Recipient/
                                                Goal
                        with the award.
```

The characterization of Actor and Undergoer does not differentiate the ergative and
transitive perspectives on transitivity. Even though the characterization of Actor and
Undergoer suggests that they correspond to the transitive pair Actor + Goal, Actor and
Undergoer are not in fact applied in this way. For instance, the Undergoer corresponds to
Actor [SFG] as well as to Goal [SFG], and in this respect, it resembles Medium [SFG];
but Actor [RRG] may also correspond to Medium, as the examples in Table 12(10)
show.

Table 12(10): Comparison of Actor & Undergoer with Agent & Medium

	Agent	Medium
Actor	[material & effective:] Colin killed the taipan	[material & middle:] The sun emits radiation [mental & middle:] The dog senses the earthquake
Undergoer		[material & effective:] Phil threw the ball to the umpire [material & middle:] The door opened [relational & middle:] Fritz was very unhappy

Contrast the characterizations of Actor and Undergoer in RRG given above with those
of Medium and Agent (Halliday, 1985: 146-7):

Medium: "Every process has associated with it one participant that is the key
figure in that process; this is the one through which the process is actualized, and

without which there would be no process at all. ... It is the entity through the
medium of which the process comes into existence."

Agent: "... in addition to the Medium, there may be another participant functioning
as an external cause. ... Either the process is represented as self-engendering, in
which case there is no separate Agent; or it is represented as engendered from
outside, in which case there is another participant functioning as Agent."

The Actor-Undergoer model in RRG, when applied to English, does not capture the
significant generalizations embodied in this notion of Medium, such as

- the Medium is restricted relative to the Process in the same way regardless of
  whether the clause is effective (+ Agent) or middle: **the door** opened : she
  opened **the door** :: **the ice** melted : she melted **the ice** :: **the milk** spilt :
  she spilt **the milk** :: **she** grieved (at the news) : the news grieved **her**

- the Medium is the participant that is most closely bonded to the Process by
  lexical collocation.

- the Medium is the element which combines with the Process to form the clause
  nucleus; it is this nucleus that determines how the process is subclassified and
  interpreted (cf. run + dog; run + factory; run + nose; cut + hair; cut + grass; cut
  + meat; kill/ die + animal; kill/ die + light; kill/ die + motion) and which carries
  the main systemic potential (contrast open + door : open + bank account; run +
  factory : run + jogger).

- the Medium is the one participant that cannot be treated circumstantially; hence
  (other than in one special kind of clause, the medio-passive) it is never mediated
  by a preposition.

12.4.3 Token-specific roles and verb classification

Foley & Van Valin (1984: 33-4) note that there are two approaches to token-specific roles
(relations):

(i) Fillmore's (1968) case grammar: Here a number of case roles is identified as a
universal set. These roles exist independently of (classes of) predicates, though
predicates (verbs) may be classified according to case frames.

(ii) Gruber's (1965, 1976) & Jackendoff's (1972, 1976) thematic relations: These
are explicitly derived from the semantic decomposition of predicates. Thematic
relations "are a function of the argument positions of abstract predicates" such as

CAUSE, and GO; for instance, GO is a three-place predicate: GO (x, y, z), where x = theme, y = source and z = goal [in the sense of destination].

Foley & Van Valin follow the second approach, but they base their decomposition not on Jackendoff's work but on Dowty's (1979) verb classification, which is in turn based on Vendler's (1967) verb classes. As we saw in Chapter 12, Section 12.2 above, Vendler's typology is based in the first instance on considerations of how the Process unfolds in time — its temporal profile. In contrast, the process types used in systemic interpretations are based on considerations of the nature of nuclear transitivity — how participants interact, what kinds of entities they are, whether projection is possible, etc. Note that semantic decomposition is a way of handling paradigmatic, systemic relations as if they were syntagmatic: general features such as 'go' and 'cause' are actually posited as constituent elements of the abstract semantic decompositions of verbs/ predicates. See further the next section below.

12.4.4 Dowty's (1979) development of Vendler's verb classes

Dowty bases his account on Vendler's four classes of verb — states, activities, accomplishments and achievements. The criteria used by Dowty (1979) for distinguishing states, activities, accomplishments and achievements, are summarized by Foley & Van Valin (1984: 37); they are essentially concerned with establishing the temporal profile of the process unfolding in time (see Table 12(11)).

The basic program quoted by Foley & Van Valin is described by Dowty (1979: 71) as follows:

> The idea is that the different aspectual properties of the various kinds of verbs can be explained by postulating a single homogeneous class of predicates – stative predicates -- plus three or four sentential operatives and connectives. English stative verbs are supposed to correspond directly to these stative predicates in logical structure, while verbs of the other categories have logical structures that consist of one or more stative predicates embedded in complex sentences formed with these 'aspectual' connectives and operators.

It is important to note that Dowty is here concerned with explaining **aspectual** properties of verbs — i.e., properties that have to do with the unfolding of the Process in time and not, in the first instance, with the Process as part of a transitivity configuration with participants and circumstances.

The operators and connectives are as follows:

DO — "under the unmediated control of the agent" (Dowty, 1979: 76)

BECOME — "where ϕ is any predicate formula and t is any time, BECOME ϕ is true at t if ϕ is true at t and false at t- 1".   (Dowty, 1979: 118)

CAUSE — a logical connective between events (cf. our enhancing sequences).

Table 12(11): Criteria for distinguishing verb classes

		states	activities	accompl-ishments	achieve-ments
examples		know, believe, desire, love; have	run, walk, swim, push a cart, drive a car	paint a picture, make a chair, deliver a sermon, draw a circle, recover from illness	find, lose, die; recognize, spot
	meets non-stative tests	--	√	√	?
temporal profile	has habitual interpretation in simple present tense	--	√	√	√
	V for an hour, spend an hour V-ing	OK	OK	OK	bad
	V in an hour, take an hour to V	bad	bad	OK	OK
	V for an hour entails V at all times in the hour	√	√	--	N.A.
	x is V-ing entails x has V-ed	N.A.	√	--	N.A.
	complement of 'stop' [i.e., in phase with 'stop']	OK	OK	OK	bad
	complement of 'finish' [i.e., in phase with 'finish']	bad	bad	OK	bad
	x V-ed in an hour entails x was V-ing during that hour	N.A.	N.A.	√	--
other	ambiguity with 'almost'	--	--	√	--
	occurs with 'studiously, attentively, carefully' etc.	bad	OK	OK	bad

The logical structures of the semantics of the four verb classes are given in Table 12(12) (Foley & Van Valin's Table 2, p. 39).

Table 12(12): Verb classes and logical structure

verb class	logical structure
state	predicate' (x)
achievement	BECOME predicate' (x)
activity	DO (x, (predicate' (x))
accomplishment	ϕ CAUSE ψ (where ϕ is normally an activity verb and ψ is an achievement verb)*

NOTE: * This statement is taken from Foley & Van Valin; in fact, however, ϕ and ψ would not be verbs but logical structures involving interpretations of verbs.

12.4.5 Verb classes in RRG

As noted earlier, the semantic decomposition illustrated here is really a way of handling paradigmatic, systemic relations in syntagmatic terms. However, the 'operators' and 'connectives', instead of being interpreted concretely as components of the logical structure of predicate (syntagmatic interpretation), can be construed paradigmatically, as systemic features: see Figure 12-11.

This systemic interpretation raises interesting questions which are not brought out in Foley & Van Valin's decompositional approach: whether the systems are strictly experiential or quasi-logical, and whether the set of features is exhaustive or should be increased to include other types of expansion (cf. Chapter 3, Section 3.2 where these are shown to be pervasive throughout the semantic system).

The status of the Vendlerian verb classes has to be questioned. Foley and Van Valin (p. 39) note:

> there are a number of interrelations among the verb classes which are not easily expressed in the Vendler four-way classification ... For example, activity verbs may become accomplishment verbs if a definite goal is added, e.g. *walk* (activity) versus *walk to the store* (accomplishment).

Table 12(13): The RRG verb classes

TYPES			EXAMPLES	ROLES
state	locational		*be in, at, on, under*	theme, locative
	non-locational	state/ condition of being	*be tall, sick, dead, happy, afraid, fat*	patient
		possession	*have*	locative, theme
		perception	*saw, smell*	locative, theme
		cognition	*know, think, believe*	locative, theme
achieve-ment				BECOME + state
activity	potential controllable	controlled	*smile intentionally; walk, swim, talk; ignore*	agent
		uncontrolled	*smile instinctively*	effector
	motional		*fall, roll, rotate*	theme
accomplish-ment			*break glass*	x CAUSE (BECOME state)

This is one important reason why these classes are not **verb** classes — the classification actually derives not only from the verb but also from participants and circumstances: whether or not they are present, and if so, whether or not they are bounded, specific, etc.. This again suggests (cf. Section 3.1) that the Vendlerian classification is not a system that is inherent in the general system of the grammar or the semantics: it is merely a possible interpretation of the profile of the unfolding of a process in time, one that is determined by many factors. Foley and Van Valin (Section 2.5, pp. 47-53) suggest how

Dowty's typology and logical decomposition can be used to derive case roles from predicate structures in a principled way. They recognize some further subclasses of states and activities. The different types and semantic relations they establish are tabulated in Table 12(13) above.

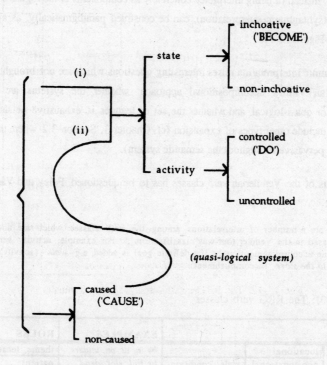

Fig. 12-11: Systemic interpretation of Dowty's verb classes

The types recognized here are interpreted in system network form (states and activities) in Figure 12-12. The semantic roles can then be introduced by means of realization statements: see Figure 12-13. As soon as they are made explicit in this way, a number of questions arise; for example:

(i) why are 'possessive', 'perception' and 'cognition' not grouped together, since they have the same structural consequence in terms of semantic roles: + Locative, +Theme?

(ii) how are the semantic roles restricted — what kinds of entities can serve as Theme, Patient, etc.? (Note that this has to be made explicit in a system network with realization statements.)

(iii) what is the entry condition to the system network fragment shown above?

(iv) what other predictions about transitivity can be made, e.g. concerning projection? (All that the account makes explicit is the distribution of roles such as Theme, Locative, and Effector.)

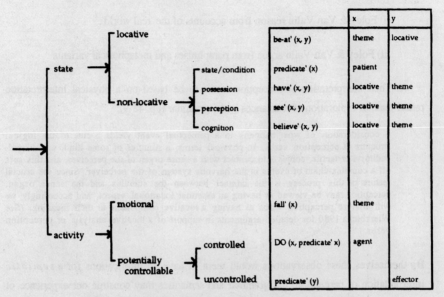

Fig. 12-12: The RRG classes interpreted systemically

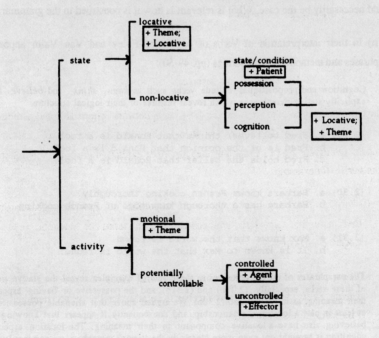

Fig. 12-13: Addition of realization statements

In their reasoning about how some of the verb types should be interpreted in terms of semantic roles, Foley & Van Valin's account differs from our systemic account of types in the ideation base in two respects:

(i) Foley & Van Valin reason from accounts of the 'real world';

(ii) Foley & Van Valin argue from paraphrases and metaphorical variants.

(i) Their interpretation of perception seems to be based on a physical interpretation rather than an exploration of reactances in the grammar (pp. 48-9):

> A consideration of what happens in a perceptual event yields a clue to the logical structure of perception verbs. In physical terms, a stimulus of some kind, e.g. visual, auditory, or tactile, comes into contact with a sense organ of the perceiver, and this sets off a complex chain of events in the nervous system of the perceiver. Since the crucial feature of this process is the contact between the stimulus and the sense organ, perception may be viewed as having an essential locational aspect, and accordingly we will analyze perception verbs as having a locative component to their meaning. (See Wierzbicka 1980 for detailed arguments in support of a locative analysis of perception verbs.)

By themselves, these observations would seem to have no implications for a *semiotic* interpretation of perception: the grammar and semantics may construe our experience of the world in the same way as (modern) science does, but there is no reason why this should necessarily be the case. What is relevant is how it is construed in the grammar.

(ii) In their interpretation of verbs of cognition, Foley and Van Valin appeal to paraphrases and metaphorical renderings (pp. 49-50):

> Cognition and propositional attitude verbs such as *know, think* and *believe* have explicitly stative paraphrases which reveal features of their logical structure.

(2.29) a. Fred believes/ thinks that Ronald is a fool.
       b. Fred is of the opinion that Ronald is a fool.
       c. Fred holds the belief that Ronald is a fool.

(2.30) a. Barbara knows French cooking thoroughly.
       b. Barbara has a thorough knowledge of French cooking.

(2.31) a. Max knows that the world is round.
       b. It is known to Max that the world is round.

> The paraphrases of the (a) sentences in these sets of examples reveal the stative nature of these verbs, especially (2.29b) and (2.31b), and the possessive or 'having' aspect of their meaning, as in (2.29c) and (2.30b). We argued above that alienable possession is at least in part a locational relationship, and consequently it appears that knowing and believing also have a locative component to their meaning. The location aspect of cognition is brought out even more clearly in the various metaphors we commonly use. ... In these metaphors and many others thinking is characterized as having something in or on one's mind. Thus an important part of the meaning of cognition verbs is locational, and from the examples in (2.29) - (2.32) we may conclude that the thought, belief, or knowledge is located with respect to the thinker, believer, or knower's mind.

This line of argumentation seems very similar to the strategy that was used in classical transformational grammar: one construction is observed to have a paraphrase (often metaphorical, as we can now see), and the construction is then analysed as if it was in this paraphrased form — derived from it, in the case of transformational grammar. The fact that we find systematic pairs of process : process + range such as (doing) *dance : do a dance* :: (sensing) *know* : (being & having) *have knowledge* is significant; but it does not mean that *dance* is semantically "really" 'do a dance' or that *know* is semantically "really" 'have knowledge'. If we argued along these lines, most of grammar could be reconstrued metaphorically as forms of being & having, realized by relational clauses (as we saw in Chapter 6); compare:

```
She is exploring the other alternative :
She is in engaged in the exploration of the other alternative

He is patrolling :
He is on patrol

They are fighting :
They are at war

It hasn't rained for seven years so forests burn frequently :
The seven-year lack of rain leads to frequent forest fires
```

Such interpretative reductions tend to obscure the multiplicity of perspectives built into the transitivity system.

Before leaving the RRG verb classes, we can intersect them with the primary types of figure we have posited here. The comparison is based on the examples discussed in Foley & Van Valin (1984): see Table 12(14).

Table 12(14): RRG verb classes and our types of figure

			being & having	sensing	saying	doing
state	locational		√			
	non-locational	state/ condition of being	√	affection ??		
		possession	√			
		perception		√		
		cognition		√		
achieve-ment				recognize realize		
activity	potentially controllable	controlled		ignore		√
		uncontrolled				√
	motional					√
accomplish-ment						√

There are some types within the ideation base where it is uncertain what the equivalent RRG classes are: meteorological, effective sensing (the 'please' type), affective sensing, saying, identifying, and causative ascriptive being & having. The absence of saying from the list conforms to the pattern we have found with other similar typologies; yet saying is significant as the key to the construal of projection and non-material experience. Let us now turn to the account of participant roles.

12.4.6 Relationship between the two sets of roles

Foley & Van Valin characterize the mapping between macro-roles and 'token-specific' ones as follows (pp. 54-5):

> Actors may be agents, effectors, or locatives, depending primarily upon the verb it (sic) cooccurs with. In any given clause, although arguments bearing more than one of these semantics relations may be present, the actor may be interpreted as only one of them, and the possibilities for interpreting the actor, i.e. the linking of NPs with argument positions in the logical structure of the verb, always follow a strict hierarchy.

> ... Thus the hierarchy of accessibility to (or interpretation of) actorhood is agent > effector > locative, when more than one of the relations occurs in the clause.

> The situation regarding the undergoer is more complex, because a given verb with a single logical structure may allow two arguments bearing different semantic relations to be undergoer. There are no such variable choices for the actor.

> An example of variable undergoer assignment is ... a. *John gave the book to Bill* b. *John gave Bill the book.*

Foley & Van Valin summarize their observations concerning the relationship between macro-roles and 'token-specific' semantic roles: see Figure 12-14.

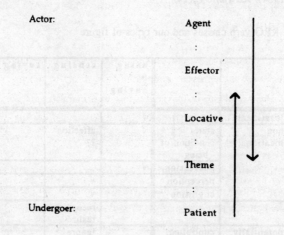

Fig. 12-14: Foley & Van Valin's mapping between the two sets of roles

As noted earlier, the macro-roles are seen as an 'interface' to syntactic functions such as Subject and Object. They facilitate the specification of a number of syntactic constructions such as voice (active/ passive).

As noted at the beginning, the RRG account at this point rests on the notion of **generality**. However, the systemic accounts of transitivity in e.g. English and Chinese rest on the notion of alternative **perspectives**. The participant roles Medium, Agent, Range and Beneficiary embody not just a different degree of generality from the process-specific participant roles Actor, Goal, Recipient; Senser, Phenomenon; etc. but, more importantly, a different perspective. They can capture different kinds of facts about the transitivity system of a language. Moreover, as Martin's (1996a) work on Tagalog transitivity shows, it is important to allow for variation in transitivity models across languages: Tagalog embodies a model that is significantly different from the models English transitivity is based on.

In RRG, transitivity is treated within the semantics: macro-roles and 'token-specific' roles are **semantic roles**, and the 'token-specific' ones are introduced with the logical structure of semantic predicates (together with the operators DO and BECOME, and the connective CAUSE). In contrast, we treat transitivity both within semantics (the paradigmatic and syntagmatic organization of figures) and within lexicogrammar (the grammar of transitivity): it is a system construed within the content plane of language — both in the ideational component in the lexicogrammar and in the ideation base. This two-stratal approach to transitivity makes it possible to model the resource of grammatical metaphor and is fundamental to work on multilingual systems for generating text.

12.5 Inherent indeterminacy, and variation in systemic interpretations

We have drawn attention at various points to the overall indeterminacy of language, something that we see as a necessary condition of its ability to function in the construal of experience. Our experience of the 'goings-on' in and around ourselves is so rich and many-faceted that no semiotic system that attempted to impose on it a rule-bound, determinate frame of reference would be 'functional' as a resource for survival.

We have tried to show such indeterminacy as a positive feature, and build it into our suggested meta-construal — not as some wayward or exceptional extravagance but as an unmarked state of affairs that is recognized to be the norm. To this extent, our grammatics becomes itself a metaphor for the grammar — that is, to the extent that we are able to enact this indeterminacy in our own representations.

In our treatment of figures in the ideation base, we stressed the fluidity of the boundaries among the various types of figure: doing-&-happening, sensing, saying, being-&-having. We construe these in the grammar as a system of process types: at primary delicacy, material, mental, verbal, relational. These are sections on a continuum — or, better, regions in an n-dimensional semantic space; but they are not demarcated by any uniquely self-selecting set of criteria. A stratified semiotic defines three perspectives, which (following the most familiar metaphor) we refer to as 'from above', 'from roundabout', and 'from below': looking at a given stratum from above means treating it as the expression of some content, looking at it from below means treating it as the content of some expression, while looking at it from roundabout means treating it in the context of (i.e. in relation to other features of) its own stratum. Adopting this **trinocular** perspective we have identified the various process types in terms of their nuclear transitivity; this seems to us the most operationally useful approach, since it takes account of what they mean, how they are expressed, and what their systemic potential is — without privileging any one perspective at the expense of the other two.

However, even if we adopt this approach, this still does not impose a single determinate form on the description. As we have already noted, Martin, in his systemic treatment of processes in Tagalog (1996a), offers a different interpretation of nuclear transitivity: he defines it in terms of orientation, rather than configuration, and hence operates with a significantly different concept of participant function. And even within our own configurational model of English there is often considerable 'play'. A good example of this is Fawcett (1987). We have referred earlier to Fawcett's work in systemic theory, especially his COMMUNAL natural language processing system; the overall architecture of Fawcett's text generation model is somewhat different from Penman, but the basic design of the grammar is the same. It differs, however, in the treatment of relational processes, and in the distinction made between relational and material.

The frontier between relational and material processes is typically fuzzy, and as Fawcett points out the grammar's construal of possession and circumstantiation (the latter prototypified by location in space and time) may be interpreted in more than one way. Fawcett incorporates into the "relational: possessive" category, processes of giving and acquiring; reduces the circumstantial to locational processes only; and includes within these, processes of going and sending (for discussion of this area, see Davidse, 1996b). As is to be expected, this alternative analysis embodies certain generalizations that are not made in our account of figures, and ignores certain others which are. (His abandonment of the distinction between attributive and identifying seems harder to motivate, since this cannot in fact be explained as a textual (thematic) system in the way that Fawcett proposes; cf. Davidse, 1996a.) The point to be brought out here is that there is no unique 'correct description' of a semiotic system, or of any phenomena that have to do with meaning. Stratal relations are not relations of cause & effect, and a stratified system cannot be reduced to constructions of content-expression pairs.

This is not to say, of course, when a choice is made among a set of alternative descriptions for representing features in grammar that are inherently indeterminate, like the types of process in a transitivity system, that the choice is insignificant, or merely random. On the contrary: it resonates throughout the grammatics as a whole (or should do, if the description has any claim to be comprehensive). Again there is the analogy between the grammatics and the grammar: just as no region of the grammar is isolated from the rest, so every descriptive statement has consequences throughout the description. Fawcett's alternative model for relational processes, with its particular features such as treating 'giving' and 'placing' as agentive possessives and locatives ('make ... have', 'make ... be at') rather than as material dispositives, has to be understood in its total explanatory context: (i) in relation to its repercussions within the transitivity system, both the trinocular perspective on transitivity itself (from above, as generalizations about meaning; from roundabout, its consequences for agnateness, delicacy and the move towards lexis; from below, as regularities in the realization) and the overall topology of the content — transitivity in relation to the semantic construal of causality, agency, disposal, and so on; (ii) in relation to Fawcett's architectural design, which differs from ours in having a single system-structure cycle for the two strata of semantics and lexicogrammar (his "syntax") and then adding a further level of description that is expressed in cognitive terms.

12.6 Conclusion

In this part, we have engaged in metalinguistic typology and comparison, trying to bring out theoretical and descriptive similarities between other approaches and our own. We have focussed on approaches that were developed in the context of cognitive science and natural language processing. Hence we have not taken up theoretical issues in social semiotics and functional linguistics within the European tradition, nor have we explored descriptive contributions such as Ernst Leisi (1955), Eugene Nida (1975), Adolf Noreen's (1904-12) monumental *Vårt Språk*, or Roget's *Thesaurus*. Among approaches that have been taken up in cognitive science and natural language processing, we have not discussed work located within a lexical perspective, such as those of Igor Mel'chuk and others (including lexical functions) and of Levin (e.g. 1993), or the various research projects in NLP of an encyclopaedic nature. We have also not been able to deal with important studies of particular topics within semantics, such as Kiparsky & Kiparsky's (1970) classic treatment of facts, or Givón's (1980) and Ransom's (1986) approaches to the semantics of so-called complementation. There are many similarities among all these approaches; but there are also significant differences, and it seems worth pointing out that these can often be traced back to the nature of the semantic system itself. There seem to be two main reasons for this.

(i) The system often embodies **complementarities** providing more than one way of construing similar types of experience — for example, construing perception either as inert sensing or as active behaviour, or construing phenomena of all kinds either congruently or metaphorically. If one is concerned with a restricted, designed semiotic system, then the appropriate strategy, when one is faced with more than one option in natural language, may be to select one canonical form; but if one's concern is with language as a whole, the only response that will hold up in the long term is to acknowledge the variation and explore its function.

(ii) The system is **polysystemic** from the point of view of contextual diversification: given a particular context type or a set of related types, some parts of the overall semantic system will be deployed in a systematic way whereas others will remain inactive. For instance, if contexts where the goal is to instruct somebody in a procedure were the only source of evidence for the semantic system, we could safely ignore figures of sensing and saying and the logical relationship of projection. And yet in the general system, which is the overall meaning-making resource deployed across all the different types of context, these figures and sequences turn out to be essential both to the functioning of the semantic system and to our own understanding of its fundamental principles.

Part V:

Language and the construal of experience

13. Language as a multifunctional system-&-process

13.1 Types of system-&-process

We are treating language as a semiotic system, and it may be helpful to locate this concept within the context of the history of ideas, albeit in a very sketchy fashion. As we conceive of it, the term "semiotic" is framed within a linear taxonomy of "physical — biological — social — semiotic"; and the term "system" is a shortened form of "system-&-process", there being no single word that encapsulates both the synoptic and the dynamic perspectives (we have referred to the term "climatic system" with the same observation on how it is to be understood).

Why a "linear" taxonomy? There is an ordering among these four types of system, which we can appreciate most readily, perhaps, at the "meta" level: this is the order in which they have come to be studied and interpreted, in the past five hundred years of human scholarship. We should add here, perhaps, that we emphatically do not equate history of scholarship with the history of western scholarship; in our own interpretation of language we have in fact drawn explicitly on other scholarly traditions besides the western one. But it happens that, for complex historical reasons, it was European thinkers who first cracked the codes — that is, who took our understanding of phenomena up one level, on to what came to be recognized as the "scientific" plane; and while this is certainly not the end of the story — there are no doubt many higher levels of understanding still to be attained — it is as far as we have got up to the present. And the codes were cracked in a certain historical order: the first to be understood, at this level, were the physical systems; then the biological, and after these the social. There was a gap of a few generations between each step: the sort of interval that separated Galileo and Newton from Lamarck and Darwin, and, somewhat shortened, the latter from Marx, Weber and Durkheim. In other words, there was a certain intellectual distance to be covered in bringing a comparable kind of insight into these different types of system-&-process.

This seems quite understandable when we reflect that there is an ordering among the phenomena themselves, in the way these systems are each made up. Physical systems are just physical systems. Biological systems, however, are not just biological systems; they are at once both biological and physical. Social systems are all three: social, biological and physical. This makes them increasingly difficult for us to comprehend. This is not the same as saying that social systems are more complex than biological ones, or biological than physical; there are too many different ways in which things can be complex, for any such observation to make much sense. But they are increasingly complex *in this particular respect;* and this means that it is increasingly difficult to recognize the essential nature of the phenomena concerned. What is problematic is the relationship between the system and the instance; or, to put it another way, what is the nature of a "fact" in these different realms of experience? A biological fact is different from a physical fact, and a social fact is different again; the relationship between that which can be observed, and the system-&-process lying behind what is observed, is significantly harder to establish when the system is a social system, because the phenomena involved are simultaneously of all three kinds.

One consequence of this (and no doubt one reason for the further time it took to crack the codes) was that each new step required a shift of perspective. For understanding physical systems, the critical approach was that of measurement; the dominant theme was mathematics, and the perspective essentially a synoptic one. But this did not serve well for interpreting biological systems; these are better understood in terms of change, so the perspective had to be altered, to become dynamic, with evolution as the dominant theme. For social systems, however, the dynamic perspective by itself lacked explanatory power, and in the present century it was overtaken by another synoptic approach, the theme of structuralism. Our conception of the nature of social systems has been largely moulded in structuralist terms.

In explaining these thematic shifts in terms of intellectual movements, the challenges presented by these different domains of human experience, we are not ignoring or denying the significance of the social and political processes that were taking place throughout these centuries in Europe. To understand the development of structuralism, like that of evolutionary theory before it, it is of course necessary to place these thematic shifts in their general historical contexts. But it would be equally onesided to ignore or deny the relevance of the intellectual agenda. These make up an essential ingredient in the overall historical picture, no part of which can be detached as a single ultimate cause of all the rest.

What then of semiotic systems? Once again with apologies for the inevitable oversimplifying, let us try and identify what it is that is added with each step in the systemic progression. A biological system is a physical system with the added component of "life"; it is a living physical system. In comparable terms, a social system is a biological system with the added component of "value" (which explains the need for a synoptic approach, since value is something that is manifested in forms of structure). A semiotic system, then, is a social system with the added component of "meaning". Meaning can be thought of (and was thought of by Saussure) as just a kind of social value; but it is value in a significantly different sense — value that is construed symbolically. Meaning can only be construed symbolically, because it is intrinsically paradigmatic, as Saussure understood and built in to his own definition of valeur. Semiotic systems are social systems where value has been further transformed into meaning.

In their earliest lectures in linguistics, our students are encouraged to think of language in precisely this multimodal perspective. It can be studied as a physical system, in acoustics and in the physical aspect of articulation (air pressure measurements and so on). It can be studied as a biological system, in the physiological aspect of articulation and in the neurophysiology of the brain. It can be studied as a social system, as the primary mode of human interaction. And of course it can be studied as a semiotic system, in the core areas of lexicogrammar, phonology and semantics. If linguistics is conceived of as a discipline — that is, as defined by its object of study (in this case, language) — then it must encompass within itself theories and methods of all four different kinds.

The students are also encouraged, of course, to acknowledge semiotic systems other than that of language: forms of art, such as painting and architecture and music, ritual and other behaviour patterns; as well as ways of presenting the self in make-up and dress. Language is set apart, however, as the prototypical semiotic system, on a variety of different grounds: it is the only one that evolved specifically as a semiotic system; it is the one semiotic into which all others can be "translated"; and (the least questionable, in our view) it is the one whereby the human species as a whole, and each individual member of that species, construes experience and constructs a social order. In this last respect, all other semiotic systems are derivative: they have meaning potential only by reference to models of experience, and forms of social relationship, that have already been established in language. It is this that justifies us in taking language as the prototype of systems of meaning.

But there is one problem with this intellectual strategy: that the code for systems of this fourth type has not yet been cracked. There are two aspects to this problem. One is that we do not yet fully understand the nature of a linguistic fact: this is the problem of instantiation. The other is that we do not yet fully understand the nature of the relationship that is the semiotic analogue of the "cause : effect" of classical physics: this is the problem of realization. It is true that Saussure, and even more Hjelmslev, took important strides towards an understanding; but we are still arguing about what Saussure really meant (to us it seems that he had not clearly separated the two concepts of instantiation and realization), and Hjelmslev has largely been ignored — Sydney Lamb (e.g., 1966a,b) is almost the only person who has tried to follow through his achievements. Probably it will be well into the next century before the picture comes to be clear.

Meanwhile what has become clear is that there is the (by now) familiar interplay between phenomenon and observer. We have talked of physical, biological, social and semiotic systems as being categories of phenomena — which in an important sense they are. But they may also be thought of as different stances taken by the observer; thus we find physical and biological systems being *interpreted as* semiotic systems, in a kind of intellectual game which turns out to reveal new aspects of physical and biological processes. It is obviously beyond our scope — and indeed beyond our capabilities — to pursue these matters here. But they add a whole new dimension to our grammatics, to the concept of a theory of grammar as a metatheory of human experience.

Here we shall simply try to summarize what we mean by interpreting a natural language in this way, as the form in which human experience is construed. But in doing so we shall also say something about its other semiotic functions. We have emphasized the ideational, because this is what the present book is about. But there is a danger that the equally important, complementary function of language as the means whereby human societies are constructed may be relegated into the background; so the present chapter will provide an opportunity to put the ideation base back into its wider social-semiotic environment.

13.2 Review of modes of meaning — metafunctional and metaphorical

13.2.1 The metafunctions

We have stressed all along that a language is a system for creating meaning; and that its meaning potential has evolved around three motifs — what we refer to as the "metafunctions" of ideational, interpersonal and textual, with the ideational in turn comprising an experiential component and a logical component. These are the multiple aspects of the content plane — the grammar (in its usual sense of lexicogrammar) and the semantics. Since the powerhouse of language lies in the grammar, we shall refer to them here as aspects of the grammar; but it is important to insist that they could not be "in" the one without also being "in" the other. It makes no sense to ask whether the metafunctions are grammatical or semantic; the only possible answer would be "yes".

Ideationally, the grammar is a theory of human experience; it is our interpretation of all that goes on around us, and also inside ourselves. There are two parts to this: one the representation of the processes themselves, which we refer to as the "experiential"; the other the representation of the relations between one process and another, and it is this that we refer to as the "logical". The two together constitute the "ideational" metafunction, whereby language construes our experiential world. The word "construe" is used to suggest an intellectual construction — though one that, of course, we then use as a guide to action.

Interpersonally, the grammar is not a theory but a way of doing; it is our construction of social relationships, both those that define society and our own place in it, and those that pertain to the immediate dialogic situation. This constitutes the "interpersonal" metafunction, whereby language constructs our social collective and, thereby, our personal being. The word "construct" is used to suggest a form of enactment — though something on which we inevitably build a theory, of ourself and the various "others" to whom we relate.

Textually, the grammar is the creating of information; it engenders discourse, the patterned forms of wording that constitute meaningful semiotic contexts. From one point of view, therefore, this "textual" metafunction has an enabling force, since it is this that allows the other two to operate at all. But at the same time it brings into being a world of its own, a world that is constituted semiotically. With the textual metafunction language not only construes and enacts our reality but also becomes part of the reality that it is construing and enacting.

In all these metafunctions, the language does not take over and reproduce some readymade semantic space. There is no such space until the grammar comes along to construe it.

13.2.2 Ideational metafunction: experiential

The basic component of all experience is change: when something changes from one state to another, it **projects** itself on to our consciousness. This may be something in the external environment; we can see this happening with small babies, who are first jerked into semiosis by dramatic perturbations such as a loud noise or a flashing light. The grammar construes this experience of change in the form of a **process configuration**: the fundamental element of grammar is a clause, and the **clause** presents the parameters within which processes may unfold.

The grammar does this by deconstructing the process into component parts. Typically, as in English and many, perhaps all, other languages, these are of three kinds: first the process itself, secondly certain phenomena construed as participants in the process, and thirdly, other phenomena that are associated with the process circumstantially.

Suppose we are standing on the shore, and there is a rapid movement across our line of vision. We construe this grammatically as

  birds + are flying + across the sea

This is obviously not the only way such an experience could be "semanticized": it might be construed as a single unanalysed phenomenon, e.g. *it's winging*. Some processes are in fact construed in this way: in English, for example, meteorological processes such as *it's raining.* But in most instances the theory propounded by the grammar is that this is a composite phenomenon, an organic construction of functionally distinct parts: here, a process *are flying,* something participating in this process, namely *birds,* and a relevant circumstance *across the sea.* This allows for other things to fly across the sea, such as insects and aeroplanes; for birds to fly in other locations, such as over the trees, and to do other things than flying, such as singing or quarrelling. The meaning potential here is clearly far greater than if a different lexical item was used to construe every possible configuration.

The significant step that took place in human grammars in this context was, obviously, the evolution of common nouns — or rather, of common words, since verbs are also "common" in this sense: that is, words denoting classes rather than individuals. It is usually assumed that these evolved out of "proper" words, prototypically the names of individual persons; the ontogenetic evidence suggests that this is one source but not the only one, another source being rather in the interpersonal function. Be that as it may, construing processes in this way clearly depends on generalizing whole classes of phenomena; the grammar sets up **classes** of process, of participant and of circumstance. There are various ways of doing this; one that is familiar in many languages is by means of a taxonomy of different kinds of word, as in Figure 13-1. The classes of word may be distinguished by their internal form, or by the way they are able to enter into larger constructions (or both). Typically the most complex is the class of circumstantial elements, because these are themselves often formed as complex constructions; there may be simple words (a class of adverbs), but there may also be constructs like English prepositional phrases, the function of which is to bring in other potential participants but to bring them in indirectly, like *the sea* in *across the sea.* The theory behind this is that there are two ways in which an entity can be involved: either directly as a participant in the process, or indirectly in a circumstantial role, such as the place where the process happens. This indirect participant is often construed as participating in a kind of secondary process tangential to the main one (grammatically, a prepositional phrase is a reduced variant of a clause).

At the same time, while recognizing a general category of "process" to construe our experience of change, the grammar also recognizes that not all processes are alike. As human beings we become aware (and again we can see this in the actions of tiny infants) that phenomena fall into two distinct types: those happening outside ourselves, which we can see and hear, and those happening within our own consciousness — thoughts and feelings, and also the sensations of seeing and hearing, as distinct from whatever is seen and heard. The grammar construes this as a distinction between "material processes" and "mental processes". Mental processes are specifically attributed to conscious beings: humans, and some of our more intimate animal consorts. Languages construe this pattern in many different ways, and draw the line at different points; as always we are relating our account to the particulars of English. Here the grammar postulates a third type of process intermediate between these two: "behavioural" processes, in which inner events are externalized as bodily behaviour, like staring, thinking (in the sense of pondering) or crying.

Language itself, of course, is a form of human behaviour; but "languaging" constitutes, for the grammar, another distinct type of process, that of "verbal" (or, better, "symbolic") processes. An act of saying is not simply externalizing inner events; it is actively transforming them, into an event of a different kind. It then resembles other semiotic events, many of which do not require a conscious information source (*your diary says you have a dental appointment, the light says stop*). And these in turn shade into something else, which the grammar again construes as phenomenally distinct: relations of identity (including symbolic identity, like *red means stop*) and attribution. Expressions of this kind, which in English often have the verb *be*, hardly seem to fit the label "process" at all; but the grammar firmly represents them as such, so we call them "relational processes". They are modelled, in fact, on the two basic relationships that characterize semiotic systems: realization (identifying processes such as *this is* ('realizes') *my sister*), and instantiation (attributive processes such as *she is* ('instantiates') *a student of law*). Finally, there is the phenomenon of existing — still construed, grammatically, as a type of process. What is said to exist may be an entity, something that persists through time, like *there's a letter for you;* but it may also, in many languages, be a happening, as in *there was a fight.* Here we have something that could alternatively be construed as a material process (*people were fighting*), which suggests that "existential" processes are another intermediate type, something between the relational and the material.

This part of the grammar, then — the grammar of clauses —, constitutes a theory about the types of process that make up human experience. In English (which is probably fairly typical), the three principal categories that we are calling the material, mental and relational are rather clearly distinct on a number of formal grounds; the other three appear as mixed or intermediate types lying on the borderlines. (In fact the category of verbal process is more clearly distinct than the other two; and in view of its central place in the semantic system, we have treated it throughout the present study as a primary category.) The total picture is of a continuum; but not between two poles — rather something that we would represent in the form of a circle. Figure 13-2 shows this in diagrammatic form.

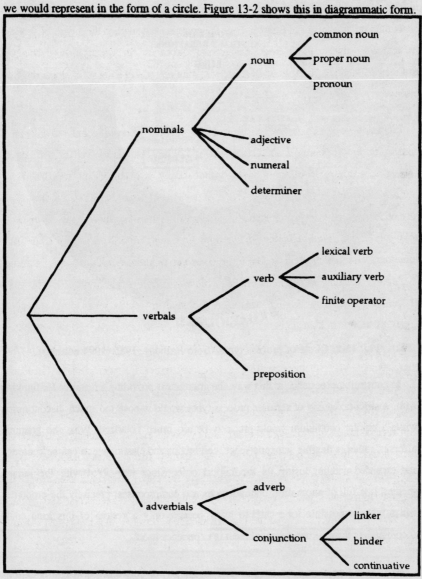

Fig. 13-1: Taxonomy of word classes in English

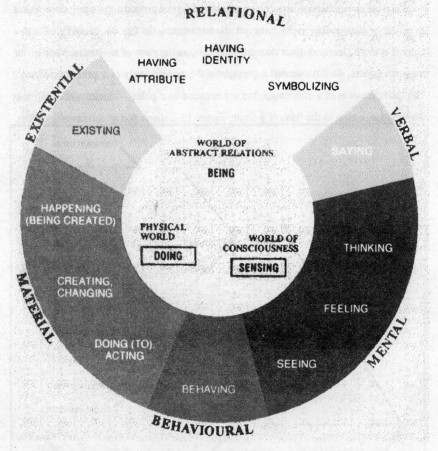

Fig. 13-2: Circle of process types (from Halliday, 1985 (1994 edition))

In construing experience in this way, the grammar is providing a resource for thinking with. A strict taxonomy of separate process types would impose too much discontinuity, while a bipolar continuum would precisely be too much polarized. What the grammar offers is, rather, a flexible semantic space, continuous and elastic, which can be contorted and expanded without losing its topological order. Since it evolved with the human species, it is full of anomalies, contradictions and compromises; precisely the properties which make it possible for a child to learn, because only a system of this kind could accommodate the disorder that is inherent in experience itself.

With each type of process, the grammar associates one or two favourite configurations of participants. These usually vary considerably from one process type to another; in English, there is a strong link between the role of "Senser" (the one who knows, thinks

&c.) in a mental process and the personal pronouns *he* and *she*, such that putting *it* in this role (*it didn't believe me*, for example) creates an anomaly — we wonder what this "it" could be? At the same time, all processes are interpreted as having something in common, in that typically there is one participant that is inherently associated with the process — without which the process could not take place at all, like *birds* in *birds are flying*. That may be the only one, in which case that participant is held accountable (even if involuntarily!) and the process is said to stop there. Alternatively, another participant may be involved; either as an external agent, like *children* in *children are flying kites*, or as a goal, like *a letter* in *I'm writing a letter*. When it comes to mental processes (and here is one of the contradictions referred to above), the grammar is uncertain whether the participant other than the Senser is doing duty as agent or not; if I'm doubtful about something, for example, I may say *your story doesn't convince me*, which makes your story look like an agent, or I may say I *don't believe your story*, which makes the role of *your story* very different — not exactly a goal, but like an expression of scope. Many languages display some such ambivalence about mental processes, which do not match up neatly with material processes in our experience in any obvious way.

As for the elements that make up the process configuration, we have seen that the foundation of the grammar's theory of experience was laid down in the simplest terms in the evolution of word classes: verbs, nouns, and others. But the constituents of a clause are not, in fact, verbs and nouns; they are more complex expressions that have expanded from verbs and nouns, which we call "verbal groups" and "nominal groups". At this point, we find a considerable difference between the two, in the kind of expansion that they engender. The formal patterns vary, as always, among different languages; but the underlying principles seem to be fairly constant.

Processes take place in space-time, which the grammar may model in a variety of different ways: the happening is upstream or downstream, past or future, real or imaginary. Typically the point of reference is the speech situation: there is some deictic feature relating what is being said to the current "moment" in time and space. In English the deixis is achieved by locating the process on a linear time-scale with 'present' as a fulcrum between 'past' and 'future', or else by locating it on one or other of a cluster of scales whereby the speaker intrudes his or her own judgment on it. There may be a wide variety of other attachments to the verb — modalities, aspects, phases and the like, which the grammar construes as features of the process; consider English examples like *wasn't going to start trying to help.* On the other hand, the processes themselves are not, in general, construed into systematic taxonomies, and the verb is expanded by grammatical rather than lexical means.

The participants, on the other hand, which represent the prototype of entities persisting in time and space, are usually not subject to this kind of modification; but they are organized in fairly elaborate taxonomies. These may be construed as systematic relations among different lexical items: thus *eyes, nose, mouth, chin* are all different parts of *face,* and *lamb, pork , mutton, beef* are all different kinds of *meat.* Something of the same sort happens with verbs, but to a much lesser extent. The other resource for constructing taxonomies of things is the expansion of the nominal group, and here the picture is very different from that with verbs. Nouns are expanded lexically as well as grammatically, so that, while entities (like processes) are located deictically relative to the 'here-&- now', they are also (unlike processes) extensively classified and described. An example such as *those two nice colourful picture postcards of Honolulu that Sandy sent us* shows these resources at work: cards are classified as postcards rather than, say, playing cards; postcards as picture postcards not plain postcards; picture postcards are described as colourful, and also (signalling the speaker's attitude to them) as nice; they are quantified, as two, and specified deictically as those. Further than that, both a circumstantial feature (of Honolulu) and even an entire process (that Sandy sent us) can be brought in as characteristics which specify more exactly the particular cards in question. Thus the grammar has the potential for construing a complex arrangement of classes and subclasses for any entity which participates in a process; or, on the other hand, of naming it as an individual, by using a "proper" noun instead of a common one. Proper nouns are already fully specific, and hence seldom expanded experientially (they are often expanded interpersonally!); but common nouns are almost indefinitely expandable, and it is this resource which organizes our universe into its elaborate taxonomies of things.

The third type of constituent of the clause, referred to above as "others" (that is, elements that are neither verbal nor nominal groups), evolved as the representation of a kind of "third party" to the process. This may be some qualification of the process in terms of its manner of occurrence (an adverbial group, in the case of English); or it may be an entity that is involved in the process but only indirectly (in English, a prepositional phrase, consisting of preposition plus nominal group). The line between direct and indirect participants is a fuzzy one, and sometimes what seems to be the same role in the process can be construed in either way, for example pairs like:

```
they gave the winner a prize        they gave a prize to the
                                    winner
he acted Hamlet brilliantly         he acted brilliantly as
                                    Hamlet
she rides her bicycle to work  she rides to work on her
                                    bicycle
the farmers chop down the trees     the trees are chopped down
                                    by the farmers
```

where *the winner, Hamlet, her bicycle* and *the farmers* appear first as direct and then as indirect participants. Here the grammar is in fact using the structural resource of plus or minus preposition to construe a different kind of contrast, having to do with status in the message. But the distinction is significant because, as we saw above, such "circumstantial" elements tend also to function as qualifications not of the process but of some entity that is itself a participant: as well as *the ice lies thinly on the water,* with *thinly* and *on the water* as circumstantial elements of the clause, we have *the thin ice (lying) on the water,* where these have now become modifiers of ice — and then *the thin layer of ice on the water.* And since the prepositional phrase has a nominal group inside it, this opens up the possibility of further expansion, like *the ice on the water in the pond by the oak trees in the corner of the wood.* Thus incorporating the circumstantial element into the representation of a participant does not merely add one feature to the specification; it allows more or less indefinite scope, particularly in combination with the incorporation of an entire process. (We have already pointed out that the prepositional phrase is in fact a miniaturized clause; so the two really constitute a single resource, that of using a process to specify a particular class of entity.) This potential was crucial to the development of science and mathematics (see further on this below).

13.2.3 Ideational metafunction: logical

Turning now to the logical part of the grammar's ideational resources: this is the part that is concerned not with individual processes but with the relation between one process and another. In calling this "logical" we are using the term in the sense of natural language logic: that is, grammatical logic, not formal logic — although, of course, this is the source from which formal logic is ultimately derived.

The changes that constitute our experience are not all independent of one another. On the contrary; our experience is that one thing leads to another, and there is in principle no limit to an experiential chain. But the exact nature of the relationship may vary from one transition to another; so the grammar construes the relationship between processes dyadically, in the form of a nexus between a pair of clauses. The first process may have a second process related to it, by a relationship such as sequence in time, or cause and effect; this in turn may have another one related to it, either by the same relationship or by a different one — in either case, the relationship is construed as holding between the members of a pair. So the logical system, within the ideational metafunction, engenders a different kind of linguistic structure from that of the experiential system. In the logical world, the parts are not constituents of an organic configuration, like the process, participants and circumstances of the clause. They are elements standing to each other in a potentially iterative relationship; and each element represents an entire process.

Two kinds of logical relationship are construed by the grammar in this way. One is that of "expansion", in which the two processes are of the same order of experience and the second one is interpreted as in some respect expanding on the first. The other is that of "projection", in which the second process is construed as belonging to a different order of experience: it is projected, by the first one, on to the semiotic plane. Each of these defines a complex region of semantic space.

Conceptually perhaps the simplest way of expanding a process is by elaborating on it: saying it over again (or something very like it, with repetition as the limiting case), or else exemplifying it, or clarifying it in some other way. The grammar represents this relationship symbolically in English by prosodic means: the same intonation pattern is repeated, for example *we're shut out; they won't let us in*. But since this does not appear in writing, various purely written symbols are used instead, typically *i.e., e.g.* and *viz.* The second type of expansion consists in extending one process by construing another one as an addition to it (with 'and' as the limiting case); or as an alternative to it, a replacement for it, or as some form of reservation or contrast. Here the grammar typically employs conjunctions, like *and, or, but, instead, besides.* The third type of expansion is one of enhancing the first process by another one setting up a specific semantic relationship, of which the principal ones are time, cause, condition, concession, and means. Here again the grammar deploys a range of different conjunctions, which mark either the enhancing clause (*when, because, by, though, if* and so on) or the one that is being enhanced (e.g. *then* 'at that time', *then* 'in that case', *so, thus, yet*).

In projection, one process is used to construe another one, such that the latter becomes a representation of what someone says or thinks. The types of process that have this power of projection are the verbal and the mental processes: *he says (that ...), he told (her to ...), she thinks (that ...), she wanted (him to ...).* Thus the projection operates at either of the two strata of the content plane: either that of the wording, where the projection is by a verbal process, or at that of the meaning, where it is by a mental process. Because the grammar can project in this way, semiotic events, both those which are externalized as sayings and those which are internalized as thoughts, are brought within the overall domain of the phenomena of experience.

Probably some such system of logical relationships between processes will be found in all languages, though as always there is great variation in the formal resources that are deployed, and also in the systematic semantic organization of the relationships themselves. In English, and many other languages, the grammar makes a systematic distinction in the relative status that is accorded to the two processes entering into such a logical nexus. Either the two are construed as being equal in status, or one is construed as being dependent on the other. In principle, any particular type of expansion or projection can be interpreted in either way, either as "paratactic" or as "hypotactic"; but in fact there is some degree of partial association: certain combinations are favoured, and others correspondingly disfavoured. For example, in English, when one process is construed as a simple restatement of, or addition to, another, the two are likely to have equal status; whereas where one is seen as enhancing the other they are usually unequal — a means is secondary to what has been achieved by it, a cause is secondary to its effect. (Note that these are overall quantitative tendencies; in any one instance the choice may go either way.) Similarly in a projecting relationship, the two elements in a verbal projection are typically equal in status, while those of a mental projection are unequal. This is not surprising: since you can hear what a person says, you give the wording the full status of a direct experience, as in *Mary said, "I will wait here for you tomorrow";* whereas you cannot observe what a person thinks, so this is more likely to be construed as dependent on the process that projects it, as in *Mary thought/ decided she would wait there for him the next day.* In the first, the deictic standpoint is that of the sayer, namely Mary; what she said is quoted as "direct speech". In the second, the deictic standpoint is that of the person speaking; what Mary thought is reported as "indirect thought". Again, it is always possible to report speech — and even to quote thought, with the speaker acting as an omniscient narrator; but those combinations are less favoured in everyday English discourse.

In its ideational metafunction, language construes the human experience — the human capacity for experiencing — into a massive powerhouse of meaning. It does so by creating a multidimensional semantic space, highly elastic, in which each vector forms a line of tension (the vectors are what are represented in our system networks as "systems"). Movement within this space sets up complementarities of various kinds: alternative, sometimes contradictory, constructions of experience, indeterminacies, ambiguities and blends, so that a grammar, as a general theory of experience, is a bundle of uneasy compromises. No one dimension of experience is represented in an ideal form, because this would conflict destructively with all the others; instead, each dimension is fudged so that it can coexist with those that intersect with it. We can illustrate these compromises with some very simple examples from English:

— between a single process and a sequence of logically related processes, e.g. she told me / she gave me to know

— between related processes and related elements within one process, e.g. they fight harder than we fight / they fight harder than us

— between the process itself (action, event &c.) and a participant, e.g. the day dawns / the dawn comes

— between two processes and one process with a circumstantial element, e.g. use a spade to dig the ground / dig the ground with a spade

— between a participant in a process and a circumstantial element, e.g. she rides her bicycle to work / she rides to work on her bicycle

— between one cluster of participant roles and another, e.g. the mistake didn't strike me / I didn't notice the mistake

> — between one process type and another, e.g. why do you grieve? / why are you sad?

Such pairs are not synonymous, because each of the two representations aligns the experience in question with a different set of other experiences. It is obvious that there is scope for an enormous amount of variation in the way different languages accommodate the innumerable possible complementarities of this kind. We have outlined the picture from the point of view of English, but doing so as far as possible in a way that would enable the relevant questions to be raised for other languages. In the last resort each language construes experience in its own way — has its own "characterology", as the Prague linguists expressed it. But every language embodies a working, and workable, schedule of compromises, that taken all together constitute its speakers' construction of reality.

13.2.4 Interpersonal metafunction

Our concern in this book is primarily with what we have called the "ideation base", the systems of meaning into which, through language, human beings construe their collective and individual experience. Usually when we talk about the linguistic "construction of reality" this is the aspect of reality that comes to mind. But at the same time as construing experience — in the same breath, so to speak — they are also, through language, enacting their interpersonal relationships; and this interpersonal component of meaning is no less part of what is constituted for us as "reality". If the ideational component is language as a mode of reflection, the interpersonal component is language as a mode of action; and reality consists as much in what we do as in what we think.

When we say that the grammar enacts interpersonal relationships, we mean relationships of all kinds from the transient exchange of speech roles in temporary transactional encounters (*How are you? — Good, thanks; and you? — Coming along. Now what can I do for you?*) to the enduring familial and other networks that constitute the structure of society. We tend to be less aware of this metafunction of language, at least in more learned contexts; partly because, as adults in a literate culture, we are conditioned to thinking of meaning purely in ideational terms (language as a means of "expressing thought"), and partly because it is less obvious that talking is a way of doing

— of acting on others (and through them, on our shared environment) and in the process, constructing society. But the interpersonal and the ideational are the two facets of our everchanging social semiotic.

The most immediate way in which we act, grammatically, is through our choice of speech function. One kind of speech function is a command; this is obviously a way of getting someone to do something, but we tend to think of it as being in this respect untypical. However all speech functions are modes of action, whether command or offer, question or statement, or any of their innumerable combinations and subcategories. All dialogue is a process of exchanging meaning, in which the speaker is enacting, at any one time, a particular interpersonal relationship, including his own role and the role he is assigning to the listener (i.e. he is specifying a network of interpretations for his own and the others' behaviour). Grammatically, each time he says a clause, he is not only construing a process (as described in the last section) but also, unless he makes it logically dependent on another clause, acting out a speech function; and this embodies two simultaneous choices. The speaker is either giving or else requiring the other person to give — that is, demanding. And the commodity being given or demanded may be either "goods-&-services" or "information". Each of the four combinations defines one of the primary speech functions:

give + goods-&-services: offer   [accept goods-&-services given!]

demand + goods-&-services: command   [give goods-&-services demanded!]

give + information: statement   [accept information given!]

demand + information: question   [give information demanded!]

If the commodity being exchanged is goods-&-services, then the action that is given or demanded is typically a non-verbal one: what is being exchanged is something other than a construction of meanings, and the meanings serve to bring the exchange about. In principle the listener need not say anything at all; but listeners usually do, typically by reversing the role, responding to an offer with a command and to a command with an offer:

```
[offer] Shall I help you find it? — Yes; please do! [command]
```

[command] Come and help me find it! - All right; I will. [offer]

If on the other hand the commodity being exchanged is information, then this is in fact made of meaning; the speaker's action, and that of the listener if responding to a question, is bound to be a verbal one, because here language is not only the means of carrying out the exchange, it is also the nature of the exchange itself.

Choosing a particular speech function is, obviously, only one step in a dialogue; what the grammar creates, through the system of "mood", is the potential for arguing, for an ongoing dynamic exchange of speech roles among the interactants in a conversation. The mood system, together with other systems associated with it, constructs a great range of speechfunctional variation; and since in principle any ideational meaning can be mapped on to any interpersonal meaning, this makes it possible to construe any aspect of experience in any dialogic form. If the ideational metafunction is language in its "third person" guise, the interpersonal is language in its "first and second person" guise; the interaction of a 'me' and a 'you'. The 'me' and the 'you' are of course constructed in language; they have no existence outside the social semiotic. Once constructed, me and you then become a part of experience and can be referred to alongside the him, the her and the it; but note that (unlike their interpersonal meaning, which does not change) their ideational meaning changes every time there is a change of speaker (this is what makes me and you so difficult for children to learn). Note in this connection that the basic distinction constructed by language is not, as sometimes claimed, that between 'me' and 'the rest'; it is that between 'me-&-you', on the one hand, and the rest — the 'third party' — on the other. This distinction is coded in the grammar at many places, for example in the system of modality (see below); there can be no "first person" unless there is a "second person" with whom these roles can be alternately acted out.

The mood system constructs the clause as a move in an argument: either as a "proposition" (statement or question) or as a "proposal" (offer or command). The system provides scope for argument by incorporating an opposition of 'on' or 'off': each clause assigns either positive or negative polarity. Every proposal or proposition selects one or the other: either *that was a snake* or *that wasn't a snake,* either *catch it!* or *don't catch it!* But at the same time the interpersonal grammar goes much further; it rejects a simple polarity of 'yes' and 'no', opening up a broad semantic space in between. This is the area of "modality", where the interactants present different aspects of their own judgments and opinions, exploring the validity of what is being said and typically locating it somewhere between the positive and negative poles.

Languages differ considerably in their construction of this space, and in the extent to which they interpret it grammatically. In English, there are four distinct grammatical traverses between 'yes' and 'no', two deriving from the polarity of propositions ('it is/ it isn't') and two from the polarity of proposals ('do! / don't!'). The former are along the dimensions of "probability" and "usuality", the first being the more elaborated of the two (because more arguable); for example,

> That was a snake.
> -- It wasn't. It can't possibly have been a snake.
> -- Couldn't it? Don't you think so? I think it might have been.
> -- It probably wasn't. But snakes can appear round here.

All of these represent probability except the final *can* which means 'sometimes' (usuality). Note that it is always the judgment of speaker or listener that is represented as a choice of modality, not that of any third party (this is one of the boundaries drawn between 'me-&-you' and 'the rest'). The latter occupy the dimensions of "obligation" and "readiness", readiness including both inclination and ability; for example,

> They ought to clean this place up. People will leave it so untidy.
> -- They can't; they haven't got the equipment. They're not supposed to clean it anyway.
> -- You mean they won't. But someone must. Can we?
> -- I don't see why we shouldn't. Will you help?

Although these are derived from the sense of proposals ('you are required / supposed / allowed; I am able / willing'), they are not restricted to clauses having these speech functions; obligation and readiness are construed by the grammar propositionally and hence are used freely with third persons. But they still represent the judgments of speaker or listener on the obligations or inclinations involved (*he ought to help, she will help*).

Modality is a rich resource for speakers to intrude their own views into the discourse: their assessments of what is likely or typical, their judgments of the rights and wrongs of the situation and of where other people stand in this regard. But there are numerous other kinds of interpersonal meaning constructed by the resources of the grammar. These include comments about how desirable or plausible or self-evident something is, expressions of attitude in referring to persons and objects, sets of words with similar experiential meaning but distinguished interpersonally by connotation (sometimes called "purr words" and "snarl words"), and numerous forms of personal address and reference (kinship terms, personal names, honorifics, endearments, insults and the like). For a recent theoretical account of the field of "appraisal", see Martin (in press); for an analysis of appraisal in casual conversation, see Slade (1996).

Unlike ideational meanings, which tend to be located at definable locations in the grammatical structure, interpersonal meanings tend to be strung throughout the discourse, by an accumulation of grammatical and lexical features or by other devices such as voice quality and intonation contours. This signals the fact that interpersonal meanings are more diffuse: they relate to the figure as a whole, rather than to one of its elements; or to a whole turn in the dialogue, or even to some more extended passage of the discourse. Some particular interpersonal colouring may inform the whole of an individual speaker's interaction with another person; and because human societies are inherently hierarchical, the interpersonal component of the grammar in many languages enacts networks of social relationships with varying degrees of inequality and of distance. Thus there may be regular lexicogrammatical variants used to maintain different alignments of speaker and listener, and even of third parties, on vectors of power and familiarity; such forms may be located at one point in each grammatical structure (for example in the endings of the verb) or dispersed prosodically throughout the wording of the clause. But even in a language such as English, where there are no such systematic speech styles institutionalized in the grammar, there is always some functional variation along these lines: we have no difficulty in recognizing what are the more formal and what are the more informal variants among different samples of spoken or written discourse.

Interpersonal meaning is mapped on to ideational meaning at all points from the most micro to the most macro: from modality and speech function in the clause (or even features built in to the morphology of the word, like the diminutives characteristic of many languages) to settings affecting the whole of a particular register, like the aura of power and distance that we associate with the language of bureaucracy. These are the various ways in which language functions as a mode of action; and these meanings, no less than ideational ones, are brought into existence by the grammar.

13.2.5 Textual metafunction

There is a third component in the linguistic construction of meaning; this is what we refer to as the "textual" metafunction. If we were trying to find a term to match the expressions "language as reflection" and "language as action" that we used to gloss the ideational and interpersonal metafunctions, we might come up with "language as information"; but this is itself not very informative. It is a difficult concept because, unlike the other two, the textual metafunction has no obviously distinct function at the back of it. All uses of language involve the creation of text.

But at the same time this is precisely the context in which the textual metafunction may be understood. The concept of a metafunction is "meta" in the sense that it refers not to functions of individual utterances — functions of the instance — but to functional components of the system of language. They are, of course, "functional" in origin — that is, they derive from the functions of language as manifested in instances of use; and if we observe children developing their mother tongue we can see how the ideational and interpersonal resources of the system gradually emerge from the earliest semiotic encounters, in a way which may plausibly mimic how the metafunctions originally evolved. The textual metafunction is different because it does not originate in an extrinsic context of this kind. Rather, it is intrinsic to language itself. The "textual" metafunction is the name we give to the systematic resources a language must have for creating discourse: for ensuring that each instance of text makes contact with its environment. The "environment" includes both the context of situation and other instances of text. Relative to the other metafunctions, therefore, the textual metafunction appears in an enabling role; without its resources, neither ideational nor interpersonal constructs would make sense.

Since these resources are oriented towards discourse, many of the "textual" systems in any language have a domain potentially higher than the clause and clause complex; they set up relationships that create semantic cohesion, and these are not restricted by the limitations of grammatical structure. But they also contribute a critical dimension to the overall grammar of the clause. In this guise, the clause functions as a quantum of information; it is construed as a message, with a range of possible structures providing for different interpretations according to the discourse environment in which it occurs. These structures have been less fully described than those of the other metafunctions; they were brought to the notice of grammarians by Mathesius and his colleagues of the Prague school in the first half of the present century. But it seems that one typical way of construing the clause as a message is as a combination of two perspectives, that of the speaker and that of the listener (the latter, of course, being also as modelled for the listener by the speaker). We can see this pattern clearly present in English.

From the speaker's point of view, a piece of information has a specific point of departure; the Prague scholars referred to this as the "Theme". The Theme, in English, always includes one element that has an experiential function, typically a participant in the process; it may include other elements as well, for example an interpersonal expression of modality if the speaker is thematizing his/her own point of view. One way of signalling what is thematic is by putting it first in the clause, as is done in English, where everything up to and including the first experiential element constitutes the speaker's chosen point of departure; for example *But surely time is defined as that which you can't turn back?*, where the Theme is *but surely time*. Here the speaker is construing a message around the theme of 'what I'm saying is contrary to what went before' (*but*); 'it's my opinion, and I'd like to challenge you with it' (*surely*); and 'the startingpoint is the topic of *time*'. The remainder of the clause constitutes the body of the message, labelled grammatically as the "Rheme".

But the "Theme + Rheme" configuration becomes a message only when paired with another one, that of "Given + New". This construes a piece of information from the complementary point of view, as something having news value — something the listener is being invited to attend to. It may not contain anything the listener has not heard before; a great deal of "news" is totally familiar, being simply contrasted or even reiterated. On the other hand, the entire message may consist of unknown information, for example the first clause of a piece of fiction. But the message is construed along prototypical lines as an equilibrium of the given and the new, with a climax in the form of a focal point of information: 'this is to be the focus of your attention'. This focal point usually comes at the end; but (unlike the Theme + Rheme) the Given + New structure is not signalled, in English, by word order — it is signalled by intonation, and specifically by pitch prominence, the point of maximum perturbation (falling, rising or complex) in the intonation contour. The principle behind this is clear: if the Theme always came first, and the New always came last, there would be no possibility of combining them; whereas one powerful form of a message — powerful because highly marked — is that in which the two are mapped on to one another, as in **no wonder** *they were annoyed* (where the focus is on the interpersonal theme *no wonder*).

All languages display some form of textual organization of the clause. How far this kind of speaker - listener complementarity, with a quantum of information being construed out of the tension between the two, is a general or prototypical feature of this aspect of the grammar is not at all clear. In Austronesian languages, for example, there is typically a much more complex pattern of interrelationship between the textual and the ideational structures of the clause (mapping of Theme on to different transitivity roles) than is found in Indo-European. Even with regard to English, where it is well established how the flow of information is engendered in the grammar, opinions differ as to how far this should be seen as one continuous movement and how far as the intersection of two different periodicities (as we are inclined to interpret it). It may be a general principle that thematic status is more closely tied to the clause (as the locus of experiential and interpersonal choices) than is the listener-oriented pattern of given and new; in English the "quantum" of information that is defined by this latter construction is not, in fact, identical with the clause and may be smaller or larger. But all discourse is organized around these two motifs, which between them "add value" to the clause, enabling it to 'mean' effectively in the context in which it occurs.

Over and above its contribution to the grammar of the clause, what we are calling the "textual" metafunctional component comprises a further set of resources, which construe clauses and clause complexes into longer stretches of discourse without the formality of further grammatical structure. These are the resources for creating "cohesion". These are of four kinds: reference (sometimes called "phora", to distinguish it from reference as defined in the philosophy of language), ellipsis, conjunction, and lexical cohesion.

Reference is a way of referring to things that are already semiotically accessible: either actually, in the text, or potentially, in the context of situation. The English reference systems are the personals, especially the third person pronouns and determiners *he/him/his she/her/hers it/its they/them/ their/theirs,* and the demonstratives *this/these that/those* and the maverick *the* (which emerged as a weakened form of *that*). Such systems evolved in a deictic function; when used anaphorically or cataphorically (that is, in deictic relation to the text), they create cohesion. There is also a third source of referential cohesion, through the use of comparison, with words such as *same, other, different, less, smaller.*

In **ellipsis**, some features which are present in the semantic construction of the clause (or other unit) are not realized explicitly in the wording, which cannot then be interpreted unless these features are retrieved from elsewhere. Here it is not the meaning that is being referred to; it is the wording that is being retrieved, usually from the immediately preceding clause (whereas reference can span considerable distances in the text). Ellipsis is particularly characteristic of dialogue, especially adjacency pairs such as question and answer. Sometimes in English a substitute element is inserted as a placeholder; e.g. *ones* in *Which lanes are closed? — The northbound ones.*

In **conjunction**, the various logical-semantic relations of expansion that construe clause-complex structures (discussed above under the "logical" metafunction) are deployed instead as a source of cohesion. There are a large number of such conjunctive expressions, ranging from single words like *however, moreover, otherwise* (many of them originally composite forms) to prepositional phrases like *in that case, in other words, at the same time* (often containing a reference word inside them). They cover more or less the same range of meanings that we referred to as "elaborating", "extending" and "enhancing"; but they do not establish any structural relationship in the grammar, and this is recognized in written English, where they regularly occur following a full stop.

Lexical cohesion refers to cohesion that is brought about by lexical means: choosing a word that is related in a systematic way to one that has occurred before. The range of semantic relations that can create cohesion in this way is very wide; but there are five principal conditions under which it occurs. These are: repetition, where the speaker simply repeats the same word; synonymy/antonymy, where a word is chosen that is similar or opposed in meaning; hyponymy/meronymy, where a word is chosen that is related by 'kind of' or 'part of' — either vertically, like *melon ... fruit* or *car ... wheel*, or horizontally, like *melon ... plum*, or *wheel ... mudguard;* and collocation, which does not necessarily imply any particular semantic relationship but means simply that a word is chosen which is regularly associated with a previous one, like *aim* coming shortly after *target*, such that a resonance is felt between the two.

As far as the textual metafunction is concerned, therefore, any one clause will typically embody two sets of semantic choices. One will be its organization as a message, a piece of information flowing from speaker to hearer, its limits defined by the speaker's point of departure and the focus of attention projected by the speaker on to the listener. The other will be the cohesion it sets up with the preceding moments of the discourse, as well as with other discourses and with the total semiotic environment. These enable the clause to function effectively as reflection and as action. But in the course of serving this enabling role, the textual component opens up a new dimension of meaning potential, in that it construes a further plane of "reality" that is as it were made of language — meaning not as action or as reflection but as information. In the modern world, when we increasingly live by exchanging information, rather than by exchanging goods-&-services as hitherto, this aspect of meaning potential is coming more and more to be foregrounded. But it has always been there; and this is not the first time in history that it has proved to be an indispensable resource.

13.2.6 Ideational metaphor

We described the clause, earlier, as a construction of experiential meaning: a configuration of process, participants and circumstances set up by the grammar in the course of its evolution as a theory of experience. We will come back to this in a moment; meanwhile we have tried to supplement and add depth to this account by bringing in the other two planes of meaning, the interpersonal and the textual. For a fuller understanding of the clause, we have to recognize that it evolved simultaneously as reflection, as action and as information: that is, not only as a representation of the phenomena of our experience but also as a means of social action, of moving around in interpersonal space (and so defining that space and those who occupy it); and as a semiotic construct, whereby language itself becomes a part of, and a metaphor for, the reality it has evolved to construe and to construct.

These three "metafunctions" are interdependent; no one could be developed except in the context of the other two. When we talk of the clause as a mapping of these three dimensions of meaning into a single complex grammatical structure, we seem to imply that each somehow "exists" independently; but they do not. There are — or could be — semiotics that are monofunctional in this way; but only very partial ones, dedicated to specific tasks. A general, all-purpose semiotic system could not evolve except in the interplay of action and reflection, a mode of understanding and a mode of doing — with itself included within its operational domain. Such a semiotic system is called a language.

We are accustomed to thinking of a language as being prototypically realized as speech; justifiably enough, since language first evolved in the spoken medium. Also, it is the spoken medium that language is first mastered in by a child — in the typical case. But, as we remarked in Part I, side by side with spoken language there has evolved another form of expression that might equally well be taken to represent language in its canonical form; namely Sign, the mother tongue in communities of the deaf.

13.2.6.1 Deaf Sign

From one point of view, as we introduced it in the earlier discussion, Sign will appear as a realizational variant: that is to say, the meanings of language — its semantic system — may be construed either in sound or in gesture. There are, in fact, sign systems that are constructed along these lines: in principle this is what is meant by "signed English". But if we consider the nature of the two forms of expression, vocal on the one hand and gestural on the other, it is clear that they have very different properties. Gesture operates in a 3-dimensional "signing space" defined by reference to the signer's body and its parts, and movement within that space is entirely accessible to the receiver; thus in addition to succession in time (which is common to both), the gestural medium can exploit a number of parameters of spatial variation: the "articulatory organs" (fingers, hands, arms, other body parts), their location, orientation, thrust (direction and speed of movement) and so on.

In the most immediate sense, as regards their potential for construing signifiers — elements of wording and their arrangement in combination — both these forms of expression, vocal and gestural, are open-ended. Neither of them imposes a limit on the inventory of morphemes or their configuration in grammatical structures. Nevertheless they are significantly different in the kinds of resource they offer for making meaning.

Perhaps the major difference between the two is their potential for iconicity. We have referred all along to the primarily visual nature of human experience: how much of it is constituted as location, and especially movement, in space. Now, both gestural and vocal resources involve positioning and moving the organs of articulation in space; but the position and movement of the vocal organs, besides being largely out of sight of the listener, is very much more constrained; and while this permits a limited degree of iconicity (association of close vowels with 'small', open with 'large', for example) this can never be more than a marginal feature of the system as a whole. Thus even allowing for the additional iconic potential of loudness and length, the expression systems of spoken languages must remain prototypically conventional. This is the familiar principle of the "arbitrariness" (i.e. conventionality) of the linguistic sign.

Gestural systems, by contrast, have a far greater potential for construing experience iconically. Thus in Johnston (1989: 16) "signs are roughly graded into four classes of **transparent, translucent, obscure** and **opaque** signs, depending on how iconic a sign is"; and while most signs fall in between the two extremes — Johnston grades them as obscure or translucent, rather than opaque or transparent — many of those he labels "obscure" have a popular explanation in iconic terms (e.g. 2388: n. CAMERA, v. TAKE A PICTURE, PHOTOGRAPH. Obscure action. Popular explanation: 'holding a camera and depressing the shutter button' [p. 301]). This suggests that even if particular explanations are "nothing more than deaf folklore" (p. 16), the system as a whole is perceived as prototypically iconic; and this feature is borne out in two important respects. One is that many of the signs construing basic categories of experience that would be learnt very early in childhood, in the transition from protolanguage to mother tongue — examples are 1291 GET; 1479 HOLD; 1824 RUN; 2473 BIRD; 2759 DRINK, CUP; 36 BED; 163 UP — are clearly iconic, and so would tend to establish iconicity as the norm. The other is that individual signs may be modified in a distinctively iconic fashion; e.g. 1471 "v LARGE, BIG, (with amplification) great, (with amplification and stress) enormous, huge, immense"; see in particular the section on "sign modification" in Johnston (1989: 494-9). As Johnston comments (p. 513), "A language which is itself visual and spatial has far more opportunities than an auditory one to map onto itself those very visual and spatial qualities of the world it wishes to represent".

Signers are also members of another language community, that of the (predominantly hearing) speakers of English, or whatever language is spoken around them; the two groups interact, and there is obviously no insulation between the two language systems. This gives rise to contact phenomena of two kinds: on the one hand, intermediate forms whereby English is realized in sign expressions (signed English, and finger-spelling), including a large number of new, "contrived" signs; and on the other hand, constant intrusion of English forms of expression, and therefore of English modes of meaning, into the sign language itself. The situation is then further complicated by the low status accorded to Sign by many members of the hearing community, often including the educational authorities, who (since they did not understand it) not only refused to see it as a potential vehicle for education and systematic knowledge but in some cases attempted to suppress it altogether.

But for children who are born without hearing, Sign performs all the functions of a naturally evolving mother tongue. It is their primary means for the construal of experience, in precisely the sense in which we are using that expression throughout the present book — the construction of their essential "ideation base". (It serves the other metafunctions as well, of course; for discussion of this see Johnston, 1992.) In precisely the same *sense*, but not in the precisely the same *way*: the semantic system that is construed in (say) Australian or British Sign is not the semantic system of English, despite its being constantly permeated by English in the ways referred to above. It is a system needing to be described in its own terms, based on detailed studies of its grammar and discourse such as now being carried out for Auslan by Trevor Johnston. Such a description is designed first and foremost for the needs of the deaf community; but it will have general significance as a source of further insight into the semantics of spoken languages, making it possible to view them comparatively in the light of an alternative construction of reality.

From Sign, we can get further insight into the construal of experience as ideational meaning because of its greater potential for iconicity in the expression. Semantic space can be construed iconically in signing within a continuous space-time, constituted as bodily experience for the signer and as part of shared visual experience for signer and addressee.

13.2.6.2 Metaphoric and congruent wordings

From a comparative standpoint, spoken languages and deaf sign languages stand to each other in a metaphoric relationship, as alternative construals of a (largely, though not totally) shared experience. What appear at first simply as different modes of expression turn out to have, associated with them, somewhat different constructions of meaning. It would be beyond our scope, and our competence, to pursue this further. But it brings us back to another dimension of metaphor to which it bears a rather striking analogy. Many "spoken" languages may be realized in two different media: in speech, and in writing. At first this presents itself just as two modes of expression; but when we look more closely at discourse in spoken and written language we find regularly associated differences in grammatical construction. We find written language constructed in nominal groups, whereas spoken language is typically constructed in clauses. And since it is in the grammar that our experience is construed into meaning, what we are seeing are different forms of the construction of experience, one couched primarily in terms of figures, the other in terms of elements that make up such figures, mainly those that function as participating entities.

Our basic approach to this is embodied in the term "metaphor", as used in the context of metaphor in the grammar. We used the expression "grammatical metaphor" to refer to a complex set of interrelated effects whereby, in English and many other languages, there have evolved what seem to be alternative representations of processes and properties. In terms of word classes, meanings prototypically construed as verbs or adjectives come to be construed as nouns instead. But, as we saw, this is simply the superficial manifestation of a wider and deeper phenomenon affecting the entire construal of experiential meanings in the grammar.

To recapitulate with a very simple example: Given a pair of expressions such as *in times of engine failure* and *whenever an engine failed,* the two are related to each other by grammatical metaphor. A particular phenomenon has been construed (i) as a prepositional phrase with a nominal group as its Complement, (ii) as a hypotactic clause introduced by a conjunction; moreover, the lexical content has been construed in two quite different ways:

	(i) prepositional phrase	(ii) dependent clause
'time'	Head/Thing in nominal group	hypotactic conjunction
'engine'	Classifier in nominal group in *of*-phrase qualifying *time*	Head/Thing in nominal group functioning as Actor
'fail'	Head/Thing in nominal group in *of*-phrase qualifying *time*	Head/Event in verbal group functioning as Process

If we take just the question of which elements function as Thing, the two are exactly complementary: in (i) the Thing nouns are *time* and *failure,* while in (ii) the only Thing noun is *engine*. This relationship is analogous to that of metaphor in its usual, lexical sense; only here the transfer is not between words but between grammatical classes.

From a purely descriptive point of view, each version is metaphorical from the standpoint of the other; there is no inherent priority accorded to either. Once we bring in considerations of history, however, a clear priority emerges; and it is the same priority whichever of the three diachronic dimensions we choose to invoke — the phylogenetic (history of the language), the ontogenetic (history of the individual) or the logogenetic (history of the text). In all these three histories, version (ii), the clausal, comes first. This form of construal evolved first in the history of English; version (i) emerged only as the result of a long process of later evolution. It comes first in the life of a child; children master version (i) only after a long (in terms of their young lives) process of becoming literate and being educated. And it comes first in the unfolding of a text; we are much more likely to be told first that engines fail and only then to hear about a phenomenon of engine failure. Once we take note of progression in time, then given a pair of such expressions we can identify one of the two as the more metaphorical. The process is one of movement away from what we referred to as a "congruent" form.

"Congruent" is of course a contingent term. What it is saying is that, at the present moment in human history we can recognize forms of language which seem to represent a common coding of experience: this is the configuration that we referred to as "process + participant + circumstance" which is construed in grammars through some version of the trichotomy of verb, noun and the rest. If we relate this to English, it is the form of English that is learnt as a mother tongue, in which phenomena are interpreted clausally, in a kind of dynamic equilibrium of happenings and things. The prototypical thing is a concrete object which can be related by similarity to certain other objects, such that taken together they form a class, like engines. The prototypical happening is a change in the environment that is perceptible to the senses, or a change in the senser's own consciousness. A process is a happening involving one or two such objects, or one object and a conscious being. When children move from their own constructed protolanguage into the mother tongue, this provides a theory which they can use to give a plausible construction to their own individual experience.

Under certain historical conditions, such a theory may come to be modified or reconstructed. No doubt there have been various more or less catastrophic changes in earlier human history which have brought about relatively rapid changes in language — relatively, that is, to the gradual evolution of the system that has taken place all the time. We have no means of knowing about these. But it seems likely that what we are here calling grammatical metaphor represents one such partial reconstruction, in which, in the context of science and technology, a rather different kind of "reality" is being construed.

It might be maintained that a pair of expressions such as *in times of engine failure* and *whenever an engine failed* are simply synonymous, and do not imply any reconstruction of experience. But there are two problems with this view. One is that of history, referred to above. If neither had preceded the other, they could simply be free alternatives (though language is seldom so extravagant with its resources as this would imply!). But since one form of wording came first, it inevitably acquired a rich semantic loading. Since nouns evolved as names of classes of things, anything which is represented as a noun inevitably acquires the status of a thing, with the implication of a concrete object as the prototype. Thus in *engine failure,* the grammar has construed a thing called *failure*; and the nominal group then accommodates classes of *failure* (with another noun as Classifier), such as *crop failure, heart failure* and *engine failure.* Thus *engine failure* and *engines fail* are precisely not synonymous, because in *engine failure* the happening 'fail' has acquired an additional semantic feature as the name of a class of things.

The second problem is that of sheer scale. If only odd, more or less random instances of this kind of metaphor occurred, they could have little effect on the system as a whole. But given the massive scale of this shift in the grammar, affecting as it does entire registers of modern English, it cannot simply be dismissed as meaningless variation. As we saw in Chapter 6, the metaphoric processes themselves are highly systematic; moreover they occur in typical syndromes, so that it is not just one aspect of the construction that is affected. Rather, the entire perspective is shifted sideways, so that each element in the configuration is reconstructed as something else. When this pattern comes to predominate throughout a large proportion of the discourse of adult life, it amounts to a fairly major resemanticizing of experience.

13.2.6.3 Origins of grammatical metaphor: the evolution of scientific discourse

Why did such a significant development take place? The most important single factor was undoubtedly the evolution of science and technology. It is possible to trace the emergence of this pattern of grammatical metaphor back to the origins of western science in ancient Greece, and to follow its development step by step; each stage in the evolution of the grammar realizes a stage in the evolution of a world view.

The philosopher-scientists of the ancient Greek world, Thales, Pythagoras, Anaximander and their successors, inherited a language with a grammar of the kind outlined above, in which experiential meanings were construed in clausal patterns as a balanced interplay of happenings and things; nouns enjoyed no special privileged status. In the course of their writings (and no doubt first of all in the course of their sayings, only we have no access to these) they distilled this into a language of learning. We do not know how much they reflected on this process; it is unlikely they engaged in any very explicit language planning. What they did was to exploit the resources of everyday Greek, its fundamental semogenic potential. In particular, they exploited two of its grammatical powers: the power of forming new words, and the power of extending grammatical structures (cf. Chatper 6, Section 6.3 above).

The first of these was their resource for creating technical terms. For systematic scholarship it is necessary to **technicalize** some of the words that are used, and this imposes two requirements: the words must be interpretable in an abstract sense, since they need to refer not to outward appearances but to the properties and principles that lie behind them; and they need to relate to one another in a regular and systematic way, so as to form stable taxonomies. Ancient Greek was a language of settlement, in which the potential for this kind of development lay predominantly in the nouns; and there existed already a number of noun-forming suffixes by which words of other classes — verbs and adjectives — were transcategorized. Two of these were particularly potent: the 'active' ending –σις-*sis* and the 'passive' ending –μα *-ma*. A number of derivatives with these suffixes had been around for a long time: for example, from πρασσω *prásso* 'do' the nouns πραξις *práxis* 'a doing, action' and πραγμα *prâgma* 'something done, a deed, act'; and from ποιεω *poiéo* 'make' the nouns ποιησις *poíesis* 'making, creation, production' and ποιημα *poíema* "something made, a product". Using these and other nominalizing suffixes the Greek scientists created hundreds of new technical terms; and by combining them with other derivational resources they developed extended series of semantically related forms, for example the following set deriving ultimately from αλλος *állos* 'other':

(1) with –σις *-sis*, αλλοιωσις *alloíosis* 'change, alteration';

(2) αλλοτριος *allótrios* 'belonging to another'; then, with –σις *-sis*, αλλοτριωσις *allotríosis* 'estrangement, alienation';

(3) αλλασσω *allásso* 'make other, change'; παραλλασσω *parallásso* 'make alternate, transpose'; then with –σις *-sis*, παραλλαξις *parállaxis* 'alternation, alternating motion', and with –μα *-ma*, παραλλαγμα *parállagma* 'interchange, variation'.

In this way they established the foundations of the lexical component of a technical discourse, and the principles on which it could be indefinitely extended.

The second of the resources that was brought into play was a syntactic one, the structure of the nominal group. The nominal group of ancient Greek was very like that of modern English: it had a similar arrangement of elements around the Head noun, allowing both prepositional phrases and clauses in modifying function (with some difference of ordering), and included among its deictic elements one which was very close to the English *the*. Thus any noun could accumulate qualifying clauses and phrases which were explicitly signalled as defining, analogous to English *the electrons in an atom, the angles which make up a triangle*. One context which demanded elaborate nominal group structures of this kind was that of mathematics, as scholars conducted more and more sophisticated measurements, for example in their attempts to understand planetary motion. Here is the English translation of a nominal group from the work of Aristarchus of Samos, sometimes referred to as "the ancient Copernicus" because he was the first to propose that the earth revolved around the sun:

```
the straight line subtending the portion intercepted within the
earth's shadow of the circumference of the circle in which the
extremities of the diameter of the circle dividing the dark and
the bright portions in the moon move
```

This has 32 words in the original Greek (fewer than the English because the equivalent of *of* is the genitive case of the noun); note that it is only the Subject of the clause, which continues ... *is less than twice the diameter of the moon.*[1]

The forms of scientific discourse developed by the Greeks were then taken over into Latin. Although Latin differed in certain significant respects (for example, it had no definite article, and it did not readily accept prepositional phrases as Qualifier in the nominal group), it was close enough to Greek, both linguistically and culturally, for this to present few problems. Most Greek derivational compounds could be calqued directly into Latin (e.g., περιφερεια *peripherêia* to *circumferens*); Latin had its own stock of nominalizing suffixes, like *-atio(nem)* and *-mentum;* and a reasonably similar potential for expanding nominal groups. As Latin took over as the language of learning throughout the greater portion of Europe, it had already developed an equivalent semogenic power. In the medieval period Latin continued to serve; but by this time, although its morphology was largely unchanged, it had taken on the semantic patterning of the vernacular European languages. So when Latin itself was replaced by these languages, the transition was not unlike that which had taken place earlier into Latin from Greek: first the Greeks developed new meanings in Greek form, then these meanings were taken over into Latin forms, then new meanings were developed in Latin, then these new meanings were taken over

---

[1] The one minor piece of linguistic engineering that had to be undertaken was to ensure that the prepositional phrases in such constructions were placed after the Head word rather than before. It was also possible for a qualifying expression to be inserted between the Deictic and the Head, equivalent to English *the in an atom electrons*; this has only a limited potential for expansion, as can be shown by rewriting "The House that Jack Built" in this format:

This is the that Jack built house.
This is the that lay in the that Jack built house malt.
This is the that ate the that lay in the that Jack built house malt rat.
This is the that killed the that ate the that lay in the that Jack built house malt rat cat.
...

With the qualifying phrase or clause at the end, the structure branches "to the right" (using the linear metaphor derived from European orthographies) and there is much less restraint on adding further elements. On the other hand, the fact that it is possible to put the qualifying element before the Head, which in English it is not, helps to avoid some ambiguity in the bracketing, as this example shows: here, both *(which is) intercepted in the shadow of the earth* and *of the circle along which* ... are qualifying the word *circumference*, and the Greek makes this clear with *the intercepted-in-the-shadow-of-the-earth circumference of the circle along which* ... . The English translation cannot follow this ordering.

into the modern European languages, then new meanings were developed within these languages. Thus there was a continuous evolution in the discourse of technology and science: in each transition, one component of the system was preserved.

This discourse first appears in English in the work of Chaucer, for example his "Treatise on the Astrolabe", written about 1391. Here we find the same linguistic resources brought into play: nouns as technical terms, and extended nominal groups. The former are partly technological (to do with the construction and operation of the astrolabe), generally Anglo-Saxon or Norman French, like *plate, ring, turet* (eye, or swivel), *riet* (from *rete* 'net', i.e. grid), *moder* ('mother', body of the instrument); and partly theoretical (from astronomy, mathematics or general methodology), mainly borrowings from Latin like *altitude, ecliptik, clymat* (climatic zone), *degree, equation, conclusioun, evidence*. The latter do not attain any spectacular length but involve the expected mixture of clauses and prepositional phrases, as in *the same number of altitude on the west side of this line meridional as he was caught on the east side*. This is clearly the discourse of organized knowledge; but it is not sharply set off from the language of everyday life.

It is with the "new learning" of the Renaissance that a distinct language of science begins to emerge, with a vastly greater dependence on grammatical metaphor. The earlier exercises in nominalization had been abstract but only minimally metaphorical; there is a trace of grammatical metaphor in expressions like *conclusion* and *the same number of altitude*, but no more than is found in the language of daily life. When we come to the writing of Newton, however, we find formulations such as the following:

> ... by these two Experiments it appears, that in equal Incidences there is a considerable inequality of Refractions.

> ... the cause of Reflexion is not the impinging of Light on the solid impervious parts of bodies, but ...

> ... if the thickness of the body be much less than the Interval of the Fits of easy Reflexion and Transmission of the Rays, the Body loseth its reflecting power.

These contain a great deal of grammatical metaphor; contrast them with more congruent forms of expression such as *light is refracted unequally (even) when it falls at the same angle; light is reflected not because it impinges on the solid, impervious parts of bodies; if the body is much less thick than the interval between the points where the rays are easily reflected and (where they are easily) transmitted, the body is no longer able to reflect (light).* Why has the mode of expression changed along just these lines?

If we look at Newton's "Opticks", from which these are taken, we find that it consists of three simultaneous discourses interspersed. In one of these phases, Newton describes his experiments; in another he draws conclusions from the experiments; and in the third he provides mathematical explanations. The language of the first phase is non-technical and non-metaphorical; e.g. *I looked through the Prism upon the hole, and turning the Prism to and fro about its Axis, to make the Image of the hole ascend and descend. ... I stopp'd the Prism, ...* The third is like the passage from Aristarchus quoted above, e.g. *The Excesses of the Sines of Refraction of several sorts of Rays above their common Sine of Incidence when the Refractions are made out of divers denser Mediums immediately into one and the same rarer Medium, suppose of Air, ...* The examples just cited of grammatical metaphor are typical of the second phase. It is here that Newton is proceeding by logical steps through a reasoned argument; and he frequently needs to summarize the argument up to that point, or in anticipation of what is to come. A typical sequence would be the following:

```
... when Light goes out of Air through several contiguous
refracting Mediums as through Water and Glass, ... that Light ...
continues ever after to be white. ... ... the permanent whiteness
argues, that ...
```

The metaphorical nominalization *permanent whiteness* summarizes the earlier sequence of inductions. There are similar contexts for expressions such as *an inequality of Refractions, the impinging of Light on ... Bodies, the thickness of the Body, reflecting power* in the passages cited above.

The nominalized forms *inequality, impinging, thickness* are not technical terms; or rather, they are so to speak technicalized for the given instance, but they do not lose their semantic status as property or event. Why then are they reconstrued as nouns? The reason is to be found in the grammar of the textual metafunction. In order to function with the requisite value in the message, which means either as Theme or as focus of information, they cannot remain as complete clauses; they have to be "packaged" into single elements of clause structure, and the only available constituent for this purpose is the nominal group. Instead of being a process in its own right, *light impinges on a body,* the phenomenon in question is construed as a participant, *the impinging of light on a body.* It can then take on a clearly defined status in the grammatical construction of the discourse.

What is beginning to emerge here is a grammar for experimental science: a way of construing experiential meaning so that it can be organized textually into a form of discourse for the advancement of learning. Again, this was not achieved by any conscious act of language planning; ironically, while the leaders of the new scholarship paid a great deal of attention to language, and recognized that their languages needed to be reequipped if they were to meet these new demands, they saw the problem in lexical rather than syntactic terms — as a problem of making their lexical taxonomies at once explicit and rigorous. The designed systems they came up with were of great interest for what they revealed about the nature of language (as embodied some generations later in Roget's English "Thesaurus"); but played no part in their scientific endeavours. The grammatical innovations, on the other hand, which were not designed at all, proved invaluable.

When the processes and properties turn into nouns, the verbs do not disappear from the scene. Scientific discourse is still written in clauses, and these clauses still have verbs in them. Let us return briefly to the examples from Newton's "Opticks":

    those Colours argue a diverging and separation of the
    heterogeneous Rays from one another by means of their unequal
    Refractions

    the variety of Colours depends upon the Composition of Light

    the cause of Reflexion is not the impinging of Light on the solid,
    impervious parts of Bodies

We might suggest a more congruent form of the first and second examples here: *colours vary because light is composed [in this way]; because those colours [appear] we know the heterogeneous rays diverge and separate from one another* ... . The verbs *depend upon* and *argue* both express a logical-semantic relation between the two nominalized processes: either an external cause, *'a* happens; so *x* happens', or an internal cause, *'b* happens, so we know *y* happens'. This is another grammatical metaphor; the congruent form of representation of a logical relation is a conjunction. The two types of metaphor work together, to construe the two processes as one: 'happening *a* causes happening *x*', 'happening *b* proves happening *y*'. It is not the case, of course, that this type of construction had never occurred in English before; it had. But it was rare; whereas from the time of Newton onwards it gradually took over, becoming the most favoured clause type of scientific language — as indeed we find it today.

We have suggested that the immediate context for this change was a discursive one: the evolution of a register of experimental science, in which certain forms of argumentation were highly valued. This is usually interpreted simply as the emergence of a particular genre, the scientific article; but that is only one side of the story — no such genre could have come into being without these changes in the grammar of the clause. At the same time, they have other significant consequences. We have already pointed out the fact that one effect of grammatical metaphor is to render many of the semantic relationships implicit: if the happening is construed as a clause, the semantic relations are spelt out in the configuration of grammatical elements, whereas if it is construed as a nominal group they are not, or only partially so (compare *his energy balance approach to strength and fracture* with *he investigated how strong [glass] was, and how it fractured, using [the idea that] the energy [...] balanced out*). On the whole, the greater the degree of metaphor in the grammar, the more the reader needs to know in order to understand the text.

But to say that the semantic relations have become less explicit is to imply that these relations themselves have not changed. In one sense, this is true: we can "unpack" the metaphor, and experts will generally agree on how to do it. But in another sense it is not true. Scientific discourse began, as we saw, with the creation of technical taxonomies and mathematical constructs; these were already modulating the semiotic construal of experience, even if only at the margins, by creating a new realm of abstract things that had not existed before. But the transformation brought about by the renaissance was a more fundamental one; not only was this realm of abstract things greatly extended, but, more significantly, phenomena hitherto construed as processes and properties were now transformed into things — they were *reconstrued*, by grammatical metaphor. We have illustrated this transformation from English; but it took place in all those languages that took over the semiotic functions of medieval Latin.

We have shown that the motive for reconstruing experience in this way was in the first instance a textual one: in the grammars of these languages, when one is developing a reasoned chain of logical argument such that complex phenomena have to be given a clearly defined status in the organization of information (the clause as "message"), such phenomena have to be constructed in nominal form. But there is no insulation between one part of the grammar and another, and this inevitably has ideational effects. Any semantic construct that appears as topical Theme has a function in transitivity; if it is formed as a nominal group, it is potentially a participant in some process, and therefore at some level it is an entity, a thing. If we say *diamond is transformed into graphite*, this is a process involving two things, diamond and graphite; if we reconstrue this as *the transformation of diamond into graphite* it has become one thing, transformation, with diamond and graphite serving only circumstantially to qualify it as a thing of a certain kind.

This reconstrual of experience is complex: what were first construed as happenings have become things, with the original things now serving merely as their appendages; but at the same time what were first construed as logical relationships between processes have been reconstrued as processes in their own right. So *the transformation of diamond into graphite is caused by ...* . It is also complex in another way: the original status accorded to the phenomenon is not lost, but enters into a metaphorical nexus with the new one. So *transformation* is still a process, as well as being a thing; *is caused by*, as well as being a process, is still a logical relation between processes. But, as we have seen, the overwhelmingly predominating effect of this reconstrual is a nominalizing one, in which other phenomena are transformed into things. This is a major shift in ideational terms, and plays a significant part in the historical semiotic.

In the world of classical physics, the flux of experience was held under control: reality had to be prevented from wriggling, while it could be observed and experimented with. The control over experience is partly a physical matter; but it is also in part semiotic, and the semiotic control of experience is achieved by the nominalizing power of the grammar. Since it is the grammar that has construed it in the first place, the grammar is able to transform it by reconstruing it in other terms. Grammatical metaphor played an important role in shaping our humanist world.

But it shaped it in a way which soon came to be felt as decidedly inhuman. Already at the end of the eighteenth century, within a hundred years of Newton's "Opticks", people were reacting against the rigidity of the world of physics; what they could not accept were the ideological constraints set up by scientific discourse, by a grammar which construed all experience in terms of things. In our own twentieth century the scientists themselves have become weary of it, finding that it prevents them from engaging with the indeterminacy and the flow that they now regard as fundamental — let alone with the concept of the universe as conscious and communicating, as something itself to be interpreted as a semiotic system-&-process. Once we conceive of reality in semiotic terms, it can no longer surprise us that language has the power to construe it, maintain it, and transform it into something else.

13.3 Indeterminacy and probability in language

We have not here explicitly foregrounded the concept of indeterminacy in language. But there is a reason for this. To foreground indeterminacy is to treat it as something special, as a marked feature that stands out from, and hence distorts and destabilizes, the phenomenon under scrutiny. Here however we take indeterminacy for granted, as a normal and necessary feature of an evolved and functioning semiotic system. Rather than being something that needs to be especially remarked on, it is something that should be built in to our ways of representing and interpreting language: part of the background, rather than the foreground, to our account of the construal of experience.

We should however make a few observations about the significance of indeterminacy in relation to our present view of the meaning base. What does it mean to say that a natural language is an indeterminate system? In the most general terms, it suggests that the generalized categories that constitute language as a system — as "order", rather than as randomness or "chaos" (let us say randomness rather than chaos, since chaos in its technical reading is also a form of order) — are typically not categorical: that is, they do not display determinate boundaries, fixed criteria of membership, or stable relationships from one stratum to another. We could refer to them as "fuzzy", in the sense in which this term is used in fuzzy logic, fuzzy computing, etc.; but we prefer to retain the term "indeterminate" for the phenomena themselves, since "fuzzy" is usually applied to the theoretical modelling of the phenomena (it refers to meta-fuzz rather than fuzz).

This issue of order vs. randomness has surfaced at various times throughout the history of linguistics, as analogy vs. anomaly, theory vs. usage, and the like; the prevailing ideology has usually been on the side of order. Part of the reason for this is simply that order is easier to describe: indeed the act of describing typically imposes order, because it involves naming, classifying and taxonomizing. This is true of any form of systematic knowledge. But part of the reason lies in the nature of language itself, or at least the kind of language that linguistics was designed to account for. The exclusive object of study in linguistics was written language; and written language gives a much greater appearance of order than does language in its spoken form.

We say "gives a greater appearance of order" because the actual picture is very much more complex. The immediate appearance of order in written language — the fact that it is presented to us in neat blocks and rows upon a page (or the equivalent, in other forms of technology), whereas speech is notorious for its hesitations, false starts, backtracking, clearing of the throat and whatever — is simply a consequence of the fact that we do not display its history: we leave out the provisional attempts and early drafts, and "publish" only the finished product. When analogous measures are taken with spoken language there is no significant difference between the two: speech is just as orderly as writing (cf. Halliday, 1985/9).

It is when we come to look at the ideation base that significant variation does begin to appear. We see this in its clearest form in grammatical metaphor, which is typically associated with writing rather than speech. Grammatical metaphor objectifies our experience, transforming its being and happening into things; in so doing, it privileges order, since experience can now be categorized into classes and hierarchies of classes, which are significantly more determinate than the processes and properties favoured by the grammar in its congruent form. But even non-metaphorical forms of writing construe with greater determinacy. We may cite two very pervasive distinctions between spoken and written discourse. On the one hand, writing construes the text into clear-cut constituents, marked off by spacing and other forms of punctuation; in spoken language there are no clear beginnings and endings in the expression (we cannot refer to pauses, since they tend to occur at transition points before something that is less predictable;

pauses seldom mark the text's grammatical boundaries). On the other hand, many interpersonal and textual systems are realized in speech by intonation, and most intonation contrasts are gradual rather than categorical. Thus both syntagmatically and paradigmatically written language tends towards greater determinacy; hence our received model of language, in the mainstream grammatical tradition, emphasizes clear-cut constituents and classes. Not that it has no tolerance at all for mixed and intermediate categories; but it treats them as the exception, not the norm.

13.3.1 Types of indeterminacy

We have tried to make the point that the human condition is such that no singulary, determinate construction of experience would enable us to survive. We have to be able to see things in indeterminate ways: now this, now that, partly one thing, partly the other — the transitivity system is a paradigm example, and that lies at the core of the experiential component of grammar. There are perhaps five basic types of indeterminacy in the ideation base: ambiguities, blends, overlaps, neutralizations, and complementarities — although it should be recognized from the start that these categories are also somewhat indeterminate in themselves. What follows is a brief characterization of each in turn:

(1) **ambiguities** ('either a or x'): one form of wording construes two distinct meanings, each of which is exclusive of the other.

(2) **blends** ('both b and y'): one form of wording construes two different meanings, both of which are blended into a single whole.

(3) **overlaps** ('partly c, partly z'): two categories overlap so that certain members display some features of each.

(4) **neutralizations**: in certain contexts the difference between two categories disappears.

(5) **complementarities**: certain semantic features or domains are construed in two contradictory ways.

Examples of these types of indeterminacy follow.

(1) Ambiguity

(i) must:

```
You must be very careful! (when you do that)
        — obligation 'it is essential that you should be'

You must be very careless! (to have done that)
        — probability 'I am certain that you were'
```

Here the listener/ reader adopts either one interpretation or the other — usually, of course, without noticing that there is another possible meaning. In (i), the Attribute suggests the choice (one does not usually instruct someone to be careless!); but cf. *you must be very sure of yourself* ('before you do that'/ 'to have done that'). Compare also (ii), where the ambiguity is one that is typical of identifying clauses.

```
(ii) home is where your heart is
        — Token ^ Value 'if you live in a place, you love it'
        — Value ^ Token 'if you love a place, it is home to you'
```

(2) Blend

```
they might win tomorrow
        — ability 'they may be able to'
                            x
        — probability 'it is possible they will'
```

Here, on the other hand, the meaning of the oblique modal *might* combines the two senses of 'able' and 'possible', rather than requiring the listener to choose between them. If the verbal group is 'past', however, this again becomes an ambiguity:

```
they might have won

        — ability 'they were capable of winning (but they didn't)'

        — probability 'it is possible that they won (we don't know)'
```

(3) Overlap ('borderline case')

PROCESS TYPE	material	(behavioural)	mental
Example	wait	listen	hear
1.	unmarked present: present-in-present *I'm waiting*	unmarked present: present-in-present *I'm listening*	unmarked present: simple *I hear*
2.	can't project **I'm waiting that they're away*	can't project **I'm listening that they're away*	can project *I hear that they're away*
3.	does not impute consciousness *it (the bus) waited*	does impute consciousness *it listened = the cat*	does impute consciousness *it heard = the cat*
4.	is probed by *do* *the best thing to do is wait*	?	is not probed by *do* **the best thing to do is hear*

Behavioural processes such as *listen, watch* share some features with material processes ('present-in-present' as unmarked tense; no projection), other features with mental processes (the Medium/ Behaver is a conscious being). They lie on the borderline between 'doing' and 'sensing' (so can be re-iterated as *do* in some contexts but not in all).

(4) Neutralization

	finite	non-finite + preposition	non-finite - preposition
I get tired ...	condition *if I run*		
		source *from running*	
	cause *because I run*		*running*
		manner *with running*	
	time *when I run*		

If the dependent clause in such an environment is finite, it selects one or other type of enhancing relation: condition, cause or time. If the dependent clause is non-finite, the distinction is partially or wholly neutralized.

(5) Complementarity

transitivity   (i): transitive perspective

dry = 'make dry' (cf. wipe)

they	'll dry/wipe		— 'What will they dry?'
Actor	Process	+ Goal	
they	'll dry/ wipe	the dishes	'the children will dry the dishes'

transitivity   (ii): ergative perspective

dry = 'become dry' (cf. fade)

		they	'll dry/fade	— 'What will dry them?'
+ Agent	Process	Medium	Process	
the sun	will dry/ fade	them		'the sun will dry the clothes'

As discussed in Chapter 4 above, the grammar adopts two complementary perspectives on agency, the transitive and the ergative. Most processes are oriented primarily within one perspective or the other; here we have illustrated the complementarity with a verb that is at home in both.

Local indeterminacies of all these types are found in all regions of the content plane, either within one stratum or at the interface between one stratum and another (including of course puns, which are formed at the interface of content and expression). Some of them involve very general categories, and hence resonate across wide stretches of semantic space, like the transitive/ ergative complementarity. We may call them "local", however, in contrast to one global form of indeterminacy which is a feature of the entire system of language, and probably of any evolved semiotic system, namely its probabilistic character. Since we have not attempted to model this feature explicitly, it is perhaps important at least to adumbrate it in a few paragraphs.

13.3.2 Probability

We have sometimes referred to the relative frequency of a particular feature of the grammar. For instance, in our two examples of the meaning base as a resource in language processing, certain patterns characteristically recurred: future tense in the weather forecasts, imperative mood in the recipes. In each case this was a special feature pertaining to the register in question: in weather forecasts, the future tense is especially frequent *relative to the other primary tenses*.

To say this means that there is a general expectancy in English discourse that, again relative to the other primary tenses, future will occur less frequently than it does here. In other words, there is some global expectation, in the grammar of English, about the relative frequency of the different terms in the primary tense system, past, present and future. Similarly there is some global expectation about the relative frequency of imperative and indicative mood. Frequency in the text is to be interpreted, therefore, as the manifestation of underlying probability in the system.

Until recently it has not been possible to establish global probabilities of this kind, because to do so it is necessary to process very large numbers of instances, far more than could hope to be achieved given the time it takes to analyse the grammar of a text. We have been familiar with lexical probabilities for the greater part of a century, because words are relatively easy to count; and it has been recognized that the global probability of a word's occurrence is an integral part of its functioning in the linguistic system (Zipf, 1935). Those who know a language are rather sensitive to lexical frequencies, and will readily gloss a rare word by a more common one if called upon to explain something not understood. It seems fairly obvious that the same probabilistic principle will hold for terms in grammatical systems, although the suggestion has often met with considerable resistance, sometimes in a quaintly self-contradictory form: on being told that he is more likely to use this feature than that, the speaker protests that he is perfectly free to deviate from the norm — not recognizing that, in that case, there must be a norm for him to be departing from.

We now have very large corpuses, of English and some other languages, readily available and able to be accessed by sophisticated programs of software. It thus becomes possible to establish grammatical frequencies to match the quantitative patterns already established in the lexis. It is still not easy, because grammatical categories are typically not realized in any consistent and unambiguous way; there has to be rather complex pattern-matching to enable the program to recognize even apparently regular grammatical categories like those of tense and mood in English. But some studies have been undertaken; with regard to English primary tense, for example, in a corpus of about a million and a quarter finite clauses, past and present were found to be very closely equal, whereas future was considerably the least common of the three (Halliday & James, 1993).

This now gives substance to our observation about the future tense in weather forecasts. What we are saying is that there is a global pattern of probabilities in English, including a probability profile of the tense system whereby the probability of future is (say) 0.1. The register of weather forecasting, however, sets up a local pattern in which the probability of future is (say) 0.5. This changes the meaning of the system of primary tense, because it reverses the marking and hence sets up a new relationship among the different terms. It construes a realm of experience in which the future becomes the familiar dimension of time, the point of reference by which both present and past are defined.

This illustrates one very powerful feature of a probabilistic system of this kind: that it accommodates systematic functional variation. We have discussed the two text types illustrated in Part III, weather forecasting and recipes, as examples of variation in register: of the way in which the meaning selections in texts tend to vary systematically with their contextual function — their value in the social process. We pointed out that this variation is seldom categorical: except in very closed registers, or "restricted languages", no major options are likely to be totally excluded. What happens is that the probabilities are reset. This may be a relatively minor skewing affecting a large number of semantic features; but one or other system may stand out by being particularly clearly realigned, as happens with tense and with mood, respectively, in our two examples. We can in fact define register variation as the resetting of probabilities in the lexicogrammatical and semantic systems, including those in the ideation base.

We observe these probabilities in the form of frequencies in the text; thus in order to investigate register variation, we need to have very large corpuses, with texts of different types covering a wide range of functional varieties. (Note that there can be no such thing as a structured sample of such variation, any more than there can be of dialectal variation; you cannot quantify the functional spread of a language.) This makes it possible to establish both the global and the local probabilities. The objection has sometimes been made that global probabilities in a language are meaningless; that since every text is in some register or other, there can be no such thing as a quantitative profile of the language system as a whole. But the two perspectives are merely different standpoints of the observer; we can vary depth of focus just as we will, subject only to the constraint of the quantity of text data available — it makes no difference to the validity of the results obtained. (It may affect their usefulness, of course; but that depends on the purpose of any particular investigation. For some purposes it is precisely the global probabilities that we need to know. Again it is interesting that no such objection is raised to the concept of global probabilities in the lexis.)

The significance of global probabilities in the grammar emerges in various ways, both historical and synchronic. Historical change in language is typically a quantitative process, in which probabilities in systems at every level are gradually nudged in one direction or another, now and again becoming categorical so that some systemic upheaval takes place. Each instantiation of a tense form, say, whenever someone is speaking or writing in English, minutely perturbs the probabilities of the system — because what we call "system" and "instance" are one and the same phenomenon, being observed from different depths in time. There are, of course, more catastrophic types of change: languages become creolized, creolized systems in turn become decreolized, or a language ceases to be spoken altogether. At the "instance" end, a single highly-valued instance may exert a disproportionate effect: quotations from the Bible and from Shakespeare are familiar triggers of this "Hamlet factor" in English (in media discourse today almost every *change* is a *sea change*, which goes into our folk taxonomy of types of change). But such qualitative effects take place against a background of microscopic quantitative pressures, the sort of nanosemiotic processes by which a language is ongoingly restructured as **potential** out of the innumerable **instantial** encounters of daily life — the "sheer weight of numbers", as we sometimes call it. And in the ontogenetic dimension of history, the growth and development of language in a human child, an analogous dialectic can be observed: highly valued instances of text (rhymes, favourite stories and the like) interact with the quantitative pressures of the talk going on around (the child's access to the global probabilities — note that children do not begin learning the grammar by sorting out functional variation!) to yield a meaning potential that is a reasonable copy of the probabilistic system shared among the community.

Synchronically (that is, viewed synoptically in this way as a meaning potential) a language is, as we have said, a probabilistic system: if we say that, in the grammar, there is a system of primary tenses past/ present/ future, we assume the rider 'with a certain probability attached to them'. But we do not, of course, speak or write with one grammatical system at a time. Systems intersect with each other simultaneously (we choose tense along with voice, polarity, mood, transitivity and so on), and they follow each other in linear succession (we choose tense in clause 1, again in clause 2, again in clause 3 and so on). Each instance has its environment, both of previous instances, and of simultaneous instances of systems with their own sets of probabilities. We shall not attempt to discuss this issue here; except to refer briefly to what is one important aspect of indeterminacy, namely **partial association** between systems. We model the grammar as if each of these choices was independent: that the choice of tense, say, is not affected by the simultaneous choice of mood. This may, in fact, be so; but when choice is made in two systems simultaneously, such that each serves as environment for the other, there is often a conditioning effect on the probabilities. This may be an indication of a change in progress, or it may be a stable feature of the overall system. Nesbitt & Plum (1988) have shown, on the basis of a quantitative study, that there is mutual conditioning in English between the systems of projection (locution/ idea) and taxis (parataxis/ hypotaxis, i.e. (in this environment) quoting/ reporting), such that there is a positive association (1) of quoting and locution, (2) of reporting and idea. In other words, the favoured combinations are those exemplified in *She said, "I understand now", She thought she understood then*. This means that, in construing people's sayings and sensing, we do allow for projecting someone's speech into our own deictic space (*She said she understood then*), and for projecting someone's thought as if we had heard it expressed (*She thought, "I understand now"*); but these are marked options, clearly contrasting with our usual representation of these familiar aspects of experience. This in turn relates to the different interpretations of *thought* in these two environments: unmarked 'held the opinion' (which may be disputed by the speaker, — *But she didn't*); marked 'said to herself'.

Such partial associations, like probabilities as a whole (and in fact like all forms of indeterminacy), are difficult to represent in an explicit way in the grammatics. This has long been recognized in computational work in text generation and parsing[2]. The fact that these indeterminacies are difficult to handle computationally is another manifestation of something we know already: that it is hard for humans to construct a machine which will perform human-like semiotic tasks. (We should not fall into the familiar trap of saying "because it cannot be accommodated by our present logic, therefore it does not occur"!) The relevant question here is, what is the place of semantic indeterminacy in our overall construal of experience? We have not taken up that issue in this book; but we have tried to embody a general awareness of indeterminacy in our overall interpretative frame.

---

[2] Nigel, the systemic-functional generation grammar of the Penman system, had probabilities attached to terms in systems right from the start in 1980. They were used in random generation when the grammar was tested. For probabilistic analysis, see e.g. Sampson (1987, 1992.)

13.3.3 The significance of indeterminacy

How would we summarize the significance of indeterminacy, from the point of view of the semantic construal of experience? It lies first and foremost, perhaps, in the general principle that is being proclaimed, if indeterminacy is a typical and unremarkable feature of the grammar: that 'this is the way things are'. Our "reality" is inherently messy; it would be hard to construe experience, in a way that was beneficial to survival, with a semiotic system whose typical categories were well-defined, clearly bounded, and ordered by certainty rather than probability. This is the problem with designed systems, including semiotic ones: as a rule, they fail to provide adequately for mess.

Secondly, systems have varying probability profiles, so that (in terms of information theory) they carry differential loads of information: the skewer the probabilities of the terms in a system, the greater the redundancy that it carries — hence the less we need to attend to its unmarked state. For example: it has been found that, in an English clause, positive is about ten times as frequent as negative (Halliday & James, 1993). What this means is that we build in to our sense of a figure the presumption that something is or something happens, rather than that something is not or does not happen; extra work has to be done if a process is being construed as negative. The same applies to future tense, as we saw: extra grammatical energy is required to assign a figure to the future.

But, thirdly, within the overall construction of experience, the diversity of spheres of social action is realized by variation in the line-up of semantic features — that is, by variation in register. The probabilities are reset; and in some cases one or two "critical systems" are strongly affected in this way, such that the local norm skews the system, or perhaps even reverses the skewing set up by the global norm. It is here that we find future taking over as the unmarked primary tense in weather forecasting. As we said above, we define register variation in just these terms, as the ongoing resetting of probabilities in the lexicogrammar, which then functions to construe the ongoing variation at the level of the social process.

Moving away from consideration of probabilities, there are also, fourthly, regions in the ideation base whose construal typically involves one or other of the particular kinds of indeterminacy that we referred to earlier in this section. Let us try to offer some very brief illustrations of this, building on the few examples that were given above. The first is concerned with ambiguities and blends. The illustration comes from the interpersonal metafunction; here the meaning that is construed in the ideation base is being assessed (judged probable, desirable &c.) at the same time as it is intersubjectively enacted as proposition (statement, question) or proposal (offer, command).

Modality, the speaker's angle on what is or what should be, is notoriously fluid and shifting in its categories, probably in every language. In English, there is a fairly clearly defined semantic region construed at the intersection of a number of grammatical systems, including (1) type: probability/ usuality // obligation/ readiness: inclination/ ability; (2) value: median // high/ low; (3) orientation: objective/ subjective; (4) immediacy: immediate (neutral) / remote (oblique); (5) polarity: positive/ negative; and one or two others (for a summary, see Halliday, 1985). These are realized synthetically in various ways, one of which is by the modal finite operators *can, could, may, might, will , would, should, must, ought-to* (and one or two other fringe members). There is a great deal of indeterminacy throughout the region; but it is of more than one kind. At one "corner", if we combine value with neutral (immediate), then the resulting wordings are **ambiguous,** as to the *type* of modality expressed: thus *must* has three clearly distinct meanings, (a) as probability (e.g. *that must be Mary* 'certainly that is Mary'), (b) as obligation (e.g. *you must wear a helmet* 'it is essential that you wear a helmet'), (c) as readiness: inclination (e.g. *if you must make all that noise* 'if you insist on making all that noise'). That these are truly ambiguous can be gathered from an example such as *she must complain,* which has to be interpreted in *one or another* of these different meanings — the context will of course usually make it clear which; for example:

following	example	systemic reading
'I wonder why they take all that trouble just for her?'	— She must complain.	probability: 'the reason is certainly that she complains'
'I don't think they'll let her return it!'	— She must complain.	obligation: 'it is essential that she should complain'
'Whatever happens she's never satisfied'	— She must complain.	readiness: 'she insists on complaining'

But at the opposite corner, so to speak, if we combine low value with oblique (remote), the result is typically **blending** rather than ambiguity: e.g. *it couldn't hurt you to apologize* is a blend of 'it would not be able to hurt you' (readiness: ability), 'it is unlikely that it would hurt you' (probability) and even perhaps 'it would not be allowed to hurt you' (obligation). In other words, looking at it from the point of view of blending, in the region of 'what I think'/ 'what is wanted', it is easiest to blend the low values 'what I can conceive of' with 'what is permitted', especially in 'remote' conditions (hypothetical, projected or tentative) [realized as *could, might*]; and hardest to blend the high values 'what I am convinced of' with 'what is required', especially when 'immediate' [realized as *must*]. This is diagrammed in Figure 13-3. This shows that, in modality, a very complex region where the metafunctions themselves overlap ('what I think is' and 'what ought to be' blending in 'what I think ought to be'), the indeterminacy even extends to indeterminacy between the different types of indeterminacy!

The next illustration is concerned with overlaps and complementarities. For this we can turn to the system of transitivity. As we saw, the grammar distinguishes a number of types of process, material, mental, verbal and relational; the distinctions are made by a cluster of syntactic variables — the valency of associated participant roles, the class of entity that takes on each role, the potential for combining with other figures, the associated tense systems and the like. But since these variables "draw the line" at different places, there are areas of overlap, with mixed categories that share some characteristics with one group and some with another. We gave the example of behavioural processes; these are a mixed category, formed by the **overlap** of the material, on the one side, and the mental or verbal on the other. Behaving is construed as a type of figure that (like the mental) typically has a conscious participant as the central role, and does not extend beyond this to a second participant; but, on the other hand, it does not project, and it has a time frame like that of the material. Thus behavioural processes lie squarely athwart a fuzzy borderline. In those figures where there is a second direct participant, some form of agency runs through all the different types of process; but agency is such a complex aspect of human experience that the grammar does not delineate it by a single stroke, but construes it by means of a fundamental **complementarity**, that between the transitive and the ergative perspectives. Thus figures involving two direct participants, such as Actor + Goal in the material, are aligned along two different axes: the transitive one, based on the potential extension of force (mechanical energy) from a doer to another entity; and the ergative one, based on the potential introduction of agency (causal energy) from another entity as external source. Thus *the earthquake shook the house* is construed *both* as 'earthquake + shake' plus optional Goal 'house', *and* as 'house + shake' plus optional Agent 'earthquake'. As always in cases of complementarity, certain parts of the region are more strongly aligned to one perspective, other parts to the other; but the total picture requires the confrontation of the two.

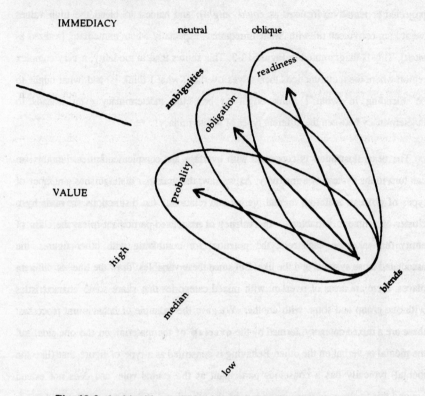

Fig. 13-3: Ambiguities and blends in the different corners of modality

Thirdly, neutralization. When two figures are linked into a sequence, by some logical-semantic relation, there is a rather wide range of possible semantic relations between the two: the relations of time and of cause and condition are particularly elaborated in this respect, but there are others besides — the manner, the matter, and so on. The distinctions among these relationships, however, may be to a greater or lesser degree **neutralized**, where one clause is construed as dependent on the other; this happens as the dependent clause moves from finite to non-finite status. For example, in *they get caught taking bribes* the distinction that would be made in the agnate finite clause, among, say *they get caught if they take bribes, they get caught when they take bribes, they get caught because they take bribes,* is simply neutralized — it is not a blend of all three, nor is there any ambiguity involved. An intermediate degree of specificity, with partial neutralization, can be seen in the non-finite clause with accompanying preposition, as in *they get caught for taking bribes*. What happens here is that the fact that there *is* a connection between the two figures is unequivocally construed by the dependency; but the nature of this connection — *what kind of* logical relationship is being set up — does not enter the picture.

There are of course many different contexts for all these indeterminacies, in different regions of the total semantic space. Certain types of ambiguity appear to be not so much artefacts of the realization (not just grammatical puns, so to speak) but rather another kind of complementarity, where the grammar is as it were "having things both ways" — both interpretations have to be accepted at one and the same time. This is sometimes the case with Token + Value structures, in figures of being. These clauses are always ambiguous, if the verb is *be*, since this verb does not mark the passive; yet some depend on being interpreted both ways — particularly, perhaps, some proverbial sayings. Thus, *one man's meat is another man's poison* is both Token ^ Value 'what one person likes may displease another' and Value ^ Token 'what one person dislikes may please another'; contrast *what's sauce for the goose is sauce for the gander,* which can be interpreted only as Token ^ Value. (That these are true potential ambiguities can be seen from the following example of popular economics, given in answer to the query about personal wealth:

```
Total net personal wealth is between two and a half and three
times Gross Domestic Product.
```

This might mean either 'personal wealth accounts for 2.5 - 3 times GDP' (Token ^ Value: that's how it's evaluated), or 'personal wealth is expressed as 2.5 - 3 times GDP' (Value ^ Token: that's how it's calculated). See the discussion in Halliday (1985: Ch. 5).)

It seems likely that all these different kinds of indeterminacy are what make it possible for the grammar to offer a plausible construal of experience — one that is rich enough, yet fluid enough, for human beings to live with. We should stress once again that the examples cited here are features of the ideation base of one particular language, namely English. No other language will be identical. Indeed the distribution of indeterminacies is likely to be precisely one of the features in which languages differ most, and even perhaps varieties within one and the same language. But every language depends on indeterminacy as a resource for meaning — even if our grammatics is not yet very clever at teasing it out.

13.4 Polysystemicness

One feature that emerges from the preceding discussion (and from our treatment throughout) is the **polysystemic** nature of the ideation base. The ideational meaning potential embodies not one single semantic system but rather several such systems coexisting; in Firth's terms, it is a "system of systems" — in two distinct but related ways.

(i) There are internal **complementarities**:

> in the congruent mode of construing experience, there is a **metafunctional complementarity**: the ideational potential offers two complementary modes for construing experience — the highly generalized **logical mode**, with projection & expansion as the dominant semantic motifs, and the more particularized **experiential mode**, with its typologies of processes, things, qualities, and circumstances;

> within this congruent mode, there is a **fractal complementarity**: the highly generalized semantic types of projection & expansion are manifested in complementary domains — those of sequences, figures, and participants; so that, for example, some phenomenon of experience construed as having temporal expansion might appear either as a sequence or as a configuration;

> still in its congruent mode, there are **systemic complementarities**: the ideational potential offers systemic complementarities such as the ergative and transitive models of participation in processes, and the mass and count (singular/ plural) models of quantity;

> beyond its congruent mode, there is **metaphorical complementarity**: the ideational model offers a complementarity between the congruent mode itself and the metaphorical mode, making it possible to take some phenomenon as already construed and then reconstrue it as if it was a phenomenon of a different kind.

Such complementarities constitute one form of indeterminacy of the system — one that allows it to be "polysystemic" in the particular sense of embodying more than one way of construing experience.

(ii) In addition, the ideation base is polysystemic in another sense: **registerial variation**. We have seen that such variation can be construed in terms of the probabilistic nature of the linguistic system, as variation in the probabilities associated with terms in systems. Seen in this light, a register is a particular probabilistic setting of the system; and the move from one register to another is a re-setting of these probabilities. What is globally the 'same' ideational semantic system can thus appear as a collection of different systems, as one moves along the cline of instantiation from potential to instance (see Figures 8-1 and 8-3 in Chapter 8, Section 8.1). As we noted above, the effect is quantitative; but it is also qualitative, in the sense that it provides different perspectives on experience within the same system. We referred to the change in the perspective on time that takes place when one moves into the realm of weather forecasting. In the limiting case, this effect may be qualitative, in that certain options may simply be absent in a system of a given register, having the probability of zero. Our accounts of the registers of recipes and weather forecasts contain illustrations of this: we noted, for example, the highly restricted construal of agency in the world of the kitchen.

The overall ideation base thus comprises many different registerial variants — register-specific systems that we called domain models. Now, just as the overall ideation base is a theory of our total experience of the world around us and inside us — the theory that is shared by the culture as a whole, so also the different registerial variants constitute different 'subtheories' of our experience. These 'subtheories' may complement one another by simply being concerned with different domains of experience — the culinary and meteorological domains in our examples in Part III. This complementarity is purely additive, although for society as a whole it constitutes the semiotic aspect of the division of labour, whereby different people construe different facets of the overall cultural experience. But such subtheories may also be concerned with more or less the same domain, bringing alternative theoretical perspectives to the construal of experience that is shared. Halliday (1971) shows how this is achieved in William Golding's novel *The Inheritors*, by means of alternative deployments of the resources of transitivity as Golding presents the world view of two groups of early humans; these different perspectives on the shared experience are constituted as variants of the same overall transitivity system.

From an educational point of view, the most fundamental complementarity is the move from the registers of everyday life to the registers of education: this is a move from folk or commonsense models to the "uncommonsense" models of systematic and technical knowledge. To say that the ideational system is polysystemic means that it can support these different theoretical angles on experience: semantic variation of all kinds is the manifestation of the different theoretical interpretations that language places on experience. In the next chapter we shall try to illustrate this point, by a consideration of the realm of human consciousness as this is construed in daily life and in (mainstream) cognitive science.

14. Construing ideational models: consciousness in daily life and in cognitive science

As a resource for making sense of our experience, the ideation base enables us to construe a range of different theories, commonsense as well as scientific. There is a cline between folk, or commonsense, theories and scientific, or uncommonsense, ones; and at any point along the cline alternative theories may be in competition. The ideation base, by dint of being polysystemic, accommodates variation along this cline, not only from folk to scientific but also across alternatives: it embodies both congruent and metaphorical construals of experience, and it provides elasticity within the overall construction space. We shall examine this variation with particular reference to those phenomena to which we are offering the ideation base as a conceptual alternative: the mind, knowledge, cognition — as the concerns of cognitive science. Drawing on our discussion in Part II, we shall suggest that the domain of cognitive science is construed ideationally within the folk model; but that this model is extended metaphorically in cognitive science itself, and this extension in fact invites the interpretation of knowledge as meaning. First, however, let us make a few comments on the cline from folk to scientific and the variation in the degree of conscious awareness that this involves.

14.1 Models embodied in the ideation base

Researchers concerned with culture have distinguished among different kinds of **cultural models** — folk models, expert models, scientific models (see e.g. Holland & Quinn, 1987). Cognitive science operates with a scientific model of the individual mind; but, we shall suggest, it is one that is based fairly uncritically on certain aspects of a folk model, in particular in its selection of, and perspective on, its own domain of enquiry. Our discussion will relate to the models we have identified within the ideation base — the general potential model, and the more specific domain models.

14.1.1 Models at different levels of abstraction

Any given model of experience exists at different orders of abstraction; see Figure 14-1. It is a configuration of higher-level meanings within the **context of culture**; at the same time, it is also construed **semantically**, in the **ideation base**. The relationship between these two orders of abstraction, contextual and semantic, is a stratal one; hence a model is a cultural construct that is construed in language (together with other, language-dependent semiotic systems such as expository drawings and diagrams).

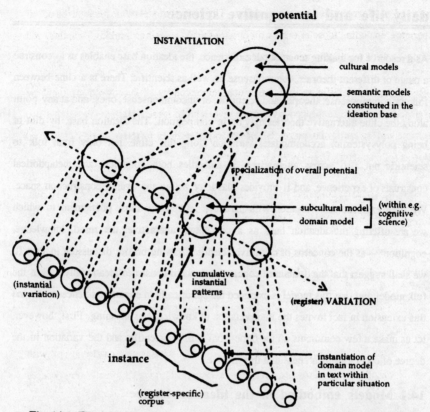

Fig. 14-1: The different orders of abstraction in a model and the different degrees of instantiation

At both these strata, models are also located along the cline of instantiation (see Chapter 8, Section 8.1 and Figure 8-3), running between the **potential** — the overall resources for making meaning, within the context of culture, and the **instance** — instantial 'texts' constituted of meanings that have been selected from this potential, within particular contexts of situation.[1] The potential end of the cline of instantiation embodies all the contextual-semantic models that the culture embraces. The everyday folk models are likely to be embraced unconsciously by everybody in the culture, because they are everyday models, instantiated in casual conversation, and because they are

---

[1] 'Text' or 'discourse' here has to be understood not just at the lowest level of abstraction in language as a realization in speech or writing, but primarily as configurations of linguistic and higher-level cultural meanings — as generally throughout this book (see Halliday, 1978a; Halliday & Hasan, 1985; Martin, 1992).

construed as congruent in the cryptogrammar. The general model of the phenomena of our experience, including those of our own consciousness — seeing, thinking, wanting, and feeling —, is of this highly generalized kind.

In contrast, scientific models are much more contextually constrained: they are developed, maintained, changed and transmitted within those situation types that we associate with scientific language. We can characterize them in terms of field, tenor and mode as follows (from Halliday & Martin, 1993: 54):

field: (i) extending, transmitting or exploring knowledge (ii) in the physical, biological or social sciences;

tenor: addressed to specialists, to learners or to laymen, from within the same group (e.g. specialist to specialist) or across groups (e.g. lecturer to students); and

mode: phonic or graphic channel, most congruent (e.g., formal 'written language' with graphic channel) or less so (e.g., formal with phonic channel), and with variation in rhetorical function — expository, hortatory, polemic, imaginative and so on.

These ranges of field, tenor and mode values define a great variety of situation types within institutions of higher education, of research and of technological development. However, these situation types are quite constrained relative to the context of culture as a whole: only certain members of the culture participate in these situation types and engage with the scientific models that are developed, maintained, changed and transmitted within them. In this respect, scientific models are clearly subcultural models: contextually they are located somewhere between the potential and the instance. If we focus on particular scientific models, such as those of the mind in cognitive science, we will find that they are even more contextually constrained. Figure 14-1 shows the dispersal of contextual-semantic models along the cline of instantiation. As the figure indicates, an inherent property of instantiation is variation; and scientific models (like other subcultural models) vary one in relation to another. Sometimes they are complementary, sometimes they conflict.

14.1.2 Models at different levels of awareness

There is thus a range of variation from our everyday folk models to scientific models, with expert models somewhere coming in between (Linde, 1987). Such models vary considerably in the degree to which we are consciously aware of them as models (cf. Whorf's, 1956, notion of critical consciousness). We are more aware of models that 'stand out' as belonging a particular subculture than of those that are part of our everyday repertoire; and we are more aware of scientific models than of folk models.

Whatever the scope and sophistication of a model, however, we are likely to be more aware of a model as a cultural construct than as a linguistic construct, since language is typically further from our conscious attention. Certain aspects of language are closer to conscious awareness than others (see Halliday, 1987): these are the more exposed parts of language, which are also the parts that tend to get studied first. In Western thinking about language, the most exposed aspect of language has been the "word": to talk is to "put things into words". The folk notion of the "word" is really a conflation of two different abstractions, one lexical and one grammatical.

(i) **Vocabulary** (lexis): the word as lexical item, or "lexeme". This is construed as an isolate, a 'thing' that can be counted and sorted in (alphabetical) order. People "look for" words, they "put thoughts into" them, "put them into" or "take them out of another's mouth", and nowadays they keep collections of words on their shelves or in their computers in the form of dictionaries. Specialist knowledge is thought of as a matter of terminology. The taxonomic organization of vocabulary is less exposed: it is made explicit in Roget's Thesaurus, but is only implicit in a standard dictionary. Lexical taxonomy was the first area of language to be systematically studied by anthropologists, when they began to explore cultural knowledge as it is embodied in folk taxonomies of plants, animals, diseases and the like.

(ii) **Grammar**: the word as one of the ranks in the grammatical system. This is, not surprisingly, where Western linguistic theory as we know it today began in classical times, with the study of words varying in form according to their case, number, aspect, person etc.. Word-based systems such as these do provide a way in to studying grammatical semantics: but the meanings they construe are always more complex than the categories that appear as formal variants, and grammarians have had to become aware of covert patterns.

It is only in more recent times that the more covert areas of grammar have been systematically studied — those that, following Whorf, we have referred to as "cryptogrammar" (see Chapter 2, Section 2.8 above). Whorf (1956) distinguished between overt and covert categories and pointed out that covert categories were often also "cryptotypes" — categories whose meanings were complex and difficult to access. Many aspects of clause grammar, and of the grammar of clause complexes, are essentially cryptotypic. It is the analysis of some of these more covert features embodied in the everyday grammar, in particular the theory of mental processes, that throws light on the domain of cognitive science.

In addition to the different degrees of their awareness of different grammatical **units**, such as words and clauses, people are also not equally aware of the different kinds of **functions** in which the resources of language are organized. In particular, in constructing and reasoning about more conscious models, people are readily aware of those linguistic resources whose function it is to interpret and represent experience, those of the ideational metafunction; but they are much less aware of those of the other two metafunctions, the interpersonal and the textual — no doubt because these do not embody representations of experience but reflect our engagement with the world in different ways. However, although they tend to be overlooked when one comes to build a 'scientific' model of language and the mind, these other metafunctions are no less important than the ideational. We will take up this issue again below with respect to the balance between ideational and interpersonal meaning (for related discussion of the textual metafunction, see Chapter 9 above).

14.1.3 Emergence of scientific registers

In the early scientific period in the West, new registers evolved as part of the ongoing reconstruction of experience in the form of systematic knowledge and experimental science (cf. Chapter 13, Section 13.2.6.3). Perhaps the earliest to evolve in these new contexts were those registers associated with the exploration, storage and dissemination of new knowledge about plants and herbs in the 16th and 17th centuries. These new contexts put pressure on the linguistic resources, and the meaning-creating power of these resources correspondingly increased. We can hypothesize a gradual evolution from the registers of ordinary language, with their folk models of the world, including folk taxonomies of plants and herbs, to more specialized scientific ones. It was at this point, as people became aware of the rapid development of new knowledge and the need for processing and storing it, that conscious design of language began, with nomenclatures and taxonomies being explicitly discussed and fixed. At the same time — but in this case without conscious design — new ways of meaning evolved in the construction of figures and sequences.

In the evolution of a more scientific approach to information about plants and herbs, it is possible to trace not only a move away from folk taxonomy towards scientific taxonomy, but also a move towards an organization of discourse that represents information succinctly and uniformly, culminating in Linnaeus' descriptions; see Slaughter (1986) for discussion. The following extracts spanning a period of about 225 years are quoted from Slaughter's account:

Banckes' (1525) *Herbal:*

> Asterion or Lunary groweth among stones and in high places. This herb showeth by night. This herb hath yellow flowers whole and round as a cockbell, or else like to foxgloves. The leaves of this herb be round and blue, and they have the mark of the moon in the middle, as it were three-leaved grass, but the leaves thereof be more [larger] and they be round as a penny; and the stalk of this herb is red, and this herb seemeth as it were musk, and the juice thereof is yellow. And this herb groweth in the new moon without leaves, and every day springeth a new leaf to the end of fifteen days, and after fifteen days it loseth every day a leaf as the moon waneth, and it springeth and waneth as doth the moon; and where it groweth, there groweth great quantity. The virtue of this herb is thus. They that eat of the berries or of the herb in waning of the moon, when it is *in signo virginis,* if he have the falling evil, he shall be whole thereof; or if he bear this about his neck he shall be helped without doubt.

Gerard (1597), *The Herbal or General Historie of Plants:*

The first of the Daffodils is that with the purple crowne or circle, having small narrow leaves, thicke fat, and full of slimie juice; among the which riseth up a naked stalke smooth and hollow, of a foot high, bearing at the top a faire milke white floure growing forth of a hood or thin filme such as the flours of onions are wrapped in: in the midst of which floure is a round circle or small coronet of a yellowish colour, purfled or bordered about the edge of the said ring or circle with a pleasant purple colour; which being past, there followeth a thicke know or button, wherein is contained blacke round seed. The root is white, bulbous or onion-fashion.

Bauhin (1620), *Prodomus theatri Botanici:*

From a short tapering root, by no means fibrous, spring several stalks about 18 inches long: they straggle over the ground, and are cylindrical in shape and furrowed, becoming gradually white near the root with a slight coating of down, and spreading out into little sprays. The plant has but few leaves, similar to those of *Beta nigra*, except that they are smaller, and supplied with long petoiles. The flowers are small, and of greenish yellow. The fruits one can see growing in large numbers close by the root, and from that point they spread along the stalk, at almost every leaf. They are rough and tubercled and separate into three reflexed points. In their cavity, one grain of the shape of an Adonis seed is contained; it is slightly rounded and ends in a point, and is covered with a double layer of reddish membrane, the inner one eclosing a white, farinaceous core.

Carolus Linnaeus (1754), *Genera plantarum:*

```
                            Urtica
Masculi flores
CAL. Perianthium tetraphyllum: foliolis subrotundis, concavis,
obtusis.
COR. Petala nulla.
 Nectarium in centro floris, urceolatum, integrum, inferne
angustius, minimum.
STAM. Filamenta quatuor, subulata, longitudine calycis, patentia,
intra singulum folium calycinum singula. Antherae biloculares.
```

Here we can see the emergence of a specialist form of discourse, as commonsense knowledge about plants is gradually turned into uncommonsense, scientific knowledge. Linnaeus' specification could be turned into a designed frame-based system of the kind used today in frame-based inheritance networks (cf. Chapter 1, Section 1.9.5).

As designed semiotic systems emerge, both the registers of everyday language and the original specialist registers continue to exist and to develop; folk models of the world will co-exist alongside the scientific ones (see e.g. Halliday & Martin, 1993: Ch. 8). A certain degree of intertranslatablity is likely to be maintained — linguistic renderings of logical or mathematical formulas, for instance; and this constitutes one of the contexts in which ordinary language is brought into explicit contact with more scientific varieties. There will always be some complementarity of function between the more designed varieties and those that are naturally evolving. They may be allocated to different spheres of activity: for example, the language of bird-watchers vs. the language of ornithologists. But in other cases the two are closely integrated as submotifs within a single sphere: for example, the use of both natural language and mathematical expressions side by side in the learning and practice of mathematics. This kind of interpenetration still entails a semiotic complementarity, but of a very sensitive kind, requiring a delicate interpretation of the context in order to bring it out.

14.1.4 The shift from folk models to scientific ones

The shift from folk models to scientific ones thus takes place over a long period of time; it typically involves several factors: see Figure 14-2.

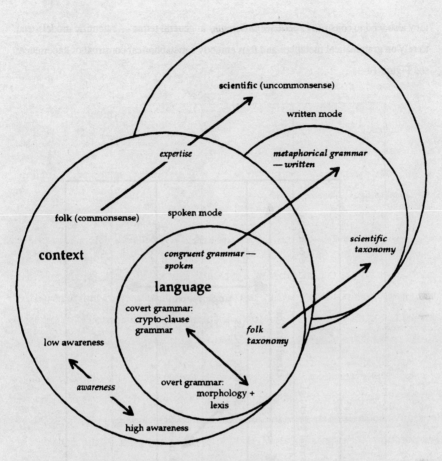

Fig. 14-2: The shift from folk models to scientific ones

As we noted above, folk models are part of the unconscious background of thinking in everyday situation types; they have *evolved* without any conscious design and are not associated with academic contexts. Folk models can also be more conscious, of course — these are the models that people talk about, that they believe they believe (cf. Figure 14-3 to be discussed below). Scientific models are consciously *designed* in more restricted situation types, usually within academic institutions, to serve as resources in reasoning about the world.

As we also noted above (cf. Figure 14-1), we can interpret folk models and scientific ones as co-existing **varieties** of the same basic system within the ideation base. In the first instance, we will, of course, be aware of them as differing in particular domains — e.g. as operating with different lexical semantic organizations (see further below); but they also tend to construe experience differently in general terms — scientific models tend to rely on grammatical metaphor and thus embody a metaphorical construal of experience: see Figure 14-3.

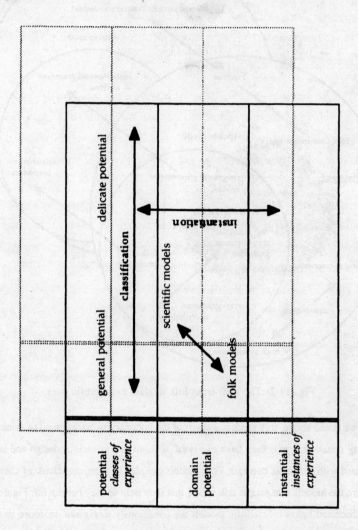

Fig. 14-3: Folk and scientific models within the ideation base

In the move from folk models to scientific ones, the first aspect of language to which scholars directed their attention was, as we would expect, the vocabulary. Thus in the early science of the 16th and 17th centuries, scholars were concerned with the taxonomic interpretation of the world; they tended to feel that ordinary language let them down, and started to explore the possibilities of artificial languages, culminating in Bishop Wilkins'

(1668) *Universal Language and Real Character.* What this meant was that scientists were moving away from folk taxonomy as a way of interpreting the world, towards a scientific taxonomy, in which further taxa were introduced and terms were more explicitly defined (cf. Chpater 2, Section 2.11.3 above). The solution to their problem thus turned out to be not, as they thought, the development of an artificial language, but rather the development of new regularities in the forms of ordinary language.

Within the grammar, there was some awareness of the grammatical construction of words; for instance, Wilkins introduced 'transcendental particles' on the model of (Latin) derivational morphology so as to be able to expand the vocabulary in systematic ways. But these scholars did not discuss the less exposed aspects of grammar — the covert categories of the clause and clause complex. They seem to have remained unaware of the part that was played by such patterns in constructing their discourse. However, by this time, the cryptogrammar of scientific English was already evolving along the lines discussed in Chapter 6; and these changes were accelerated in the discourses of Newton, whose work marked the end of purely taxonomic science and laid the foundation of a new model based on experimentation, general laws and predictions, and in work of later 18th century and 19th century scholars. The most central aspect of the various changes that took place was the **reification** of experience — the grammatical metaphor whereby processes were reconstrued as things. In the language of everyday commonsense, *A attracts B, so B moves* — a complex of two clauses; in the language of science, *attraction causes* (or *is the cause of*) *movement* — where the everyday clause complex, the sequence of two processes of action, has been 'compressed' into one clause with two nominalized elements, and a single process of being (*cause* 'be causally', or *be*). When they are reconstrued as things, processes lose their location in time and often also their participants; for instance, *A attracts B* is likely to be reconstrued simply as *attraction*. Attraction, repulsion, motion, gravity, acceleration, etc. can then be taxonomized in the same way as ordinary things such as plants and animals; they become part of an explicit taxonomy of metaphorical things. These basic resources were already in place in ordinary language — the nominal group for representing things and for organizing them into taxonomies,[2] nominalizing suffixes for reconstruing non-things as things, and so on; but

_____

[2] The nominal group offers the resources for taxonomizing things but the verbal group does not offer any equivalent resources for taxonomizing processes (cf. Chapter 4 above). Thus if

their potential was being exploited to a greater extent and in significantly different ways. This change in the grammar entailed a change in world view, towards a static, reified world — so much so that Bohm (1979) complains that language makes it hard to represent the kind of flux that modern physics likes to deal with. Bohm's dissatisfaction is directed at language in general; but his real target is — or should be — the language of science. The everyday language of casual speech is, by and large, a language of flux, construing experience in much the way that Bohm seems to demand (see Halliday, 1987).

Over the last decade or so, detailed work on the semantic patterns of the registers of different disciplines has shown how scientific models are construed not only in physics but also in other disciplines at secondary and tertiary level. Unsworth (1995) shows how the resources of the ideation base are deployed in physics to reconstrue commonsense experience — e.g. sounds that we can hear are construed into microscopic and macroscopic sequences of processes, and these are then 'condensed' by means of grammatical metaphor into 'things' such as vibration, contraction, and rarefaction. Wignell et al (1990) show how taxonomic order is built up in geological models (cf. Chapter 2, Section 2.11.3 [1] above) and how sequences of geological processes can be 'distilled' into metaphorical 'things' such as lithification. In these models, technicality is a salient feature. In contrast, Eggins et al (1993) show that models of the past in secondary-school text books of history do not rely on technicality (with the exception of a few technical terms for periods, such as "the Renaissance"), but rather on metaphorical reconstructions of the past. Instead of people taking part in processes unfolding over time, these processes are reconstrued as things (such as famine, war, migration) having temporal location. This makes it possible for historical models to generalize over particular events that people might observe, and to construe long-term patterns and tendencies.

We now turn to another area of human experience — our experience of taking part in seeing, thinking, wanting, and feeling, i.e. in processes of consciousness. We begin by

---

'remember' is reified, it can be construed as a thing which is easily taxonomized — 'memory: short term memory/ long term memory; semantic memory', and so on.

reviewing the general folk model of such processes, and then explore how this folk model has been reconstrued in cognitive science.

14.2 Sensing: the folk model

We have shown how the system of the ideation base construes consciousness: as conscious processing by a conscious being. Conscious processing can create a higher-order world of ideas (or, as we would say, meanings), comparable in certain respects to Popper's World 3; this defines the essential distinction between projection and expansion as ways of relating one figure to another (Chapter 3). Conscious processes themselves appear as the central figures in the construal of experience (Chapter 4), and they are pivotal in differentiating among the various types of participant (Chapter 5). This folk model is constituted in innumerable encounters in the course of casual conversation; and it is instantiated again and again in contexts of everyday life.

Conscious processes are of two kinds: sensing, and saying. Since what we are exploring here is the modelling of "mind", our concern in the first instance will be with sensing. Processes of saying will be implicated later on. Let us first review the folk model by exploring some text instances of how speakers and writers construe consciousness. In the following passage from a dialogue, one speaker refers to her own conscious processing:

Text (1): Extract of casual conversation (backchannelling omitted)

When I feel really depressed, I **think** "what a horrible lot", and
I call them to myself — I **think** "they're absolutely horrible".
"What other parent ever had such children?" I **think**; "I've simply
devoted my life to that lot". But when I'm feeling in a good mood,
and I **see** them sort of more or less as individuals, I **think** to
myself "I don't **care** whether they're sort of particularly devoted
or not." "They're so lovely" I **think**. (Svartvik & Quirk, 1980: 319.)

Processes of sensing are shown in the extract in bold. The following are some notes on our analysis.

(i) *feel.* The two clauses *I feel depressed, I'm feeling in a good mood* are on the borderline of sensing and being; we treat them here as processes of being, sinc they seem agnate to *I am depressed*   (relational: ascriptive, with *feel* as non-salient syllable); cf. the proportion

```
I feel depressed : I am depressed :: I don't feel depressed : I am
not depressed
```

rather than to *I feel that I am depressed* (mental: cognitive, with *feel* as salient), where the proportionality does not hold:

```
I feel depressed : I feel that I am depressed ≠ I don't feel
depressed : I don't feel that I am depressed
```

— where the last is not contradicted by *but in fact I am.*

(ii) *see.* The clause *I see them as individuals* could be either mental: cognitive + projection 'I consider that they are individuals' or mental: perceptive + Role 'I see them in their guise as individuals'. The latter interpretation is agnate to *I look at them as individuals,* which seems more plausible here. But in either case the *see* figure is one of sensing.

(iii) *care.* The clause *I don't care* is grammatically mental: emotive. The following clause *whether they're ... devoted or not* is a projection; but it is one of the 'fact' type, not projected by the mental clause itself (see the second paragraph below).

The speaker construes her processes of thinking as (1) a figure of sensing, realized by a mental clause (*I think*), and (2) a projected figure, realized by a clause representing the 'content' of that clause — the idea projected by her thinking (*they're absolutely horrible; I don't care whether they're sort of particularly devoted or not; they're so lovely;* and so on). The figure of sensing is a configuration of a Process (*think*) and the participant engaged in sensing, the Senser (*I*); that is, consciousness is construed as a complementarity of change through time and persistence through time — as a conscious participant involved in an unfolding process.

In the grammar, the 'idea' is a separate clause that combines with the 'sensing' clause in a clause complex, through the relation of projection; see Figure 14-4 for a structural interpretation. In our analysis (unlike that of the mainstream grammatical tradition), the projected clause is not a constituent part of the mental or verbal clause by which it is projected. There are numerous reasons for this; some of them are grammatical — for example, it cannot be the focus of theme-predication [we do not say: *it is that they're absolutely horrible that I think*]; it cannot be the Subject of a passive mental clause [we do not say: *they're absolutely horrible is thought by me*]; it is presumed by the substitute *so* , which is also used to presume conditional clauses in clause complexes: *I think they're absolutely horrible and my husband thinks so too*]. But these, in turn, reflect the semantic nature of projection: this is a relationship between two figures, not a device whereby one becomes a participant inside another. We can thus show the difference between these and 'fact' clauses, those where the idea clause is a projection but it is not the accompanying mental clause that is doing the projecting; such readymade projections do function as constituents. An example here is *I don't care whether they are devoted or not;* compare *it's not whether they are devoted or not that I care about.* Figure 14-5 shows how the proposition construed by the idea clause is projected, as the "content of consciousness", by the Senser involved in the process of sensing. This content is brought into existence by the sensing process, as actualized through the Senser; and it is construed as being of a higher order of semiotic abstraction than the process of sensing itself (i.e. it is always at one further remove from the instantial context).

I	*think*		*they're absolutely horrible*
1		——>	'2
mental clause			projected clause
Senser:	Process:		
nom. gp.: conscious	verbal gp.		

Fig. 14-4: Clause complex of mental clause projecting an idea clause

In the conversation above, the 'ideas' projected by the figures of sensing are **quoted** — a kind of interior monologue. Typically, however, figures of sensing project ideas as **reported**.[3] The potential for projection, and the contrast between these two modes of projection, indicate a similarity between figures of sensing and figures of saying; interestingly, one of the figures of sensing in this extract includes a participant that is

---

[3] A number of these figures, if we consider just their wording, could be interpreted as reported. However, the context of the discourse, and their realization in phonology, makes it clear that all are in fact quoted projections.

more characteristic of figures of saying — a Receiver: *myself* (in *I think to myself*). We shall return to the relationship between sensing and saying in Section 14.4 below.

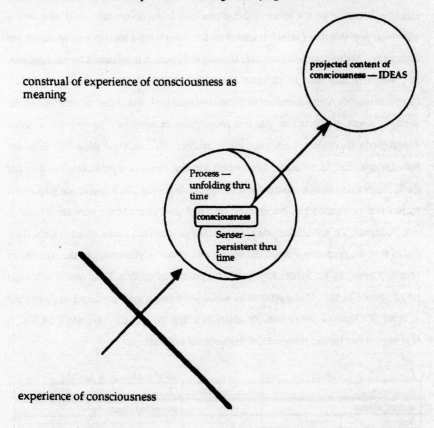

construal of experience of consciousness as meaning

projected content of consciousness — IDEAS

Process — unfolding thru time

consciousness

Senser — persistent thru time

experience of consciousness

Fig. 14-5: The grammar's construal of consciousness as meaning

Speakers in casual conversation are often concerned with construing their own consciousness. Indeed, Painter (1993) documents how one child first learned to construe mental projection: he began with figures in which he himself was the Senser. The system made it possible for him then to generalize his own experience of consciousness by construing other persons in the Senser role, as he built up a model in which this role could be occupied by any conscious (prototypically human) being. Thus in narrative, the writer often construes his or her characters' consciousness on the same model as in Figure 14-4 above. Projected ideas are typically reported rather than quoted. For example:

Text (2): Extract from *A first time for everything*

Jessica Steele, *A first time for everything*. Mills & Boon.

projection	text
"β	If she were to be truthful,
<<α>>	Joss **owned**,
"β	she didn't feel very much like going out that Monday evening.
α	She **could not have said**
"β	why particularly it was that the Beacon Theatre Group had no appeal that night,
	though, as she poured herself a second cup of coffee,
α	she **didn't think**
'β	the dull and gloomy weather had very much to do with the way she was feeling.
	Silently she sipped her coffee,
	and a few minutes later she carried her used dishes from her dining-room and through to her smart cream and pale green kitchen,
α	**knowing**
'β	that she would go out
	It wasn't in her nature to let anyone down,
	and Abby, her closest friend, was at present *smitten* with Fergus Perrott
	and, for some reason, seemed to need her along
	to boost her confidence.
	Joss set about tackling her washing up,
α	**reflecting**
'β1α	that Fergus **had not asked** Abby
'β1"β	to go out with him yet,
'β+2	but that these new and frequent visits to the Beacon Theatre Group — an offshoot of the Beacon Oil Sports and Social Club — seemed to be paying dividends.
	She was **sure** she **had seen** a gleam of interest in Fergus's eyes last Friday
	as he'**d watched** Abby during rehearsals.
	All three of them worked for Beacon Oil at Beacon House, London —
	she and Abby both on the secretarial side,
	while Fergus worked in Personnel.
	Thinking of last Friday,
α	Joss **pondered**
'β1	that she *must have been feeling* a bit like today's weather then —
'β+2	or maybe *started to feel* in the need of something more stimulating than her present job,
α	for she **had realised**
'βα	that she had been only half joking
'βxβα	when she'**d asked** Fergus then

'βxβ"β	if his department had been notified of any interesting secretarial vacancies.
	...
	Leaving her neat and tidy kitchen,
	Joss went
	to get ready to go and pick up Abby.
	They **had known** each other for three years now.
	[] The whole time in fact
	since, at twenty years old, Joss, with her feet well and truly on the secretarial ladder, had started to work at Beacon Oil.
	In an attempt *to lift her glum spirits*, Joss tried to count her blessings.

Here Joss's conscious processing is construed as part of the sequence of her activities. The figures of sensing are often accompanied by the content of her thinking, represented by a projected idea. The figures of sensing are also often construed as simultaneous with figures of doing & happening, involving Joss as Actor, as in *as she poured herself a second cup of coffee, she didn't think the dull and gloomy weather had very much to do with the way she was feeling.* Here enhancing sequences are used to construe figures of sensing and figures of doing & happening as unfolding in parallel, with the same person in the pivotal roles of Senser and Actor respectively. In addition to deploying figures of sensing to construe Joss's consciousness, the writer has also drawn on a lexical metaphorical motif of (vertical) movement in an abstract mental space: *boost her confidence, lift her glum spirits.* We will return to the lexical metaphor below.

Like Text (1) above, Text (3) provides an example of a speaker construing his/ her own processes of consciousness:

Text (3): Extract of casual conversation

A: Oh dear, (sighs) one **forgets** how time runs [?]. I **think** Malcolm's twenty-seven, twenty-eight, perhaps a bit more. I **don't know**.

B: I eventually **estimated** twenty-eight, twenty-nine. I must have looked at him for some time.

A: He went —

B: He's not, he's not easy to **guess** actually.

A: No. He got a brilliant first when he was twenty and it meant he couldn't graduate till he was twenty-one. They wouldn't give it to you. And he stayed — did he stay at Oxford to do a postgrad year or did he come immediately here? I **can't remember**. He's working for a Ph.D. here I **think**.

B: m

A: But I **think** he gets so involved in his computer business that I **don't know** how his Ph.D. is going.

B: **Shouldn't think** he had much time left.

A: I **shouldn't think** so. (Svartvik & Quirk, 1980: 153)

Here also the projected figures are reported rather than quoted (for example, *one forgets how time runs* rather than *one forgets: how does time run?*): as already noted, reporting is the typical mode of projection for figures of sensing. The figures of sensing are again realized congruently by mental clauses. However, some of these mental clauses are metaphorical: they also stand for interpersonal assessments of modality. Thus the projecting clause complex *I think* ——> *Malcolm's twenty-seven, twenty-eight, perhaps a bit more* is agnate to a simple clause with either a mood Adjunct (*Malcolm is probably twenty-seven, ...*) or a modal Finite within the Mood element (*Malcolm will be twenty-seven, ...*). A projection mental clause such as *I (don't) think*, since ideationally it realizes a figure of sensing, **construes** the speaker as 'Senser at the time of speaking' (it occurs metaphorically only in simple present tense); at the same time, it **enacts** the speaker's own 'intrusion' into the dialogue — his or her judgment about how much validity can be attached to the proposition contained in the projected clause.

Interpersonal metaphor is thus the hinge between the ideational and the interpersonal modes of constructing the self. In the ideational mode we *construe* ourselves as conscious Sensers, while in the interpersonal mode we *enact* ourselves as speakers interacting with addressees; the metaphor brings the two together in such a way that *the ideational construal stands for the interpersonal enactment* (see Figure 14-6). The grammar of everyday discourse thus clearly points to the significance of interpersonal meaning in the way that we construct ourselves — the self is not only construed but it is also enacted. Cognitive scientists, however, have derived their object of study, and their model of this object from the ideational perspective alone, failing to take the interpersonal perspective — that of enacting — into account.

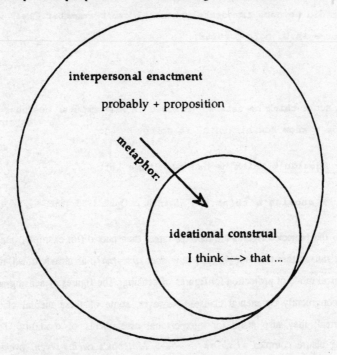

Fig. 14-6: Ideational construal standing for interpersonal enactment

The everyday grammar's contribution to the construal of sensing is thus both rich and varied. Some features of it are particularly significant to the uncommonsense model of mainstream cognitive science. The grammar separates out consciousness from the rest of our experience in the form of mental processes, capable of projecting ideas; but in addition, consciousness may also be 'externalized' in the form of verbal processes, capable of projecting locutions. This 'world view' can be depicted using the conventions of comic strips: see Figure 14-7. The conventions of comic strips clearly differentiate between figures of sensing and saying on the one hand and figures of being & having and doing & happening on the other (cf. Chapter 3, Section 3.3.1 above, esp. Figure 3-5): the latter are represented graphically, whereas the former are represented linguistically, in terms of their projected content. Comic strips thus codify the higher-order nature of projections and their constitution in language.

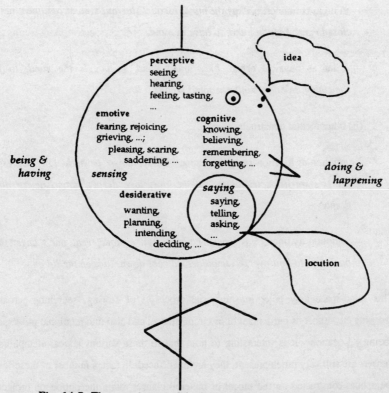

Fig. 14-7: The container model of the mind of lexical metaphors

The grammar thus construes sensing as a bounded semantic domain within our total experience of change. This picture is further enriched through lexis, prominently through lexical metaphors (cf. Chapter 6, Section 6.2.1 above). Metaphors relating to space, with the mind as a container (Reddy, 1979; cf. Lakoff & Kövecses, 1987, on Anger), a finite space or a physical entity reinforce the grammar's construal of a bounded domain of sensing. We cited the lexical metaphors *boost her confidence, lift her glum spirits* from Text (2) above; other examples of lexical metaphors include:

(i) mind:

— mind as space: *cross one's mind, broaden the mind, be out of one's mind, to be driven out of one's mind, get something out of one's mind, search one's mind, at the back of one's mind, to put at the back of one's mind, at the front of one's mind*

— mind as container: *occupy the mind, escape/ slip one's mind, an open mind, a closed mind, keep in mind, to have in mind,*

— mind as physical organ: *blow one's mind, to boggle the mind, to have something on one's mind, the mind recoils*

(ii) other mental constructs:

— emotion as location in vertical space: *be up/ down, be high/ low, depress sb, lift sb's spirits, spirits soar; fall in love, love deeply, abhor/ detest/ dislike deeply*

— emotion as liquid/ gas (contained in body): *explode, vent one's anger, blow one's top, to boil over, to smoulder, to cool down, to keep the lid on,*

This mind-space may enter into material processes of storing, searching, crossing, escaping etc., either as participant or as circumstance, and also into relational processes of "being + Location". It is interesting to note that in these various lexical metaphors the Sensers are still very much present; they are not effaced. In fact, a number of these lexical metaphors constructed on the model of material clauses retain the option of projecting; see Figure 14-8.

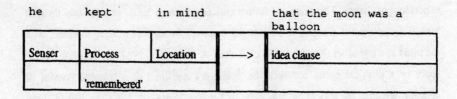

he	kept	in mind	——>	that the moon was a balloon
Senser	Process	Location	——>	idea clause
	'remembered'			

Fig. 14-8: Projecting combined with material lexical metaphor

Let's now consider how this folk model informs the models of consciousness in (mainstream) cognitive science.

14.3 From folks to scientists

What is the nature of the move from our everyday construal of the experience of consciousness — our folk theory of Sensers sensing phenomena or projecting ideas — to

the way cognitive scientists construe that experience? We can see the essential nature of
this move when the folk theory is reconstrued as if it was a scientific one. When Dennett
(1981) tries to characterize folk psychology, he has in fact already made the move (our
bolding):

> What are beliefs? Very roughly folk psychology has it that
> **beliefs** are information-bearing states of people that arise from
> **perceptions** and that, together with appropriately related
> **desires**, lead to intelligent **action**. That much is relatively
> uncontroversial, but does folk psychology also have it that
> nonhuman animals have beliefs? If so, what is the role of language
> in belief? Are **beliefs** constructed of parts? If so, what are the
> parts? Ideas? Concepts? Words? Pictures? Are **beliefs** like speech
> acts or maps or instruction manuals or sentences? Is it implicit
> in folk psychology that beliefs enter into causal relations, or
> that they don't? How do **decisions** and **intentions** intervene
> between **belief-desire** complexes and actions? Are **beliefs**
> introspectible, and if so, what authority do the believer's
> **pronouncements** have? (p. 91, 1990 reprint)

Instead of saying *people believe that ...*, *people want others to ...*, etc., as people do
in everyday discourse, Dennett writes *beliefs, desires,* etc.. Here mental clauses with a
Senser, a Process of sensing (believing, wanting, desiring, etc.), and either a
Phenomenon entering into (or being created by) the Senser's consciousness or an idea
projected as a separate clause, have been reconstrued as nominal groups with a
nominalized mental process as Thing/ Head and (typically) neither participants nor
projected ideas. This reconstrual is brought about by grammatical metaphor: meanings
that are normally construed by clauses are construed as if they were meanings that are
normally construed by nominal groups. If Dennett had tried to constitute the folk theory
as it is, instead of construing it as if it was a scientific theory, he might have written:

> Very roughly, when people believe something, they believe that
> something has happened because they have seen or heard it happen;
> and if they believe that something has happened and they want
> something else to happen, they do something about it.

The two modes of construing our experience of consciousness are compared in grammatical terms in Figure 14-9.

(1) Folk model (congruent construal):

| they | believe | | that some- thing has happened | | because | they | | have seen or heard | | it happen |

αα:		—>	α'β:	—>	χβ:				
mental: cognitive & metaphenomenal: idea			clause: project- ion (idea)		mental: perceptive & macrophenomenal				
Senser	Process					Senser	Process		Phenom enon
nom. gp.: consc.	verbal group					nom. gp.: consc.	verbal group		clause: act

(2) Scientific model (metaphorical reconstrual):

Beliefs (= information- bearing states)	arise from	perceptions
relational: identifying & circumstantial		
Token	Process	Value
nom. gp.	verbal gp.	nom. gp.
Thing: nominalized process of cognition	Event: verbalized conjunctive relation of cause	Thing: nominalized process of perception

Fig. 14-9: Congruent folk model reconstrued metaphorically as scientific model

The scientific model is metaphorical; and it stands as a metaphor for the congruent folk model. As the figure makes explicit, there is a considerable loss of ideational information as one moves from the congruent mode to the metaphorical mode: grammatically, a clause complex is compressed into a clause, and the clauses that are combined in the clause complex are compressed into nominal groups. As a result, the subtle distinction between the cognitive projection of ideas (sb believing that ....) and the perceptive sensing of acts (sb seeing sth happen) is lost, and participants can be left implicit. (The mental clause's capacity for projection is echoed in Dennett's definition of *belief*: [Token/ Identified:] *beliefs* [Process:] *are* [Value/ Identifier:] *information-bearing states* ... .) The possibility of leaving participants implicit means in practice that Sensers are effaced in the scientific model and, as a result, the consciousness we experience in the living of life is also construed out of the picture, being replaced with unconscious processes not accessible to our experience.

The move from the congruent mode of the folk theory to the metaphorical mode that provides the resource for theories within cognitive science can often be found in introductions to accounts of how people sense the phenomena of their experience, as in the following passage from Restak (1988: 242), an introductory book on "the mind" (our bolding, underlining and italics):

> ... to explain the mind's operation in thinking. Here, for example, is an everyday situation: two people meet on a beach. Michelle **recognizes** that she's encountered Michael before, but can't *come up with* his name. But she does **recall** that he's a doctor, specializes in paediatrics, and lives in New York City.
>
> Michael **remembers** Michelle's name but can't *dredge up from* **his memory** any biographical details about her. He **recalls** they met previously at a party given by a friend to celebrate the completion of his residency. Michael can *bring* vividly *to* **mind** what Michelle was wearing and how attractive he found her.
>
> Ordinary **experiences** like this raise important questions about how **thinking** is organized. Why is it that Michelle can **recognize** Michael's face, **remember** significant facts about him, but can't *come up with* his name? In Michael's case, the organization would seem to be different: he can **remember** names but specific life details are only a blur. What kind of mental organization in Michael might account for these differences?
>
> The most popular metaphor for the human mind is that of a huge and intricate filing system. When Michelle and Michael encounter each other, **facial recognition** sets off an elaborate *search* through "files" *stored* within billions of neurons. ... (Restak, 1988: 242)

Restak begins by giving a common-sense account, using the congruent grammar of mental clauses with projected ideas: *Michelle recognizes* ——> *that ..., she does recall* ——> *that* .... He then uses a lexical metaphor for remembering that is part of our everyday lexicogrammar — *dredge up from memory, bring to mind*. Here the 'mind' is construed as an object with extension in space — a container. The mind is also construed as a circumstance (*from memory, to mind*), in a mental clause that is partially constructed on the material model of manipulating an object but which is still mental, since it is configured with a conscious participant (the Senser) and since it can project (*bring to mind* ——> *what Michelle was wearing;* cf. *bring to mind* ——> *that she was intelligent, dredge up from memory* ——> *that she was a physician*). When he has finished this commonsense account, he raises general issues for an uncommonsense, scientific account by using the metaphorical mode: *experiences like this* (rather than *people experience similar situations* or the like), *thinking* (rather than *how people think*), *facial recognition* (rather than *people recognize faces*), and so on. (When later he harks back to the illustrative account of a particular situation of everyday experience, he returns to the congruent mode.)

Restak also deploys the lexical metaphor of a mental space that we find in the commonsense model — a space in which 'objects' can be stored, which can be searched, and so on: *facial recognition sets off an elaborate search through "files" stored within billions of neurons*. The spatial metaphor of the commonsense model is taken over by cognitive scientists. It serves as the sources of processes in their model of the mind — processes of storing, searching, retrieving etc. within figures of doing & happening and processes of being located at/in within figures of being & having. That is, processes of sensing are reified, and processes of doing & happening and of being & having take their place. The spatial metaphor also opens up the way for modelling the mind along computational lines: human memory can be modelled on computer memory.

This shift in the passage quoted from Restak is representative of what we think happens with respect to how mainstream cognitive scientists construe their object of study. To illustrate further some features of cognitive models, we have included a short extract from a book on the psychology of cognition. It is the very first paragraph of the book. We have analysed each clause in terms of the major types of figure — doing, sensing, saying and being-&-having: see the columns to the right of the text in Table 14(1).

Table 14(1): Analysis of passage on cognition[4]

TEXT (Processes in bold)	Type of figure			
	doing	sens-ing	saying	being & having
[1] Semantic <u>memory</u> **is concerned** with the structure of <u>knowledge</u>, with [[how <u>knowledge</u> **is** stored, cross-referenced and indexed]]; it **is concerned** with the organization of everyday world <u>knowledge</u>, and with the representation of meaning.				√ [[√]] √
[2] Semantic <u>memory</u> **is** not just an internal dictionary [[in which linguistic terms **are listed and defined**]]				√ [[√]]
[3] The elements **are** <u>concepts</u>, and although most <u>concepts</u> **are defined** by their properties not all concepts **are** verbal ones.				√ √ √
[4] <u>Facts or propositions</u> **are represented** by <u>concepts</u> [[**linked** in particular relationships]], and sets of <u>propositions</u> **combine** **to form** related areas of <u>knowledge</u>.				√ [[√]] √ √
[5] Although there is a common core of culturally shared <u>knowledge</u>, semantic <u>memory</u> **is** personal because each individual's <u>knowledge</u> and <u>experience</u> **differ**.				√ √ √
[6] It is not just a static mental encyclopaedia, but a working system, in which new <u>facts</u> **are constantly being incorporated**, stored <u>knowledge</u> **is being updated and reclassified**, and particular items of information **are being sought, located, assembled and retrieved**.	√ √ √			√
[7] It **represents** one of the most important, interesting and difficult areas of study in cognitive psychology today.				√

---

[4] The excerpt is taken from the introductory paragraph to Chapter 1, Semantic memory and the structure of knowledge, of Gillian Cohen, 1977. The psychology of cognition. New York: Academic Press.

[8] Semantic organization is especially important because it is one of the most powerful and pervasive determinants of performance in mental tasks.				√ √
[9] [[How knowledge is arranged]] **determines** [[how *we* **speak** and how *we* **understand**, how *we* **solve** problems and how *we* **remember**]]	<-- [√]</br>	 [√] [√]</br>	[√] 	[√] √
[10] It is worth [[analysing in some detail the reasons [[why semantic memory is especially intractable to study]]]] because many of these problems are endemic in cognitive psychology generally, and because the limitations [[which are inherent in our methodology]] are quite strikingly illustrated in this area.	[√] 			√ [√] √ [√] √
[11] Methodological problems will form a recurring theme throughout the book.				√
[12] The validity of theories of cognitive function depends on the power of the research methods, so that we cannot hope to assess the value of the evidence, nor the truth of the conclusions unless we scrutinize the methods, probing their weaknesses, and trying to evaluate the advantages and disadvantages of different approaches.	 √ √ √ √			√

Note: *how we speak* in (9) is verbal activity; it is on the border between verbal processes and material ones: we can interpret as verbal (but it cannot project), or as behavioural (here simply treated as a subtype of material).

Figures of sensing are realized not as mental clauses but as nominal groups taking on roles in clauses of various process types (predominantly relational; cf. below). We can contrast this scientific excerpt with a fragment of ordinary speech: see Table 14(2).

The dominant process type in the psychology text is relational — being, representing, defining, and so on. There is one short passage of doing, sentence number [6]; it describes possible operations on memory. There are only two congruent mental processes with Sensers (*we*), one of understanding (*how we understand*) and one of remembering (*how we remember*); but both of them occur in a rankshifted (embedded) clause complex:

   [[How knowledge **is** arranged]] **determines** [[how *we* **speak** and how *we* **understand**, how *we* **solve** problems and how *we* **remember**]]

Moreover, the sentence says that how we sense is determined by how we arrange knowledge.

Table 14(2): Contrast between folk model of people thinking and scientific model of people sensing

	material	mental	relational
folk model: clause:		you would see her ...; I've known her come in and say ...; I'd forgotten I'd been ill; I remember now when she carried Walter ...; I think she deemed I wasn't big enough ...	
scientific model: nominal group serving in clause:	in which new <u>facts</u> are **constantly being incorporated,** stored <u>knowledge</u> **is being updated and reclassified,** and particular items of <u>information</u> **are being sought, located, assembled and retrieved.**		Semantic <u>memory</u> is concerned with the structure of <u>knowledge</u>, ... <u>Facts or propositions</u> are represented by <u>concepts</u>...

In figures of doing, mental constructs serve as the Goal being manipulated in the mental space:

Location:	Goal:	Process:	Actor:
in which	*new facts*	*are constantly being incorporated*	?
	stored knowledge	*is being updated and reclassified*	?
	and particular items	*are being sought, located,*	?
	of information	*assembled and retrieved*	

These figures are realized by passive clauses, where the Actor is absent. This makes it possible to construe sensing without any explicit personal agency; the processes are initiated at a subpersonal level. Edelman (1992: 237-8) comments on the general tendency that the example above illustrates:

> Human memory is not at all like computer memory. ... In whatever form, human memory involves an apparently open-ended set of connections between subjects and a rich texture of previous knowledge that cannot be adequately represented by the impoverished language of computer science — "storage", "retrieval", "input", "output". To have memory, one must be able to repeat a performance, to assert, to relate matters and categories to one's own position in time and space. To do this, one must have a self, and a conscious self at that. Otherwise, one must postulate a little man to carry out retrieval (in computers, it is we, the programmers, who are the little men).

The text extract in Table 14(1) above is quite representative. Let us cite just one additional example. The following extract is from the opening chapter of a recent text book in cognitive science (Stillings et al, 1987: 1; our bolding = processes in congruent mental clauses, underlining = figures of sensing metaphorized as nominal groups or names of sensing):

1. What is Cognitive Science?

One of the most important intellectual developments of the past few decades has been the birth of an exciting new interdisciplinary field called *cognitive science*. Researchers in psychology, linguistics, computer science, philosophy, and neuroscience **realized** that they were asking many of the same questions about the nature of <u>the human mind</u> and that they had developed complementary and potentially synergetic methods of investigation. The word *cognitive* refers to <u>perceiving</u> and <u>knowing</u>. Thus, cognitive science is the science of <u>the mind</u>. Cognitive scientists **seek to understand** <u>perceiving</u>, <u>thinking</u>, <u>remembering</u>, <u>understanding</u> language, <u>learning</u>, and other <u>mental phenomena</u>. Their research is remarkably diverse, ranging from **observing** children, through programming computers to do complex problem solving, to **analyzing** the nature of meaning.

1.1 The Nature of Cognitive Science

Cognitive scientists **view** <u>the human mind</u> as a complex system that receives, stores, retrieves, transforms, and transmits information. There are four important <u>assumptions</u> to this information-processing view.

Formal Information Processes

The first corollary is that information and information processes can be studied as patterns and manipulation of patterns. To clarify this <u>assumption</u>, let us **look** at an example. **Consider** the following longhand multiplication problem: [...]

As in the examples above, the object of study of cognitive study is constructed by ideational metaphor, as reified sensing (*perceiving, thinking*) or as names of sensing (*the mind, mental phenomena*). There are also a number of congruently realized figures of sensing — mental clauses with Senser + Process, with the potential for projecting. But these figures of sensing are *not* what cognitive science studies; rather they construe the processes of doing cognitive science: the Sensers are (cognitive) scientists. This is quite a normal use of congruently realized figures of sensing in scientific discourse; but here they are rather striking, because of the disjunction between the congruent construal of the scientists' own mental processes and the incongruent construal of those they are trying to understand.

14.4 The model in mainstream cognitive science

To sum up the discussion so far: while the domain of scientific theorizing about cognition is determined by the grammar of processes of sensing, the model is depersonalized, and sensing is construed metaphorically in terms of abstract "things" such as knowledge, memory, concepts. This suggests that mainstream cognitive science is basically an elaborated variety of a folk model, rather than a different scientific alternative (cf. Matthiessen, 1993a):

(i) The congruent ideational system separates out consciousness from the rest of our experience and construes it as a domain of sensing, embodying a Medium + Process complementarity where conscious beings (Medium) perceive, think, want, feel (Process). Sensing is thus 'mediated' through the Senser; and this process may project ideas into semiotic existence. This domain of Sensers sensing (that ...), which is construed in the congruent system, is taken over in cognitive science. However, it is not taken over as being itself a theory of conscious processing; instead, it is treated as a phenomenon — that is, sensing is turned into the **object** of study.

(ii) Since it is not taken over as *a theory*, the fundamental insights of the folk theory are ignored: figures of "Sensers sensing (that ...)" are re-construed through grammatical metaphor as participants. In particular, the domain of sensing is **reified** as the "mind", so that instead of somebody perceiving things happening, or somebody thinking that the moon was a balloon, the model of cognitive science has *perception, vision, cognition, learning, memory, ...* .

(iii) Since figures of sensing are reified as participants, the processes of sensing are likewise turned into things, and the participants in sensing, the Sensers, are typically **effaced**. The Senser/ sensing complementarity of the folk model is thus lost, as is the feature of Sensers projecting ideas into existence.

(iv) Since figures of sensing are reified as participants, they can themselves be construed in participant roles. Here another feature of the folk model is taken over: its spatial metaphor is retained and further elaborated. Thus the mind is construed as a space where the metaphorical participants of sensing are involved in processes of doing & happening and of being & having: thoughts, concepts, memories, images are stored, located, retrieved, activated and so on.[5]

(v) Since figures of sensing are reified as participants, the path is opened up to the **taxonomic** interpretation of sensing, in the form of scientific taxonomy: *memory —long-term/ short-term memory, sensory memory, semantic memory; recall — free recall; learning — associative learning/ cognitive learning/ classical conditioning; ... .*

(vi) Since Sensers are effaced, and projection is lost as a feature of the Senser/ sensing complementarity, the gateway to the interpersonal realm — where Sensers are enacted as interactants in dialogic exchange — is closed, and the interpersonal element in the ideational/ interpersonal complementarity is lost.

Figure 14-10 represents the central motif in the metaphorical reconstrual of sensing: sensing is 'extracted' from figures of sensing as a domain, and reified to become one of a variety of participants that take on roles in figures of being & having and doing & happening, taking place in the mind construed as a container.

The 'scientific model' in mainstream cognitive science is centrally concerned with **information located in the individual's mind.**[6] This information is organized in some way as a conceptual system. The definition given in a newsletter produced by the cognitive science panel of the Australian Research Council, October 1989 (our italics) was as follows:

> Cognitive science is the systematic study of *mental processes*. Amongst the disciplines commonly involved are cognitive psychology, linguistics, philosophy, computer science and neuroscience. Cognitive science seeks to elucidate the information-acquisition and information-processing mechanisms underlying cognitive

---

[5] The widespread lexical metaphor of memory as a kind of space predates cognitive psychology by many hundreds of years; see e.g. Yates, 1966, on medieval notions such as the "memory theatre" used as aids to remembering.

[6] Alongside this cognitivist approach, there is a material one embodied in formal approaches to semantics, where the 'aboutness' of linguistic expressions is taken as central and these expressions are interpreted in terms of models of possible worlds: see Sections 10.1 and 10.2 above. However, in this respect there is a formal-cognitivist alliance: meaning is interpreted not as something in its own right but as something outside language, either a mental construct (concepts, ideas etc.) or a material one (referents in the real world or a formal model of a possible world).

tasks like *perception, recognition, storage of information and its retrieval from memory, problem-solving, language acquisition, language comprehension and language production.* Cognitive scientists seek to construct and test explicit theories of *the mind,* specifying the kinds of information processing that occur in cognitive activity, and to model the ways in which the ability to perform such tasks are acquired, changed or impaired. It is common for cognitive scientists to express models of mental processes in explicitly formal and/or computational terms.

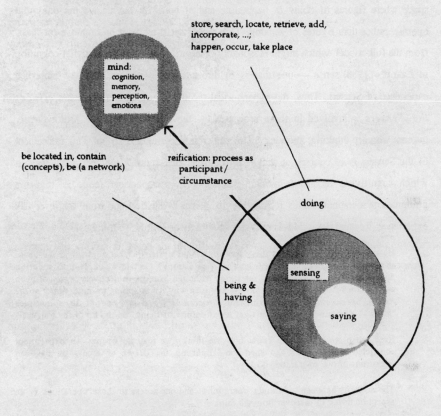

Fig. 14-10: Scientific reconstrual of the mental domain

Other definitions include Simon & Kaplan (1989: 1):

Cognitive science is the study of *intelligence and intelligent systems,* with particular reference to intelligent behavior *as computation.* Although no really satisfactory intentional definition of intelligence has been proposed, we are ordinarily willing to judge when intelligence is being exhibited by our fellow human beings. ...

and Wortman & Loftus (1985: 129):

To cognitive psychologists ... the *thought processes going on in a person's mind* are just as important as the overt behaviors we can see.

The mainstream cognitive science model is thus basically derived from a variety of the commonsense model. It creates a *metaphorical distance* from experience as construed in our congruent grammar, so that the conscious processing that we experience can be reconstrued as a 'subconscious' domain that we do not have access to — an abstract space where figures of doing & happening and of being & having are the ones that operate, rather than figures of sensing. This would seem to be at one remove (at least) from the folk model, which might reasonably be seen as one of experientialist cognition in Lakoff's (1988) sense — one that is in direct contact with the everyday, embodied experience of Sensers. Thus, the metaphorical reconstrual of mental processes *effaces the Sensers* involved in these processes — the conscious beings, prototypically human, who are thinking, knowing, believing, remembering and so on. This effacement of the Sensers is of course not accidental: in fact, one central feature of the way in which cognitivists reconstrue mental processing in metaphorical terms is that the grammatical metaphor makes it possible to distance the account from our everyday experience. Restak (1988: 243-4) puts this succinctly as follows (our italics):

> How does the mind construct this representational system? What goes on in the brain so that the word beach evokes a host of associations? Certainly simple introspection doesn't offer an answer to this question. Although you are subjectively aware of each association when it arises, you haven't any idea why it has sprung to mind. *Many of the mind's operations remain permanently inaccessible.* Every one of us sometimes "knows" a certain word, yet can't get it out despite its being "on the tip of the tongue."
>
> Even when we believe we know how we think, we may be wrong. An experiment conducted several years ago shed some light on the degree of access we have to operations of our own mind. [...]
>
> The disparity between the mind's operations and our access to those operations is an aspect of trying to discover how we think.

Here a contrast is construed in the grammar between the congruent *we think, we believe, we know* and the metaphorical *the mind's operations*. This contrast represents the conflict between our everyday experience of ourselves seeing, feeling, thinking, remembering, and so on, and the "scientific" model of cognitive science. Indeed, Dennett (1988) makes the generalization that "every cognitivist theory currently defended or envisaged ... is a theory of the sub-personal level". Given this orientation, it would thus seem that the unified senser existing as a person who "senses" is an illusion construed by the grammar as part of a folk theory of our own sense of conscious processing.

D'Andrade (1987) discusses two 'scientific' developments of the folk model, academic psychology and psychoanalysis; he suggests that "though the academic and psychoanalytic models modify the folk model, it is clear that these are modifications of an already existing conception of the mind". These two models move away from the folk model in two directions. (i) They reinterpret figures of sensing as figures of doing or being-&-having; that is, they interpret mental phenomena in material terms. With the growth of cognitive psychology, this situation has changed, of course; it is no longer disallowed to talk about mental processes. (ii) They emphasize motivation as an important unconscious psychological factor; thus they introduce unconsciousness in the account of the workings of the human mind. In the systems of process types in the grammar, there is no 'unconscious' type of sensing distinct from the conscious ones that can project ideas. D'Andrade summarizes these differences as follows:

> Thus, even though the academic and psychoanalytic models have their origins in the folk model, both are deeply at variance with the folk model. That is, the folk model treats the conscious mental states as having central causal powers. In the folk model, one does what one does primarily because of what one consciously feels and thinks. The causal center for the academic model is in the various physical states of the organism — in tissue needs, external stimuli, or neural activation. For the psychoanalytic model, the causal center is in unconscious mental states. Given these differences in the location of the causal center of the operations of the mind, the three models are likely to continue to diverge.

14.5 Beyond sensing — folk & scientific

In a way, the two directions away from sensing that D'Andrade identifies in the unconscious folk model — material reinterpretation and 'unconsciousness' — are opposites: the first reconstrues sensing in terms that are more readily observable by scientific method (i.e., method other than introspection), while the other introduces a factor that is even less readily observable than conscious sensing: unconscious motivation. But they share the characteristic that they construct the 'mind' as remote from our everyday experience with sensing.

At the same time the 'scientific' models of the mind fail to extend consciousness in the way it is extended by the grammar of English. There are, in fact, two complementary perspectives embodied in the semantic and grammatical systems of English; and together they point towards an alternative interpretation both of 'information' as constructed in cognitive science and of the individualized 'mind' that is its object of study.

(i) **Ideational: Sensers and Sayers.** The ideational resources of language are primarily a theory of experience, so they are reflected fairly directly in consciously designed theories such as those of cognitive science. If we stay within the ideational metafunction, where mental processes are **construed**, we also find other processes that are complementary to these: those of **saying** (verbal processes) and those of **symbolizing** (a type of relational process).

(ii) **Interpersonal: interactants**. If we move outside the ideational metafunction to the interpersonal, the resource through which we interact with other people, we find that here we are acting out our conscious selves — "modelling" consciousness not by construing it but by **enacting** it. Since this kind of meaning is **non-referential** it is not taken account of in scientific theories at all.

Both these perspectives — that of **the construal of processes other than the mental** (saying and symbolizing), and that of **meaning as enacting as well as meaning as construing** — are absent from the cognitive science modelling of mind; and in our view they could with advantage be brought into the picture when we try to understand these complex and central areas of human experience. To do so would both enrich the cognitive model and steer it away from obsessions with information, with knowledge as a separate 'thing' divorced from meaning, and with mind as the exclusive property of an individual organism bounded by its skin.

What is common to these two further sources of insight is that both depend on **projection**. (i) The potential for projecting is shared by sensing and saying; and (as we have seen in Chapter 3), when they are considered together, they reveal a very powerful principle that is embodied in the folk model: that through projection, we construe the experience of 'meaning' — as a layered, or stratified, phenomenon, with 'meanings' projected by sensing and 'wordings' projected by saying. (ii) Projection also brings the ideational and the interpersonal aspects of consciousness together. Ideationally, projection is an mode of construal — in figures of sensing and saying, sensers and sayers construe meanings and wordings. Interpersonally, projection is an mode of enactment — in moves in dialogue, interactants enact propositions and proposals. Interpersonal metaphors of mood and modality bring out the relationship between the two: here interactants simultaneously both **enact** propositions and proposals interpersonally and **construe** this enacting in such a way that the ideational construal comes to stand as a metaphor for aspects of the interpersonal enactment (see Figure 14-6 above).

The two extensions of scientific and folk models are contrasted in Figure 14-11.

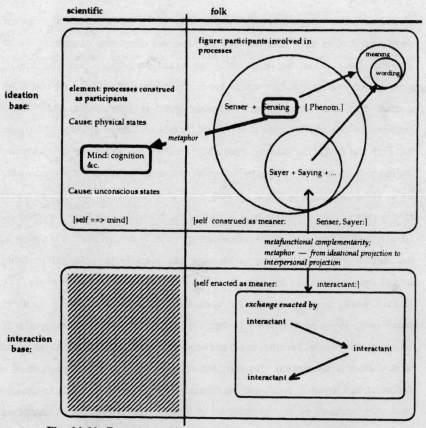

Fig. 14-11: Extensions of 'sensing' in folk and scientific models

Both of these paths leading beyond the figures of sensing embodied in the folk model, beyond the ideational domain of sensing, are of fundamental importance to our conception of the individual mind and hence of the domain of cognitive science. By implication, cognitive science should not only be 'cognitive', it should also be semiotic, because it is the notion of *meaning* that enables us to see the connection between sensing and saying, and between theory and enactment of consciousness. The folk model — developed unconsciously and collectively out of shared experience over hundreds of generations — construes and enacts the complexity of being a person by bringing to it a multiplicity of perspectives. It extends the 'mind' by refracting it through language, the resource that makes the "cognitive operations" possible and by the same token ensures that they are not subjective but intersubjective.

15. Language and the making of meaning

Throughout our discussion of language and meaning (and it may be useful to stress here once again that we have described only the ideational component of meaning — the **ideation base** — not the interpersonal and textual perspectives), we have tried to present a comprehensive picture with language at the centre of the stage. Language is not a second-order code through which meanings created in some higher-order realm of existence are mysteriously made manifest and brought to light. To borrow the conceit that Firth was fond of caricaturing, there are no "naked ideas" lurking in the background waiting to be clothed. It is language that *creates* meaning, in the sense that meaning has for us as human beings (which is the only sense of it that we can know). Language is able to create meaning because it is related to our material being (ourselves, and our environment) in three distinct and complementary ways. In the first place, it is a *part of* the material world: the processes of language take place in physiological (including neural) and physical space and time. In the second place, it is a *theory about* the material world: language models the space-time environment, including itself (cf. Matthiessen, 1991a; Matthiessen & Nesbitt, 1996), in a "rich" theoretical mode: that is, both construing it (our **ideation base**) and enacting it (our **interaction base**). In the third place, it is a *metaphor for* the material world: the way that language itself is organized, as a stratified, metafunctional system, recapitulates — acts out, so to speak — *both* the make-up of this environment in natural (physical-biological), social and semiotic systems-&-processes (our **metafunctions**) *and* the internal contradictions, complementarities and fractal patterning by which all such systems-&-processes are characterized (our **stratification**).

In other words, language has evolved as part of our own evolution. It is not arbitrary; on the contrary, it is the semiotic refraction of our own existence in the physical, biological, social and semiotic modes. It is not autonomous; it is itself part of a more complex semiotic construct — which, as we have tried to show (Part I above), can be modelled in stratal terms such that language as a whole is related by **realization** to a higher level of **context** (context of situation and of culture). This contextualization of language, we suggested, was the critical factor which made it possible to relate language to other systems-&-processes, both other semiotic systems and systems of other kinds.

15.1 Language and other semiotic systems

In the last chapter we reviewed the "scientific" model of the mind that informs cognitive science, looking at it from our point of view of construing experience through meaning. We showed that 'mind' is a construct of the ideation base, owing much to the commonsense picture of the world that is embodied in everyday grammar; but problematic because it draws on this account onesidedly. The scientific model takes off from the grammar of mental processes (seeing, feeling, thinking), but ignores verbal processes (saying) — although the two are both processes of consciousness, are closely related grammatically, and share the critical feature of being able to create meaning by projection. It takes off from the ideational metafunction, but ignores the interpersonal — although our folk perception of consciousness derives from both. Our sense of ourselves as conscious beings comes as much from the fact that we talk as from the fact that we think and feel; and owes as much to the nature of meaning as social action as it does to the nature of meaning as individual reflection.

Others have also been critical of the established academic view of mind; and some recent book titles suggest the kinds of alternatives that have been offered: "embodied mind", "social mind", "discursive mind". These suggest that the concept of 'mind' should be brought into close relation with other phenomena — biological, social, or semiotic. We will return to these in a moment. But once this has been done, the mind itself tends to disappear; it is no longer necessary as a construct *sui generis*. Instead of experience being construed by the mind, in the form of knowledge, we can say that experience is construed by the grammar; to 'know' something is to have transformed some portion of experience into meaning. To adopt this perspective is to theorize "cognitive processes" in terms of semiotic, social and biological systems; and thus to see them as a natural concomitant of the processes of evolution.

15.1.1 The representation of meaning in language, in relation to other semiotic systems

We have located ourselves, throughout the book, in a certain region of metasemiotic space: that is, we adopted a particular perspective on what we are trying to explain. Our central concern has obviously been with 'meaning': our interpretation of meaning is immanent, so that meaning is inside language, not some separate, higher domain of human experience. (For meaning-making systems other than language, see Section 15.1.2 below.) The central meaning-making resource in language — its "content plane" (within which the ideation base, which has been our focus of attention, is one part) — is stratified into two systems: that of lexicogrammar, and that of semantics.[1] The semantic system is the 'outer' layer, the interface where experience is transformed into meaning. The 'inner' layer is the grammar, which masterminds the way this transformation takes place. This deconstrual of the content plane into two strata, referred to in the first chapter, is a unique feature of the post-infancy human semiotic, corresponding to Edelman's (1992) "higher-order consciousness" as the distinguishing characteristic of *homo sapiens*.

Since we are interested in how experience is construed, we have focussed attention on the semantics: concepts like "figure", "element", "process", "thing" are categories of semantic theory. But in modelling the semantic system we face a choice: namely, how far "above" the grammar we should try to push it. Since the decision has to be made with reference to the grammar, this is equivalent to asking how abstract the theoretical constructs are going to be. We have chosen to locate ourselves at a low point on the scale of abstraction, keeping the semantics and the grammar always within hailing distance. There were various reasons for this. First, we wanted to show the grammar at work in construing experience; since we are proposing this as an alternative to cognitive theories, with an "ideation base" rather than a "knowledge base", we need to posit categories such that their construal in the lexicogrammar is explicit. Secondly, we wanted to present the grammar as "natural", not arbitrary; this is an essential aspect of the evolution of language from a primary semiotic such as that of human infants (see Section 15.2 below). Thirdly, we wanted to explain the vast expansion of the meaning potential that takes place through grammatical metaphor; this depends on the initial congruence between grammatical and semantic categories.

But in any case, it is not really possible to produce a more abstract model of semantics until the less abstract model has been developed first. One has to be able to renew connection with the grammar. Other scholars working in systemic semantics have

---

[1] Thus semantics, as a field of study, is located within linguistics. We should therefore make it clear that it is not being used in the traditional sense that it has had within linguistics, of the study of the meanings of words. It is used in the sense it has always had in systemic theory, namely the total meaning-making system of a natural language. Semantics thus relates to the lexicogrammar as a whole. We can talk of "lexical semantics" if we want to foreground the meanings of words (lexical items functioning in open sets), and of "grammatical semantics" if we want to foreground the meanings of closed grammatical systems; but just as the lexicogrammar itself is a continuum, so — even more so, in fact — is there continuity between these two aspects of semantics, so we have not found it necessary, except in one or two instances, to make this terminological distinction.

been careful to maintain this connectivity, making clear how the semantic categories are construed in grammatical terms; for example, Hasan's (1996) semantic networks, Martin's (1992) discourse semantics, and Fawcett's (e.g. 1994) text-generation model "GENESYS" (Fawcett describes his model as "cognitive" but it is firmly anchored in the grammar). Functional linguistics generally is moving in the direction of more abstract representations of semantics; but there is no comprehensive description available yet.

15.1.2 Socio-semiotic and bio-semiotic systems

We need now to orient our immanent conception of meaning with respect to semiotic systems other than language. This notion of "other semiotic systems" is a rather complex one; there are many ways of indexing such systems, but we can perhaps try to locate them according to their relationship with (the semantic system of) language. This relationship may be of different kinds. Let us first of all distinguish the broad categories of "socio-semiotic" and "bio-semiotic", and consider the socio-semiotic first.

(i) Socio-semiotic systems

(a) Socio-semiotic systems that are **realized through** language. This category corresponds to Hjelmslev's (1943) concept of a "connotative semiotic": a higher-level system that has language as its plane of expression. These include theories: every theoretical construction, scientific, philosophical, aesthetic, and so on, is a higher-level semiotic realized in language. They also include the codified aspects of social institutions such as the law, the financial system, constitutions and codes of practice. Martin interprets both genre and ideology in this light, as social activity structures and ideological formations that are realized in language (e.g. 1985, 1992; for a critique of Martin's view, see Hasan, 1995).

From a semantic point of view, such systems constitute **contexts** for language; they can thus be modelled as part of a general linguistic theory, being interpreted as a higher stratum of language itself. That is to say, we can extend the series:

the system of **phonology** realizes that of lexicogrammar;

the system of **[lexicogrammar realized in phonology]** realizes that of semantics;

the system of [**semantics realized in** [**lexicogrammar realized in phonology**]] — which is what we call "language" — realizes the system of context (i.e. the "culture", considered as a semiotic potential).

Such higher-level systems (theories, institutions, genres), since they are realized in language, are realized as subsystems within the semantics and the grammar. These subsystems are what we have referred to as registers; cf. our examples of cooking and weather forecasting in Chapter 8.

(b) Socio-semiotic systems that are **parasitic on** language, in the sense that they depend on the fact that those who use them are articulate ('linguate') beings. These include the visual arts, music and dance; modes of dressing, cooking, organizing living space and other forms of meaning-making behaviour; and also charts, maps, diagrams, figures and the like. Many socio-semiotic systems are combinations of types (a) and (b); for example, religious ceremonials and most types of dramatic performance.

These systems enter into relation with language in two ways. On the one hand, they are metonymic to language: they are complementary, non-linguistic resources whereby higher-level systems may be realized (e.g. ideological formations realized through forms of art; theoretical constructs realized through figures and diagrams). On the other hand, they relate metaphorically to language: they are constructed, stratally and metafunctionally, in the image of language itself, and hence can be modelled on language as prototype, being described "as if" they had their own grammar and semantics (Kress & van Leeuwen, 1990, 1996; van Leeuwen, 1988, 1991; Steiner, 1984, 1988b; Winograd, 1968; O'Toole, 1994, 1995; Matthiessen, Kobayashi & Zeng, 1995; Lemke, in press). (See especially in this connection O'Toole's analysis of painting, architecture and sculpture in stratal and metafunctional terms.)

(ii) Bio-semiotic systems

(a) Bio-semiotic systems through which language interfaces with its biological environment

(1) Systems that interface with the content plane. These are the systems and processes of human perception, tactile, auditory, visual, and so on. They are themselves semiotic, in that what the organism "sees" is what is construed by the brain into meaning; this then becomes the "input" to the semantic system and is transformed into higher-order meaning of the linguistic kind.

(2) **Systems that interface with the expression plane.** These are the physiological systems and processes of the production and reception of speech: motor systems of articulation (air stream mechanisms, constrictions and oscillations of the larynx and other organs, movements of tongue and lips, shaping of the buccal cavity) and receptor systems of auditory perception in the various regions of the ear. When language comes to be written, analogous systems come into play for the production and reception of visual expressions.

(b) **The brain as bio-semiotic system.** The neural events that constitute the various interface systems are themselves in the broadest sense semiotic: terms such as "communication", "exchange of information", that are used to characterize the activities of the brain are less abstract variants of the concept of "semiotic systems & processes".

At the same time, the neural networks can be thought of as "realizing" the system of language, in the sense that it is in the brain that language **materializes** as a process of the bio-physical world. In this perspective the relationship between language and the brain is itself a semiotic one, analogous to that between the content plane and the expression plane within language itself; and by the same analogy, there is no necessary or "natural" relationship such that certain parts of the neural network (certain locations within the brain) are dedicated to language or to any particular subsystem within it. The analogy is relevant here because it is the fact that language and the perceptual systems share a common "realization" in neural networks and neural processes that enables language to function as a dynamic open system, one that persists in time by constantly being modified through ongoing exchanges with its environment.

15.1.3 The evolution of reality construction

Neurobiologists interpret the evolution of the brain in vertebrate species as the evolution of the species' potential for constructing reality (Jerison, 1973 (1992); Edelman, 1992). Evolution brings about a constant change in the organism's relation to its environment; this relationship becomes increasingly complex, so that the organism's *model* of the environment has to become increasingly complex in its turn. This, it is suggested, is what "drives" the evolution of more and more complex brain structures.

Edelman (1992) relates this evolutionary perspective to the emergence of consciousness, which he explains in terms of a neurological account of brain structures. He interprets consciousness in what we can think of as semiotic terms, making a distinction between primary consciousness, which depends on the construal of scenes or images, and higher-order consciousness, which depends on the construal of meaning in language:

> Primary consciousness is the state of being mentally aware of things in the world — of having mental images in the present. But it is not accompanied by any sense of a person with a past and future. It is what one may presume to be possessed by some nonlinguistic and nonsemantic animals ... (p. 112) ... Obviously, primary consciousness must be efficacious if this biological account is correct. ... primary consciousness helps to abstract and organize complex changes in an environment involving multiple parallel signals. ... Primary consciousness provides a means of relating an individual's present input to its acts and past rewards. By presenting a correlative scene, it provides an adaptive way of directing attention during the sequencing of complex learning tasks. (p. 121) ... Primary consciousness is required for the evolution of higher-order consciousness. But it is limited to a small memorial interval around a time chunk I call the present. (p. 122)

> In contrast [to primary consciousness], higher-order consciousness involves the recognition by a thinking subject of his or her own acts or affections. It embodies a model of the personal, and of the past and the future as well as the present. It exhibits direct awareness — the noninferential or immediate awareness of mental episodes without the involvement of sense organs or receptors. It is what we as humans have in addition to primary consciousness. We are conscious of being conscious. (p. 112) ... How can the tyranny of this remembered present [i.e. the restrictions of primary consciousness, MAKH & CM] be broken? The imprecise answer is: By the evolution of new forms of symbolic memory and new systems serving social communication and transmission. In its most developed form, this means the evolutionary acquisition of the capability of language. Inasmuch as human beings are the only species with language, it also means that higher-order consciousness has flowered in our species. (p. 125) ... Long-term storage of symbolic relations, acquired through interactions with other individuals of the same species, is critical to the self-concept. The acquisition is accompanied by the categorization of sentences related to self and nonself and their connection to events in primary consciousness. (p. 132) ... An inner life, based on the emergence of language in a speech community, becomes possible. ... Higher-order consciousness adds socially constructed selfhood to this picture of biological individuality. The freeing of parts of conscious thought from the constraints of an immediate present and the increased richness of social communication allow for the anticipation of future states and for planned behavior. (p. 133-4)

Edelman's account indicates the evolutionary value of the human potential for construing processes of consciousness, discussed in Chapter 14 above. In contrast with mainstream cognitive science, Edelman makes language the central resource and relates it to the social construction of the self.

Our conception of the "meaning base" is fully compatible with this line of interpretation (cf. Halliday, 1995a): the human brain has evolved in the construction of a functioning model of "reality". We prefer to conceptualize "reality construction" in terms of construing **experience**. This is not so much because it avoids metaphysical issues about the ultimate nature of reality — we are prepared to acknowledge a broadly materialist position; rather, we have three more specific considerations in mind. (i) One is that what is being construed by the brain is not the environment as such, but the impact of that environment on the organism and the ongoing material and semiotic exchange between the two. (ii) The second is that we want to emphasize the evolutionary perspective, since this allows us to start from what human beings have in common with other species rather than always insisting on our own uniqueness: when we talk of "construction of reality" it is almost impossible to avoid taking our own construction as the norm, whereas parakeets, pythons, and porpoises have very different experiences to construe — different both from each other's and from those of people. (iii) The third point is that the concept of experience is, or can be, a collective one: experience is something that is shared by the members of the species — construed as a "collective consciousness", in Durkheim's classic formulation.

This last point needs to be clarified. Edelman's interpretation of higher-order consciousness referred to above suggests that this form of consciousness (unlike primary consciousness) is constituted in language. Language is a socio-semiotic system, so it follows that higher-order consciousness is constituted *socio*-semiotically; and since socio-semiotic systems are collective, it follows that higher-order consciousness must also be collective. Collective consciousness is an attribute of human social groups — the members of a given culture. But we need to distinguish between the consciousness of a social group and the consciousness of a species, whose collective construal of experience is codified in the structure of the brain. All human populations have the same brain, and to that extent all construe experience in the same way. But humans live in social groups, and their local environments vary one from the other; to that extent, different groups construe experience in different ways. The significance of this for us is that language is the resource for both: both what is common to the species as a whole, and what is specific to the given culture. In the way these two components are construed in the grammar, we cannot tell them apart. But it is the role of language in the construction of experience as meaning — as shared activity and collaboratively constructed resource — that gives substance to the concept of collective consciousness as an attribute of the human condition.

It has been found that, among the higher primates, those species that live in social groups have more complex brain structures, other things being equal, than those that live apart as individuals (Dunbar, 1992, quoted in *New Scientist*). This, too, is something which resonates with our interpretation with language. In our account of the ideation base, we have stressed the interactive, dialogic nature of the construal of experience. But we have also stressed that the ideation base is only one component of the total semantic resource: as well as construing our experience in language, we also use it to enact our interpersonal relationships. Because we are social animals, there is an added dimension of meaning for language to cope with (cf. our discussion of the ideation base and the interaction base in Chapter 9, Section 9.1.2.1). We cannot observe how these resources have evolved in the history of the human species. But we can observe how they grow in the development of the human individual. In the final sections (15.2 and 15.3) we will give a very brief sketch of our topic from an ontogenetic point of view.

15.1.4 Biological, social and socio-semiotic environments for the "individual"

The human individual is at once a biological "individual", a social "individual" and a socio-semiotic "individual":

> as a biological "individual", s/he is an **organism**, born into a biological population as a member of the human species.

> as a social "individual", s/he is a **person**, born into a social group as a member of society. "Person" is a complex construct; it can be characterized as a constellation of social roles or personae entering into social networks (see Argyle et al, 1981, for a discussion from a sociological point of view; Firth, 1950, relates personae to language, and Butt, 1991, develops further his theory from a systemic-functional point of view, in the light of sociological models of social networks).

> as a socio-semiotic "individual", s/he is a **meaner**, born into a meaning group as a member of a speech community. "Meaner" is also a complex construct. For the socio-semiotic construction of the individual subject, see Thibault (1993); for the modelling of the individual subject by reference to concept of 'meaning potential', see Sefton (1995).

These different levels of individuality map onto one another: a meaner is a person, and a person is a biological organism. But the mappings are complex; and at each level an individual lives in different environments — in different networks of relations. Lemke (1995, in particular Ch. 5) provides an insightful "dissection" of the "notion of the individual human subject":

> The biological organism and the social persona are profoundly different social constructions. The different systems of social practices, including discourse practices, through which these two notions are constituted, have their meanings and are made use of, are radically incommensurable. The biological notion of a human organism as an identifiable individual unit of analysis depends on the specific scientific practices we use to construct the identity, the boundedness, the integrity, and the continuity across interactions of this unit. ... The social-biographical person is also an individual in so far as we construct its identity, boundedness, integrity and continuity, but the social practices and discourses we deploy in these constructions are quite different. We define the social person in terms of social interactions, social roles, socially and culturally meaningful behavior patterns. ... We obtain the common sense notion of a human individual only by a complex process of conflation: mapping the social-biographical person onto the physical-biological organism. This, too, is accomplished by our cultural patterns of discourse, and the associated actional practices. Because the classical notion of a human individual is constructed in this way, if we no longer make the traditional metaphysical presumption of a single 'real object' to which each of these discursive systems 'refers' or 'on which' it acts, there is no longer any reason to suppose that 'the individual' constructed by each of these systems of practices coincides with those constructed through the others. (p. 81)

Lemke then goes on to explore material, social and semiotic constructions of "individual" and to suggest where we need to depart from the received notion of individuality (cf. Ch. 14 for the mental aspect of this notion). Towards the end of his discussion he writes:

> We need some latter-day Jean Piaget to write *The Child's Construction of the Sense of Self*. It should tell us how the child (and later the adult), enmeshed in semiotically and materially mediated interactions with other members of a community and with the material environment, progressively recapitulates (always to some degree individuating) a trajectory of development that leads to our constructing the sense of a Self, a Self that looks out through the windows of the eyes, that initiates motor actions by 'will' and 'intention', that 'feels' the sensations which impinge on a body in which it sits, but of which it is not truly a physical part. It will tell the story of how we are taught to think of ourselves as Selves.

This is part of the process whereby children learn how to mean.

15.2 Construing experience: ontogenetic perspective

15.2.1 Protolanguage and language

A human infant is a social being from birth (cf. Trevarthen, 1987). Newborn children can exchange attention with their mothers, addressing them and recognizing that they are being addressed by them; the infant's whole body is actively involved in the exchange.

This is "pre-language" ("pre-meaning", even "pre-text"); but it is not language — no distinction is yet being made between symbolic and non-symbolic acts. Then, as they become aware of themselves and their environment, children feel a tension building up between two facets of their experience: between what they perceive as happening "out there" and what is happening "in here", within their own borders so to speak. We can watch babies of around 3 - 4 months struggling to reconcile these complex sensations: they can see a coloured object, reach out, and grasp it and pull it towards them. The inner and the outer forms of this experience have to be brought into line; in order to achieve this, children begin to act in a new, distinctively symbolic mode. A typical example of such an "act of meaning" is the high-pitched squeak a child of around 5 months may produce when some commotion takes place that has to be assimilated. Adults interpret these proto-signs as a demand for explanation: "Yes, that's a bus starting up. Isn't it noisy!" Thus meaning arises out of the impact between the material and the conscious as the two facets of a child's ongoing experience.

Children gradually build up an inventory of such proto-signs, and towards the end of the first year the signs begin to form **systems**, sets of contrasting terms in particular proto-semantic domains or **micro-functions**: typically, the instrumental (e.g. 'I want/ I don't want'), regulatory (e.g. 'Do that!/ **Do that!!**'), interactional (e.g. 'I'm here/ where are you?'), and personal domains (e.g. 'I like that/ I'm curious about that'). These already foreshadow the semantic motifs of the adult language, the experiential and interpersonal metafunctions, although they are not in any direct correspondence with them; thus the "personal" signs expressing curiosity, or pleasure/ displeasure, constitute the beginning of the semiotic exploration of experience and open the way to naming and classifying phenomena, while the interactional signs are the ones whereby a child enacts social relationships with caregivers and others who are close (Halliday, 1975; 1984b). Here we see the earliest context for the later emergence of types of process within the grammar (Halliday, 1991). But the immediate significance of the protolanguage is that by acting semiotically in these particular contexts children construe the fundamental distinction between "self" and "other", and the further distinction of "other" into persons and objects (cf. the discussion and figure in Halliday, 1978b). The consciousness of the self arises at the intersection of the various semiotic roles defined by each of these systems[2] — as well as, of course, from awareness of being one interactant in the general dialogic process (Halliday, 1991).

The protolanguage is typically associated with the stage of crawling, when children are mobile, but not yet walking and running: typically about 0;8 - 1;4, but with wide variation around these times. The elements of the protolanguage are "signs" (that is, content/ expression pairs); they are thus formally identical with the semiotic resources of higher mammals (primates and cetaceans) — but with one important difference: the signs of other species become *codified* as the form of communication among adults, whereas those of human children are *transitional* to a system of a different *kind*, and hence do not stabilize into a settled pattern but are constantly shifting on both semiotic planes.[3]

How, and why, do children discard their functioning protolanguage and move on to "language" in its adult form? To take up the "why?" first: because the protolanguage sets limits on both dimensions of meaning. You can converse in it, but you cannot build up a dialogue: that is, it allows exchange of meaning, but it precludes any form of an interpersonal dynamic, in which meanings expand on the basis of what went before. You can point with it, but you cannot refer: that is, it allows focus on an object, but it precludes any form of ideational systematic, in which phenomena are construed as configurations and in taxonomies. For these to be possible you need a semiotic of a different kind, one that allows for a purely abstract level of representation "in between" the two faces of the sign. To put this another way (as we did at the beginning of the book), the sign has to be deconstructed so that, instead of content interfacing directly with

---

[2] There is a sense in which these roles anticipate the functions in the transitivity structure of the clause: proto-Beneficiary (instrumental), proto-Agent (regulatory), proto-Carrier (interactional), and proto-Senser (personal).

[3] It is clear that animals such as chimpanzees and gorillas, whales and dolphins, communicate with signs in this defined sense, and it appears that these are in some way organized into sign systems. It is possible that some of these species have already moved towards a human-like, stratified form of language; but this has not yet been demonstrated, as far as we know, by any of the available evidence.

An interesting case is that of domesticated cats and dogs. They communicate with signs to their human companions, but apparently not, or only very rarely, to each other. The affinity often felt between such pets and small children is not merely one of a shared material plane (they are more like each other in size) but also one of a shared semiotic plane: they share a common form of language.

expression, the relationship is mediated by a systematic organization of form (a lexicogrammar). In other words, the semiotic has to become **stratified**.

Children make the transition from protolanguage to language typically in the second half of the second year of life. The transition has been described in detail elsewhere, based on intensive observations of individual children (see especially Painter, 1984, 1989; Oldenburg, 1987); we may assume that in general terms they are recapitulating the phylogenetic evolution of language, although of course we can only speculate about the way that evolution took place (it is important to say explicitly that all human languages known today are equally far removed from that phase in our semiotic history). During that stage they learn to construe elements and figures, and in this way "semanticize" both the construction of experience and the enactment of interpersonal relations. In terms of the grammar, they learn to form groups and clauses, and to select systemic options simultaneously in transitivity and in mood.

Since our concern in this book is with the ideation base, we have not been considering interpersonal aspects of meaning, and we have not put major emphasis on dialogic patterns in discourse. So in this final glance at ontogenesis we should foreground very clearly the fact that meaning is an interactive process and that children learning to mean construe their semiotic resources through dialogue. This is not simply an optional extra, something that makes the learning processes easier; it is an inherent property of semiosis itself. Semiotic systems are social systems, and meaning arises in shared social consciousness; this is evident already in the protolanguage, when infants depend on being treated as communicating beings, and those within their "meaning group" are tracking them — unconsciously creating the language along with them (see Halliday, 1979b). We find this manifested also in the forms of discourse, in the way children participate in constructing narratives of shared experience (see Halliday, 1975: 112; Painter, 1989: 55). When we talk of "construing experience" as the metafunctional realm of the ideation base, we are referring to the shared experience of the group, the culture and the species; it is by means of dialogue that children gain access to this shared experience and are enabled to construe their own experience with reference to it. And the dialogic nature of discourse serves the child also as a metaphor, as the semiotic manifestation of the social conditions of human existence.

15.2.2 Generalization, abstraction and metaphor

A prerequisite for the semiotic construal of experience is **generalization**: the move from "proper" to "common" as the basic principle of referring. The protolanguage, as already remarked, is non-referring; children move into reference by gradually deconstruing the proto-linguistic sign in a sequence of steps such as 'I want Mummy to ...', 'I want Mummy!', 'Where is Mummy?', 'Mummy' (see Halliday, 1992). The sign has now become a word, functioning as a proper name. Typically one or two other signs have been deconstrued at the same time in similar fashion, e.g. 'I want my (toy) bird!', 'Where is my bird?', 'My bird'; and by a further step these then become common names 'bird(s)'. The child has now learnt to name a class of things; this then opens the way (i) to constructing hierarchies of classes — a 'pigeon' is a kind of 'bird', and so on, and (ii) to naming other kinds of element, processes and qualities, which can be construed only as "common" terms. Since these other elements have distinct and complementary functions it becomes possible to combine them into organic structures, as complex elements or as figures, such as 'blue bird', 'birds flying', 'tiny bird flew away'. The resources are now in place for construing experience in lexicogrammatical terms.

This principle of generalization — that is, naming general classes rather than specific individuals — is what makes it possible to construct an ideation base. When they have reached this stage, children can make the transition from protolanguage to mother tongue, building up figures and sequences of figures, and simultaneously structuring these as moves in dialogic exchanges (question, statement, etc. — the interaction base), and as messages or quanta of information (the text base). In other words, they learn "how to mean" according to the metafunctional principle of adult human semiosis. But there are two further developments to come before the ideation base can take the form it has to take if it is to produce discourse of the kind we have been assuming throughout the book (and illustrating with weather reports and recipes); and there is some elapse of time before children take these further steps. The first of these developments is abstractness; the second is (grammatical) metaphor.

General terms are not necessarily abstract; a bird is no more abstract than a pigeon. But some words have referents that are purely abstract — words like *cost* and *clue* and *habit* and *tend* and *strange;* they are construing some aspect of our experience, but there is no concrete thing or process with which they can be identified. Small children simply ignore them, but by the age of about four or five they begin to cope with abstract meanings; in literate societies, this is the time we consider that children are "ready to start school", no doubt because you have to cope with abstractness in meaning in order to be able to learn to read and write (cf. wordings like *spell, stand for, beginning of a sentence*). But it is not only the written medium; rather it is the whole world of educational knowledge that demands such abstractness in meaning. Consider examples taken from primary text books such as *Some animals rely on their great speed to escape from danger*, or *The time taken by the earth to rotate once on its own axis is a day*.

What happens here is that experience is being **reconstrued** in order to build up a form of knowledge that is systematically organized and explicit. Children already know that animals run away because they're frightened, and that the sun goes round the earth once in a day; but they have to learn these things over again in a new, more abstract semiotic frame. When Nigel was 4;11 he had the following conversation with his father:

Nigel: Why does as plasticine gets longer it gets thinner? (*sic*)

Father: That's a very good question. Why does it?

Nigel: Because more of it is getting used up.

Father (doubtfully): Well ...

Nigel: Because more of it is getting used up to make it longer, that's why; and so it goes thinner.

Here Nigel displayed a clear understanding of the principle of conservation. Some years later in school he was studying the following passage:

Put a label on each [container] to show two things:

(a) The quantity it holds.

(b) What fraction of a litre in it. (*sic*)

Put all that measure 1 litre together. Some will be tall, some short, some rectangular, some cylindrical for milk or drinks, some wine bottles or carafes. But they all contain 1 LITRE. A litre is a litre, whether long, round or square. ... So all kinds of shapes can be made to have the same capacity.

K. Perret & G. Fiddes, *New Primary Maths*, Book 5. Sydney: School Projects, 1968/ 1977. (p. 71)

Note the difference in the way the grammar construes the same domain of experience, first in its everyday commonsense form, as spoken by a child, and then in its reconstruction as educational knowledge.

But there is a further transformation still to come, when experience is once again reconstrued, this time as **technical** knowledge. This reconstrual too is institutionalized, in the transition from primary to secondary education: when children move into secondary school, as adolescents, they learn to organize their experience according to the disciplines — mathematics, science (chemistry, physics, biology), geography, history, and so on. Semiotically, the critical factor is that of metaphor; the semiotic bonds that had enabled the child to learn the mother tongue in the first place, bonds between figures and their elements on the one hand and clauses and their transitivity functions on the other, are systematically (and more or less ceremonially!) untied. The categories of experience are deconstrued, to be recategorized over the remaining years of schooling in the "objectifying" framework of grammatical metaphor. We have described these effects in Part II above (Chapter 6) and will not repeat the exposition here (cf. Derewianka, 1995, for a longitudinal study of one child). By the time children reach the 11th and 12th year of education their experience is being construed in terms such as these:

> Every similarity transformation, if not a translation, reflection, rotation, or enlargement, is the product of two or more such transformations.

> A. McMullen & J.L. Williams, *On Course Mathematics* 4. Advanced Level. Melbourne: Macmillan, 1965/ 1975. (p. 153)

> What would be the order of magnitude of the moment of inertia of the Earth about its axis of rotation?

> E.D. Gardiner & B.L. McKittrick, *Problems in Physics.* Sydney: McGraw-Hill, 1969/ 1985. (p. 58)

The elements are processes and qualities that have been metaphorically reconstrued to become participants: *rotation, magnitude, enlargement,* and so on; together with the relation of identity construed as a process by the verb *be.* When our adolescents' ideation base comes to accommodate a meaning potential of this technicalized kind, we consider that they have reached semiotic maturity.

The developmental dynamic of "generalization — abstractness — metaphor" provides the semiotic energy for the grammar, enabling it to serve as the powerhouse for construing experience in the form of scientific knowledge. Presented in this very sketchy fashion the movement may seem catastrophic and discontinuous; but this is misleading. Rather, it is a steady progression, marked by three periods of more rapid development at the transitions: from protolanguage to language (generalization, associated with bipedal motion), from commonsense (spoken) language to written language (abstractness: the move into primary school), and from non-specialized written language to technical language (metaphor: the move into secondary school). There is a clear grammatical and semantic continuity between the various versions of experience, which we can bring out by analysing the grammar of particular instances (such as those cited above). At the same time, the ontogenetic perspective shows that in fact our experience is being ongoingly reconstrued and recategorized as we grow from infancy to maturity. This is the outcome of processes taking place in human history — evolutionary events that are at once both material and semiotic, and that cannot be reduced to either purely physical processes driven by technology or purely discursive processes driven by ideology. There is no point in asking whether the ideation base of our technologized natural languages necessarily had to evolve the way it did. But it is extremely pertinent to ask, given the enormous demands now being made on both the material and the semiotic resources of the human species, what the options are for the way it may evolve in future.

References

Allen, J. 1987. *Natural language understanding*. Menlo Park, CA: The Benjamins/ Cummings Publishing Company.

Amsler, R. 1981. A taxonomy for English nouns and verbs. *Proceedings of the 19th Annual Meeting of the Association for Computational Linguistics*.

Anderson, J. 1983. *The architecture of cognition*. Cambridge, Mass.: Harvard University Press.

Argyle, M., A. Furnham & G.A. Graham. 1981. *Social situations*. Cambridge: Cambridge University Press.

Bach, E. 1968. Nouns and noun phrases. E. Bach & R. Harms (eds.).

Bach, E. 1989. *Informal lectures on formal semantics*. Albany, NY: State University of New York Press. [323]

Bach, E. & R. Harms (eds.). 1968. *Universals in linguistic theory*. New York: Holt, Rinehart and Winston.

Ballim. A. & Y. Wilks. 1991. *Artificial believers: the ascription of belief*. Hillsdale, NJ: Lawrence Erlbaum.

Barr, A. & E. Feigenbaum. 1981. *The handbook of artificial intelligence*. Menlo Park, CA: Addison-Wesley. Barwise, J. 1988. On the circumstantial relation between meaning and content. Eco et al.

Barwise, J. & J. Perry. 1983. *Situations and attitudes*. Cambridge, Mass.: The MIT Press. Bateman, J.A. 1985. *Utterances in context: towards a systemic theory of the intersubjective achievement of discourse*. Ph.D. Thesis, Department of Artificial Intelligence / School of Epistemics, University of Edinburgh.

Bateman, J.A. 1989. Dynamic systemic-functional grammar: a new frontier. *Word* 40.1-2 (*Systems, structures and discourse: selected papers from the fifteenth international systemic congress*).

Bateman, J.A. 1996. *KPML development environment — multilingual linguistic resource development and sentence generation*. Manual for release 0.9, March 1996. IPSI/ GMD, Darmstadt, Germany.

Bateman, J.A. , Kasper, R., Moore, J. and Whitney, R. 1990. *A general organization of knowledge for natural language processing: the Penman Upper Model*. Research report, Information Sciences Institute, University of Southern California.

Bateman, J.A. & C.M.I.M. Matthiessen. 1993. The text base in generation. K. Hao, H. Bluhme & R. Li (eds.), *Proceedings of the international conference on texts and language research, Xi'an, 29-31 March 1989*. Xi'an: Xi'an Jiaotong University Press.

Bateman, J.A. & S. Momma. 1991. *The nondirectional representation of Systemic Functional grammars and semantics as Typed Feature Structures*. Technical report, GMD/ Institut für Integrierte Publikations- und Informationssysteme, Darmstadt and Institut für Maschinelle Sprachverarbeitung, Universität Stuttgart.

Bateman, J.A., C.M.I.M. Matthiessen, K. Nanri and L. Zeng. 1991. The rapid prototyping of natural language generation components: an application of functional typology. *Proceedings of the 12th international conference on artificial intelligence, Sydney, 24-30 August 1991.* San Mateo, CA: Morgan Kaufman.

Bateman, J.A., C.M.I.M. Matthiesssen & L. Zeng. forthc. *A general architecture of multilingual resources for natural language processing.* MS, Macquarie University & GMD/ IPSI.

Becker, J.D. 1975. The phrasal lexicon. R. Schank & B. Nash-Webber (ed.), *Theoretical issues in natural language processing,* Association for Computational Linguistics.

Benson, J.D. & W.S. Greaves (eds.). 1985. *Systemic perspectives on discourse: selected papers from the ninth international systemic workshop, Volume 1.* Norwood, NJ: Ablex.

Benson, J.D. & W.S. Greaves (eds.). 1988. *Systemic functional approaches to discourse: aelected papers from the twelfth international systemic workshop.* Norwood, NJ: Ablex.

Benson, J.D., M.J. Cummings, & W.S. Greaves (eds.). 1988. *Linguistics in a systemic perspective.* Amsterdam: Benjamins.

Berger, P.L. & T. Luckmann. 1966. *The social construction of reality.* Garden City, NY: Doubleday.

Berlin, B. 1972. Speculations on the growth of ethnobotanical nomenclature. *Language in Society* 1.

Berlin, B., D. Breedlove, & P. Raven. 1973. General principles of classification and nomenclature in folk biology. *American Anthropologist,* 75.

Berlin, B. & P. Kay. 1969. *Basic color terms: their universality and evolution.* Berkeley, CA: University of California Press.

Berry, M. 1981. Systemic linguistics and discourse analysis: a multi-layered approach to exchange structure. M. Coulthard & M. Montgomery (eds.), *Studies in discourse analysis.* London: Routledge & Kegan Paul. Berry, M., C.S. Butler, R.P. Fawcett & G. Huang (eds.). 1996. *Meaning and form: systemic functional interpretations. Meaning and choice in language: studies for Michael Halliday.* (Volume LVII in the series Advances in Discourse Processes.) Norwood, NJ: Ablex.

Biagi, M.L.A. 1995. Diacronia dei linguaggi scientifici. R. R. Favretti (ed.), *Proceedings of the international conference "Languages of Science", Bologna, 25-27 October 1995.* In press.

Bickhart, M.H. & R.L. Campbell. 1992. Some fundamental questions concerning language studies: with a focus on categorial grammars and model-theoretic possible world semantics. *Journal of Pragmatics* 17.

Bohm, D. 1979. *Wholeness and the implicate order.* London: Routledge & Kegan Paul.

Boole, G. 1854. *An investigation of the laws of thought: on which are founded the mathematical theories of logic and probability.* London: Macmillan. [New York: Dover. 1958.]

Brachman, R.J. 1978. *A structural paradigm for representing knowledge.* BBN Report No. 3605, Bolt Beranek and Newman, Inc. Cambridge, MA.

Brachman, R.J. 1979. On the epistemological status of semantic networks. N.V. Findler (ed.), *Associative networks: representation and use of knowledge by computers*. New York: Academic Press. Reprinted in Brachman & Levesque (1985).

Brachman, R.J. & H.J. Levesque. (eds.) 1985. *Readings in knowledge representation*. Los Altos, CA: Morgan Kaufman.

Brachman, R.J., R. Fikes & H.J. Levesque. 1983. KRYPTON: A functional approach to knowledge representation. *IEEE Computer*, 16.10. Reprinted in Brachman & Levesque (1985).

Brachman, R.J. & J. Schmolze. 1985. An overview of the KL-ONE knowledge representation system. *Cognitive Science*, 9.2.

Brew, C. 1991. Systemic classification and its efficiency. *Computational Linguistics* 17.4.

Brill, D. (1991). *LOOM: reference manual*. Technical report, Information Sciences Institute, University of Southern California.

Bundy, A. (ed), 1986. *Catalogue of artificial intelligence tools*. Second, revised edition. Berlin & New York: Springer-Verlag.

Bursill-Hall, G.L. 1971. *Speculative grammars of the Middle Ages: the doctrine of partes orationes of the Modistae*. The Hague & Paris: Mouton.

Butt, D.J. 1983. Semantic "drift" in verbal art. *Australian Review of Linguistics* 6.1.

Butt, D.J. 1987. Randomness, order and the latent patterning of text. D.I. Birch & M.L.M. O'Toole (eds.), *Functions of style*. London: Pinter.

Butt, D.J. 1991. Some basic tools in a linguistic approach to personality: a Firthian concept of social process. F. Christie (ed.), *Literacy in social processes: papers from the Inaugural Australian Systemic Functional Linguistics Conference, Deakin University, January 1990*. Darwin: Centre for Studies of Language in Education, Northern Territory University.

Caffarel, A. 1990. *Mediating between grammar and context: a bi-stratal exploration of the semantics of French tense*. B.A. Honours thesis, Department of Linguistics, University of Sydney.

Caffarel, A. 1992. Context projected onto semantics and the consequences for grammatical selection. *Language Sciences*, 14.4.

Cann, R. 1993. *Formal semantics: an introduction*. Cambridge: Cambridge University Press. (Cambridge Textbooks in Linguistics.)

Chafe, W.L. 1970. *Meaning and the structure of language*. Chicago: Chicago University Press.

Chafe, W.L. 1979. The flow of thought and the flow of language. T. Givón (ed.), *Syntax and Semantics 12: Discourse and Syntax*. New York: Academic Press.

Chafe, W.L. 1987. Cognitive constraints on information flow. R. Tomlin (ed.), *Coherence and grounding in discourse*. Amsterdam: Benjamins.

Clark, H.H. 1975. Bridging. *TINLAP-1*. Reprinted in P.N. Johnson-Laird & P. Wason (eds.). 1977. *Thinking: readings in cognitive science*. Cambridge: Cambridge University Press.

Conklin, H. 1962. Lexicographical treatment of folk taxonomies. F. Householder & S. Saporta (eds.), *Problems in lexicography*. Bloomington, Ind.: Indiana University Research Center in Anthropology, Folklore, and Linguistics. (Publication 21.)

Cook, W.A, 1977. *Case grammar: development of the matrix model (1970 - 1978)*. Washington, DC: Georgetown University Press.

Cross, M. 1991. *Choice in text: a systemic approach to computer modelling of variant text production*. Ph.D. thesis, Macquarie University.

Cross, M. 1992. Choice in lexis: computer generation of lexis as most delicate grammar. *Language Sciences*, 14.4.

Cross, M. 1993. Collocation in computer modelling of lexis as most delicate grammar. M. Ghadessy (ed.), *Register analysis: theory and practice*. London: Pinter.

Cruse, D.A. 1986. *Lexical semantics*. Cambridge: Cambridge University Press. (Cambridge Textbooks in Linguistics.)

D'Andrade, R. 1987. A folk model of the mind. Holland & Quinn (eds).

Dahlgren, K. 1988. *Naive semantics for natural language understanding*. Dordrecht: Kluwer.

Davey, A. 1978. *Discourse production: a computer model of some aspects of a speaker*. Edinburgh: Edinburgh University Press.

Davidse, K. 1991. *Categories of experiential grammar*. Ph.D. thesis, Catholic University of Leuven

Davidse, K. 1992a. Existential constructions: a systemic perspective. *Leuvense Bijdragen* 81.

Davidse, K. 1992b. A semiotic approach to relational clauses. *Occasional Papers in Systemic Linguistics* 6.

Davidse, K. 1992c. Transitive/ergative: the Janus-headed grammar of actions and events. M. Davies & L. Ravelli (eds.).

Davidse, K. 1996a. Turning grammar on itself: identifying clauses in linguistic discourse. Berry et al. (eds.).

Davidse, K. 1996b. Ditransitivity and possession. R. Hasan, C. Cloran & D. Butt (eds.).

Davidson, D. 1967. Truth and meaning. *Synthèse* 17.

Davidson, D. 1970. Semantics for natural languages. Reprinted in D. Davidson & G. Harman (eds.), *The logic of grammar*. Encino, CA: Dickenson, 1975. Davies, M. & L. Ravelli (eds). 1992. *Advances in systemic linguistics*. London: Pinter.

de Beaugrande, R. 1980. *Text, discourse, and process: toward a multidisciplinary science of texts*. Norwood, NJ: Ablex.

de Beaugrande, R. 1994. Function and form in language theory and research: the tide is turning. *Functions of Language* 1.2.

de Beaugrande, R. in press. *New foundations for a science of text and discourse*. Norwood, NJ: Ablex.

Dennett, D. 1981. Three kinds of intentional psychology. Healy (ed.), *Reduction, time and reality*. Cambridge: Cambridge University Press. Reprinted in J.L. Garfield (ed.), *Foundations of cognitive science: the essential readings*. New York: Paragon House, 1990.

Derewianka, B. 1995. *Language development in the transition from childhood to adolescence: the role of grammatical metaphor*. Ph.D. thesis, Macquarie University.

Dik, S. 1978. *Functional grammar*. Amsterdam: North-Holland.

Dik, S. 1986. Linguistically motivated knowledge representation. *Working Papers on Functional Grammar* 9. Amsterdam.

Dik, S. 1987. Generating answers from a linguistically coded knowledge base. Kempen (ed.).

Downing, P. 1980. Factors influencing lexical choice in narratives. W. Chafe (ed.), *Cognitive, cultural and linguistic aspects of narrative production*. Norwood, N.J.: Ablex.

Dowty, D., R. Wall & S. Peters. 1981. *Introduction to Montague semantics*. Dordrecht: Reidel.

Dowty, D. 1979. *Word meaning and Montague grammar*. Dordrecht: Reidel.

Dunbar, R. 1992. Quoted in *New Scientist* 1850, 5 Dec. 1992. (Supplement Number 4: Secret Life of the Brain.)

Eco, U., M. Santambrogio & P. Violi. (eds.) 1988. *Meaning and mental representations*. Bloomington, Ind.: Indiana University Press.

Edelman, G. 1992. *Bright air, brilliant fire: on the matter of the mind*. New York: Basic Books.

Eggins, S. 1990. *Conversational structure: a systemic-functional analysis of interpersonal and logical meaning in multiparty sustained talk*. PhD thesis, Department of Linguistics, University of Sydney.

Eggins, S. 1994. *An introduction to systemic functional linguistics*. London: Pinter.

Eggins, S., P. Wignell & J.R. Martin. 1993. The discourse of history: distancing the recoverable past. M. Ghadessy (ed.), *Register analysis. Theory and practice*. London: Pinter.

Ellis, J.M. 1993. *Language, thought and logic*. Evanston, Ill.: Northwestern University Press.

Ehrich, V. 1987. The generation of tense. G. Kempen (ed.).

Fang, Y., E. McDonald & M. Cheng. 1995. On Theme in Chinese: from clause to discourse. R. Hasan & P.H. Fries (eds.), *On subject and theme: a discourse functional perspective*. Amsterdam: Benjamins.

Fawcett, R.P. 1980. *Cognitive linguistics and social interaction: towards an integrated model of a systemic functional grammar and the other components of an interacting mind*. Heidelberg: Julius Gross; Exeter: Exeter University Press.

Fawcett, R.P. 1981. Generating a sentence in systemic-functional grammar. M.A.K. Halliday & J.R. Martin (eds.). Fawcett, R.P. 1984. System networks, codes and knowledge of the universe. R.P. Fawcett et al (eds).

Fawcett, R.P. 1987. The semantics of clause and verb for relational processes in English. M.A.K. Halliday & R.P. Fawcett (eds.).

Fawcett, R.P. 1988a. The English personal pronouns: an exercise in linguistic theory. Benson, Cummings & Greaves (eds.).

Fawcett, R.P. 1988b. Language generation as choice in social interaction. M. Zock & G. Sabah (eds.), *Advances in natural language generation*. London: Pinter.

Fawcett, R.P. 1994. A generationist approach to grammar reversibility in natural language processing. T. Strzalkowski (ed.), *Reversible grammar in natural language processing*. Dordrecht: Kluwer.

Fawcett, R.P., G.H. Tucker & Y.Q. Lin. 1992. The COMMUNAL Project: how to get from semantics to syntax. *Proceedings of the 14th International Conference on Computational Linguistics*.

Fawcett, R.P., M.A.K. Halliday, S.M. Lamb & A. Makkai. (eds). 1984. *The semiotics of culture and language*. 2 Volumes. London: Frances Pinter.

Fawcett, R.P. & D.J. Young. 1988. *New developments in systemic linguistics. Volume 2: theory and application*. London: Pinter.

Fillmore, C. 1968. The case for case. Bach & Harms (eds.).

Firth, J.R. 1950. Personality and language in society. *Sociological Review* 42.2. Reprinted in Firth (1957).

Firth, J.R. 1956. Linguistic analysis and translation. *For Roman Jakobson: essays on the occasion of his sixtieth birthday*. The Hague: Mouton. Reprinted in F.R. Palmer (ed.), *Selected papers J.R. Firth 1952 - 1959*. London: Longman, 1968.

Firth, J.R. 1957. *Papers in linguistics 1934-1951*. London: Oxford University Press.

Fischer-Jørgensen, E. 1975. *Trends in phonological theory: a historical introduction*. Copenhagen: Akademisk Forlag.

Fodor, J. 1975. *The language of thought*. Cambridge, Mass: Harvard University Press.

Foley, W.A. 1986. *The Papuan languages of New Guinea*. Cambridge: Cambridge University Press (Cambridge Language Surveys).

Foley, W.A. & R. Van Valin. 1984. *Functional syntax and universal grammar*. Cambridge: Cambridge University Press.

Fox, B. 1987. *Discourse structure and anaphora: written and conversational English*. Cambridge: Cambridge University Press.

Frake, C. 1962. The ethnographic study of cognitive systems. T. Gladwin & W. Sturtevant (eds), *Anthropology and human behavior*. Washington: Anthropological Society of Washington. Frege, G. 1879. *Begriffsschrift, eine der arithmetischen nachgebildete Formelsprache des reinen Denkens*. Halle: Nebert.

Frege, G. 1892. Über Sinn und Bedeutung. *Zeitschrift für Philosophie und philosophische Kritik* 100.

Fries, P.H. 1981. On the status of theme in English: arguments from discourse. *Forum Linguisticum* 6.1. Reprinted in J. Petöfi & E. Sözer (eds.), 1983, *Micro and macro connexity of texts*. Hamburg: Helmut Buske (Papers in Textlinguistics 45).

Fries, P.H. 1992. Structure of information in written English text. *Language Sciences* 14.4.

Fries, P.H. 1995. Themes, methods of development, and texts. R. Hasan & P.H. Fries (eds.), *On subject and theme: a discourse functional perspective*. Amsterdam: Benjamins.

Fries, P.H. in press. Towards a discussion of the flow of information in a written English text. M.J. Gregory, M.J. Cummings & J. Copeland (eds.), *Relations and functions in and around language*.

Givón, T. 1979. *On understanding grammar*. New York: Academic Press.

Givón, T. 1980. The binding hierarchy and the typology of complements. *Studies in Language* 4.3.

Goldman, N. 1974. *Computer generation of natural language from a deep conceptual base*. Ph.D. Thesis, Stanford University.

Goodenough, W. 1956. Componential analysis and the study of meaning. *Language* 32.

Grosz, B. 1978. Discourse knowledge. D. Walker (ed.), *Understanding spoken language*. Amsterdam: North Holland.

Gruber, J. 1965. *Studies in lexical relations*. Ph.D. thesis, Massachusets Institute of Technology.

Gruber, J. 1976. *Lexical structures in syntax and semantics*. Amsterdam: North-Holland.

Haack, S. 1978. *Philosophy of logics*. Cambridge: Cambridge University Press.

Haiman, J. (ed.) 1985. *Iconicity in syntax*. Amsterdam: Benjamins.

Halliday, M.A.K. 1956. Grammatical categories in Modern Chinese. *Transactions of the Philological Society*. Abridged version reprinted in Halliday (1976).

Halliday, M.A.K. 1959. *The Language of the Chinese "Secret History of the Mongols"*. Oxford: Blackwell (Publications of the Philological Society 17.)

Halliday, M.A.K. 1961. Categories of the theory of grammar. *Word* 17.3. Abridged version reprinted in Halliday (1976).

Halliday, M.A.K. 1963a. The tones of English. *Archivum Linguisticum* 15.1.

Halliday, M.A.K. 1963b. Intonation in English grammar. *Transactions of the Philological Society*.

Halliday, M.A.K. 1966. Some notes on "deep" grammar. *Journal of Linguistics* 2.1. Abridged version reprinted in Halliday (1976).

Halliday, M.A.K. 1967. *Intonation and grammar in British English.* The Hague: Mouton (Series Practica XLVIII).

Halliday, M.A.K. 1967/8. Notes on transitivity and theme in English. *Journal of Linguistics* 3.1, 3.2, & 4.2.

Halliday, M.A.K. 1971. Linguistic function and literary style: an enquiry into the language of William Golding's *The inheritors.* In S. Chatman (ed.), *Literary style: a symposium.* New York: Oxford University Press. Reprinted in Halliday (1973).

Halliday, M.A.K. 1973. *Explorations in the functions of language.* London: Edward Arnold.

Halliday, M.A.K. 1975. *Learning how to mean.* London: Edward Arnold.

Halliday, M.A.K. 1976. *System and function in language: selected papers,* ed. G.R. Kress. London: Oxford University Press.

Halliday, M.A.K. 1977. *Aims and perspectives in linguistics.* Applied Linguistics Association of Australia (Occasional Papers Number 1).

Halliday, M.A.K. 1978a. *Language as social semiotic: the social interpretation of language and meaning.* London: Edward Arnold.

Halliday, M.A.K. 1978b. Meaning and the construction of reality in early childhood. In H.L. Pick Jr & E. Saltzman (eds), *Modes of perceiving and processing information.* Hillsdale, NJ: Erlbaum.

Halliday, M.A.K. 1979a. Modes of meaning and modes of expression. D.J. Allerton, E. Carney, and D. Holdcroft (eds), *Function and context in linguistic analysis: essays offered to William Haas.* Cambridge: Cambridge University Press.

Halliday, M.A.K. 1979b. One child's protolanguage. M. Bullowa (ed.), *Before speech: the beginnings of interpersonal communication.* Cambridge: Cambridge University Press.

Halliday, M.A.K. 1984a. On the ineffability of grammatical categories. A. Manning, P. Martin & K. McCalla (eds), *The Tenth LACUS Forum* 1983. Columbia: Hornbeam Press. Reprinted in Benson, Cummings & Greaves (eds.).

Halliday, M.A.K. 1984b. Language as code and language as behaviour: a systemic-functional interpretation of the nature and ontogenesis of dialogue. Fawcett et al (eds).

Halliday, M.A.K. 1984c. *Listening to Nigel.* Department of Linguistics, University of Sydney.

Halliday, M.A.K. 1985. *An introduction to functional grammar.* London: Edward Arnold. Second, revised edition 1994.

Halliday, M.A.K. 1985/9. *Spoken and written language.* Geelong, Vic: Deakin University Press. Reprinted London: Oxford University Press.

Halliday, M.A.K. 1987. Language and the order of nature. D. Attridge, A. Durant, N. Fabb & C. MacCabe (eds), *The Linguistics of Writing.* Manchester: Manchester University Press. Reprinted in Halliday & Martin (1993).

Halliday, M.A.K. 1988. On the language of physical science. M. Ghadessy (ed.), *Registers of written English: situational factors and linguistic features.* London: Pinter. Reprinted in Halliday & Martin (1993).

Halliday, M.A.K. 1990. New ways of meaning: a challenge to applied linguistics. *Journal of Applied Linguistics* (Greek Applied Linguistics Association) 6. Reprinted in Pütz (ed.).

Halliday, M.A.K. 1991. The place of dialogue in children's construction of meaning. S. Stati, E. Weigand & F. Hundsnurscher (eds.), *Dialoganalyse III: Referate der 3. Arbeitstagung,* Bologna 1990. Tübingen: Niemeyer (Beiträge zur Dialogforschung, Bd. 1). Teil 1.

Halliday, M.A.K. 1992. How do you mean? Davies & Ravelli (eds.).

Halliday, M.A.K. 1993a. Towards a language-based theory of learning. *Linguistics and Education* 5. Halliday, M.A.K. 1993b. Systemic theory. R.E. Asher (ed.), *The encyclopedia of language and linguistics.* Oxford: Pergamon Press. Volume 8.

Halliday, M.A.K. 1995a. On language in relation to the evolution of human consciousness. S. Allén (ed.), *Of thoughts and words: proceedings of Nobel Symposium 92 "The relation between language and mind", Stockholm 8-12 August 1994.* London: Imperial College Press; Singapore: World Scientific Publishing Co.

Halliday, M.A.K. 1995b. Computing meaning: some reflections on past experience and present prospects. Paper presented to PACLING 95, Brisbane, April 1995.

Halliday, M.A.K. 1996. On grammar and grammatics. Hasan et al (eds.).

Halliday, M.A.K. in press a. Things and relations: regrammaticizing experience as technical knowledge. J.R. Martin & R. Veel (eds.).

Halliday, M.A.K. in press b. The grammatical construction of scientific knowledge: a the framing of the English clause. In R.R. Favretti (ed.), *Proceedings of the international conference "Languages of Science", Bologna, 25-27 October 1995.*

Halliday, M.A.K. in press c. Grammar and daily life: construing pain. Bessy Dendrinos (ed.), *Proceedings of the fourth international symposium in Critical Discourse Analysis, Athens, December 1995.*

Halliday, M.A.K. & R.P. Fawcett (eds). 1987. *New developments in systemic linguistics. Volume 1: theory and description.* London: Pinter.

Halliday, M.A.K. & R. Hasan. 1976. *Cohesion in English.* London: Longman.

Halliday, M.A.K. & R. Hasan. 1985/89. *Language, context, and text: aspects of language in a social-semiotic perspective.* Geelong, Vic.: Deakin University Press. Reprinted London: Oxford University Press, 1989.

Halliday, M.A.K & Z. James. 1993. A quantitative study of polarity and primary tense in the English finite clause. J. M. Sinclair, G. Fox & M. Hoey (eds.), *Techniques of description: spoken and written discourse.* London: Routledge.

Halliday, M.A.K. & J.R. Martin. (eds.) 1981. *Readings in systemic linguistics.* London: Batsford.

Halliday, M.A.K. & J.R. Martin. 1993. *Writing science: literacy and discursive power.* London: Falmer Press.

Harvey, A. 1997. Equivalence and depersonalisation in definitions: an exploration of lexicogrammatical and rhetorical patterns in English technical discourse. Ph.D. thesis, University of Sydney.

Hasan, R. 1978. Text in the systemic-functional model. W. Dressler (ed.), *Current trends in textlinguistics.* Berlin: de Gruyter.

Hasan, R. 1984a. What kind of resource is language? *Australian Review of Applied Linguistics* 7.1. Reprinted in Hasan (1996).

Hasan, R. 1984b. The nursery tale as a genre. *Nottingham Linguistic Circular,* 13. (Special Issue on Systemic Linguistics.) Reprinted in Hasan (1996).

Hasan, R. 1985a. Lending and borrowing: from grammar to lexis. J.E. Clark (ed.), *The cultivated Australian.* Hamburg: Helmut Buske.

Hasan, R. 1985b. Meaning, context and text — fifty years after Malinowski. Benson & Greaves (eds.).

Hasan, R. 1985/9. *Linguistics, language and verbal art.* Geelong, Vic: Deakin University Press. Reprinted London: Oxford University Press.

Hasan, R. 1987. The grammarian's dream: lexis as most delicate grammar. M.A.K. Halliday & R.P. Fawcett (eds.). Reprinted in Hasan (1996).

Hasan, R. 1989. Semantic variation and sociolinguistics. *Australian Journal of Linguistics,* 9.

Hasan, R. 1992. Rationality in everyday talk: from process to system. J. Svartvik (ed.), *Directions in corpus linguistics: proceedings of Nobel Symposium 82, Stockholm, 4-8 August 1991.* Berlin & New York: Mouton de Gruyter (Trends in Linguistics Studies & Monographs 65).

Hasan, R. 1995. The conception of context in text. P.H. Fries & M. Gregory (eds.), *Discourse in society: systemic functional perspectives.* Norwood, NJ: Ablex. (Meaning and Choice in Language: studies for Michael Halliday [Advances in Discourse Processes L])

Hasan, R. 1996. *Ways of saying: ways of meaning,* ed. C. Cloran, D.G. Butt & G. Williams. London: Cassell.

Hasan, R., C. Cloran & D.G. Butt (eds.). 1996. *Functional descriptions: theory in practice.* Amsterdam: Benjamins.

Havránek, B. 1932. The functional differentiation of the standard language. P. Garvin (ed.), 1964. *A Prague School reader on esthetics, literary structure, and style.* Originally in B. Havránek & M. Weingart (eds.), Spisovná cestina a jazyková kultura.

Hendrix, G. 1978. Semantic knowledge. D. Walker (ed.), *Understanding natural language.* New York: North Holland.

Hendrix, G. 1979. Encoding knowledge in partitioned networks. N.V. Finder (ed.), *Associative networks.* New York: Academic Press.

Henrici, A. 1966. *Some notes on the systemic generation of a paradigm of the English clause.* Working paper, O.S.T.I. Programme in the Linguistic Properties of Scientific

English, Communication Research Centre, University College London. Reprinted in Halliday & Martin (eds., 1981).

Henschel, R. 1994. Declarative representation and processing of systemic grammars. C. Martin-Vide (ed.), *Current issues in mathematical linguistics*. Amsterdam: Elsevier.

Hjelmslev, L. 1943. *Omkring sprogteoriens grundlaeggelse*. København: Akademisk Forlag.

Hobbs, J.R. 1984. Building a large knowledge base for a natural language system. *COLING 84*.

Hobbs, J.R. 1987. World knowledge and world meaning. *TINLAP 3*.

Holland, C. & N. Quinn (eds.). 1987. *Cultural models in language and thought*. Cambridge: Cambridge University Press.

Hopper, P. & S. Thompson. 1980. Transitivity in grammar and discourse. *Language* 56.

Hopper, P. & S. Thompson. 1985. The iconicity of the universal categories 'noun' and 'verb'. Haiman (ed.).

Hopper, P. & E. Traugott. 1993. *Grammaticalization*. Cambridge: Cambridge University Press. (Cambridge Textbooks in Linguistics.)

Hovy, E. 1988a. Planning coherent multisentential text. *Proceedings of the 26th Annual Meeting of the Association for Computational Linguistics*.

Hovy, E. 1988b. *Generating natural language under pragmatic constraints*. Hillsdale, NJ: Lawrence Erlbaum.

Hovy, E. 1991. Approaches to the planning of coherent text. C. Paris, W.R. Swartout & W.C. Mann (eds.).

Hovy, E. &. K. McCoy. 1989. Focussing your RST: a step towards generating coherent multisentential text. *Proceedings of the 11th Annual Conference of the Cognitive Science Society, Ann Arbor, Agust 1989*.

Huddleston, R.D. 1969. Some observations on tense and deixis in English. *Language* 45.

Jackendoff, R. 1972. *Semantic interpretation in generative grammar*. Cambridge, Mass.: MIT Press.

Jackendoff, R. 1976. Toward an explanatory semantic representation. *Linguistic Inquiry* 7.

Jackendoff, R. 1983. *Semantics and cognition*. Cambridge, Mass.: MIT Press.

Jackendoff, R. 1988. *Conceptual semantics*. In Eco, Santambrogio & Violi (eds.).

Jackendoff, R. 1991. Parts and boundaries. Levin & Pinker (eds.).

Jacobs, P.S. 1985. PHRED: a generator for natural language interfaces. *American Journal of Computational Linguistics*, 11.

Jacobs, P.S. 1987. KING: a knowledge-intensive natural language generator. In Kempen (ed.).

Jakobson, R. 1949. On the identification of phonemic entities. *Recherches Structurales, Travaux du Cercle Linguistique de Prague* V.

Jerison, H. 1973. *Evolution of the brain and intelligence.* New York: Academic Press.

Jespersen, O. 1924. *The philosophy of grammar.* London: Allen & Unwin.

Johnson-Laird, P.N.. 1983. *Mental models: towards a cognitive science of language, inference, and consciousness.* Cambridge: Cambridge University Press.

Johnston, T. 1989. *AUSLAN dictionary: a dictionary of the Sign Language of the Australian Deaf Community.* Petersham, N.S.W.: Deafness Resources Australia Limited.

Johnston, T. 1992. The realization of the linguistic metafunctions in a sign language. *Language Sciences* 14.4.

Kasper, R. 1989. A flexible interface for linking applications to Penman's sentence generator. *Proceedings of the DARPA Workshop on Speech and Natural Language.* Information Sciences Institute, University of Southern California.

Kasper, R. 1987. *Feature structures: a logical theory with application to language analysis.* Ph.D. Thesis, University of Michigan.

Kasper, R. 1988. Systemic grammar and functional unification grammar. Benson & Greaves (eds.).

Katz, J.J. & J. A. Fodor. 1963. The structure of a semantic theory. *Language* 39.

Katz, J. & P. Postal. 1964. *An integrated theory of linguistic description.* Cambridge, Mass.: M.I.T. Press.

Kay, M. 1979. Functional grammar. *Proceedings of the fifth annual meeting of the Berkeley Linguistic Society.*

Kay, M. 1985. Parsing with functional unification grammar. K. Sparck-Jones & B. Webber (eds.), *Readings in natural language processing.* Los Altos, CA: Morgan Kaufman.

Keenan, E. & A. Faltz. 1985. *Boolean semantics for natural language.* Dordrecht: Reidel.

Kempen, G. (ed.) 1987. *Natural language generation: recent advances in artificial intelligence, psychology, and linguistics.* Dordrecht: Kluwer.

Kiparsky, P. & C. Kiparsky. 1970. Fact. M. Bierwisch and K. Heidolph (eds.), *Progress in linguistics.* The Hague: Mouton.

Kittredge, R. & L. Lehrberger (eds.) 1982. *Sublanguage: studies of language in restricted semantic domains.* Berlin: de Gruyter.

Kittredge, R. 1987. The significance of sublanguage for automatic translation. S. Nirenburg (ed.), *Machine translation: theoretical and methodological issues.* Cambridge: Cambridge University Press.

Klose, G., E. Lang, Th. Pirlein (eds.) 1992. *Ontologie und Axiomatik der Wissensbasis von LILOG.* Wissensmodellierung im IBM Deutschland LILOG-Projekt.

Kneale, W. & M. Kneale. 1962. *The development of logic.* London: Oxford University Press. Knowlson, J. 1975. *Universal language schemes in England and France 1600-1800.* Toronto: Toronto University Press.

Kobayashi, I. 1995. A social system simulation based on human information processing. Ph.D. thesis, Tokyo Institute of Technology.

Kobsa, A. & W. Wahlster (eds.). 1989. *User models in dialogue systems.* Berlin: Springer.

Kress, G.R. & T.J. van Leeuwen. 1990. *Reading images.* Geelong, Vic: Deakin University Press.

Kress, G.R. & T.J. van Leeuwen. 1996. *Reading images: the grammar of visual design.* London & New York: Routledge.

Labov, W. 1973. The boundaries of words and their meanings. C.-J. Bailey & R. Shuy (eds.), *New ways of analysing variation in English.* Washington: Georgetown University Press.

Lakoff, G. 1972. Linguistics and natural logic. D. Davidson & G. Harman (eds.), *Semantics for natural language.* Dordrecht: Reidel.

Lakoff, G. 1987. *Women, fire and dangerous things: what categories reveal about the mind.* Chicago: Chicago University Press.

Lakoff, G. 1988. Cognitive semantics. Eco, Santambrogio & Violi (eds.).

Lakoff, G. 1992. Metaphor and war: the metaphor system used to justify war in the Gulf. M. Pütz (ed.).

Lakoff, G. & M. Johnson. 1980. *Metaphors we live by.* Chicago: Chicago University Press.

Lakoff, G. & Z. Kövecses. 1987. The cognitive model of anger in American English. Holland & Quinn (eds.).

Lamb, S.M. 1964. The sememic approach to structural semantics. *American Anthropologist* 66:3.

Lamb, S.M. 1965. *Outline of stratificational grammar.* Washington DC: Georgetown University Press.

Lamb, S.M. 1966a. Prolegomena to a theory of phonology. *Language* 42.

Lamb, S.M. 1966b. Epilegomena to a theory of language. *Romance Philology* 19.

Lamb, S.M. 1992. *Outline of a cognitive theory of language: a work in progress.* Mimeo.

Lang, E. 1992. Linguistische vs. konzeptuelle Aspekte der LILOG-Ontologie. In G. Klose et al.

Langacker, R. 1978. The form and meaning of the English auxiliary. *Language* 54.

Langacker, R. 1984. Active Zones. *Proceedings of the tenth annual meeting of the Berkeley Linguistic Society.* .

Langacker. R. 1987. *Foundations of cognitive grammar.* Stanford, CA: Stanford University Press.

Large, A. 1985. *The artificial language movement.* Oxford: Blackwell.

Leech, G. 1974. *Semantics.* Harmondsworth: Penguin. Second, revised edition 1981.

Leisi, E. 1955. *Der Wortinhalt.* Heidelberg: Quelle u. Meyer.

Lemke, J.L. 1984. *Semiotics and education.* Toronto: Toronto Semiotic Circle (Monographs, Working Papers and Publications 2).

Lemke, J.L. 1990a. *Talking science: language, learning and values.* Norwood, NJ: Ablex.

Lemke, J.L. 1990b. 'Technical discourse and technocratic ideology'. M.A.K. Halliday, J. Gibbons & H. Nicholas (eds.), *Learning, keeping and using language: selected papers from the 8thWorld Congress of Applied Linguistics,* Volume II. Amsterdam: Benjamins.

Lemke, J.L. 1995. *Textual politics: discourse and social dynamics.* London: Taylor & Francis.

Lemke, J.L. in press. Multiplying meaning: visual and verbal semiotics in scientific text. J.R. Martin & R. Veel (eds.).

Levin, B. 1993. *English verb classes and alternations: a preliminary investigation.* Chicagor & London: The University of Chicago Press.

Levin, B. & S. Pinker (eds.) 1991. *Lexical and conceptual semantics.* Cambridge, MA & Oxford: Blackwell.

Linde, C. 1987. Explanatory systems in oral life stories. Holland & Quinn (eds).

Lockwood, D.J. 1972. *Introduction to stratificational linguistics.* New York: Harcourt Brace Javanovich.

Longacre, R. 1974. Narrative vs other discourse genres. R. Brend (ed.) *Advances in Tagmemics.* Amsterdam: North-Holland.

Longacre, R. 1976. *Anatomy of speech notions.* Lisse: Peter de Ridder Press.

Longacre, R. 1985. Sentences as combinations of clauses. T. Shopen (ed.), *Language typology and syntactic description. Volume II Complex constructions.* Cambridge: Cambridge University Press.

Lounsbury, F. 1956. A semantic analysis of Pawnee kinship usage. *Language* 32.

Malinowski, B. 1923. The problem of meaning in primitive languages. Supplement I to C. K. Ogden & I. A. Richards. *The meaning of meaning.* New York: Harcourt Brace & World.

Mann, W.C. 1982. *An overview of the Penman text generation system.* Information Sciences Institute, University of Southern California: ISI/RR-83-114.

Mann, W.C. 1983a. The anatomy of a systemic choice. *Discourse Processes* 8.1.

Mann, W.C. 1983b. Inquiry semantics: a functional semantics of natural language grammar. *Proceedings of the First Annual Conference of the European Chapter of the Association for Computational Linguistics.*

Mann, W.C. & C.M.I.M. Matthiessen. 1985. Demonstration of the Nigel Text Generation Computer Program. Benson & Greaves (eds.).

Mann, W.C. & C.M.I.M. Matthiessen. 1991. Functions of language in two frameworks. *Word* 42.

Mann, W.C. & S.A. Thompson. 1987. *Rhetorical Structure Theory: a framework for the analysis of texts.* Information Sciences Institute, University of Southern California: ISI/RS-87-185.

Mann, W.C., C.M.I.M. Matthiessen & S.A. Thompson. 1992. Rhetorical Structure Theory and text analysis. Mann & Thompson (eds), *Discourse desription: diverse linguistic analysis of a fund-raising text.* Amsterdam: Benjamins.

Martin, J.R. 1985. *Factual writing: exploring and challenging social reality.* Geelong, Vic.: Deakin University Press (Sociocultural Aspects of Language and Education). Reprinted London: Oxford University Press, 1989.

Martin, J.R. 1992. *English text: system and structure.* Amsterdam: Benjamins.

Martin, J.R. 1996a. Transitivity in Tagalog: a functional interpretation of case. Berry et al. (eds).

Martin, J.R. 1996b. Metalinguistic diversity: the case from case. R. Hasan, C. Cloran & D.G. Butt (eds.).Martin, J.R. in press. Beyond exchange: appraisal systems in English. S. Hunston & G. Thompson (eds.), *Evaluation in text.* London: Oxford University Press.

Martin, J.R. & C.M.I.M. Matthiessen. 1991. Systemic typology and topology. F. Christie (ed.), *Literacy in social processes: papers from the Inaugural Australian Systemic Functional Linguistics Conference, Deakin University, January 1990.* Darwin: Centre for Studies of Language in Education, Northern Territory University.

Martin, J.R., C.M.I.M. Matthiessen & C. Painter. 1997. *Working with functional grammar.* London: Edward Arnold.

Martin, J.R. & R. Veel (eds.). forthc. *Reading science: research, popular culture, industry and schooling.* London: Routledge.

Matthiessen, C.M.I.M. 1987. Notes on the environment of a text generation grammar. G. Kempen (ed.).

Matthiessen, C.M.I.M. 1988a. Representational issues in systemic functional grammar. J.D. Benson & W.S. Greaves (eds.).

Matthiessen, C.M.I.M. 1988b. Semantics for a systemic grammar: the chooser and inquiry framework. J. D. Benson, M. J. Cummings & W. S. Greaves (eds.).

Matthiessen, C.M.I.M. 1990a. Two approaches to semantic interfaces in text generation. *Proceedings of COLING-90, Helsinki, August 1990.*

Matthiessen, C.M.I.M. 1990b. *Metafunctional complementarity and resonance.* Department of Linguistics, Sydney University.

Matthiessen, C.M.I.M. 1991a. Language on language: the grammar of semiosis. *Social Semiotics* 1:2.

Matthiessen, C.M.I.M. 1991b. Lexico(grammatical) choice in text generation. C. Paris, W. Swartout & W.C. Mann (eds.).

Matthiessen, C.M.I.M. 1992. Interpreting the textual metafunction. M. Davies & L. Ravelli (eds.). Matthiessen, C.M.I.M. 1993a. The object of study in cognitive science in relation to its construal and enactment in language. *Language as Cultural Dynamic* (*Cultural Dynamics* 6.1-2.).

Matthiessen, C.M.I.M. 1993b. Register in the round: diversity in a unified theory of register analysis. M. Ghadessy (ed.), *Register analysis. Theory and practice.* London: Pinter.

Matthiessen, C.M.I.M. 1993c. Instantial systems and logogenesis. Paper presented to the 3rd National Chinese Systemic Symposium, Hangzhou University, Hangzhou, July 1993.

Matthiessen, C.M.I.M. 1995a. Fuzziness construed in language: a linguistic perspective. *Proceedings of FUZZ/IEEE, Yokohama, March 1995.*

Matthiessen, C.M.I.M. 1995b. *Lexicogrammatical cartography: English systems.* Tokyo: International Language Sciences Publishers.

Matthiessen, C.M.I.M. 1995c. Theme as a resource in ideational 'knowledge' construction. M. Ghadessy (ed.), *Thematic development in English texts.* London: Pinter.

Matthiessen, C.M.I.M. 1996. Systemic perspective on tense in English. M. Berry et al. (eds).

Matthiessen, C.M.I.M. & J. Bateman. 1991. *Text generation and systemic linguistics: experiences from English and Japanese.* London: Pinter.

Matthiessen, C.M.I.M. & M.A.K. Halliday. forthc. *Outline of systemic functional linguistics.*

Matthiessen, C.M.I.M., I. Kobayashi & L. Zeng. 1995. Generating multimodal presentations: resources and processes. *Preprint of Artificial Intelligence in Defence Workshop, Eighth Australian Joint Conference of Artificial Intelligence (AI '95), Canberra, November 13-14, 1995.*

Matthiessen, C.M.I.M., K. Nanri & L. Zeng. 1991. Multilingual resources in text generation: ideational focus. *Proceedings of the 2nd Japan-Australia Symposium on Natural Language Processing, Kyushu Institute of Technology, October 1991.*

Matthiessen, C.M.I.M. & C. Nesbitt. 1996. On the idea of theory-neutral descriptions. R. Hasan, C. Cloran & D. Butt (eds.).

McCawley, J. 1973. Syntactic and logical arguments for semantic structures. O. Fujimura (ed.), *Three dimensions in linguistic theory.* Tokyo: The TEC Corporation.

McCoy, C. & J. Cheng. 1991. Focus of attention: constraining what can be said. W. Mann, C. Paris & W. Swartout (eds.).

McDonald, E. 1994. Completive verb compounds in Modern Chinese: a new look at an old problem. *Journal of Chinese Linguistics* 22.2.

McKeown, K. 1982. *Generating natural language text in response to questions about database structure.* Ph.D. Thesis, University of Pennsylvania.

McKeown, K. 1985. *Text generation: using discourse strategies and focus constraints to generate natural language text.* Cambridge: Cambridge University Press. McKeown, K. & W.R. Swartout. 1987. Language generation and explanation. *Annual Review of Computer Science.* 2.

Mel'chuk, I. 1982. Lexical functions in lexicographic description. *Proceedings of the Eighth Anuual Meeting of the Berkeley Linguistic Society.*

Mellish, C. 1988. Implementing systemic classification by unification. *Journal of Computational Linguistics,* 14.1.

Miller, G.A & P.N. Johnson-Laird. 1976. *Language and perception.* Cambridge, MA: Belknap Press of Harvard University Press.

Miller, G.A. & C. Fellbaum. 1991. Semantic networks of English. B. Levin & S. Pinker (eds.).

Mitchell, T.F. 1957. The language of buying and selling in Cyrenaica: a situational statement. *Hesperis* 26. Reprinted in T.F. Mitchell, *Principles of Neo-Firthian Linguistics.* London: Longman, 1975.

Montague, R. 1974. The proper treatment of quantification in ordinary English. R Thomason (ed.), *Montague, R.: Formal philosophy.* New Haven: Yale University Press.

Nakamura, J-I. & N. Okada. 1991. Modeling, accumulating and evaluating machine dictionary of Japanese noun concepts. *Proceedings of the 2nd Japan-Australia Symposium on Natural Language Processing, Kyushu Institute of Technology, October 1991.*

Nesbitt, C. 1994. *Construing linguistic resources: consumer perspectives.* Ph.D. Thesis, University of Sydney.

Nesbitt, C. & G. Plum. 1988. Probabilities in a systemic grammar: the clause complex in English. R.P. Fawcett & D.J. Young (eds).

Nida, E. 1975. *Exploring semantic structures.* Munich: Fink.

Nordenfelt, L. 1977. *Events, actions, and ordinary language.* Lund: Doxa.

Noreen, A. 1904-12. *Vårt språk.* Lund.

O'Donnell, M. 1990. A dynamic model of exchange. *Word* 41.3.

O'Donnell, M. 1994. *From theory to implementation: analysis and generation with systemic grammar.* Ph.D. thesis, University of Sydney.

O'Toole, L.M. 1989. Semiotic systems in painting and poetry. M. Falchikov, C. Poke and R. Russell (eds). *A Festschrift for Dennis Ward.* Nottingham: Astra Press.

O'Toole, L.M. 1992. Institutional sculpture and the social semiotic. *Social Semiotics* 2.1. O'Toole, L.M. 1994. *The language of displayed art.* London: Leicester University Press (Pinter).

O'Toole, L.M. 1995. A systemic-functional semiotics of art. P.H. Fries and M.J. Gregory (eds), *Discourse in society: functional perspectives.* Norwood, NJ: Ablex.

Oldenburg, J. 1987. *From child tongue to mother tongue: a case study of language development in the first two and a half years.* Ph.D. thesis, University of Sydney.

Padley, G.A. 1985. *Grammatical theory in Western Europe 1500 - 1700. Trends in vernacular grammar I.* Cambridge: Cambridge University Press.

Painter, C. 1984. *Into the mother tongue: a case study in early language development.* London: Pinter.

Painter, C. 1989. Learning language: a functional view of language development. R. Hasan & J. R. Martin (eds).

Painter, C. 1993. *Learning through language: a case study in the development of language as a resource for learning from 2 1/2 to 5 years.* Ph.D. thesis, University of Sydney.

Painter, C. 1996. The development of language as a resource for thinking: a linguistic view of learning. R. Hasan & G. Williams (eds), *Literacy in society.* London & New York: Longman.

Paris, C.L., W.R. Swartout & W.C. Mann. (eds.). 1991. *Natural language generation in artificial intelligence and computational linguistics.* Boston: Kluwer.

Parker-Rhodes, A.F. 1978. *Inferential Semantics.* New York, NY: The Humanities Press.

Partee, B. 1975. Montague grammar and transformational grammar. *Linguistic Inquiry* 6.

Pattabhiraman. T. 1992. Aspects of salience in natural language generation. Ph.D. thesis, Simon Fraser University.

Patten, T. 1988. *Systemic text generation as problem solving.* Cambridge: Cambridge University Press.

Patten, T. & G. Ritchie. 1987. A formal model of systemic grammar. G. Kempen (ed).

Paul, H. 1909. *Prinzipien der Sprachgeschichte.* Halle.

Pawley, A. 1987. Encoding events in Kalam and English: different logics for reporting experience. R.S. Tomlin (ed.).

Phillips, J. 1985. *The development of comparisons and contrasts in young children's language.* M.A. Honours thesis, University of Sydney.

Phillips, J. 1986. The development of modality and hypothetical meaning: Nigel 1; 7 1/2 - 2; 7 1/2. *Working Papers in Linguistics* 3. University of Sydney, Linguistics Department.

Platzack, C. 1979. *The semantic interpretation of aspect and aktionsarten: a study of internal time reference in Swedish.* Dordrecht: Foris Publications.

Pollard, C. & I. Sag. 1987. *Information-based syntax and semantics. Vol. 1: Fundamentals.* CSLI Lecture Notes No. 13. Stanford University, Center for the Study of Language and Information.

Pollard, C. & I. Sag. 1993. *Head-driven phrase structure grammar.* Chicago & London: The University of Chicago Press.

Postal, P. 1966. On so-called "pronouns" in English. F. Dineen (ed), *Report of the Seventeenth Annual Round Table Meeting on Linguistics and Language Studies*. Washington, DC: Georgetown University Press. (Monograph on languages and linguistics 19).

Postal, P. 1970. On coreferential complement subject deletion. *Linguistic Inquiry* 1.4.

Pütz, M. (ed.), 1992, *Thirty years of linguistic evolution*. Amsterdam: Benjamins.

Quillian, M.R. 1968. Semantic memory. M. Minsky (ed), *Semantic information processing*. Cambridge, MA: MIT Press.

Quirk, R., S. Greenbaum, G. Leech, & J. Svartvik. 1985. A *comprehensive grammar of the English language*. London: Longman.

Ransom, E. 1986. *Complementation: its meaning and forms*. Amsterdam: Benjamins.

Ravelli, L. 1985. *Metaphor, mode and complexity: an exploration of co-varying patterns*. BA Honours thesis, Department of Linguistics, University of Sydney.

Ravelli, L. 1988. Grammatical metaphor: an initial analysis. E. Steiner & R. Veltman (eds.).

Reddy, M. 1979. The conduit metaphor: a case of frame conflict in our language about language. A. Ortony (ed.), *Metaphor and thought*. Cambridge: Cambridge University Press.

Reinhart, T. 1982. *Pragmatics and linguistics: an analysis of sentence topics*. Bloomington: Indiana University Linguistics Club.

Renton, N.E. 1990. *Metaphors. an annotated dictionary. A concise overview of 3800 picturesque idiomatic expressions normally used subconsciously*. Melbourne: Schwartz & Wilkinson.

Restak, R.M. 1988. *The mind*. New York: Bantam.

Roget, M. 1852. A *Thesaurus of English Words and Phrases, Classified and Arranged so as to facilitate the Expression of Ideas and assist in Literary Composition*.

Rosner, M. & R. Johnson (eds.). 1992. *Computational linguistics and formal semantics*. Cambridge: Cambridge University Press.

R.R. 1641. *An English grammar: or, a plain exposition of Lilies Grammar. In English, with ease and profitable rules for parsing and making Latine: very usefull for young scholars, and others, that would in a short time learn the Latine tongue. Which may serve as a comment for them that learn Lillie's Grammar*. London, Printed by Felix Kyngston for Mathew Walbank and Laurence Chapman.

Salmon, V. 1966. Language-planning in seventeenth-century England: its contexts and aims. C.E. Bazell, J.C. Catford, M.A.K. Halliday & R.H. Robins (eds.), *In memory of J.R. Firth*. London: Longman.

Salmon, V. 1979. *The study of language in 17th-century England*. Amsterdam: Benjamins. (Amsterdam Studies in the Theory and History of Linguistic Science 3.17.)

Samlowski, W. 1976. Case grammar. E. Charniak & Y. Wilks (eds.), *Computational Semantics*. Amsterdam: North-Holland.

Sampson, G. 1987. Probabilistic models of analysis. R. Garside, G. Leech & G. Sampson (eds), *The computational analysis of English: a corpus-based approach.* London: Longman.

Sampson, G. 1992. Probabilistic parsing. J. Svartvik (ed.), *Directions in corpus linguistics: proceedings of Nobel Symposium 82, Stockholm, 4-8 August 1991.* Berlin & New York: Mouton de Gruyter (Trends in Linguistics Studies & Monographs 65).

Schank, R. 1972. Conceptual dependency: a theory of natural language understanding. *Cognitive Psychology* 3.4.

Schank, R. 1982. *Dynamic memory: a theory of reminding and learning in computers and people.* New York: Cambridge University Press.

Schank, R. & R. Abelson. 1977. *Scripts, plans, goals and understanding: an inquiry into human knowledge structures.* Hillsdale, NJ: Lawrence Erlbaum.

Schank, R. & A. Kass. 1988. Knowledge representation in people and machines. In Eco. Santambrogio & Violi (eds.).

Schneider, K. 1977. *Aktionsart och aspekt i svenskan och danskan jämförd med tyskan och nederländskan.* Turku.

Sefton, P. 1995. *State-potentials and social subjects in systemic-functional theory: towards a computational socio-semiotics.* Ph.D. thesis, University of Sydney.

Sheldrake, R. 1988. *The presence of the past.* Glasgow & London: Fontana.

Shieber, S. 1986. *An Introduction to Unification-Based Approaches to Grammar.* Stanford University: Center for the Study of Language and Information.

Sigurd, B. 1977. Om textens dynamik. *Papers from the Institute of Linguistics, University of Stockholm* 34.

Simon, H.E. & C.E. Kaplan. 1989. Foundations of cognitive science. M.I. Posner (ed.), *Foundations of cognitive science.* Cambridge, Mass: MIT Press.

Sinclair, J.M. 1992. The automatic analysis of corpora. J. Svartvik (ed.), *Directions in corpus linguistics: proceedings of Nobel Symposium 82, Stockholm, 4-8 August 1991.* Berlin & New York: Mouton de Gruyter.

Slade, D. 1996. *The texture of casual conversation in English.* Ph.D. thesis, University of Sydney.

Slaughter, M. 1986. *Universal languages and scientific taxonomy in the seventeenth century.* Cambridge: Cambridge University Press.

Sowa, J. 1983a. *Conceptual structures.* Menlo Park: Addison-Wesley.

Sowa, J. 1983b. Generating language from conceptual graphs. *Computers and Mathematics with Applications* 9.1.

Sowa, J. (ed.) 1991. *Principles of semantic networks: explorations in the representation of knowledge.* San Mateo, CA: Morgan Kaufmann.

Starosta, S. 1988. *The case for lexicase: an outline of lexicase grammatical theory.* London: Pinter.

Steiner, E. 1984. *Language and music as semiotic systems: the example of a folk ballad.* Trier: LAUDT.

Steiner, E. 1988a. Describing language as activity: an application to child language. R.P. Fawcett & D.J. Young (eds.).

Steiner, E. 1988b. The interaction of language and music as semiotic systems: the example of a folk ballad. J.D. Benson, M. Cummings & W.S. Greaves (eds.).

Steiner, E. 1991. *A functional perspective on language, action and interpretation: an initial approach with a view to computational modelling.* Berlin & New York: Mouton de Gruyter.

Steiner, E. & R. Veltman. (eds.) 1988. *Pragmatics, discourse, and text: some systemically inspired approaches.* London: Pinter.

Stillings, N.A. et al. 1987. *Cognitive science: an introduction.* Cambridge, Mass.: MIT Press.

Sugeno, M. 1993. Toward intelligent computing. *Proceedings of the 5th IFSA World Congress, Seoul 1993.*

Svartvik, J. & R. Quirk. (eds.) 1980. *A corpus of English conversation.* Lund: Gleerup. (Lund Studies in English 56.)

Talmy, L. 1985. Lexicalisation patterns. T. Shopen (ed.), *Language typology and syntactic description. Grammatical categories and the lexicon.* Cambridge: Cambridge University Press.

Taylor, J. 1989. *Linguistic categorization: prototypes in linguistic theory.* Oxford: Clarendon Press.

Teich, E. 1995. *A proposal for dependency in systemic functional grammar: metasemiosis in computational systemic functional linguistics.* Ph.D. thesis, Universität des Saarlandes, Saarbrücken.

Teich, E. & J.A. Bateman. 1994. Towards an application of text generation in an integrated publication system. *Proceedings of the 17th International Workshop on Natural Language Generation, Kennebunkport, Main, USA June 21-24.*

Thibault, P.J. 1992. Grammar, ethics, and understanding: functionalist reason and clause as exchange. *Social Semiotics* 2.1.

Thibault, P.J. 1993. Using language to think interpersonally: experiential meaning and the cryptogrammar of subjectivity and agency in English. *Language as Cultural Dynamic (Cultural Dynamics* 6.1-2.).

Thompson, S.A. 1988. A discourse approach to the cross-linguistic category 'adjective'. J. Hawkins (ed.), *Explaining language universals.* Oxford: Blackwell.

Thomson, J.J. 1977. *Acts and other events.* Ithaca & London: Cornell University Press.

Tomlin, R. 1987. Linguistic reflections of cognitive events. R. Tomlin (ed.).

Tomlin, R. (ed.). 1987. *Coherence and grounding in discourse.* Amsterdam: Benjamins.

Trevarthen, C. 1987. Sharing making sense: intersubjectivity and the making of an infant's meaning. R. Steele & T. Threadgold (eds), *Language topics: essays in honour of Michael Halliday, Volume 1.* Amsterdam: Benjamins.

Trubetzkoy, N. 1939. *Grundzüge der Phonologie*. Prague. (Travaux du Cercle Linguistique de Prague 7.)

Tung, Y.-W., C.M.I.M. Matthiessen & N. Sondheimer. 1988. *On Parallelism and the Penman Language Generation System*. University of Southern California, Information Sciences Institute: ISI/RR-88-195.

Unsworth, L. 1995. *How and why: recontextualizing science explanations in school science books*. Ph.D. thesis, University of Sydney.

Vachek, J. 1964. *A Prague School reader in linguistics*. Prague: Academia.

van Leeuwen, T.J. 1988. *Music and ideology: towards a socio-semantics of mass media music*. Sydney: Sydney Association for Studies in Society and Culture. (Working Papers 2.)

van Leeuwen, T.J. 1991. The sociosemiotics of easy listening music. *Social Semiotics* 1.1.

Vendler, Z. 1967. *Linguistics in philosophy*. Ithaca: Cornell University Press.

Ventola, E. 1987. *The structure of social interaction: a systemic approach to the semiotics of service encounters*. London: Pinter.

Verkuyl, H.J. 1972. *On the compositional nature of the aspects*. Dordrecht: Reidel.

Waddington, C.H. 1977. *Tools for thought*. Frogmore: Paladin.

Webber, B.L. 1987. Event Reference. *TINLAP: theoretical issues in Natural Language Processing -3. Position Papers*. Computing Research Laboratory, New Mexico State University (Memoranda in Computer and Cognitive Science).

Whorf, B.L. 1956. *Language thought and reality: selected writing of Benjamin Lee Whorf*, ed. J.B. Carroll. Cambridge, MA: The MIT Press.

Wierzbicka, A. 1975. Why "kill" does not mean "cause to die": the semantics of action sentences. *Foundations of Language* 13.

Wierzbicka, A. 1980. *Lingua mentalis*. New York: Academic Press.

Wierzbicka, A. 1985. Oats and wheat: the fallacy of arbitrariness. J. Haiman (ed.), *Iconicity in syntax*. Amsterdam: Benjamins.

Wierzbicka, A. 1988. *The semantics of grammar*. Amsterdam: Benjamins.

Wignell, P., J.R. Martin & S. Eggins. 1990. The discourse of geography: ordering and explaining the experiential world. *Linguistics and Education* 1.4. Reprinted in M.A.K. Halliday & J.R. Martin, 1993.

Wilkins, J. 1668. *An Essay Towards a Real Character and a Philosophical Language*. London.

Winograd, T. 1968. Linguistics and the computer analysis of tonal harmony. *Journal of Music Theory*. Reprinted in M.A.K. Halliday & J.R. Martin (eds.), 1981.

Winograd, T. 1972. *Understanding natural language*. Edinburgh: Edinburgh University Press.

Winograd, T. 1983. *Language as a cognitive process, Volume 1: syntax.* Reading, Mass: Addison Wesley.

Witherspoon, G. 1977. *Language and art in the Navajo universe.* Ann Arbor: University of Michigan Press.

Woods, W. 1975. What's in a link: foundations for semantic networks. D.G. Bobrow & A. Collins (eds), *Representation and understanding: studies in cognitive science.* New York: Academic Press.

Wortman, C.B. & E.F. Loftus. 1985. *Psychology.* New York: Knopf.

Wurm, S.A. 1987. Semantics and world view in languages of the Santa Cruz Archipelago, Solomon Islands. R. Steele & T. Threadgold (eds.), *Language topics. essays in honour of Michael Halliday, Volume 1.* Amsterdam: Benjamins.

Wuthnow, R. et al. 1984. *Cultural analysis: the work of Peter L. Berger, Mary Douglas, Michel Focault, and Jürgen Habermas.* Boston: Routledge & Kegan Paul. Yates, F. 1966. *The art of memory.* London: Routledge & Kegan Paul.

Zadeh, L.A. 1987. *Fuzzy sets and applications: selected papers by L.A. Zadeh,* ed. R.R. Yager, S. Ovchinnikov, R.M. Tong, H.T. Nguyen. New York: Wiley.

Zeng, L. 1993. Coordinating ideational and textual resources in the generation of multisentential texts in Chinese. *Proceedings of PACLING 93, Vancouver, April 1993.*

Zeng, L. 1996. *Planning text in an integrated multilingual meaning-space: a systemic-linguistic perspective.* Ph.D thesis, University of Sydney.

Zipf, G.K. 1935. *The psycho-biology of language: an introduction to dynamic philology.* New York: Houghton Mifflin Company.

Index

西方语言学与应用语言学视野

第二语言习得前沿书系

Gass, S. M. et al. *Linguistic Perspectives on Second Language Acquisition*
第二语言习得的语言学视角

Brown, H. D. et al. *Readings on Second Language Acquisition*
第二语言习得论著选读

Haley, M. H. et al. *Content-Based Second Language Teaching and Learning: An Interactive Approach*
基于内容的第二语言教与学——互动的思路

Carrell, P. L. et al. *Interactive Approaches to Second Language Reading*
第二语言阅读研究的交互模式

Singleton, D. *Exploring the Second Language Mental Lexicon*
探索第二语言心理词汇

Koda, K. *Insights into Second Language Reading: A Cross-Linguistic Approach*
洞察第二语言阅读——跨语言途径

Robinson, P. *Cognition and Second Language Instruction*
认知与第二语言教学

Cook, V. et al. *Second Language Writing Systems*
第二语言文字系统

Boxer, D. et al. *Studying Speaking to Inform Second Language Learning*
口头话语分析与第二语言习得

Jessica, W. *Teaching Writing in Second and Foreign Language Class-rooms*
第二语言与外语写作教学

Dodigovic, M. *Artificial Intelligence in Second Language Learning: Raising Error Awareness*
人工智能在第二语言教学中的应用——提高对偏误的意识

Wong, W. *Input Enhancement*
输入的强化

VanPatten, B. *From Input to Output*
从输入到输出

Macaro, E. *Learning Strategies in Foreign and Second Language Classrooms*
外语与第二语言学习策略

Macaro, E. *Teaching and Learning a Second Language*
第二语言的教学与学习

Chapelle, C. A. *Computer Applications in Second Language Acquisition*
计算机在第二语言习得中的应用

Oxford, R. L. *Language Learning Strategies: What Every Teacher Should Know*
语言学习策略——教师必读

应用语言学专题

Hunston, S.　　　　*Corpora in Applied Linguistics*
　　　　　　　　　应用语言学中的语料库

McCarthy, M.　　　*Spoken Language & Applied Linguistics*
　　　　　　　　　口语与应用语言学

McCarthy, M.　　　*Issues in Applied Linguistics*
　　　　　　　　　应用语言学论题

Rose, K. R. et al.　*Pragmatics in Language Teaching*
　　　　　　　　　语言教学中的语用学

Schmitt, N.　　　　*An Introduction to Applied Linguistics*
　　　　　　　　　应用语言学入门

西方语言学系列

Harris, A. C. et al.　*Historical Syntax in Cross-Linguistic Perspective*
　　　　　　　　　历史句法学的跨语言视角

Steinberg, D. D. et al.　*An Introduction to Psycholinguistics*
　　　　　　　　　心理语言学导论

Schiffrin, D.　　　*Discourse Markers*
　　　　　　　　　话语标记

Heine, B. et al.　　*World Lexicon of Grammaticalization*
　　　　　　　　　语法化的世界词库

Firbas, J.　　　　*Functional Sentence Perspective in Written and Spoken Communication*
　　　　　　　　　书面与口语交际中的功能句子观

Palmer, F. R.　　　*Mood and Modality*
　　　　　　　　　语气·情态

Lass, R.　　　　　*Historical Linguistics and Language change*
　　　　　　　　　历史语言学和语言演变

Fauconnier, G.　　*Mental Spaces: Aspects of Meaning Construction in Natural Language*
　　　　　　　　　心理空间——自然语言中的意义构建

Levinson, S. C.　　*Space in Language and Cognition: Explorations in Cognitive Diversity*
　　　　　　　　　语言与认知的空间——认知多样性探索

Vilém Mathesius　　*A Functional Analysis of Present Day English on A General Linguistic Basis*
　　　　　　　　　普通语言学基础上的当代英语功能分析

Campbell, L.　　　*Historical Linguistics: An Introduction*
　　　　　　　　　历史语言学导论

Jesperson, D.　　　*The Philosophy of Grammar*
　　　　　　　　　语法哲学

Norman, J.　　　　*Chinese*
　　　　　　　　　汉语

Halliday, M. A. K. et al.　*Construing Experience though Meaning*
　　　　　　　　　通过意义识解经验

全国独家购权影印原版外文学术期刊

世界图书出版公司北京公司

世界图书出版公司隶属中国出版集团公司，是由国家新闻出版总署批准的国内最大的国际版权贸易公司。世图北京公司为广大高校师生以及相关机构研究人员提供 600 余种国外原版期刊（2009 年），其中语言学类期刊共有近 40 种，相当数量为核心期刊，订价相当于原版的 50%，相信这些期刊会对研究人员、学者、师生的科研和教学工作提供重要的帮助。

2009 年语言学期刊：

世图刊号	英文刊名	期次	原版参考价	世图价
BW701	ELT Journal	4/Yr.	1690 元	970 元
BW702	Applied Linguistics	4/Yr.	2790 元	1600 元
BW703	The Modern Language Journal	4 + 1/Yr.	1830 元	1260 元
BW704	Language Learning	4 + 2/Yr.	3970 元	2740 元
BW705	Review of English Studies	5/Yr.	2990 元	1340 元
BW706	Forum for Modern Language Studies	4/Yr.	2230 元	1280 元
BW707	Language Teaching Research	3/Yr.	3590 元	2060 元
BW708	Language Testing	4/Yr.	4880 元	2810 元
BW709	Child Language Teaching and Therapy	3/Yr.	3300 元	1900 元
BW710	Second Language Research	4/Yr.	4310 元	2480 元
BW715	Yearbook of English Studies	2/Yr.	1710 元	980 元
BW716	Modern Language Review	4/Yr.	1880 元	1150 元
BW717	Annual Bibliography of English Language & Literature	1/Yr.	3630 元	2090 元
BW718	The Year's Work in Modern Language Studies	1/Yr.	3370 元	1940 元
BW719	International Journal of Lexicography	4/Yr.	2430 元	1400 元
BW720	Journal of Semantics	4/Yr.	2560 元	1470 元
BW721	Translation and Literature	2/Yr.	1570 元	900 元
BW722	Gender and Language	2/Yr.	1390 元	800 元

世图刊号	英文刊名	期次	原版参考价	世图价
BW723	Journal of Applied Linguistics	3/Yr.	2080 元	1200 元
BW724	Linguistics and the Human Sciences	3/Yr.	2080 元	1200 元
BW725	International Journal of Applied Linguistics	3/Yr.	2420 元	1670 元
BW726	Journal of Sociolinguistics	5/Yr.	4600 元	3180 元
BW727	Linguistics Abstracts	4/Yr.	17140 元	11880 元
BW728	Studia Linguistica	3/Yr.	3870 元	2670 元
BW729	Syntax	3/Yr.	3130 元	2160 元
BW730	Transactions of the Philological Society	3/Yr.	7010 元	4830 元
BW731	World Englishes	4/Yr.	8860 元	6110 元
BW733	Corpora	2/Yr.	1060 元	610 元
BW734	Word Structure	2/Yr.	1110 元	640 元
BW737	Discourse & Communication	4/Yr.	5110 元	2940 元
BW738	A Journal of Language Teaching and Research	3/Yr.	2710 元	1560 元
BW739	Discourse Studies	6/Yr.	8100 元	4660 元
BW740	Journal of Language and Social Psychology	4/Yr.	5150 元	2960 元
BW741	Written Communication	4/Yr.	5200 元	2990 元
BW742	First Language	4/Yr.	4500 元	2590 元
BW745	International Journal of American Linguistics	4/Yr.	1860 元	1070 元
BW746	Classical Philology	4/Yr.	1610 元	920 元
BW756	English：Journal of the English Association	3/Yr.	1680 元	970 元

更多期刊信息请访问我们的网站 www.wpcbj.com.cn。如果注册成为会员，就可以进行网上订购。订购全年期刊或免费索取目录，可以通过以下方式：

1. 通信地址：北京市朝内大街 137 号，世界图书出版公司北京公司期刊部，邮编100010

2. 联系电话：（010）64038378　64038344

3. E-mail 地址：qkb2@wpcbj.com.cn